DAVY HARWOOD BOXSET

1-3

TIJAN

Copyright © 2014 Tijan

To my readers and those who have continued to love Davy through the years.

PROLOGUE

I wasn't supernaturally inclined to know when vampires were around, but I knew anyway. I was empathic and that meant that I could feel what others felt, I felt what was going on around me. And right now, as I was on top of the Heffler where I volunteered for a crisis hotline, I knew there were eight nearby. I'd been the unfortunate one to answer the call and now I stood there, teetering on the edge with a 'jumper' before me. I was keenly aware of the two vamps behind me and the six on the ground. Vampires didn't usually care about death. I had no idea why they were there, but it didn't matter at that moment.

"Okay." I took a deep breath and tried to inch forward.

The jumper was a frail looking girl with inflamed cheeks. Her red curls whisked around her from the wind, which didn't help our situation at all. She turned, saw me, and her eyes widened. She was the deer in my headlights, but I hoped that I wasn't the oncoming car to push her over the edge.

"Hi—hello—how are you? No—I mean..." I should have stopped then, but I was the only one from the hotline there. I'd been the last to leave and because of that, I was the only one that heard the phone, answered the phone, and figured out where the girl had called from.

I took another breath, and then said more calmly, "My name's Davina, but you can call me Davy—if you want." A part of me waited for the normal 'Stay away from me or I'll jump!', but it didn't come.

She didn't say a thing. I saw the tears and that's what made me pause. She'd been hysterical on the phone. I'd heard the words 'a guy', 'kill myself', and 'love.' My mind leapt to the natural clichéd conclusion. I thought she was going to kill herself over a guy and a part of me felt a little contempt for her. I know, I know — she's suicidal. I should be sympathetic, but really—a guy?!

That had been my first reaction, but now I thought differently. This girl wasn't the suicidal virgin with a love gone reality. I looked into her hazel eyes and saw true agony in this girl. It was real and it blew my breath away for a moment. That was saying a lot.

"Okay." I needed to settle myself. I needed to plant both feet on the ground and I needed—I looked at her again. The pain was crippling. I could feel it. There was a sense of contentment and resolve in her too. This girl was done. What she was done with, I had no idea, but I felt it. She'd fought a battle, she'd lost, and she was done with it all.

For a moment, I stood in awe of her. I'd had my fair share of trauma and struggle, but I still had hope. This girl had none.

I closed my eyes and opened every sense I had. Every empath I knew would scream against this, but I needed to know what this girl had gone through. Something told me that I *needed* to know. I lowered my bridge, and I felt myself slip inside of her.

Turmoil. Desolation. Agony.

Worst of all, I felt the surrender. It slammed against me like waves of sleet in a downpour. It actually hurt and I bit my tongue. I wanted to feel more. I wanted to understand so I pushed further. Empaths are advised against this for a reason. If we touch too deep inside a person sometimes a part of us doesn't come back.

There was something inside of her, something that promised me that it'd be worth it. I needed to uncover it. Surging forward, I fought past the hopelessness and defeat. Then I reeled back when I touched the core.

There had been a guy. He had loved her. She had loved him... and then... I felt devastation, betrayal, and an end.

I gasped abruptly.

I don't know what happened, but something had happened. She had loved this guy. She found something and then... It was her decision, which was important. She decided when she'd die... not... I couldn't feel it anymore.

She gasped. My eyes flew open and I felt a wind propel me backwards. It was as if the universe didn't want me near this girl. I couldn't look away. Her eyes wanted to tell me something, something that she didn't even realize she wanted to say, but she didn't have the words or she didn't have the will. Then a single tear rolled down to join the rest and she smiled. It was haunting. Then she let go of the railing. I watched, stricken, but already in expectation as she soared downwards.

Something was off, something reeled inside of me.

Something had not gone according to plan and I'm the kind of girl where I knew that plans should go according to plan! It was usually highly essential, but this—this wasn't good. Not only for the fact that some part of me still felt connected to her, but there was a universe-world-future issue at stake. I had no idea why I felt that, how I felt it, but I did. I was panicked.

The girl had jumped, and it was like the world was now going to end

I gulped.

1

"**M**r. Moser is not happy."

That was my greeting as I dropped my books on the library table and plopped down next to my roommate. She was the originator of my stupid hotline volunteer career. The career that was *finito*, done, and over with. I snuck inside that morning, slipped the envelope underneath the door, and bolted.

There are occasions where I'm very much a coward, and this was one of those times.

"I'm not surprised," I muttered and bent to grab a pencil out of my bag. The location of the bag was just opportune. It was on the floor so I was able to turn and present my back to my roommate. I hoped she'd take the hint.

"What do you mean you're not surprised? Why aren't you surprised?" Emily hadn't taken the hint. Then again, she never did.

She had been my roommate for the last three months. Her entire life plan was written in detail with bulleted expenditure costs, but it all revolved around her career choice in social work. She was the one to volunteer at the hotline. She was the one who dragged me there. She was even the one that pointed out Adam. Emily wasn't the reason why I stayed. Adam was that reason.

I like boys. Most people would say that I'm boy-crazy, but the truth is I just find them entertaining. I would never ever kill myself over a guy. They're not worth that much, but they are worth a fun activity or a cuddle during a movie. When I saw his rich chestnut hair and almond eyes, I knew that Adam would make a great movie-cuddler.

"Davina!" Emily called out sharply. She was being ignored. That made her pissy.

I sighed and fought the urge to bury my head in my book. No. Why fight it? I buried my head into my book and groaned dramatically. I knew one thing. It would make Emily shut up. If there was one thing that made her uncomfortable, it was when someone was in need of emotional reassurance. I once saw her spill a drink and use that as an excuse to leave a group when one of the girls started crying. I highly doubted Emily's social work career would make it past the paper it was written on, but I wasn't going to be the one to tell her.

On another note, I hated being called Davina. It's Davy. It'll always be Davy. It'll never be Davina. Then I realized there was silence. Emily had quieted. I risked a look, and saw that her eyes were downcast on her own pile of books. I thanked my own quick wits for this reprieve.

"Davina."

I stiffened at the name, but when I looked over my shoulder I melted into a gooey feeling inside. Adam was approaching with an eager stride. His almond eyes sharpened with warmth, and I saw the earnest grin on his face. Tall, dark, and just pretty. That's how I'd describe my perfect guy, and Adam easily fit the bill. Plus, he wore Abercrombie. What girl didn't like that? Well, probably a lot, but it looked yummy on him.

"Hi, Adam." I was warm. I was always warm around him.

He stood at the end of our table and seemed riveted by me. I wondered why and then let it go. Obviously, the guy had woken up and realized his love for me.

"I heard about the suicide last night. Are you okay? You were there, right? That's what Shelly said."

Shelly. All the gooeyness dried up. Shelly was my competition. I cheated on my empath rules and took a peek inside her once. The feeling was mutual. She hated me even more and I didn't need to be psychic to know that she planned to murder me.

I was only joking. Somewhat.

I was a short girl at five foot six inches with an average build, not slim, but not big either. I had brown curls on a good day, and a frizzy fray on a bad, but I knew my dark brown eyes and my full lips were my best features. Guys liked to stare at both of them, but Shelly was a tall willowy blonde with absolutely beautiful blue eyes. I always felt like I was swimming in a lake when I looked at them.

Shelly liked Adam. I liked Adam, but I wasn't sure who Adam liked.

"What else did Shelly say?" I couldn't hide my sarcasm.

Adam's smile dimmed slightly, but he pressed, "Is it true? You answered the phone and she was on the roof?"

The boy was goal oriented. "Yes. I was there, but she jumped."

Emily looked up with wide eyes. Adam shifted a little and his eyes skirted from me to Emily. "Are you okay? Shelly said that you quit the hotline."

Emily harrumphed.

"Um."

"I can't believe you quit." Emily had to put her two cents in.

"Yeah." Adam took the seat next to mine and lowered his voice. It was soothing and seductive to my ears. "The place won't be the same without you, you know?"

Of course I knew, but that was the point of it. I wanted to get as far away as possible. It would always remind me of the girl from last night. I wasn't freaked out with agony and so forth, but the truth was that I was freaked out by the gut-wrenching feeling that something worldly awful had happened and that it was connected to me. "I just... it's too much, you know? I can't handle—she died in front of me. It's just too much for me."

I saw the sympathy in Adam. He placed his hand on mine. "I

know exactly what you mean. If you ever need anything, call me. Okay? I want to help you through this tough time."

Emily fled the scene. I almost caught a back draft from her sprint. "I'd really like that, Adam."

He squeezed my hand. "Any time. Remember that, Davina."

I'd remind him another time not to call me that name.

Then the happily-ever-after feeling was gone as I felt a vampire walk past us. A cold wind slapped my insides and I looked up. Normally, vamps ignore me. They can't feel me like I can feel them so they just believe that they're not noticed.

Not this time.

I gasped when I saw a pair of coal-black eyes staring right back at me. The vamp was tall with jet black hair. He wore a white buttoned-down shirt over jeans. He kept going, but I still felt his eyes after he turned the corner.

"Davina," Adam said sharply, confused.

"What were you saying?" His hand was gone. I wanted his hand back.

He frowned again and asked, "Are you okay? You pushed me away and I mean, that's okay if that's what you need right now. I just thought..." He trailed off and looked away.

I didn't have to be empathic to see his insecurity. "It's not that. That guy scared me just now. I'm sorry. I want your help, I really do."

His eyes twinkled.

I sighed again. How could any girl not fall in love with how adorable he was?

"Can you two stop with the sappy moment?" Emily returned with a storm at her backside. She slumped in her seat. "I'm trying to study."

"Oh, yeah," Adam laughed, a little embarrassed. "I-uh—I'll talk to you later, Davina?"

I nodded. Hell yeah, we'd talk.

"Good. See you later then."

I glanced at Emily as he left and saw her sharp green eyes on me. She narrowed them in disgust.

"You make me sick."

"What? Why?" I was innocent.

"You totally lied to him just now. I had to run to the bathroom to keep from barfing. Really?! You can't handle it? She died in front of you? Mr. Moser told me that you need to get back to the hotline. You broke protocol and that's why you quit, not because you're 'emotionally shaken.' Seriously, Davina."

Maybe my roommate knew me a little better than I realized.

"Can you blame me?! Adam is to die for." I could not believe I just said those words.

"I can't believe you said that." Emily reiterated my thoughts.

I flushed, embarrassed, and leaned back in my chair. "What am I supposed to do? I didn't quit because of protocol, okay? And I need any advantage with Adam. You know Shelly Whistworth has her claws in him."

Emily was annoyed. "You have to go and talk to Mr. Moser. You did break the rules and he's worried about a lawsuit. And Adam Darley is not worth your time to lie and lower yourself. If he's a stand-up guy, he'll recognize that you're much more fun to be with than Shelly Witless. If he's not and he goes to her, he's not the guy that you'll want anyway."

"I'm not lowering myself," I remarked, and crossed my arms. "I'm just being manipulative."

Emily looked at me knowingly. "Well, stop. It's annoying."

"It's fun."

Emily opened her mouth and started to say something, but I felt the blast of cold race through me. My heart slowed as the vamp walked towards me from the opposite direction. His eyes were on me again. He seemed to look right through me, but he didn't slow his pace. He walked right past.

I hated vampires. I knew what they could do from personal experience. However, there were a lot of good vampires that liked to hang out on campus. Some of them even took classes and wanted to learn. This guy looked like a regular college student and he walked like one. Right to the computer lab, and back out again for a Mountain

Dew. Typical college behavior, but I was betting he wasn't one of the 'good' vampires.

"Do you know who that is?"

"You interrupted me. I was talking."

I watched as he returned from the vending machines and sat back down at a computer. "That guy. Do you know him?"

"We're at a school with six thousand students. Really?! We're freshmen, Davina. How can you expect that I'd know him?"

I turned and regarded her. "Do you know him or not?"

She shifted uncomfortably in her seat.

"Who is he, Emily?" I leaned closer and hoped he couldn't hear us. There were two glass walls between us and the computer lab always buzzed with conversations and printing papers. If he tuned in, he could hear us, but for once I hoped that I wasn't a speck on this guy's radar. Correction—make that his vampire's radar.

"He's in my social work class."

"Intro?"

"Yeah. He's a junior and he's fulfilling a requirement." She sounded like she'd practiced that. Something felt off with her. She liked to share her opinions on people, but she didn't with this guy.

"You like him." I couldn't fault her. Vamps had seductive appeal down to perfection. Emily was a girl. Even *she* would fall under their power whether they intended it or not. The only way you could fight against their pull was if you knew what they were.

"I do not!" Emily cried out. She started to gather her books back up, but I laid a hand on them.

"It's okay. He's dreamy. I understand." I glanced back over, but sighed in disgust.

He just sat there at the computer. His hands didn't move on the keyboard. "Who is he?" I asked again, still watching the back of his head.

He sat rigidly.

"Luke Roane," Emily sighed. She'd be mortified at how dreamy it sounded.

"Roane?" I arched my eyebrows.

What kind of name was that? I'd heard of a Roane back home, but the name was only spoken about as a legend. Most of the vamps didn't believe he existed. I didn't like this new twist. My college life wasn't supposed to deal with supernatural things like this. I wanted an Adam in my life, not a vampire named Roane.

"He's really intelligent." Emily had opened her floodgates. Now her opinions flew freely. "He cares about the world and he's got some super insights into humanity."

I bet he did.

"Even Professor Sulls asks his opinions on matters. Luke's like no other guy that I know. I mean, I respect him. I have really high standards and I only respect two other guys," she said, casually.

"I know." I said dryly, "Jesus and Martin Luther King Jr."

"Can you believe it?" Emily sighed again. She was on the fast track for her first college lovecrush. It was my little name for those crushes when a girl thinks she's in love. They were annoying... to everybody.

Lovecrushes aside—or maybe front and center—I hadn't moved my eyes off Roane's back, but then my eyes slid past his shoulders to his black computer screen. I found myself staring smack head-on with him. I gasped in mortification. He'd been staring right at me the whole time. This was not good, not at all. He knew that I knew. I knew that he knew I knew. I could've pretended that I didn't know he was listening to us, but now all bets were off.

He'd seen.

I smiled smugly and whispered, "I know what you are."

His face didn't move. His eyes didn't react, but I knew I'd made him angry.

2
—————

I called my empath sponsor and planned to meet her for coffee. When I pushed through the glass doors of Coffee Java, I inhaled the freshly brewed aroma and felt like I'd just touched a piece of heaven.

Blue looked up and waved an arm from a back booth tucked into the corner with bookcases and empty tables surrounding it. I liked how private it was. Blue got her name for her graying hair that she dyed with blue highlights. She liked that it gave her an out-of-this-world quality although she was very much an earthly woman. Every one of the bracelets jangling on her wrist stood for a cause – pollution, cancer, save the forests, happiness from an orgasm.

I smiled widely as I weaved my way through the book cases. "Blue-cheese, how are you?"

She laughed with her raspy deep-throated voice. "That never gets old." Nudging forward a coffee, she added, "Take it. You know it's for you."

I nabbed it and closed my eyes when the liquid touched my lips. It was so good, so yummy, and I knew I really *was* in heaven.

She closed the novel she'd been reading and pushed it to the side. She wasn't one for idle talk. "Okay, girl. Out with it."

"I have a problem."

She arched a perfectly outlined eyebrow and rested her chin on her hand.

"I have *vamp* problems," I said further.

Understanding dawned in her grey eyes. All empaths understood that statement. Sometimes we felt too much, but when we felt a vampire our senses went haywire from what *they* felt. "Are you still practicing your blocks?"

I nodded. I'd upped my level since I joined the hotline.

"That's good. Keep at it. Now, tell me about the vamp problem."

What could I say? "It's nothing really, but a feeling. He saw me in the library today with my roommate. I asked her about him and he heard the whole thing."

Blue frowned. Her purple lips rubbed together. "What's the problem? Vamps are used to that."

"I was watching him when I asked her about him. I didn't realize that he'd been watching the entire time."

"What do you mean 'watching'?" She narrowed her eyes.

"He knew that I knew what he was. It was like a challenge or something. I didn't like it."

"Oh, girl." Blue frowned deeply this time. "What'd you do?"

I took a sip of my coffee, but the flavor didn't taste heavenly anymore.

"Girl."

"I might've said something like 'I know what you are' ...or something."

She pursed those purple lips together and reached for her coffee. I felt her disapproval coming at me in waves. "You did what?"

"I couldn't help it, alright? It was like he was challenging me or something."

Blue sat her coffee down and leaned forward in a matronly way. "You know better, Davina. You have issues with vampires. We all do, but you've got more. You gotta fight that. Now what's gonna happen? You know vampires. They love challenges. He's going to be all over you now. *Then* what? How are you going to get away?"

In a small voice, I murmured, "I could always do what I did before."

Blue let out a disgusted sound and rolled her eyes. "I would not recommend lighting a vampire on fire. It didn't help you back home. It won't help you this time. Learn from your mistakes, child."

My back stiffened at that. I hated being called Davina and I *really* hated being called 'child'. "You know, maybe moving here and having you so close isn't all that great."

"I'm being your sponsor. You know the steps. If you've got vamp problems, you've done step one. You've told me. Good job, but you need to be held accountable for the next step. Which is?"

She knew I knew it, but I cringed when I had to say it. "I have to attend an empath meeting."

"And?"

"And—" This was so freaking hard. "—I have to tell the group."

"About?"

I growled deep in my throat. "I have to tell them about Craig and how I lit him on fire because he was stalking me."

Pride gleamed from Blue and she smiled blindingly. "That's my girl. You know the deal. Vampires have their twisted thing for us. The good ones avoid us out of respect and the bad ones—you know more than most."

I swallowed tightly. Craig had reveled in my torment. He'd become obsessed with me. He stalked me and he loved that I couldn't block him. Vampires were overpowering, much more so than humans. An empath could easily block humans at a level four, but it wasn't until level six that we could easily block vampires. Craig met me when I was on level five. Luckily, the night that I'd snapped and lit him on fire was the night that I broke to level six. I remembered that night. I saw him on fire and I remembered the pain that engulfed him while I stood back to watch.

"Girl." Blue's calming voice brought me back. She had opened herself up and I could feel some of the pain taken from me.

"Don't do that," I murmured huskily. I didn't want her to feel my pain. No one should be burdened with that.

She reached over and placed a hand on mine. It instantly calmed me and I turned my palm upwards to link our fingers. Blue smiled gently. "There's a reason why we're empaths, Davy. You know that. I like to help a little bit, every now and then."

'Every now and then' was the empath community's motto. We all learned that we could help every now and then, but not too much to kill ourselves. Too many had died because they tried to help too much.

"Now," Blue squeezed my hand. "What are you going to do with your current vampire?"

"Oh." I took a deep breath. "I don't know. I'll have to see what kind of vampire he is. He might be one of the good ones."

Blue twisted her lips in disbelief.

"I mean, he seems to be one of the student vampires." The chances were fifty-fifty. The bad ones pretended to be college students to hunt.

"There's a meeting next week. You should go."

I'd have to go — it'd be good for me.

"So, tell me about your crazy uptight roommate." Blue's eyes rekindled with gentleness. She knew I needed a lighter topic. The 'Craig topic' was deep enough for me. So I sat back and entertained her with Emily stories. By the end of our meeting, I hadn't said a word about the suicidal girl. I knew I should have, but I was still uneasy thinking about it. Some things were too hard or too scary to put into words.

When I returned to campus that evening, I faltered as I got out of my car. The air was chilled, but there was something else, something supernatural in it. Looking over my shoulder I only saw a parking lot full of cars. There was a clump of trees at the north end of the lot, but I'd go south to my dorm. I held my breath as I walked underneath two tall oaks and an arched overhang that led into the quad of my dorm.

Throwing my bag over my shoulder, I marched forward. No shadows moved and none seemed to watch me in return. I breathed easier when I neared the main doors. Once inside, excited voices came from the television room.

We were allowed boy visitors, but a lot of girls used the lounges for their study groups. It wasn't unusual to look inside to see books and papers sprawled across the beige carpeting right alongside sleeping students. This is what I saw as I peeked inside, but I wasn't ready for the sight of my roommate in a corner chair with a wistful smile on her face. She glowed.

I was floored. There was no Roane. There was no professor. There were no school books and yet, Emily glowed. Her straight blonde hair fell freely over her shoulders and she even had a tint of lip gloss on.

Had we all gone to hell and I missed the bus?

Then I felt the cold flare inside again. I felt him behind me before I looked, but when I did I found myself staring into the blackest coal eyes that I'd ever seen. Craig had looked at me with those same eyes the night he died. I shivered at the memory.

Luke Roane saw the tremor. His eyes raked me up and down and it was like we were caught in a heated debate, but there were no words. It wasn't my first vampire face-off, but this was different than the others.

I should've been able to easily block this vamp, but I felt the curtain slowly lift and I couldn't do anything about it. I always felt their cold, but usually it was just a tickle. This time I felt the full blast of his darkness. It worked its way up my feet to my legs, past my knees, and over my waist. I fought it off, but it kept coming. The evil started to wrap itself around me. I felt its tentacles grasp my arms and start to squeeze me tight.

All the while, he watched me with no emotion.

Not me. I couldn't hide my struggle. My teeth started chattering. When I felt the first poke in my chest, I shoved past him and hurried to my room. After I burst through the door to my room, the spell lessened immediately, but I was panting to catch my breath.

I heard my phone start to ring and knew it was Blue. She'd be the first to feel my panic. At that moment, I hated the lack of privacy with empaths.

I ignored the phone and slid down the door to breathe in and out.

I'd felt evil before. I'd felt it from Craig many times, but not to this extent. I'd never felt like it wanted to squeeze the life out of me, have it wrapped around my heart. It felt like it wanted my soul.

I shuddered again. I needed warmth. I needed a distraction. Hell, I could use this to my advantage.

I pulled out my phone and dialed Adam's number since I'd programmed it in the first day when we'd gotten the Hotline Volunteer Directory.

Adam picked up on the second ring. "Hello?"

I purposely didn't fight the slight tremor in my voice. "Adam?"

"Davina? Are you okay?"

"Yeah, yeah, I mean—I think—"

"What's wrong? Did something happen? Do you need to talk?"

"I..." I sighed to myself. I needed to be honest. It was Blue's motto. I was about to use this boy, but I liked him. He was normal. He was human. My hands tightened around the phone. "Can you come over?"

His answer was swift. "I'll be there in ten minutes."

"Thanks, Adam." I hung up and fell back against the door. And the strange thing, I really was thankful.

When I heard a knock at the door, I screamed and shot to my feet. I knew who was on the other side, although I couldn't feel him. "Go away." I flinched when I heard my voice. It was raw and vulnerable. *I* was raw and vulnerable.

He knocked again, but slower this time. I snorted. Really?! Did he think it would be more dramatic that way?

"Go away!" I yelled this time. I wasn't scared of vamps. I was just scared of *this* vamp. The door seemed large and luminous. I watched as it seemed to grow before me. It was like it was just waiting for me to answer it.

I don't know how long I stood there.

"Davina? It's me." I jumped when I heard another abrupt knock, but relaxed instantly. It was Adam. A whole host of relief, warm fuzzies, and other feelings rushed through me at the sound of his voice. Nice and normal.

Flinging open the door, I launched myself at him. He even smelled normal. If I knew I wouldn't scare him away, I would've wrapped my legs around his waist. "I am so glad you're here," I jumbled out with my nose pressed into his masculine-smelling sweater.

Adam laughed, caught off guard, and held me up. "I'm glad that you're glad."

Right. Human. I needed to act human. I unglued myself and pulled back. "Sorry. I...uh...sorry. I'm just..." I felt stupid.

"Emotional," Adam offered.

He was awesome.

"That's okay. Mr. Moser said it's good to let yourself feel. Let it flow naturally, Davina. Really. That's the only way you can start healing." Adam enfolded me tighter and tucked his chin in the crook of my neck. "Let it out, Davina. Let it out."

His blue sweater felt warm against my skin. He smelled of pine trees and musk. I inhaled deeper and smelled a little vanilla in there too. This is what it would be like if we were boyfriend and girlfriend. I might need him. He'd come to hug me and the world would melt away.

"Ahem."

We turned to see Emily glaring at us with her arms crossed and annoyed.

"What?" I was having a moment.

She rolled her eyes. "You have a visitor downstairs."

"Who?"

Emily shrugged impatiently and pushed past us to her closet. She flung open the door and grabbed a brush. As she combed her hair and reached for some lipstick, she remarked, "Some girl who looks like a stripper."

That could have been anyone according to Emily's standards. "She didn't give a name?"

"What am I—your receptionist?" Emily gave me a disgusted look, slammed her closet door shut, and stormed past me. Adam whistled underneath his breath.

I didn't know why Emily was so pissed, and at that moment I didn't care. She'd go back down, make crooning noises with the vampire, and be her oddly gushing self in a moment. I had three things on my mind: visitor, vampire, and Adam.

"I guess the news got out, huh?" Adam stuffed his hands into his front pockets, which made him look leaner and taller. The soft shadow from our poorly lit dorm room seemed to soften his features and his blue eyes looked adorable. My tongue might've just fallen out.

Then I heard what he said. "Wait. What news?"

"The girl that jumped – it's all over the news."

That didn't bode well with me. "Uh." I ran a hand through my hair and cringed. My hair must've looked like a bird's nest.

"You look fine," Adam reassured me.

"Thanks." I still turned and found a mirror. Not bad. My normally frizzy hair actually looked shiny and healthy. Wonders never ceased.

"So I guess...your visitor, huh?"

"Want to walk down with me? Make sure it's not someone creepy?"

Adam looked relieved and concerned at the same time. I chose to think he was concerned for my benefit. When we reached the stairway, I was surprised when I felt Adam grab my hand. He looked embarrassed. "Just in case it's someone you don't want around."

"You're going to play my protective boyfriend?" I teased.

His cheeks turned pink. Adorable. I squeezed his hand and said in all honesty,

"Thanks, Adam. It means a lot."

When we moved through the bottom doorway, I stopped dead in my tracks. My focus zoomed in on the petite blonde who had wrapped herself around Emily's vampire. One of her leather clad legs rubbed up and down against his calf and her cleavage was barely hidden underneath a tight black lace tank top poised perfectly for his viewing pleasure. Her crystal blue eyes snapped up and latched onto mine.

I knew why Emily was so furious.

Kates Heath, a childhood *nostalge*— another one of my words that I used to describe childhood friends that you remained friends with because of nostalgic memories and nothing else — was the epitome of every man and boy's fantasy of a bad girl. Vampires ate girls like her for breakfast or they would if they could.

"Heya, celebrity," Kates drawled in her husky voice and whipped her dusky blonde hair around.

"Kates." I refused to look the vampire in the eyes.

Slowly, with hypnotizing grace, Kates unwrapped herself from him and stood to cross the room towards me. I felt the tension in the air. The entire room had been watching and now everyone held their breaths at our next move.

I flicked my gaze to Emily. She looked like a bomb ready to explode so I latched onto Kates' arm and yanked her behind me. Dragging her outside, we circled around the corner and through an alcove of trees in the far corner before I whirled and snapped, "What are you doing here?"

Kates looked taken aback, but her smoky laugh rang out. "I can't believe you. Look at you. You're all College Barbie."

"What are you doing here, Kates? You're not supposed to be here."

Kates chuckled. "You're too much sometimes, Davy. Get over it. You know exactly why I'm here."

"No. I don't."

She groaned and placed her hands on her hips. "Steven saw you on the news. He called me and I headed here. You're on the freaking news, Davy. You know how bad that is for you."

"Nine o'clock news. That was a half hour ago. There is no way that you drove from home in thirty minutes." We lived five hours away.

"It was on the five o'clock news, Barbie Doll."

Did it even matter? "You can't be here," I hissed.

Kates smiled smugly and shifted comfortably back on her heels. "You've got me, whether you want me or not. Who's the hottie vampire, by the way? He's delicious."

I grimaced, but warned, "Stay away from him."

"Why?"

"What do you mean 'why'? He's a vampire."

Kates shrugged. "He's hot. I caught a peek at his marking. He's a Hunter."

"Kates." I shook my head, and sighed. Nothing was going how it was supposed to. I didn't even know what to think about him being a Hunter.

"What?" Kates piped up, dumbfounded. "Look. I'm just here to watch your back. When I think you're covered, I'll head out. Promise."

"I don't need this. I can't."

"You were on the news. They talked about that suicidal girl and that someone from the hotline was there. They didn't say your name, but it won't matter. They're going to get calls from people wanting their five minutes of fame. It's only a matter of time before you're hunted down. Let's hope that no one finds out about your special gifts."

Kates was right. Things were going to get bad, really bad. Here I was, concerned about Emily's vampire and Shelly Witless. This reminded me— "Adam is mine."

"Ooh—who's Adam?"

"None of your business." I was adamant.

"It might become my business. I'm bunking with you until it all blows over."

Oh no.

3

___

The next morning, I opened my eyes and instantly groaned. When Kates and I had returned to the dorm last night, I'd been ecstatic to find the vampire gone, but disappointed to find Adam gone too However, Emily *had not* been happy to meet our newest roommate. Kates ate it up. She loved causing drama and I could see that Emily was her newest target.

I woke Kates up and made her promise to play nice, which she did with a gleam in her eyes.

Later, when I let myself in my dorm room, I knew Kates had found a loophole. Emily jumped on me and crowded me against the door. "She has to go! Now."

"What? I don't—" Although, I could guess.

Emily shot up a hand. "Or I'm calling the cops on her."

Sadly, I wasn't surprised. This was just how Kates got her jollies. "What'd she do?"

"What'd she do? What didn't she do?!" Emily laughed in outrage. She crossed her arms and I almost saw a cloud of smoke puff out of her ears.

Kates sauntered in with a towel and a thong dangling from her hand. A coy smile was outlined by ruby red lips. "Heya, you're back."

I moved Emily aside and hung up my bag. "I'm tired. I'm hungry. And," I looked at Emily. "I'll deal with Kates later."

A look of disgust flashed over her face before she harrumphed once and left.

"So... how many vamps did you see? I've seen fourteen and I haven't left this building."

"Uh huh." When I sat down, I didn't want to deal with vamps, my roommate, or my nostalge.

Kates dropped into Emily's chair beside me. "I want to know what's going on with the vampire population. I've been to colleges before. I've been to *this* college before and I remember seeing four, not fourteen."

"So what?" I sighed as I glanced at the message machine. Twenty-three messages. Apparently, the word got out that I'd been on that roof. "What am I supposed to do?"

Kates threw a toned leg on the desk. "It's weird that you're famous. I would love to be famous, but not you. We all know your deal—"

"Emily doesn't," I intervened quickly.

"Really? She doesn't know? No wonder she's pissy at me. I know something she doesn't and she knows it. Anyways, let's hope the reporters don't find out you think of yourself as an empath."

"I am."

"They won't think that." She waved it off. "They'll paint you as some psycho and you'll be blamed for that girl jumping. So the question is how long can you avoid them? Or is that going to make them hungrier?"

Everyone in the psychic community had grown up with strict guidelines on how to handle possible exposure. Some followed and some didn't. The ones that the media reported on, they either didn't care or they wanted their moment of fame. I could handle the media.

"Why so many vampires?" I wondered out loud instead. I didn't want to discuss my current celebrity status.

Kates shrugged and stood up. She dropped the towel and bent

over to look through my closet. I was relieved to see that she wasn't naked. "I know you're all demure when you're around me, but you have some rocking clothes. Like this one!" She produced a pair of black leather pants.

"That's for a Halloween costume." Not really. They were for Adam. The when and where was still up to debate.

Kates snorted and slipped the pants on. She chose a near-see-through cream colored shirt. "I think we should go and 'interview' that hottie from last night."

"No, we won't."

Kates heard the emotion and whipped around. Her crystal blue eyes pierced straight through me. "Out with it. Now."

"I don't like him. That's all you need to know."

"Right, because the last time you slammed this wall between us things were just *peachy* then too."

I glowered. "There was a reason I wasn't feeling so friendly towards you. You were dating the guy that I was daydreaming about. I'd be stupid to have trusted you back then."

She flipped her blonde hair over her shoulder. "I only dated him because that bitch told me you were into Chris. I thought *you* were the backstabbing whore." That bitch would never be named. She'd driven a wedge between two best friends and she'd paid for her crimes, but we were still bitter.

I stood slowly. "We both know that I wasn't into Chris."

"I know now."

"Yes, you do."

Kates snorted in disgust. "I really hate her for what she did."

Warily, I looked at the blinking voice messages. "Food? Or drink?"

Kates snorted again. "Do you have to ask?"

Kates and I always had fun on our night outs. Sometimes that was the only time we had fun. A flood of memories rushed through me and I turned to snatch my fake license. For the night I'd be Silvia Dellawoy, a ripe twenty-two year old from Hillsfield, Illinois. I just hoped that I wouldn't meet a bouncer from Hillsfield, Illinois. "Let's go, Tammy."

Kates laughed huskily as she reached for the door. "Oh honey. You might not like that vampire, but I know a place where the were-wolves hang out. You'll love them."

Did Kates know me or what? I loved werewolves. They worked so hard at suppressing their own urges I didn't have to block them. They blocked themselves.

"But you're changing clothes," Kate announced and scoured my closet to pull out a pair of blue jean tights with a sparkly low cut v-neck top. I eyed the clothes, but knew it was a lost battle. Kates always had her way and it had been a long time since I'd let my hair down, not literally though.

When we left the dorm, I made sure we took the back stairway. It was easier and no one needed to stare from the front television lounge, no one that we wanted. Kates reached for the exit door, but paused when the bottom door opened. I heard a familiar tap of heels on the stairs and cringed. That's when Emily rounded the stairs and blinked in surprise at the sight of us. She carried a steaming bowl of oatmeal in her hands. I saw her stiffen.

We were dressed for a nightclub, a top notch nightclub, and Emily was dressed for oatmeal. She wore a pair of flannel pajama pants with a baggy sweatshirt and rabbit slippers. The white ears drooped over and touched the floor.

"We're... uh..."

"We're going out." Kates smiled and looped her elbow through mine.

I felt like we were the popular beautiful girls as we stared down one of the unpopular, dowdy girls. I hated it.

Removing my elbow, I smiled nervously. "You want to come with us?" I didn't want to be one of those girls. I liked oatmeal too. Kates gasped. Emily was floored. I insisted, "You must. Kates will even do your hair!"

Kates snorted abruptly.

"Okay." Emily didn't sound too sure.

As all three of us slowly traipsed back to the room, I only hoped that Emily wouldn't realize we were going to a werewolf bar. If she did, holy crap.

When we got out of the car, much later, outside the local were-wolf bar, I glanced at Emily as she smoothed her pressed shirt down and nervously checked the rest of her clothes. She looked uncom-fortable. Kates had wound Emily's hair into a braid that wove around her head. With the make-up job Kates provided, Emily looked a little hip hop, but she held strong with the clothes. We wanted her to wear a pair of tattered tight blue jeans and a loose-fitting pink and silver tank top, but Emily was adamant. She wore khaki pants with a buttoned-down pressed pink shirt. She looked like a librarian with costume make-up.

She would stick out like blood to sharks. Luckily, we weren't going to a vampire bar. They would've been all over her. Werewolves stuck to their own kind and they looked human. It was only when their fur started to grow that a human would freak out. I hoped our night would not end with a freaking Emily.

"Okay. Let's go!" Kates yanked me forward. Emily followed at a sedate pace, but when I looked over my shoulder I saw she was biting her lip. She was warily eyeing the bar's sign and I felt her nervousness. It pounded me like hail.

Once inside, Kates dragged us to get drinks, but Emily hung back. Three shots were ordered and when Kates tried to give one to Emily, it was declined. Then I saw the evil delight turn my way. She pushed the shot at me and I downed two right away. I wasn't even going to fight Kates. I needed to save my energy for Emily. Someone would have to make sure she didn't end up dead. Not Kates, she laughed in delight and turned to order another four shots.

We were in for a rough night.

Then I looked over Emily's shoulder and gulped when I saw a muscular guy with blonde dreadlocks lick his lips as he eyed Emily's backside. Blood to sharks. He nudged his buddy and both of them turned to lap her up. Then their eyes slid to mine and I sucked in my breath horrified. We weren't at a werewolf bar. Bud's was a vampire bar.

I grabbed Kates.

"Hey! Watch the beer!" I saw the brimming pitcher and felt the cool liquid splash on my arm, but I was infuriated. I could give a damn about beer and I don't normally think blasphemous thoughts like that.

Beer was holy.

"I have to talk to you. Alone."

Kates saw my fury. I realized that she'd known the whole time.

"What's going on?" Emily spoke up.

"Nothing. I have to go to the bathroom."

"Oh. I have to go too," Emily gushed out, relieved.

"No!" I barked. I saw that Emily was taken aback so I gentled my tone, "I meant alone."

"Oh. Okay."

"We'll be back," I hurried out and yanked Kates behind me.

"But, alone?"

Storming off and dragging Kates with me, I roughly pushed our way through the crowd. I felt each of them when my arms or shoulders made contact, but I just gritted my teeth against the pain. Vampires felt too much hatred for me. I should've been able to automatically block them, but I was angry. Plus, I hadn't been prepared.

An entire bar of vampires was not my night of fun.

When I pushed into the bathroom, I saw two vamp girls at the mirror. "Get out! Now."

They turned, annoyed, and stopped short. One of them gasped, but the other looked like she was going to argue before the other dragged her outside. I knew that I should've cared about what I'd just seen since vamps don't follow orders unless there was a reason, but I didn't.

Flipping the lock, I rounded on Kates. "How could you?!"

She rolled her eyes and approached the mirror. As she primped her hair, she shrugged. "You have to get over this hang-up with vamps, Davy."

"Hey," I pointed a finger at her. "You should have just as much of a hang-up with them. I mean—"

Kates rounded and stared at me. I saw the warning, but I didn't heed it. "Your mother used to kill vampires. We all know what they did to her."

"You don't talk about that. Ever!" Kates seethed.

"They branded you—"

"Shut up!"

"I know your mom was a slayer, but they slaughtered her, Kates. How can you be okay coming here?"

Kates slapped me. I fell against the wall and tasted blood on the inside of my cheek, but I rounded back and exclaimed, "You had no right bringing me here. You *really* had no right bringing Emily."

Oh god. I gulped. Emily had been left alone. Throwing open the door, I hurled myself through the crowd. I know that I jarred a bunch of them, but I didn't care. I just needed to find my roommate and get out of there. We were like sitting ducks in Dodge.

Then I stopped in my tracks and my mouth fell to the floor. Emily sat, squashed in a booth, with three vampires around her and at the end sat her Luke Roane vampire. He looked relaxed, lounging back in the booth, but I saw the way his eyes darted over his men and Emily. He didn't share in the conversation, but he was in control of it. They glanced at him occasionally, like they were waiting for a signal from him to change the subject.

He didn't. He looked content and yet, he still looked like the predator he was even though he dressed like a normal college student with tight-fitting shirts and trendy blue jeans. He wore a black shirt that molded to his lean form.

I could tell Emily was miffed that she didn't sit beside him, but she was still all smiles. Vomit came up in the back of my throat, but I swallowed it back down. He didn't deserve her gushy fuzzies.

"That's why I brought you here." Kates paused behind me. "He's a Hunter, Davy. You know what they do. You want to know why all those vampires are on campus, ask him."

I watched how the vampires instinctually felt Kates' approach.

They all looked up with eager eyes, but not him. He turned and looked straight at me. I met his gaze without a flinch, even though I felt my insides snap. I had to hold it in, he couldn't know. Then I glanced to his collarbone where a corner of his shirt had fallen to the side and saw the beginning of his mark.

I didn't need to see all of it because I'd seen it before. It was the mark that all Hunters were branded with once they'd gotten their first kill. It was a symbol of interlocking crosses with the Hebrew inscription for remembrance in the middle. Craig told me once that the symbol stood for their humanity. They were branded to remember what it was like to be human, so they could keep a reverence for the humans that they'd sworn to protect. The Hunters were an elite league and a vampire had to be invited by the Elders. Only a handful roamed and guarded each state.

As I watched Emily's smile slip at Kates' arrival, I knew that they were both safe. Hunters guarded against the Craigs of the vampire world. They hunted their own, the ones that refused to accept the new decree not to harm humans. Two Hunters had arrived and ripped Craig to shreds with no jury or bargain when I'd lit him on fire. They were judges in themselves and those two Hunters had made their judgment on Craig.

Suddenly feeling nauseous, I pushed through the crowd to a side door and found myself in a back alley.

The door hadn't closed behind me before I heard him. "You're running away."

He leaned against the door, relaxed and primed for attack. His fangs didn't show, but I wondered if he'd had them ready for me. Something told me this vampire wouldn't mind violating his decree with me.

"You're using my friend." I thought I caught a flash of amusement, but it disappeared just as quick.

He remarked, emotionless, "They're using me."

Kates was. Emily wasn't.

'You're not good with your own shield.' I heard him in my mind and gasped before I shoved him out. I was more irritated he'd gotten in

without me realizing because I was better than that. He smiled and I bared my teeth. "You don't get to read my mind."

"Not anymore. You just blocked me," he spoke, bored, and had the nerve to stretch in front of me.

"You're an asshole." He was getting harder to block, not from my mind but from feeling him. Though, it wasn't like the last time. I didn't feel the evil reach inside of me.

He laughed, but his eyes were so cold. "You've never spoken to me and this is our first exchange? Oh wait, you taunted me, right? 'I know what you are.' Isn't that what you said or did I get it wrong? You think I'm some animal."

I lashed out, "Been taking trips in my mind?"

"I haven't needed to," he shot back. His eyes sparked a bit. "You read loud and clear. I'm surprised you've gotten away with it for so long."

I frowned. "What are you talking about?"

"Lying. All you do is lie. I've known about you for a couple of days, but I could tell right away."

"I don't lie." I reacted, tersely, and my hands formed tight fists.

He looked down at them, but he smirked. "Yes, you do. That's all you do. You lie to that boy you've got dancing to your tune. You lie to your roommate. She doesn't know who we are. You're lying to yourself when you think you don't want Kates here."

I stiffened at his proclamations. He had no idea. "Get away from me and stay away from my friends."

Something went flat in his eyes. The look had been there, but I hadn't seen it till it was gone. It vanished completely now and I knew he was furious. "Your friends won't stay away from me."

"How do you know Kates?" I asked. He'd mentioned her by name, which meant something. I remembered the two vampire females in the bathroom. They'd either known me or they'd known Kates. I needed to know why...

I suddenly felt sick. I felt actual vomit surge up in my throat, but I clamped a hand over my mouth and whirled to a corner. It spewed out before I could stop it. He was quiet behind me. I expected some taunting, but there were none.

"What?" I asked weakly as I wiped at my mouth. "No words to insult me with? Maybe I'm just drunk."

"You could be. You drank what? Four shots?"

So he'd been watching from the beginning...

"I highly doubt it." Something was off in his tone, like he knew something that I didn't. I wasn't pleased with it. I felt that he wasn't pleased either. That's when I gasped further and wretched again.

I had been feeling him. Somehow, I'd slipped inside without the evil lashing at me. As I glanced at him through watery eyes, I saw that his mind was elsewhere. He didn't know I felt inside of him. I took a small breath and stilled, concentrating to explore what else was in him. Duty. It blared at me. I was startled by that, but then I surged further and tentatively touched what was beneath it, pain. It was blistering. It reminded me of the girl on the roof. She'd felt the same pain, but unlike her surrender this vampire was firmly and completely devoted to something. He defied death or maybe death retreated from him. I'd never felt what I felt from him.

"Stop that!" He hurled me out of him.

I gasped and fell against the bricked wall. My arm scraped against the roughness and I watched, frozen, as his coal eyes took on a keen alarmed look. The air was charged around him. I sucked in a breath and smelled what he did. My skin had torn from the wall and even I could smell the blood in the alley.

"Are you an animal?" I whispered my challenge and waited for his response. It was like something inside of me had uttered those words, something that wasn't from me—and he knew it.

He blocked me. I shielded him. And yet—there was something else, some entity, that felt the other between us. Suddenly, it was too much and I gutted out, "Get away from me!" The connection was destroyed and I felt it reel inside of me.

"Gladly." Acid dripped from him and he was gone in the next second.

The door slammed behind him and I was left to gasp for breath at his abrupt exit. It was too much. His presence had been too much. Too many things swirled around inside of me, but I closed my eyes and concentrated on breathing. I remained there until I felt my feet beneath me, until I was able to stand and breathe at the same moment.

Then I remembered my question. He'd known about Kates, but I didn't know how. I needed to know for her safety.

4

______

I went back inside, but the moment I approached their booth Roane jerked his head towards the door. The other vampires stood and followed him. Kates frowned at the abrupt exit, but Emily gushed with a glazed look over her face.

She smiled at me with stars in her eyes. "Did you see him, Davy?"

I had more than seen him, but I wasn't about to share that with her. I asked Kates, "What happened to her? She looks drunk." There were no empty glasses in front of Emily.

"What do you think?"

Kates was still annoyed with me, but my stomach rumbled and I pressed a hand over it. I had worse things on my mind. With a closer look at Emily, I saw the glazed eyes, flushed lips, pink cheeks, and then I saw her neck. There was a small red mark over her artery. "What did they do?"

"What do you think?" Kates asked flatly, bored. Hell, she probably watched the whole time.

Vampires weren't supposed to feed off humans, but I knew a few of them used lovebites to sneak a taste. It was frowned upon by the Elders, but not strictly prohibited—especially when it happened in a bar. It was considered the same as making out to them.

"I'm bored," Kates announced.

Emily smiled, drunkenly. "Did you see him, Daveeena? He was here and then he was out there and now he went that way." She swung her hand towards the door and smiled sleepily.

"Maybe we should go."

Emily protested. "But... he's..."

"Not coming back, wino." Kates snorted and stood. She stretched and pretended to heave a big yawn—her boobs arched in the air.

I rolled my eyes. "Come on, Emily. I'll get you home."

Kates dropped her arms abruptly. "You had four shots. You can't drive anywhere."

"I'm fine. Really." I could've told her about the nausea, but she was mad. I wasn't feeling all friendly and soul-confessing.

Kates raked us up and down and then glanced over her shoulder. "I think I might stay. I'll give you a call."

Emily stumbled, but I caught her. Then I frowned even more when I saw her cheeks pale abruptly. Lovebites are just that—they're little nips. They don't take too much blood, but she was reacting as if they drank her empty.

"Did you drink?" It would explain a little.

"She had some beer. She'll be fine. Take her home, get her in bed. She'll be the same tomorrow."

I didn't bother to ask Kates how she'd get back. I knew she'd be fine or sleep somewhere else. She was still branded and a lot of vampires held a grudge. "Just, be safe."

"Yeah. Whatever."

"Seriously, Kates. Safe, not stupid, remember?"

"Yeah. I know," she grumbled and shoved through the crowd. I watched as she disappeared into the bathroom until Emily stumbled in the opposite direction. Someone caught her and pushed her ahead. I tried to grab her, but someone else bumped her further ahead. Pretty soon, I watched helplessly as Emily managed to fall out the front door backwards.

Talk about exits.

I darted through the crowd and found Emily on the wet sidewalk, ashen, and with mud on her khakis. If the girl could see herself, she'd be mortified. She looked like every other drunkard.

"Come on. Let's go."

I bent forward to help her stand. Fishing the keys out of her pocket, I guided her to the car and in the backseat. My inner empath alarm was going off when we drove off. There were an inappropriate number of vampires. My home town had a population of 2,000. Southdale wasn't big, but it wasn't a three hundred bump in the road. We averaged five or six vamps. Benshire was at least 12,000. That meant there should be around 200 hundred vamps around. I knew the vampire population would be significantly more compared to home, but as I drove past Bud's, I saw more than I should've trolling the streets and alleys.

Emily puffed out a snore and there was a speck of drool at the corner of her mouth. Of course. She'd be one of those slobbering drunks when she drank. Then I remembered the red mark. The vampire drank from her. That meant some of him was in her. It was a small bit, but it was something. My stomach rolled over on itself as I considered the possibilities.

Too many vampires. That girl had jumped from my building and eight vamps had been there. A Hunter was here and he looked like he was permanently staying. Something was going on.

No—forget it! I did not want to get involved with the local vampire political crap. They had their own community. As long as they stayed away from me..., but they hadn't stayed away from Emily. I was worried they wouldn't stay away from Kates. She'd been branded as a slayer's daughter. It was known that a vampire slayer's strength passes to her daughter at the slayer's death. The vamps hadn't hurt Kates then, but if they saw the burned mark in her skin they'd know that Kates had the strength of a slayer. She could handle her own, I knew that, but I knew that a lot of them still held resentment towards slayers of all kinds—the good and bad. If there was an overabundance of vampires in the area, which I was pretty sure there was, chances were good that some of those with chips on their fangs would be in town. If they ran into Kates, who knew what would happen.

I had to know. It was for Kates' safety.

Suddenly, I felt like I would vomit again. I pressed my arm over my stomach, but it didn't help. I felt the first gag and veered the car over to the edge. Bursting through the door, I upchucked my entire stomach contents on the side of the road. When I leaned back on my knees, I warily eyed three vamps in the alley. I waited, since I didn't know what they would do. If it came to it, I could probably obliterate a vampire just from my breath. It was rank.

"Davy?"

"Yeah?" I wiped my mouth and moved back to the seat.

Emily peered at me through foggy eyes, haphazard hair, and pasty white cheeks. Talking about vampires.

"Where'd you go?" She frowned, confused.

I held the steering wheel in my hands, but I needed a breath to settle my stomach. "Nowhere. You fell asleep."

She giggled. "Did you see him? He was there. He didn't talk to me, not really, but he was there. Am I pathetic? I think I need to do something. Maybe I could—what kind of girls do you think he likes? I bet he likes girls like your friend. She's a little skanky, sorry. I'm not able to stop what I'm saying before I say it. But she is."

"Don't worry, Ems. I know what you think about Kates, but there's more to her. Trust me. She's a good friend."

"Not to you." Emily poked the air with her thumb. Not her hand, her thumb. It was comical to watch.

Then I heard what she said. "What?"

Emily heaved a deep sigh and pressed her cheek against the window. "Yeah, yeah. You were somewhere and she wasn't saying nice things about you tonight. Said you were crazy, obsessive, and there were other words. I know there were other words."

"I wasn't really nice to her when we went to the bathroom."

"Don't matter." Emily was firm. She shook her head in a circle. "A friend is a friend, no matter what's been done between you. I know that much. I have some good friends. Of course, they'd never go to

Buds, but they're good friends. I don't like 'em sometimes, but still, I don't say bad things about 'em."

There was some merit in what she was saying. "What about when you just have to vent about something?"

"She ain't vented. Or, no. She didn't vent. That's it. She's seen me at my ugliest times. She's still around. Bethany Ann saw me one time with a green foliage mask on. That wasn't pretty."

"See." I flashed a grin. "You know exactly how I feel." Except what she had to say wasn't sitting well with me. It didn't feel good. None of it.

"Yep, yep." And she was back to sleep.

I heaved a sigh of relief. Emily drunk was almost as annoying as Emily sober. Turning back to the steering wheel, I pulled onto the road and it didn't take long before I saw the campus. When I parked the car, I considered how heavy my roommate was. She was a little taller than me, but my weight.

I could handle her.

Hefting her up the stairs a few minutes later, I regretted my decision. Her head hit not one, but two doorways. Then she hit our doorway. When I caught sight of the couch, I knew I'd never be so glad to see that paisley thing in my life. Grunting one last time, I dropped Emily on the couch. Then I shut the door and sat watching Emily sleep, weighing what I needed to do. There was no real question, though. Deep down, I knew Kates was in danger.

I rubbed my hands together and knelt on the ground by Emily. Then I closed my eyes and I reached out... I broke through Emily's first layer. It was sluggish, but that was no surprise. It was the booze, but immediately underneath was a swirl of emotion. Adrenaline. I felt excitement, passion, rigidity, and a firmness inside of her. All of it was jumbled together. Then I went further and I gasped silently.

I'd always known she had a black and white perspective on life, but she was harder on herself. I felt like I was being suffocated inside of her, but I pushed further down. That's when I was hit with a wall of pain. It was masked with jealousy and insecurity. A blast of emotions hurled at me and I could almost hear the snarl. They hit me like a downpour of sleet. When I caught onto them, the hatred was physically painful. I knew I sobbed, but I just held on. I couldn't do anything else.

Hatred. Evil. Turmoil.

The adrenaline was mixed with eagerness. I knew the feeling would haunt me, but I'd found what I was looking for. The vampire was in her. Taking my time, I waded through each strand. They were all entangled together. This vampire might've spent time with a Hunter, but he was cruel. I felt how much he loved to be cruel, but then again, a Hunter was sometimes the cruelest of them all. It made sense what company he'd keep.

I managed to search through each strand. Sometimes I just got a feeling. Sometimes I got a name. Other times, I got a place or a memory. Certain emotions centered on a specific time or memory with him. Then I got an image of his cruelty, a little girl. When I heard her defeated whimper, I shed some tears. The pictures, feelings, thoughts, memories—everything swirled together and then out of the middle the word 'slayer' lashed at me.

I bolted upright and jerked away from the couch. I was hurled out of Emily. Curling into a fetal position on the floor, I was helpless to stop the tears. They just trickled down. Some of it came from the vampire. Some from the little girl, but I knew the majority were from my own wounds.

I was bleeding and raw, but I needed to find Kates.

5

I tried to call Kates, but there was no answer. Then I thought about calling Blue, but before I could, my own phone rang. I slapped it against my ear and heard, "It is about time you called me!"

Blue sounded like she was at her wits' end.

"Girl, you need to tell me that I'm off-racket. Tell me that my senses are going sky-rocket into nomad's land. Tell me... tell me that I'm high and I've got a debt to the peyote drug lord. Please."

Blue knew better.

I sighed softly and murmured, "You should've blocked me."

"Oh, hell." Blue groaned. "How am I supposed to block you? You're mine."

She was my sponsor. It was a bond that we weren't supposed to impede, but situations could run amok and who knew where both of us would be. A person always hears how the 'team' is there for them, how it's all for one and one for all—it's literally true when you're empathic.

"I know," I sighed.

I could hear those wheels in Blue's head and I knew she was turning them rapidly.

She asked, "You said you were going to call me. What were you calling me for?"

"Can you feel someone for me? My old friend, Kates." I didn't need any other introduction. Kates was well known, by my sponsor and the rest of the empaths. When a vampire slayer is slaughtered, empaths feel and remember it for years.

"Oh girl," Blue whispered, brokenly. "Are you sure?"

"Yes." I sat up straighter. "I can't. I'm really weak right now."

"I will, but you have to promise me."

Oh God. I waited in dread because I already knew what she was going to say. She always harped about it.

"You have to go to the next Empath meeting with me."

"Fine." I'd figure a way out of it later.

Emily grunted a snore behind me. It sounded like a train warning of its arrival, but she flipped on her stomach and the snore was muffled by the couch. I groaned and sat up straight to stretch a little, but was distracted when I heard Blue humming. I cracked a grin. I'd forgotten she did that when she needed to search for her person.

Some empaths, the really skillful ones, could close their eyes and have the person immediately. Those were the best of the best. The rest of the upper middle class could do it, but much more slowly. Blue had told me that when she first trained for this skill, she learned by feeling every person, in every room, every building, down every street before she found her target. It sounded exhausting to me and completely ludicrous. For some reason, most of the empaths liked to have this skill. They liked working on their gift (curse—as I say) and expanding it. The curse can drive a person crazy if you're unable to shield and block others.

"Oh... oh... oh... OH..... oh..."

Blue was not having an orgasm.

"Oh..... uhhuh.... uhhuh..." This was followed by some grunts. "Ummmmm." Blue went back to her humming. "Oh, child. You're in some trouble, aren't you?" Then she said, "Davy, you need to help that girl."

"What'd you feel?" I felt a knot in my throat.

"You know that I can't tell you. What I felt within Kates is private and she chooses when to tell her friends, if she does. But I will tell you who you can call to help. She trusts him. I felt that and I already felt that she's told you."

I groaned. I already knew who she was going to say and then I heard my worst fear. "There's a Hunter in town. She trusts him. He can help you. He can help *her*."

"Why did I ask in the first place?" Holy man, I really hated that vampire.

Blue chuckled gravely. "The most gifted always search. It's an automatic radar, Davy. It continually scans without causing you the normal pain. But only the most gifted are able to do that."

I didn't need to hear that. I did not want to be one of the 'most gifted.' I couldn't keep the disbelief out of my voice. "Right."

"It's true. I haven't said anything because I'm aware of how you feel, but it's true. You are very gifted. What you can do… takes my breath away sometimes."

It took my breath away too—and not in the good way.

Emily moaned in her sleep, which was followed by another train arriving at the station. Okay, I needed to face facts. I couldn't do anything about my most cursed gift, but I could do something about Kates. "The Hunter, huh?"

"He's who you need to contact. Do you know how?"

Do I know how? I scoffed at that thought. There's always a few venues to search out a Hunter, but lucky for me—I had my roommate.

"Yeah. I'll be fine," I reassured her.

"Alright." I could sense her unease now. "I'll lower my shield to you so you can reach me if you get in trouble. I'll alert the community immediately."

That was not what we needed. If she alerted our community, the empathic community, then it might be war between the empaths and vampires.

"No, no. I'll be fine. I'll find the Hunter. We'll be fine."

"Okay. Well, I'll be feeling you." And Blue hung up with her slightly eerie parting.

After that, I needed to wake Emily. The idea was not appealing, but I reached forward and gently patted her shoulder. "Emily. Em."

Nothing.

"Hey!" I shoved her this time.

"What? Huh?" She blinked, dazed, and struggled to focus. "Davy?"

"Do you have Roane's phone number?" She just looked at me. I snapped my fingers in front of her face and I saw the fog separate.

"Huh?"

"Luke Roane."

"Luke? Is he here?" She started to sit up, but I pushed her back down.

"He's not, but I have to call him. Do you have his number?"

"Uh."

I saw the wheels turn slowly, but I knew she was starting to wonder why I'd need his number. And why I needed to call him. "Where's his number? I wanted to warn him about Kates. I think she might like him."

"It's in my cell phone." Her answer was predictably instant.

"And where's that?"

"My purse." She lifted her arm weakly and it dropped back down with a plop.

I saw that her arm was still through the pink purse straps. I hadn't even noticed when I carried her inside, but then again, I was a little distracted by carrying her entire body. After I snagged her phone from inside, I thumbed through the contacts and found him. It took four rings before I heard his abrupt greeting, "Who is this?"

My mouth was dry. "Emily's roommate."

"Who?"

He didn't remember my roommate? "You know, the one that your buddy bit tonight."

There was silence on the other end, long tense silence. "What do you mean?"

"I need your help. I think my friend is in danger."

"Who is this?"

Good God. "The empath!"

"Oh." He understood now. He was quiet for a moment, a long moment, and then he asked, "Your friend is in danger?"

"Yeah. I need your help."

"The slayer." He seemed to choose his words carefully.

"Kates. She's not the slayer."

"She has the powers of a slayer."

"There's a difference. She's not a slayer," I defended, heatedly. I shouldn't care this much, but being a slayer according to the new decree was illegal and it warranted instant death as punishment. The Hunters replaced the slayers. The slayer elders had agreed with the decree and so it was born.

Roane didn't respond to my argument. "Where are you?"

"At my dorm."

"With your roommate?"

"Yes." Why was this so confounding to him? "I got your number from her."

"From Emily?"

"Nevermind. Where do I meet you?"

There was silence again on his end.

"I can come to you," I cried impatiently into the phone. Why did he need to consider this? He was a Hunter. He had to help, didn't he? Although, truthfully, I wasn't sure what their job requirements were. I mostly just knew they hunted the bad vampires. I waited for a long breath and then he said abruptly, "I'll come to you. Don't leave your dorm."

He hung up immediately and Emily snored from the couch. Ignoring her, I programmed the vampire's phone number into my phone before I stood up—then I felt awkward. I didn't know what I was waiting for, but I sat at my desk and waited... and waited ...and waited some more. It'd been an hour before I growled to myself. I couldn't stay in the room any longer so I left and went downstairs to the lobby. Of course, when I got there I noticed two things. It was two in the morning and Shelly was wrapped around Adam in the television lounge.

6

I tried to slip outside, but no luck.

"Davina!" Adam called out, hurried, and did my ears detect a little bit of guilt? I was pretty sure they did.

"Hey," he called again and eagerly waved a hand.

Shelly unwound her tentacles around him, but one of her arms remained on his hip. It was intimate and I knew her smirk wasn't coincidental. They both looked dressed up, but Adam had on a sleek buttoned-down black shirt that looked like it'd been ironed. He always looked nice, but this was a pay grade above that. Shelly wore a leather shirt fastened together by one big pearl button underneath her breasts. It added cleavage. Lots of cleavage. The girl knew how to dress. Even Kates would've been appreciative.

"Hi, Davy." Shelly's ruby red lips formed a perfect, unfriendly, smile.

Adam was blind. He beamed. "Where are you going this evening?"

"More like morning, Adam." Shelly laughed and patted his arm.

If I were a vamp, my fangs would've already been out.

"Oh yeah. I didn't realize how late it was. We were just talking. Time must've gotten away from us both." Adam smiled nervously and shuffled on his feet.

He was uncomfortable. Good. He should be.

"Are you just going out?" Shelly asked this time. Her quick eyes skimmed me up and down. I wasn't exactly dressed for a nightclub, but I knew I looked alright. How could a person go wrong with black? And it was tight. Tight always seemed to be good with guys, though that wasn't why I wore it.

I opened my mouth, but closed it. I wasn't sure what to say. I couldn't tell them the truth, but I was a horrible liar.

Shelly's eyes smarted. She asked, quick on the prowl, "Do you have a date?"

"A date?" Adam sounded taken aback, but he tried to hide it.

Oh yeah, bucko. I have a life besides you. Wait. Was this what I wanted my future boyfriend to think? I wasn't sure.

"Davina."

I stiffened at that word and not because it was the name I started to loathe (no one can remember Davy), but because I was hit by the same cold blast as all the other times. It was followed by a host of shivers up and down my spine. Roane was able to make my name sound like a lover's caress and as I turned to look at him, the way he strolled towards us, he looked like the perfect bad boy lover that all the good girls obsessed about. Plus, the whole supernatural predator thing molded to his form perfectly. He dressed like me all in black, but he ventured into leather land. He wore a black tee shirt over a pair of black leather pants. I never noticed how high his cheeks were, the angles seemed sharper and I realized it was because he had nearly shaved all of his hair off. He now sported a clean buzz cut and it made him look even more dangerous. I understood why Emily had a thing for him, but then again all vampires had an unnatural sex appeal.

Judging by Shelly and Adam's reactions, both were aware of it. Adam seemed to stand taller while Shelly's mouth could've dropped to the ground from her drool. Her eyes quickly darted back and forth from Roane to me. "Is this your date?"

I sucked in my breath as I waited for Roane's response, but to my surprise there was none. I twisted back, prepared to see fury or something in those emotionless coal black eyes, but there was no reaction. He watched me steadily. So I gulped again and opened my mouth, but as I met Adam's uncertain eyes I closed it with a snap. I had no idea what to say. If I said it wasn't a date, they might ask where we were headed and then what? I couldn't tell the truth. These two didn't know about that world and I didn't want them to know. Anyone who got involved with that world got hurt.

So I lied through my teeth and my fingernails cut into my palms, "Yes. It's a date."

Something slammed in Adam's eyes and I felt effectively shut out.

Shelly's smile lit up, but there was a calculating sheen there. I didn't know how I felt about that, but I wanted to know exactly what she felt. I really, really wanted to know and before I realized it, I was already inside of her. Whoa—talk about multi-layered. The girl had it all, but the top emotion was selfishness. She wanted Adam, much more than me. Underneath that, she wanted to have sex with Roane, really badly and I even felt some of her calculation how to make that happen. She planned—no! I blinked, shaken, as I ripped myself out.

Shelly had plastered a fake smile on as she oozed, "...wonderful place. I highly recommend it. Right, Davina?"

I was a little mortified to realize that they'd had an entire conversation. "Yes. Exactly, but maybe not." I learned long ago to always be vague when someone catches you at something. It never mattered what, just be vague. I'd never gone wrong yet and Shelly immediately supplied my question.

"The Shoilster. It's a great club, right? Your friend said that's where you're going."

The Shoilster? That place was awful. The booths were plastic and cheap. The food looked decadent, but tasted like fish. All of it tasted like fish. Shelly was crazy. I smiled politely. "Well yes, it's wonderful at times, but not all the time. And really, we might not even go there."

"Oh. I thought." Her eyes jumped to Roane, but to my shock, Shelly didn't say a thing.

When I turned, I saw that Roane stared long and hard at her and I recognized that look. They did that when they wanted the other person to shut up. Craig had turned that look on me enough times. I couldn't tell him to stop, not with Adam there, but I needed to do something. I might really hate Shelly, but even my enemy didn't deserve to be on the other end of one of those stares. They just held a person immobile, like their thoughts were frozen in time. In my opinion, it violated their right and so I did the only thing that I could. I violated Roane's right to privacy. I narrowed my eyes and I pushed through his shields. He had a lot of them, too many, but I got through and I read the first emotion. He was annoyed and exasperated, but I didn't think it was with me or Shelly. I pushed further and found the same fierce determination to stand and stare death down.

I blinked, belatedly, and wondered where he got his motivation from. It might come in handy with a new diet I might need.

I shook my head slightly and pushed even more.

Vampires were a mass of swirling emotion. I'd been in enough to get a general feel, but this felt different. There was something. I couldn't put my finger on it, but there was something different inside of him. He ran by a different set of codes than the others. I felt that and in that moment, I understood why he was the one to call. Blue hadn't said it, not directly, but Kates respected this one. There was a reason. Then I felt a cold firm hand grasp my arm and I was wrenched out of him, physically and mentally. I gasped and blinked back abrupt tears—it happened sometimes when an empath was too deep. Then I looked up into Roane's coal eyes.

He was furious. He'd been unemotional before, but he let me see that fury free and clear now. I gulped and my hand clamped onto his hand. Intending to try and yank his hold free, I couldn't. I just wrapped my fingers around his arm. He was stronger than me. He wasn't moving and I couldn't make him move. We were deadlocked and then he said tersely, underneath his breath, "Stay. Out."

"Davina?" Adam called from a distance. He was five feet away. I was the one far far away, still locked in a battle of wills with the vampire. "Davina!" Adam called again, more insistent this time.

Roane held my gaze captive. He held a dark promise in his if I didn't adhere to his warning. Well—two could play at that game. "Then don't use your eye radar thing on my friends."

He blinked slowly and released my arm, but it felt like some force still held me close. If he moved his arm an inch we would've been in an embrace. He murmured, almost sensually, "She's not your friend."

"I know that. It doesn't matter. You don't do it."

His eyes judged me, like he wanted to call me a liar. "Fine. It's your back for her knife." Then he moved back, just an inch, and I felt like I could breathe.

"Davina!" Adam called again.

When I looked at Adam, I think my heart stopped. He looked utterly and completely concerned for my welfare. Shelly looked pissed off with her arms folded. Her eyes darted from Roane, to myself, and then to Adam.

"Hey." Adam gentled his tone, but he stepped forward and touched my arm. "Are you okay?" He raised cautious eyes to Roane and quieted his tone. Little did he know that there was a vampire five feet away. "That didn't look friendly. You know?"

"I'm fine." I patted his arm reassuringly. "I promise. That was just a little misunderstanding."

Roane snorted behind me.

"So, you guys are going to the Shoilster? I haven't been there. I'd like to come!" Adam exclaimed suddenly and a little bit shrilly.

"What?" Shelly was startled, but she recovered instantly. She linked her elbow through his and turned a charming smile towards us. "I mean, that'd be great. Let's go. It could be, like, a double date?"

"A double date?" Adam asked, confused, as he shook his head. "No. We'd just be hanging out, right?"

I sent Roane a helpless look, but he just smiled tightly and turned his back. Bastard vampire. "Okay, but I don't know. I think. I guess, I—um—we could go for a little while?"

"Great." Shelly was all for it.

"Great." I echoed Shelly's sentiments and surprised both of us when I slammed a hand on Roane's (very) chiseled chest. We both jumped under the contact, but I gritted my teeth and grabbed his hand.

"We'll meet you there."

"Uh," Adam muttered.

Shelly locked her hands with his. "We'll meet you there! Sounds like a plan."

They were out the door before I could blink, literally. Once they were gone, it was just me and Roane. I gulped painfully. My hand was still on his chest and I felt him laughing. "What?" I turned, dazed, when I saw an actual smile on his face.

I think I just wet my pants. "Stop!"

Roane just laughed harder and shook his head. Did I mention that my hand was still plastered to his chest? I didn't think I could move it. "A double date? We're on a date? I thought you were all about keeping your friend safe, but now I don't know what's more pathetic. You and this boy that you're infatuated with or that I came here?" He chuckled again to himself and moved away.

My hand abruptly fell to my side. "Really? I'm pathetic?"

His laughter dissolved quickly and he sobered while he studied me a moment. Then he shook his head, almost gently, and chided, "No, it's just your pursuit of being normal."

My mouth went dry and my body went numb.

He added, impervious, "You're not normal, but you're so blind to who you are that you're willing to do anything for that boy. And he is a boy, trust me."

"I'm not blind." I didn't say anything about the 'boy' factor. "I *am* too normal."

"No, you're not." He stepped closer, unnervingly so. Then he murmured and this time it was fully sensual, "You're above normal. You just don't want to admit it."

"I have a roommate. I go to college. I skip classes. I volunteer at the hotline and I hate it! That's normal. How can that not be normal?"

"And the fact that you're telling a vampire all this?" Amusement flared in his depths, but it mingled with something else, something that sent a shiver down my spine and not one of those good ones.

"You're not normal. When you accept that, you'll accept your destiny."

My destiny?

He turned to leave, but he seemed to glide from the room. I was left behind to echo, "I'm a college student. That's my destiny... what destiny? I'm like everyone else."

But there was no one in the lounge.

"Hey!" I called out, sharply.

7

———

"Your boyfriend thinks I'm the bad guy," Roane spoke up when we parked outside of the Shoilster.

I didn't even spare him a glance. It wasn't worth it. "You are. You're a vampire. You're evil."

"He's clueless and he's in danger." Roane turned to look at me and this time I met his gaze, but my eyes quickly filtered over his shoulder to where Shelly and Adam waited beside the front entrance—talk about an imposter nightclub. It was one of those clubs that had the nicest décor, but the food wasn't cooked properly, never tasted good, and hardly ever filled a person. Yet, they arranged it nicely, complete with a garnish on the very tip of the plate so it seemed like it was worth the lavish price. It was Shelly's wet dream. It had all the trimmings, but none of the quality.

"Watch it. You're broadcasting again," Roane warned with a hint of amusement.

"Shut up!" I lashed out, harshly. "You're evil and get out of my head." I reached for the door handle, but Roane slapped a hand over mine.

I froze. I didn't dare move because his hand had a cemented hold over mine. His body brushed against mine and if he'd been human, I would've felt his breathing against my cheek. I kept my eyes down, anywhere but his. Then he remarked, "I'm not in your head and that goes both ways, Empath. You stay out of mine and I'll return the favor."

"If you call me that again, I will—" I threatened, but I caught my words.

'Don't let them know you. Don't explain anything to them!' That had been Kates' first lesson to me when I confessed I was worried a vampire was stalking me. The other lessons... I hadn't been the one to think of setting Craig on fire, but I'd been the one to throw the match. And this one—this vampire...

"Vampire," I snarled in return and turned to let him meet my stormy eyes. "I didn't want to call you, but your name popped up in my magic eight ball. There's a reason, and I'm thinking you know what it is, so let's figure out a few ground rules."

He let go of my hand and a rush of blood swept through it. I could've sobbed from the release of pressure, but my eyes hardened. "I will not 'feel' you. You will not listen to my thoughts and after we've ditched Adam and Shelly you will help me with Kates. After that, you and I go our very separate ways."

"Gladly." It was the second time he used that word with me and the same acid dripped from his tone.

"Fine."

"Fine." Then he reached for his door and was outside before I could blink.

I took a deep breath and muttered to myself, "Okay. Calm down. Be cheerful. And just fake your way till the end." That'd been another lesson from Kates, but it hadn't pertained to vampires. I liked to be adaptable and as I strode out into the cold air, I found I could breathe a little easier. Adam gave me a tentative smile. He moved away from Shelly and stepped close. "Are you okay? You don't look like you're up for this tonight. We could always—"

"Double date some other night?"

"It's not a date or a double date, not for me anyway." Adam frowned and stepped even closer. The air was cold enough to block his body heat, but I shivered as I imagined myself pressing against him. I felt a flush in my cheeks and ducked my head. I didn't want him to see how red I was, but I caught a movement from the corner of my eye. Roane shook his head with a flash of scoffing amusement. He made a point of turning his back to me.

My cheeks were aflame now, but not from eager anticipation. I held my breath and focused hard. I wanted to piss him off. I only knew one way to do it, but I'd just made a promise. I couldn't sneak my way inside again or I'd have to suffer the consequences.

"Davina?" Adam distracted me when he reached out to touch my arm.

I jumped from the cool touch, but exclaimed immediately, "Oh, I'm so sorry, Adam."

"Hey," he started to say, reassuringly, but he looked furtively at Shelly and Roane. He stopped as his eyes caught and held with Roane's.

Oh god. Roane was doing the same thing with Adam that he'd done with Shelly. He had the eye radar thing going and I could feel Adam's body freeze, immobile, as the vampire took his leisure time searching through Adam's thoughts.

I only had a few options, but I reacted without thinking. I covered the space between myself and Roane before my brain had time to scream 'Be rational!' As if I had no control over my actions, I watched my own hands grasp the front of his shirt roughly. Roane didn't have time to react before I pushed against him and slammed my lips over his. After that I felt like something unlocked inside of me. Adam was released from Roane's distraction. My eyes snapped shut and I pressed harder against Roane.

As kisses went, it was forced and impersonal.

Then I felt Roane's hand slide around to the back of my neck and he took a breath before he took over the kiss. After that, all force and impersonal formality was gone within an instant. Roane's lips opened over mine and he parted mine expertly. I felt his tongue sweep inside and I gasped from the molten intrusion. He switched our places. I was lifted up and pushed against the wall as his head tilted us so our backs were partially hidden. His hand cupped the side of my face and his thumb ran over my lips as he pulled away to nip at them gently. My eyes were still closed, but I couldn't control my body. Every time he leaned close to nip at my lips, I arched into his touch, begging for more. When I heard a soft chuckle resound from him, I opened my eyes bleakly and saw a smug vampire staring at me.

All the heat, the passion that I didn't want to admit to myself, was instantly replaced with coldness. I snapped and shoved him back.

Roane went, but he went slower than I'd wanted.

I swung horrified eyes to Adam, but I saw that he was gone. Shelly must've gone with him. "They're gone."

"After that display, I doubt your boyfriend is going to show his face again."

"He's not my boyfriend." I had really wanted him to be though.

Roane said smugly, "You kissed me in front of him. You can't explain that away, Empath."

Empath! I swung my fists at him. My hand was two centimeters away from slapping his face when it was caught and held in his powerful grip. The smug smirk was replaced by cold anger. "Don't do that again."

I felt a slow shiver from his words, but I was beyond caring. "Don't ever call me that again!" I waited in thick silence before he released my hand. It dropped with a thud to my side, but I still fought from swinging my other hand.

"Fine, then you can stop calling me Vampire. My name is Luke, not Roane."

I shrugged and sniffed, "Whatever."

"Why did you kiss me?"

"Because we made a deal. It was the only thing I could do to stop you from doing that thing again."

"That thing?" Roane—Luke—echoed with a twinge of laughter in his voice. "What do you mean by 'that thing'?"

I knew this test. It was more about me than him. He just wanted to know what I knew. "It's what you, vampires, do when you want to search inside someone's head. It's worse than what I can do. You put your eye radar on that person and they can't move so you can take your time looking through their brain index. I hate it and I really hate that Adam doesn't even know what you did."

I felt like I could vomit.

"He saw you kiss me," Luke finished for me.

"Now he'll think—" I didn't know what exactly he'd think, but with a sinking heart, I knew there was nothing I could do now.

"Want to know what he thinks? I can tell you."

It must've been my imagination because I detected a small bit of sympathy in his tone. Vampires weren't sympathetic. I'd gone crazy. I lied, "No."

"He likes you. He thinks I'm a bastard, but he's worried about your welfare. He won't be deterred from the kiss. Trust me."

"Really?" The vampire was a complete contrast of emotions. I hated him, I needed him, and now—I was grateful to him.

He sighed and then swung towards the door. "Let's go."

"This place?" I still disliked this place. "We don't have to go here now. They're gone. We can go and find Kates now."

"This is where Kates is." Roane moved towards the door and a bouncer swept it open. Roane passed through like he owned the place. I was forced to reluctantly follow and when he turned down into a back hallway I knew this night had gone from bad to worse.

"Let's go!" he commanded down the hallway and then I saw him open a door.

I sighed and quickened my pace even though this went against how I usually operated. I liked to slowly wade in and get my surroundings before I made rash decisions. It hadn't been a rash decision to light Craig on fire. I'd thought and planned for weeks in advance and then the night came along. This was different. I'd been to the Shoilster, but I'd never been down a back hallway and certainly not a basement. The door was left open, but Luke was already downstairs and out of my eyesight.

"Get down here, now!"

My foot reacted first and I fumbled my way down the stairs.

What I saw when I got to the end brought my jaw to the ground, almost literally.

The main floor of the Shoilster was used for dining and dancing. Not the basement. The basement looked like another secret gathering of vampires. They were everywhere. Some sat on plush red couches that lined the walls. Some stood in the middle, between two ponds that shown a sparkling reflection on the ceiling. I wondered if there were crystals or diamonds in the ponds, but then I forgot my question as my gaze caught and held on a girl in a back corner.

Kates.

She stood with a sultry smile on her face and her body was leaning suggestively towards a guy who looked like he'd love to ravish her that night. They both held crystal goblets with red liquid and I had a fleeting thought that his might hold blood, but Kates' would've had merlot. For all her dressings, she was a wine girl through and through.

I didn't know how long I stood there, but when a few vampires started to send glances my way, I decided it was time to mingle—or just move. I moved. Like any other bar patron, I found myself at the crowded counter with no chance of heralding a bartender. It was packed. I was surprised that I'd even noticed Kates in the first place.

"Are you alone?" The question came out smoothly, too smoothly, and the blonde vampire stood tall. He was over six feet with a square jaw and sparkling blue eyes.

I smiled for different reasons. Roane had disappeared so I was alone. Then I smiled because this vampire thought I was a lost, misdirected little human who had no idea he thirsted for my blood. I felt a wave of confidence sweep through me and I relaxed for the first time in awhile. Leaning back against the counter I slipped into Silvia's persona. I held a hand out. "What's your name? You look like a Ben? No. Maybe a Royce. Are you a Royce? Are you the sixteenth heir in a line of royal blue bloods? You dress the part. Is that custom fitted?"

I gave the vampire credit. He was startled, but he rolled easily on his heels and he returned with charm,

"It is actually. I can order something for you, if you'd like."

"But, wait—you'd have to get my measurements first, right?" My smile dazzled. "I know this gig, forwards and backwards. You're not getting my blood."

That got his attention. If he'd had breath, I would've given myself a pat on the back for stealing it away. He didn't so I didn't pat myself on the back, but it didn't matter. I saw his nostrils flare and my heart sunk. I'd just become the next big challenge for this vampire and I knew how that road traveled.

"Don't," I said sharply as I held a hand up. "I lit the last vampire on fire who thought I was a challenge for him to bleed. I'll do it again and it won't take nearly as long this time. That's my warning to you."

"Kade," Roane decided to join the conversation from... I glanced around. I had absolutely no idea where he materialized from, but his presence snapped Kade into order.

"Lucas," Kade returned as he waited for his leader to speak. The blonde Casanova instantly stood straighter and waited for his command.

"Leave." That was all Roane said and Kade turned to leave, but he stopped mid-turn and raked his eyes over me. "I like you." He pounded Roane on the chest before he finally turned to leave.

Roane studied me intently. "Do I dare ask what that was about?"

"No."

"Okay." Roane was easy.

"I saw Kates."

Roane narrowed his eyes, but he didn't say anything. Instead, he signaled for a drink and just like that—he got one. I glowered. "Could get me one, but no..."

He lifted a second finger and I felt better when a beer was pushed into my hand. I didn't bother to say thanks. "What's the plan?"

"You wanted help. I brought you to your friend. I thought you were worried about her."

I flushed and raised my beer to him. "You know that's not all there is to the story. I thought she was in trouble." I hesitated. "My source said to contact you so I did."

"Your magic eight ball. Tell me, how'd your magic eight ball mention me? Was it by name?"

"You're making fun of me."

"No," he rejected quickly. "Unlike you, I know why you contacted me, but I'm just wondering how much you actually know."

"I know." I didn't, but I wasn't about to let him know that. "I know plenty."

Roane chuckled. "You know nothing."

"Oh, really?" I turned to face him squarely. I even put my beer on the counter to let him know that I meant business. "You think I know nothing? I know enough, Vampire."

I said the word and I said it hotly. I dared him to call me on it. Oh yes, I'd call him Vampire if I wanted.

Roane smiled coolly and returned, "What do you know, Empath?"

I felt hot, angry, but I'd started us down this road. I'd see it through. "I know something big is going down. There's a whole crap load of vampires here and I don't think that's normal for Benshire. I know that there was a girl who killed herself the other night and a whole host of too many vampires were in attendance. There were two on the roof with her and six on the ground. I think whatever's going on has something to do with why Kates is here because I'm not stupid enough to think she's actually here for me."

There. I was out of breath. I'd said it all. I felt my skin starting to crawl before Roane replied cautiously, "You're smart for an empath., but maybe too smart? Maybe you know too much for your own good?"

My eyes bulged and my throat went dry, but what did I do? I took a drink of my beer when I heard the very words that I'd feared coming from a vampire. Those words were never followed by anything good.

What do you do when you're in a room of vampires and the most dangerous one tells you that you know too much? You bolt. What did I do? I hyperventilated. "Oh yeah? You think I can't handle all of this?"

"Relax," Roane chided softly as he moved closer.

I tensed, but he only placed his drink on the counter behind me. I waited for him to move back, but he didn't. Then I hyperventilated a little bit more...

"I told you, relax." Roane shifted closer and his chest was nearly pressed against me with an arm tucked around me. To the outside observer, we were a couple on the quick way to a dark corner. To my inside observer, I was pretty sure I might've wet my pants.

'It's not him. It's not him,' I chanted to myself.

Roane chuckled softly against my cheek. "You're right. It's not me. It's your ex."

My eyes flew wide open—I'd closed them without realizing it, but I caught my breath when I saw Roane watching me knowingly, amused, and did I detect some sympathy too? My hand tightened around the beer bottle. It was my only weapon of defense.

"You're freaked out about all vampires because of one bad seed."

"You're all bad seeds."

"True, but most of have us enough control and self-discipline. We have carnal desires, but we don't act on them. If we did vampires wouldn't be a secret to 90% of the world's population."

True, but... they were still evil. I took a nervous sip of my beer, but I didn't taste it. In fact, as I felt the lightened bottle, I realized that either it had evaporated or I'd drunk most of it already. I wet my dry lips and hoped it had evaporated. "What... what did you mean before when you said that I know too much?"

"You do." Roane tucked his hand that had rested on the counter behind my back and pulled me close. We were now flush against each other.

Craig was the reason why I was feeling this jittery, hot flash, shivering reaction. It had nothing to do with this vampire.

Roane's breath tickled my cheek. "There are a lot of vampires here and there is a reason. You're right. I'd been hoping your friend was here for you. I doubt it, though. That's why I brought you here."

I was dumbfounded... and a little woozy.

"Do you see her?" Roane urged me forward. We were embracing now, but he tilted my head to his shoulder where I was able to prop my chin up and then my eyes went wide when I saw what he wanted.

Kates was grinding against her vampire, but I didn't see lustful Kates. She was on the prowl and I saw a predator glint in her sapphire eyes. She didn't move thick with desire. She was alert, primed and it didn't sit well with me.

Roane felt my tension and he nuzzled underneath my ear. "She's not here for you. She's not even here for the same reason the rest of us are here. She's here because she's about to do something that I don't want her to do."

"Why?" My whole body grew numb from the shock.

"You know the decree that was approved by both boards."

It was the one where hunters replaced slayers. Gulping, I knew where this was going.

"Her mother was ripped to shreds because she violated the decree. That power went to your friend. She was branded because of that. Every vampire will know she's got slayer power, but if she does what I think she's here to do—you know what will happen."

That was the problem. "Please? Just..." '*...don't kill her.*'

To my surprise, Roane didn't respond right away. His hand cupped the back of my neck. "You dropped your shield."

I had, but I hadn't done it on purpose. '*Please don't hurt her. Please... she's... she saved my life.*'

His eyes bore into mine. "I'm a marked Hunter. You know I can't."

"What do I do?"

"You save her life. You return the favor and you make sure she doesn't do what her carnal desires are thirsting for. Make sure she doesn't kill any vampires or you know what'll happen to her." He moved back an inch and signaled for two more drinks. He replaced my empty bottle with a full one. "You've seen up close what Hunters will do to anyone who violates the decree."

I closed my eyes as I saw Craig on fire, his face twisted and angry. I could still smell the charred skin and I couldn't repress a grimace. My eyes flew open when I felt Roane tip my bottle up. My mouth opened automatically and the cool liquid helped wash some of the bad memories away. I swallowed and held my breath when Roane brushed his thumb over my lips. He held my gaze, but I knew he wasn't doing the eye radar thing on me. I'd put my shield back in place, but he wet his lips. "I have enough on my plate. I can't worry that a slayer is going rogue. Take care of her, take care of your friend or... you know what I'll have to do."

Talk about no pressure. Save your friend or she'll die a horrible violent death. Yeah... I downed the rest of my beer. "Yeah... yeah, I can do that." I highly doubted it.

My eyes wandered to Kates, but when I couldn't find her, Roane supplied, "She just took a guy out the back door. If you hurry, you can get there before my guys."

I was forced to do what he bid so I shoved away from him and swept through the crowd. My body calmed a little as I moved further away, but it also grew cold. I hadn't realized how I'd been cocooned by Roane.... I caught sight of the red exit sign and pushed past three vampires that stalked towards it. I hardened my jaw and vowed to do what I needed to do, but when I pushed out the back door I stopped dead in my tracks.

Kates was sharing a smoke with the vampire and laughing. I'd expected—not this. Before I could react, the door slammed shut behind me.

"Davy?"

Oops. I smiled sheepishly. "Uh... hey. I didn't know..."

Kates stared at me, long and hard, and then flicked her cigarette on the ground. "If you tell me that you didn't know I was here, I will skin you alive."

"I knew you were and there are three vampires on the other side of this door that know you're here too." I'd be awful under torture.

Kates rolled her eyes. "Honey, every vampire in that bar knows I'm here. I'm a branded slayer, remember?"

Okay. This wasn't going how I thought it would.

"This is Cherry," Kates introduced with a back wave. "Cherry, this is my best friend, Davy."

"You're the Empath."

The way he made it sound, it was like I was the only one. There were nearly a hundred thousand of us in the world, but I was probably the only one stupid enough to meander into a vampire bar twice in one night.

Kates frowned at him. "Yeah, she's empathic. What of it?"

His quick eyes snapped to hers and read the warning. He straightened and ran a hand through his auburn curls then he flashed a charming smile. "No, she's not just empathic. She's the empath that was cozying up with the Hunter."

"What?" Kates whirled to me. Her mouth didn't drop, but I felt her bristling in shock. Kates hated being surprised.

The Hunter. That made him sound like he was famous or something, but then I realized he was famous in the vampire community. All hunters were known. "I—it wasn't like that."

"Sure," he scoffed with a knowing smirk.

Kates looked between us. "Okay." She turned and pressed a kiss to the corner of his mouth. "I'll be seeing you."

He didn't respond, but seemed to melt into the shadows as Kates grabbed my elbow and walked me out to the street and across to the next block. "Kates, I—" I started.

She hissed, "Not yet. Not here."

I was left with little choice but to follow. After we walked down another three blocks and hailed a taxi, Kates started as soon as the taxi's door was shut, "What were you thinking? You don't show up at a bar like that, not alone."

"I wasn't alone and hello—you took me to the first one, remember?"

"I was there! You weren't alone. And what do you mean, you weren't alone?"

"I went with the Vam—," I shot a fevered look at the taxi driver. "I went with Roane."

"Who?"

"Luke Roane, you know... the one that you wanted me to talk to in the first place."

Comprehension flashed and she sat back, slightly appeased. "Why?"

"Um... I thought you were in trouble. I felt it. I did my thing and his name came up. I was told to get a hold of him and he'd know what to do. He could help you."

"I'm not in trouble. What do you mean you did your thing? You didn't—that's private, Davy!"

If the taxi driver was listening, he'd think we were both crazy. "I didn't! Blue did and she told me to call Roane."

"What? Why?"

I shrugged. "She said that you respect him or something. I don't know. She said he was the one to call about this."

I waited for more confusion, but to my surprise there was just silence. I stole a look and saw that Kates looked contemplative. "Do you? I mean, do you respect him?"

She threw me a cold look. "That's private. It's not your business or your silly sponsor's. I think that whole thing is just... you don't need their help anymore. You're doing fine just by yourself. Why do you keep talking to her?"

"Not this again." I crossed my arms and scooted low in the seat.

"You don't need help. They get in your head and mix everything up. It's not good, Davy."

"You're just pissed off because someone might know a little more of your inner workings than you do, Kates."

Silence. Complete, utter, death defying silence.

"How dare you!" Kates seethed. I felt her body bristling from unspent fury.

I'd done the deed. I'd gone where both of us knew I should never go again. The truth is that Kates had more baggage than I could ever feel my way through. I suspected that Blue had only done a quick sweep of what made Kates go boom.

"Emotional baggage? I'm not the one who lit a vampire on fire!"

The taxi jerked. I met his gaze in the rearview mirror and he looked panicked. Correction: he looked like he was about to kick us out. "Ex-nay on the ampire-vay."

"Screw that! And screw you, *Daveeena*. Do you even know what you were doing coming to the Shoilster? I thought you hated Roane. You hate all vampires and then I hear that you're snuggling up to one? And it's a Hunter! Really? Of all of them?"

"Kates," I tried to assuage, but I already knew it wouldn't work. "I'm sorry, but I'm not sorry. I don't think you're here to be my friend. I'm not stupid, Kates. I know that a crap load of vampires are in town. You didn't come because I saw that girl kill herself. You came for all of the vampires."

The taxi slammed on his brakes and neither of us was surprised. Normal people would've slammed against the seats from the abrupt stop, but not us. We reached out, held ourselves in place, and continued the argument.

"You're telling me what kind of friend I am? Is that what this is about? Is that why you came to the Shoilster? Because I'm a shitty friend?"

"No…" Good gracious. For such a kick ass tough chic, she was sensitive. "Look, I'm just…"

"Get out! Get out! Get out!" The driver twisted around in his seat and gripped a steel bat in his right hand.

We didn't blink. We got out and as the taxi shot off, Kates yelled, "You're right. I didn't come for you. I came because all the freaking blood-thirsty vampires are here, but do you even know why they're in town? You have no idea because this isn't your world. It's my world, Davy!" She breathed in and out raggedly.

"What are you talking about?" I asked, perplexed. Our arguments never made sense. "I don't even… What?"

"You're right! I didn't come for you. You were just my excuse. I'm a horrible, horrible friend," Kates nearly screamed.

She was irrational. I wasn't much better when I said things like this, "No, you're not. You're just… your mom was a slayer and you saw her die. All that power went to you and they all know you're a slayer, but you can't do what you're supposed to do and you can't do anything about it—except you have this weird thing with hooking up with vampires. I don't get that. You're protective about that world, which you can be because you know how I hate vampires, but…" What else could I say? I didn't know what I was trying to say. "I'm rambling. I ramble when I have an idea, but I lose the idea and you're here and I'm here and… I don't know what we're fighting about."

Kates snorted. "Just call someone to pick us up, would you?"

I took out my phone, but I caught myself. Who could I call?

"What?" Kates growled.

I waved the phone around. "Who do I call? If you're going to haul off on me again, I don't want to call Adam or…" I had no one else.

"What happened to Love Bit and Twice Not Shy?"

I groaned at the name, but it was fitting. "Emily's out for the count."

"She passed out?"

"She passed out."

I caught a fleeting grin before Kates turned her back to me and eyed the empty street. We were nowhere. We were somewhere, but I had no idea where we were so we were nowhere. Kates gestured to a street sign. "We're at Emerson and Keeley Ave. Call someone and tell them to pick us up here."

I sighed and I had no choice. I called The Vampire.

9

"**E**mpath," he greeted as he pulled over and unlocked the doors of his black car. I was horrible with recognizing makes and models, but I knew it was black. As I got in the front seat, I saw that it was new, like new new, like next year new. The seats were made up of black leather and they were still slippery. I almost wooshed off when Kates climbed into the back seat.

"Thanks." I felt stiff as I reached for the seatbelt. "I see our truce is over with, Vampire?"

"You don't have to bother with the seatbelt." He shifted gears and shot back onto the street. "I'm taking my cues from you. You called me 'Vampire' in your head when I pulled up."

"Huh?"

Kates just snorted.

"I have vampire reflexes, Empath. We won't get into an accident."

"What does that mean?"

"It means that he can go fast and still land on his feet, just like a freaking cat. Didn't you know? All vampires have nine lives," Kates drawled from the back. She was still pissed.

I sighed.

Roane murmured, "Vampires have one life. It's called immortality."

Kates met his gaze in the rearview mirror. "Is that so? Here I thought you were the one that took away their immortality, right? You hunt them. Or did I get that wrong?"

"Takes one to know one..." The words were so smooth, so chilling, and deadly...

I had no idea what that was, where that came from, but something else was in the car with us. As I looked between Roane and Kates, I knew it was something between them and it was something specific. I held my tongue, though. I knew that I did not want to step sideways into whatever they were in...

"You have something against vampires, Kates? I wasn't aware of that."

I needed to give him his due. He could hold his own against my nolstage.

Kates choked on something. "Please. We both know what I have against vampires and it ain't a grudge, Hunter."

"That's right. You and Cherry go way back. How long exactly?"

Kates was silent, the very scary quiet when I knew she was about to explode... any second now...

Roane slowly rolled his knuckles over the steering wheel. He was in control, perfect control. "You don't know him. You met him tonight and you had every intention of killing him."

"You don't know that! You don't know anything!" Kates came unhinged. She jerked upright and slammed against my seat. She was so furious. Kates always looked sultry. She was the sexy one of us, but just then her heavily made up make-up looked clownish on her. It looked wrong. That's when I knew that what Kates was doing was wrong.

Their argument passed over me, but I tuned back in to hear Kates shout, "—who made you judge and jury? You're a Hunter. You kill them and you enjoy that. That makes you an animal in my eyes. You're no more above the rest of them, but you like to think you are—"

"—an animal?" Roane narrowed his eyes dangerously and replied, silkily, "I'm the animal, Kates? I died. I came back as a vampire. You're a human. You have a choice in the matter. You have a soul."

"A soul." Kates threw herself back in the seat, disgusted. She glanced to the window and muttered underneath her breath, "What is that anymore?"

"Okay." I sat up and ignored the chilling glance from the vampire and turned around. I even ignored how Kates refused to look at me and how her back was perfectly poised to make me feel insignificant.

"You're stupid."

I caught the slight jerk of Kates' eyebrows.

"You can sit there and ignore me, but I know you're listening."

"Tell me, o wise best friend, why am I so stupid?"

"Are you killing vampires?"

"Like I'm going to have this heart to heart with you when *he's* in the car. Not to mention, why did you call him? I thought you hated the guy. Now you've got him on speed dial? I still can't believe that you showed up with him."

I ignored that. "Are you killing vampires? And we've been over that—I had to."

Kates scorched me with those sapphire eyes and I gulped. "I am not talking about this with him in the car—with him in any close vicinity at all. And what if I was? I'm not saying that I am, but what if I was? So what, Davy! I'm a slayer. It's what I was born to do. You don't know what it's like to have this thing inside of you, this darkness or something. I am programmed on the inside to do one thing. Kill vampires. I'm not allowed because some stupid decree made a decision that they could patrol their own. Well, that's just..." She trailed off, almost sad.

"You don't think I might know a little bit about that? I can feel inside of people. Remember what it was like in the beginning, before I upped my blocking levels? It was hell, Kates. You should remember that. I had this thing that came from inside of me and I couldn't control it. I do understand a little bit about what you're talking about." I felt wrung out just talking about it, but I remembered those first few years. I would do anything to not remember them.

The air was thick. I heard the swish of the car's wipers and a part of me realized that it had started to rain, but I concentrated on Kates, just Kates. She was so still with her face turned towards the window. I glanced at her reflection and wasn't surprised to see a lone tear trickle down the side of her face.

"I don't care what you're doing. I just can't lose you and I know that if you are doing what I feel is taboo to talk about right now— then just stop it. Okay?"

Kates sniffed. That was rare.

"Fuck off." That was the real Kates.

I fell back in my seat and glimpsed my dorm through the window. Roane turned the car into the parking lot and slowed to a halt just before the quad's archway. As soon as we had stopped, Kates scrambled out and slammed the door. The car rocked from her force.

"That went stupendous." I sighed.

Roane shifted the car into park and turned it off.

I didn't care if the car sprouted roots and became a tree. I just knew that my butt had no desire to follow a pissed off vampire slayer, especially when my roommate was probably still sleeping.

"She heard you. That's all that I really hoped for the night."

Huh?

Roane added, "She knows that I know what she's doing. She knows that you know and that you're worried for her. That's all we can hope. If she stops, then good for all of us. If she doesn't, then it's my problem. Not yours."

"I didn't follow anything you just said."

"You don't need to. You tried. That's all you can do."

"You're very supportive for being a vampire." I couldn't stop the sneer. Then I felt the same coldness from before. I looked up and gulped when I felt his coal eyes on me. They were colder than normal.

"You need to get over your ex. Things will go a lot smoother for the both of us when you do."

"What are you talking about? I felt that Kates was in trouble and for some screwed up reason, I got you to help me. We both saw how well the 'slaying intervention' just went. You and me, that's never going to happen again." I felt brave and bold, but a part of me trembled on the inside. I just didn't know what or why. Then I burst out, "Why was your name in her head? Why did I have to call you? You're the one..." I called her executioner. That's what I did. So... why? That question burned me.

I was surprised to hear sympathy in his voice. "I know that she's breaking vampire law. I was in her head because she fears me and she needs me. I'm the one that has to stop her."

"But..."

"You're the friend who can help me do that. No one else can do that."

That explained some of it, but there was other weird stuff going on too. "Why are there so many vampires?"

"Because..." He trailed off. For the first time, I didn't sense all of his attention on me. It felt liberating and yet, I got a sudden sick feeling. He was the primal predator. When their attention wasn't on the prey that meant it was on some other prey, something worse.... He blinked, once, and the spell was gone. His fierce eyes turned back on me and I felt all that attention once again. "Does it matter?"

"I think it does." My throat was dry.

"Talk to your friend. Plead with her again and maybe you and I won't have to do this again."

He'd dismissed me. Just like a flip of a switch. "And here I thought you were a little more human than most vampires. You proved me right. You're just as much of a dick as most guys I know. Thanks for that, it's very human of you." I threw open my door and stalked off. When I reached my dorm I glanced over my shoulder and saw that he was gone. Ass.

As I moved through the first lobby and darted up the stairs, I paused before my dorm door. I didn't know if I could handle what was on the other side. I was tired. The hallway smelled of moldy toast and I grimaced when a bad aftertaste formed in my throat. I stood there for awhile and took a deep breath.

The moldy toast had nothing on Kates.

When I bolstered up the courage and opened my door, I wasn't surprised to find Kates packing a bag. I didn't even comment when I saw a pair of my jeans in her bag. Instead, I closed the door, sat by my desk, and heard the snores from Emily.

Kates clenched her jaw tighter and threw more clothes in the bag. After a minute of silence, she screamed. "Nothing? Really? Nothing?"

"Are you leaving town?" It was all I asked because I wanted her gone. I wanted her away from him. It didn't bother me one bit if she was mad at me. This was for her own good.

Kates studied me as she twisted her hands in a sequined halter top. She loved that shirt and I knew she'd regret ripping it so I stood and gently took it away. She let me, which surprised me. "Are you doing what he says?"

"...yes..." She turned away as the admission slipped out.

I knew it, but hearing it was different. I already felt like I needed a time out. "Can you stop?"

"No."

"Why not?"

"Because..." Kates turned back to face me. I saw the tears swimming in her eyes and I blinked back my own. "...because they killed my mother, because they're trying to tell me that I can't be who I am, because they're my whole world. I know what'll happen to me if I'm caught and he knows that I am. I finally know that he knows. There are others like him. There are other hunters."

"You can go to one of my meetings with me. It might do you good."

"I'm not empathic." She dipped her head and I heard a chuckle.

I nudged her toe with mine. "It doesn't matter. The meetings are supposed to help anybody and everybody. Why do you do it? Do you know why, I mean, really why? It might help if you understand it."

"Right. I'm going to go to a shrink and tell them that I can't stop killing vampires. I won't get thrown in an asylum at all."

"What about Blue? She knows about this stuff. She makes me talk to her about my stuff all the time."

"Oh, I can see that one. Your sponsor and me as roommates, because she doesn't know how much I hate all that crap she makes you do."

Blue did know. Blue knew a lot more, but I wasn't going to voice it. "Try it."

When I heard my phone peel, I already knew who was on the other end. "Hello, Blue. You know we were talking about you."

"I'm not a damn mind reader. I felt a question. What's the question?"

Blue would never cease to amaze me. "Can Kates come and stay with you for awhile? She's got... some things to talk about."

"I'm making breakfast. Have her pick up some coffee on the way. I like the pumpkin spice latte."

"Blue says—"

"I heard." Kates didn't look too sure... "I go and talk to her and this is how I'm supposed to get help? It's just like that? That's too easy, Davy, even for you."

It was all I could think of. "He won't know where you are."

"If he wants to know, he'll know."

"Kates." I wasn't sure if I should ask, but another question kept nagging me. "Why are all the vampires here?"

"Because they have fairy tales just like us. We have Santa Claus or the Easter Bunny, but they have the Immortal."

So much of that statement made no sense. "They *are* immortal."

"Not *their* immortality. It's the Immortal, as in a human who has immortality."

Huh?

I was dumbfounded and clueless and I *still* hadn't moved from my desk chair, even after my butt had gone numb an hour ago. That was how long it took for Kates to explain about the Immortal. Then she explained again. And again.

I was still confused. "So you're saying..."

Kates threw up her hands. "You're not normally stupid."

The insult bounced off of me. "They think this Immortal—"

"—a human who has immortality." Kates rolled her eyes.

"—has blood that they want? I don't... why the fairytale analogy?"

"Oh my God! For real? You can understand my sick twisted insides, but you don't get this?"

"Explain it again." And this time, I'd pay attention and not get lost on the idea of a human who has immortality or the fact that the vampires want immortality. They already had it so why... I was lost again.

"I'll break it down. Vampires need blood to live, right?"

I nodded, but it wasn't entirely true. They could go without, but would go crazy.

"There's only one Immortal in the world at a time and they have special fluids inside of him/her/whoever."

"Okay." Still confused.

"When a vampire drinks the blood of an immortal, they get the juice of life."

"Juice of life?"

Kates threw herself backwards on my bed. "I had no idea this would be that hard."

"Again." I nodded emphatically with knowledge-absorbing eyes. I'd lap up the information like I was a dog drinking water. Something told me that Kates was ready to storm out of there, whether I understood or not. It was that same something that told me I needed to know this stuff.

"Vampires need blood. The Immortal has life in its blood. When a vampire drinks her/his/its blood they don't need blood to survive anymore. They've got the juice that keeps that Immortal alive. They won't thirst for blood anymore and that has some serious consequences."

I couldn't worry about the consequences or what the significance meant. I was still wrapping my head around a vampire's fairytale. "So if they drink the Immortal's blood, they don't need blood? At all? They're not hungry? How many times do they have to drink from the Immortal?"

Kates shrugged and stretched languidly. "I have no idea. No vampire has ever drunk from the Immortal that I know of. We need food, right? It's like if we took one big bite of some magical Wheaties. The magical cereal would stay inside of us and we would never need to eat again, ever."

"I'd still want to eat other things." Spaghetti. Lasagna. Anything with pasta or chicken... I loved burgers too. I should love salads.

"We're human. They're vampires. I'm sure not all blood tastes the same, but think of it this way. They're supreme meal is human blood. The decree says that they can't drink humans anymore, except when they sneak a taste like from LoveBit and Still Passed Out Here." Kates lazily gestured to Emily, who rolled over and snorted a snore in response. "But that's wrong too. If they get a taste of the Immortal's blood, they no longer need to lavish up whatever crappy blood they have to drink now. They're not like us. We like food. A lot of vampires have a love/hate thing with blood. Ask your new buddy, Roane. I bet he's one of the vampires who detests having to drink blood or detests how much he misses human blood. Get the tragic stuff?"

Not at all, but I nodded anyway with wide eyes. And he wasn't my buddy. He'd never be my buddy.

"I'm surprised your sponsor hasn't called to check on me or something."

"She knows that we're still talking," I mumbled automatically as my mind was still trying to wrap around Kates' magical Wheaties metaphor.

"Say that again?"

I blinked and saw the stillness in Kates. She looked... well, she looked like Kates again: pissed, tired, and raring for a fight. "She probably figures that we're still talking and that's why she hasn't called." I was a bad liar.

"Is she permanently in tune with you?"

I couldn't ignore that Blue had called before when we'd both been thinking of her. Blue was my sponsor. She was always alerted towards me, but that didn't necessarily mean she was inside all the time. Actually, she was hardly ever inside of me. I had some superior shields to the best vampire or empath, but I couldn't tell Kates that. If Blue wasn't tuning into my radio, that meant she was tuned into Kates'. Judging by the stormy expression in Kates' cobalt eyes—I swallowed what I'd been about to say and lied, "Yes, she is."

Relief and pity flashed in Kates' gaze, but the tension quickly left her. "I should go..." Kates stood reluctantly and glanced uneasily towards the door.

It took a few more minutes, but after she left I glanced at the clock and saw it was close to five in the morning. With a long drawn-out yawn, I used the bathroom and readied for bed. Then I closed my eyes in blissfulness as I crawled into my bed. Heaven. Emily snorted, but it didn't faze me. Nothing fazed me.

I felt sleep creep into my limbs and before long; I knew I drifted off to sleep...

I felt the heat first. It blasted me and my eyes shot open to see that I was back on the roof and the girl who had jumped to her death was in front of me. I felt a shiver travel down my spine and then glanced over my shoulder for the vampires, except there were none. I closed my eyes and sensed out, but I didn't feel any beneath us either. It was also warm out. I'd been on that roof that night and it hadn't been warm.

"Davina," she called to me.

I don't know why, but I clamped my eyes tighter together. Something told me not to open them. If I did, I'd see something I didn't want to or hear something I didn't want to...

"Look at me," she commanded and my eyes popped open. I had traitorous eyes.

She had stood on the edge with tears glistening on her cheeks that night. There was no sadness now. Instead, I saw urgency, but she was calm. She had been turned half away from me, but she faced me squarely. She wore the same white dress that billowed around her slender frame. A warm gust of wind teased the ends of her auburn curls, but she didn't have inflamed cheeks this time. They were pale, as they might've always been. Her hazel eyes were framed by thick, rich eyelashes, but that's not what mesmerized me.

She spoke with her eyes.

"You don't... you can't talk to me normally?" I was fascinated, but a little weirded out.

She smiled softly, but her mouth didn't move. "This is your dream. You make up the rules."

I blinked. "What?"

She smiled gracefully. "Reach out to me, Davina. Reach out to me."

"I did that night."

"Reach out to me." Her eyes were misted now, haunted.

I couldn't breathe.

"You know what I'm trying to tell you. Reach out to me so you can understand now."

"Understand what?" Chills blasted me. I felt goose bumps up and down my arms. A cold breeze wafted against my neck and the hairs on my back stood upright.

She glided closer to me with a hand outstretched.

I got one of those creepy feelings as if I was watching a horror movie play out in front of me. Or if I was in a horror movie and I was the next victim to die.

"I chose."

I snorted. "You chose to die that night. Good for you."

"No." She shook her head and those perfect lips still didn't move. "I chose you."

I gasped and jerked upright. I couldn't breathe. Something wasn't letting me breathe. My eyes popped open and I found myself in bed, heaving frantically for air. I was drenched in sweat with my blankets on the ground. Sunlight blinded me and I gasped, covering my eyes. It didn't help the splitting headache that had formed at the back of my head.

"Morning."

I saw Emily at her desk, wearing her white terry-cloth robe with her bunny slippers. She'd just showered, but she looked like she'd been hit by a bus that reversed and did it again. Judging by the bags underneath her eyes and the drooped shoulders, I knew my roommate was feeling her first hangover.

"Morning," I rasped out and lifted my arms. I felt like anchors were tied to both of them and they fell abruptly back on my lap.

"You had a nightmare. You were screaming and you threw all of your covers off. I covered you up three times, but you kept kicking them off. I gave up." Emily lifted a wary shoulder and turned back to the book she had opened in front of her.

It was worse than a nightmare, but I wasn't in the sharing mood. I wasn't even sure if my voice sounded normal. I just hoped that I hadn't wet my pants. Then I sniffed the aroma of coffee and quickly saw her mug beside her. "What is that?"

"Huh?" Emily sounded like a zombie, sluggish and nearly catatonic.

"You have coffee?"

She looked at it, but pushed it away. "You can have it. I'm not feeling all that great." Her cheeks pinked and she ducked her head in shame. Oh, my very sheltered roommate.

"What are you doing all day today?" I asked when I finally got the energy to get out of bed and grab the mug. The mug warmed my hands, which was good. They were sickly cold and covered in sweat, but my pants didn't smell so I knew I hadn't messed myself.

"I think I'm sick. I'm just going to stay in and watch movies all day. You?"

"I'm huh..." I was dumbfounded. Emily never took sick days, even when she was sick enough to be admitted to a hospital.

She coughed. "I'm supposed to work at the hotline booth at the convention today. Do you think you could fill in for me?"

I was completely speechless. Me. Hotline. Convention. Not happening. "I quit, remember?"

"You still have to make that official with Mr. Moser so you didn't. Besides, I'm supposed to work with Adam today."

"Sold!" I was a whore. Not really, but now that I knew Kates was safe I could get back to my first objective: Adam. After what he'd witnessed last night, I knew I had damage control to do.

"Besides, I don't want to take the chance that I'll see Luke at the convention. I look awful today."

I looked at her, horrified. It was a good thing she wasn't looking back otherwise she would've seen the guilt that I had branded on my entire face. Oh god. With everything that had happened last night, I'd almost forgotten about Emily's ramblings. She'd been in an altered state, but the truth came out and I knew she had a thing for him.

"Hey, Emily..." Really? What was I going to say? Don't like Luke Roane because he's a vampire and he's a dick? Don't like him because he hunts other vampires and kills them? Or maybe... don't like him because I kissed him in front of Adam and Luke Roane knows that I'm empathic?

I'm sure they'd all go over well.

"What?" Emily asked, impatient.

"Uh… nothing. I'll go to the convention for you."

"I know." She made it sound like it'd been inevitable. "You gotta be there in twenty minutes."

That's when I looked at the clock and thought my heart stopped beating. It was 1:39. I hit the ground running.

Our school held a volunteer convention on the main lawn of the campus. It was surrounded by brick buildings and a few ponds on three sides. Statues were displayed randomly over the lawn, but I knew it wasn't by accident when the crisis hotline booth was placed next to the angel statue. She was in gray stone, her two eyes watched wherever you went, and her tight curls were in dire need of a new perm. The wings had been sculpted to arch upwards as if she were about to push into the air and fly away.

She freaked me out.

I dropped into one of the vacant seats behind our table and announced when someone sat beside me, "I named her Eileen."

"Uh... okay."

Did my ears detect? I looked and was rewarded. Emily had sweetened the pot with Adam, but I hadn't let myself hope. Now, I did.

Adam looked refreshing in a soft blue sweater and a pair of tan corduroys. Both molded to his tall form while his chestnut curls accentuated his yummy almond eyes. I almost wanted to eat him. If I'd been a vampire, I might've ignored the decree.

"You named her Eileen?" He smiled and ducked his head. "Uh...

oh… kay. Um, where's Emily? I'm not complaining or anything, but I thought I had the afternoon block with her."

"Emily's sick." I turned and stared at Eileen for a moment. Was it my imagination or did she seem to grow before me?

"Oh. Okay. So… um… you and that guy, huh?"

Just like that, Eileen lost her appeal. I closed my eyes and cleared my throat. I knew I had damage control to do, but I hadn't known it would start this soon. The need to deceive was itching and so I itched it. "He has a girlfriend that was there. They had a tiff and he wanted to make her jealous. I wanted to tell you, but then all of the sudden she was in front of the club and I kissed him. I know, I know. It wasn't smart of me or anything, but when a friend asks for a favor who am I to say no?" I held my breath. When I saw the instant relief flash in those adorable almond eyes, I expelled it.

"Oh so… you and him aren't…?"

"No. God no! No." I couldn't emphasize that enough.

"That's good to hear because…"

I watched in disbelief as Adam opened those perfectly formed lips and spoke in slow motion. It took a moment before the sound hit my ears, but I heard, "…go on a date? Maybe tonight?"

"Yes!" I shouted and instantly cowered back in my chair. Never appear too eager. Kates hadn't taught me that lesson. I'd learned it on my own, but sometimes I couldn't control myself.

Adam looked taken aback. He paused a second before he nodded. "That sounds great. I was thinking of the Alexander Restaurant. It's supposed to have good food."

I hoped my drool was kept in check. I had no idea where the Alexander Restaurant was and I didn't care about good food. We could go to the Shoilster for all I cared. A date with Adam! I'd die happy when I told Shelly Witless.

"Are you guys from the hotline? Do you have any pamphlets?"

Adam immediately started his perfect volunteer thing. I was content to sit back and daydream about our perfect date, listening to his voice drone on until the guy was done with his questions. A few more people came over and Adam was eager to answer questions. I was eager not to. I considered us a good team.

"...that girl died, right? Wasn't someone there?"

My chair tipped forward and I almost went flying into the table. My eyes shot open to see whoever was talking with Adam. The guy looked like an average student. He could've been Adam's twin dressed in Abercrombie, but it wasn't the sight of him that sent my alarms buzzing. I felt him. He was a vampire. In fact, the girl who had stopped before him and the first guy had been vampires too. I just hadn't really noticed or cared. I cared now and I sat up straighter in my chair to scan the lawn. Six out of ten students were vampires. Those were not good odds. A normal statistic should've been one out of ten.

"Why are you asking questions like that?" I glared at the vampire. "If someone was there or not is none of your business. A girl died. You should be considerate."

Of course, he wasn't.

"Hey, hey, I meant no disrespect." The guy held his hands up in mock surrender and made a show of backing up two steps. He grinned charmingly towards me, but I shot out of my seat and leaned closer to him. "A person died that night. I don't care that you're not a person... of virtue. A human being died that night. It makes me wonder why she did. She was *only* human after all... maybe she was pushed into it. Maybe someone who isn't human did it?"

"Davina." Adam stood and touched my shoulder.

I ignored him and held the vampire's gaze steadfast. I wanted to make sure he heard my real meaning. "I know enough about humans and those who like to think they are. I know which category you fit in."

"That's enough, Davina."

"You should go—you and your friends."

The vampire hated it. He caught every nuance of my threat and probably more, but I didn't care. I was trembling so hard. Slowly, too slow for me, he turned and walked away, but he looked over his shoulder and met my gaze. Then he smiled. Damn vampires.

"Davina! What was that? You can't talk to customers like that! He might've joined up as a volunteer."

"Trust me," I muttered underneath my breath. "You don't want him answering that phone."

Adam said something, but I didn't hear it. A figure was weaving lithely through the crowd. Roane. My eyes narrowed when I noticed that he looked like he was on the prowl.

"I'll be right back," I said briefly and pushed off through the crowd.

When Roane stalked his prey, he did it well. I lost him eight times before I finally saw him at the corner of our admissions building. I sprang forward and would've lost him again if I hadn't jumped over two bushes and thrust my way through four groups of students. I stepped on toes and banged against private parts, but I didn't care. I landed with a huff at Roane's feet and bent over gasping. "We need to talk about the Immortal and all of these vampires here."

Roane wrapped a firm hand around my arm and yanked me behind him. I didn't have time to blink before I found myself pushed up against a building wall as Roane glared at me.

"Huh?" I was still focused on breathing.

"You better think long and hard before you start throwing out words like that to me." Roane glared at me with deadly intent.

Oh. Whoa. I blinked as I took in the sight of him again. The shadow from the building hit his face to accentuate his angular cheekbones. His tight shirt molded against his form, highlighting his lean muscles that would've had any A-List actor drooling in envy. Then there was the air surrounding him. He looked capable of killing. He might've been a forceful dick, but I'll admit he was hot. He even smelled of danger. My eyes shifted to see his teeth showing. I knew that his fangs could elongate out from their gums and he could jump nine feet at times. That's how far the other hunters had jumped on Craig. Their fangs had been bared to the flames before they sunk them into his flesh.

"Davy!" He hissed and clamped his other hand to my arm. He had me trapped in place now.

"Wha—huh?"

"What are you talking about?"

I shrugged out of his hold. "Kates told me about your fairytale. Whatever. But there are *way* too many vampires at this convention for it to be a coincidence. What is going on?"

He relaxed slightly—which unnerved me. "They're harmless."

"I don't want them here. This is my world. I go to college here. I'd like all the vampires to just leave!"

He laughed.

He laughed.

The lethal Hunter that scared me the most laughed at me. "Hey!" I hit his shoulder, but vampire bodies are sculpted and hardened to withstand anything. My hand literally bounced off of his shoulder and I was the one that gasped from the pain.

"What?"

I cradled my hand to myself and gritted my teeth when it started to throb. "Don't laugh at me."

"I'm not. Yes, the Immortal is in town. They're here for her. It's like when humans flock to wherever the pope shows up. I can't make them leave so you're going to have to deal with their presence."

"They hurt people."

"That's my problem. Trust me, I can handle my job." Roane turned and gestured towards the hotline booth with his head. "I thought you quit that place."

"What? Huh?" I looked over and sure enough, I could see the booth through a line of pine trees that blocked us from the convention. There he was, hard at work. My Adam. My hero. And he was currently answering some more vampires' questions. His hand didn't tremble. He didn't sweat. He had no idea those things were vampires. I saw how eager he was. He thought he was recruiting future volunteers. Unlike those vampires, his heart was in the right place.

"I saw you over there. I thought you quit."

Roane pulled me back to our conversation. I felt off balance from my Adam daydreams and then Roane's presence was a world in itself. The force that came from him was sweltering and it seemed to suck a person in. I shook my head again and tried to get past a little dizziness.

Oh... no... no. I realized with horror that the dizziness wasn't going anywhere. In fact, the world was starting to circle around me at breakneck speed. I felt myself falling and I shot out a hand for balance. The building in front of me felt sturdy as I leaned my head against it. It was really nice to touch.

And then...

Double crap. Everything went black.

12

I found myself in a dark secluded room and on top of an uncomfortable couch when I woke up. Where the hell was I?

"We're in a professor's office."

I jumped abruptly and let out a shriek. Then I saw a shadow detach itself from the wall and stroll forward. Roane.

"You fainted." His voice was curt.

"You caught me before? I thought it was the building."

He leaned back on the desk and asked, "What's going on with you? You were vomiting the other night and I know you weren't drunk. Now you fainted. You look like you've been sick since last night. Cold sweats?"

"Why do you care? It's none of your business. How did you know about the cold sweats?" I didn't think I wanted to hear the answer.

"I can smell the perspiration on your skin."

I'd been right.

"It's got a sweet aged smell to it. Not many vampires can place it."

"Too much information."

"You asked."

"Well, I wish I hadn't now." My voice sounded like I'd just sang the lead in an opera—as a novice.

"Your throat hurts?" Was there sympathy in that voice?

"Yeah." It felt like I'd swallowed bark and then vomited it back up, still fully formed.

Roane crossed and sat in the chair beside my head. He leaned forward on his knees and regarded me intently. Why did the chair have to be positioned so close to the couch? Why did Roane's hands brush slightly against my shoulder and why didn't I suppress the shiver this time? I swallowed tightly and grimaced from the pain. The shivers were becoming normal to me. Somehow, I was certain that wasn't a good thing.

"You might be able to ignore that something's going on with you, but I won't."

I slowly and achingly sat up. "Why do you care?"

"Because I might need you if Kates goes against the decree again. You're still the only person she'll listen to and contrary to what you think; I really don't want to kill your friend."

What every girl wants to hear. "Well... thanks for not wanting to kill my friend." What every girl wants to say.

"Have you talked to anyone about your symptoms?"

"You sound like a counselor or a doctor. It's annoying. And no, I haven't said anything. You know that, it's why you brought me in here from the convention—the convention! Adam! Did you—"

Roane stood and crossed to the window. He peeked through the drawn blinds. "Your boyfriend thinks you had an emergency and that's why you were called away. Don't worry; I had someone pass along the message." Did I detect a slight smirk at the corner of his lips? I could only imagine what that might mean... "Can you stand?"

"Uh... yeah... I mean... can I have a minute here?" I swallowed underneath those impenetrable eyes of his.

"I can help, you know."

I knew instantly what he meant and I felt myself pale. "No, no, no. I am not drinking your blood. I don't care if it'll heal whatever wrong's with me."

"I thought I'd offer."

"Again. No."

Roane stood up. The chair didn't even creak. It looked old,

uncomfortable, and pink. I felt the couch creak underneath my weight so I knew that if I'd been the one to stand up from the chair, it would've sounded like a falling tree. Not Roane with his supernatural grace. Not even Kates could move how he did. Something told me that Roane was not the vampire to be pitted against. I shivered at that thought and for once I was thankful the Hunters were on my side.

"You should go home and rest for the night."

I could rest, yes, but not for the night. "I can't. I have a date tonight."

"With your boyfriend?" He said it so calmly and evenly. I frowned when I couldn't discern what he might be thinking—and why the hell did I care about that?

"With Adam. He's taking me to the Alexander Restaurant. It's supposed to be divine eating." I almost tripped on my own self-righteousness.

"I own it." His voice was flat. Emotionless.

"Let me know how that makes sense. I didn't know that vampires were such 'divine' chefs."

"You should stop stereotyping us. You know that we're not all the same, Davy."

I heard the seductive promise and I hated how my body reacted. "Is it hot in here?"

"I'm not Adam either. You like him because you can control him. You don't like me because you can't manipulate me. You can't control me."

"You're not very normal for a vampire either." Had I just admitted to being manipulative?

"Truth hurts. Deal with it." Roane turned back towards the window.

"What's out there? You keep looking out there. Are you looking for something in particular?"

"More like *someone* in particular."

"And that makes sense." Sarcasm.

Whatever Roane was going to say was interrupted as his eye

caught and held on something. I saw a slight grin appear and vanish just as quickly, but his eyes remained on whatever spot he watched. He withdrew abruptly from the window and crossed to the office door. It wasn't even a second before he opened it and another giant vampire stepped through. It almost looked coordinated, but who coordinates that? *Vampires would.* I snorted at that thought. Roane ignored me, but the other vampire lifted a pair of shrewd dark eyes my way. They were cold. No—scratch that. They were freezing. And they didn't want me there.

"Who is this?" Even his voice sounded like the tundra.

"No one. Did you find something?"

He drew up to his fullest height, which was impressive. I guessed he might've been over six feet and five inches, but I'm terrible at guessing that stuff. With his broad shoulders and his rich golden curls, the vampire could've passed as a member of the royal Viking family. "Raitscliff and Lucan have both found a female that might be the next."

"Their families are here?"

The Viking nodded and waited for Roane's command.

Roane nodded once. His shoulders were made of stone. "Call the rest. I can't fight both families alone."

"You are not alone." The Viking sounded sincere. He laid a gentle hand on Roane's shoulder and I was more surprised when it wasn't shrugged off. Roane seemed to get strength from the simple touch.

"I know I am not alone, Gregory, but I would fear for your life too heavily. Raitscliff has vowed your death since Hartsdale."

"He can try." Gregory puffed up as his hand formed a tight fist.

He had meaty hands. I could only imagine the damage one of those hands could inflict. Just... impressive...and horrifying.

"Find Wren and I'll meet you back at the house."

"And her?" He sneered at me.

I straightened and fixed him with one of my glares. I could do the frostbite thing back at him. I think my glare bounced off him how my hand had bounced off of Roane before.

"Go." Roane ignored Gregory.

Gregory clamped his jaw tight and abruptly disappeared from the room. He didn't literally vanish, but the effect was the same. He was there. He was gone. And the door clicked in his wake.

"Boyfriend?"

Roane ignored me as he moved back to the window and peered through the blinds. Then he heaved a deep unnecessary breath.

"Why do you do that?"

"What?"

"Breathe. Sigh. Why do you do that? You don't actually breathe, you know. You don't need air."

Roane studied me for a moment. "It's habit. It's the body's habit. I try to grant the wish of the body."

"It's not like you're a demon that inhabits it. It was your body before you became a vampire."

He measured his words, but I caught the slightest inflection of... remorse? "To me, I was taught to respect the soul and the vessel of the soul. My mind might be similar, but I am not human, Davy. I don't have that soul anymore. The body misses the soul. It's a unique relationship that can't be described, but there are vestiges. There are little remains that tell me what the body used to do with the soul. Breathing is just one of them."

Well—that was... very philosophical. I wasn't sure I was glad that I had asked. "Oh."

"You're a human, Davy. And yet, you're more than the others. You know of us. You know of our world. You look down on us, but I'm human enough to know that you fear us. You went through a terrible thing with one vampire. I understand that his scars are still in you, that you think and feel because of them. They have power over you and yet—I think you're above those scars. I think you *can* be above them."

I was blown away and infuriated by what he said. I was also pissed, though I wasn't sure why. "You're a Hunter. You're a vampire. You own a restaurant. I'm guessing that you own a few of them. You go to college. Why do you even bother going to classes? Why pretend to be one of the lowly creatures we are?"

Roane took a step forward.

I leaned forward on the edge of the couch.

He studied me like he was absorbing my image into his brain.

I let him. I soaked up the attention—I'm not above admitting that. I wanted that attention. I wanted his attention. And I held my breath.

"Why pretend? That's your question? You shouldn't ask it that way. You shouldn't put us above you. Because it's not like that, Davy. The new decree is supposed to remind us what it's like to be human. Humanity. That's what everything is for us. Some forget. Some want to forget. It's about us not forgetting what we used to be. We used to be human. We used to have that soul inside of us and we cling to anything that will help us keep that reminder." Roane surged forward. "Education is the right for any soul. There is a potential that is only granted freedom through education. To not learn, that's to forget a soul's humaneness."

And that was said by a vampire. "Good thing I'm in college then..."

"Don't joke this off. Don't cover up what you are."

"I..." I opened my mouth, but what was there to say? I didn't know... I couldn't even formulate a thought. I just knew that my heart was pounding like a thundering racetrack.

Roane opened his mouth, but closed it abruptly. He glided forward.

I couldn't think.

He was only an inch away.

I couldn't.

His hand swept upwards.

I closed my eyes.

His hand cupped the side of my cheek. Then, his lips touched mine.

13

His lips held mine softly, sensually, for a brief moment before his mouth opened over mine. He didn't demand entry, but I gasped and his tongue slid sweetly inside.

My hand held weakly onto his shoulder. Roane slid a hand down my arm to my waist and over my thigh. He lifted me in the air and sat me down on the edge of the desk. As my legs parted, he fit perfectly. A bubble burst inside of me and the remnants coursed through my entire body. I felt the heat fill my fingers, my toes, and even my neck where his thumb caressed lightly.

My body melted, but Roane held me up. As my neck fell backwards, his hand held me still and his lips pressed fluttering kisses down to my throat. His belt buckle rubbed against the inside of my leg and then his hand lifted my leg to dangle it over his. I felt his body stiffen and surge against me. He paused once and I knew what he wanted. Every muscle stood out, prominent, from his skin. I saw the struggle in his stormy eyes. They were always coal black, but there was a silvery haze over them this time. He was hungry.

And then...Roane drew in a ragged breath and I saw the decision jerk through his body. I felt the shudder against me, between my legs, and then I felt cold. Roane moved back and I felt the magic rip out from inside of me. I ached. It was like I was starving and been given something to eat, only to have it taken away after one taste. I wanted more and I reached forward without thinking.

Roane weakly batted away my hand, but I caught his instead and hauled him forward. He was back between my legs, where he was supposed to be. This time I took control. I felt the indecision shudder through his body. My hand slid up his back and over each of his chiseled muscles to his corded neck, then down around his arm. I felt over his chest and explored the dip between each muscle in his stomach.

My eyelids were heavy with desire as I looked up at him, but I didn't know what to say. I felt like I'd been woken to life for the second time. I wasn't about to go back to sleep. With that thought in mind, I drew him closer and met his lips. It was all he needed. Roane took control. His hands wrapped around me and pulled me on top of him.

I wanted the barrier gone, but Roane ripped away from me again to slam a hand over the door. The door tried to open, but Roane barked out something. It sounded unintelligible to my ears, but I saw that the door remained shut after that.

I gasped for breath. Cold air slammed against my insides. Oh god.... Oh... god....

"Turn your shield on."

What? I looked up, but struggled to see Roane. It was like a black veil had fallen over my eyes. I knew he was there. I heard him, but I couldn't see him. Then my body twitched and I drew in a panicked breath. I felt the desk underneath me. It was rattling and I realized, as if I were in the distance, that it was me. I was making the desk shake uncontrollably. I didn't...

"Davy!"

Roane's voice was so far away.

"Roane," I heard myself whimper.

"She's going into shock, Lucas."

That wasn't Roane. I frowned, but I felt myself falling backwards and then something caught me. I knew it was Roane, but I couldn't see him. I opened my mouth to talk to him and ask him who had come into the room, but no sound came out.

"Her heart is going crazy. You have to put her out."

"Shut up, Wren!" Roane snarled.

"Her body is changing, but she's still with us. Put her out, Lucas! She's scared right now. Put her out and she'll be fine when she wakes up."

I felt Roane's chest jerk upwards, as if he couldn't make the decision. I heard the struggle in his voice. "I... the dreams, Wren. I can't... you don't know what they go through."

"No." The girl was cold. "This girl is not Talia. This girl is the new one and you have to put her out. She has to have those dreams, Lucas. They *all* have to have those dreams. She has to know what she is. Put her out."

I felt the surrender in Roane's arms before he bent over my body. His hand wrapped around my throat and then...

"Welcome." The voice was harsh and sarcastic, but also upbeat.

I looked up and saw nothing. I was in a black hole.

"You know you're dreaming. We know you're dreaming. Everyone knows you're dreaming." The words came again. They rushed at me from behind this time.

I sat up, shaken, but was surprised to find strength surge through my body. I flexed my hand slowly and held it in front of me. My hand wasn't my hand. I saw through my hand, through my skin and my blood. Everything was silver. It ran through my entire body and was pumping into my heart.

Oh my god—Roane! Kates! Anyone!

"Stop whining." It whipped around me again. I heard a laugh this time.

"Who—what are you?"

"This is the circus, didn't you know? We're in Alice's Wonderland with the seven berry gummy bears. Exciting, right? I know you're on the edge of your seat. I would be if I had a seat, but I don't. I'm shapeless. I have no form. I have no solid. I'm the gray in between." The voice bounced around me.

"You're psychotic. That's what you are." I drew in a breath.

"I like you. I didn't like the last one. She was weak."

"Weak?"

"Yeah."

Suddenly, the girl from the roof stood in front of me. She wasn't poised on the edge of the roof, not like that night or in my dream. This time she wore a yellow sweater over white jeans. Her red curls hung loosely down to her waist.

"Her." The voice was disgusted.

"I was there that night."

"She died because you were there. If you hadn't shown up on that roof, she couldn't have died. She could've stabbed herself in the artery and she would've lived through it. But you already knew that, didn't you?"

I closed my eyes, but I saw the same thing. Blackness. I opened my eyes and the girl was gone.

"It's annoying when you do that."

"Do what?" But I didn't want to know. I wished that I would wake up.

"When something happens that you don't like, you try to escape it. You should stop. It's a bad habit. Freaky Cinderella needs to see her toad or she might step wrong and squash him."

"I'm in a psych hospital, right? I'm having hallucinations and I'm actually schizophrenic. That's what you are. You're me talking to me and this doesn't exist."

"Little Jack can't run without his Jill. The pail won't let them."

Yep. I was insane. "I need to go right now. I can pinch myself. I'll wake up. Or I can kill myself. You always wake up before you die, right?"

"There are rules, Jackass." It screamed this time and with a blink of the eye I saw the girl again. She stood in front of me, looking through me, and I saw the hazel eyes from before. They weren't sad or content this time. They were terrified and she quaked beneath my stare. Then someone passed me and I saw that she didn't tremble because of me. She knelt as a black form loomed above her. It was a person, but the shape was too blurry. I couldn't see who it was. I really wanted to know who it was. "Trees stand on the ground. The sun sets and rises again. The moon beams down. Waves roll back and forth and what's underneath it all? Rules."

"Who is that?" I gestured to the black shape. Something was before me and I needed to know what it was. I felt the urgency shoot through my body and I glanced from the corner of my eye to my arm. I screamed as I saw the silver course through all of my body and explode outwards into a blinding light. The black shape was illuminated a man with a scar that ran from his eyebrow down his face to end below his neck. He held a jagged dagger in his hand and blood dripped from the tip.

"Who is that?"

"Would Jack and Jill have run up the hill if they had no pail?"

I felt a poke in my side. "Stop it."

The voice laughed. "That wasn't me, Freaky Cinderella."

"Don't call me Freaky Cinderella," I snarled and whirled around. Nothing. Darkness. As I whirled the other way I saw the same girl, but the scarred man was gone. She held the dagger this time and I watched, frozen, as she took the knife to her arm and gritted her teeth. As sweat beaded over her eyebrows, she started to cut her own skin.

"She was the Freaky Cinderella," the voice whispered in my ear.

"Who are you?"

"The water."

"Who's the pail?"

"You."

Not the answer I was expecting. "And Jack and Jill are...?"

"Wrong answer, Freaky Snow White."

I was Snow White now. "Could you pick one fairy tale and keep with it? I'm getting confused."

"You haven't been kissed yet. The seven berry gummy bears won't let you be kissed. I wouldn't like them if I were you."

"Thank goodness that you're not me then," I snapped back.

There was a pause. I felt surprise in the air. "The seven berry gummy bears need to die."

"I'll eat them. How about that?" I was nearing the end of my rope. The voice was starting to irritate me. I liked gummy bears and I hated fairy tales. "Reveal yourself. Now." I felt the resistance in the air. It swirled around me. As I pulled one way, it pulled the other way. Then I screamed, "Reveal!"

The air exploded. I blinked from the force of it and then I saw myself staring back at me. The real me was annoyed. "Who are you?"

"The water."

Oh yes. I was a sarcastic brat. "No riddles. Who are you and who am I?"

The other me smirked. "I'm the water. You're the pail, but you need to figure out who Jack and Jill are."

"Humans and vampires."

"Try something more elemental than that. Those are species. Look at yourself."

I glanced down to my arms and lifted them high. I still saw the silver color pumping through my skin. I saw the tendons and ligaments attached to my muscles and bones. The silver ran through it all. I was a little unnerved, but I gritted my teeth. There had to be a message in all this nonsense.

"You're life."

"I'm Davy."

"That's what we can call you, but that's not what you are. Not anymore."

"I'm..." I looked up, somber. "Jack and Jill don't exist. You're the Immortal. You're life and you're in me now. It's not about Jack and Jill. It's about running up the hill and falling down. It's about fetching the pail. They wouldn't have to run up the hill if they didn't need to fetch a pail of water."

"You're starting to get it. She never got it."

"The hill is..."

"The hill is the pursuit. You're the golden prize."

I was going to wake up. I felt it slowly coming.... My other self disappeared in a flash, but the voice haunted me, "You're the Immortal now, Davy. Welcome to the Land of Never Death."

Then I gasped as the dagger flashed towards me. Blood dripped down and it was mine this time. The dagger swept closer and embedded itself in my chest. I opened my mouth to scream, but no sound came out.

14

---

y eyes snapped open and I let loose a shrill scream. My hand clamped on my chest, but it took a moment before I realized that there was no dagger. There was no blood. My hand shook as I held it out and saw there that was no silver blood. My hand was normal. Pale. I looked around and there was no Alice's Wonderland. I breathed a sigh of relief.

"You're awake."

I turned towards the voice and was dazed to see a hooker leaning against a grand oak door. She wasn't really a hooker, but she looked like one. She smiled coolly and straightened from her post, then stalked towards me with one precisely placed black boot in front of the other. She was a vampire. That was obvious, but she wasn't like the other vampires around Benshire. They dressed like regular folk. She wore a black leather corset held together by silver safety pins. The leather looked like it cut into her skin, but I doubted she cared. It's not like she really needed to breathe. It gave her some massive cleavage.

The corset looked like it was tucked into her pants. The ends were tucked inside those high-heeled black boots that started below her knees.

Uncomfortable. Dangerous. Sexy.

Her dark eyes flickered and I almost expected to see a drop of blood at the corner of her mouth. It would've blended with her lipstick and the auburn curls that hung down to her waist.

"Welcome back." She clipped those words out.

"You say that, but I don't think your heart's really into it," I replied with a raspy voice. I frowned and glanced down—that's when I saw where I was. Black satin sheets. I was in a massive bed placed on a pedestal in the center of the room. The bed was, whoa. That's all I could say and the rest of the room.... I took a second look at the doors since they were my only exit. They were massive too and made of oak with little swirls in the frame around the doors, like an artist had custom-made the frames just for the room. The swirls in the frame matched the two window frames, bed posts, and head-board. Someone was more decorative than me. Then I looked at myself and saw I was dressed in my jeans with only my thin camisole. That was it. No socks. I always wore socks. I loved my socks. "Where am I?"

"Lucas wanted to make sure you were safe."

"What happened to me?"

Her body is changing...

My body shook as I remembered those words and I focused on her again. "You know who I am? You were there. You said—" I fell silent, confused. How had she known? I hadn't even known.

She was smug. "Do I know who you are? Yes. I'm one of three who knows. And yes, I was there when your body started changing. You were seizing. I had to put you out of your misery."

I sat further up in the bed. "You told Roane to do it. You told him that I needed 'to know.'" My throat was sore so I started to massage it.

"Now you know, don't you?" I saw a flash of dislike in her eyes and knew this vampire *really* loathed me.

I threw my legs out from underneath the sheets and stood weakly.

"He's not going to want you to leave. Lucas said to keep you here no matter what." There was a warning in her dark eyes. So I made sure there was a wide berth as I rounded to the door. When I reached it, I held her gaze. That's when I saw that she had no intention of stopping me. Why? Did she really hate me that much? Was it about Roane?

As those questions formed in my mind, I was inside her. Her shields were like air for me. She had no idea. She was frozen in place, like I had paralyzed her. I could easily slip through now whereas I would've broken a sweat before.

"No, Davy." A hand wrapped around my arm and jerked me out.

So many things flashed through my mind, but I watched as she blinked. She was slowly coming out of her trance. Then comprehension flashed and loathing quickly followed. It had been there before, but this time it was tenfold and she bared her fangs. If Roane hadn't been there, she would've killed me.

Roane pulled me against his chest and tucked me to the side at the same time. He moved and stood between the two of us. "Wren, walk away. She doesn't know her powers yet. Go."

Wren straightened to her full height. She didn't spare Roane a glance, but she promised so many lethal things in her eyes. If Wren had been at Kates' bar, I knew I would've tucked tail and just left Emily to fend for herself. Not now. I felt something in my gut. I held a hand over my stomach and the feeling instantly speared into my skin, like I had called it there. It's on the other side of my skin and I watched horrified and amazed as a spark came out of it. "Oh my god!"

"She's going into shock again. She can't handle it." Take a guess at who said that.

"Not now, Wren," Roane snarled as he swept his arms underneath me and I felt myself being lifted in the air.

"Put her out again. She can't handle it, not yet. It's too soon. Her body changed too fast, Lucas. Put her out."

"No!" I struggled in Roane's arms, but he laid me on the bed and held me down.

"Calm down, Davy. You have to calm down. I know it's hard. I know the adjustment is disconcerting, but please stay with me."

"She can't handle it. She'll be another kicker before the week's end."

"Out!" Roane roared this time.

I slammed back into reality and felt Roane's body on top of mine. I heard his ferocity. He was tense and hard like a rock, but his attention was focused on her.

My palm itched. I looked at it, detached from myself, and saw it jerk. It was like it knew I watched it, like it had something it wanted to do. I wasn't sure what was going to happen, but I knew something was going to happen. It closed on itself and I felt a searing heat flare through my body. My hand trembled, but it remained fisted and then the heat surged through my body again and soared to my hand. The heat burst out of my body and shot through the air. It aimed perfectly.

Wren saw it coming. The heat slammed against her chest and she crashed backwards through the doors. She was there. She was gone.

"Where did you send her?" Roane scrambled off the bed and looked through the opened doors.

"I wanted her gone." We still hadn't heard her fall.

"Gregory!"

"She's okay. She landed in the lilies." Gregory's voice echoed through the house.

Roane swung his impenetrable eyes my way from the doorway. "Wren hates lilies. Did you know that?"

My eyes went wide as I realized that when I'd been inside of her, I'd done a quick scan. It was like I was some ultra-charged empath now and I was the internet inside of humans, well, vampires. I shrugged. "Lucky guess. She didn't look like the flower type."

Roane studied me intently. The silence stretched out. One second. Five seconds. Thirty—a minute—five minutes. Ten minutes. That's how long we stared at each other. Ten freaking minutes. Then, "You don't even need a shield anymore."

"That's all? I heat-rayed your girlfriend out of this house. All you say is that I don't need a shield anymore?"

Roane didn't change expressions. "You're changing, Davy. You know that you're changing and you know what you're changing into. Talia needed a shield and you don't. It's... remarkable."

I didn't like that name. In fact, I loathed that name. "Who is Talia?"

"She was the Immortal before you."

"I KNOW THAT LOOK," Roane announced a few hours later as he strode back into the room and closed the doors behind him. I knew he'd left to deal with Wren, but I didn't care to ask what had happened. She was gone. I was glad and then I thought better of it when I watched him close those doors. It might've been his slow movements or how he paused before he pulled those two doors shut, but the entire movement was ominous.

I sat up slowly and swallowed tightly. My hands fisted into the satin sheets, but it was all I could do. I was afraid to move. I was afraid to breathe. I was even afraid to think. He looked long and hard as if to see inside of me. He might've been. He knew more about me than I did.

"What look?" I wasn't sure I wanted to hear his answer.

Roane gestured with a nod. "You don't want to be here. Are you thinking of your little human boy? Are you hoping that he'll take you away from here? You want to forget everything that's happened this last week?"

He had no idea how right he was. "Just because you can read other people's thoughts doesn't mean that you can read mine."

"I can't anymore, but I could before. Now there's no way to get into that head. She wasn't like that."

'She.' Something about that word did not sit well with me. I didn't want him to know, though, so my voice didn't tremble when I asked, "She? Talia?"

Roane did his thing again. He measured me up and down for thirty seconds. "Yes. She was a good person."

"She wasn't really a person, was she?"

"You're right. She wasn't really a person."

"Even though that's what the lore says about Immortals. That they're human, but they have immortality."

"They?"

"I'm the last in a long line, right? Wren said that I'm not going to make the week before I'm on that rooftop."

Roane took one of those habitual small breaths and leaned against the wall. He was across the room and yet, I felt suffocated by his presence. He was too close. He wasn't close enough. I was on his bed. I wasn't in his arms. I sucked in a harsh breath and shook my head. I couldn't think like that—I couldn't feel like that. It was wrong. Everything was wrong.

"I understand it, you know." He sounded raw, scraped open.

Something relaxed inside of me. I didn't feel so alone. "Understand?"

He moved closer. I didn't see it, but I sensed it. I felt him move beside the bed, but he didn't sit down. He stayed beside me, but just out of reach.

"You're going through it again. You were empathic. You couldn't control your gifts. I heard you with Kates, how horrible it must've been. I'm a vampire, Davy. I understand the complexities between Empaths and Vampires. I know you must've been tortured."

'Hey, little girl, little girl, little girl. Come out and play… come out and play. I have some toys for you.'

"Do you really?" I strangled out. "Do you know what he did to me? The things that he said and that was just, those were words. Do you really understand what he did to me?"

I looked up and was caught by Roane's gaze. In the span of knowing him, he was usually so unemotional. There were times that I knew I'd infuriated him. There were times I'd been intimidated by him. I'd felt what it was like to be inside his arms, but I'd never seen this from him.

He was haunted.

"Were you tortured?" I don't know why I asked.

"I did the torture, Davy."

'It's about us not forgetting what we used to be. We used to be human.'

"That must've been..." I wasn't sure what to say. That must've been *hard* for him? He did the torture and I'd been tortured. I was suddenly angry, really angry at him even though he hadn't been my torturer. Not to mention that I wasn't human anymore. Would I turn into the same monster?

"That's not..." Roane stopped and turned away, but paused before he had completely turned his back. He raised a hand and ran it over his head.

I drew my knees to my chest and hugged them. I could see he was upset, but so was I. "I'm not human anymore, Roane. You can't—" He couldn't understand. He'd been a vampire for so long.

"What? I can't understand? I have no idea what it's like to suddenly wake up and not be human, with powers that don't make sense. You're right, Davy. I have absolutely no idea."

I shrunk back from his stinging words.

Roane pressed, "I know more about you than you do right now, Davy. I know what the Immortal is. I know that you're empathic and you're still human. You've just got other juices flowing in your blood."

"Can I get rid of them?" I kneeled on his bed. A part of me was desperate. I didn't want this.

Roane sucked in his breath, but didn't move away. He didn't move closer either, but he couldn't look away. I felt my power over him. It was blinding and I knew that he couldn't turn away. He wanted to. A part of him really wanted to turn and walk away. He didn't.

I moved closer, just close enough without touching him. If either of us moved an inch, we would've felt the other. I wanted to feel him. I needed it. It was the same hunger that I'd felt in that professor's office. Something inside of me—or maybe it was me—needed him. It was like I was starving for him.

Roane searched my face, but his eyes flickered and held on my lips. He wrung out, "You don't know yourself right now. This isn't what you want."

"This isn't what happened in the office? That was both of us."

"You were starting to change. You weren't yourself. You won't be, not for a long time."

"Are you trying to save me, Roane? Is that what this is? You're trying to be compassionate? Maybe feeling your human self right now?"

I felt the whiplash from his eyes. He was furious, but he clenched his jaw tight. "You don't want me to save you or you don't want to be saved? You want me to be a vampire, Davy? Is that what you want? Maybe you want me to drink your blood? Davina."

Davina.

Vampire.

I lifted stormy eyes to his. "You have this decree to stop yourselves from being what you are. It's the same thing as Kates. She's meant to be a slayer and that decree says she can't be herself. You're evil. Be evil and she can do what she's supposed to do. She gets to kill you."

His lip curled upwards, mocking and lethal. "And that's what pisses you off, because you don't know where you fit in. You've never known, have you? You're a human. You're not supposed to know about us, but you do. You're empathic and that made you a freak. You found out things you weren't supposed to and now what are you? You're more of a freak than Kates or I will ever be. Only one can exist and you're all alone."

Those words hit me, but he was right. "I am alone and I don't know who I am—what I am."

"Davy."

"Kates said that you want my blood? I have life in me and you want that life?" Everything was blaring inside of me. "You…"

"It's not that simple."

"Then make it simple!" I cried out, infuriated. There was something inside of me, something that I didn't understand. I wanted it out. I wanted it gone because it didn't belong there. It wasn't me and

I only wanted to be me. "I don't want this, Roane! I don't want this thing inside of me. Take it out. Drink it out. Drain me—do whatever you need to do. I want it gone!"

'Welcome to the Land of Never Death.'

"Get it out of me!" I grasped Roane's shoulders and pressed myself against him. I felt him stiffen. He was so rigid.... "Please, Roane."

He sighed in surrender and wrapped both arms around me.

Just then, we heard a cough and I nearly wept, but I couldn't name from what emotion. Roane lifted his head and I felt the coldness where he had rested his cheek against mine. He turned towards the intruder. "What is it, Gregory?"

"The Family is here. They need to know about her."

Her—me. I felt the reluctance in Roane and though he didn't move I still felt a part of him tear away from me. I almost gasped from the pain. "They can't know, Gregory. No one can know." It was like he'd spoken about death, about his death.

"Raitscliff and Lucan both think the new Immortal is a different girl."

"Do you know this girl?"

"Yes."

"Then go and get her. They can't hurt her if we have her."

"You'll bring war to this household," Gregory warned.

I glanced towards the Viking vampire and was surprised to see the gravity in his eyes.

Roane wrapped his arms tighter around me. I closed my eyes as his cheek brushed against mine and felt his words against my shoulder. "Find the other girl. Bring her here."

When Gregory left, I looked up. "What'll happen to the other girl?"

Something broke inside of Roane at my question. A part of me realized that I was in there because I felt it break. I hadn't purposely gone into him, but I was. He either didn't care or didn't know. "They'll drain her. They'll kill her thinking she can't die. But even if she was the Immortal, I would still need to stop them."

"Why?"

"No vampire can drink the Immortal's blood. It can't be allowed to happen."

I lifted my head and searched his eyes with mine. '*How?*'

"I'll fight them."

I pulled away and out of him at the same time. Everything was too much. "This is all too overwhelming."

"It's going to get more overwhelming."

"What do you mean?"

"You should sit down, Davy."

That didn't sound ominous at all. "Okay..." I sat slowly and took a breath. I knew I'd need to ready myself for whatever was coming my way.

He stepped back and leaned against the wall "In all my life, no Immortal has been known."

"What do you mean? You knew the other girl. You said she was a good person."

"I did know her, but I was the only one, Davy. I knew Talia when she was little and I protected her. That was my job. I wasn't always a Hunter. I became one because certain Elders questioned me."

I straightened. "You're not telling me everything."

"No, I'm not. That's not important at this time. You need to know about the Immortal and you need to understand the situation. You're the new Immortal. I suspected before, but I wasn't sure."

"Why do the other vampires think it's someone else? I was on that roof with Talia. They saw me."

"But they didn't see her touch you. There was no contact between you two."

'Yeah, but I felt inside of her.'

Roane read my thoughts. "The Immortal thread goes from one human to the next. She didn't touch you. They don't know about the psychic contact between you. No one else knew about that possibility. It's always been documented in the Immortal lore that one Immortal needs to physically touch the next Immortal. *I* knew that it didn't need to happen that way, but no one else knew."

"She touched someone else?"

Roane nodded. "Another girl left the building when Talia went inside. Talia held the door open for her and their arms brushed against each other."

Too many questions. Not enough answers. "What did you mean when you said that no Immortal has been known?"

"You said before that the Immortal was a fairytale and you're somewhat right. There's always been the belief that an Immortal existed, but no one knew for certain. There were theories, but Talia was hidden by my family. I was entrusted to protect her, but I failed."

I felt how his words hurt him. This was his duty. It's what I felt inside of him the first time we spoke. "You were supposed to protect her and hide her?"

Roane nodded, his jaw tight.

"What happened? How'd the other vampires find out?"

Something told me that Roane wasn't going to share the details unless he absolutely had to. "I'd been sent on a different mission for one of the Elders so I wasn't even there. But there was an argument and the wrong person overheard. Talia made a choice—she ran that night. She knew she needed to find another Immortal and hoped the Immortal would remain hidden. She did what she needed to do."

"She chose me?" He still wasn't telling me everything.

"The Immortal thread chose you, not Talia. You were supposed to work late that night. She knew you'd come upstairs and she knew you were empathic. She needed to let go of the thread without them seeing it. When you went inside of her, the thread came back with you."

"We aren't supposed to touch too deep in a person." I wet my dry lips. They felt like they were bleeding. "If something went wrong, a part of us could stay inside. I never thought that a part of them could come inside of me. That's not how it's supposed to happen. There are rules, universal laws of nature stuff."

"The Immortals can bend those rules."

That meant... "I can bend those rules."

"You can't think that way, not yet. You don't know all of your powers and we don't have time for you to get acquainted with them."

Roane surged forward. "That's why I'm giving you this crash course. Gregory's right. I *am* bringing war to this household, but I have to keep you hidden. No vampire can drink from you. If they did, they would have your powers. Any vampire would be unstoppable. I can't let that happen."

I'm back to my dislike for vampires. Evil creatures, the lot of them, well, the possible exception might be in front of me. "Let me guess. When that happens then the world might end?"

"Hardly. It just means that vampire has too much power. No creature should have that power."

"Except a human."

"Except someone with a soul. Yes."

We're back to that conversation. Souls, humanity, forgetting or not forgetting what it's like to be human. It was all connected. I jerked my head up and down and hoped it resembled a nod. I wasn't holding my breath. "What now?"

Roane paused for a second. It was one of those seconds where you felt your heart was going to explode. "You have to walk away from me and be normal."

"What did you say?" My heart skipped a beat.

Roane stepped towards me, but stopped abruptly. It was like he wanted to come closer, but didn't dare. I completely understood and found myself swaying towards him, but I forced myself to stay on the bed.

"I'm the Hunter here. They know that they can't drink from a human, even if they think she's the Immortal. I have to stop them. They won't think twice when they see the girl here, but they'll start to wonder if you're here too. I know some of these vampires. Each of us has a Family and some Families are more powerful than others. Some extremely powerful Families are coming here and all of them want the Immortal. I can't worry that they'll discover who you are if you're here. You need to go. You need to hide and you can do that by being normal. Don't use your powers. They can't sense your power."

"Where's your Family?"

"They're coming."

He was being vague and I didn't like that. My eyes sharpened. "Gregory said war. He wasn't exaggerating."

"He wasn't." Roane looked away and rubbed a tired hand over his jaw. My hand itched to cover his.

"I came here to be normal. I wanted to go to college because that's the normal thing to do. Kates didn't understand it, but she's not like me. She likes being unique or abnormal. She doesn't understand. I wish she did sometimes." I looked up and held his gaze. It was alluring, seductive, but I saw the anger that was repressed. It simmered under the surface. "I have a date tonight. I should go on that date, huh?"

He clenched his jaw for the briefest of seconds. "It would be the 'normal' thing to do, yes."

I wondered if it cost him to say that. It cost me to hear it. "Okay. I'll go on that date, then."

Roane stayed where he was.

I couldn't bring myself to walk out those doors. "I should go."

He nodded again. "Gregory will be back with the girl shortly. Hopefully, after awhile, things will go back to normal. You should... stay away from Kates. Stay with your roommate, with that boy. Go to classes. Do your normal thing."

I frowned as a thought came to me. "You said that you needed me to help Kates. Did you? Or was that whole thing just a lie because you thought I was the Immortal?"

'Did he use my roommate?'

"I used them both, yes." Roane read my mind again.

I thought my shields were up against him? "And my powers?"

"Try not to get angry. Talia told me that she used to 'pack it away'. She said some days she was human and the others, she was the Immortal. You could try that."

"What about the other girl? What are you going to do with her?"

Roane answered swiftly and I caught a glimpse of the Hunter he was. I had felt how fierce he could be, how determined and devoted to his duty he was when I'd been inside of him. I had marveled at his motivation and I saw it again when he replied, "We'll hide her.

When they demand to know where she is, we'll fight. We'll win. And then she'll be seen in another state, another city, and rumors will be told again. They'll all go there."

They'd leave Benshire and the real Immortal behind. It was brilliant, but something told me that was just Roane doing his job. It was another day in the office for him.

"This is what you do, isn't it." I glided across the room until I stood right before him, within touching distance.

Roane closed his eyes and struggled not to reach out. The same battle was within me. A part of me was starting not to care about the consequences. Were there consequences?

Roane caught my hand. I hadn't been aware of lifting it, but he caught and held it immobile in the air. There it was—the connection between us, again. Both of us looked at our hands. His hand wrapped around my wrist. Slowly, hypnotically, I bent my fingers and caressed his finger, just slightly, but it was enough. Roane drew in a ragged breath. I held my own. Then he growled as he hauled me to his chest and lifted me in the air. I wrapped my legs around his waist and we fell on the bed. His weight pressed me down and I searched for his mouth, desperately.

He found it and claimed me.

Roane slid his hands down to my waist. I arched my back to press against him and wrapped my arms around his neck. It seemed like I couldn't get any closer, but I needed to.

I couldn't get enough of him.

And then a phone ring peeled through the air. I cursed under my breath as Roane ripped himself away from me. Instantly, I felt the cold blast against my body and I would've done anything to have him back. The phone rang again and Roane paused when he found it. A third time. "I can't answer this." Roane sounded like he had one last nerve of willpower and the phone was quickly eating it away.

I lifted my head and saw that he had my phone. I'd completely forgotten that I *had* a phone. It seemed like something from a different world, not a world where vampires and Immortals existed.

It rang a fourth time and I felt the impatience across the line. "It's my roommate." I held out a heavy hand and snapped it open. "What?"

"What? You just say it like that? What? Your boyfriend is here. He said something about a date. And you ditched out on the convention today. Thanks a lot. Mr. Moser trusted me and I was stupid enough to trust *you*."

"Emily…"

"Get back here from wherever you are and deal with Adam. I don't want him here."

I sighed in surrender. "I'll be right there."

"Thank you. I'm going to make Adam wait in the lobby for you."

Before I could reply, she'd already hung up.

Roane peered out the window and then looked back. "Gregory's back. I'll have him take you to your dorm."

I wondered if my exhaustion was from the Immortal's change in my body or knowing my life wouldn't be the same again. A third option was the desire that literally throbbed inside of me. My guess —the Immortal had nothing on Roane. When I started towards the door, he stopped me. "Stay away from Wren. Make sure you're never alone with her."

"Why?"

"There are some things that you don't know about her and she knows about you. Avoid her if you see her."

I nodded and left with a heavy heart.

"We have seven different types of chairs in the room. Why do we have seven different chairs? It's insane. It's a complete lack of chair-efficiency. I can't handle all these chairs."

This is what greeted me as I stepped inside my dorm room.

Emily was frantic. She had placed every chair in a line, which wasn't long because our dorm room wasn't big. Now she paced with frantic hands in the air.

I frowned and shut the door. "What's going on?"

"He called! Can you believe it? He called. He's downstairs. Right now!"

"Who?"

"That guy from the bar." It was endearing how my roommate hung her head and blushed. "I made out with. I've never done that, Davy." Her eyes were wide and horrified. "I can't believe I did that and now he found me. He's downstairs."

I wasn't sure what my role was here, but I improvised. "What does he want?"

"Dinner," she blurted out.

Horrifying. A slow smile started to spread on my face. "Dinner?"

"Can you believe it? He wants to sit and eat and talk. I don't know what to do."

"Apparently you're categorizing our chairs." I frowned as I looked over the room. There *was* an inordinate amount of chairs. Both of us had desk chairs. There was a pink bean bag that sat beside an inflated purple bean bag. Not to mention the couch, plus another lawn chair—I wasn't sure where that came from. Then there were our regular desk chairs that came with the dorm room. She was right. I counted seven.

"I still feel like crap. Why do I feel like this? I hate being sick. I have too much work to do." Emily moaned and fell into one of the chairs.

A thought occurred to me. "You can come with me and Adam."

Disgust first flashed over her features, but then a bright smile lit it up. "You're right. It's not awkward then. I won't even have to talk. You like to talk. You and Adam can talk, but no mushy stuff. I don't think I can stomach that tonight." She pressed an open palm over her stomach and I feared she was going to *actually* throw up.

I remembered my night of vomiting and grimaced. My stupid body had been changing and I felt a tingle in my palm. My body was *still* changing.

When I turned towards the closet, I muttered to myself, "I don't know if I could stomach it either."

"What's he wearing?"

"Who?"

"The guy!"

"I didn't go through the lounge. I snuck up the back stairs." I shrugged and grabbed my shower bag. Then I toed off my shoes and slid on my flip flops.

"Where are you going?" Emily gasped with a hitch in her voice.

"I'm going to take a shower and then get ready. Adam can wait."

"What about the guy?"

"He can wait too. We're worth it." Then I proved how overjoyed I was with a long yawn.

Emily narrowed her eyes, but didn't comment.

Was I overjoyed? Not anymore. *Could* I be overjoyed with the idea of a date with Adam? I was hoping. I wanted normalcy before and I still wanted normalcy. What was messing it all up was Roane and the Immortal stuff. I shook my head to clear my thoughts. I was a human now. I'd be the Immortal another day. Human. Date. But first, a shower.

When I entered the room after a quick cleaning, I saw that the chairs all remained the same and Emily was dressed now in a pair of khakis and a red sweater. I considered making a joke about Target, but thought better of it. In her state, Emily wouldn't register the joke or she would've been even more horrified.

"I'm freaking out," Emily rushed out.

"Yes. Yes, you are." I nodded to myself.

"What kind of guy comes to a girl's dorm? How did he even know who I was?"

I had one answer for that. He was a vampire. They could sniff down their adversary. "I'm pretty sure Kates introduced you guys or Roane did. It's not that big of a campus. There are only a few dorms for freshman girls."

"Roane?" Emily asked, confused.

"Oh—Luke, right? That's what you call him."

Emily sighed wistfully, "I wish he were downstairs."

My hand stilled as I reached for a black lacy shirt. My stomach flipped on itself, but I took a deep breath and pushed past the moment of shame. My roommate had a crush on Lucas Roane. I knew that and I still kissed him. Could I take it back? I don't think that was the question I needed to ask myself. I should've asked—did I want to take it back?

"But he's not and this guy is. I like this guy—he's... I don't know how to explain it."

I'd heard it so many other times. Emily wasn't the first to have fallen underneath a vampire's attraction. It was ensnaring and powerful. We were both doomed.

"Okay, I'm ready!" Emily announced and I turned to see that she was glowing.

"What happened to the 'we have too many chairs?'"

She blushed again. "I don't know. It's silly, right? I should be excited that a guy is here. He took the time to find me and wants to have dinner. It's dinner. That means something, right? Right?" The glow quickly slipped to show befuddlement.

"It means something, yes."

She smiled and her panic lessened again. I'd never seen her so frazzled. It was so *human* of her and I found that refreshing. "Are you ready to make him eat his heart out?"

Emily smoothed a shaking hand down her shirt and chuckled.

I grabbed my purse and posed. "How do I look?"

Emily blinked. "You look great. Wow, you really do."

I chose a cream silk shirt that hugged my body. A layer of black lace had been sewn over it and the shirt rested low on my hips where I felt the snug fit of my jeans. I had eyed the high heeled black boots, but the black ballet slipper shoes won. I felt comfortable. I knew I wouldn't be mistaken for a Target employee.

As we left the room, I tried not to ask myself the question of whether I was dressing for Adam or the hope of Adam? I sucked in a breath. I didn't want that—I didn't want to start thinking about things like that. I was normal for the night.

Emily had walked ahead, but turned back. Her eyes widened dramatically and she stopped abruptly to place a soothing hand over my arm. "Are you okay?"

"I'm good. Thanks." I was a taken aback at the concern in her voice. It was real. I always thought Emily ran in the opposite direction of emotion. I squeezed her hand in reassurance and then we both turned towards the boys who were waiting.

Adam straightened from the wall and smiled that adorable grin.

I felt a calming breath go through me and remembered the reasons why I had liked Adam in the first place. He was sweet and kind. He wasn't evil. There was no hidden agenda.

"You look great, Davina."

"It's Davy." Emily clarified, "She likes to be called Davy."

Score one in the friendship category for my roommate—and from the looks of her leering vampire, she scored a point with him. Unlike Adam's golden curls, this vampire's blond locks looked greasy. Some went for that dirty sex-craved look, but I was glad this one wasn't there for me.

"Emily." The vampire moved from across the room and took her hand gently to rub against his black tight-fitting shirt.

Emily blushed. "Oh my."

"You look beautiful," he crooned as he pulled her towards him and placed a hand around her waist. Well well well... Emily had more than a devoted vampire on her hands.

I eyed him questioningly and wondered if I should slip inside. Then I remembered Roane's words. I was human with human traits and that meant no powers, not even my empathic ones.

"Are you ready to go, Davy?" Adam emphasized my name this time.

"I am and you look good too." And he did, wearing a white pressed shirt over a pair of dark blue jeans.

Emily squeaked when the vampire bent his head and whispered something in her ear. Whatever he said produced another blush and she sounded breathless. "We're going with them."

"We are?" The vampire lazily lifted his head and smiled charmingly.

"We are."

Adam coughed to cover up his surprise. "We're going to the Alexander Restaurant."

"I heard that's divine eating." The vampire was smooth. I had to give him that.

"I don't know if you remember Davy, but this is my roommate. Davy, this is Bennett. He was at that bar we went to with Kates."

"It's nice to meet you this time." I made sure to be polite, but Bennett had no interest in me.

When we got to the cars, Emily insisted all of us go together. As we started off, I sat in the front passenger seat and moved the mirror so I could watch Bennett. I started to realize that something about the vampire bothered me. Of course, it might've been the fact that he was a vampire, but there was something else. He had his hands all over Emily—which I wasn't surprised she allowed. Vampire charm meant vampire addiction. Not many girls could fight the lure once bitten. I knew Emily had no chance so I was secretly happy about the driving status. I could keep an eye on Bennett and make sure he didn't sneak anymore lovebites against Emily's wishes.

Then as we neared the restaurant, I caught some furtive glances that Bennett kept shooting towards Adam. His hands were on Emily, but his eyes were on Adam. What the—? "Bennett, did you and Adam know each other before?"

Bennett lifted his eyes to stare long and hard at me through the rear view mirror. Adam had a look of confusion. He had no clue. So that meant the vampire was up to something. I switched my gaze back to Bennett's in the mirror and wasn't surprised to see him reassessing me.

"Did you guys?" Emily rasped out. "I guess we never introduced you two."

Adam looked like the idea had never occurred to him.

Bennett lied, "We have a class together."

"We do?"

"Yeah. Social work."

"Oh, yeah. The class with Moser?" Adam played into Bennett's hand.

"That's great!" This new Emily was easily satisfied.

I wasn't, but I quieted when Adam pulled into the parking lot. As we got out of the car, I found myself alone with Bennett. Somehow, in the blink of an eye, Emily and Adam had approached the restaurant without us.

"What?" I managed out before Bennett stepped right in front of me.

"You know who I am." He tried to pierce me with his blue eyes. They reminded me of Kates, how fierce and crystal blue they could be at times.

I recovered quickly and snapped out, "I know *what* you are."

"If you're smart, you'll keep that to yourself," he threatened.

"I'm not smart. A lot of people think I'm dumb, really dumb, bimbo dumb." I backed down quickly when I remembered Roane's warning. Loathing vampires drew attention and it certainly wasn't normal. They were used to being feared.

He ran an aggravated hand through his greasy hair. "What do you want?"

"Stop taking lovebites out of my roommate." How many times does a person get to say that?

"Fine. You won't say anything to her? She doesn't know what I am. I'd like to keep it that way."

"You had to have realized that I'd know what you are. Kates was at the bar that night." I knew every vampire knew who and what Kates was.

"What?"

"Kates. She's one of my best friends. She's a slayer, remember?"

"Oh yeah... I never thought... Kates is one of us. She's loyal to Lu —there's a lot of humans that know our secrets and a lot that don't. I'd like Emily to be one that doesn't know."

Whatever he'd been about to say, I wasn't sure I wanted to hear it. By the look of his sudden nervousness and quick catch, I knew Bennett wished that he hadn't slipped what he had.

I stepped closer. "She's loyal to who?"

"Lucas Roane. The Hunter. She's loyal to him like everyone else."

I knew that was a load of crap. He hadn't been about to say Lucas. "She's loyal to him, huh?" I told myself to let it go. My insides screamed that this vampire was bad news, but I was a human that night. Roane made me promise. I couldn't do anything, absolutely anything, to give any suspicion. So that meant I needed to accept that Bennett had lied through his fangs to me.

"She is and so am I. There's no problem, right? I won't hurt your roommate. If I do, I'd have to be killed, remember?"

Right. The whole decree thing. And yet, as he turned and left me behind my gut didn't agree with him.

17

"I wasn't sure where you went." Adam pulled my chair out for me.

"Uh, yeah." I didn't think I could tell him a vampire had threatened me.

Adam frowned, but sat beside me as Bennett arrived behind me. There we were. Two couples based on lies and supernatural coincidences. As I looked around, I realized that we were at the best table. The restaurant was nice and by nice—I meant expensive. A fountain was in the middle of the restaurant and each table had a crystal goblet with three small goldfish swimming inside. Our glasses were diamond encrusted.

"Did you request this table?" I asked Adam.

"What?"

"This is the best table in the restaurant. Did you ask for this?"

Bennett lifted his whispering head. Emily fanned herself.

"No. I mean, I called and asked for the availability tonight. They weren't doing reservations. We just got here. I couldn't have... what was the question?"

"Nothing." I shook my head with an easy smile. It didn't matter, but I wondered if Roane had anything to do with the table. I hoped not. It didn't help my confused emotions.

"Shall we order?" Bennett suggested.

I fixed him with a glare. "Right. You're a big fan of, what? Salad?"

"Davy." Both Emily and Adam reprimanded me.

I was nonplussed. "Maybe you can order the meat rare. You can tell them not to cook it, just slap it on a plate for you."

"Davina." Emily had remembered her prim and proper standards. She looked nauseous.

I arched an eyebrow, ready for whatever Bennett threw back, but Adam caught my hand and dragged me from the table.

"What is going on with you?" Adam tried to be nice, but he still sounded aggravated. It was somewhat endearing. He was like a gentleman that needed to ask something ungentlemanly, but couldn't figure out the words.

"I don't like him."

Adam sighed and scratched the back of his head. A surge of warmth speared through me. He really was unlike everything else in my life. Stable. Honest.

"Hey." I caught his hand and pulled it between us. "I like you."

He was startled, but delight spread over his features. "Really?"

I squeezed his hand and moved closer. "I know that it's sudden and fast and this is our first date, but I just wanted to tell you that. I like you."

"I like you too." An anchor seemed to have lifted off him. "Wow. That feels good to have that off my chest."

This is what I wanted, right? I wasn't sure, but I held tight to his hand anyway. Adam glanced from my eyes to my lips and back again. I held my breath. I knew what he was going to do—he waited for a signal, any signal. If I moved just an inch he would've been a happy boy. I was stricken. Adam was what I wanted. I'd taken one look at him at the hotline and knew he would be mine. I enjoyed the chase and now the chase was done. Adam was mine. So why wasn't I happy? Giddy? I was just...nothing.

Then I glanced over Adam's shoulder and knew it would have to wait. Kates was at our table.

"What the—?" I straightened away from Adam and stepped around.

"What?" He looked too and froze in place.

I wasn't sure why he seemed paralyzed, but I know that the sight of Kates whispering into Bennett's ear wasn't going to make my life any easier. What in the hell was she doing here? I didn't wait to ponder and marched across the room. "What are you doing here? And with *him*?"

Kates gasped, "What are you doing here?"

"I'm on a date." I jerked my thumb over my shoulder. Adam looked like he was caught in a pair of headlights.

"With him?"

Why was this so surprising?

"Yes. That's Adam. I told you he was mine." My chest puffed up a little bit.

"*That's* Adam?" Why was Kates so incredulous?

"Yes." I felt like a broken record.

A myriad of emotions flashed across her face. Shock, bafflement, disdain, and horror. I didn't care about the others, not really, but the horror caught me. I zeroed in and felt inside of her. What I felt made my toes curl.

Kates had a secret, a very shameful end-your-life type of secret. Bennett had told me that she was one of them, but I hadn't given him credit. I did now. The Lu— that she was loyal to wasn't Lucas. It was a vampire named Lucan. I remembered that two Families had arrived in town, ready for a war. Lucan and Raitscliff. I highly doubted it was a coincidence. There were no coincidences when it came to the supernatural or to anything that regarded my life.

"Kates." It was all I could mutter. I was still dumbfounded by what was planned and I saw the veil fall over her eyes. She knew that I knew. She knew *how* I knew. That's when she grabbed my arm and held tight. Each of her fingers tightened over my elbow, but I couldn't look away.

"What are you going to do?" The question choked me.

"You weren't supposed to be here. You weren't supposed to be a part of this."

"But I am."

Her fingers tightened again. They would've hurt if they'd been from anyone except my best friend. "Don't."

She hung her head, but her fingers still held my arm immobile. Then she made a decision and barked at Bennett, "Take him."

Bennett nodded with an eager look in his eyes and rushed around me. He grabbed Adam and hauled him out of the restaurant.

"What's going on...?" Emily started to run after Bennett, but stopped and looked at us. She looked confused as she saw Kates. "Davy? What's going on... Kates?"

"Don't," I pleaded with Kates. I knew what was happening. I knew that Emily had seen too much, but I still tried.

Kates shook her head and strode forward. She clamped a hand on Emily and dragged both of us behind her. We burst into the cold air where a black van waited for us. The doors were open—beckoning and dark.

"Oh my god. No!" Emily cried out and dug her heels in.

She was no match for a vampire slayer. Kates tightened her hold and merely lifted Emily across the pavement and into the van. She let go of my arm in the process and I wasn't sure if it was accidental or not. It didn't matter. Kates started to climb into the van, but stopped and looked at me. I stood on the cold pavement, the chill bounced off my adrenaline, and I held my best friend's gaze steadfastly.

Emily cried behind her and Adam groaned in pain.

I could bolt and I knew Kates wouldn't chase after me. This was my best friend giving me a chance. I rubbed where she had held my elbow. It was a dull throb, but it didn't matter.

"Davy." Kates wanted me to run. She didn't want me to be a part of this—little did she know how much I *was* a part of it all.

I made my mind up in that second and strode forward. Kates dropped into a chair and I crossed over her to drop into the chair beside her. Emily and Adam shrank back in their seats. The door slammed shut and the van shot off down the street.

"We got him?" Bennett turned around from his front seat. I

wasn't surprised to see a handgun in his hand, but did vampires even need weapons? I thought they were a weapon in and of themselves.

Kates reached to the floor and slammed a cartridge into her gun. "We got him, Benny."

"Alrighty tighty, man. That was fresh." Bennett grinned wolfishly, caught my look of disdain, and winked. "Come on, babe. You know our race. You've gotta appreciate how tight that was run."

"How tight that was run? Your race? Babe?" I questioned dully and leaned forward. "You really want to ask my opinion?"

Bennett cut an uneasy look towards Kates. "You hopped in all by yourself. No one made you come."

"Right, because when my friends are being kidnapped, I'd really appreciate the opportunity to run and hide. I'll remember that next time."

"You don't have to be such a bitch," Bennett muttered underneath his breath and turned back to look out the front window.

"What is going on? I don't understand—my arm really hurts," Emily moaned from the back.

Bennett smiled wolfishly.

"You like this, don't you." I was starting to *really* hate this vampire.

"Davy," Kates hushed me.

I shook off her restraining hand and narrowed my eyes. "You're like all the rest. You enjoy hurting people. You get off on it?"

Bennett chuckled and shook his head. "You mean like your ex-boyfriend? I knew him, you know."

"He wasn't my boyfriend," I snarled.

"That's what Craig used to say too." He didn't believe me at all.

"Bennett," Kates tried to hush him. It hadn't worked with me.

"You have horrible taste in men. Craig was fun to hang out with, but he was off his radar."

Emily squeaked. "What are you talking about, Bennett? What is he talking about, Davy? Kates?"

The only one not talking was Adam. I wondered why... and then

I heard my answer from Kates as she turned to look at me. "We were sent to get the Immortal's boyfriend."

Adam seemed to shrink underneath her gaze. His hair was messed and his shirt was wrinkled. Then I saw the guilt in his eyes, in those adorable pure-kindness almond eyes. The anchor dropped. "What is she talking about?"

Bennett started to laugh.

"Shut up, Bennett!" Kates swiftly punched him.

Bennett seemed shocked and then he growled. It was an unearthly growl, a sound that only the undead could produce. The sound sent shivers down my back.

Emily shrieked.

I wanted Bennett dead, not silenced, but it didn't matter in that moment. I turned around, placed a hand on my seat, and felt the cold plastic material underneath my fingers. "Boyfriend?"

Adam flushed and hung his head in shame. "Shelly and I are dating."

Shelly and him—they were dating. The words met my ears, but I sat back, dazed, as I let them comprehend I liked Adam. I actually did, but I didn't too. And I was so confused. Was this remorse that I was feeling?

"What'd I tell you? Bad taste in men. You should stick to my kind."

"Bennett, I swear that if you don't shut up, I will slice your head off!" Kates grated out.

"Your kind?" Emily moaned, tearful.

My throat burned, but when didn't it? I felt the first tingle in my stomach, deep inside, but I sucked in a ragged breath. Roane told me no Immortal stuff, certainly not with my current company. I wanted so badly to do something, to follow through with Kates' threat.

"You're one of us, Kates. Don't get all twisted and holy. You're in this all the way. Just like the rest of us. It's a tough break your buddy got brought along, but that's what you get for living in two worlds. You can't have it all, Katie."

"Do not call me Katie," Kates warned. Lethal.

Bennett laughed and turned back around.

I glanced at the driver. He'd remained quiet the entire time. I couldn't see his face at all, except a small side section. He was dressed in all black. A black baseball cap was pulled low over his eyes. It overshadowed the side of his face, but I caught a prominent cheekbone. Whoever he was, he had angular cheekbones. That was Kates' type. She liked her men lean and with those hollow cheeks.

"You said that you were sent for the Immortal's boyfriend. That's Adam?"

"Yeah." Kates frowned in sympathy. She raised a hand and I watched, immobile, as it descended in the air.

That's when I snapped. I gasped and caught her hand. "Don't you dare have pity on me. Don't you *dare* try to comfort me like a friend. You don't have that right. Don't you dare."

Kates blanched.

I gripped harder.

I felt the pain slice through her arm. It flared in her sapphire eyes, but I didn't care. I sunk my fingers tighter in her arm until she cried out, "Davy, stop. Please." She whimpered the last word.

Disgusted, I flung her arm away and sat back in my chair. I turned towards the window as I watched the scenery fly by.

In the back, Emily whimpered right alongside my betrayer. "Have we been kidnapped?"

"Yes, Emily," I murmured dully. "We've been kidnapped."

18

W e drove through town and stopped once to put blindfolds on. I thought Emily was going to hyperventilate, but Bennett skimmed a kiss over her forehead and she quieted. Even as the 'bad guy', he still had power over her. Then Kates turned and handed me the blindfold. I looked at it dumbly for a moment, but saw the appeal in her eyes. If I fought it, I wasn't sure if she would've overtaken me and put the blindfold on or if she would've allowed Bennett to do it. It didn't matter either way. I tied it behind my head and waited for Bennett to finish tying Adam's.

Adam. What could I even say about him? I couldn't think about him, not yet. I didn't even know what I thought anymore. Kates. Adam. Myself. Emily—betrayal was running rampant in these parts of Benshire.

After the blindfolds were checked a second time the van pulled ahead and we drove in silence the rest of the way. It slowed and turned upwards onto a gravel road. It wasn't long until we stopped and not one word was spoken.

The air felt heavy.

Suddenly, the door was thrown open and the cold blasted us. I flinched once, but refused to do it again.

"Come on, Davy," Kates urged softly.

I swallowed tightly and jumped out of the van. I felt Kates' alien touch as she grasped my arm and aligned herself to walk beside me. Emily whimpered behind me. Bennett shushed her in a seductive voice and then a door opened ahead of us and classical melodies greeted us. It seemed like an odd contrast, but the music echoed around us as we stood there. The place was large. Then I felt another ominous feeling start to tingle in my gut. Murmurs of conversation stopped when we stepped further into the room and I heard people, vampires?, stand up.

It was our entrance. Our hostage entrance—the thought struck me as amusing. I grinned, but I was instantly revolted at the idea that I might find something like this entertaining. Nothing was funny about the situation. Then I heard Emily's sobs of terror and sobered completely.

"Come on, Davy," Kates' restrained murmur hit my ears. Her request was unwelcome, but I couldn't fight back. I wanted to do something, to use my powers in someway.

And then suddenly I was.

I gasped silently as I saw the room. My vision was slightly blurry with a dark reddish tint to it. I felt Kates look to her right and I saw that side of the room. That's when I realized that I still had my blindfold on. I wasn't seeing this through my eyes. I saw through Kates. I had slipped inside of her and was viewing the room through her eyes.

I had been right. The room *was* full of vampires. All of them stood and watched our slow trek. I instantly knew these vampires weren't from Benshire. They were dressed differently. Some wore leather vests. Some wore long flowing velvet red coats, fringed at the ends. Some dressed in feather tunics. Still others wore nothing except tight jeans. The one thing they had in common was a symbol that ran over the left arm and left shoulder. It was the letter L. That was the entire symbol, but it spoke volumes.

This was Lucan's Family.

I counted thirty on that side of the room before Kates glanced to the left and there I was. My head was bent. The blindfold was perfectly placed. I had a sneer of anger on my face. I smiled and watched as my lips tried to curve upwards, but failed. It didn't look pretty. I sighed and saw myself sigh. I wished Kates would look somewhere else.

She didn't and I felt remorse blast throughout Kates as we walked forward.

I tripped when my foot hit against a step and I saw nothing anymore. I stumbled out of her and concentrated on the stairwell. It curved upwards for two flights of stairs. We went down a hallway and then climbed another set of stairs. It felt more like a mausoleum. There was a dull swish across the floor ahead of us and I knew it was the sound of a heavy door being opened.

Kates led me inside and released my arm. A second later the door closed and I waited, holding my breath. When nothing else happened, I lifted my blindfold. I rapidly blinked as my eyes adjusted to our surroundings. The room was dark so I crossed to the wall and felt for a light switch. As my fingers ran across a cold plastic box, I felt the outline of a switch and flipped it up.

Light surrounded us.

We'd been put in a room that looked like a museum display. A huge king-sized bed stood in one corner with gold posts that led and hooked to a sheer canopy. It dipped halfway to the ground.

I counted six chairs that looked like thrones. Each of them was upholstered with red velour material. It reminded me of medieval times and I almost expected a court jester to dance out from behind one.

"What?" Emily gasped and whirled in a tight circle with her blindfold still on.

I rolled my eyes and reached to remove it. She shrieked until she saw that I held the blindfold in my hand.

"Oh." She sounded a little disappointed.

"You need to drop that guy, Em." It wasn't a suggestion. She flushed and hung her head. "I know, but I'm weak and I think I'm on a little something."

Think? She was.

Adam groaned from the corner and I turned to see that he had sat on a chair. He gripped his blindfold tight in his hand and didn't look at us. No one said anything for a moment. It was almost as if there was too much to say that we didn't know where to start.

Then Emily exclaimed, "We've been kidnapped! I can't believe it. Why? Are they doing it for ransom? What's going on? Why are you so calm, Davy?"

I ignored Emily for the moment and stood in front of Adam. He saw the tips of my ballet slippers and gulped. His jaw clenched before he lifted his eyes to mine. There it was. I saw it in his eyes. I knew a cheater when I saw one.

"You're with Shelly?" I asked it quietly, but so damning.

Guilt was all over him, but he rasped out, "I didn't... I didn't mean for any of this to happen. Shelly was lonely and crying the other night when we went out with that guy. You kissed him and I got so jealous. I kissed Shelly. Your friend, Kates, saw us. She was going into the Shoilster and caught us."

I frowned. That explained some of it.

They'd said the Immortal and the Immortal's boyfriend. Adam had looked guilty. None of this made sense. "Adam, they took us because of you. You know that, right? They grabbed you first."

"Because Kates is psychotic!" Emily laughed hysterically. She rounded to perch precariously on a dark purple velvet couch beside Adam's throne. She shook her head and her hand lifted to pull at the ends of her hair. "She was probably so angry that he was two-timing you that she seduced Bennett. She persuaded him to kidnap us all. It's all because of her."

My roommate was crazy, stupid, *and* under the influence of vampire lust.

Adam frowned, but didn't address Emily's weird ramblings. Instead, he sounded sincere. "I am so sorry, Davy. The thing with Shelly happened so quick and then I asked you out yesterday. I never thought you'd actually say yes. You were with that guy, even though you said that the kiss was just because of his girlfriend. And then you said you liked me and I liked you too—I *like* you. I still like you, but this happened and I was going to break up with Shelly tonight. I just didn't call her yet."

Well, if my math added correctly, I highly doubted he would've gotten in touch with her. Kates and the Lucan Family thought Adam was the Immortal's boyfriend. I knew that Roane had the Immortal. Everything should've added up so that meant—Shelly was the girl that Talia had brushed arms with the night before she jumped. They thought Shelly was the Immortal.

"But why kidnap you?" I asked the question out loud to myself, but I jumped when Emily answered.

"Kates is behind all of this. I already told you that. She's doing this to get even with Adam because she thinks he cheated on you. She's crazy. Your friend is crazy."

The crazy one was the one talking. I sighed and closed my eyes. My insides were a whirlwind. Everything was happening too fast and not fast enough. "None of this makes sense."

"What guy?" Emily must've finally heard Adam.

"Huh?" Adam looked at her.

"You said that Davy kissed a guy. Who? She only likes you." Could my roommate be more blunt?

"Emily," I hissed. "Shut up."

Adam frowned, ever so helpful. "I never got his name. We were never introduced, but he was tall."

"These people," Emily murmured, tearful. "What kind of people could do this?"

Kidnappers. Heartless soulless people. Vampires.

I watched as my roommate tried to make sense of what she couldn't understand. She really thought Bennett was a person, someone with a soul. She didn't understand the power he had over her. She clung to what she wanted to believe. And Adam—he just saw his own guilt. I felt a tear at the corner of my eye, but I swallowed painfully and brushed it away. Adam was the guy that I had thought he was all along. He was so human that he was—human. He got jealous. He made a mistake. Then he got caught up in the situation. Neither of them had a clue what was really going on. I was envious of their naiveté. It was my fault Emily was crying. It was my fault that Adam looked so shameful. Both of them were innocent in this entire thing.

I was the Immortal.

Then the door was pushed open. Emily jumped, but she didn't squeal this time. Thankfully.

Adam looked up.

"Davy," Kates called me. A strand of her dirty blonde hair had slipped down to frame the corner of her cheek. Her sea blue eyes were bright and clear. She fully knew what she was doing. There was no vampire lust that filtered her decisions.

I took a small breath. I needed to accept the inevitable. Kates had betrayed me, but the sad part was that she didn't know she betrayed me. I did know one thing, though. Kates wasn't there to kill vampires. She was there for an entirely different reason.

"Come on," she beckoned and I went.

19

We didn't go far. We went down one set of steps and past four doors before Kates opened the fifth. After she shut the door and I glanced around, I realized that this was her room. There was a giant bed that had a canopy, just like the one in the other room. There was a sensual feeling to the room until I caught sight of the opened closet door. I saw the hooker boots, leather halter tops, and frayed jeans.

That was all Kates.

"This is where you stay?" I asked, hurt.

Sorrow flashed in her eyes, but she nodded before she perched on another velour throne chair. She only had two. It looked like they kept the good stuff for the hostages.

"Let's start this by you telling me why you *really* came to Benshire." I deadlocked my eyes with hers. This was the showdown. Truth time.

Kates swallowed once. "I came here because I fell in love with someone."

"Someone or something?" I couldn't keep the disdain away.

Anger flashed briefly in her eyes, but she pushed past it. "I fell in love with a vampire. Your contempt's not new so could you stop with the attitude? It's not helping."

"It's helping me."

"You want some answers and I'm trying to tell you them. I won't be so inclined if you piss me off."

"Listen to you. 'So inclined'—who've you been talking to? You don't talk like that on a good day, Kates. Drop the act. I want my friend here, not whoever you are when you're with this *thing* you love."

"Thing?"

Had we just not gone over this? Contempt. Me. For vampires. Not a surprise. I raised my chin and glared.

"What is your problem? You're acting like I've lied to you!" Kates shouted.

"You have!" I shouted right back. "You just kidnapped me."

"You weren't supposed to be there!"

"Well, I was. And my roommate is in that room. And Adam—it had to be Adam?"

Kates snorted again, but laughed hollowly. "Don't come crying to me because you have crap taste in guys."

My eyes went red. "Excuse me?"

"You didn't like Craig, but he sure liked you. Maybe it's something about you that attracts these losers?"

"Losers? Me? Are we really not considering your vampire? He's a creature of the night, Kates. I don't think Adam is worse than that."

"Creature of the night? So am I, Davy!"

"You're a human." Unlike myself.

"So are you."

"This isn't about me."

"This *is* about you! I'm sorry that you're mad that Adam cheated on you. You could do better. He looks like a pussy."

She'd been the one to interrupt Adam and Shelly while I'd been pressing Roane against the wall around the corner.

Was it hot in here or was it me?

I fingered my shirt's collar and pulled it away to fan myself, but to no avail—I was burning up. I hoped my Immortal stuff wasn't acting up.

"You're going to be fine anyway."

"What do you mean?"

"Look," Kates continued. "I came to Benshire because of the Immortal."

"The fairytale Santa Claus for vampires?" Her words exactly.

Kates grimaced and I caught a flash of embarrassment. "That girl that killed herself, she was the Immortal."

Tell me about it.

"I was sent here to find the new Immortal."

At her look of expectation, my eyes widened and I sat up straight. I was supposed to be confused. I was supposed to be shocked. I was supposed to be... I didn't care. "Like I'm going to believe anything you say right now anyway."

"Oh my god, Davy!"

"You kidnapped me!"

"I did not!" Kates surged to her feet.

"Evidence. I'm in a vampire castle! Against my will!"

"By chance! By chance. It was an accident. You're not supposed to be here. You're not supposed to be a part of this at all."

I wasn't supposed to be a part of this? She had no idea. "I'm still here, aren't I?"

"Could you be more dramatic? I'm here. I'm going to protect you. Obviously."

"Right," I scoffed and crossed my arms. "Because you're a slayer?"

"Because I'm your best friend," Kates pointed out. "Idiot."

"How'd you even know where we were?"

She grimaced. "Bennett knew. He followed Adam to your dorm and overheard him talking to Emily."

Oh holy hell.

She added, "For what it's worth, I think Bennett actually has a thing for her."

"What else should I know about, Kates? You were supposed to be at Blue's this whole time. Did you even go? What happened with that?"

Her eyes widened and I held my breath. This was not good.

"I went," Kates murmured quietly, reluctantly. "But you told me that she'd gone inside and did her empathic thing. I couldn't have that, Davy."

"*I did it*," I wrung out, hoarse.

"You're my best friend. That's different and I know you, Davy. You don't really—you're not really detail-oriented, you know. You only go so far. I haven't been worried about you, but Blue—she—she knew things that she shouldn't have."

"What did you do to her?" My hands started to tremble. I felt my voice quiver and I felt something become unglued inside of me. It was starting to rise, starting to choke me. I stopped breathing. "Is she alive?"

"Barely." She whispered the word and refused to meet my eyes.

Blue was family. "What did you do?"

Roane said not to get upset—too late for that. I was upset. I was more than upset. Kates said nothing and I jerked forward a step. "What did you do, Kates?!"

I felt her guilt before I heard it. I closed my eyes and whirled away as I saw what she'd done. She'd hit her. I flinched as I heard the punch. I felt the fist crunch against Blue's jaw. My sponsor hadn't stood a chance. "She respected your privacy. She wouldn't tell me what she'd felt. She was worried about you and she wanted you to get help. She wanted to be the person to help you. I trusted you to go to her! What did you do, Kates?!"

"You know!" Kates screamed back.

I felt the slap of her words. I doubled over and gasped for breath. Tears came to my eyes and I rapidly blinked them away. "You don't know what you've done."

Kates looked like she'd just been slapped by my words.

"Where is she?"

"She's in the hospital. Coma."

"You're a first class bitch."

'*I am.*'

I heard Kates' thought.

'*I deserve so much worse. I should be the one in the coma. I should be*

—no, Lucan needs me. He said that I'd have to do things I wouldn't want to. He always knows. He said this would happen and Davy would react like this. He knows.'

"Who the hell is Lucan?"

Kates jerked her head up and her eyes widened. "You can—no, you can't!"

I stalked forward, one step at a time.

She backed away. "You can't, there's no way. You never could before."

"I'm gifted, remember?"

"You're not *that* gifted, Davy."

I pierced her eyes. I wanted her to feel me deep inside, so deep that she'd never feel privacy again. "Maybe I've never been this furious before. Maybe I never had a reason to do what I can do now. She was like a mother, Kates. She was like my mother!"

She wanted to deny what I said. She wanted to not believe me, but it didn't matter. "Are you going to tell me who Lucan is? Or am I going to go inside of you and figure it out myself?"

She blanched at my meaning. A cruel smile curved at the corners of my mouth. I wanted to see her squirm some more.

"I'm Lucan." I heard the answer, but it came from the doorway.

I swung my gaze and stopped short. He was Roane's complete double. He had the same coal eyes that held too many promises. Some of those promises sent shivers down my back. It was the same angular cheekbones, strong jaw line, and full plump lips that begged to be touched. He even had the same cocky, yet saddened, shrug to his muscular shoulders. They were strong shoulders. Both of them stood the same. Confident. Leaders. Sure that their way was the right way.

Except, there were differences too. Roane kept his hair buzzed short. Lucan wore his black hair sleek and straight to where it touched the tips of his shoulders. I watched as he lifted a graceful hand and tucked it behind one ear and knew that was his habit.

Kates watched in yearning and her hand jerked. She wanted to be the one to tuck that strand of hair behind his ear.

"She loves you."

Kates jerked her gaze to me and instantly looked away, but I already saw it. I saw everything.

I breathed out, "You weren't thinking of Roane before. You were thinking of him. Blue got it wrong somehow. Then in the car, you and Roane, you two looked like you wanted to murder each other." I swung my gaze to Lucan. "Who are you?"

He smiled, almost tenderly, but I still saw the killer in him. "Lucas is my twin brother—my *human* twin brother."

'Raitscliff and Lucan have both found a girl… their families are here'

Lucan strolled forward. "We're both vampires, yes. We were sired from different families."

"What do you want from me?" I wasn't sure how to react. In fact, I wasn't sure how to even breathe around this Roane look-alike. Lucan smiled again and I saw another difference. They lived by different codes. Roane defied death. He stood in the way of death and Lucan, he merely thought death couldn't touch him. I wasn't sure which one was the safest for company, but I'd soon find out.

"You're Kates' best friend. You got mixed up in this by accident. She says that you know Lucas, so I have a mission for you." He really didn't think I'd decline the proposal, little did he know about who I was.

I tilted my chin up. "What do you want?"

He turned and held Kates' gaze for a moment, but neither of them needed to communicate their thoughts. I read the look and knew it was a lovers' connection.

"Lucas has the Immortal at his home. I want you to go there and give her a message. I want you to tell her that we have her boyfriend. If she doesn't want him to die, she needs to come to us by tomorrow night."

"And if she doesn't?"

"We'll have a meal. That's all."

Kates jerked in reaction.

I stepped forward. "And what makes you think that 'Lucas' will let me talk to her?"

Then he smiled one of those intimate I-know-your-secret smiles. "Because I know that this Adam character isn't your boyfriend."

"How do you know that?" I already knew. I *so* already knew. Though, I needed to hear it.

"Because I smell my twin brother all over you. You'll have no problem getting in to see the Immortal and we both know it."

Well, hell.

20
___

"You know what to do, right?" Kates asked as she walked me to the van.

"Lie to the Hunter and tell Shelly that her boyfriend's going to die if she doesn't give her blood up to the longest fang."

Kates sighed, annoyed. "Come on, Davy. This is some serious stuff here."

Oh, believe me. I knew the gravity of my situation. "I wouldn't want anyone to end up in a coma. Yeah, I get how serious this is."

"I know that you're upset about what happened with Blue, but things just happened. I didn't mean for that to happen, but it did and I'm going to do everything I can to make sure your friends are okay."

Oh gee, thanks for the consideration. "You're right. I *am* more than upset about what you did to Blue. You didn't mean for it to happen? What'd you mean for, Kates? You have a temper. You don't think I know that? I should probably be grateful that you didn't just kill Blue. That would've solved your problem, right? She peaked inside you and saw the real you, so you kill her."

'Lucan knows. He knows me. He told me to kill Blue and I couldn't, but it's okay. It worked out. He said that no one could make the connection. He said everything would be alright. I have to trust him. I love him.'

I watched as Kates calmed herself down. Lies. "Wow, Kates. You take the cake. Is this about you loving this guy or is this about you not being alone?"

She'd been the one to introduce Craig and me. She'd told me to set Craig on fire. She'd been the one who told me that fire wouldn't kill him, but it'd hurt him. I had wanted to hurt him. I wanted to hurt him still. A stab of nausea surged through me. All my regrets, shadows, the darkest time in my life—and Kates had been right beside me the entire time. She'd been the one to encourage me, but now that I thought about it, she might not have encouraged me in the right way.

I expected blistering rage from Kates. I got patience instead and I blinked, startled, as she relayed almost warmly, "I love him. He's going to change things, make things how they're supposed to be. I know you can't understand because you don't know anything about this world and you shouldn't. It's a dark world, but Lucan's going to change things, make things right."

"So that you can kill vampires again?" I scoffed at the idea. The decree was finalized and it swept over the entire vampire nation. There was no reversing that baby.

"Maybe."

I saw her belief and couldn't believe it. She thought that, she *really* thought that. I didn't know some stuff about the vampire world, but I knew enough to know that the decree was set in stone. There'd be a few world wars within the vampire community before that decree was overthrown... unless....

'It just means that vampire has too much power. No creature should have that power.'

I sucked in a choking breath. I suddenly, very suddenly, needed to get to Roane. This was the 'world at stake' feeling that I felt the night on the roof with Talia. Something had happened, something very, very wrong had happened and I felt it. I had ignored it. Now things might've gone too far to stop it.

"I have to go," I rushed out and darted to the van. The door was open so I hopped inside and slammed it behind me. I never stopped to look at who drove me. I just needed to get to Roane, but I'd need to go to the dorm first.

Once I hurled myself through the lobby, up the stairs, and down the hall, I burst through the door. I was grateful that I'd been the last out the door and not Emily because I never locked the door. Emily had been too frazzled by her date, she'd forgotten her purse—that meant her phone.

I scrolled through until I found Roane's number. It took a few rings, but he answered, "Is this Emily?"

"No, it's me. I lost my phone, but that's not why I'm calling. I have to see you, now!" Please, please don't ask for any explanation. I didn't have time.

Roane hesitated a second and then asked, "Where are you?"

"My dorm room."

"I'll send Gregory."

"Thank you, thank you, thank you." I needed to calm down, but I was bursting at the seams. As I waited, I couldn't sit still. I paced. I jogged in place. I did jumping jacks. I even rearranged the furniture. Afterwards, I cringed. Emily wouldn't want the couch by the window.

"Davy? It's Gregory. Lucas said to knock on your door."

"Coming!"

Gregory greeted me with a polite nod and I tried to ignore the attention this *very* large Viking vampire was attracting. His voice could've rumbled through the entire building. Heads popped out from nearly every door, but while some squeaked in fear, a lot squeaked from excitement—the sexual kind.

Vampire. Horny freshman girls. What else needed to be said?

Gregory swept around me in the lobby and held each of the doors open until we got to the car. It was the same black SUV that he'd driven before. "Can't you drive a car with some color? Why does it always have to be black?"

"Davy?"

"Nothing. Nevermind." I shrugged it off and slipped inside. From there, it was all foot tapping, knuckle breaking, and counting my breaths again.

I felt like I needed to burst, like something inside of me finally knew something—or felt something was going to happen. I was going to burst from the inside out. I just knew it. Then Gregory pulled the car over and I burst out of the car to sprint inside. I swept past Wren and a whole host of other vampires.

They were all arriving for the war.

I darted up the stairs and spotted Roane's closed bedroom doors. I threw them open, prepared to unburden my soul, but I braked abruptly. Nothing. Roane wasn't there. The sheets were in the same place. The window was open and a cool breeze swept in.

"Oh my god! Vampires are so unreliable!" I cried to myself.

Then I heard a soft chuckle behind me and I whirled around—my jaw dropped. There he was, buttoning a black shirt that looked custom-fitted and straight from the dry cleaners. He wore a pair of light blue jeans underneath, which also looked custom fitted and dry-cleaned.

"You've got money. I can see that," I stated as my greeting.

"That's what you had to say and why you called with your commanding 'now!'?" Roane drawled as he slipped past only to drop the shirt off his shoulders—oh whoa. I had assumed he'd been buttoning it up, but nope. He'd been unbuttoning it.

"Wha—why—what are you doing?" I quickly turned around. I wanted to look. I shouldn't. It was bad to look, but I peeked anyway. Roane was all muscles. Perfect, chiseled, hard ridges, muscles up and down and all around. My fingers itched to touch them and my mouth went dry, but I twitched to keep myself back.

"I was out. I had to make sure you and Gregory weren't followed."

"That would've been bad, huh? If they had followed me..." I trailed off as Roane was in front of me in a flash... in all his shirtless glistening chest gloriousness.... Fans. Vampires should keep fans everywhere they were... for all those hot, passionate, and overheated humans like myself....

"They?" Roane caught my shoulders and jerked me back to him. I'd been absentmindedly looking for a fan somewhere.

"They?" he barked again.

"They." I needed to remind myself who 'they' were. Oh—"Yes. Your twin brother." I growled that last bit and shoved Roane back. "You could've told me that you had a twin brother. They have Emily and Adam."

"You met Lucan?" Roane grilled. "You talked to Lucan?"

I nodded. "I met him. I talked to him. I found out that Kates is in love with him, thanks for that heads up and yes—he sent a message for the Immortal. I'm supposed to deliver it because *apparently* he can smell you all over me. That's gross. I really don't like being sniffed."

"I've almost forgotten what he smells like," Roane confessed as he moved around me and back into the bedroom. He flicked his wrist out and shut the door on his way. As I turned to watch him, the door shut behind me with a click.

"How can you forget what your twin smells like? Wouldn't he smell like you?" I couldn't believe I was having this conversation.

Roane stopped, stared at me for a moment, and then crossed to his closet. He pulled out a grey shirt, but only held it as he hung his head. "Lucan and I were sired by different Families. That means that we have the same face now. Nothing else remains the same with the two of us. I have different blood than he does."

"Because you were sired by different Families?"

"Lucan was sired first." Roane still hadn't put the shirt on. He only held it and now his hand wrapped tightly around it. He looked at the floor and I heard the suffering in his voice. "He was the louder one of us. Everyone thought he was the leader. When he was sired, I felt it happen. I felt him and then suddenly—I thought he was dead. It was almost two weeks before he came to me. He said that he couldn't control himself before that and he wanted to make sure he wouldn't hurt me. I didn't see much of Lucan after he became a vampire. I lived another year as a human until this man came to me."

I felt the history swirl around us, like it was another entity in the room.

Roane continued, haunted, "He told me that Lucan had become a problem with the vampires. He was uncontrollable and defying a lot of their rules. He said that I was once his twin brother. They wondered if I could help them with their problem. That's what they called him. My brother was 'their problem.'"

I heard his hollow laugh and bit my lip from crying out.

"He turned you into a vampire because of your brother?"

"No. He took me to Lucan—as a human. Lucan was the one who decided I should be a vampire. He missed me. He wanted me beside him. He wanted things to be how they were. The man who had come to me realized what Lucan was about to do. He did it instead. To say Lucan was furious is an understatement. He ripped my Master's head off."

"You didn't have a Master?" I had no idea what that meant, but I guessed that it meant something.

He cleared his throat. "I joined Lucan for awhile. I became a part of his Family, even though I wasn't from their bloodline. The rest of the group didn't like that, but Lucan was their leader. They did what he said and I'd been his twin brother—it still meant something to Lucan and me. We were how we used to be, for a time."

Inseparable. I heard it before he said it. I felt it from him. Roane wished things were how they used to be.

"As I learned things, I started to change. Lucan didn't like it at first, but I don't know—I think his Family were the ones who stepped in."

"You said Lucan was the 'louder' one of you. They thought he was the leader."

Roane shook his head and sat. His shirt was still fisted in his hands before him. "I'd been the leader when we were human. Lucan was just loud, but he didn't think things through. He acted for me sometimes. I liked controlling from behind the scenes and it worked for us. We were starting to get back to that and I think his Family didn't like the idea that one of their own wasn't the leader anymore.

They didn't like being led by an outsider. Lucan loved it. I took them to new heights. I told you that I'd done the torture with their Family I'd done worse than that. I didn't know who I was. I felt a separation between me and Lucan. I hated it. I went dark, really dark as a vampire."

"Until they kicked you out."

"Lucan was forced to kick me out." Roane closed his eyes. "I found my Family and things changed for awhile."

"Was that the last time you saw him, when he kicked you out?"

He shook his head, his jaw clenched. "I wish, but no. Lucan and I, we still both liked to defy laws, even vampire laws. That was in us from when we were human. We still saw each other until..."

"Lucas," I whispered, but held back. He was going to say something, but hesitated. And something in me didn't want to hear it.

He swung his eyes to mine and I couldn't look away. He was starving. I was starving... something was in the air—I couldn't move. I couldn't breathe.

I couldn't think.

"You called me by my name," he wrung out. Hoarse.

I nodded with a tight throat. I couldn't form any words. I had gravitated to him and I stood above him as he sat. I didn't know what to say, how to react. I needed to be by him. It was something in me or maybe it was just me. I could only breathe. That was all I focused on until I felt his hand lift and the back of his finger wiped a tear away from me.

"Davina," he whispered as he arched upwards, but he didn't seek my lips. Not yet.

I grasped the side of his face and I was the one to press my lips to his. A part of me knew that I needed him and I wouldn't ever stop needing him. I just hoped it wasn't the end of both of us.

I pressed against him, as close as possible. His hand slid slowly up my back and lingered at my shoulder. He traced his finger down my arm, to my wrist, my hand, my fingertip, until it rested warmly on my stomach. He spread his palm wide and held me in place for a second.

I gasped and surged upward against him. I needed air.

Roane groaned as he pulled his lips away. "Your shield's down."

I pressed my lips against his and moaned when I felt the struggle inside of him. He paused. He wanted to say something, but my tongue gently touched the tip of his. Then he lost the battle for control. Both his hands claimed my head and he tilted it so his tongue swept further, deeper.

I was so lost in his exploration that I hadn't realized when Roane lifted me in the air. As I felt the satin sheets underneath my bare skin my eyes shot open.

When had I gotten undressed?

Roane's lips settled on my neck and I felt the throb pound furiously inside of me—it didn't matter when I'd gotten undressed.

He rested just above me and cradled the back of my neck. He lingered just over my collarbone, but swept his lips gently back and forth before he settled down to suckle lightly. I swept a hand up into his hair and the other explored down his chest to rest on his belt buckle. My fingers paused and then dipped inside. Roane growled as he surged upwards.

I laid there on the bed as he stood between my legs and both of us froze in place.

Then I felt something come over us. I didn't know what it was, but I knew I didn't want it there. My hand fell away from his jeans with lightning speed. He caught it and held it. My eyes locked with his and I found myself thinking, '*What?*'

'*Your shield shouldn't be down.*' How could a thought be so accusing?

'*We're in the middle of something and you want to lecture me on my shield? Really? Is this the time?*'

'*Your shield should always be raised. You don't know who could get in.*'

'*Besides evil vampires who want to drain my blood? I have no idea.*'

"Enough," Roane snarled. I jumped from the sound. "Raise your shield now! I shouldn't be able to read your thoughts."

"What's the deal?" I sat up, but Roane didn't move. The movement brought us closer, only a few inches separated us. I swallowed tightly. My body reacted so quickly.

"The deal is that someone else, someone who doesn't want to protect you could get inside and read your thoughts," Roane leaned over and whispered, intimately.

A shiver sent goose bumps over my skin. '*Why would I worry about some evil vampire getting in my head when you're already there?*'

Roane didn't react—outwardly. He didn't show a thing, but I felt him. He was all fury. It blasted against me. Acid dripped from his voice. "Right."

"I..." I scrambled up, but stopped abruptly.

Roane jerked his head back and to the side.

I jumped in reaction from his quickness. When he didn't move back, I waited—something needed to be said or done or exploded.

"You're angry."

I hadn't expected that. I blinked in shock at the understanding in his voice. "Uh."

Roane turned his head back and his dark eyes caught mine. "You don't understand this. You, me, and you're angry."

"Are you serious?" I snarled back at him, but I felt a traitorous tremor build in my body. It wanted release. It demanded release, but, nothing.

"This attraction we have for each other—it's like a pull."

How quaint. "Is that what it is? I hadn't noticed."

Roane moved back a step. I felt his hands leave my thighs where they'd been resting. The cold invaded. "You were hunted by a vampire, my kind. I feel it too, Davy. We can barely be in the same room without touching. It's been there since the beginning and it's been growing every minute. It's almost uncontrollable lately, but— this is new to you."

And it wasn't to him?!

I sat up straighter and stood slowly. "So are you the big bad experienced vampire lover and I'm the virgin? Are you here to teach me what I need to know? Or maybe your job is to guide me correctly, make sure I don't fumble along. Right? Am I getting this wrong?"

"You're hearing me wrong," he said faintly. Defeated.

I stood tall, shrugged my shoulders back, and firmed my jaw. "I hope so because you're sounding pretty damn superior."

"That's not what I'd intended."

"That's not what you intended? This whole thing wasn't intended. I shouldn't have gone up to that roof. I shouldn't have answered that phone. I shouldn't have a best friend who's a brainwashed bunny by your 'human' twin and I really shouldn't be here with you. None of this should've happened. I shouldn't have even come to Benshire, but I listened to Blue."

I stopped and gasped for air, my eyes wild. Then I choked out, "She should've picked someone else. I can't be this Immortal. I don't want to have this on my shoulders. I can't—someone else should be the Immortal. I haven't had this for a few days and already my roommate was kidnapped. My best friend is in love with a vampire that wants to drain me and my empath sponsor is in a coma. I don't even know what to say about you."

Something happened and I felt like I could breathe again.

Roane moved closer, but he paused. "I hurt your pride before. I'm sorry. All I meant is that you know *of* my world, but you don't *know* my world. Now you're the Immortal and your entire life needs to change. You're right. Being the Immortal is a lot to bear. It's a great burden, but you're also wrong. Talia didn't choose you. The Immortal thread chose you. Talia trusted the Immortal thread to choose the right person—it did. It chose you for a reason, Davy."

"I really don't want to be the Immortal, Lucas. I want—can't I pass it along?" I was still a little miffed.

He didn't answer for a moment. "You can't. Once the Immortal thread is linked with your body, you'll die when it passes to the next carrier. The body goes through a withdrawal that's lethal. Talia didn't want—she didn't want to suffer like that."

I closed my eyes swiftly and felt everything from that night again. She'd chosen her death. Now I understood, but I still wished I hadn't. I wrung out, "I just want to wake up and hear Emily snoring. I don't want this. I can't have this."

I slowly dropped back down on the bed and cradled my head in my hands. My fingers slid through my hair and clung to each strand. I wanted to pull them out. I wanted to feel something other than what I was feeling.

I couldn't deal with it.

Roane reached forward and delicately moved my knee aside. He knelt before me.

I held my breath.

He moved his hand from my leg and slowly reached to untangle my hands from my hair. I gasped as the last finger was detangled and then my fingers desperately sought his shoulders. He slid in and I surged forward to wrap my arms tighter around him.

"You have to bear something that you didn't choose. I understand, Davy. I understand it more than you think." Roane tucked his head against mine. His lips brushed the tip of my ear. "I know what it's like to have your life suddenly change and it's not what you decided. I do understand that."

I frowned.

His hand curved around my neck and I felt the cool touch of his lips when he pressed a kiss to my ear. "You can do this, Davy. We'll figure everything else out."

Did I dare believe him? I wanted to—badly. I lifted my head, met his black eyes, and smoothed my thumb over his cheek. "I'm a little moody right now. I'm not used to being so powerless. I hate it."

He didn't say anything. Then he dipped and touched his lips to mine.

I closed my eyes and felt it again. It had been rushed and fevered, but the wave of lust swirled slowly throughout me. The heat spread from my fingertips, up my arms, down my sides, around my toes, and back to settle in my center.

I entwined my arms around his neck.

Roane grazed his lips against mine, hypnotically back and forth. I arched upward, needing more. As my neck was stretched to the fullest, he slid his mouth down my neck and settled on my collarbone where he started to suckle.

My hand cradled the back of his neck and my other slid over his shoulders, feeling the hard dip between his muscles until it rested on his hip. Roane continued to suckle and I pressed down on his head, just lightly.

It inflamed him. He swiftly lifted me up to place me on the bed.

I laid there; dazed at how quick he'd reacted, but Roane didn't wait for my brain to catch up. He shucked his pants and quickly unzipped mine. As they slid down my legs and past my toes, I panted for breath. After he dropped them on the ground, Roane crouched over me. His eyes met mine, captive and fevered.

Then with a tug at his lips, he slid a hand up my leg. Sharp desire pierced me, but I could only gasp for breath and lay there, nearly paralyzed. I watched, entranced, as his hand slid to my waist, caressed my stomach for a moment, and then dipped between my legs. As a finger entered me, my paralysis was gone. I shot up from the bed and wrapped my arms around his shoulders. I threw one leg around his hip. Roane grasped it and raised it higher. His finger slipped further inside and I could only cling as it started to move in and out.

The sensations built quickly. He kept moving, in and out, until I gasped and turned my mouth towards his shoulder. My lips grazed his skin and in a drunken state I pressed my teeth against his skin.

Roane groaned roughly.

I nipped his skin—he shuddered. I licked him and he slid two fingers inside of me.

My fingers dug into him, starving. Then I bit—quickly and savagely. I needed more, but I didn't know of what.

Roane arched his head and growled. I felt the reverberations between my legs and then I moaned as Roane quickly positioned himself and entered smoothly. At his first thrust, I wrapped my legs around his waist and hooked my ankles.

The pleasure intensified and I couldn't think. I couldn't do anything except hold on as the fever built and built.

Roane bent his head down and found my collarbone again where he started to suckle. His teeth grazed against my skin and he nipped lightly when he thrust deep at the same time. The pace quickened, in and out, back and forth.

I groaned, but bit my lip to silence my moans.

"No," Roane gasped and lifted himself off of me so his weight didn't press down anymore.

I protested and tried to draw him back down.

He held me off and I bit down harder on my lips as he pistoned into me. Deftly, Roane slid his thumb between my lips and bent down to whisper, "Bite down on me, not on yourself."

I didn't register the desperation in his voice, but I felt the pleading through my body. And, answering something carnal, my teeth pierced his skin.

Roane cradled my head and quickened his pace. We were both lost, only feeling each other.

I felt his blood slide down my throat and gasped, needing more.

Roane held me tighter against him, almost crushing me, but I welcomed it. I needed it. I was starved for more—and then the fever built. I was on the edge—Roane grasped my hip, pulled out, and slammed back inside. Both of us went hurdling over the edge. The waves took over my body. I collapsed on the bed and was powerless as the ripples coursed through me.

Then slowly my eyelids fluttered shut.

"It's the three ring circus. There are clowns, tigers, one legged elephants, and for a bonus feature: we've got a white zebra. You in for the count? You want tickets with that heaping bowl of popcorn? Deal's going once, twice, too late."

Only one voice said things like that—I sighed and sat up in the darkness. "I'm sleeping again."

"Again—you mean 'finally'!" It chided me, "You've been awake for a very long time. It's about time you fell off to nanaland. I can only amuse myself so much here. You're not that entertaining of a person."

"Thanks for that."

"Keeping it real, Bearded Lady."

Oh, lovely. A circus theme.

"Fairytales are overdone. The court jester wants his turn."

"Last time you told me I'm the Immortal. I've adjusted. I'll do whatever I need. What else can you hit me with? I'd like to wake up or go back to normal dreams. You're a little hard to handle sometimes." If I tried to reason with it, would it work?

The voice laughed. Shrill. "Would you like a comb for your beard?"

No reasoning would be had. "So what are you here to enlighten me with?"

"You lie really well." The voice had been maniacal before, but it was calm, eerily calm now.

I felt shivers go down my back. "What are you talking about?"

"Ask your lover."

Roane's words lashed back at me before I could stop them. *Lying. All you do is lie.*

I flinched and murmured, "No. You're wrong."

"I haven't said anything," the voice gloated.

"I know what you're going to say. You're going to say what he said. I don't lie. I'm not a liar."

"Tigers spawn earthlings on their back. Sometimes they ride on the backs of elephants, but only the ones with roller skates."

"Make sense, for once!" I shrieked into the darkness. It was an abyss.

"Silly Bearded Lady. They don't ride on the one legged elephant. That'd be dangerous."

"I'm not lying to anyone."

"And stupid. Who'd want to ride on the back of a one legged elephant? You'd fall right off." The voice ignored me and continued, amused, "And then rolling hula hoops that are on fire would burn you. Why are they always on fire? I've never figured that out."

"Enough!" I'd forced it before and I was willing to bet that I could do it again.

A black wind shrieked in protest and swept around me. I blinked, startled, and tried to stand still as a tornado picked up from underneath my feet. It rushed upwards, enveloped me, and as it started to settle—I found myself staring back at—what a shocker— myself. Except that it wasn't me. My brown curls looked sleek and framed my shoulders. My eyes weren't innocent. They were know- ing, wise, and a little crazy. And still, I looked sultry. I was dressed how I had dressed for Adam's date, in my lace shirt and snug jeans, but there was a different aura that surrounded the Immortal me. Confidence.

She grinned and winked. "Bet this isn't what you wanted, huh?"

"How'd you know?" I returned, sardonically. "It's not as if you're a part of me or something."

"You're sarcastic."

"Just because you're inside of me doesn't mean that you understand me."

The Immortal me smiled sweetly. "I know a lot more about you than you know about yourself. I know all about Craig. I know about Kates. I know how you're heaping a whole pile of denial poop on a burning house because you did the deed with a vampire. And not any vampire, Bearded Lady. You did it with *thee* vampire. There are ramifications that you can't handle right now."

It wouldn't stop. "Please, please. All this nonsense—I can't handle it. I might go insane."

"Every circus must pitch a tent and entertain."

"Let me guess, I'm your audience?"

"You're the tent, Beardy, but you'll do. The tigers might not think so. They might want to shave off your beard or burn the tent. I haven't decided which."

"I'd really like to wake up. I need to tell Roane something and I can't when I'm asleep."

"That's right, Horny Bearded Lady. You didn't stop to think. The tigers think it's funny how the Bearded Lady forgets her beard when she's around The World's Strongest Man."

"Oh, please. Roane is not the world's strongest man." I felt foolish saying that. Who said things like that?

"You might be surprised." The Immortal laughed it off and vanished.

Great—back to the dark abyss. There were no winds this time. It was just darkness, no mocking voice, and no uneasy feeling inside of my stomach.

I looked down and choked out a gasp. I lifted my arm and like before, I saw the same silver color underneath my skin. I watched in fascination as the silver color seemed to melt into a thick rich paste that sparkled like diamonds. I liked diamonds, just not inside of me.

"You're every girl's best friend. You're the prize, Davy. You're the one that everyone wants."

"Tell me something that I don't know," I challenged.

"Craig wanted to make you a vampire. He told you how he'd do it, how much he'd enjoy it, and that you'd thank him in the end. And now—vampires, vampires all around the shiny prize. What's a scared little girl to do? The hungry monsters keep circling, but they won't be kept at bay for long. A shark's going to bite soon—or maybe one did."

"Roane didn't bite me. I bit him."

"You liked it. You'd do it again. I can feel the thirst inside of you. What's that mean? Are you going to become a vampire?" The Immortal laughed hysterically and spun around me in tight circles.

I looked down at my arms and watched, detached, as the sparkling paste thinned and became like blood. "Roane said you chose me, did you? Did you actually choose me or did you get stuck with me?"

"The divorce will have collateral damage that no fortune teller can foresee."

That was a cheerful thought. "What do you want from me?"

I felt the Immortal slow to a stop, instantly, and sensed its calm. "Stop lying to yourself. You're only hurting yourself."

"Fine," I gritted out. "You invaded me! You had no right."

"He's thee vampire. You should sit up and pay attention."

"How can I? Your riddles are a bit mind twisting," I snorted out.

Then it answered another one. "As long as you're the Immortal, you are unable to become a vampire."

I clasped my eyes closed in relief. Maybe there were some benefits to being the Immortal.

"You drank his blood. There are ramifications for that—ones that won't be foreseen until much later, but they'll still be there when you've forgotten your worry." Relief, release, and now doom.

"I'm tired. I want to wake up."

"Every circus has a snake charmer. Who's yours? What snake slithered in your tent?"

I gasped awake and bolted upright in bed. I didn't need to find my bearings. Everything rushed back at me at breakneck speed. I was in Roane's bed. His sheets were a welcoming cool touch against my naked skin and I turned to see him at his window, gazing outwards. His black pants rode low on his hips. There was no shirt in his hand this time, only worry in his eyes.

I swallowed tightly because I felt what he felt inside.

Resignation and fatigue. Underneath that was determination. He was going to win. He'd always known it and now it was time to remind everyone else.

"What'd you dream about?"

I curled against the headboard and wrapped the sheets around me. I felt exposed. "A lot of ramblings and crazy talk. There was a circus theme this time."

"Circus?" Roane frowned, but never moved away from the window.

The fairytale wasn't worth mentioning. "The Immortal told me that there was a snake charmer in my tent."

"You talk? You have conversations?" Roane looked taken aback.

"Yeah, anyway—the snake charmer sent a snake inside the tent."

He crossed to sit beside me on the bed. He sat with his back towards me and I watched the corded muscles on his back. He was primed and ready to go.

"I think I'm the tent. The Immortal told me that, but someone was inside of me."

Roane swung his hypnotic eyes toward me.

I grinned and rasped out, "No, not you. She meant like an empath was inside of me. It's been known to happen. If an empath is skilled enough, they can find someone and look outward—look at where they're at. I did it. I had Blue do it to Kates for me."

"You think that someone was inside of you to see where you are?"

"I know it." The moment my eyes had opened, everything flooded to me. "Kates told me that Blue was in a coma. If I'd gone further inside of her I would've seen that Kates hadn't put Blue in a coma. She took her captive. Blue was being held in the same castle where they took me with Emily and Adam. I didn't search inside of her enough."

Roane stood and crossed to his closet. I watched as he flung open the doors and quickly rifled inside. "Tell me more." The command was thrown over his shoulder.

"Blue was inside my head. They made her go in when I had my shield down."

Roane paused and looked at me.

I swallowed painfully. "She got inside and they're coming here."

"That's what he intended the whole time." Roane suddenly stopped and straightened to his fullest height. Each muscle on his back stood out, primed and livid.

In that moment, I was suddenly aware of how Roane was a vampire. He was a predator and now he'd go against another predator. Roane was a Hunter. Their skills went unmatched by other vampires. It was why they were chosen to be the hunters of their own kind, but Lucan was his human brother. And he led, what Kates believed to be, a revolution.

"They had no intention of you delivering a message to the Immortal. Let me guess, they have her boyfriend and they hoped she'd give herself up for him?"

I nodded. "How'd you know?"

"I can read thoughts. The girl they think is the Immortal has no idea what a shield is—and your shield was down too, Davy. I read that they'd taken Adam and Emily. I know that Kates used you."

"Did you read inside of my head what your brother really intends to do with the Immortal?"

Roane paused.

"He wants my blood because he wants his Family to have the Immortal's powers. He's hoping to have an army of unstoppable vampires so that they can reverse the decree. The one that states they can't hunt, bite, or kill humans. The one that started the Hunters in the first place and the one that'll allow Kates to do all the slaying she wants."

I looked at my hands, lifted them upwards, and gasped as I saw a glimpse of the sparkling diamond blood that I'd dreamt about. My eyes closed and then my normal skin was back.

"No," Roane clipped out. "My brother doesn't just want to reverse the decree. My brother wants to rule the entire Vampire nation." He lifted his eyes once again to me. Then he reached inside his closet and pulled out a lethal sword. He strapped the sword diagonally across his back and lifted a gold necklace over his head. It hung on the apex of his chest. I wondered at the significance when I saw that a small leaf emblem that dangled from the chain.

I searched for something to say. "At least he's ambitious."

Roane clipped out, "His 'ambition' just sealed his fate." Then his jaw clenched, unclenched, and clenched again. "He wants you. He can't have you."

23

———

Gregory came for me. He knocked once and announced his presence through the door.

"Give me a second." I glanced around with a heavy head, drooped shoulders, and my heart was not in my chest, but I moved my body as if it still belonged to me. Gregory knocked once more before I opened the door. "Okay. I'm ready."

He nodded with that same look in his eyes that I'd seen the first time. They were shrewd and he still looked at me in distaste, but I might've detected a small bit of sympathy. I wasn't sure. I was just happy that it wasn't Wren.

Gregory led me out. As we passed a circular stairwell in the middle of the hallway, I heard the buzz downstairs. The floor shook underneath my feet. The excitement in the air was addictive. I felt their thirst for blood. Every muscle in their bodies was stretched to the fullest from their anticipation.

A war was brewing.

As soon as we hit the outside air, something reeled inside of me. I felt another frenzy of excitement, rage, and carnal desire. Unlike inside, this frenzy was twice as bad. I looked out and saw one thing. I shouldn't have been able to see Roane, but I did. He stood on a hill, a dark figure among the shadows around him. He was a vampire and at that moment, I felt with confidence that he was the best.

There was no wind. The night was still, eerily so, but I felt the frenzy of activity from Roane's Family behind me. I felt it from the oncoming army too. Roane stood between the two armies and I wondered why he stood where he did.

As I got into the back seat, Gregory shut the door. As he slid beside me from the other side, I grasped his hand and shot inside before I realized what I had intended.

He wanted revenge. It was what he thirsted for, almost more than anything, but he'd been given an order. He intended to fulfill that order and I choked back tears as I heard Roane ordering him to protect me, keep me safe, and fulfill that duty above anything else. It cost Gregory, but he intended to see it through.

I almost shot back out of him, but I gritted my teeth and remembered my mistake with Kates. I looked further and saw the reason he wanted revenge. Raitscliff.

I remembered Roane's words. *'Raitscliff has vowed your death since Hartsdale.'*

Now I understood.

Raitscliff had turned Gregory's daughter. He sought revenge by murdering Raitscliff's second in command. Both vampires wanted the other's throat now.

I shuddered from the rage inside of Gregory, but I went further and got a rush of memories, emotions, and even worse, I heard his little girl. She laughed softly, delicately when he crooned as a proud father for her to sleep. They were both human in this memory. Then there was another memory where he held his arms out for her as she took her first steps.

She had golden curls and the warm brown eyes like her father. Then I saw when she'd been changed into a vampire for an enemy Family. As I started to pull out of him, I brushed against another thread of emotions. This one was his belief. He believed in Roane. He believed so fully, it brought tears to my eyes.

I gasped again and this time, I was inside of Roane. I saw through his eyes and felt inside his body. I felt his strength and fierce resolve. I didn't stop to wonder how I was inside of him, but I was. I stood on that hill, cloaked in darkness. I felt freed as an animal of the world, possibly the best.

Roane didn't relish his darkness. I felt a surge of sadness, but I didn't search through that. I couldn't, not yet. I looked out through his eyes. Unlike the dark reddish tint that I'd seen through Kates' eyes, his were crystal clear. His vision was magnified to make out a single droplet on a blade of grass. He saw everything.

He was chillingly patient as an army of vampires approached with the symbol of a lion painted on their bodies. They were on foot, silent and lethal. Their bodies weaved in and out of the shadows that were overcast from the woods surrounding Roane's home. They hoped for a surprise attack.

They failed.

He sniffed the air—Raitscliff. Roane took another long shuddering sniff and something pricked inside of him. There was no Lucan in the approaching army. Sixty beasts led by Raitscliff. He had forty behind him. The odds were favorable for the Roane Family.

"Get out of me, Davina!" Roane snarled and then shoved me out.

The car had pulled away, but I hadn't noticed. Gregory watched out the windows.

"What does Lucas intend to do?" My voice was scratchy.

Each muscle in his thick neck shifted until Gregory peered at me squarely. He had no idea that I'd been in there and that I knew what made him tick. "Lucas has a plan. He always has a plan. It should not matter to a human such as yourself."

I straightened in my seat. "I might be human, but I'm the reason all of this is happening. I don't care what you think of me. I care about what happens tonight. I want to know what Lucas is planning."

Gregory stared at me. "We both know what he plans."

Lucan's death.

"Lucan isn't back there. He's not going to Lucas' house. It's just Raitscliff—"

Gregory didn't move. He did nothing and yet, I felt his attention snap. It was now solely directed on me.

I continued with a dry mouth, "I... you know what I am." It wasn't the time to waste words. "You know what I can do. I was inside of you. I know what he did and I know what you did doesn't measure against what he did. It was wrong. I'm not a vampire. I don't understand you people. To be honest, I don't care to ever understand, but I have a proposition."

Here we go—

"It's the luck of the Irish. Don't do it, yee lads."

I clasped my eyes close and cried out, "I'm not dreaming. There are rules. You can't invade my head now."

The Immortal laughed. "I don't have to be lucky to be Irish. I'm the Immortal. I'm you, Davy. You've got the luck of a lass."

"Go away!"

"Now, now," it tsked me. "Ye caun't go tound screaming tah yaself. Peeple tink ya crazy, that's wat tey tink."

I glanced at Gregory. He thought I was crazy.

"You can't do this to him. You will not take away this man's last purpose."

I turned away and tried to whisper into my hand, "He's a vampire."

"The soul isn't kept in a neat locked box. The soul is imbedded into the body. The body remains and part of the soul still remains. He has a purpose. You will not tempt him and you will not remove that last purpose for his being."

Gregory had stilled.

I whispered back to the Immortal, "His purpose is to kill. That's what vampires do."

He growled deep in his throat. Then the Immortal lashed at me, "You are ignorant. That is unforgivable! His purpose is hope. He has hope in Roane, at what he believes Roane will achieve. You will take that away."

Huh?

"His daughter and enemy are his weaknesses. You will not take his hope by exploiting his weakness. You are not that type of person."

"I'm not a person."

"You are wrong. You are the last person I need."

Talk about hearing my own doom. I sighed and said instead to Gregory, "Can you just take me home?"

His big beefy hand jerked at my question. "Did you mean what you said? Is it really just Raitscliff back there?"

I jerked a shoulder up. "I lied. I wouldn't know that anyway." I wondered if he bought my lie and I, for once, had no idea what he wondered in return. A moment later he relaxed beside me. Then I heard the slight crunch of gravel beneath the tires and the wind against the window.

Absentmindedly, I noted, "The wind's picked up."

Gregory turned his thick neck. "I've known a few Immortals. It took them years, some lifetimes, before they could do what you've done in two days."

Something told me he hadn't bought my lie. I didn't reply back. What could I say?

'You're the last human I need.' The words haunted me and a fresh shiver crawled down my spine. I felt it all the way through my body and to my gut. Something didn't bode well for me... but I'd have to figure it out later. A war was about to break out and I knew that I needed to do something about it. I had to stop it, but I had no idea how to do that. Pre-Immortal age, I would've sought out Blue... .and then the light bulb turned on. Blue was awake. Blue was not in a coma. And I could talk to Blue—but not in the physical sense.

"Stupid!" I should've thought of that before.

Gregory didn't spare me a look. It was a good feeling. We had become acclimated to each other.

I closed my eyes, hunkered down, and sought out Blue. It only took a second before I found myself in her head. She was not so blue, though. She was furious and seeing red wherever she looked. Her arms were jerking in rhythm, scraping away at something, and her teeth were gritted. Then I remembered that Blue wasn't a vampire. I couldn't communicate with her.

'They can't know about Davy. I can't tell them.'

I sucked in a panicked breath.

'Jacith sent me for a reason. I can't let them know Davy's the one.' Blue continued, 'I told them Lucas' position. He can handle them. Everything is not lost. They still think the other girl is the Immortal. Everything is still safe. They cannot be divided.'

How did Blue know? What did Blue know? What did she mean when she said we couldn't be divided? We already were.

Before I pulled completely out of Blue, I heard a different voice from inside of her. It was deep, ominous, and I almost felt the immortality from it. 'He will need her at the end otherwise all will be lost.'

The deep voice sent shivers down my spine and something took root inside of me. I needed to be there, at whatever it was. I needed to be beside Roane. With that thought, the decision took over my body. I looked down and watched as my body turned into a glowing beacon. I was faintly aware of Gregory's jerk in reaction.

The Immortal was taking over.

I swallowed tightly as I didn't know if I wanted it or if I was just along for the ride. Either way, I closed my eyes tightly, and knew the next second would decide my fate.

Something burst inside of me and I felt my body shoot into the air. Gregory twisted around me like I was in the eye of a tornado. He was quickly replaced with the car, the surrounding road, and the other cars. I was in the air and everything started to circle around me. Looking down, I saw the Raitscliff Family beneath my feet. I could barely make out the symbol of the lion until they suddenly started to circle so fast it was a constant blur. It was like a colorful wall and I gasped when a lion burst out of the blurred wall. It lifted its head and let loose with a deafening roar. It closed its massive mouth and then hung its head before it vanished.

For the first time in my sanity, I reached out for the Immortal. "Please stop this. I mean it! I can't—I just want this to stop. Please stop."

And for the first time, the Immortal didn't answer.

I closed my eyes and felt my body slam to the ground. My legs were unsteady, but I looked up to see the surrealness around me. Kates and Lucan stood in front of me. I squeaked in panic, but when they didn't react, I relaxed slightly.

Lucan was in the front, perfectly straight and with confidence in his shoulders. His black eyes were intense as he looked at something in the distance. He thirsted for what he thought was next to come.

His jaw was clenched tight. I watched, horrified, as his nostrils slowly flared. It was like he smelled blood in the air. Then I saw patches of his skin break out to form a puzzle. He was the puzzle, but the pieces were off. It was like something had been put together wrong.

Kates stood with her head half bent towards the ground and a hand outstretched to touch the back of his. An air of intimacy swirled around them. But while he stood with no regrets, I saw a shadow in Kates. Her hair had slipped down her cheek and lifted in the air. It moved slowly, so slowly. I realized that time still moved forward, but crawled at a snail's pace. Not me.

'There are rules, universal laws—The Immortals are able to bend those rules.'

I was bending time—no. The Immortal was bending time or... I was. It didn't matter who was doing it because it was happening. Then I saw Kates bite the corner of her lip. If I'd been any other person, I wouldn't have caught that gesture. She was having second thoughts—and something else flooded inside of me. There was still something in her that knew her path was wrong. Hope flared in me.

Then something else exploded inside of me and I was hurtled through the same tornado of time as before. When I stopped again, I saw Shelly huddled in a far corner. She was pale and tears were frozen in midair on her cheek. Wren grasped her shoulder tightly. The two looked in complete contrast with Shelly's yellow sweater and Wren's hooker outfit. Then something prickled the back of my neck and I turned around.

Roane stared directly at me. His eyelid twitched and I almost screamed when he hurled himself at me. When Roane's hand touched my arm, I was thrown out of my time-loop thing. It felt like we both tumbled out of invisible glue and fell roughly against the opposite wall.

Wren and Shelly both jumped, but Roane pressed against me. "What the hell are you doing here?"

I couldn't really tell him that it was a deep and foreboding voice inside of Blue's head that sent me to him. In fact, I couldn't even explain how I'd gotten to him, but I had.

"Are we in your restaurant? Weren't you just outside of your place?" There were three tables set up in a corner. Diamond-encrusted glasses sat on top of them. I recognized those glasses. They were from the Alexander Restaurant.

"I'm every girl's best friend," I said faintly, echoing the Immortal's words.

Roane frowned fiercely, but pressed closer. He shifted and blocked me from Shelly and Wren. I wasn't even sure if Shelly knew I was there. It had all happened so fast, but I figured that Wren could smell me.

"I sent you with Gregory." He was enraged. A shiver passed through me—it was one of those sorts that I always got around him. What was it about this guy?—vampire. What was it about this vampire? My legs forgot they had bone in them whenever he was in the vicinity.

I needed to be distracted. "I zapped away from him. Don't worry. You can't blame him. He couldn't stop me... and how could you? That's annoying."

Roane replied swiftly, "You drank my blood. I'm connected to you."

I wasn't sure if I was comfortable with that thought.

"You didn't answer me. Why are you here?" Roane pressed.

I looked towards one of the walls, the north wall, and I felt what was on the other side. "He's here. He's out there. And he knows that you're in here."

Roane followed my gaze, but he never questioned what I said. "How far?"

"Across the road. Kates is with him."

Roane narrowed his eyes and quickly crossed to a window. As he moved away, the cold replaced his warmth.

Shelly gasped in surprise. "Davy? What are you—How? Oh thank god!"

I attempted a smile, but just sighed in the end. She shouldn't have been grateful to see me. I was the reason she was here and yet —I couldn't not appreciate the irony. Shelly Witless was happy to see me. Only the supernatural could do something like that.

Shelly frowned, confused. When she moved toward me, Wren held her back. "Wha—Davy, are you... do you know these people?"

There it was again, just like Emily and Adam. All three of them thought they were held captive by people. If only it were true. I didn't say anything. What could I say?

Roane moved away from the window. "They've got us surrounded."

Wren growled. "How many?"

"Lucan's army. They split up."

"Our Family?"

"We should be okay." Roane hauled me behind him as he strode through the door. I heard Shelly cry out and knew Wren did the same with her. He led the way down a narrow hallway and out onto a slight perch. We were on a third floor that I hadn't known existed in the restaurant. I glanced down and saw the fountain in the middle of the room. Our table must've been right underneath where we stood now, but I hadn't had time to study the restaurant's interior before.

I studied it now and saw that the fountain was larger than I thought. Giant goldfish circled in the clear blue water. Then I looked at the bottom and blinked twice before I realized that there was no bottom. The fountain fell to a depth that I couldn't see. I glanced at Roane and briefly thought about slipping inside. His eyes could see it.

"Don't even think it."

"How do you do that?" It was becoming annoying. I had my shield up, with the little bit of effort that I needed now, but it was up. He could still read my mind.

"I don't have to be a genius to know what you were thinking," Roane muttered before he turned and swept us down a narrow stairway to our left. I said swept, but we really flew downwards. It only took a second before our feet landed with a swoosh on the main floor.

I heard another swoosh behind us.

"Oh—!"

"We're going underground?" Wren's voice was tightly restrained.

I looked over my shoulder and gulped when her eyes landed on me. She hated me. I saw it. But she was like Gregory. She followed Roane. She believed in him. And for the second time, I wondered what vampire could inspire loyalty like that.

She growled a warning and Roane jerked me in front of him. His hand fell from my arm and planted itself on my waist. He steered me in front of him and answered Wren at the same time, "Yes, we'll go underground. A tunnel connects to the mansion. We can regroup and head out of town."

"We're running." I heard the distaste in her voice.

"No." Roane stopped and looked behind. He stared her down. "We are being smart. There are two armies to our one. Right now, we have an entire army behind us."

"It's a Family," Wren retorted.

"Yes, a Family of vampires. It's an army to our two, Wren. I won't chance it."

"Vampires!" Shelly squeaked. I heard another cry of pain a moment later and knew Wren must've tightened her hold.

Wren bit out, "You wanted to send the replacement away. I understood that, but I knew you were going to come and fight. Now we're running. You would've chanced it if she hadn't shown up."

Oh—we all knew who she meant.

Roane had already been stiff before, but now he was like cement. My finger twitched. I fought against the urge to trail it down his arm, just to feel him. It wasn't the time or place.

I closed my eyes and mentally repeated that to myself. I'd said it a third time when I felt Wren back down from Roane. I didn't know what he'd said, but it must've worked. I felt the surrender in the air and then Roane turned to steer me forward again.

He wasn't as rigid as before. I wondered if he knew what had passed through my mind when I felt one of his fingers dip underneath my waistband and started to rub back and forth.

My legs started to turn into jelly and I leaned back against him once before he realized what was happening. He chuckled underneath his breath, for my ears only, and removed his hand.

I bit my lip to keep from crying out in protest, but it was the right thing to do. An army was coming and we were on the run. It was definitely not the time for my legs to melt into the ground.

Roane directed me around the main floor, through a myriad of tables. As we passed the fountain, I glanced down again and caught a swish of a tail from the deeper depths.

"Focus, Davy," Roane murmured into my ear. "We'll be fine."

"She will be. She can't die, but the rest of us can," Wren snarled. I heard the swift swish of her leather as she strode behind us.

Roane steered us to a back door and as his hand reached out, glass shattered behind us. He stopped, but I watched in fascination as his hand flexed momentarily. He fought against an urge and then decided something as he turned slowly. My heart was effectively in my throat. I tried to peak around him, but Roane kept me in place behind him.

Wren growled. I jumped when I heard another deeper undertone that she hadn't added before. It had been from Wren before, but this sound was from the vampire.

All of the sudden, Shelly and Wren moved away. Shelly screamed in protest and Roane's hand slipped behind me. He grabbed the doorknob, but didn't turn it. I watched, confused, and then as another explosion occurred, Roane pushed the door open. I was quickly on the other side before I realized what happened and the door was shut behind me.

Not good.

I turned and looked at the closed door. Roane didn't want me in danger. I got that, but what he didn't know is that we couldn't be divided—for whatever reason. The scary voice inside of Blue's head said so.

I heard another explosion on the other side followed by a loud thump. I pressed my ear against the door and heard a lot of growling, a bunch more thumps. When I heard a shrill scream, the pain blasted me. I could've blocked it, but I didn't want to—I sighed in relief when I realized it wasn't Roane. Then I slipped inside their pain and nearly choked as they died. The body's coldness quickly became cemented. It had been a vampire, but now it was just a body. His eyes were open. I looked through him at the room from the ground. His head was turned to the right and I had a perfect view of the action.

Wren had shoved Shelly into a corner with a table to block her.

Roane warned me never to be alone with her. Now I knew why.

She swept forward, dodged a vampire, grabbed his leg and another's leg and rolled to the ground. She used her body's momentum and both vampires fell to the ground. Their necks snapped as she completed her roll. Somehow, she grabbed a knife in each hand and quickly stuck them into two more vampires who were focused on Roane.

My mouth went dry watching her. All of the sudden, I felt another searing pain in my chest. I gasped and clutched my chest. When I pulled it away, I was surprised to find there was no blood. I'd expected blood and then I cursed underneath my breath. I quickly slipped back into the dead vampire and looked for Roane. I couldn't see him. The pain must've been his.

When I tried to get inside of Roane, he lashed at me, '*Stay out!*'

I tried again—nothing. Roane had completely locked me out.

The dead vampire was turned the other way now. He wasn't a help and so I did what I probably shouldn't have. I slipped inside of Wren. She was boiling with adrenalin, excitement, and wrath all at once. Complicated.

As she bent forward, I reeled, and suddenly she was back up with her legs in the air and her fists between them. I felt like I was on a roller coaster. Then another scream punctured the air and everything froze.

Wren whirled around, her insides surging.

Lucan held Shelly in front of him with his mouth turned towards her neck. He lowered his teeth, but looked up—Wren followed the gaze—and there stood Roane with two vampires in his hands.

It was a direct challenge.

Roane straightened, deftly flexed his hands and snapped the vampires' necks. Their bodies fell to the ground and he stepped over them, calm and assured.

Wren stretched her hands, ready for Roane's command. None came. He held his human brother's gaze steadily. "Do you want to drink? Go ahead. You know what will happen."

Lucan grinned, lethally, and nipped lightly at Shelly's skin.

She shuddered against his chest, but Lucan only had eyes for Roane. "Is this how you thought it'd end? After all this time and I've got the girl in my arms. You had your chance, brother. Too bad you forgot who you were when you went to them."

"Do you want the Immortal or do you want me?" Roane threw out the challenge.

For a moment I saw indecision in Lucan's eyes. Roane was right. Lucan did want his brother back, but something had gone wrong between them, more than the ready-to-kill-each-other type of wrong. "Is that what it would take, Lucas? If I let her go, would you remember who you're supposed to be? Do you think I'm *still* the stupid one?" A hard glint appeared in Lucan's black eyes. "Or maybe if I drink from her, you'll have no other choice. You'll have to come back to my side."

"That's what you want, isn't it?"

I felt Roane's confidence. It was sweltering, sexy, and entirely too alarming. I felt what was on the other side—the acceptance of what was to come.

Lucan hesitated, but an emotion quickly stormed in those blackened eyes. His hand grasped Shelly's neck tighter and a vein jerked in her neck.

Wren wetted her lips. She wanted a taste too, but her fear and loyalty to Roane held her back.

For a moment, just a moment, I was tempted to slip inside of Shelly, but I knew the fear would paralyze me. I didn't know for sure if I could withstand it, but then another thought came to my mind. With a gasp, I was inside of Shelly. The terror was suffocating, but I tried to wade through it. It was like hardening cement. I felt Lucan pressed behind me. I felt my neck, Shelly's neck, trembling and weak. Then a box opened behind me. There was a light, but it quickly shut off.

The terror was gone. The trembling had stopped. Shelly had gone into a back corner of her mind where she could escape. She was no longer in control of her body. I would've done the same thing. Hell, I *had* done the same thing in my recent past.

Then I slipped into every pore of her body. Lucan stilled at the sudden change, but then Shelly's body jerked when I took control. He continued, "You had your chance, brother. You could've been beside me through eternity. You chose the wrong side. I've got her now and I'll reign in your defeat."

My eyes—Shelly's eyes—snapped to Roane. His eyes narrowed as he sensed the change. He paused, studied me/Shelly, and comprehension flared in his eyes. He looked towards the closed door where my body stood, but swung back to Shelly.

He knew—and he was pissed.

Roane chose his words carefully. "You need to be careful, Lucan. Things aren't as they seem. Things are... undecided."

Wren frowned and glanced to her leader.

Roane took a purposeful step forward. He didn't step forward, he stalked forward.

Lucan stilled—I wasn't inside of him, but I felt his body's answer to the sudden shift in Roane's body. Roane had been cautious, held himself back before and now there was no holding back. Lucan registered it all and I wondered how long it would be before he realized who exactly he held in his arms. It wasn't my body. It wasn't my blood, but I still didn't want to feel his fangs rip through Shelly's skin.

"What's undecided, brother?" Lucan enjoyed the back and forth. "You led with me. You were the one who had this grand idea. It was just because she was a child. That's the only reason why you stopped. You're weak. You were weak then and you're weak now. You protect her even though this one means nothing to you."

Roane's attention snapped to his brother. For the first time since the battle had started, Roane wasn't focused on me. I frowned as I wondered who Lucan referred to....

He sounded malicious. "You hunted the first one. You were supposed to have the first drink. It shouldn't have meant anything that the thread jumped to her child."

"Shut up, Lucan!" Roane growled.

"It's the truth. And the thread's not in Talia anymore. Your lover died. You weren't even there to protect her. That's what you had chosen. You chose her over me." Disdain and bitterness dripped from Lucan, but I watched horrified as something glazed over Roane's eyes at the words.

Her? Lover?

Roane and Talia, the previous Immortal, had been lovers. From the clenched jaw, I judged that he still loved her. I closed my eyes tightly as tears stung them. They were a knee jerk reaction.

Lucan continued, "You fell in love with a child. Only a vampire can be that sick, but I understood. I did, Lucas. I'm your brother. I understand things like love at first sight. You fought me for her, but that's over. She's not alive anymore. You can forget this charade and take up my side again. I need my brother beside me. It hasn't been the same without you."

"I didn't fall in love with Talia until she was an adult. I fought you that day because she was a child. We don't hurt children."

"Yes, we do. We're vampires. Why do you keep denying what we are?"

I opened my eyes, Shelly's eyes, a crack and glimpsed the pain in Roane through her tears—my tears that her body produced from my suffering.

Roane shook his head. "I'm no longer your brother, Lucan. That ceased when Jaleathus sired me. The Roane's Family blood became mine. We live with different standards in our blood."

Lucan snorted in contempt. "Don't tell me about your different standards. They come from Jacith. He brainwashed your entire

Family, but you're still vampires. You try to pretend you aren't. I'm *insulted* that they did this to my brother."

A bitter laugh wrung out of Roane. "You were nothing without me, Lucan. I told you how to act. I told you how to think. I told you everything. You wouldn't have done anything if I hadn't been there."

Lucan froze behind me. I felt rage build inside of him. His fingers tightened on Shelly's throat. His other hand gripped her arm until I felt a trickle of blood seep downwards. It trickled over his hands, but he didn't realize it. Roane's nostrils flared at the smell. So did Wren's. I glanced around the room. All of them except Wren and Roane eyed the blood. It was Immortal blood, or so they thought.

"You're wrong," Lucan whispered. "I lead my Family. I've found the Immortal. I have her in my arms. You failed, brother."

Roane smiled. It was a confident, too smooth, type of smile. Lucan gripped harder on Shelly's arm—more blood slipped downwards. It trickled over her palm, down her finger, and hung just off the tip of the nail.

My heart pounded heavily as I waited.

It let loose and splattered on the floor.

Still no reaction from Lucan.

He was focused, almost crazily focused on Roane. "Now what is your Family going to do? You were supposed to protect the Immortal and you couldn't do that, could you?"

"I'm a Hunter, Lucan. Are you forgetting what that means? I'm connected to all of the other Hunters. You rip into that girl and I can call on them. You won't be fighting just me. You'll be fighting all of them."

"I'll have the Immortal's blood. I'll be unstoppable." Lucan was so sure, so confident in his own words. I knew instantly when he smelled the blood. His body jerked in reaction and I/Shelly was slammed against a wall. His fangs clamped onto Shelly's neck and sunk further. He drank—oh—I fought against it. The blood was pulled out at breathtaking speed. I tried to slow the draining, but it was useless.

Lucan was a starved animal. Shelly whimpered from inside of

her box. She felt her body's death. I saw the box open and the light shone briefly before she crawled out of the box. There she was, terrified, but calm. She knew her death was almost there.

I almost wished that Shelly had been a vampire. I could've talked to her, comforted her in that moment, but she wasn't. She was just a human, but it was a good thing that Shelly was a human. Life was simple for her.

I felt her heart slowing… thump… thump… she closed her eyes and fell. Her heart had stopped. Lucan let go, confused, and Shelly's body really did fall to the ground.

"She's dead," he muttered, stricken. "But…"

Kates had been silent the entire time. She gasped now, "It's not her. She's not the Immortal, but—"

I could still hear from Shelly's body, but I couldn't see anything anymore. I didn't want to stay inside of her and then I heard Kates again. "Lucan, what do we do?" Panic trembled just on the tip of her tongue, but I wondered where that had come from. Kates never panicked. I left Shelly and found Kates easily.

'It can't be, but I wonder… it can't be,' Kates thought. I caught an image of myself and knew my nolstage was connecting dots faster than I was comfortable with.

'You can't, there's no way. You never could before.'

Kates knew I'd been on the roof with Talia. She'd known that Talia was the Immortal.

'She's the empath that was cozying up with The Hunter.'

Kates had been surprised when I'd shown up at the Shoilster with Roane. Now it was starting to make sense.

'She's the Immortal.' Kates cursed to herself.

I slipped out of Kates before I felt whatever she was feeling now. I shouldn't have. I should've stayed inside of her because I knew my nolstage had power over Lucan—therefore over my livelihood, but I was a coward. I drew in another shuddering breath as I opened my own eyes and stared at the same door. I lifted a hand and tentatively touched the wood with my palm. It was so sturdy, but just on the other side everything was barely hanging in the balance.

'Your lover died.'

I pressed a knuckled fist against my mouth. Talia and Roane had been lovers. He had loved her. I remembered the stricken expression in Roane's eyes as Lucan had said those words. It had been pure love, the kind that was meant for the rest of a lifetime. He had loved someone else like that... and me... I realized that there had been nothing between us.

My stomach turned over suddenly. I could've thrown up in that moment. I glanced downwards, distantly, as I looked at my stomach. Roane was drawn to the Immortal inside of me. A part of Talia was inside of me. He was drawn to her. He needed her—not me. I was just the body.

'Davy,' Roane called to me with his thoughts.

I jerked my head to the side. I didn't want to talk to him, not at that moment, but it was irrational. I didn't want to deal with what was really happening on the other side of that door. He had no obligation to me. We'd only been together one time.

Just once.

That was it. Right? There had been no words of affection, no nothing. He had loved her. How was I supposed to compete with that? I couldn't. The answer was so bleak to me.

'Davy!' Roane was more urgent this time. *'Davy, you need to get out of here. There's a hallway that goes down. Follow it, keep going. You'll pass the fountain below us. Keep going. You need to get out of here, away from Lucan. He knows it's not Shelly. It's only a matter of time before he figures it out. He's already looking at the door. You have to hurry.'*

It hurt to even hear his voice. *'Kates knows. She figured it out.'*

There was a pause. *'Yeah. I can see that. You have to hurry, Davy. The tunnel will go all the way to the mansion. It should be safe by the time you get there. Find Gregory.'*

I was supposed to run. My childhood best friend, my vampire—I didn't know what Roane was—and so many others were in the room behind me. Shelly was dead. I knew I wouldn't die. I was the Immortal and I had a strong feeling the thread wasn't going to jump to anyone else—if it did then I was dead anyway.

I was stuck.

Run, not run, hide, not hide. What could I do? I knew what I wanted to do. I always ran. I pressed sweating palms to my pants and tried to wipe them off. I turned, faltering, and stared at where Roane urged me to go. The tunnel was dark, but it didn't seem ominous. The room behind me was too ominous, but the sound of the water calmed me slightly. It ran through the wall beside my ear. Before I knew what I was doing, my foot had stretched outwards and I found myself slowly passing through the darkness.

I kept going and the water grew louder.

The tunnel dipped forward. I felt gravity on my body and knew I was heading downwards.

I took a harsh breath and clasped my eyes tightly together. I needed to be honest with myself. I was escaping. It wasn't because Roane told me to go. He loved someone else, someone that was inside of me now. That hurt—it seared deep down, almost too far for my empathic abilities to comprehend. Well, that's not true. I could comprehend it, I just didn't want to. I wanted to run from it. He was behind me. Kates was in that room. She had the knowledge to change my life forever. I could be hunted if Lucan found out who I was.

I stopped in the tunnel and drew in a ragged breath.

I could go back, but to what? Why? Lucan wanted my powers. He couldn't have them. I knew that no matter the odds, Roane would best his brother. What was I afraid of? I could run... there was no danger.

I remembered the voice inside of Blue's head. Roane and I could not be separated.

"Are we on a pity party? Is this what the staggering amount of suffering and confliction is about?" The Immortal chose to announce its presence.

I sighed in contempt. "Now is not the time. Why can I hear you like you're here?"

"I'm the Immortal. Have you forgotten our first trip around the merry go round? You're the pail. What do you carry? Who are Jack and Jill? You should know this by now!"

"Stop it—"

"—THINK!" The Immortal screamed. "Who's Jack and Jill? You are the Immortal! You think I was the one pulling all those strings back there where you catapulted yourself out of that car and behind your sidekick? I didn't do that, Davy. I wasn't the one in the drivers' seat. That was all you. I was riding shotgun. You were the Immortal. You, not me, not this voice you keep hearing. It was all you."

My throat went dry at those words. The thread was inside of me. The thread jumped from person to person, body to body. I wasn't—there was no way, but everyone had been shocked by the speed my body had acclimated to the Immortal thread. Gregory said some took years to do what I'd done in two days, but none of it made sense. What did it mean that I had done what I had? If it hadn't been the Immortal... it was me? Who was I?

"Cut out the Buddha bull. You can ponder the eternal question of your identity later. You've got to stop moaning in your own piss and get back to that room."

"Are you my conscience? Are you the good angel now?"

"That's the issue, honey bunny. I'm neither. I'm the in between. I'm the go between. I'm the reason that your devil is on the left and the angel is on the right. That's me—that's you now so you better start deciphering it!"

The Immortal was pissing me off. "Get out of me!"

She chuckled. "Are you angry? You're more than clueless. You're choosing your ignorance. You can't walk away when you know you're needed in that other room."

"Shut up! I don't care. I'm doing what Roane wants."

The Immortal laughed. "You're doing what you want. You're running away because you got your feelings hurt. You're being a sissy. The boy likes someone that's not you. Boo freaking hoo. Wake up! You're more than that and all that romance crap is nothing compared to what's going to happen if you don't get your butt back there. Stop feeling with your emotions and think with your head."

I was empathic. Feelings *were* my thing.

"Well, they aren't anymore," the Immortal snapped. "You want to know a little about yourself? A long *long* time ago a visionary realized what vampires could do. He saw how dangerous they could be so he went and created a 'prophecy' that said one day, a person who was interwoven with the essence of life would take *their* life from them.

You're feared by vampires, but also desired. Some think you were created as an ultimate weapon against them, but then rumors started going around that they could drink from you. If they drank your blood, they could get your powers. That's the prophecy, Davy. The prophecy *was* created and the Immortal thread came to be. You've got the essence of life flowing through every particle of your body.

All the other girls, yes—even Talia—they weren't the Immortal. They were just the carriers for the thread. One would come and become the Immortal. That's you—not them. And if you want to sit and mope that Roane loves Talia, someone who was less than you, you disgust me."

As shocking revelations came, this one was big.

It continued, "Every vampire out there thinks they can drink from you and they'll have your powers. That's what they've been taught. You're the toad to their Cinderella. They're wrong. If they'd bitten any other carrier then they would've gotten the powers. The thread would've jumped to them, given them a flare of power, but immediately attached itself to the first human they would've touched. No vampire can handle the essence of life inside of them. It goes against their grain as a vampire. They thrive on pain. They thrive on suffering, on darkness, on death. We are the light. We are life. You are life, Davy, and you're the prophecy."

How could this help now?

"It'll help because you know something they don't. The prophecy states that when the Immortal becomes one, instead of giving them powers, you will give them life. You'll strip them of their immortality, Davy."

"They'll be human?"

"You'll make their heart beat. Again."

The answer was so quaint.

"But what about Blue? What the voice inside her head said? Roane and I aren't supposed to be divided?" I'd been running when I knew that the ancient voice had commanded otherwise. I should be ashamed.

"That was Jacith. He's a moron who believes he's got way more power than he does. You have that power now. Not him. You have the knowledge. Not him, but you are needed back there. Get back there! NOW!"

The decision slammed into my chest.

The sound of water tickled behind the back of my head. I focused on it again. It was louder than before. Roane had said the tunnel would pass the fountain. I moved forward and as the water grew louder, I knew what I needed to do. Determination rang through me when I felt the tunnel dip dramatically below my feet and the sound of rushing water slammed against my ears.

A rock wall was beside me. It was dank to the touch and I closed my eyes because I could feel the water on the other side. It was swirling angrily, ferocious to hear. When I'd been upstairs, I had tried to look for the bottom of the fountain. I hadn't been able to see it, but now I wondered if I was nearing the end. I pressed further and the sound grew louder and louder.

The water slammed against the rock. As I turned a corner, there it was. I'd come to an opening in the tunnel. The water rushed past me and dramatically turned to the left, but not before some of it splashed over a small hedge that separated the water from the tunnel. It disappeared from there, but there was a small walking path beside the water.

I watched the water, saw deep into the blue depths, and before I knew it—I had raised my hand above the water. Something sparked inside me and I watched from outside my body. The water lifted out of the fountain and held still in the air. It waited for my hand's command, my command.

I had no idea if I was doing it or the Immortal, but I held my breath as I raised my hand. The water followed. It lifted from the floor before I settled it back down, gently. That's when I stepped on top of the hedge and before I knew it, I'd stepped on top of the water. A part of me screamed inside, but I watched my face from outside my body. I looked calm, in control, and confident.

She knew what she was doing. She knew where she was going. She was secure. Then the water rose around her and shot upwards.

I watched from a distance as my body rode that water upwards. It surged, rolled, and seemed to thunder as gravity was flipped upside down. I couldn't take my eyes off of myself. Something totally alien took over my body. My normally frizzy brown curls were sleek as they lay against my shoulders. The curls perfectly framed my face and my lips seemed to form a small heart.

As we—me and myself—neared the top, I watched my eyelids lift and I froze in shock.

I had brown eyes, but they were silver. They seemed to see everything at once. Then they turned towards me and seemed to zap me. "Get back. Now!"

I felt myself sucked through the air and crashed into my body. I gasped, choked, and struggled against what was happening.

"Accept me. Accept yourself," The Immortal me told myself. This voice was me. I wondered, belatedly, if I could have three different personas inside of me and still be sane. Maybe. I doubted it, though.

"Accept—now!" With that last command, I threw back my head, my arms jerked upwards, and I gasped as something flowed down my throat. It molded to my body. Then the world rushed at me with breakneck speed. I lifted high and over. The water fell away and I looked around the room.

Kates was frozen beside Lucan. Her blue eyes were wide, terrified, but what drew my eye wasn't how she looked at me. It was the knowledge that burned bright. She'd known, but seeing it was a different matter. Still... that wasn't the knowledge that I saw. She knew something else was going to happen, something that she didn't want to admit to herself. I saw it so bright. It was like a candle that flickered behind her.

"You!" Lucan growled. His hair was pushed back, carelessly, but it molded to the sides of his face. His eyes gleamed cruelly and he sneered as if knowing he'd won.

I felt Roane jerk forward. He stepped to move between myself and his brother, but I stopped him. When I lifted a hand, the room rattled. "No."

"Wha—" Kates gasped and jerked her head around.

"Holy fu—" Even Wren was amazed as she took in the scene.

"Davy, stop," Roane said, but it was too late.

I moved around and stepped in front of Lucan. As I looked down at him, I realized that I was floating in the air. Something prickled the back of my wrist and I looked around.

Every glass, every champagne flute, every crystal dish floated in the air. All those diamonds sparkled furiously. They were blinding, but I saw them through my silver eyes. They looked like air particles to me.

"What—you're the Immortal. You!" Lucan took a step forward.

"Lucan!" Roane shouted a warning.

I spoke above Roane. "Yes. I am she. I am the Immortal."

My voice was different. It wasn't just mine, but all the Immortals before me. Something ancient poured through me. It was frightening, but I felt the power. "I am not what you want, Lucan. That is my only warning."

"Davy, don't do this," Kates whispered this time. "Please. Please don't do this."

I merely looked at her. The candle started to burn brighter.

Lucan growled ferociously this time. He reached for my wrist, but two things happened in the blink of my eye. Kates stepped in front of him, her back to me. And Roane flung himself forward.

I stopped everything.

Time stood still, but Roane jerked me behind him. As I fell to the floor, I raised my head. "That's right. You're connected to me."

"My blood is in you." Roane turned and glared at his brother.

"He's frozen. I stopped time."

"So I see," Roane breathed harshly. He raked a chilling glare over his brother again before he turned and regarded me.

I stood to meet him and tilted my chin for respect. "You don't approve of what I've done."

"This isn't you, Davy. This is the Immortal. You're not..." He gestured to my body. "This isn't you. I want you back."

I could've told him that this was the new me, but instead I stepped around him. I stared at Kates and breathed out in awe, "Look at her."

The candle now shone brightly behind her. The blinding yellow flame encompassed her body. She was a mere black shadow in front of it.

"Do you see it?" I wanted him to see it.

Roane frowned, but looked. "It's the slayer. She's trying to save Lucan."

She wasn't. She wasn't doing that at all. My hand rose of its own volition, but it dropped now, saddened. "You don't see it."

"She doesn't want me to hurt him. She's in love with him, what do you expect?"

"She's not saving him. She thinks she's saving me. It's so bright around her. It's her hope." The candle burned even brighter now. It looked like it was going to explode. "She's saving herself."

"She's not, Davy." Roane was firm. "Kates is smart. She knows that I wouldn't let him touch you. She's making her move against me, not for you."

He was wrong. Roane didn't realize what had happened. He didn't really understand who I was anymore. Everything he knew was limited. All the vampires thought wrong.

It didn't matter, not right then, but I turned and gazed at my lover. He looked fierce with murder in his eyes. Every part of him screamed that he was an animal, but I remembered what he'd said before.

"There's a soul inside of you."

Roane frowned, jerked off balance for a moment.

I moved forward and lifted a palm to his chest. His muscles jerked in response from my touch, but he held still.

I continued, "You told me before that you don't have a soul, but your body remembers what it did with the soul. That's why you breathe sometimes. The soul is imbedded in every part of a person. You're still a person. You still have a soul. And you honor it, even now when you want to kill your brother."

'He cannot divide them.'

I understood them now. I glanced over my shoulder at Lucan. "He's not put together right. I saw that before, but I didn't understand it. I knew you'd win today. I felt your strength. What you said was right. You have the strength of all the Hunters inside of you. You'd overpower your brother too easily, but that's where it'd rip away your humanity. You'd become the animal that you loathe inside of you."

Roane stiffened at my words. He started to pull away, but I clasped the back of his arm. I wouldn't let him move and his eyes widened at my strength. "If you had killed your brother today, that would've destroyed you. He's still a part of you. You love him and you'd be the end of him. It would've been the end of you as well. I can't have that. I need you."

His eyes clung to mine.

I touched his lips. They were perfect, cool to the touch, and I leaned forward to nip at them.

Roane grasped the back of my head and deepened the kiss. I felt his love with that kiss, but I pulled away. Haunted. "Do you love me or do you love who is inside of me?"

His eyes shuddered closed and he withdrew. "I loved her, yes."

"That's why you're drawn to me."

"That's why you're drawn to me too!" Roane whipped back to me. I was taken aback by the loathing in his eyes. "You don't think I've thought of this? Something takes control of you when you're around me. It's not you, either, Davy. You might think you feel something for me, but you don't. A part of Talia is inside of you. It's always her reaching out for me, taking control of you."

Oh god. I couldn't understand.

I started to slip inside of him, but he shoved me out. "I don't want you to know the mess inside of me."

I respected his wish. I couldn't solve the problem between us, but I knew a problem that I *could* resolve for him. So I looked back at Lucan. "You can't help your brother, but I can."

"Wha—"

I rushed forward and stepped in front of Kates. My back was to Lucan. And then I unlocked time.

"No!" Roane shouted, but I snapped my fingers. Every glass, every diamond, every champagne flute exploded in the air. They all ducked from the exploding shards of glass.

I whispered to Lucan, "I want to give you what you want."

He licked his fangs and grasped my arm. That was all he needed and he jerked me forward to clamp onto my skin. I tensed as my skin broke underneath his fangs, but I grasped his head. I willed him to drink all he needed.

"No!" Roane leapt across the room and pulled his brother from me. Lucan fell against a wall, bewildered and triumphant. Then his back arched dramatically. Only his head and toes touched the floor. He sucked in a ragged breath and pounded at his chest frantically. Desperate.

Roane stopped in front of me. He held me back with an arm around my waist and watched in confusion. "What?"

I watched Roane as he watched his brother. "He can be right again. I saved your brother for you."

"What did you do, Davy?" The words were wrung out from him. Roane stared as Lucan howled in pain and rolled on the ground.

My words were for his ears only. "I gave him life again. He can be right."

Lucan continued to writhe on the floor, but Roane suppressed a shudder and abruptly turned so he couldn't watch anymore. He pulled me tight against his chest and wrapped both his arms around me. He buried his head in the crook of my shoulder and I watched for him. One of my hands lifted to cradle the back of his head.

Everyone watched in the room. No one dared to speak. Then Lucan's body lifted off the floor, his back arched, and a dark light ripped out of his mouth. It slammed to the ceiling and settled there. Waiting. I'd kept the crystals floating in the air and now I turned my wrist. Each little shattered particle of crystal all moved as one.

"Be gone," I whispered.

Immediately the crystals surrounded the black light and an explosion occurred.

Roane jerked. Everyone gasped. Kates fell to the floor with a wrangled moan. Wren cursed softly, but savagely. After another moment of holding me, Roane lifted his head to turn towards his brother. Lucan was unconscious.

"He's sleeping."

"Davy, what did you do?"

"His soul is intact."

Roane looked anguished. "He's human?"

I nodded.

"How?"

I couldn't tell him, not really. So I closed my eyes and when I opened them again, I let Roane see my true self. He saw the silver eyes. "I'm the Immortal."

EPILOGUE

"Welcome to our last conversation."

I sighed in irritation and turned, but stopped in surprise. I looked around. "We're not in the dark anymore. I think I'm sleeping again."

The Immortal me stood before me. "No, we're not because this is the end."

I tilted my head questionably. "What are you talking about? I thought we were immortal, together for eternity?"

Silver eyes flashed back at me. "Stop thinking about trivial things. You don't need to distract yourself anymore."

"It's what I do." I shrugged it off, but something prickled at me. It was in the Immortal's voice—my voice. Then my eyes widened. It was *my* voice talking back to me. It wasn't the annoying Immortal or the lecturing Immortal. It was me.

Finally.

"What have I done again?"

The Immortal me smiled, assured and strong. "I did choose you, Davy, but I didn't go to you. When you reached inside of Talia, you pulled me out and inside of you. There's a part of you, a part that is noble. Your strength is more than I've ever encountered in a being before. You pulled me into you."

"That'd been my plan the whole time." My attempt at self-sarcasm was pathetic.

The other me continued, "There's a lot about being the Immortal that you don't understand. It's too much for you to know everything now, but things will be revealed as you go. You have a destiny and others will help you as you go. My part is done."

"What part was that?"

"My job was to help you accept who you are, who we are together. You accepted the Immortal, but you don't know the consequences. You will learn them as you go. I won't be the voice for those lessons."

I wasn't sure how I felt about this. What would I get instead?

"You've changed, Davy. You've become something new. This world is yours for the taking and you can make it better. There is a reason why the Immortal was created. You're not a fairytale. You're real and you are a force to be reckoned with. Do not let anyone take that from you. Do not!" She gutted out the last words, forcibly and urgent.

I had so many questions, so many new revelations, so many of everything. I wanted to know it all, but then she said, "Welcome to your destiny. It is the beginning."

'Welcome to our last conversation.'

Then I woke up with a gasp. I was disoriented at first, feeling something warm around me. Then I heard cars honking in the distance. Slowly, I sat up and looked around. I was on the roof with a blanket draped over me. When I sat up, I smiled at the couch cushions that I'd been laying on.

"I brought you up here. Kates needed to sleep and I wanted some privacy. You both must've fallen asleep as soon as you got back to the room." Roane moved from the building's edge.

His eyes were still the same coal black, but there was something searching in them. He seemed softer, but he was dressed as such. Black pants with a crisp black shirt that wasn't tucked in. With his hardened jaw, he looked ruthless—and he was.

His hand fell to his side and something flashed in the moonlight. It was his necklace.

I stood and gestured, half-heartedly. "You took that before. It's a leaf thing? What's it mean?"

He lifted it and stared at it long and hard. He murmured, "It was my brother's. I took it from him when I fought him. It was when Talia became the Immortal."

Oh. So much of that statement didn't sit comfortably with me. "I see."

Roane took a deep breath and turned back to gaze over the city. The lights spread out for miles and as I moved beside him, the sight made me smile. Cars honked in the distance. People laughed. More lights flickered, but there was a stillness in the city.

I wasn't sure if it was Benshire or if it was me.

"I need to meet with the Roane Elders and give them this necklace."

"Why?" We'd just dealt with Lucan. I'd finally shown Roane that I was the Immortal. He was right when he said that Kates and I were tired. We both collapsed as soon as we got to the room. Everything had *just* happened. I wasn't ready for him to leave me. Not yet.

"I have to tell them what happened. My brother is gone. After you left, some of his men took him. I have to tell them that my brother is human again and then I'm going to ask for the job of finding him. The necklace will be used to hunt him, for whoever is given the assignment."

Again.... Oh. I felt a sense of dread.

"Davy, things have happened that aren't understood."

Everything about that statement didn't bode well with anyone. I knew that things went smoother when they were understood. "How long do you think it'll take for you to find Lucan?"

How long was he going to be away?

"I don't know. It might take a few hours or months. He's human, but he still knows everything. He'll be dangerous. Lucan *liked* being a vampire. He'll want to become one again. I need to stop that from happening."

I nodded jerkily.

"They're not going to understand how you turned him human. That's not known by anyone and my Family were the ones entrusted to protect the Immortal. This will not sit well with the Elders."

"Am I in danger from them?"

"I don't know. When word gets out what you can do, you'll be feared by vampires. There aren't many who'd like to be human again. And you're Immortal. They can't kill you, which is what their first reaction will be. My Elders might want that too, but I'll argue on your behalf. I think they'll realize the foolishness of that."

I frowned as a different question formed in my head. "Roane, who is Jacith?"

His shoulders stiffened. "Where did you hear that name?"

"He was in Blue's head. The Immortal mentioned something about him."

Roane didn't like hearing any of that. "He's a *very* powerful witch, possibly the most powerful I've known."

"What does he have to do with the Immortal thread?"

Roane didn't answer right away, but eventually he did. "He created it."

Oh—whoa. I blinked in shock, but remembered the Immortal's words. Jacith thought he was powerful, but I was more. Somehow, I didn't think this Jacith would enjoy learning that information.

"Did he create the prophecy? Or just the Immortal thread?"

Roane had looked back over the city, but he whipped around once more to me. He had an accusing look in those dark eyes. "What are you talking about? Jacith created the Immortal. You talk as if the prophecy and the thread are separate. They are not. I assure you. My Family has volumes of Immortal lore. We were entrusted to protect the thread."

Except, they didn't know all of it and they didn't need to protect me. I knew about the separation from the Immortal. "You didn't know that I can turn vampires human."

Roane opened his mouth, but he couldn't argue my point. He closed it again as a look of mysticism crossed over his face.

I never thought I'd see that. I loved it.

"I thought I knew everything there was to know about Immortals. I'm starting to wonder if I know just a *little* about Immortals. It's unsettling."

"You don't understand, Roane. There's a prophecy that I think you don't know about. Someone created the prophecy and later someone else created the thread. I came to be before Jacith created the thread. I don't know why that's important, but it is. I know this because the Immortal told me. I told you before that we have conversations. She/it/me told me this... and someone else is going to guide me."

Roane turned and touched my shoulder. He turned me towards him. "Davy, the Immortal thread was created by Jacith. I know this, but you're correct. He has never spoken about the ability for an Immortal to turn vampires into humans. If, in your conversations, you learn more then you must tell me. The Immortal is crucial to the vampire nation. We *must* know everything you know."

Something else didn't sit well with him. "What is it?"

Roane lifted up his head and gazed over the city's lights before he answered. "I was with Talia for years. I watched her grow and she never once talked about a conversation with the Immortal. It's so different. I don't know what to make of it. She would have odd dreams sometimes, but that was it."

I wasn't sure what stung me more: Talia and Roane or the lack of conversations. I could've done without those conversations. "I'm the last, Roane. The Immortal told me. I'm the last to be the Immortal. I'm not a carrier for the thread. I *am* the Immortal."

'Do not let anyone take that from you.'

Roane was silent.

I continued, "It's just the beginning, Roane. I know that your next step is finding your brother, but it's just the beginning for me. There's so much more. I can feel it. I know it."

Roane looked at me gravely. He stared long and hard. He didn't try to slip inside. I didn't try to slip inside of him. We remained in our own bodies. No powers. No thought reading.

"Are you looking for my soul?"

Slowly, he shook his head and took my hand. His fingers slid against mine and locked in place. I closed my eyes and savored the feeling. Strength radiated off of him, perhaps for what was to come.

Then he whispered, "I'm looking for mine."

To continue, Davy Harwood in Transition

DAVY HARWOOD IN TRANSITION

TIJAN

CHAPTER 1

I felt stupid.

There was no other way around it; no way could I justify my emotions. I just felt stupid.

Emily had hounded me for the last two months. She wanted me to talk to Mr. Moser. Finally, after she'd held my cell phone hostage, I'd had to succumb. So this is how I found myself back in the infamous building where I used to volunteer with the hotline.

I suppressed a shudder. I really hated working at the hotline and it wasn't because of the last time I'd been in this building. Although that moment had changed my life, the real reason was because I hated talking on the phone. Only a select few got on my 'I'll talk to you on the phone' list.

"Davy Harwood," Mr. Moser boomed as he entered his own office. If he was trying for intimidation, it would've worked three weeks ago.

Mr. Moser did not qualify for my phone list.

I waited until he rounded his desk and sat. His leather chair squeaked underneath his weight, but his two beady green eyes weren't amused and didn't care. His orange tie had flapped over his shoulder and it stayed there, caught between the wrinkles of his green buttoned dress shirt. His khaki pants hadn't fared any better. I wasn't a wrinkle-noticing person, but I wouldn't have been surprised to find out they'd been rolled up and stuffed in the back of a drawer for the last two years.

He lifted an eyebrow. "Do you have anything to say to explain your actions three weeks ago?"

I was more concerned about how his tie still hadn't moved off his shoulder. He looked like an idiot. Was I supposed to tell him?

"My actions, sir?"

"You broke protocol."

Oh, that. The night that had changed my life. If only Mr. Moser actually knew I was supposed to go up to that roof.

"Oh," was all I said. I tried to sound apologetic. I folded my hands and when I looked down, I even fiddled my thumbs.

"I'm not buying it, Davy." Mr. Moser was very smart.

"Buying what, sir?"

"You answered the phones after we'd already closed. You broke protocol. You identified the caller's location; chose to intervene without any communication with your supervisors, and then you had the balls to resign by sneaking a letter under my door. I am not buying your act right now, young lady."

He said 'balls'. I loved that.

"Yes, but." I really had no defense. I'd claimed what had happened was too traumatic for me to continue working with the hotline. Things *had* been traumatic, but he was right. I'd chosen the coward's way out so that I wouldn't get in trouble.

I eyed Mr. Moser up and down. The beady eyes had a glaze of anger in them. "I had hoped better of you, Davy."

Wow. Guilt.

He sounded disappointed as he took a deep breath. "Emily is an outstanding Listener. She spoke highly of you, but perhaps she was biased since you are roommates. Still, even Adam seemed to have taken a liking to you. He respected you, Davy."

I had so many corrections to Mr. Moser's rose-colored perspective. One, Emily was an awful listener. She might be a wonderful Listener at the hotline where she was fulfilling a requirement for a social work class, but she didn't listen to anyone in real life. And two, Adam had taken more than a liking to me. Adam had asked me out on one date. The date had failed miserably and I didn't think being kidnapped had been the problem.

"What are you thinking?"

"Well, under the circumstances I do not support your actions. You broke protocol and you should have the correct discipline. Then there's the item of your resignation. I know that you didn't really mean to resign and because of Miss Whistworth's death, the hotline is in need of any willing volunteers so I've decided to look past your actions."

What? Did he mean … ? There was no way.

Mr. Moser beamed. "You can start tonight. Adam needed a replacement since he's taken two weeks of vacation. You can take his desk."

I had no words. I couldn't even feel my toes and I felt everything, literally.

Mr. Moser was already up and out of his office before any thoughts could form in my brain. And when I realized I'd been duped, I groaned and dropped my forehead on the desk. Not only did I feel stupid, but I felt like a complete moron.

When my phone vibrated, I snapped it open. "Yeah?"

"What's wrong, slick?" Kates drawled. I heard music in the background and that meant one thing.

"Are you at the Shoilster?"

I'd been there twice and hated both times. Plus, it was a vampire bar. I wasn't the biggest fan of vampires.

"Hell no." Kates barked out a laugh. "Listen, I'm going to be out of town for awhile. I need to figure some stuff out."

My childhood friend had been camped out in my dorm room for two weeks. The news was met with varying shades of relief and concern. I knew if Emily was the type to shout for joy, my roommate would've been screaming at the top of her lungs. I was growing tired of the tension between the two. Of course, Emily had reason for her dislike. Kates had been the one to kidnap us, but Emily wasn't privy to the fact that Kates had tried to save me from her psychotic vampire boyfriend later that evening.

"Where are you going?" She might be a vampire slayer, but she'd find trouble. She always did.

"I'm not going to find Lucan."

I relaxed, just a little.

Kates added, "There's something I gotta do on my own. Trust me, slick. You can talk to Blue if you want. She agrees that I should go and do this thing."

"I don't know, Kates." I wasn't too concerned about what my Empath Sponsor had to say since I'd been avoiding her ever since I found out she was connected to my immortal enemy.

"What don't you know? You don't even know what I'm doing."

I opened my mouth.

Kates beat me to it. "I'm not telling you because you'll just worry. I've talked about it with Blue. She agrees that I should go and do this. And she thinks I shouldn't tell you so I'm not. Besides, you have enough to worry about. You're the freaking Immortal, Davy. I have no idea why you're still in college, much less going to see that idiot supervisor."

I was going because Emily made me, but I couldn't say that to Kates. "I'm living a normal life because I'm going to be living for a long time. Are you sure that you're not looking for him?"

Kates' boyfriend had been a psychotic vampire, but he was human now. So that made him a psychotic human with all this knowledge about vampires and how to become a vampire again.

Kates was silent for a couple beats. "I don't really have to, remember?"

I flushed and shut my mouth. The reminder was duly noted. If anyone was going to find Lucan, it'd be Lucas Roane, his twin.

"Have you heard from him?" Kates asked, gently.

I rolled my eyes. I didn't need kid gloves. "I haven't seen Roane since he took off."

That had been ten days ago. And since he was hunting Lucan, I had no idea how long it would take. Lucan was human, but he thought as a vampire. Roane was not only a vampire, but a hunter. I was surprised he was still gone actually. Hunters had the skill and jurisdiction to hunt and kill any vampire that broke the decree that stated no humans were to be bitten or harmed by vampires. They were the elite of their race and Roane was one of the best.

Lucan didn't stand a chance.

"Your roommate has been buzzing around the room like she's on meth. You sure she's a sober saint? She ain't acting like it."

"Did you say something?" I was so thankful to Kates' attention deficit. No more questions about Roane.

"What? I've been perfect."

"Kates, no," I groaned.

"The chit needs to toughen up, seriously. I've gotta go, Davy. I'll be in touch. Don't worry about me. I love you. I'll be fine." And my childhood friend hung up.

I sighed and dropped my forehead on the desk. What else could I do?

"Okay, Miss Harwood, we've got you back in the program!" Mr. Moser broadcasted as he strode back into his office.

Yes, my life could get weirder. I lifted my forehead from the desk. "Mr. Moser, I hate phones. I'm not good on the phone. I'm not good at this work."

"Nonsense! You're perfect."

Meaning, he was desperate. Adam's two weeks to mourn his girlfriend of one day must've put the hotline in a dire spot.

"When is Adam coming back? Maybe I could fill in until he gets back?"

Mr. Moser squashed that idea as he slapped a file on his desk. "We'll figure that out when the time comes."

I winced from the slap and resigned myself to my fate. I had an entire six hour shift answering a phone in my future. You'd think I would've seen this coming since I was the Immortal and empathic, but I was lame.

CHAPTER 2

"No, Anne, you shouldn't let your roommate eat your peanut butter. If it bothers you, you could ask her not to eat your food. And don't feel foolish calling the hotline about this issue. Sometimes the smallest arguments stand for the bigger problems."

I was bored. Five hours and fifty-eight minutes had passed and my eyes gleamed in excited anticipation. Two more minutes and I could hang up the phone. No after hour calls would lure me back. I'd gone that route and see where I was—in the exact same spot! Never again. And I fought back a yawn.

"Davy."

I glanced over and saw Holly Brightner waving. She leaned across our desks and tapped my Dialogue Reassurances sheet.

I rolled my eyes and shooed her away. Still, I recited like a sympathetic moron, "Anne, the peanut butter probably stands for something more. What does the peanut butter really stand for?"

Shoot me, one more minute.

Holly gave me a smile in approval and I resisted the urge to kick her underneath our desks. Her pasty white skin and round brown eyes were enlarged underneath her glasses. When she blinked, I swear that her lips formed a small oval and the image of an owl flashed in my mind. And her brown hair was pulled back into a tight bun. If Holly had a spirit animal, it would've been an owl.

Thirty seconds and I no longer cared what Anne had to say. I'd used my empathic stuff on her and felt the normal jealousy and insecurities that so many girls suffered. The girl wasn't homicidal or suicidal. That was all I cared about.

Five seconds, four, three, two, one . . . I hung up and grabbed my bag.

Holly stopped me. "Davy, you didn't cite the proper farewell greeting. It's very important to the callers. You never know what they're going to do after they end their call with us."

"It was peanut butter, Holly. Peanut Butter."

"We have the guidelines for reasons. I know you've been away for a few weeks, but—"

My phone cut her off, which was a mixed blessing. I was ready to eviscerate Holly.

The phone rang again and I looked at the clock. My shift was over.

Rang a third time.

Holly's mouth fell open.

The fourth ring seemed demanding. I knew what I should do, but my shift was over and Mr. Moser had said no calls after hours. When Holly saw that I had no intention of answering the phone, she reached over and did it for me. She listened for a moment and then held the phone away from her ear. "They hung up."

I wouldn't have wanted to talk to Holly either.

My bladder was screaming for attention so I made a trip to the bathroom before heading home. When I popped back in for my bag, I saw that Holly had left. I'd never been so happy in my life.

Then my phone rang again.

Doom and gloom settled on my chest. I knew who was on the other side. Consider it my empathic curse.

It rang again. And again. And again.

I knew it wasn't going to stop.

I dropped my bag, plopped down in my chair, and picked up the phone.

"You're right. That other girl has the attitude of an owl. I don't blame you for being irritated."

Welcome to my world of craziness and the supernatural.

"So you're not in my head anymore, you're on the phone now?" For being my next Immortal guide, I wasn't sure I liked this new route of communication.

"I'm on the roof. Be there in five."

When I heard the dial tone, I stared in disbelief. Not only was I going to meet my next guide in person, she hung up on me. I hoped that she meant five minutes, not five seconds. Who could get up there in five seconds. That's right, me. I squared my shoulders, nervously smoothed out my jeans and pressed my yellow tee shirt tighter around me. I shouldn't be nervous. Whatever I looked like didn't matter. The Immortal was already inside of me, it's not like the guide was going to take one look at me and yank it out because I wasn't pretty.

Still. I wished that I had used my anti-frizzy curl gel when Emily had chucked it across the room at Kates. Kates had laughed. I had laughed. Emily had stormed off and my gel had been left underneath my bed.

I trekked out of the office and headed towards the roof door. As I started up the sparse stairs, I heard my footsteps echo all the way down to the basement. Each echo made my heart pound. By the time I got to the top, I felt like I was going to explode, like a bomb was ticking underneath my skin.

Then the door was open and I stepped onto the roof.

For a second, just a briefest of moments, I saw Talia on the edge again with her hair waving in the air and her white dress billowing from the wind. The same sad acceptance railed against me.

But I blinked and the image was gone. Instead, a different girl was there and this one was a doozy. Red eyes, black and blue sleek hair that fell past her waist, and ivory skin that any vampire would've marveled at. She stood at my height, a little slim with her hipbones sticking out, and a mark that covered the entire left side of her face.

I gulped and froze. There was no way I was getting closer.

She snorted, rolled her eyes, and her disgust blasted me.

I was safer where I was.

And then in a flash, she was in front of me.

Oh man, those red eyes looked like they were on fire. That mark was an intricate symbol of weaving lines. I wondered if it meant something and then cursed my foolishness. Of course, it meant something. Everything meant something in my insane world.

"You're right. It does mean something, but it's nothing for you to know. Not yet." She was smug as she leaned closer.

I gulped again. The red in her eyes that looked like fire was fire. An actual flame was in her eyes. It moved in perfect rhythm with the wind that swirled around us on the roof.

"What are you?"

She laughed. "I'm not a vampire."

"Are you a werewolf?"

"I'm not a werewolf either. And no, I'm not anything that your precious vampire is going to know either. I'm beyond his knowledge. I'm beyond a lot of people's knowledge."

"Are you a witch?"

The flame glowed brighter for a moment and then settled back down. "Very good, Davy, but as I said I'm not anything that your lover knows. He knows witches."

There was a riddle there, but I retorted, "He's not my lover."

"He was. He will be again. And he's much more than that." As she spoke, her head tilted to the side and smoke swirled in her eyes to cover up the flame.

"You're a fortune teller witch. You see the future, don't you?" I hated fortune tellers. And, even though I've never met a witch, I was pretty sure I didn't like them either.

She laughed again and the smoke vanished with a swift pop. Her fire was back. "I come from a witch, but I'm no longer a witch, Davy. I'm much, much more and I'm here to help you."

"Help me with what? The last one who told me that needed me to accept the Immortal inside of me. What's your agenda with me?" They always had agendas.

"The other one annoyed you, yes?"

She already knew the answer to that.

She had a smug smile on her face. "I'm here to piss you off."

I barked out a laugh. "It's not hard to do that—"

"No." she stepped closer. The fire tripled. Her jaw was so strong, so poignant, and it told me that she meant every word she uttered. "Stepianhas annoyed you. She was sent to you to help you accept who you were, but I know her methods. She used riddles. I will not use riddles. I will tell you bluntly and directly. And I will piss you off. I will not annoy you. I will make you angry. I will make you furious and if so be it, all the better."

Okay.

One, Stepianhas? Two, what did she mean by making me furious? And three, I was already pissed off.

"You're already doing a good job. Who the hell is Stepianhas?"

"My name is Saren. Stepianhas was your last messenger. I will not talk further about my sister. My job is to challenge you and help you learn your powers."

Stretching. Learning. Powers. All I could hear was a name. "There was a name to the annoying voice in my head? That was a person? That wasn't me?"

"She was sent to you as I have been sent to you. We are not of your world, but we will help guide you among this world."

"I thought you said no riddles." Dumbass.

She paused, thought, and then smiled sheepishly. "It seems that my attempt at directness has different meaning in your world than mine. I apologize. I believe that I should've said that I am not my sister. I am the one to teach you of your consequences."

"You suck at this job." I was tired of all this Immortal stuff. "Why now? It's been two weeks."

"Uh—" Her mouth gaped open for a second and I saw the thoughts fly through her head. Literally.

I watched them for a moment before it hit me what I was doing. The last one said something about 'She's the Immortal, she will know. She mustn't know. If she shall ever find out, it will be catastrophe. Remember the vampire. It's about the vampire.'

It was like reading words on a page. "What do you mean when you say that it's about the vampire?"

Saren's eyes widened as she saw me inch closer, but she didn't say anything for a moment. "He is important."

"Why?" I wanted to intrude on her personal space. It worked on me, it should work on her.

She grinned and lifted a palm in the air. I felt the air being sucked into her hand and knew she was going to use it against me to shoot me away from her. To a normal person, this would've happened in an instant. To me, I felt the air swirl around me and halted the speed. When I saw her slam the force at me, I lifted my own hand and waved it. It bounced off me and shoved her backwards.

She hadn't fallen down, but it pushed her to the edge of the building. She lifted her head in shock. "You are better than I expected."

I lifted my chin. "You can't bully me. I'm the Immortal." As I said it, I knew I shouldn't have. Saren straightened upright and her eyes changed from a flame to a bonfire. The outline disappeared around her eyes. Flames leapt from outside of her eyes and smoldered the air. I smelled the burning in the air. Then she lifted a hand and flames shot at me.

"No!" I held up my hand. Something charged out of my body and met the flames full force. Instead of coming at me, they shot in the air. The entire sky lit up in flame. I looked up and thought three things. It looked pretty, there was no way that was inconspicuous, and holy crap! Sirens sounded in the distance and I looked over. Saren was gone.

What a surprise.

I turned towards the exit and wished I knew how to transport myself by snapping my fingers. Some Immortal perks still needed to be learned. When I got to the street, I ducked into an alley as the fire truck braked in front.

I cut across the middle of the campus and was almost to my dorm when I felt the air change. The hairs on my back stood up. There was a shift in the atmosphere. It was like if I'd been walking with a blanket on me and someone ripped it off me. I knew someone was there and I was out in the open. When I heard a slight growl, I reacted without thinking and twisted my body around. I bent backwards.

Bennett leapt at me. His eyes were shocked as he went over me. His dirty blonde locks had grown longer since I'd seen him last, but he was dressed in a black leather vest and jeans. His boots clipped my chin and I fell to the ground.

"Ouch!" I snapped up and held my chin. I felt blood against my fingers. "What'd you do that for?"

His eye gleamed with a purple shine. His chest heaved up and down and his hands fisted together as he stood there. "You turned him." Then he charged and caught me. With my back against his chest, he lowered his head to my neck and growled. "Turn him back."

"Bennett, stop that!"

He clamped me tighter against him and his teeth touched my skin. They didn't break the skin or draw blood, but he wanted me to know he could. I was starting to wonder how demented he'd become. Didn't he remember the last time a vampire drank from me? "Bennett, you will become a human if you drink from me."

"You're the Immortal. You can turn him back."

"Turn who?" Then it clicked in place. "You want me to turn Lucan? Are you crazy? I don't even know where he is or if I can do that."

"You're the Immortal. You can do anything."

A part of me puffed up in pride. I was the Immortal. Of course, I could do anything. Then reality set in. "Bennett, I turned into the Immortal two weeks ago. I wouldn't know how to do it."

"Think it and it happens!" he growled and lifted me in the air.

"Oh—" Not good. My feet dangled for a second before he slammed me back down. This time I fell all the way to the ground and laid there. Bennett was on top as he whispered in my ear, "You will change him or I will hurt you."

Then the air changed again. Something was coming and they were coming fast. Before I could look, Bennett was off me. I scrambled up in time to see Roane throw Bennett into the building across the yard. The brick cracked from the force. Before Bennett could fall to the ground, he caught himself and jumped from the building at him.

I sat there with my mouth open as I watched Roane stand in place with his shoulders ready. His knees didn't look like they moved when he caught Bennett, twisted, and slammed him on the ground. Instead of catching his throat to hold him in place as I expected, he impaled him to the ground and flicked a lighter on him. Bennett's eyes got wide and he gasped. He started to kick, trying to scramble away, but whatever Roane had impaled him with kept him in place. Before the lighter hit his chest, Roane swept a hand around me and lifted me in the air. I felt myself being carried away, but I tried to watch Bennett. Roane tucked my head into his shoulder. He wouldn't let me look. When he moved past a building, I saw the air light up.

"Block him. Block him now."

I hadn't realized that I'd been trying to feel him when I closed my eyes and did it. Not a second later, Bennett's screams filled the air. I clasped onto Roane tighter and wound my legs around his waist. No matter the circumstances, it was good to feel him again, maybe too good.

CHAPTER 3

Roane carried me to the roof of a building. When he set me back on my feet, he went to the edge and looked down. A red glow lit the sky from where Bennett had been and I grabbed his hand to help steady myself. My knees were shaking so loudly, I was surprised Roane didn't hush them.

"I want to see who comes." Roane gripped my hand.

Instead of Bennett, a fire burned in his place. "His body's gone?" There was a citrus smell in the air that mixed with the fire. Both odors made my stomach churn.

A small smile flashed over his face, but it was gone quickly. His face contrasted in a myriad of shadows from the glow. The tops of his cheekbones and nose were highlighted, but everything else was dark. It gave him a supernatural look, but then again, he was a vampire.

"It burned faster than normal. He drank from someone who'd overdosed on heroin. It speeds everything up."

"That explains the purple eyes." I was about to ask more when Roane touched my shoulder and nodded at the quad below. I didn't see anything, but he spoke in my head, *"Let the Immortal see."*

Everything switched.

The fire felt like it was all around me and Roane's inner tension lashed at me like a whip. I could taste the heroin from the human's blood in Bennett. That was the citrusy feel in the air. Wrinkling my nose, I started to share how weird that was, but closed my mouth as I sensed movement from all corners of the quad. They were vampires. They moved at a slow synchronized pace and made sure no one could see them. With my human eye, I wouldn't have. But as the Immortal, I knew what they thought and knew their arrogance. As I closed my eyes, I felt into them. They were used to doing what they wanted. They thought they were above everyone else, including other vampires.

"*Who are they?*"

Roane gripped my hand and shook his head.

And below us, they froze as one entity. Their black forms, masked from the shadows, melted backwards. They were gone in the next instant.

He expelled a deep breath.

I knew I messed up, but I had no idea how.

"You twitched when you asked me that. Your hand twitched."

"They could see that?"

"They felt it." He sounded disappointed.

"They felt my hand twitch, but they didn't know we were here? How's that possible?"

"They didn't know we were here because as they move in, they blanket their surroundings."

"We're above them."

"Doesn't matter." Roane sat on the edge. He dropped his head in his hands. "They have sonar that sends pulses all around them. They map the ground. One disturbance or change in their 'map' and they go away. It could be as little as a bird or a rock that fell. One movement, a hand twitch, and they leave."

Talk about anal. "They're scared of a bird?"

"They aren't scared. They're powerful, stronger than the hunters' bloodline."

"They're vampires." No one was stronger than the hunters.

"They're more. They're a different species of vampires."

"You guys have species?!"

Roane chuckled and found my hand with his. "Each vampire is born from the bloodline of the vamp that turned him or her, but those guys are different. They were born as vampires. There's magic in their blood that lets them reproduce. They give birth just like humans."

"Baby vamps." Holy crap.

"Baby vampires." He nodded.

"How do they do their sonar stuff?"

"No one knows. They stick to their own. We don't even know if they follow the decree. We know about them only because Lucan found a baby girl one time. He had a thing for anything unusual. My brother was obsessed with anything more powerful than us. It's why we found Talia when she was so little."

Every hair on my body stood upright. I shuddered. "How did you know they'd be here tonight?"

"I didn't. I knew Bennett was obsessed with having you change Lucan."

"You think Bennett knew where Lucan is?"

He shook his head. "I know he didn't, but he knew where you were. I think Lucan found that girl and her line has taken him in. If I were him, I'd have them find you. You're an unknown to him now. He thought he knew everything about the Immortal, but he now knows that he doesn't. He didn't take your power. You made him human instead. That's never been in the lore. You're going to become his new obsession now."

And that was alarming on a whole other level. "They were following him to find me?"

He nodded and clenched his jaw.

My eyes got wide. "That's why you killed Bennett, isn't it?"

"As much as I'd love to follow them back, I won't risk you."

"How would you be able to follow them? It sounds like they're living ghosts to the vampire community."

Roane looked at me and tilted my head up. His hand cupped the side of my face and his thumb caressed my cheek. "I'd follow you, not them."

There went my heart. It stopped its pitter pattering.

"I could follow you anywhere."

Now it took off like a horse race.

His hand dropped and he stood up. "I drank from you before you fully became the Immortal. I can smell you from a continent away."

My shoulders slumped down. The pitter patter race ground to a halt. "You know just what to say to a girl."

"It's the aroma. Your blood overwhelms me at times."

My nose wrinkled. "So I'm smelly?"

He looked out over the quad and murmured, "Yes. Exactly." Then he abruptly looked down. "No, not in a bad way. It's a good way. We were lovers. It's an intimate aroma, like perfume."

"Were?"

Roane laughed and took my hand. He pulled me to my feet and then hugged me tightly. "We will be again. I'm hoping." His eyes held mine captive and the Derby race started once more.

"I'd like that too."

He rested his forehead against mine. "Bennett is dead."

"Yeah. And the fire is gone already." The burning smell and glow had both vanished.

"Don't you want to check on your roommate?"

"What? Why?" Talk about curveballs.

"He nipped from her. That means she was under his spell. Now he's dead—"

"I can't believe I didn't think of that already. She's going to be flipping out. She thought she was in love with him." I surged upright and then stopped to glower. I used to hate vampires. Roane and a few others had redeemed them in my eyes, but now I remembered why I hated them so much. Their stupid little spells they could put on humans. "I have to get home right now. The abrupt break will be sending her off the deep end."

Roane nodded and kissed my forehead. "I'll be at the Alexander tonight."

"Okay. I'll come by after she's calmed down."

Roane walked me back to my dorm and left with one last kiss to my forehead. I watched him leave and sighed. I was glowing. How could I not? I just hoped my roommate wouldn't notice.

When I walked into my room, Emily took one look and threw a book at me. I ducked, but the second one hit my chin. "Ouch!"

"What? Did you just see Adam? You're happy!" Her chest heaved up and down. She was seething. Then she twisted her hands in her hair and pulled at it. "I'm going crazy, Davy! I don't know what's wrong with me."

I did, but I wasn't going to tell her. "Do you have your period?"

"I just had it."

"There's a full moon tonight. That makes people go crazy."

She stopped pulling her hair and her hands dropped against her legs. "Really?"

I shrugged in my head. "Sure. Unless you really are going crazy."

"No, no. It must be the full moon. It has to be. It came out of nowhere."

"What does it feel like?"

"Like my reason for living just died. I have no purpose anymore. I should kill myself."

She answered so quickly, my eyes popped out. "Okay. You shouldn't work at the hotline until this is gone."

"Why?" she asked with a blank face.

"Because." You're crazy. "Trust me. It's the full moon effect. You're not normal right now."

"Will this go away?" Desperation flashed over her face and her hands started to go for her hair again.

I rushed forward and caught her hands. "It will go away. Promise."

"How long does the full moon last?" Her voice hitched on a hysterical note.

"There's the pre moon stage and the post moon stage. Plus, you have the half moon and partial moon. I'm sure all of that makes it go longer."

"Oh." She sounded dejected as she sat on the couch. "What am I supposed to do? I felt like I lost my husband, like he was brutally murdered and slowly ripped to pieces."

"Uh." I saw some wine coolers in the corner and grabbed them. "Drink."

She pushed it away. "That won't help. It'll make it worse."

"Okay." Then I sat beside her. "What can I do to help you?"

"I don't know. Take my pain away."

Oh no. I swallowed tightly. I knew Emily wasn't serious. She didn't know I was empathic and her request was an actual possibility, but I didn't know if I wanted that madness in me. "How about a sleeping pill? You'll sleep right through it and wake up refreshed for a month?"

I settled for a second best option.

"I don't feel like that's a healthy thing to do. I feel like I should go through this. I should feel this torment."

"You're crazy. Why would you want to do that? This isn't your fault. You're feeling this because of—" I clamped my mouth shut. "Because of the moon."

"Yeah."

I watched Emily and saw she was determined to feel this thing through. Sometimes she amazed me and other times she made my head spin around. Who would want to feel this type of madness? Emily would.

She hugged a blanket around her. Tears coursed down her cheeks and she sneezed a few times. I handed over a tissue box. "You're determined to stay awake for this?"

"Yes." She sounded determined, but I heard a waver in her voice.

It was all the permission I needed. "I'll get you some juice."

She looked at me with grateful tears in those eyes. "I'd appreciate it so much. Thank you, Davy."

I grabbed one of the cups from our dirty bin and went to the door to wash it. Emily didn't spare me a look as she huddled into the couch and I grabbed my purse. When I went to the bathroom, I cleaned the cup and pulled out some sleeping pills Kates gave me awhile ago.

I dumped three in Emily's drink and stirred it so the powder dissolved. And when I handed over the juice to her trusting hands, I felt no guilt. I was drugging my roommate out of love. If I left her alone with the madness that came when a love bite was broken, she would have tried to commit suicide. I'd seen it before and I wasn't going to let Emily do something stupid like that. "Drink all of it. Your body needs those vitamins."

She guzzled it down and wiped at her chin. "Thanks, Davy. You're the best roommate."

The jury's out on that one. I popped in a movie, grabbed my blanket, and settled beside her. Emily's eyes kept watering through the movie until I reached over and grabbed her hand. She would quiet right away and I allowed myself to pull some of that pain out of her. I felt the madness trying to get through my barrier, lashing at me, snarling, but I kept it at bay. Emily's pain was pushed underneath the craziness and it streamed into me like a calm river. If I hadn't been the Immortal, I couldn't have separated the threads. An hour later, I opened my eyes and saw that she'd fallen asleep with both hands clenched on mine. There was a feel of desperation in her body.

When my eyelids started to feel heavy and drop, I realized some of the sleeping pills must've gotten into my system too. Roane was at the Alexander and I wanted to see him, but my eyelids refused to stay open. After five minutes, I gave up the fight and moved to my bed. It wasn't long until I found myself dreaming of vampires with rabid purple eyes. And then a voice screamed in my head, "Davy! Wake up!"

I shot upright and banged my head on Emily's bunk. I rubbed my head, expecting to see someone in my room. There was no one and I started to lie back down.

"Get up! Get up! You're needed at the Alexander NOW!"

Alexander. Roane. Crap.

CHAPTER 4

When I got to the Alexander, I wasn't surprised to find it filled to the maximum. It had always been the hotspot for the showy and shallow. And those were just the humans. The basement was filled as well, but with vampires.

"Davina."

I turned and saw Gregory. He stood by the bar with a drink in hand. His face was stiff and his thick square-like jaw seemed cemented in place.

"Hi, Gregory." I held a hand out and the blond Viking vampire took it for a handshake. He had never warmed up to me, but as one of Roane's loyal followers he was forced to be nice. He smiled thinly and offered his drink. "Lucas is in his office. I'll take you there."

As I followed him into a narrow back hallway, I was startled to hear Roane's given name. I'd grown so comfortable thinking of him as his bloodline's name that I'd forgotten it wasn't his first name. As we continued through a few more hallways, I was surprised how Gregory fit through them. Then, at the end of one, he knocked on a black door. I would've walked past it and not known it was there, but it opened to Roane's office. He sat behind a massive mahogany desk. While the entrance was plain, everything inside the office was not.

The desk was large enough for a king to lie on. Leather couches and chairs sat beside it while a painting was mounted on the wall. I watched the smiling woman in the painting and half expected her to speak to me. She looked too life-like.

Roane lifted his head and his coal eyes flickered when he stood. "Davy. You came. Thank you, Gregory."

"Lucas."

Roane gestured towards a chair when the blonde giant left. "I need a few minutes to finish some paperwork."

"So I better get comfortable, huh?" I looked at the door as I sat down. "For being Hulk Hogan, he's quiet like a ghost. It's scary."

"He's a vampire."

"Again. Scary."

Roane shifted some papers and piled them on a corner of his desk. "Vampires can't hurt you anymore. You can get that chip off your shoulder you have against us."

I shuddered in my chair. "And yet, they keep coming after me."

"Because some of us are dumb." Then he smirked. "We're like humans in that way."

"Was that a joke?" I arched an eyebrow. "Where's this new Roane come from? I thought everything was serious, the world is ending, and the Immortal needs to be protected."

"Maybe this is the real me? Maybe I'm a funny vampire underneath everything?" His hands paused as they shifted some papers into a folder. Then they continued and a smile flittered over his face. It was gone in the next instant.

I narrowed my eyes as I watched him. He might be joking about being funny, but I'd felt inside of him. He was all resolve, determination, and death bended beneath him. Then I smiled. "You've missed me."

His hands paused again and gripped the folder before he closed it and lifted his head. His eyes sparkled.

I was across the desk in an instant and in his arms. He gripped me tight as I settled on his lap, straddling him in the leather chair. I clasped behind his back and breathed him in. His neck trembled slightly and then I pressed a kiss against it. He groaned and stood up with his hands underneath my legs. He held me tight against him and lifted to carry me to a nearby couch. As he laid me down, he held himself above me and studied me. His eyes were intense. Something shifted in them when he traced my face with a finger, down my cheek, around my lips, and back up the other cheek to brush some hair from my forehead. It was a loving touch and my eyes started to water as I felt the tenderness.

"What's wrong?" he asked in a gentle voice.

I tugged him down on top of me and hugged him with all my might.

"You missed me too." His voice was muffled against my neck. It teased my skin and shivers broke out over my body. I felt him smile as he added, "A lot."

It was more than that. Something in me would always yearn for Roane. When I saw him again, that something woke up. It was as if I'd been asleep till he got back and now he was back, everything else woke up too. Did he feel the same? The old question burned in the back of my head, or did he feel it for Talia?

Roane pulled away and sat up. "What's wrong?"

"Talia." I didn't hesitate. I didn't see why I should.

Roane shut down. His eyes had been open and alive. "What about her?"

"You loved her. She held the Immortal thread before me. I can't help but feel that there's a part of her inside of me and that's who you want." Most girls wouldn't have managed the first words, but I was more now.

Roane stood and crossed to a bar. After he poured himself a drink, he offered me one. I shook my head, suddenly cold. Roane moved back to lean against his desk as he regarded me. His eyes were dark. "I loved Talia. I won't deny that."

There it was. I didn't flinch.

Roane added, "I've never lied about that. I did love Talia, but I don't love her anymore."

My eyes shot to his.

"I don't know what you're really asking me, but I can guess. It's not the right time for that, but what I can tell you is that what's between us is between us. You may think Talia is a part of you, but she's not. There's nothing in you from her. She held the Immortal thread inside of her and gave it to you. You've taken the thread and you've become the Immortal. If anything, it should've been that Talia held something of you inside her when I loved her." He studied me when he was finished and then sipped his drink. His throat swallowed in a slow motion.

I gulped. When those eyes were focused on me and intense, when he said words like that, I had to grip the couch to keep myself from launching at him. I wanted to beg him to take me then and there, but I didn't. Then I fought to calm my trembling voice. "Okay."

Roane flashed a smile. "Okay? That's it?"

Someone knocked on the door at that moment. Roane turned his back to me when it opened and I expelled a ragged breath. I tried moving off the couch, but my legs were jelly.

Then Gregory spoke from the doorway, "We have an impending."

Roane didn't move at all, but everything changed; danger emanated from him. An alarm bell went off in my stomach and my jelly legs were suddenly sturdy as stone. I stood, but stayed by the couch. I wanted to go to his side, but Roane wasn't a vampire who enjoyed the comforting damsel. When he nodded with his jaw clenched, Gregory looked at me and then closed the door behind him. He said it all in that one glance. Something was wrong and Roane wasn't telling me any of it.

"What's going on?"

He took my arm and led me to the door. "It's time for you to go."

Hello, I thought we were going to have sex. Now I was really alarmed. "What was that about? Gregory looked at me before he left. He felt bad about something. What is it?"

I dug in my heels and looked directly at him. He had his shields up, he always had them up, but I went through them like vapor. His manner had been a show. He'd been flirting and forcing himself to feel relaxed, but it was the opposite. He had lied about Talia. He still loved her, but there was more. Something had gone wrong with the Roane Council and his insides were on edge, murderous edge, because of it. I slipped out and saw he hadn't a clue that I'd been there.

"You never told me about the council meeting. What happened there?"

His eyes flared in anger. "You stay out of me."

"Then tell me the truth. Tell me what's going on."

"You need to leave." He pushed me towards the door, but stopped to grab two daggers and a 9mm. He strapped a sword over his back and when he turned back to me, I didn't recognize the hunter who stood there. I'd seen him in fighting mode, but this was different. There was no emotion, just business. That business was killing.

When he took my arm again, my head snapped back and I felt the Immortal rush through me. She coursed through my arms, toes, veins, and into my eyes. I knew Roane saw my white eyes when he cursed.

"Do you know?" he asked.

I closed my eyes and lifted into the air. The room swirled around me. Everything moved around me as if I was in the eye of a tornado and then I looked out and saw who approached.

They were a group of vampires. All were heavily armed with weapons, similar swords as the one Roane wore. Wren was with them, but two large Goliath vampires held her arms. Her wrists were bound in greenery. Her eyes were strained and teeth clenched against the pain. I didn't know what was going on, but I knew what side I stood with. Before the thought entered my mind, I was already behind Wren and the two giant guards.

Everyone was in a time warp so no one saw me when I took a knife from one of the guards and cut through Wren's bandages. Her shoulders lifted up as if refreshed. The pain left her and she sprang into action. I pulled back from the group, watching her take the sword from one of them and plunging it into their heart. As they fell, she whirled around and decapitated both of them in one movement. Then she landed on her feet, primed for attack as the rest of the group turned in shock. Only a few reacted. The rest paused a second to wonder how she got free. They paused too long.

Roane was already on them. Wren saw him fighting and a crooked smirk flashed over her face before she began fighting with renewed energy. She fought freely without pausing as she sliced and diced through the vampires. Roane killed the same way. He cut down every vampire in his trail, but gave no feeling or thought to any of them. When they were both done, each stood in the middle of the wreckage and looked at the other. Wren smiled shakily as her body trembled in excitement. Her coral eyes looked wild, hyper. Roane felt nothing. There was no emotion in his eyes. Then he turned towards me and I vanished.

I was waiting in his office when they arrived a few minutes later. Wren burst through the door and her adrenalin blasted against me. She was on a high, but when her eyes caught sight of me all that energy faded. It left her depleted and she snarled, "You."

"Me."

She looked the same. I hadn't noticed when she'd been held captive, but now her attention was focused on me. It was intimidating, or should've been, as I studied her in turn. She wore the same leather corset with silver snappings and leather boots. Her eyes snapped in disgust when she felt my appraisal and she flipped those long auburn curls over her shoulders to purse her lips together. "Like what you see?"

"You still look like a hooker." Disdain oozed from my pores.

She drew to her full height and took a menacing step towards me. That's when Roane passed around her to his desk and murmured underneath his breath, "She can make you human."

She stopped, snarled again, and swept out of the room. The door slammed shut with enough force to shatter glass.

Then I looked up and met Roane's gaze. Any smart comment I might've made about Wren's departure died in my throat.

His eyes snapped at me. "You want to tell me what you were doing out there when we're still trying to keep your identity a secret?!"

CHAPTER 5

"**W**hat are you talking about?"

"The Elders know that the Immortal is alive, but they don't know your name. Anyone who knows it's you is either loyal to me or dead."

"Except Lucan and Kates."

"Yeah," he sighed. "Except those two, but Lucan won't say anything. He'll want to keep that information to himself. And Kates is loyal to you, right? She is, right?"

"Yeah." I gulped. "She's loyal to me." And now she'd left for some reason that she wouldn't tell me. He didn't need to know that bit.

"You need to stay away from me."

"What?" I cried out. "You told me to come here tonight. You told me that you wanted to see me and now you're telling me to stay away?!"

Roane looked resigned. "I have to protect you and one way I can do that is if you have no connection to me. They might know the Immortal is here—"

"Who?!"

"Vampires, Davy! All the vampires." He sat now as if surrendering. "The secret's out. Everyone knows the Immortal exists and she's here. I tried to tell the Elders that you left, but they must not have bought it. They know you're here. They might not know who you are, but they know the Immortal is here."

"What does this mean for me?"

He shrugged. "I have no idea, but it's not good for you. My guess is that they'll try to kill you first. When they realize that won't work, they'll capture you and they'll figure something else out. They aren't friendly, Davy. They're scared of you and vampires don't handle fear very well. Everything else is supposed to be afraid of us, not the other way around."

"They can't kill me. Can they?"

"I don't know. Do you even know?"

"No." I looked away. Saren hadn't been helpful with any information. Riddles. Everything was riddles. "So I go and do the normal thing that you wanted me to do before?"

"I don't see any other way right now." Roane's hand rested on the desk and then he clenched it into a fist. "It'd be good if you go. I'm sorry."

With a knot in my throat, I nodded. "When will I see you again?" He looked up and sorrow flashed for a moment before it was replaced with regret. Guilt came next. I knew he wasn't going to answer me so I said, "I know you still love Talia. I saw that inside of you."

He tried to smile, but failed. "I hate that I can't keep a secret from you."

"Trust me. I wished I didn't know half the stuff I do." Then I turned and started to leave. As I reached the door, Roane stopped me.

"Davy."

I turned and my heart jumped.

He smiled, but it was haunted. "Gregory can drive you back. After that you need to stay away from me."

My heart fell back in place. "Okay."

The Viking vampire was silent as he took me to my dorm. Roane had sent me away. He didn't want to see me anymore. I knew the reason behind it, but it stung. A part of me, the little girl inside of me wanted to fall into his arms and live happily ever after. The rest of me knew better.

"We're here," Gregory said as he put the car into park.

As I was about to get out of the car, I reached over and grabbed his arm. Gregory didn't react. He made no movement, but I knew he was guarded against me. That's when I realized the sound of his little girl's laugh had been tickling my empathic abilities since I'd gotten in the car. I just hadn't noticed it till then.

The laugh came from his unconscious and my empathic sense had reached for it. I met his gaze. "I will turn your daughter back. She can be yours again."

Something shifted inside of him and he jerked his head in a nod. "Thank you."

I nodded back and climbed out.

"Davy," he called after me. I looked over my shoulder. "Please don't make a promise like that unless you can fulfill it."

"I have no doubt that no matter what Roane promises, there's going to be another war. I'll be at the center of it and I will meet your daughter. I will turn her human again."

He smiled, shaken.

Then reality clicked with me. "Don't tell Roane I said any of that."

He shook his head. "He'd advise me not to believe you. For some reason, I do."

I wasn't sure how old Gregory was, but he looked old for a vampire. And when he smiled, I wondered when he had last smiled. His face looked cracked until the smile disappeared. Then all the cracks fell back in place and it was smooth again.

"Okay." I waved goodbye before I headed back inside. When I got to my floor, I saw a girl standing outside my room with her nose pressed against the door.

And I thought I was coming back into the world of normal. "Hey, what are you doing?"

She turned with wide eyes. She was a petite girl with reddish hair that was separated into two braids. They hung over her shoulders and touched the suspenders of her blue jumpsuit.

"Who are you?"

"Um." She bit her lip and looked back at the door. Then she looked at me again. Panic filled her eyes and she bolted. A door slammed shut down the hallway almost as soon as I blinked.

"I don't see that every day either." I took a deep breath and opened my door. The vision of Emily tangled in a ball of blankets on the floor greeted me. She snored happily and some drool trailed to the floor. I checked the clock and realized that I'd need to put another dose of sleeping pills in her juice.

As I went to the bathroom to mix the concoction in the glass, I heard someone behind me.

"What's wrong with her?"

The weirdo stood in the bathroom doorway. She blocked me from the hallway." I can tell something's wrong with her. What is it?"

I stared at her and then started giggling. When I couldn't stop, I realized something was making me laugh and I looked at her with tears in my eyes. "It's you. You're doing this to me."

"Doing what?" She frowned.

"You're tickling me! What are you? You're a werewolf!" It was their constant sniffing. They sniffed out everything in the air, even if they didn't know they were doing it. It was as natural to them as breathing.

Her eyes bulged out. "I smell vampire on you, but you're not. What are you?"

I bent over, giggling.

"What can I do? This has never happened before." She looked panicked as more giggles erupted from me.

"It's because—" I couldn't even talk.

"Should I leave?"

Still giggling, I nodded with tears running down my face. The door slammed shut and almost immediately the laughing fit lessened so I was able to stand upright. I breathed out and wiped the tears from my eyes.

"Are you better now?" she called from the hallway.

"Yeah," I called back. "How far down the hallway are you?"

"A few doors away. I'm sorry?"

"That's okay. It's not really your fault."

"I feel ridiculous talking like this. What's your phone number?" Her voice trembled.

My phone? I felt in my pockets and tried to remember the last time I had used my cell phone. "My phone's in my room. Leave your number on my board. I'll call you when I can. I have to check on Emily first."

"Okay. I'll do that."

When my eyes stopped tearing up, I finished mixing the sleeping pills with some orange juice and headed back to my room. There was no werewolf lingering in the hallway and when I got inside, I woke Emily enough until she drank the juice. As soon as she was done, she groaned and rolled over. Snores came from her soon after.

I heard a knock on my door and a piece of paper slid underneath. *'My name is Pippa. The number is 555—. Call me!'*

I didn't recognize the area code. I frowned at the paper.

"Are you going to call me?" she asked through the door.

"My roommate's fine. I don't have to explain anything to you."

"What? Something's wrong with her. I need to know."

"No, you don't. I'm not hurting her. I'm helping her. She'll be as good as new in two days. You can ask her yourself then."

Good luck getting a real answer.

"What? Come on. Please! I need to know." Her voice hitched on a note, like she was about to cry.

An empath could only deal with so much. I sighed and crossed to the door. I pressed against it and whispered, "I am not trying to be mean. I just can't do this right now. Leave, please?"

She whimpered on the other side. "I have to know."

"If you don't leave, I will have this building streaming with vampires. I know your kind doesn't like them." As far as threats went, I thought it was a solid one.

She was silent for awhile. "I have to know what's wrong with your roommate. If she doesn't get better in two days, I'll call my pack."

I had no doubt she would. "This isn't your business."

Again, she was quiet for a little bit. "My inner wolf is telling me otherwise."

Oh—ugh! I was tired of everything supernatural. "Whatever. Just go away."

I felt her leave. I didn't feel the slight tickling anymore, but I knew she'd be back. Anything supernatural always came back. They were always ominous. Then I watched Emily snore into the floor.

Nope. Nothing supernatural with her.

She wouldn't wake again for a long time, so I fell into my bed. At last.

Halfway through my first dream, a bloodcurdling scream woke me up. I bolted upright in bed and saw Emily in the middle of the room. She was pulling at her hair. Her hands had formed fists and were entangled in her hair. "AHHHHH!"

"Hey, hey!" I tried to soothe her. "It's okay."

"It's not okay! What's wrong with me?" Tears cascaded down her face and she looked at me. The pain was so powerful, it staggered me back. "What's wrong with me, Davy? I am going crazy, aren't I?"

"No, no you aren't." I hugged her close and made soothing sounds. I rocked her back and forth.

"Do something. Make this stop. I can't handle it anymore," she sobbed into my chest.

I closed my eyes and held her tighter. Then I took a deep breath because I already knew what I was going to do. God help me, I went inside of her. I didn't control it like I had before. I didn't have the time. I went all in and choked on the emotions. It felt as if a bucket of vipers had been let loose. They were everywhere. Slithering. Biting. Angry.

Once I managed to stand my ground in the midst of the madness, I reached out and grabbed one of the emotions. It was hopeless. I gathered it to me and reached for another. I kept going until I had enough clasped to me that she could calm down. I wasn't sure how long this had taken, but then I enveloped the emotions into me. They passed the barrier of our bodies and I took them into me.

As they bounced around inside of me, I opened my eyes and saw that Emily had calmed. I managed out, strained, "Go to the bathroom and come back to bed."

Emily nodded, still trembling. I'd taken what I could, but there was still Bennett's madness inside of her. When the door opened, I wasn't shocked to see Pippa there with concerned eyes. She looked from Emily to me and her eyes widened. She knew what I'd done.

They had never met, but Pippa extended an arm to Emily and she went to her. The two walked together.

I knew it wouldn't be long until they came back and I tried to hurry and get another potion of sleeping pills ready for Emily. My hands were shaking, but I only spilled a little bit before the door opened. Emily came in. She was calmer than when she had left.

I looked at Pippa and saw she must've done the same thing I did. I had no idea wolves could do that, but it didn't matter at that moment. I held out the glass to Emily. "Drink!"

She did and it wasn't long before her eyelids started to droop. When she curled into her bed, I looked at Pippa who had remained in the hallway. She watched me in sympathy.

"What are you?" she asked.

I jerked a shoulder up. It looked more like a twitch. "Does it matter? How'd you help her?"

"I did what you did. Wolves can go inside of other wolves. We can take their pain too."

I frowned as I still twitched. "Emily's not a wolf."

"Her soul is entwined with one."

"What does that mean?"

She gave me a sad smile. "You'll see."

Then she left and I closed the door. As I slumped on my bed, I shook my head. That was weird, even for me.

CHAPTER 6

The next few days were the same. I went to class, the hotline, and checked on Emily as I could. At first I'd been reluctant, but Pippa won me over. Her wolf's sniffing didn't tickle me as much and she wanted to help with Emily. She made a good argument. There was something unnatural about Emily's willingness to go to Pippa that night. I wasn't sure what to believe about the wolf thing, but I couldn't sense any bad intentions from Pippa. So Emily found herself with one more friend when she finally sat up three days later, weaned from Bennett's love spell.

"Who is she?" Emily asked an hour later after Pippa had come with coffee and left again. "She lives on our floor? I've never noticed her before and I notice everything."

Well, not everything.

I shrugged and reached for a coffee. "I don't know. She likes you."

Emily went still at my words. "What do you mean?"

I frowned at her. "I don't mean that!"

"Oh." She relaxed in her seat.

"I just meant, I don't know. She likes you. I think she needs friends and can tell you're one of the good ones." I hurried towards the door since I was late for the stupid empath meeting that Blue kept making me promise to go to.

"Davy." Emily halted me when my hand reached for the handle. I glanced back and she smiled. "You're one of those too."

Awkward. "Sure. Have fun with your new girlfriend!"

"She's not my girlfriend," Emily shouted after me as I rushed down the hallway.

I couldn't stop my grin, but it vanished as Pippa came out of the bathroom. Judging by the look on her face, she'd heard Emily's comment. "Girlfriend?"

I slammed on my brakes, right in front of her, and spoke in my mind, *'If you hurt her, I will hurt you and trust me, I can. If you tell her anything about this, I will come after you and your whole pack. I don't need a slew of vampires. I can do a whole lotta damage by myself.'*

Pippa's eyes widened when she heard my voice. *'You don't know what you just did. The Mother Wolf knows about you now.'* Then she spoke, "How can you do that? What are you?"

A part of me regretted my impulse, but I covered it up and gave her a smug smile. "I think you should be asking 'who am I?' Don't say anything to Emily."

Pippa turned and watched when I started to inch towards the hallway's door. "It's not for me to say anything. She's linked to another wolf. It's his place to say it."

I paused in the doorway. "Good then." Was it? As I turned and left, I knew I needed to learn as much as I could about werewolves. I knew they repressed their emotions, but they were different from vampires, a lot different.

I'd gotten as far as my car before my skin started to tingle. Talk about annoying and then everything rushed at me. I'd been about to open my car door when the Immortal took over. Everything flew around me and I was lifted into the air. My eyes narrowed as I looked out and saw another approaching vampire group. There was no captured Wren with them and these vampires didn't seem bent on war. I hoped not. Then I closed my eyes and found myself in Roane's office. Everything still circled around me, but I saw him and Wren at his desk. Their voices were muffled when I heard her say, "—for her. Why can't we let that happen?"

Roane straightened. "If you're loyal to me, you're loyal to my decisions. Are you not, Wren?"

She stepped away from the desk and sighed with her head bent. "You know I am. You know what I gave up."

Roane narrowed his eyes. "Then trust me."

Gregory swept through the door in that moment. "They're here."

Wren's eyes widened and Roane shut down. He clipped out, "Let's get ready."

Gregory and Wren left the room, but Roane stayed behind for a moment and scanned the room. His eyes were narrowed and lingered where I stood, but then he left with a guarded look over his face.

When his door shut, I was back at my car. I gasped and bent over to rest my forehead on my car. What had just happened?

"You're transitioning."

Saren materialized on the other side of my car. Her eyes were still the same smoldering flames, but she was dressed as a normal college student in a white sweatshirt and jeans. The black hair was swept up in a simple braid.

"You look normal except for those things." I pointed at her eyes.

They burst into flame, but quickly sizzled as if someone had thrown a blanket over the fire. "I'm not here to play with your mind. I'm here to help you."

"What's the catch?" I eyed her in suspicion.

She held up her hands in surrender. "I'm here to help. What did you just see?"

"Really?" There was no catch?

"I'm to help you."

"What'd you mean when you said that I'm transitioning?"

"Your powers. When you accepted the Immortal before, it was only the start. Everything molded to your body, but you don't know your full power. You don't know an eighth of your powers and you have to learn them one at a time. You can't learn it all at once. It's too much. Your mind would be overwhelmed. I'm here to help and explain things to you."

"So what was that just now? Any time that I've been around Roane, even when I slowed time, he always knew I was there." And why did she seem so much nicer than the last time?

Saren smiled. The flames lit again, but they were small embers. "I'm not nicer. I'm here to do my job and that's to tell you what's going on. When I need to make you angry, I won't hold back. You need gentle guidance and answers right now."

I still didn't like her. "About what just happened?"

"The Immortal sensed something that you needed to know. It/you sent yourself there."

"Why didn't he know I was there?"

"He's powerful, too powerful, but if you don't want him to know you're there, he won't. That was you, not the Immortal. You didn't want him to know you were there. What did you see?"

"A group of vampires are coming to town. Roane is going to meet them."

She nodded. "What does that mean to you?"

"They're coming for me. I'm guessing that they'll try to kill me."

"Try."

"Try." I nodded.

Saren nodded too. "Who were the vampires?"

"I don't know—" I started to say, but Saren shook her head. She stepped close. "You know who they are. Who are they?"

I didn't even consider it. I just answered. "They were Roane vampires. They were sent by his Elders."

"And?"

I had no idea how I knew it, but I did. "They're here to usurp Roane from his position as their hunter."

"Are they going to succeed?"

"No." I spoke so quickly, my eyes widened in surprise. I hadn't known that I knew any of that.

"Why not?" Saren knew. She measured every thought I had. "Why not, Davy?"

"Because he's powerful," I blurted out. The knowledge simmered beyond my reach. Now I grabbed it. "He's powerful because his blood is in me. He's connected to me."

Saren smiled and stepped back. "You're doing well. You might not need my help."

I frowned. I wasn't sure how I felt about that.

"He's more powerful than all the hunters." She still watched me.

I nodded. I hadn't known that, but it made sense.

"You don't like that?"

"Like what? That he's connected to me?"

She took a stalking step towards me. "That bothers you. You don't like that he's connected to you, do you? You *really* don't like it."

I looked away, but I couldn't ignore what she'd said. Did I like it? No. I'll be honest. Everything was too much. I wasn't ready for this, much less ready for my abilities to help someone else. Roane was something personal, too personal to me. I didn't enjoy that I helped him become more powerful. At least, I didn't enjoy that I hadn't made that decision. It was taken from me.

"He doesn't know how powerful he is." Saren glided close behind me. "He knew you were the Immortal, but he didn't know your power would go to him. That's not why he wanted you to take his blood."

"Then why?" I turned back around. "No riddles. I need to know."

"Because he was answering something inside of him. Something in him beckons to him just like I beckon to you. It doesn't make sense, but it will. Someday. And as for what you heard just now, you needed to know they were here. You're the Immortal. You'll start to know everything that happens, whether you want to know or not. Right now, I'd be less worried about the Roane Elders and more worried about that Mother Wolf. She's a bitch."

And I needed more on my plate. "I'm supposed to go to an empath meeting. My sponsor is making me go."

Saren laughed. "I'm your sponsor, Davy. Don't go. You'll overwhelm them. They'll feel inside of you and most won't make it to the hospital. Trust me. And dump Blue as your sponsor. She doesn't mean well in the end."

My eyes snapped to her. "What do you mean by that? She's like a mother to me."

Saren smirked and stepped back. I felt her absence before it happened so I reached out and grabbed her arm. "Don't go."

She glared at my hand. I felt like it had been scorched and I let go. I didn't have another second to react. Saren was gone. I almost expected a puff of smoke to linger where she'd been, but there was nothing. Just air. Now I was really frustrated.

"Davy?" Emily called out behind me. "I thought you were leaving for something? Where do you go all the time?"

My roommate was such the inquisitive one. I wasn't too worried. She'd forget about it in two seconds, but I was relieved to see that her normal coloring had come back to her cheeks. In the broad sunlight, she almost looked like nothing had happened. She had changed to a similar outfit that Saren had worn, but her hair was pulled back in a ponytail. Pippa was dressed in something that made her look like a hippie, complete with the same two braids as before. The shirt was full of flowers and her pants were brown suede?

"Davy," Emily spoke again.

"Oh. Right. I'm not going anymore. I changed my mind."

"Oh. Well, we're going to get some breakfast. Did you want to come with?"

Pippa shifted behind my roommate, but the movement was so small. I wouldn't have noticed it four weeks ago. When she refused to meet my gaze, I shook my head. "I'm going to head to the library instead. There's something I need to look up."

Emily frowned. "You're going to do homework?"

"Yeah."

"By yourself?"

"Who else would I go with?"

"I'm the one who usually forces you to do homework. With me. And you're going alone?" My roommate looked too speculative for my taste. "Are you sick?"

"Ha ha. That's funny. See you." Then I hurried away. I didn't like that Emily was with Pippa, but I knew the wolf would keep her safe and I needed information on werewolves. I couldn't ask Roane. I didn't think to ask Saren. I was advised against seeing Blue. Kates was gone. So that left the library. Fun times.

CHAPTER 7

I wasn't sure the library would have literature on werewolves. I expected cartoons, teen romance novels, maybe some articles, but I was surprised they had an entire selection of older books. When I looked for where they were, I wasn't surprised. They were on the sixth and creepiest floor.

The book was gone when I got there. So I hoofed it back to the main floor and requested to check it out whenever it was due back. The guy looked like I had three heads when he informed me that the book was not allowed to be checked out. I gave him a blank look in return. Then he sniffled up his nose, lifted his arms like he was a tyrannosaurus rex, and proceeded to walk me back up six flights of stairs. As soon as we got there, he looked dumbfounded when he saw the book was gone. I enjoyed that.

"Well," he sputtered. "I have no idea. That book isn't allowed to be checked out. No one knows where it is. No one cares about where it is unless . . ." He gave me a meaningful look. "Why are you looking for it?"

I gave him a blank face. "I'd like to be a werewolf. You?"

He rolled his eyes and dismissed me with a hand. "I thought you were looking for a class. Perhaps one of your classmates has it, but I can see that I'm wrong. Hmmm?" Then he threw both hands in the air. "It'll show up."

"You're not very helpful."

He shrugged. "It's my last week. Do your worst."

As he left, I glowered at his back. When it didn't burst into flame, I gave up. I must not have really wanted to hurt him. Then I turned for the bathroom and as I walked past an aisle, I caught sight of someone bent over a table with a very large, very old, book in front of her.

I approached with caution at first, but the girl was oblivious to anything around her. Her nose was pressed into that book and I wondered how she could handle the dust from it.

I drew closer to her table and checked the book. It was the one I wanted. "How long are you going to be reading that?"

She shrieked and fell from her chair.

"I'm sorry."

She pulled herself back up and studied me. "Who are you?"

"Who are you?" I narrowed my eyes. The girl had long brown hair that fell to her waist. She had a heart shaped face and glasses that covered dark eyes. Though she was dressed in a baggy sweater and jeans, I knew she was stick thin. Her feet peeked out from underneath her jeans in red ballet shoes. "I like your shoes."

She blushed. "Thanks. My sister didn't want them so I got them. I was over the moon when my mom sent—wait—Why do you want to read this book?"

"Werewolves."

She blinked and pushed up her glasses. "I didn't expect that answer."

"Why are you reading it?"

"Not for the werewolves." She laughed and turned back to her page. "This book has one of the best chapters on witches from Caduna. Do you know where that's at?"

I didn't.

"It's a secret place the Quakers first settled, but there was an abolition of witches so they moved and decided no one should know of the place."

"How do you know of it?"

"My family. One of the witches was my great-great-great-great-well, one of the founding witches was in my family. The secret was passed down."

"So you know all about that place?"

She frowned and scratched behind her ear.

"What's wrong? The secret didn't go to you?"

Tears welled up in her eyes as she shook her head. "It's always passed to the oldest daughter and I'm not the oldest. Tabitha doesn't care about this stuff, but she got everything. The stone. The books. The pendant. I got nothing" She sighed heavily. "I'm the witch of the family. I can do magic. The most magic she can do is with guys. She can get any of them. Not me. What's your name again?"

I extended my hand. "My name's Davy. What's yours?"

She placed her hand in mine. "I'm Sarah, but you can call me Brown. I prefer that name. I feel like I'm part of the earth and that's the natural color of the earth. Brown."

"It's blue. The oceans cover most of the planet."

Something sparked in her and shot through me. "I know, but my connection is to the land, not the water. Maybe Tabitha has that connection."

I heard her voice, but it came from a distance. When that something sparked through her, I was bombarded with images. One was the ocean as if someone was riding over it to us. The other was of a girl in a field. She was watching me. Slim. Long brown hair. Blue eyes. Another image was at night. Brown was standing in front of me and she held her hand out to me. She was trying to warn me about something.

"Davy?"

Brown stared at me. "Are you okay? Wait! Are you a witch too?"

"No." My voice came out hoarse. "How long have you been one?"

She sighed in disgust. "I've felt like I've been one all my life, but I didn't start doing spells until now. I was forbidden to talk about it or do anything with magic in high school. Tabitha's the chosen one in my family and that's only if she chooses to become a witch. All the family powers will go to her. Not me."

"Is your mom a witch?"

"No. She chose to pass on her powers. You can do that in my family. You can get all the powers from our ancestors."

"And if you don't? What then?"

She shrugged. "You just live a normal life."

"And if you choose the powers?"

Her voice trembled. "Then you have the responsibilities of all the other witches in my family."

"What are those?"

"I don't know. You don't know until the powers pass onto you."

"What if your sister decides she wants to be normal?" I flushed as I realized I was jealous. The girl had a choice.

"Then the powers will go to the next oldest daughter, hers or mine, or Kendra's. Not me."

Her eyes looked like she was seeing something far away, remembering something painful. She bit her lip for a moment and more tears welled up in her eyes. When she brushed one away, I realized that she'd forgotten about my existence.

I felt magic in her and she was just beginning, but the power in her was enormous. I felt it. It reached out to me. It was why she told me any of this. And I knew her magic would grow the more she trained and reached for it.

A wave of sadness swept over me and I knew it was hers. My empathic abilities had gone inside of her. I wanted to heal her. When she didn't react, I knew she couldn't sense my powers. I decided to push a little further inside of her.

When I found the thread of her magic, I followed it deeper inside. It stopped and I felt it was boxed in. That's when I realized that though she was blocked from her own magic, it still seeped out slowly. She was pulling it out the more she learned and she was determined to get it all.

"You really want your powers, don't you?"

Brown jerked her eyes to mine. "What? Oh, yeah. Is it that obvious?"

"I can feel it from you." I frowned. "What happens if your sister gets the powers and you do too? Can there be two?"

"There never has been before so I'm not sure. Why?" Then her eyes popped out again. "I can't believe I've told you all this. I'm usually—I never talk to people. What is it about you? Do you have a special power over me? That's the only thing that would make sense." As she spoke, she shot to her feet and started stuffing papers in her bag. When she shoved the book in too, I opened my mouth to remind her it wasn't supposed to be taken home, but she rushed away before I could say anything. It wasn't long before I heard the door alarms sound.

Then I sat back down. I knew I should've been curious about her powers as a witch, but anything magical or supernatural didn't surprise me anymore.

"Your thoughts are transmitting so loud, I could've heard them on a radio."

Roane glided out from one of the book shelves and sat where Brown had left.

"I thought we weren't supposed to see each other?" I frowned when my voice came out raspy, but I couldn't help it. There was something about Brown that made me sad. I didn't think it came from her anymore because I still felt it and then Roane showed up.

It was me. I was sad.

'Were you in my office before? I felt you, but I couldn't place you.'

'I know about the Roane Elders, about the other vampires.'

'What do you know?'

'They want to take away your huntership and they want to kill me.'

'What else?'

'That they can't. You're too powerful because your blood is in me.'

He looked away and swallowed. Roane kept his emotions in check, but I felt his fear for a second before it was taken away the next moment. He didn't want me to feel what he felt. I chose not to comment how that hurt, but was it my place to know those things? He loved her, not me.

He thought, *'The Elders sent a sorcerer. He felt your presence, but he can't narrow it down to where you are in town. I shouldn't be here. They might be tracking me—'*

'They're not. You know they aren't. You're better than them.'

Roane frowned for a moment. "I wanted to ask if I had been imagining things or not. I should be going now."

I wasn't going to say good-bye. I didn't want to do that anymore, but I watched him. He didn't move. Then he looked around, and still didn't move. "Was that a witch you were talking to?"

I nodded. "She's powerful, but something's blocking her. She has a weird family thing. She was telling me about it."

"She's a Bright. I've heard of their line, but I've never met one before."

"You know of them?"

He nodded. "Lucan was lovers with one of them when we first became vampires. She stirred a lot of his thirst for the unknown. The Bright women are powerful witches, but most of them don't use their power. No one knows why."

"It only goes to the eldest daughter."

He shrugged. "Regardless, they all have the ability, but they don't want their power or they don't use it. The Vampire nation would be more curious about them if they did. I'm glad they don't. We have enough problems with witches and sorcerers. Your friend doesn't have power? I thought I felt some from her."

"She has power, but it's blocked to her. She can't access it. A curse was put on their bloodline. I could remove what's blocking her, but I don't know if I should. I'm afraid what might happen."

"Don't. It'll draw more attention to you. You need to stay hidden. Do normal things." Roane stood up again and looked around. A flash of emotions crossed his face. "Are you doing okay? It's been a few days. How's Emily?"

"She's normal again. Bennett's love spell was nasty. I went in her a few times and removed some of that madness. Horrible. I hate vampires." I cringed and then realized what I had said. "I'm sorry! That's not what I meant."

Roane smiled gently. "It's fine. I'm not too fond of my race right now either."

Oh right. "Is it bad for you? What are they going to do to you?"

"They tried to kill me. It didn't work. They left and they'll send hunters this time."

"You'll be going against what you are?" But he was better. He was more powerful because of me. He'd be fine. Right?

His eyes sought mine and held them. "I'll be fine. Gregory, Wren, and others are loyal to me. They'll help me, but yes, I am more powerful than them."

I was relieved to hear that. I knew it, but it seemed more real when he said it.

"Davy, why didn't you let me see you today? I felt you. I wanted to see you," Roane spoke in a soft voice.

"It wasn't really me. It was what I am. It didn't want you to know I was there. I was confused too." That was when I realized that I'd never told him about Saren. Then I realized that I didn't have any intention of telling him. I trusted Roane, but something held me back from telling him. I wasn't sure why and that bothered me. I didn't want to always feel alone.

"You're transitioning into your powers. You don't know them, not fully."

Saren had said the same thing.

Roane looked towards where he had come from. He still didn't move so I asked, "Is there something else? Is something bothering you?" Was it her? Was he thinking of Talia?

His eyes whirled back to mine. I saw her in them. He *had* been thinking of her and that hurt more than I ever wanted to admit. "Do you miss her?"

Everything in him shut down. "I'll check with you every now and then. I don't want you to worry about me. I'll be fine and if something happens, Gregory and Wren will come for you. You'll be protected by one of us if you should need it."

He left abruptly and I couldn't help but think more should've been spoken between us, but she changed everything. The memory of Talia would always come between us and I had to accept it. He loved her, not me. A part of me wanted that to change. That same part of me clung to the idea that it would, that he'd turn his love to me, but I wasn't so sure now.

CHAPTER 8

I tried to be normal after that day. Blue called me a few times, but I never answered. I knew she called because I skipped that meeting and the next two, but I couldn't tell her why. Saren told me not to speak to Blue anymore and for some reason, that didn't bother me. It should've, but it didn't. Maybe I had sensed what she was trying to warn me about my sponsor?

"Hiya, roommate!" Pippa called out when she came through the door. My actual roommate followed behind carrying a shopping bag.

"Hey guys." I tried to sound cheerful, as much as Pippa, but I didn't have the heart. And I didn't think her greeting was that funny. She had become like a roommate since she and Emily had become best bosom buddies. "You guys look happy. Why?"

Emily frowned. "What's wrong with you?"

What was wrong with me? What was wrong with her? More and more my roommate had started to transform into someone who was direct and dare I say it? She met problems head-on? Was this possible?

I narrowed my eyes. "You're changing. Why?"

Pippa's eyes widened and she grew silent. I felt her melt into the background.

Emily dropped her bags. "Excuse me if I'm changing. I don't feel right, if you really want to know. And who are you to talk? You've changed too, Davy. It's like you're moping. You ignore calls from that purple lady and you don't go anywhere except for class." Then her eyes got wide. "Is this about Kates? Did you guys have a fight and I didn't know? Am I being a bad friend?"

Pippa glanced at Emily. Her nostrils flared and I felt the wolf sniffing the air. It felt like she was trying to sniff her way into me. When I felt the tickling, the giggle rose up and I stood from the desk. "This has nothing to do with Kates. This is about you. You were going crazy and now you seem off. I don't know why, but it's different."

"Bad different?" I heard the caution in Emily's voice.

"No." The tickling hadn't stopped. "It's a good different. I don't feel like I've been a part of it and that makes me a little sad, I guess." Then I laughed.

Emily frowned.

I laughed harder and glared at Pippa.

"What?" My roommate looked between us two. "Davy, do you think this is funny?"

"Not at all." I couldn't stop giggling.

"You're laughing. That's not polite."

She sounded so offended, which only made me giggle harder. Pippa was sniffing like crazy. It felt like her nose was pressed into my butt.

"I'm sorry." I bit down on my lip, trying to silence the laughter. Then I snapped at Pippa, "Stop it!"

She squeaked and rushed out of the room.

"What?" Emily's mouth hung open. "What is wrong with you? She wasn't doing anything."

She was, but I couldn't tell that to Emily so I shrugged. "I'm jealous of her. She's your new best friend. You two are always together and it's like you're attached at the hip. I'm sorry. I'm human. I felt left out."

I was going to hell. A very bad, dungeons-with-fire type of hell.

Emily melted. "Oh, I'm so sorry, Davy. I didn't think you cared.

You seem so aloof sometimes, like there are things bothering you, but you never tell me. I had no idea it was me." She put her hand on her chest. "I'm touched, I really am."

I saw that she was genuine and my self-loathing kicked up a notch. Emily was a good person. She was human. She was a bystander and she'd already taken a few hits from the life I lived. Vampires. Being kidnapped. Now a werewolf was her best friend.

"Oh. Don't feel bad. Really."

"But I do." Then she threw her arms around me and hugged me tight. "We will hang out. You. Me. Pippa. All three of us. I want the two of you to become friends. It'll be great."

This was the last thing I wanted, but she was right about one thing. I had been moping. I had no real life. I was pathetic so I plastered on a bright fake smile. "Okay! Let's do it. Us three. We should go drinking."

Emily's smile disappeared. "What? Drinking? Nooo."

"It won't be like the last time. I promise." There was no Kates this time. We'd be fine.

"I was hungover for three days and I don't even remember drinking." Emily shook her head. "I don't think that's a good idea."

"Oh, come on. It'll be fun."

Emily still didn't look convinced.

"You need a pick-me-up, right?" I clasped her shoulders and smiled again. I even showed my teeth. I blinded her. "Let me give that to you. You need something to help jump-start your life."

"Not really," Emily murmured. "I thought that was you?"

"You. Me. What's the difference? Let's go out, have an adventure, and laugh about it over coffee tomorrow."

"I don't want to be hungover," she mumbled.

I shoved her towards the closet. "Pick out a hot outfit. I'll go tell the dog and then we'll head out. It'll be fun. Trust me."

"Dog?"

But I was already out the door. By the time I knocked on Pippa's door, I had another fake smile on. "Hiya, neighbor!" I even waved cheerfully.

Pippa stepped back. "Hey."

"Emily and I are going out for a drink. Come with."

"I don't know." She glanced up and down the hallway. "I might stay in."

"You're coming with us. No debate. We'll have a grand time."

Pippa tried to grin, but it faltered. "Are you sure?" Then she drew me into the room and shut the door. "What about, you know, me being a werewolf and whatever you are. I still haven't figured it out. You're not a witch, are you?"

Images of Brown flashed through my brain. "No. I'm not a witch."

"Oh." She visibly relaxed.

"You don't like witches?"

"No. Not at all. They don't like us."

I couldn't imagine why. My smile went up a notch. "So are you coming?"

She bit her lip and twisted her hands together in front of her. "Can you tell me what you are? It's really been bothering me."

I fought against the urge to roll my eyes. "I'm empathic."

"What?" There was confusion first and then understanding dawned. "Oh, I get it. Vampires go crazy about empaths. No wonder you smell like them so much. Or, used to. You don't smell like vampires much lately. Are they leaving you alone?"

A part of me felt like she bought that half-truth too easily, but the other part condemned me to hell again. "Are you ever going to tell Emily about you?"

Then Pippa shrugged. "It's not my place to tell her what I am. Her mate will tell her. It's his place."

Mate. I didn't like the sound of that. "Who is this guy?"

Pippa smiled again and tugged at the ends of her two braids. "I have no idea, but she'll meet him. I feel it in my blood. So does she. She feels the promise of him through me. It calms her when she's near me."

I'd seen it in Emily. If Pippa went away, the old Emily would be back within a week. I wasn't sure how I felt about that. The new Emily seemed stronger, but if I had learned anything through my ordeal with the vampires it was that if something was being kept hidden, it wasn't a good thing.

I wasn't a good thing.

Ugh. The guilt flared inside of me again. Lies and secrecy. Both words weren't good and my life was all about them now.

"You know what? Nevermind. We can go for a milkshake instead."

Pippa frowned. "Are you sure?"

"Yeah. That'd be better." I was kicking myself as I went back to my room.

Emily had already changed for the night out. She was dressed in a shimmering white shirt over gray slacks. She looked good, very good. She smiled and waved towards my desk chair. "You didn't tell me about Brown. She should come with us."

My eyes popped wide when I saw the witch at my desk with a book in her hands. She smiled politely and stood. "Hi, Davy. Remember me from the library? I've thought a lot about that day and decided that you'd been sent to me for some answers. I can give you those answers." Then she extended the book to me. "You can read as much about werewolves as you want. It's not my place to stand in your way."

What?!

Emily gushed, "She's a witch! Can you imagine that? We know our own witch."

Oh. Not good.

Then my roommate murmured, "I didn't know you liked werewolves?"

"What?!" Pippa squeaked from the open doorway.

"Pippa, this is Davy's friend, Brown. She's a witch."

Brown smiled and lifted the book again. "And I brought this for Davy. She wanted to learn about werewolves."

"She did?" Then Pippa seemed to regroup. "You're a witch?"

Brown lifted her shoulders and preened. "I'm a new witch. I don't have much power, but I can feel it. It runs in my family and I know, I just do, that someday I'm going to be a great witch. I know it."

"Oh."

While the wolf was at a loss for words, I stepped in. "That's wonderful, Brown. You'll be a great wol—witch. You'll be a great witch."

"I'm going to be sick," Pippa whimpered behind me.

Brown's chest puffed up and her cheeks got red. "Thanks, Davy. That means a lot and you barely know me too, not like that vampire that was watching us until I left. I saw him, you know. I felt him, I should say. He was a hottie. I didn't know you knew any vampires."

"Oh my—" Pippa crashed to the floor behind me.

"Vampire?" Emily questioned.

I checked behind me and Pippa gave me a weak wave. One of her shoulders was propped against the wall. "I'm okay."

"Did you say vampires?"

Brown turned to Emily and nodded. "You couldn't guess how many go to this college. They're everywhere. Well, they were everywhere, but I didn't notice them much for awhile. Now they seem to be everywhere again. I don't know what's going on. My family doesn't practice witchcraft enough to be considered a threat or an asset by the vampire world. I think that's a good thing. How about you? Do you know any vampires?"

Emily bristled. "There are no such things as vampires."

Brown laughed. "Next you're going to tell me that you don't really think I'm a witch, right?"

"No. I believe in Wiccans. I had a friend who became a Wiccan in high school, but there are no vampires, except in movies."

Brown stood tall and straightened her shoulders. She seemed miffed. "Excuse me? I am not a Wiccan. There is a big difference between a Wiccan and a witch. Wiccan is a way of life for normal humans. It's a religion, but they're not born with magic. Witches are. I was. There's a difference."

Emily fought back a grin and glanced sideways to me. "I'm sure you are."

The air instantly sizzled around us and Brown lifted a hand. "You don't think I'm a witch?"

"What?" Emily was at a loss for words. "Davy?"

I jerked a shoulder up. "So what if she's a witch?"

Pippa melted to the floor and Brown perked up. "That's right." The air lost its sizzle. The witch had been appeased. And then something came over me. I picked the sizzle back up, but it was louder.

Emily glanced around. "What's going on?"

Pippa stood up and looked around me.

Brown glowed as she looked around.

My body hummed. I felt it all over and remembered when I had changed Lucan back to being human. My body hummed at that time too. I had snapped my fingers then, but this time I merely narrowed my eyes and the microwave exploded. Sparks flew from it and Emily jumped back, screaming.

Brown clamped both hands to her cheeks. "Oh my gosh. I don't even know how I'm doing that."

Emily swung horrified eyes to her, but I grinned. "What were you saying about the difference between Wiccans and witches?"

Then I glanced at Pippa from the corner of my eye and stopped cold. She wasn't amused. My stomach dropped. She knew I was more than empathic.

CHAPTER 9

I made a quick dash for the shower. A half hour later, I found our room sparkling with cleanliness. I sighed internally as I dropped my shower caboodle. Emily only cleaned when she was nervous.

"Did the witch leave?"

Emily's eyes shot to mine. "Do you believe in that stuff?"

I shrugged as I pulled a shirt on. "Our microwave is kapoot. I think we better." It was meant as a joke, but when her eyes widened and she paled, I thought better of it. So I sighed again, pulled on some jeans, and quickly combed my hair. "Come on, let's go out."

"What?"

"Let's go out. I know somewhere we can get some drinks, maybe even free drinks."

Slowly, she stood. "We're going for a drink?"

"Yeah. We went before."

"That was with Kates. I met Bennett that night." Something flashed over her face and Emily crumbled in front of me. Her face fell. Her shoulders slumped and she dropped like a stone on my bed.

My mouth dropped with her. "Hey. Come on. It'll be good for you."

"I haven't seen him since that horrible night, when we were

kidnapped. I know the police said there was nothing we could do about it and that he skipped town. I know you said that Kates was working undercover and went after him, but I still feel like I lost him. I constantly have this sense of being cheated. It's like he died and I felt it." She stopped and a few tears came to her eyes.

One, he had died. Two, you're better off. Three, Kates hadn't been working undercover. None of that was going to make her feel better, so I patted her shoulder instead.

"I feel like I'm grieving for him." She turned and started to sob in my shoulder.

Awkward.

I kept patting her shoulder and then switched to brushing her hair from her forehead. That was always soothing.

"I still think we should go out." I tried to sound cheerful. The wolf would've been handy in this moment.

"Why am I like this?" She kept crying and pulled away to stare at her hands. She held them up with her fingers spread out, and stared down at her palms. "I feel so dirty. I feel like I'm going crazy. I know you said it had something to do with the full moon, but I still don't feel right. I keep up a good front in front of Pippa, but I'm a basket case."

"Oh come now." I shook her shoulder. "You're normal. The guy did a number on you and you have to go through what every other girl does. They're called crushes for a reason, Em. This is the time you jump back up and keep going. Hell, let's invite Pippa. Maybe the witch too? We have friends. We should celebrate."

Her eyes popped out. "Not the witch. Do you believe in that? Really? I couldn't believe it, but then there's the microwave. She's loony."

"Ah. She's harmless."

Emily dropped her voice to a whisper, "I think she's actually a witch. She seemed sure of it and I don't think she's crazy. She said there are vampires. Do you believe in them? Maybe she's delusional. I don't believe in that stuff, but then I never believed in witches." She shuddered.

I laughed on a forced note. "Vampires? Next thing you're going to say that werewolves exist, maybe even were-cats."

"Davy." Emily stood and stared down at me. She was too serious. "I think she does have magical powers. Our microwave is destroyed. We have to get a new one because of her."

I stood and patted her hand. "It'll be okay. Promise. Witches can't hurt humans."

"Really?"

"Really." I smiled at my lie and toed on some sandals. "Are you going like that?"

"We're really going out?"

"Why not? Neither of us have early classes. Let's go. Did you want to invite Pippa too?"

"Really?" Emily stood uncertainly in the middle of the room. Then she gasped and dove for her closet. When she pulled out a red shirt, she stopped, and glanced at me. She looked at my simple white tee shirt and took out a green one of hers. Then she reached for her khaki capris, but veered to her jeans instead. We now looked like twins. Super.

"I'm going to see if Pippa wants to come." Emily darted out the door.

I took a deep breath, but it wasn't long before I heard a knock at our door. Pippa popped her head around the door. "Emily said we're still going out? Is it okay if I come?"

"Why wouldn't it be?"

She glanced over her shoulder. "Emily went to the bathroom. I wanted to make sure it's okay with you if I come. I don't really think you and I get along?"

"Which is funny because we're both lying to the same person. You'd think we'd be best friends." I tried not to sound so bitchy, but I failed.

Pippa cringed.

"Sorry. That was unfair. I don't like lying to her, but I have to. I'm taking my stuff out on you. I know you said that her kindred will tell her, maybe then neither of us will have to lie to her."

Pippa narrowed her eyes. "I don't really know what powers you have or what you are, but I know you're more than empathic. If she finds out about me, why would that mean you're caught too?"

I opened my mouth and then shut it. The wolf had a point, which was irksome. Emily might not ever find out about me. That should be good news, but it was then that I realized I wanted my roommate to know about me. I didn't want to lie anymore. I didn't want to hide anymore.

So I closed my mouth. 'Well. Fuck me.'

Pippa kept winding a finger around one of her braids. "Where are we going? She mentioned Buds before? That's a vampire bar. I don't want to go there."

I cringed. "You're not the only one. I want to stay as far away from vampires as much as you."

She flashed a relieved smile. "Oh good. I didn't know. I mean, I assumed, but you smelled like vampires so much before. Nevermind. That sounds good to me."

Then Emily came in, excited and scared at the same time. I knew Pippa sensed it too because her nostrils flared and she shot me a look.

"Looking good, roomie." She flushed, but she was happy. That was all I cared about. "Ready to go?"

"Yes, I am. You guys?"

Pippa nodded, dressed in her overalls and a pink shirt this time. I was starting to wonder if she ever changed her outfit or her hair. She still had the same two braids that hung over her shoulders as she had the first time I met her.

"My pick?" I took my car keys and purse. I started for the door.

"I was wondering if we could go to the Shoilster? Some girls on our floor told me it's supposed to be awesome."

Pippa and I both froze.

"Please?"

The wolf and I shared a shaky look. "Sure."

"I call shotgun!" Emily bounced out the door and we followed at a sedate pace. This night was definitely going to be interesting.

The drive over was tense. Emily fully welcomed the idea of going out so she couldn't sit still in her seat. Pippa and I were much less excited. As we got out of the car and headed towards the bar, I saw Gregory at the door in all black with sunglasses over his eyes.

"They have bouncers?" Pippa looked at me.

I shrugged and burst ahead of the girls. Gregory saw me and froze. I felt suspicion and caution come over him as I slapped a hand on his huge bicep. It twitched under my hand and my hand shot away. I felt scolded somehow and let out a nervous giggle. "Hi! So, I'm Davy. I had a friend that used to come here all the time. Kates? Do you know her? She said we'd be welcome to get in. This is my roommate, Emily, and her friend, Pippa."

They drew beside me as Gregory's gaze slid over both girls and then back to me. He sniffed the air as Pippa was trying not to and turned back to me. I felt his meaningful look. Oh yes. He was aware I had a werewolf in my company. So my fake smile spread wider. "Can we get in? We go to school here and want a fun night out. My *roommate* heard a lot about this place." My smile slipped.

There was no reaction from the giant vampire, but his mouth flattened into a small frown. "You girls need to stay on the main floor. No one goes into the basement."

Emily was gleeful and skipped through. "Thanks!" Pippa hung her head and dragged her feet behind. Once they were out of hearing distance, I murmured, "Please don't kill me."

He harrumphed. "You wait till Roane hears about this."

"Davy! Come on. What are you doing?" Emily called from inside and I hurried ahead. A sense of doom washed over me.

As we went in, waves of vampires rushed over me. They were everywhere. Before they'd always stayed to the basement, but this time they were in each corridor, in every booth, and on the dance floor. And these weren't normal vampires that went to our university. I glanced around and my eyes went wide. I didn't know what type of vampires they were, but they weren't the normal kind. If they were at the Shoilster and Gregory let us in, they must've been loyal to Roane.

Two vampire males strolled by and eyed us up and down. I scowled at them as Emily gushed. "This place is amazing. The bright lights. Is that smoke on the floor? And what kind of music is that? Is that techno? Don't they listen to that in Europe? Where did all these gorgeous guys come from?"

"It's not smoke, Em. It's dry ice."

It was supposed to make the club more mysterious and it worked. I kept eyeing all the nooks and crannies. I wondered what was happening in those shadows that no one could see. She was right about the guys too. Most vampires were good looking, but these seemed to be the crème de la crème. Some of them were tall and lean while others were a little stockier, built like Gregory. The females resembled Wren, complete with the hooker outfits. They wore lace corsets and leather. A few of them narrowed their eyes at us, and watched us with something that resembled hatred.

Pippa shifted beside me. Her hand touched mine. *'I can't be here. A werewolf can't be here.'*

'You're with two humans. They won't say anything.'

'I can't risk it. I'm sorry, Davy. I have to leave. Make up an excuse for me, please?'

'But—'

But she was already gone.

Then Emily looked around, wide eyed. "This was the best idea you've had, Davy. Wait. Where'd Pippa go?"

"Her cousin was sick." It wasn't my best lie.

"Really?" But then Emily was back to basking in the glow of the vampires.

"Excuse me, misses. I have a table ready for you." A server appeared with a black buttoned down shirt tucked in black slacks with two menus in his hand. His hair was slicked back in gel, giving a smooth Casanova look to him.

A smirk appeared on his face as his eyes shifted from Emily to me. At first he looked at my roommate in anticipation, but then he saw me and read my eyes. *'Back off, buddy.'*

He looked away as he led us through the crowd. We kept going upwards, which was surprising. I knew the Shoilster. Customers didn't get preferred seating unless they called ahead for reservations. It was the type of club where VIPs got private boxes, but we went past even those. He took us to a back corner where the music could barely be heard, but we were tucked at an angle where we could still see most of the activity and dance floor.

As we sat, Emily took the offered menu and leaned across the table. "This place is so pretty and we got a great table. It's everything the girls were saying. Oh, thank you so much."

The server took our order and left quietly.

Emily whispered after he'd gone a few steps, "He's cute."

"He's off limits," I growled and opened my own menu.

I hated the Shoilster. The food was made to look pretty on the plate, but the quality wasn't taste-worthy. However, what do you expect from a club/bar/restaurant that's geared towards the vampire customers. They didn't care about the food. As long as it looked pretty, appeased the humans they brought with them, and allowed a lot of drinks to come in dark colored glass, they were satisfied. They could consume their blood in front of any stupid human.

Emily gaped. "What? Why? He's cute."

"You're fragile right now. You need to go out a few more times before dating again. Bennett did a number on you."

"But," she sputtered. "Didn't you say the best thing was to go out and get over him?"

I closed my menu. "No. I said going out, but not going with a guy. It is okay to go out, let yourself soak up the fun, maybe even some attention from some guys, but that's it. Guys are dangerous. You need to get your head on straight in order to handle them."

My roommate made a disgusted face. "You make them sound like they're predators."

If the shoe fits.

Then she added, "What happened to you? You were crazy about Adam before and he wasn't a good guy."

"Adam was a cheater and a douchebag."

"Oh." She fell silent because we both knew she agreed with my sentiments about him. She'd been the first to tell me. Eyeing my roommate, I saw the confusion in her eyes. Maybe if she knew about vampires, about what they could do? Maybe if I told her?

Just then someone appeared at our table and Emily gasped, "Luke?"

My stomach fell and I looked up. Sure enough. There he was, glowering down at me. Emily just smiled at him. I realized she still had her crush for him from before.

"Um, hi."

"Emily, right? You're in one of my classes?" Roane put on a polished façade and seemed happy to see her as he pushed into my side of the booth, shoving me over. As his arm touched mine and I felt how tense he was, I knew he was pissed.

When he continued to chat with my roommate, I tried to sense inside of him. I hadn't gone far before he lashed at me, *'Get out! You shouldn't be here.'*

Oh yes. He was pissed.

I hung my head for a moment because he was right. I shouldn't have been there, but I couldn't even deny it. I had wanted to see him. I wanted to go there to maybe see him. When Emily suggested the Shoilster, I hadn't argued, at all. Then I looked back up. My eyes skimmed over his chiseled features that seemed more mysterious from the shadows dancing over his face and I caught a glimpse of Gregory in the background. He'd taken point behind a post with a drink in hand. His eyes met mine for a second before he shifted and looked away. I knew he agreed with Roane, I had been stupid to go there.

I also knew he was our bodyguard for the rest of the night.

It was then that I felt Roane's hand grip mine underneath the booth and he squeezed tight. I didn't know if it was to convey how angry he was with me or if he was trying to warn me about something. Either way, I was fearful of sharing thoughts with him. Other vampires were too close, they might hear them. So I was forced to sit there as Luke talked with Emily because I knew what he was doing. He was making her feel like she was the focal point of his arrival so she wouldn't suspect a thing. I saw how her eyes lit up. She was eating it up and lavishing in it.

I was in hell.

CHAPTER 10

Roane never spoke to me as he sat with us. And once he left, Emily gave me a dreamy smile and sighed. "He's a great guy. Doesn't seem to like you much, but he's nice."

I cleared my throat and sat up straight, but she stopped me with a wave. "Don't worry. I'm not going to chase Luke Roane. He's way out of my league. I'm not completely stupid. Besides, he's probably already devoted to some beautiful creature."

"What do you mean by that?" What did she know?

Emily shrugged. "That's the fourth time he's ever talked to me, but he never once flirted with me. He's always been nice, polite, and stand-offish. Trust me; he's one of the good ones."

"Right." I breathed easier. I wasn't sure what I was going to say, but our food came at that moment. Roane had been there when our orders were taken so the server was the epitome of professional now. I caught him glancing over his shoulder at Gregory too.

I ordered a salad. Emily ordered chicken. Then our drinks started coming.

Emily's face lit up again. "What is this?"

"They're on the house." And he placed two fruity cocktails in front of us, followed by our own pitchers of the same liquid.

Roane had done this. He sat us where we were and he was paying for everything.

Then the server slipped me a note. I slid it on my lap and opened it to read. *'If you're going out, stay here where I can protect you. Enjoy. Don't come back here again. Why are you keeping company with a werewolf?'*

Talk about being blunt and hurtful at the same time. I ripped it to shreds and dropped the pieces in our candle throughout the rest of the evening. Anybody with magic could've put them back together, but I made sure each piece was destroyed when Emily went to the bathroom.

A few hours later, I learned that alcohol had no effect on me and that Emily was the same drunk as before.

Still giggling, she slapped a hand on the table. "Thank you for this. It means a lot. I don't have a lot of friends. My close friends are all home, but then I met you. You're a close friend now too, Davy. You were right. I needed to get out. I needed this."

"You did."

"You're right. I feel like a new woman. I feel like I can go to all my classes alone now. Maybe I'll even tackle this feeling of grief I have. I know—" She snapped her fingers. "I'll go to a grief counseling group. That's what I'll do. It'll help me get Bennett out of my system."

I froze with my straw in my mouth.

"What do you think?"

What did I think? She'd have a place to talk and an outlet for her emotions. A smile spread on my face. "I think that's a great idea."

"It's decided. Tomorrow I'm looking for one on campus." She bent over, giggling. "How in the world are we going to get home? I can barely sit up."

"Ladies." Gregory materialized at our table. "There is a car ready for you downstairs. We will give you a ride home."

"Oh!" Emily was taken aback. "That's so nice of you. Is there money you need? I mean, do we pay? How much is it? I'm sorry. I'm a little drunk." Then she giggled a bit more, blushing behind a hand over her mouth.

Gregory swept his detached eyes over us both. "It's free of charge. It's part of the service."

"That's wonderful." She clapped and then frowned. "This isn't normal? We're getting such great service. Why? Davy, do you know?"

I smiled and patted her hand. "The owner is a friend of Kates. I dropped her name before."

"Oh!" Then her eyes narrowed and disgust flared over her face. "I think I'm going to throw up." And then she scrambled out of the booth and to the bathroom.

Gregory's face twitched and then cleared again. He sat in her seat. "I don't think she'll be coming back soon. Her levels of intoxication are massive for a human."

I sighed and threw the last piece of Roane's note in the candle. Gregory studied me as I watched it go up in smoke and a small smile appeared on his face. He looked softer for a second. "You came to see him."

My heart sank and I shook my head. "Emily suggested this place. I couldn't say no. This night was about her."

"His office overlooks this table."

My head shot up. "What?"

He nodded and gestured upwards. "You can't see through the glass, but he hasn't moved from that spot all night since you'd been here."

Hope flared in me for a moment, but I shook my head and turned it off. I couldn't get excited at the idea he might have feelings for me. Talia still remained in his heart. He was just confused.

I looked where he had pointed and saw glass mirrors. At one section of the wall, they jetted out and around, framing an office above the entire club. I could tell Roane stood on the other side of them. Able to make out his silhouette, I pushed through and it opened up to my eyes. Gregory was wrong; I was able to see through them. My eyes met Roane's, his narrowed as he mouthed the word, *"Stop."*

I narrowed mine in defiance and sensed into him. It was so easy to slip in him now and I was met by his same boiling anger. He snarled at me in his head, *'What are you doing? You're not supposed to use your powers.'*

'I'm in your head, your head only. No one can hear our thoughts here.'

'My shields are too hard. You're right. No one can read my mind, except you.' And I felt how he hated that.

I sparked back at him, 'Sucks, doesn't it? When someone might be more powerful than you.'

'Shut up. Return to your table. Gregory is annoyed that you're ignoring him.'

'He'll get over it.'

'He's grown a soft spot for you. He wanted to be the one to take you home tonight.'

'I like Gregory. He's nicer than Wren.'

Roane bit back a laugh. *'Go, Davy. Emily is returning to the table.'*

I looked and saw her approaching. *'I'm sorry for bringing her here. I wanted to see you. I'm sorry again.'* Then I slipped out of him and saw that Gregory had a perturbed look on his face. I was afraid to ask what that meant, but Emily had arrived.

She was pale with a green tinge and held a hand to her stomach. "I just threw up eight times. I don't ever want to drink again. Davy, don't let me drink again."

I stood and held a hand to her back. "You can still drink, just not that much next time."

Gregory led the way out of the club. As we followed behind, Emily groaned and clutched her stomach. I saw how the other customers turned and stared as we passed. Some of them were interested because we were humans. They knew Gregory protected us. A few others smelled Emily's nausea and turned away in disgust. Still others watched and their eyes lingered on the right hand of Lucas Roane.

As we climbed into the backseat of a car, I caught sight of my own car parked not far away. I could've driven, but Emily thought I was drunk. I had as much as her. I should've been affected. If I told her the truth, that I was stone cold sober, she would've wondered why. So I burrowed into my seat and waited as Gregory drove us back home. When we got to the dorm, she stumbled out first and headed in without a second look.

I remained in the car and looked out my window.

Gregory got out, closed Emily's door and returned to his seat behind the steering wheel. He tilted the rearview mirror, but then turned in his seat.

A wave of sadness swept over me. "I finally realized and accepted tonight that I am completely alone. I've been fighting it, but I have to accept it now."

I didn't see his reaction, but I felt his acceptance. It was okay to speak to him about this.

I stared out the window, but I wasn't seeing anything. Saren told me to stay away from Blue, so I did. Roane told me to stay away and I tried. My roommate thought I was something I wasn't. The witch was too alarming and Pippa couldn't ever know.

I was supposed to be normal, do normal things, and that's what I had wanted in the first place.

"I feel like I'm in a prison. Every lie I tell is another door that I've shut around me. I can't talk to anybody about this."

Gregory didn't say anything for a moment. "Roane is building an army. All those vampires have declared their loyalty to him. He is going against the Roane Family line."

"What?"

"The Roane Elders are coming with their Family of vampires. They know the Immortal is here and they're going to fight their way in. Roane has declared war against them. He is no longer a part of the Roane Family. He is doing this to protect you."

"I'm the Immortal. No one can hurt me."

Wariness flashed in his eyes. "Yes, they can. They can torture you. They can imprison you with magic. No one knows how powerful you are, even us, but there's always a way to contain something. Roane fears that Lucan is with the Mori, that he is studying their ways to find a way to take the thread from you."

"Who are the Mori?"

"The ancient vampires. They have magic in them. Roane said you had an encounter with them earlier. He thinks his brother is with them."

"The ones who can have baby vamps? That's not good."

I didn't know how magic could affect me, if I was immune, or if there was something that could be used against me. I knew that the Immortal thread no longer existed. It had dissembled when my body molded to the Immortal.

"Why are you telling me this? Why didn't Roane?" And could I still call him Roane if he wasn't with that Family anymore?

Gregory smiled. "You talk out loud sometimes. You should not do that so much."

Oh, yeah. My smile felt a bit foolish. "Why did you tell me this?"

"Because you should know. Roane chose not to because he is trying to let you live as normal a life as possible. If he needs to take you away from this place, you would never be able to be a normal human again. You would be on the run for the rest of your life."

And that would be forever. I shuddered.

Then he continued, "You can always call him Roane. His given name is Lucas, but he prefers his Family name even if he is no longer associated with them. He has their standards in his blood. It is why he is making this stand against them."

I felt his trust and belief in Roane again. It was so powerful; it was almost stifling to me, but I could sympathize. Roane had a way of pulling that loyalty out of everyone, human or not.

"Okay." I nodded and reached for my door. "I know what to do. Be normal. Right?"

"It's what he wants for you."

"Then I will do that." And I needed to put a cork in my self-pity talk. Seriously. People had worse problems than mine, like Brown. Everyone would think she was crazy.

As I got out of the car and walked around, Gregory wound down his window. "If you really need to talk to someone, here's a number you can reach me. I warn you that Roane will be told every detail that we discuss, but I can be a sounding board for you."

I took the piece of paper he offered and tucked it away. "Thanks, Gregory. And tell him thanks too. I know he said you could do this."

He jerked his head in a nod, a sign of respect from him. "He cares more for you than you might think."

When I finally went inside, I was a mass of emotions. I'd been rejuvenated, but when I heard Emily in the bathroom, guilt flared in me too. Pippa rushed out of the bathroom. "What's wrong with her? She won't stop puking."

"She had too much to drink. I should've stopped her." But I'd been distracted.

Pippa rolled her eyes. "She's actually green from vomiting so much, but she still says she had fun tonight. What did you guys do?"

"Nothing. We stayed there and drank. That was it."

"I can smell vampires all over both of you. It's disgusting." She wrinkled her nose and then went around me. "I'm going to grab some medication for her."

When she left, I went into the bathroom and found Emily in a back stall. She was bent over the toilet and gave me a weak grin. "I feel horrible."

"I'm sorry, Em." I patted her back as I sat beside her. I drew my knees against my chest.

As she felt another spell coming on and bent forward over the toilet again, I closed my eyes and drew some of her illness into me. It was there—ugly, slimy, and icky stuff. Along with it remained some of her love spell from Bennett. It still hadn't fully left her system. As it flowed into me, I felt Pippa's presence and then I felt her surprise. She knew what I was doing and I could sense that Emily was starting to feel better. After a few more minutes of drawing the illness into me, Emily was able to sit up straight and she sighed.

"I feel much better." She panted and gave us a stupid grin. Sweat soaked her hair. Some of it clung to her forehead in clumps and she brushed it back. "Much better."

I smiled and squeezed her hand before I stood up.

Pippa helped me up and met my gaze for a brief second. She studied me hard. Then she murmured, "You're not even affected."

I turned away from Pippa. It wasn't any of her business. "Emily, you want to watch a movie to end the night?"

"Pippa, you want to watch too?"

The wolf stood with a dazed look. Her mouth opened and closed. "I . . . uh . . ."

"Grab your blanket. We'll crawl in our beds and fall asleep. You can have the couch." I made sure there was a welcoming tone in my voice, but my eyes sent their own message. She knew not to say anything.

Then she closed her mouth and nodded in surrender. "I'll get my stuff. I have a stuffed animal."

"You do?" Emily mumbled as she cleaned her mouth.

"Let me guess? A little wolf?"

Pippa grinned before she went out the door.

"How'd you know that?" Emily asked, but she didn't care. Now that I'd taken the illness away, the exhaustion was evident in her. She was going to be asleep before her head hit her pillow. And as I put the movie in and she crawled into her top bunk, she was snoring before I even curled up in my own blankets. Pippa came through the door and stood in the doorway with her hand on the doorknob. "She's already asleep?"

"Yeah."

She fidgeted with the door handle. "Should I go?"

Emily's snores roared through the room.

I gestured to the couch. "I already put the movie in. If she wakes up and doesn't see you on the couch, she'll wonder why you didn't come. She's going to swear that she never fell asleep and watched the whole time."

Pippa grinned. "I guess I can stay a little bit."

Then I pressed play and nestled back.

Twenty minutes into the movie, she asked. "What are you?"

I'd been tired, but I jerked awake now.

She hesitated. "I mean, you're not just empathic."

"I can't tell you and if you ever find out, you can't say a word to anyone."

Pippa didn't comment for a while. "The wolves know you exist. They know there's something different about you. I'm sorry. We don't have an open channel for our thoughts with each other, but we're highly in tune with the other wolves. The matriarch knew about you. She sensed my unease."

At her words, everything froze inside of me. I knew about the mother wolf, but I hadn't given her enough thought. First Brown had distracted me, then Roane came, and then Saren.

"Are they going to do anything?" My heart stopped.

She shook her head. "No. They're just waiting and watching right now. If you do something against us, then they'll act. They're protective of Emily, you know. Her kindred is important to the pack. They consider her one of us."

I grinned at that thought. "Can you imagine when Emily finds all that out?" I whistled under my breath. "I'd like to be a fly on the wall that day."

She giggled. "I think everyone in the pack will feel her kindred's emotions. I'll tell you how it goes."

I shook my head. Emily's world was going to split wide open. She was still uneasy about the possibility of witches. I had quieted her questions about vampires, but all the folklore was going to become real to her soon. Except me. I wasn't in the folklore.

I settled back and tried to watch the movie.

WREN PAUSED in his doorway and saw Roane with his back to the desk. He gazed over the club below him. She couldn't see from below, but she knew he'd be there and he was.

Gregory had passed the message that Davy was there. The ones who knew what she meant to Roane felt her presence immediately. They understood why a sudden intensity swept around the club and most of them waited. They watched warily to see what might happen next. Wren knew that her master wouldn't be leaving this spot for the rest of the night.

"Are you going to stand there and watch the whole night?"

Roane didn't turn around. He'd known she was there before she opened the door.

When he didn't answer, she took a seat on one of his leather couches and swung a leg over the armrest. "So what's the plan? Are you going to kick her out? She's here with her roommate and a wolf. She's here under her cover. Sneaky little bitch."

He tossed his drink back. "Gregory is going to watch her."

Wren snorted. "I bet he loved that assignment. Let's all watch the Imm—"

Roane was in her face before she finished. He grabbed her jaw in one hand and lifted her in the air. "You do not say that word. Ever."

Wren's eyes flashed in anger, but she managed a tight nod. She couldn't speak.

Roane placed her on her feet, but he didn't let go. "I get that you don't like her. I don't care. You will treat her with respect or you will be sent away. Let's not forget the last time you tangled with one of them. Talia wasn't as forgiving, was she?"

She shrugged off his touch. "That wasn't about you. Let's not forget that either or what I lost to be loyal to you."

He rolled his eyes and moved to refill his drink. "If that's how you think of this, you can leave. You made your choice long ago."

She growled, but didn't move. Her hands remained against her sides as she clenched and unclenched them into fists. With fevered eyes and a tight jaw, she struggled not to lash out and then gave up the fight. She burst out, "Tracey's coming here! She's marching with the new Roane hunter. I found out from some soldiers who defected to Gavin's Family. What are you going to do when they get here? We aren't ready for an entire army."

Roane glanced back. "Am I supposed to be surprised by this? We've known they would send an army. We've always known. They *already* captured you with a small clan, but Davy released your bonds. Did you know that?"

She froze for a second, and then shrugged. "So what?"

He turned back to the window and found Davy below; laughing with the girl who'd had a crush on him. Then he murmured as he sipped his drink, "I'm sorry that Tracey is coming here. I truly am. I know what she meant to you."

With those words, her anger was gone. She groaned. "Why do you do that? You make me so mad and then, nothing. It's all gone. You're a dick sometimes."

Roane grinned, but didn't look back. "We will deal with the army. Look around, Wren. Everybody here has come to join us. We're not powerless."

"She should be testing her powers. She should be figuring them out so she can control and use them. We will need her in the end. We won't win without her."

His jaw hardened. "She's living a normal life. That was the deal. We stay and hold this off as long as possible and she can be normal. It's what she's always wanted."

"We should be running."

He whirled back to her and pinned her against the wall. His face was inches from hers. "You didn't want to run before. You wanted to fight. Wish granted. This is what we're doing. Now you're going to bolt? Are you going to go to Tracey when she gets here?" He waited a beat. "Are you going to betray me, Wren?"

"NO—I—" She closed her mouth and looked away. "I don't think we'll win, Lucas."

His eyes softened and he let her go. "Trust me?"

With a sigh, she closed her eyes and hung her head. "I always have."

"Then please continue."

It broke her and she lifted her eyes back up. A renewed determination was in them. "Until I die."

Roane didn't respond, but clenched his jaw. It meant more than he had expressed to her, but he knew that Wren was terrified. She wanted to fight, even when the odds were against them. For her to come and request for them to run meant others were scared as well.

Fear was dangerous. It was intoxicating and maddening. And he knew he'd have to do something to diffuse it.

"For the record, the reason why I don't like her isn't because she took Talia's place." Wren moved to the door.

He lifted piercing eyes to her and waited.

She finished, "Because you don't think clearly when it comes to her. And for god's sake, if you want to see her, just go! Make up some excuse."

Roane didn't tell her that he already had.

As Wren shoved through the door, it swung open and revealed an athletic looking vampire with golden curls. His blue eyes smirked in amusement. "You don't have to knock me unconscious, Wren. I'm yours for the taking."

She brushed past and growled, "Get lost!"

Gavin chuckled as he walked inside and helped himself to a drink. He cast a cursory glance over the vampire at the window. "Hope you don't mind, Lukey dear. I was a bit parched. I haven't fed in a long while with how fast we were urged to get here. Really, Luke. It was breakneck speed. I think I should earn some points for being the bestie I am to you. How many other complete armies have gotten here? What's that? Oh, right. One. Me. No welcoming hug? No hello? No, 'what's up mate?' Nothing? I'm hurt."

A grin teased the corners of Roane's mouth. "You can have Wren for the night."

Gavin burst out laughing. "Oh yeah. I can imagine her reaction at that order. Even if you did try to enforce it, I wouldn't make it through the night alive or with my balls intact."

"You're interested," Roane shot back.

The blonde vampire shrugged and poured a second drink. "Who wouldn't be? She's hot under all that black leather. Has no one told her the vampire cliché look is outdated? Look at me; most humans think I'm a professional athlete. I get more pussy looking like this than I ever would wearing leather chaps. No vampire magic needed."

"You did wear leather chaps. Assless."

"Still." Gavin shuddered and crossed to stand beside Roane. He looked out the window. "What are we looking at? Is that her down there?" He gestured with his drink and Roane glanced down.

His eyes fell on Davy, who was laughing with a hand over her mouth. Her mate had been telling a story with hand gestures that grew bigger with each drink she had. By the look in Davy's eyes, she knew her roommate was properly drunk, but she didn't mind. Roane knew that had been Davy's intention, to make her friend forget her troubles. And he wondered if she had wanted to do the same thing.

Gavin watched the two in the booth and then watched his best friend of five hundred years. When Roane's eyes shifted and darkness replaced the shimmer of emotion that had been too brief to be caught, he already knew what the real story behind this war was.

He decided to change the subject. Further investigation would need to be had. "Tracey's coming, you know. What are you going to do about that?"

"She's the enemy."

Gavin choked on his drink. "The enemy? Are you dense? Tracey's not the enemy. She's Talia's sister. Oh no no no. She is not the enemy. She'll *never* be the enemy."

"She defected to the new Roane hunter. She's coming with their army."

Gavin rolled his eyes. "And you have Wren. She's the ace up your sleeve. Use her to get Tracey back with us. They were bosom buddies for years. Best friends, right?"

"I won't use Wren that way." Roane's voice was hard. "If she chooses to pursue a relationship with Tracey, then so be it. If she wants to bring her to us, then that is her choice."

"Oh hell, buddy." Gavin sat down his glass and grabbed the bottle. "You still have that stick up your ass, huh?"

A smile flashed over Roane's face. "I've named it. It's called Gavin."

"And your humor is piss poor. You know what your problem is? You're too noble. You need to not be so damn noble. Screw up once in awhile. Make a mistake on purpose."

"I did make a mistake."

"Not that, you didn't. You had to leave. You were ordered to leave." Gavin sighed as he saw how Roane's eyes hardened. There was no getting through to his best friend now. "Leaving Talia wasn't a mistake."

"She died because of it."

"There was more to it and you know it." He swung his eyes and watched the girl below. She had an aura around her. Gavin understood why Luke was captivated. "No one really knows what happened to bring that about, do we? It probably would've happened even if you had been there and you might've died because of it."

"Or I might've saved her life."

"Lucan found this one, didn't he? He would've found Talia. He would've bit her and he would've gotten her powers. This one stopped it. She was supposed to get the thread when she did."

"Maybe." Roane tossed the rest of his drink down his throat. Gavin handed him the bottle and soon the two were going back and forth, sharing drink for drink. When Luke excused himself, not long after the two girls left, Gavin resolved to meet this new Immortal. She had too much power over his best friend, more than he was comfortable with.

CHAPTER 11

Over the next weeks, Pippa and I became friends. Emily started attending a grief counseling group and I persuaded her into taking over my hours at the hotline. Heaven forbid. I shuddered at the thought of spending more time in that building. Everything seemed normal until Emily left Pippa and me at the library.

"Hi, guys!" Brown drew next to our table. She panted and brushed a chunk of her sweaty hair off her face. She wore a bohemian dress that clung to her, all the way to her little toes that were in brown leather sandals. "Man, it's hot. Are you guys as hot as me?"

Pippa looked at me for a second. "I'm actually a little cold."

Brown laughed. "You're so funny. Werewolves aren't ever cold. At least, I didn't think they were."

We both sat up straight at that statement. "You know what she is?"

"Of course." Then she looked alarmed. "Wait, you didn't know? Oh my gosh. I am so sorry." She looked at Pippa and bit her lip. "You aren't going to eat me, are you?"

The wolf's mouth hung open. Not only did Brown know who she was, but she just blabbed it like it was the weather. Then she slammed her with a stereotype right after.

I laughed.

"I can't do this." Pippa gathered up her books and left. Her back and shoulders were rigid at she went to the door.

Brown took her seat. "I did something wrong, didn't I? I have this problem. I speak without thinking sometimes."

"Really?" I tried to hold back my sarcasm.

She nodded. "I do and sometimes I overstep boundaries that I should know are there. I had no idea you didn't know. I'm sorry to you too. You're handling it really well. Do you know what that means, that she's a werewolf? They exist. Trust me."

"Brown." I leaned across the table. I wanted to make sure she heard me. "You need to stop talking about being a witch, or about werewolves, or about vampires. Ninety percent of the population doesn't believe in that stuff and the ones who do are going to be uncomfortable around you. You're going to get a reputation as being crazy and no one will talk to you or someone is going to hurt you." I leaned back. "So shut up."

Her eyes went wide. "Really? They'd think I was crazy?"

"I'm surprised it already hasn't happened."

"But it's just the truth. I lived in a community where witches and all that stuff were common. Everyone knew about it. People really don't know about it here?"

I shook my head. The girl was going to be an outcast.

"Oh my gosh. I have to tell you this. I haven't seen you since that last time I was at your room and by the way, here's the book I meant to take to you that day. Everything got so chaotic with my powers that day; I was in such a rush that I forgot to leave it for you."

"You brought that book to me?"

Then she produced it from her bag and it fell with a thud on the table. "Here it is! And don't worry. I did a little spell so you can walk through the door. The alarms won't go off. Promise. I've been in and out with this book many times since then." She caressed the tan dusty book in a loving gesture. "It has so many interesting tidbits in here. But you wanted it to learn about wolves, right? Probably because of the one that was just here, right?"

I shifted in my seat. Even I was uncomfortable. "You did a spell, huh?"

"Yeah." She tucked some of her curls behind her ears. "I know it's supposed to stay here, but that clerk really made me mad that day. I decided to take it with me and if he gets in trouble, he deserves it. Plus, I took it to my mom's business and made copies of it. I have three copies, just to be safe." She giggled. I could see she was proud.

"How illegal of you." I grinned and reached for the book. The cover had a velvety feel to it, but she was right." Thank you for the book. I have to head home now, though. Thanks a lot, Brown. Really." As I stood up and grabbed my bag, Brown stood in front of me. She looked uncertain and there was something swimming inside her. I could feel it. It wanted to come out at me, but I didn't know what it was.

Then she folded her hands in front of her. "Do you think you'd like to hang out sometime?" She laughed and her voice hitched higher. "You were right. I don't have any friends. I think it's because of what you said before. I talk too much, about things that I shouldn't. You're the only one who hasn't shunned me."

Oh goodness. She needed a friend.

"I thought, maybe, we could go for ice cream or something? Maybe coffee?" She gave me a tight smile. "I'll pay."

I closed my eyes. I couldn't believe I was going to do this, but there was something about her that I liked, even if she pushed the boundaries. "Okay. Maybe. I don't know. Tomorrow?"

She perked up. "Tomorrow would be great. Awesome! Thanks. I can't wait."

What had I gotten myself into? She flashed a radiant smile and grabbed her bag, which was filled to the brim with books. Then she waved over her shoulder as she ran out of the library. "Thanks, Davy! I'll see you tomorrow." A clerk appeared in front of her, but Brown turned and as she did, her bag bounced on her back and decked the clerk in the face.

She hurried away and he held a hand to his face.

I shook my head and strolled past him with the book in my own bag. No matter what kind of a person she was, Brown was a witch. And she was right. Once that box inside of her that anchored all her magic was unlocked, she'd be a very powerful witch. Until then, I was glad it only let her do a little. She'd be lethal and out of control if it wasn't the case.

As I was walking to my dorm, a sudden wave of urgency washed over me. I stopped in the middle of the sidewalk and gasped. I bent over until my head touched the tops of my knees. I gasped again and felt like I was drowning. Wave after wave crashed over me and I heard a small voice in the distance, "Tell him, please. Tell him."

I gasped against the onslaught of waves. "Tell who? Tell him what?"

Another set of waves rocked my body. The sense of drowning increased. As I closed my eyes, I felt as if I was in the ocean and something held me down. It kept me from getting to the surface. Then, in the break of the waves, I heard the same voice. It was weaker than before. "Roane. Tell him about my daughter."

"What? What daughter?" He had a daughter?

As sudden as it had come upon me, it was gone. I stood there, gasping, and blinked away tears as I felt the campus around me. The air was calm, too calm. There was no ocean. There was only the sidewalk, a few buildings, and green lawn all around me. Then I looked to the side and saw Irene watching me. The angel statue hadn't aged a day since I'd sat beside it. She gave me the same expression she had that day.

I flicked her off. She made me feel crazy and it wasn't any of her business.

When I got in my room, I had closed the door when a voice murmured behind me, "Would you like to tell me why my best friend has declared war against the very Family he has only declared his loyalty to for the last five hundred years?"

My mouth fell open and I saw a vampire dressed in gym clothes. He had blonde hair that was cut short with tight curls. His blue eyes warned of depths and ominous promises and he was graced with a lean build that professional athletes had. Something told me this guy wasn't a professional athlete.

"Who are you?" I shut my door with a bang. "Your element of surprise doesn't work with me. Nor do you scare me. If your best friend is Luke Roane, we both know he has no idea you're here because he wouldn't be okay with that. And the fact that I know that means that anything else you might try to scare out of me is useless."

He snapped his mouth shut and clenched his jaw. It was a very manly looking jaw, rigid, tight, but his blue eyes had taken on a lethal look.

Craig had instilled a loathing for all vampires in me. Some of them, like Roane, promised me they weren't all the same. This vampire was like Craig. He wanted to scare me. He wanted to make me quake in my pants. Hell no. I was not going back to that person.

I felt the room shake as my rage built.

He glanced around, but he still seemed nonplussed.

"Get out." My eyes snapped their own warning.

He watched me and studied me intently for a moment, and then something shifted in his eyes. "You're the reason why he's doing this. It's not because you're the Immortal, it's because he cares about you."

The room stopped shaking, but then I heard footsteps in the hallway. People were running. This guy didn't seem alarmed. He looked resigned.

"Who are you?" I clipped out and my eyes flashed. I knew he saw the Immortal's whites.

He scratched his forehead and shook his head. "You're not anything like her. I like that. That's okay with me." Then he held out his hand. "I go by Gavin. I'm Lucas' best friend. How are you?"

I stared at his hand like it was an alien limb that he extended. I had no plans to touch it. Since he knew who I was and didn't seem to be bothered with it, I smiled. "Wanna have a drink?" We both knew I didn't mean a normal beverage.

He drew his hand back in a heartbeat. "Ah no. I enjoy living how I am. That was a good one. Good trick." He bent forward as if tipping his hat to me. "You're a sneaky one. You've gotta be sneaky in this life. You'll do just fine."

The room started to shake again. This guy was pissing me off. He treated me like I was some newbie. But then I stopped. I was a newbie.

Then the door burst open and Brown panted, "I had a premonition. Sorry, I can't breathe." She bent over and took deep breaths. Once she had, she looked back up and smiled. "Why do you have a vampire in here?"

His eyes shifted again and he drew back. "You're a witch."

"Really?" I was dumbfounded. "You're scared of *her*?"

Brown hissed and then frowned at me. "Why shouldn't he be?"

Gavin withdrew to the window. "You won't hurt me whereas she could. Plus, I don't like witches."

"Only because you loved one once," Brown snorted and then clamped a hand over her mouth. "How did I know that? It must've been my powers."

All of this was annoying. I rolled my eyes and flicked a finger so the windows locked. I didn't want Gavin to escape so easily. Then I turned to her. "What was your premonition?"

"That you were drowning. But you look fine? Did you take a shower?"

"No."

Gavin's eyes darted from her to me. "You know her?"

I nodded.

Then he turned to her. "You know what she is?"

Her eyes leapt. "What? What is she?"

The room shook again, but he smirked back at me. Brown bounced around in a circle. Her eyes were wide as she looked around.

"She's dating my best friend." He smiled. "Luke Roane. Do you know who he is?"

"No." But she frowned. "Should I? I should, shouldn't I? You said it like I should've."

"Ah. No." I was starting to believe I lived in the insane asylum.

"You're dating Luke Roane?" Emily asked from the doorway. She looked as if she'd seen a ghost.

Oh, shit.

CHAPTER 12

Emily stumbled forward, but grabbed Brown as if she were about to fall. "You know Luke?"

I closed my mouth and glanced at Gavin, who winked at me.

'Bastard vampire.'

"Ooh, I heard that!" Brown squeaked.

Gavin looked at her, surprised. So did I, oh hell. If she could hear thoughts, this wasn't good.

"I just heard a thought! Someone thought, 'Bitch?' Is that right? Who would—" Then she jumped and looked at Emily, whose hand was now fisted into her sleeve. "Oh. Nevermind!" She sent us an impish grin. "My bad."

"What's going on?" Pippa stood in the doorway. Her hand stayed on the frame as if she was going to bolt any moment.

Emily turned to her. "Davy is a liar and a cheat. And a backstabber."

Pippa looked at me. Her mouth fell open and the questions flew over her mind. 'What happened? What is Davy lying about? I didn't know she was dating anybody—wait—she's not dating Emily, is she? That wouldn't be good. Oh no. Davy's looking at me! I forgot she can hear my thoughts. Davy, don't listen to me!'

I heard Gavin chuckle behind me and glared at him. I couldn't do anything to Emily or the other girls, but I could hurt him and before I realized what I was doing, a surge of power burst through me. My eyes shifted to the Immortal's whites.

'*Get out!*' I roared in my head.

The window flung open behind him, the screen disappeared and his body flew backwards, through it. It happened so fast, no one gasped before the screen had reappeared and the window was closed again.

A beat of silence filled the room. Then a thud was heard behind me. I whirled to find Emily on the floor.

Pippa screamed and dropped to her knees. "She fainted! Oh my goodness." Then she glared at me. "This is your fault."

Brown bounced up and down where she stood. "Did you see that?! That was amazing. I'm way more powerful than I thought!"

Pippa's mouth fell open and then closed it with a snap. "I cannot believe any of this."

"Is she okay?" I asked. I hesitated before I crossed the room and knelt beside my roommate.

"She fainted. She's not dead," Pippa snapped at me and stroked Emily's cheek. Then she went still and gasped again.

"What? What?" I reached out and clamped a hand on the wolf's arm. Instantly, I heard her thoughts and was in the swirl of her emotions. They were memories intermixed with images. I saw Pippa as a little girl with the same two braids and overalls. Then I saw her as a puppy. She had a coat of tawny-colored fur. She was running around, stumbling from paws that were too big for her. Then there was another image of a young man. His face was round in shape with brown hair that looked messily rumpled. His eyes stared straight at me, as if he could see me.

I ripped out of her, but not before I heard her shock, '*She's already met him. It's Pete!*'

As I sat back on my heels, I knew Pippa was hurt that she hadn't been told this. Something in her had assumed she would've known right away.

She looked at me, dazed. "He saw you. He knows who you are. And he's going to tell her."

My throat had a knot in it. "Who is he? Who is Pete to you?"

"He's no one. He's another wolf. That's all." She jerked upright and grabbed our dresser for balance.

'Like hell he was no one to her.'

I stood, slower, and watched the wolf. A myriad of emotions were flashing across her face, one after another. I knew Brown saw it too and she came to stand beside me. Then Pippa shook her head again and muttered, "I can't handle this."

She rushed from the room. The door remained open behind her and a second later, hers slammed shut.

Brown jumped from the sound. "Oh wow. Geez." She looked at me. "Are all wolves like that? She's jumpy for how quiet she seems. They repress too much for their well-being."

"Werewolves repress a lot. They're very secretive."

"I know. It's not healthy. Humans have a better balance of their primal and logical side. Vampires are all about the primal and were-wolves are all about the logical. It's not right. There should be some-thing that fixes it and everyone can be happy. Hmmm. Maybe I could do a spell?"

I shuddered at the thought before I started to lift Emily to the couch. Brown picked up her legs and we placed her gently down. After I covered her with a blanket, I sat at my desk with no idea how to repair anything. There had been too much damage done.

Brown sat the edge of my bed. I felt her presence trying to comfort me. "Who is Luke Roane?"

What did I even say about him? "He's complicated."

"Are you two dating like that guy said?"

Hell. Were we? "No. We're not dating."

"But you want to?"

I glanced up and felt strangely vulnerable.

She smiled to reassure me. "It's okay if you said you want to. You wouldn't be the first girl to fall for a guy they couldn't have. It's common." Her eyes saddened.

Then I stopped thinking. I let it out. "It's not how Emily thinks. I didn't meet him through her. We met because, it's complicated, but it has to do with something that happened to me, something that no one knows about. He's been helping me with it or he did help me with it until recently. Things happened. We crossed the line, did things, but we haven't since—" I took a deep breath. "Since I found out that he's in love with someone else who is dead and who died because of—he still loves her and she's still dead. Then he has this other friend who hates me. Roane's come to see me a few times, but it's never just to see me. It's always to check on me. He wants to make sure I'm okay. He feels like it's his duty that I'm okay. And Emily knew him from a class. I knew she liked him, but I didn't realize how strong her feelings were until now."

"Who's Pete?"

I shrugged. "I have no idea. She hasn't told me about him."

"Do you blame me?" Emily asked. She sat up, looking pale. "I fainted, didn't I?"

Brown and I nodded.

Emily rolled her eyes. "That's so embarrassing."

"It happens to me all the time, especially when I try a powerful spell." She shrugged. "Or when I do any spell."

My roommate caught my gaze. "Is that true? Everything you just said?"

I nodded. I couldn't shake that vulnerable feeling.

She groaned and fell backwards. "How am I supposed to be mad at you now? You sound like you're in love with him and can't be with him. I hate this. I hate it."

Brown sighed, "I think it's romantic. She loves him, but he loves someone else. He still wants to make sure she's okay."

"Shut up," Emily said at the same time I did.

We glanced at each other and both grinned. Then I cleared my throat. "I'm sorry about Luke. I really am."

Emily dismissed me. "Don't worry about it. I'm not even that upset. I'm hurt. I feel like you went behind my back, but it's not like you're the only one keeping secrets. You know about Pete?" She blinked then. "How do you know about Pete?"

Uh, hell. "Pippa knows him and she figured it out. Don't ask me how. I have no idea." I gestured towards the door. "She took off. I think she's pretty hurt you didn't tell her about him."

"Why would I? I wanted to keep him to myself for a little bit. I hadn't even told you and I would've told you first. You're my closest friend here."

Warmth spread through me when I heard that. I felt so touched, honored. I realized then Emily had become one of my best friends. She might not know as much about me as Kates did, but she defended me at times. "Thanks, Em."

"I want friends like you." Brown blinked back tears. "You guys are so awesome to each other. You both are so understanding. It's so much. This is so great."

Emily sat back. "Do you do drugs?"

"See. Like that! You're so honest with each other, with me too." Brown laughed to herself. "And I don't do drugs, but I can see why you might think that."

Emily asked me, "Was she hurt that I hadn't said anything? I didn't know she knew Pete."

"I think," I chose my words very carefully. "I think she feels like she's closer to you than you think you are to her and yes, it looked to me that she knew Pete. It looked like there was some history between her and him."

"Who is Pete?" Brown plopped down between us. Emily looked down at her hands. Then Brown added, "Don't be shy now. We all know. You heard about Davy and this Roane character. Your turn."

Emily looked back up and glared. Then she gave up the fight. "I met him at the grief group I've been going to. It's so amazing. He's so amazing. He's funny and smart and nice and just wonderful." She smiled to herself with a dreamy look on her face. "He's there because he lost someone close to him and needed to talk to people who understood. He said no one understood. When I went in and sat down at the first meeting it was love at first sight." She sighed. "I love him, Davy. He's so amazing. I feel like a part of me is home now. It's like I'm complete with him."

I smiled. "That's wonderful, Emily. It really is." I kept the sharp retort that she'd felt the same with Bennett in the back of my mind.

Brown's head swiveled between us. "If you're in love with this Pete, why were you mad at Davy about this other guy?

The dreamy look vanished.

I sighed. It was now awkward again.

Emily stood up. "I wasn't mad about the guy. I was mad because she lied to me."

"What did she lie about? I mean, she just didn't tell you, did you?"

"It's different." I placed a hand on Brown's arm.

"It's not different. She's falling in love with some guy and never said a word to you, but she's mad at you. You never told her about this guy you fell in love with even though he's with someone else? So you're not even with him. You met him separately from her."

I gave a small shrug. "There were different circumstances, but Emily feels I betrayed her because she knew him and I never told her that I did."

"But you didn't because it was too painful to say anything. Who wants to tell someone that you like a guy she knows too, but he's with someone else? What's the point then? That's humiliating. I'd keep that to myself too. I don't think you did anything wrong."

Emily stood in front of her closet. Her head was bent. Her door was still closed and she didn't move.

Brown looked at me. "You didn't do anything wrong. If Emily can fall in love with someone and not tell you, she wouldn't say a thing if she liked someone who loved someone else. She wouldn't want to be embarrassed in front of you and she would be because you're more—"

I clamped a hand over Brown's mouth. Whatever she was about to say did not need to be said. After she quieted and sat back on the couch, I let go and watched my roommate. What was she thinking and why was I so hesitant to read her thoughts?

Then I closed my eyes. I had to go in there. I had to violate my roommate. And I heard, *'Pete said she wouldn't understand. No one would. He said that she couldn't know. Am I wrong in not telling her? I didn't lie because—yes I did. Who am I lying to? Myself? That stupid girl is right. I wouldn't have told Davy if Pete hadn't felt the same as me. What do I do now? Pete, come help me.'*

Suddenly the whole room shook again. The ferocity of it shocked even me and I stood. This wasn't me. This wasn't Brown. What was coming?

Brown gasped, excited and scared at the same time.

Emily looked around, but there was a waiting look in her. That's when I realized that she knew what he was. She had asked for him to come and she thought it was him coming.

Pippa ran to our door and braced herself. "What's going on?"

Brown screamed, "Something's happening!"

Then it stopped and the air felt eerie. I had a moment to wonder what stood outside our door before three bursts of light exploded from the hallway. Pippa fell to the ground. Emily crumbled. And Brown dropped. All of them were unconscious.

"What?" I gaped at them.

Saren stood in the doorway, in blue leather this time. The fire in her eyes was blazing and it smoldered in the air. A burning smell filled the room. "We have to go. Now."

"What did you just do?" I couldn't look away from their fallen bodies.

"They aren't dead, but they will be soon if I don't get you out of here."

"But—"

She grabbed my hand and both of us teleported. The room wrapped around us and we were on our feet in an alley somewhere.

I threw down Saren's hand. "What just happened?!"

She ignored me and scanned our surroundings. "We're safe. For now."

"Saren!" I clipped out. "Fill me in on what's going on or I'm going back. I'll figure it out for myself."

A burst of fire exploded from her eyes. It zapped and burned me before she retracted it. "Don't threaten me. I am still your superior and you need me if you're going to survive the near future."

"What?!" My mouth hung open. Again. "What are you talking about?"

She stopped and turned to me. "Do you know what kind of wolf your roommate is mixed up with?"

"Like Pippa? She's harmless."

"The girl is. He's not. Pete Young is the next leader of the were-wolf nation. He's at your school to unite the werewolves for an uprising against the vampires."

"They're going to war with them?"

"The werewolves have laid low for thousands of years, but they're strong. Their power is ancient, more ancient that the vampires and it's rising again. Pete Young is meant to bring them together. They don't want to replace vampires, but they want to usurp them. And this guy is the equivalent of your vampire to their species."

A part of me was proud of Emily. "But what does that have to do with me?"

"She called him. He was going to her, fast. The second he got there he would've felt your power and tried to drain you from it. He wouldn't have been able to stop himself."

"Vampires can't sense my power. Why could he?" Pippa hadn't sensed my powers.

Saren sighed in frustration and paced up and down the alley. She was tense, ready for a fight. "We should be moving and not talking. He probably sensed your trail and could be coming after us."

"Stop!" I held onto her shoulders. "He's just a werewolf, right? Right?"

Saren shook her head. "He's not *just* a werewolf. He's got power, magic in him. He was created using the essence of the Immortal thread from a dead Immortal."

"Talia?"

"Her mother. The wolves took her mother after Lucan and Lucas left her. They took the essence of the thread that was still in her body with magic."

I had no idea how to figure this all out. "What? Huh?"

She rolled her eyes and sighed in disgust. "It's like a boat that makes waves in the water. They caught the waves that remained after the boat had left. Does that make sense to your human brain?"

"Hey! Back off, fiery witch from hell! You think I like this? You think I like running from magical beings?" I snapped at her and then ran a hand through my hair. "You said that my friends would've died if we hadn't left. Why? What would've happened?"

"When he tried to drain you, you would've defended yourself. You still don't know your powers. Your reaction would have been stronger than you wanted and would have killed him. You would've killed your friends too. I stopped it from happening. I stopped him from figuring out who you are, at least until we can figure out how to blanket your powers to him."

"Oh! So I can go back?" At her dark look, I added, "Sometime?"

Saren rolled her eyes. They looked like sparklers waving in the air. Then she stalked off with her leather-clad legs rubbing against each other.

I took in the sight of her black hair flowing behind her, sleek and shiny with her blue leather outfit. "You look like a superhero right now. Did you go for that on purpose?"

She sighed in disgust. The blue leather transformed into a black-colored outfit. The fabric was loose and flowed behind her, billowing in the wind. She kept going.

"Can I do that? Can you show me how to do that?"

She barked over her shoulder, "We have work to do."

CHAPTER 13

"Not to be a nag, but where are we going?" I followed behind Saren as we walked down another set of streets. We'd been walking in circles for the last hour. I wasn't sure if she was aware of the attention she was attracting dressed like a rich person in the back streets that accumulated the back street type of person. A few homeless. A few drunks. More than a few illegal activities were going on around us.

Saren kept trudging around and cursed underneath her breath.

She whipped back to me now. "What do you think I'm doing? I'm mixing your scent with all these other things. He's good. He's going to be able to pick your scent out of all these places, but I want him confused."

"I get that, but where are we going? Shouldn't we go?"

She rolled her eyes. "You are so human, it annoys me." Then she grabbed my hand and we were whisked into another teleport. When we stopped, I looked around and saw only cement floors. There were no windows, just open areas in brick walls. A tree had grown in the corner of our room with vines that climbed up the wall and onto the ceiling. A few flowers intermingled among the vines.

"Where are we? Is this some magical place?"

"It's an abandoned castle, used by a coven that was killed off in the early 1800s." Saren left for another room.

I followed, wide eyed. "Castle? Are you serious? I didn't think we had castles in America."

She stopped and glanced over her shoulder. "We're not in America anymore."

My eyes went even wider. "What?"

Then she kept going, down some steps that looked like they had been put together with brick and cement by hand.

"Where are we?"

"It doesn't matter." She strode through another opening and then paused before an altar. A moment later, she lit candles on it. A banner hung from it with a sign that looked like a hand surrounded with weaving loops of rope. A tiny blade of grass grew out of the middle of the hand.

"What does that mean?"

Saren stopped and looked where I pointed. The hand seemed to turn till it was pointed at me. It looked like it was stretched for my own to take it in a hold. Her voice was quiet. "It's the sign of the Immortal."

"The sign of me?"

"No. It's the sign of its creator, the true essence of the Immortal, what created it from the thread."

I swallowed. "You told me before not to talk to Blue. Then before that, I was told that Jacith wasn't the real creator. The vampires all think he is. They think he's some super powerful sorcerer. I don't know, but Roane told me before that Jacith created the Immortal. What's the real story?"

Saren watched me for a moment and then the air circled around her. It picked up speed and her eyes gleamed. Dust rose up from her feet and moved upwards. It covered her entire body until I couldn't see her through it. Then it stopped and everything fell back in place.

Saren didn't look like Saren anymore. The black hair was gone. The fire eyes had been replaced with soft almond ones. The black outfit was now a white robe wrapped around her body. Her hair was a golden wheat color, braided in crowns on top of her head. She smiled and I knew then this was not Saren.

"My name is Sireenia. I am a sister to Saren and Stepianhas, your last guide."

"Are you my new guide?" I wasn't sure I'd miss Saren.

She smiled again. It was a tender look. "No, but I will help you along the way. Saren is your guide for a reason. She will fight when you are unable to. No one will harm you and many will try. She is here to help you embrace your powers because you are very powerful, but you need to become your powers."

"Who is Jacith? How is my old sponsor involved?"

"You are ready for some answers. We can tell that you know more than you think." She gestured to the side where a chair carved in rock appeared. Another was beside it and we both sat in them. Sireenia folded her hands in her lap. All her movements were graceful. "Your empathic sponsor was assigned to you for a reason. She came from a long line of witches that worshiped their original sorcerer Jacith. Her attributes matched yours. You needed someone who was motherly, but aloof. She was that, but she also had a sense of purpose that you respected. She had humor that met yours. She was picked for you and her assignment was to bring you to Jacith when the thread went into you."

My eyes were wide and my soul felt like it had a hole in it. It was gaping open. Everything she said was true.

Sireenia had been watching me and then took my hand. I felt her calm enter me and the peace soothed over everything, all my agitation, panic, and it even seemed to lick other wounds inside of me.

"You're very beautiful." She held my eyes. "They've told me of your will, your spirit, but they haven't shared your looks. Do you know how beautiful you are?"

I looked away. Then she squeezed my hand and I looked back.

"You're not normally bashful. Why are you now? You know you're attractive."

I had no idea. "You're so direct. No one's told me like that." I knew I wasn't ugly, but I never thought about my looks. I wasn't known for them. I was the carefree, funny one.

"Oh. Maybe they should've." Then she winked and sat back. "But you're right. We're not here about your looks. I'm here because you wanted to learn about Jacith and Saren didn't want to be the one to tell you. She wanted me to explain it to you so here we go."

My fingers dug into the armrests of my chair and I braced for what I was about to hear.

Sireenia looked at me warmly. "Jacith used to be Jacob Withering. It's an old name with old roots and he wanted a new one. He didn't want ties to where he came from so he changed it to Jacith when he became a vampire. He lived and ruled under the normal hierarchy that each vampire does, with their Family that might be allied with other Families and so forth. This was all fine until Jacith met a witch one day. He fed from her and she turned him human. Jacith was fascinated by this. He loved the power it gave him and he had her turn him back into a vampire.

This began his long fall into sorcery and dark magic, but he kept his darkness from his vampire Family. They thought he used his magic for good, but he didn't. Even then his Family strove to protect the humans; they felt it would restore their own humanity so they wouldn't forget their true beginnings. They knew if they did forget it would only be a matter of time before all was lost. Madness and chaos would ensue. The slayers were created for this reason and then the decree occurred and hunters now hunt their own. Jacith wanted to win favor with the ruling Queen. He wanted to use her power for himself. He could use it for more magic so he created the Immortal prophecy.

He had hoped the legend of the Immortal, which would balance all powers in the universe, would make her happy. It did. She fell in love with him and he's slowly been draining her of all her power. He only created the thread of the Immortal, which vampires could get power from. He thought this was the Immortal."

There was so much I didn't understand, but I asked the one question that burned in my mind. "Is he still alive?"

She smiled, saddened. "He is and he is protected still by the Romah Family, the most powerful of all vampire Families. The Roane family is second to them, but they protect the Romah Family. They are their guardians. It's an alliance that has never been broken. Your vampire is hoping to destroy that alliance, but it'll create a divide instead. The Romah and Roane Family will bind together against him and they'll never see reason. They believe to this day that Jacith is a good sorcerer. They believe he created the Immortal for balance and equality."

"Why does the thread only go from human to human?"

"The Romah Family felt humans were sacred so Jacith made the thread to remain solely in humans. If a vampire did take on the thread inside of them, it would jump to the first human they encountered. He didn't inform the Queen that once the vampire fed from an Immortal, that vampire would have enormous power. They found this out after the first human and then protected the Immortal from that day forward. Of course, Jacith said that he hadn't known it would do that. After a hundred thousand years, they entrusted the Immortal to be defended by the Roane Family, which is why Lucas, their best hunter, became Talia's protector."

But I was the Immortal. I didn't have the thread. Jacith didn't intend for a true Immortal to ever come. The first guide had told me that.

She held my hand and squeezed it. "Jacith thought that a human with the mere thread of the Immortal would be the Immortal. He never realized the thread would take a life of its own and become an actual entity. That is what you are. You have been infused with the essence of life; this is why you make the undead alive. You take away their death."

I shook my head. There was so much information. I couldn't understand all of it. Then Sireenia whispered, "You will in time. You will know all. You will understand all."

"Why are you telling me this now?"

Her hand cupped my cheek. "You are so beautiful. You need to know this because Jacith is going to be your enemy. He is going to try and take the Immortal out of you. He will try to destroy it all."

"Why?" I felt gutted.

"Because you are not what he created. He cannot control you. He cannot control us. And he will fear you once the Romah and Roane Elders realize what you really are. "

"What do I do then?"

"You will fight him. You were created to destroy him. We were created to help you. He is too powerful for the world to have. He is the unbalance, not you."

When she put it like that, I wanted to crap my pants. "I'm not ready for that! I'm not ready for him! What if he comes tomorrow? What if he already knows? What am I going to do?"

My heart started to race and everything swirled around me. I tried concentrating on Sireenia, but she looked as if she were swimming around me. She flailed her arms at me. When I asked what was happening to me, my voice sounded in the distance and a baritone tone had taken root in my throat. Then my body felt like it was falling backwards.

I heard Saren in the distance, "Snap her out of it, Sire. We need her with us, not in the Orca."

"If she goes, then Stepianhas will calm her down."

A burst of energy zapped me. I felt like my insides had exploded, but I jerked upright from the chair, gasping and pounding my chest. My heart had stopped. When I didn't hear the constant beat again, I looked up, terrified. "What—what—what just happened?" I fell off my chair and scrambled to my feet. I pounded on my chest. "My heart stopped. My heart isn't beating. I don't—"

They stood before me. Sireenia had her hands folded in front of her. Saren had her hands on her hips. Then she snapped, "You're immortal. You're not going to die. Ever. Your heart is the least of your problems right now."

"Wha—but—my heart!" I gasped with each word. They didn't understand. They weren't human anymore. "I need to be normal. I need my heart to beat!"

They glanced at each other and a look was shared between them.

"Stop that! Stop looking at each other about me. Do something. You're all magical things. Make my heart beat again. Please." I nearly sobbed the last word. It felt like my world had changed. It was irreversible. Everything shifted in that moment and I didn't want it to happen. I didn't want to fight this guy. I didn't want to have to deal with the fact that my heart didn't beat like Emily's, Brown's, or Pippa's.

Then Saren stepped forward. She spoke with authority, "You're doing this to yourself. You stopped your heart. Only you can make it start again. Calm down. CALM!"

Everything stopped.

I stopped and I felt my body jerk upright. I stood at my highest height.

She took my shoulders then in her hands and looked me straight in the eyes. Her fire was mesmerizing. "You stopped it. You can make it start." Then she kept repeating that until I found myself mouthing the words with her. After a few minutes, I felt my heart start again.

Thump, thump, thump

"It's okay!" I exclaimed. "I'm okay. I'm going to be okay." But I wasn't. I had so much more to do and I wanted to cry. I wanted to bury my head in a pillow and make everything go away.

"I think that's enough for sharing time." Saren released my shoulders and sat in my vacant chair. She threw a blue-leathered leg over the side and pursed her lips.

"Hey, you changed your outfit back."

She shrugged. "It's my favorite. I don't care what you think."

"Oh."

Sireenia watched me during our exchange and glided forward now. "Are you okay, Davy?"

I jerked my shoulders in a casual shrug. I could be casual about this. They were. I could be one of them. Then I broke. "No! No, I'm not!"

She sighed.

Saren waved her away. "She'll be fine. She's a fighter. Besides, I have to work with her now."

"Are you sure that's a good idea? She seems fragile right now." Sireenia bit her lip as she watched me.

"She's fine. Go. Brood up something so we can disguise her power to that wolf. The sooner we can get her back, the better."

"Okay." But Sireenia glanced at me over her shoulder as she left.

"Catch!" Saren called out to me as I looked back at her. Something slammed into me and I flew against the wall.

I glared at her. "What was that about?"

She smirked and gestured at me. "Look at yourself."

I did. I was flat against the wall in mid-air. My mouth fell open. "Are you doing that?"

"You caught yourself. I bet you didn't dent the wall."

I let my body glide downwards. I asked as my feet touched the floor, "Was I supposed to?"

"Someone normal would've gone through three buildings. You barely touched the first wall. You're good, better than you think." Then she reared back to throw her power again. This time I saw it coming.

The power radiated from her toes and rose through her body. It built in power until she released it at me.

CHAPTER 14

"**D**o my eyes deceive me or is that your missing girlfriend's roommate down there? And is she sitting with a wolf?" Gavin glanced over his shoulder where Roane was sitting at his desk. Then he looked back down at the booth below.

Roane glanced up from his paperwork and stood beside his best friend. The view was massive, writhing bodies below, flashing lights everywhere, but he saw where Gavin had his eyes trained and there she was, Emily. She looked different, serious and gaunt, but there was a glow about her too. The guy next to her had a lean build with a round baby face, but his eyes weren't babyish at all. They had seen too much. He was scanning the nightclub, on the prowl with an intelligence that told Roane he wasn't there by accident.

Gavin grunted. "He's got balls being in your establishment."

Roane narrowed his eyes and watched how the wolf leaned over and placed a kiss on Emily's jaw. He lingered there, sending a possessive claim to the rest of the club. "He knows that he's being watched right now."

"Of course he's being watched. He's a wolf in enemy territory."

Roane walked back to his desk and grabbed a small dagger that he tucked into his pocket. "Come on. Let's get this over with." As they walked to the door, Roane held it open and then murmured in Gavin's ear as he passed by, "You know he's the Alpha, right?"

Gavin halted and wheeled around. "What? Why didn't you say something before?"

Roane shook his head with a small grin. He kept going and made his best friend follow at a slower pace. "He's here trying to get her scent. And I'm guessing that he knows who I am too."

"The roommate knows about you and Davy. I spilled the beans the last time I was there."

"You told me." And he had, followed by an apology every day since Davy had gone missing. It'd been three months and no one had a lead where she'd gone to. Gavin had included a detailed account of what had happened, but promised that she'd been fine when she shoved him out of her window. The roommate and a witch had been there with her, but no one could figure out what happened. Roane had listened to all the testimonies they gave to the police. Emily and the witch, along with another wolf, had been knocked unconscious. None of them could explain how Davy had gone. No vampire caught her scent. No wolf could either, but Roane had a very strong hunch that the Alpha had been persuaded to try again. If the Alpha wolf was in his club, he was at the end of the rope.

"You think he's here for a brawl?" Gavin asked in his ear, treading close behind him as they both weaved around vampires and drunken humans. Some were laughing. Some were drinking. Others were doing more.

"He might be the Alpha, but he's not stupid. He's outnumbered five hundred to one. Emily's desperate to find Davy." Then they turned one last time and the Alpha sensed them immediately.

He could smell Talia's blood, or the blood of her mother on him. It clung to the wolf like a third skin and it made his own stomach churn.

As they drew near the booth, Roane waited till Emily looked up. As soon as she did, she gasped and shrunk back in her seat. Gavin smiled brightly and slid in next to her. Roane sat beside him. They pushed the couple to the far end of the circular booth till the Alpha was directly across from Roane. Both of their gazes were locked on each other.

Emily glanced between them. She was nervous. Roane could smell it. He also felt her desperation. Her hand fell to the Alpha's lap and was gripped by his. He held it in a comforting hold and Roane grinned. "Should I give congratulations to the happy couple?"

Emily flushed and skirted further underneath the table.

He broke eye contact with the wolf and locked onto Emily who wanted to look anywhere, but at him. It was then, seeing a blush on her cheeks, that he knew she still had feelings for him.

The wolf's nostrils flared, smelling her desire, but he didn't comment. Both Gavin and Roane smelled it.

"Emily," Roane said softly, but with a twinge of authority in his voice. She shouldn't avoid this and he wanted to remind her of that. When she looked up and held his gaze, he knew she registered his meaning. She even sat up straight and squared her shoulders back. Her hand still held onto the wolf's hand with a death grip. "You know about Davy and me."

She cleared her throat and took a deep breath. "Yes. Yes, I do."

Gavin looked between them and then at the wolf. He rolled his eyes. "This is boring and awkward. Someone start talking or I'm leaving."

"Uh." Emily seemed at a loss for words. She shook her head and shrunk back in the seat.

Roane was taken aback. He remembered an assertive nerd from his classes on campus. He knew she'd taken a liking to him, but he also remembered how she was never at a loss for words. Davy had respect for her roommate, how she never feared tough situations or what to say, even if the truth was the hardest to deal with. This was not that girl. Then the Alpha held out his free hand and sat forward.

"My name is Pete Young."

Roane shook his hand, feeling strength and confidence. The Alpha was strong, the strongest he'd ever met in a wolf, but he was young. And he didn't know all the pieces, though he knew too much for Roane's liking.

"Lucas Roane. I own this nightclub."

"I know. We know. It's why we came here." Pete glanced around, a sense of unease teased at the edge of his surface. "I know that you and Emily know each other from college and that you were somewhat dating her roommate, Davy?" He looked to her for reassurance and she sighed and sat forward again.

"Do you know where Davy is?" Emily asked in a husky voice.

"I'm your last resort, aren't I?"

She jerked her head in a nod. "No one knows where she is. I can't get a hold of Kates. I don't know Davy's family and that blue lady can't find her either. She was freaking out the last time I talked to her. She said that no one could 'feel her on this world's aura' whatever that means."

"So you came to me." Roane nodded and caught Gavin's eye in the same movement.

'What are you thinking?' Gavin thought in his head.

Roane spoke to Emily, "And you've called the police?" He looked at Gavin. *'We need to get the Alpha out of here. He has the Immortal essence in him, Talia's mother. He can't know what we know about Davy.'*

Gavin's eyelid twitched, but no other muscle moved on his face. *'Didn't the police report say that he showed up at their room the day Davy disappeared? Do you think he has something to do with it?'*

Emily frowned, playing with a napkin on the table. "The police have no idea what happened. Davy was in the room with us and then it's like she just disappeared. Our dorm has video surveillance on all the exits and she's not in any of them."

Roane knew all of this. He read over every document, every witness testimony that the detectives had gotten from the event. None of it made sense to him except one item. It was tied to the Immortal. It was the only thing that made sense. If a vampire had been able to take her, he would've known by now. If another supernatural species had found out about her, he would've known too. He was linked to her and he agreed with the 'blue lady'. Davy wasn't nearby, maybe not even in the country or in their time line. The Immortal had infinite powers. She could be in another universe and he had no idea how to find her.

He smiled politely. "Unfortunately, I haven't heard from Davy for awhile before she went missing. We'd called things off because of, well for various reasons."

Emily ducked her head down and sucked in her breath. Pete glanced at her, but then understanding dawned. He jerked his eyes back up and stared at Roane. Lucas knew it was coming, felt the wolf sniffing through every layer of thought and emotion he had in him, but he steeled himself against the investigation. Yes, Pete knew there was history between Emily and Roane, but he was just now starting to guess the true nature of that history.

Then with a distant smile, Roane thrust Gavin from his head and met the Alpha full force. *'She didn't tell you the truth, did she?'*

Pete sat back, shocked and enraged. His lip started to quirk upwards in a growl. *'She told me you two were friends, nothing of what I'm getting from her now. Were you lovers? Did you throw her away once you were done as vampires always do? You discard people who care for you, treat them like garbage.'*

Roane's eyes narrowed. *'Emily had a crush on me. That was it. Your mate has never had any sort of relationship with me other than that of a classmate. That is all. We were not even friends. Search her mind. You'll find the truth.'*

'I don't go in her head unless she wants me to. I respect her privacy.'

A cruel smirk came over Roane and his eyes mocked. *'That's the biggest piece of bullshit I've ever heard a wolf tell me. You bulldoze your way through her head and heart, sniffing under every emotion she has, any memory from her past. You didn't find me because I'm telling you the truth. She had a school girl crush on me, still does apparently. And it means nothing to me.'*

Pete's eyes went feral and he surged to his feet.

Roane stood to meet him, calm as he smiled in his adversary's face. Gavin followed at a slower pace, but grinned in excited anticipation. He had a cocky glint to his eyes as he waited for the wolf to pounce. He thirsted for it even.

Emily sucked in her breath. The blood had drained from her face.

Gavin winked at her. "Don't worry, love. The two baddies need to figure out which is the alpha and who's the loser." Then his eyes found Pete's and he said with more promise, "Because there's always only one Alpha."

Pete drew back his thoughts and his fury was quickly gone. He forced a smile and looked down to grab Emily's hand. After he pulled her up and wrapped an arm around her shoulder, he laughed and forced a carefree note. "I can tell that Roane cared for Davy. If he knew where she was, he'd tell us. He misses her as much as you do." A sinister smile came over him as he thought, *'You're right about one thing. I can tell that Davy meant more to you than you want to admit. It's all over your thoughts. You're as desperate to find her as Emily is, but you're not as scared as her. You know more than you're telling. I intend to find out what that is.'*

Gavin narrowed his eyes. *'Go and pee somewhere else. This isn't your territory. It'd be a shame if a vampire decided to sneak a little taste from your lover. You know how powerful those spells can be, don't you? Or have you already tasted the last vampire that's been in her?'*

Pete snarled and showed his teeth.

"Pete!" Emily gasped as she clutched onto his arm.

Alerted by the sounds of a werewolf, the vampires surrounding them dropped their conversations and turned. They squared off against the werewolf.

Gavin taunted, "Everyone here knows what you are. They stayed away because you seemed that you were under friendly terms. Those terms are gone and even a wolf as powerful as you can't take everyone here, not when there's a hunter in the room."

Emily squeaked and fell down. Pete caught her with one arm as he glared across the table at both vampires. "I could kill both of you in a heartbeat, then thirty more before any of them could touch me."

"They'd get her." Roane narrowed his eyes and watched as Emily seemed to swoon unsteadily on her feet. *'She doesn't know who we are. If you hope to protect her, you need to tell her everything.'*

The Alpha drew back. *'You talk now as if you care for her. Before, you were disrespectful to her.'*

"Not everything I do will make sense to you," Roane chose his words carefully. He wanted the wolf to feel unbalanced. He didn't want the Alpha to start connecting dots.

Pete stood at his fullest height. "I think we should leave. I've gotten the answer that we came for anyway." He watched the vampires around them cautiously as he edged out of the booth and then down the aisle.

Roane caught Gregory's gaze, who had been standing in a far corner. He nodded and then gestured towards the wolf. Gregory bent his head.

Gavin watched Gregory follow them and chuckled. "Let's hope the Viking can jump rooftops. That's the only way he's going to be able to follow that wolf."

"He can." Roane turned away and saw Wren in another corner. She was wrapped around another female vampire.

Both stopped and watched the display for a second and then Gregory burst out laughing. Wren looked up, but then bent back to her lover's neck, sucking on it. The other vampire seemed unaffected, unaware that Wren had ever stopped and clutched the back of her head. She moaned as she pressed closer against her.

As they went back to Roane's office, Gavin helped himself to a drink. "What do you think of the wolf? He's a powerful young pup."

Roane went to his tinted windows and watched below. "He is strong, stronger than the old Alpha, but he's young."

"Human age, he's what? 30s?"

"At least." Roane frowned as Wren grabbed another female vampire and included her in their embrace. All three were quickly caressing, kissing, licking, and gaining more attention than Roane wanted his second right-hand vampire to obtain. When a male pressed into the group, Roane saw that Wren grabbed his head and shoved it against her breast. He latched on and kneeled with one of the other women.

Gavin stood next to him and lifted his glass in a salute. "Here's to Wren getting an orgy. She knows how to fulfill that need, huh?"

"Most of these vampires have crossed the world, pledging their loyalty to me. They came because of my reputation of an honorable hunter. That's not honorable. That's primal. We're above that."

"Oh come on. Looks to me that Wren's just stressed. She's letting out some of her tension. When's Tracey supposed to arrive?"

"You mean with my sworn enemy?" Roane couldn't stop a smile as he regarded his best friend.

Gavin opened his mouth, but it hung there, suspended. Then he laughed and shut it. "I forgot about that little detail. Sorry, mate. You know what you're going to have to do, right?"

"What's that?"

"Just rip the new hunter's head off his body and take his army as yours. It was yours anyway. The Elders forced a new hunter, because they want to kill the Immortal and you want to protect her. Such a trivial little difference, you know? I think all those vampires will be thankful that you're making them follow you. You're a much better leader than they could ever get and you know it. They know it. Hell, even the new hunter knows it."

Roane grew somber, but then a hard glint appeared in his eyes. "They chose what side they were on, as all of these vampires here have. They've chosen my side."

"Because they believe in what you believe in." Gavin finished his drink and spoke with gravity. "There's a civil war brewing in the vampire nation. Every one of us knows it and the Immortal is the reason for it. Half of them don't even believe she exists. They're here because you stand for the new age, for a different standard of our living. That's why they're here. For you, not for Davy. They don't even know who she is or why you've stood your ground against the Roane Elders."

"Don't forget the Romah Elders."

"Forget those old bastards. They're so ancient; I could snap them in half. They've grown rusty, gotten too used to being protected by the Roane Family."

"Jacith is aligned with them."

Gavin narrowed his eyes at his best friend, who stared at the club below. "Maybe it's time for Jacith to end, huh?"

Roane smirked and now looked at Gavin. "And who's going to do that? Jacith is old. He's powerful as a vampire and he's powerful as a sorcerer. He'd snap you in half."

"I'm not saying that I have all the answers. I'm just telling you my opinion of them. I'm sure I'm not alone. If you were to declare war against the Romah Family, I'm sure you'd have more than my Family behind you, maybe even every vampire Family in the nation."

"Not the Mori Nation."

Gavin opened his mouth, but snapped it shut. "They don't count. They're freaks of nature."

Roane barked out a laugh, but stopped. "Are you serious? You know that's where Lucan is hiding. He might even be one of them by now."

"The birthing baby vampire magic circus? No. He's not one of them." Gavin's eyes grew dangerous. "No, no. He's not one of them. He's human. And he wants them to kidnap Davy and force the thread from her. Everyone knows the lore. It'll attach to the closest human. Oh no. Lucan will stay human because he wants to be the next Immortal."

Roane closed his eyes as he heard his worst nightmare. Davy would die. His brother would become the Immortal and he'd have too much power than any being should have in a lifetime. There was a reason why it chose the next holder of the thread, but according to Davy, she wasn't the thread. She was the Immortal, a prophecy no vampire had been foretold about. And that was one of the reasons why his former Family's Elders refused to believe what he had told them. There was no prophecy stating the thread would become an actual entity. The thread was just there. It jumped from human to human and they were always protected by it so no vampire could obtain that power.

"They're stupid. They refuse to listen to me," Roane bit out. "You're right. A new order has to come in power. They refuse to hear what I've told them and it'll be the death of them. She's not a thread. She is something we know nothing about."

Gavin's finger clenched around his glass and it shattered. He was unfazed by the broken shards of glass in his hands. "She might be missing right now, but she's coming back. And something tells me that she's coming back with a vengeance. Your girl will be okay, no matter how long she's away."

Roane closed his eyes. He wanted to believe what he heard. "Let's hope."

"No matter what we think, we have another problem on our hands. That Alpha has to be dealt with."

"He's a complication that I didn't foresee," Roane admitted as he remembered Emily's haunted eyes. No, he saw how she had trusted him. He'd been her last resort and she thought he could produce Davy, no matter how unrealistic that wish had been.

Gavin chuckled and turned for another drink. "Takes a strong man, wolf or human, to bring your lover to a place and ask for help from someone she's got her 'knight in shining armor' fantasy with. I'm surprised he took it that well."

"He didn't know." Roane felt his stomach twist. "She lied to him about her feelings and she kept them hidden from him. He thought I'd had a few classes with her. He didn't know about her feelings or how she'd handled the truth about Davy and me."

"Which she still hasn't." Gavin turned back and looked out the window with Roane. They stood shoulder to shoulder. "She heard about it before Davy went missing, but she hasn't seen it. It's not a reality with her, not yet. And, mate, she had more than a crush on you. I think the girl thought she was in love with you."

"Most humans have stupid idealistic fantasies. They live in a delusional world."

"Regardless, the lass was hurt. I wonder how the wolf is going to handle that. It can't be easy, knowing that your mate has feelings for someone else and a different species too."

"They're not real." Roane turned away and grabbed a bottle of bourbon.

"They're not real to you, but they're real to her."

"Shut up."

Gavin grinned. "Oh come on. You've never had your heart shattered by someone that you only fantasized about? Fantasized so hard that you tricked yourself into thinking she was real?"

"Maybe when I was human?"

"She *is* human. So is Davy." Gavin watched his mate and saw that Roane gave nothing away. He never did. Then Gavin clinked his glass with Roane's. "Here's to us. Breaking hearts and breaking blood. There's going to be a load spilled with this war coming on."

Roane didn't comment, but gripped his glass tighter. Gavin was right, something that Roane tried not to think about every day, but he couldn't get Wren's voice out of his head. She told him that they'd need Davy and that they'd need her powers. He knew it was true. If they were going to survive the future, they'd need a miracle. They'd need the Immortal.

CHAPTER 15

Saren was crouched in the corner of the room. I was on the opposite side and we stared at each other, waiting for the other to attack. My eyes were locked on her. I watched every breath she took, every twitch the hairs on her arm made, even how the iris in her eye widened a bit. When the skin at the corner of her mouth stretched out, I flung myself in the air and tucked my feet in to spring off the wall as I flew down to her.

She was ready. She ducked her head down and rolled over till she was on her back. Then her hand came up and zapped me, just as I was about to tackle her.

"Ouch!" I glared as I thrust my body through the air and back to my corner. I rubbed my stomach. "That one hurt."

"You were trying to hurt me."

"I wanted to tackle you."

"You wanted to overtake me." She stood, her body fluid, gliding upwards till she walked towards me. The fire in her eyes had vanished, but two small embers had been ignited. I watched, always amazed, as it built slowly at first until it was a rolling fire. Then she blinked and shook her head. "You can't think about how you're going to sneak up on me. It won't work with me. It won't work with Jacith."

"Why do I have to be the one who fights him? You're better than me. You should do it." I stood and brushed off my pants. The room we had been training in hadn't been cleaned from the animals that had been in there before. Piles of straw were everywhere and they clung to my pants. Not Saren's. Her pants were spotless. "Are you sure there isn't poop in here from before? You said animals were kept in here."

She rolled her eyes and led the way out the door and through a tunnel. "I already told you that it had been cleaned a long time ago. The straw was put in there for the same reason we use that room, training. It's an old castle. There's a lot of history. Knights used to go in there. And no, you're the Immortal. I am not. You are supposed to be better than me."

Just then we passed another hallway where a display of armor was hung on the wall. I could never stop the shivers when I went past it and I felt them again. The place was old. Saren was right, the history hung in the air. It suffocated me at times, but I missed my own history. I missed my old life. "When can I go back?"

Saren pushed open a wooden door with her back and glared at me. "I told you, when you can hide from the Alpha. He came earlier than we anticipated and you were supposed to be further along in your powers."

Sireenia looked up from a counter as she stirred something in a bowl. A bright smile lit her face and she tucked a long braid behind her ear. She left a trail of flour on her cheek. "How's she doing?"

"She's blocking me. She's blocking herself. It's like she doesn't want to progress," Saren grumbled as she hopped on a stool at the counter. "What are you making?"

"Chocolate chip cookies. Davy, you like these, don't you?"

My finger had been raised in the air, ready to swipe some of the batter when I was caught by the look in Sireenia's eyes. The uncertainty and eagerness shook me for a moment. Those were human emotions and I'd grown used to not seeing Saren or Sireenia as human. Magic oozed from them in every word, emotion, or look. They told me that they were once human and it surprised me when I saw moments such as this one that showed their humanity.

I smiled back. "I love these cookies. Kates used to buy the premade batter and that's all we would eat sometimes."

"The batter?" Sireenia paled. "You mean you didn't bake them? I thought you were supposed to bake them?"

Saren swore under her breath. "Don't worry about it, Sire. You're fine. You're being more amicable than she is."

"Hey!" I stole some batter and turned as I tasted it to glare at my trainer. It seemed that was all I did with Saren now. "What's that supposed to mean?" It felt like an insult.

"You know what that means. Why won't you transition? It's like you don't want to be the Immortal. Why don't you want to be the Immortal?" She shot to her feet and rounded the counter. Her body had stiffened, ready for a fight.

I stared at her. "Wha—huh? I don't want to be the Immortal? Why do you say that?"

"Because you don't! You hold back on every training exercise I've put you through. The only thing that you don't hold back is protecting yourself. I've sent missiles at you and you evade them. You've acclimated inside. Your power is complete, but you don't want to admit it. Are you blocking yourself? You must be. I don't understand you. This is why the Immortal should never have ascended into a human being."

"I don't agree with that." Sireenia put down the bowl and spoon. "Saren, please watch what you're saying."

"Why? It's true. We've done so much for her, fought so much, sacrificed, bled for her. And this is the end result? A human who doesn't want it? I lost my humanity for the thread, but—" Saren threw her hands in the air and bolts of fire slammed against the walls. A mural caught fire, but Sireenia waved her hand in the air and it was extinguished immediately.

"The Immortal chose her. Davy is the one who will stop Jacith. She can make everything correct. She *will* change it all."

With narrowed eyes, I watched as Sireenia held Saren's arms and tried to calm her, but Saren shook her head and broke free. As she walked to the door, I realized something that I had never even considered. "You guys had the thread before, didn't you?"

They weren't witches, but they came from witchcraft. Saren had told me before. And they weren't vampires or werewolves or anything else. She said that Roane wouldn't know who they were, but the way they talked about the Immortal, as if they had first-hand knowledge. That meant only one thing. They had been the humans who had held the thread before me.

I gulped.

That meant that I could meet Talia at any moment. And the idea sent my heart racing.

Both stopped and looked at me. It was like a blanket had been pulled off and I saw the relief in both of their eyes. Sireenia was the first one to respond. "It changes you, when you've had the thread in you for so long. I had it in the beginning of time. Saren had it in the 1800s. You go through a vortex when it leaves you."

"It feels like you're getting your heart pulled out of you through your throat when the thread jumps out of you."

"Or when it's forced out of you." Sireenia grew quiet as she looked down at her hands.

I saw the pain in her and wondered who had taken the thread from her, but Saren distracted me. "How did you know that? About us?"

How could I not, but then I realized that I wasn't sure how I knew it. "I don't know. It was just a feeling. You both talk about the Immortal as if you've had first-hand experience."

Before I finished talking, Saren zapped me. The bolt of power hurdled through the air, but I looked up and everything slowed in that instant. I saw it coming, but at a snail's pace. I deflected it and sent it into a wall. Then I looked up again and saw Saren in the air, soaring at me. Her hands were outstretched and ready to let loose two more bolts of power at me. I sidestepped her too. When she landed on the floor, her bolts shattered the floor beneath her, and I grabbed her collar. The floor crumbled underneath her while I lifted her in the air and kicked off the ground. I sent us both through the air to land in the opposite corner.

Sireenia watched where we had been. Her mouth hung open and her hands had lifted to her cheeks. Then it all stopped. Everything snapped back in place. They were no longer in slow motion and Saren stumbled backwards as she fell to the ground.

"Oh my goddess." Sireenia rushed to Saren's side. Both of them looked at me.

I grimaced as I saw the questions and shock in their eyes. Then I saw their mysticism and knew they had never thought I would transition, not completely. I swallowed that back. Their lack of faith in me shouldn't have been surprising.

"You *have* transitioned!" Saren shot to her feet. "When? How? Have you been like this the whole time? Has this been a waste of our time?"

Sireenia grew quiet.

"Are you kidding me?" How could she even think those things? "I didn't know until now. I had no idea when whatever happened. I just knew that something clicked in me and I knew both of you had been thread-holders. That was it and then you're throwing yourself at me. What am I supposed to do? I thought you wanted me to defend myself."

"Can you control it?" Saren stood with her hands ready at her side.

Sireenia stood beside her and tightened her robe. She glanced from Saren to me. Then she stepped forward. "Davy, it is very important to tell us, can you control your powers?"

"You mean: can I do this stuff at will? Not really, but sometimes. Sometimes I can do it and sometimes I can't." I shrugged. "When I really want something to happen, it happens. I wouldn't bank on it, though."

"Why could you stop me now and you couldn't before? I've been training you for three months. I've been hitting you with my powers for that long and you've been taking it?"

"They didn't really hurt." Even though they had and my body

had been swollen the entire time. "I don't know, maybe I was just tired of it. Maybe I was distracted by something else. I have no idea."

"What were you thinking before Saren tried to attack you? I saw a look on your face. What was it?" Sireenia stepped forward. Her gaze was intent on me.

"I have no idea. I thought about you guys, what you were, and then I looked up and Saren's coming at me. That's all I remember."

"No, you had a different look. When you thought about us, you were surprised. When Saren attacked you, you were annoyed. She distracted you from a thought. What was it? What were you thinking between those two things? Think, Davy."

"I wasn't. Really. You guys were talking about vortexes and the thread being taken out of you. Then," I shrugged. "I have no idea."

"I felt pain from you." Sireenia tilted her head to the side. "I can feel emotions, not as well as you, but I felt sadness from you. Then panic. What were you scared of?"

"Or who."

"Who are you scared of?"

Both of them watched me. I wondered if they could hear thoughts too.

I shrugged again. "I have no idea. I just know that I haven't felt normal for a while." Not since the last time I had seen Roane when we had talked in the library and he left me.

"There! What are you thinking right now?" Sireenia surged towards me and her hands grabbed my arms.

The moment her hands touched me, a surge of memories rushed through me. The first time I saw Roane in the library, when I saw him in my dorm. Then he stood behind me when Sheila asked if he was my date. A rush of adrenalin went through me as I remembered our first kiss, when I slammed my mouth against his. And then I remembered when we made love. I'd never felt such a desperate fever before him.

"Oh dear." Sireenia wrapped me in her arms before she turned towards Saren. "It's him. It's the vampire."

I tensed and expected a biting comment from her, but it never came. Instead, I heard the door close a second later and felt Saren's absence more than I'd ever felt her presence. I pulled away from Sireenia. "What was it? Is she upset?"

"No, she's not. She's feeling her own memories." She moved to hold my face in both of her hands and then she closed her eyes.

Warmth started to pulsate through me. It spread from her fingertips into my skin, down my neck, arms, waist, and all the way to my toes. She was taking away my pain and giving me a different emotion, one of fondness. It felt good and I closed my eyes before I pulled away. "No. That's not real. It's not right that I take that from you."

"You do it all the time. You take away others' pain so I'm taking yours."

"You can't have my pain. You have enough of your own."

"I don't take it into me. Watch."

As I did, Sireenia moved back and held out her arms. She smiled and then closed her eyes. A moment later a coat transformed over her skin. It was a second layer of skin, but white. As soon as it was done growing over her it cemented to her skin and she opened her eyes with that same smile. Then she shook her body. The white skin fell away and left behind her normal skin with a rosy glow over it.

"See?" she asked. "I have some tricks up my sleeve too."

"I don't even know what I would look like if I could do that. I'd be like a quilt or something."

"I was empathic when I was human. My ability has progressed since I held the thread in me and since I lost the thread."

"What happened to you when the thread left you? Roane told me that every person dies once the thread leaves them."

"I did die, but I didn't. The human soul died, as it should, but we passed on to a different realm. There's a part in us, all of us, that connected with the Immortal and the essence of it gave us a different life. This is where we all go. This is where you will go too, I suppose."

"How many are there of you?"

"The older threads, what I call myself, have developed themselves into these bodies. I chose this body to look like this, the way

Saren also looks how she wants to. We don't have real bodies. You can touch us and see us, but no one else can; only someone who is connected to the Immortal thread can. The magic is unparalleled. It is unimaginable, but we do know certain rules and one of them is that the Alpha werewolf cannot know who you are. You must be able to hide yourself to him."

So I needed to fight an ultimate sorcerer-vampire. I was being trained by some type of witch spirits and I needed to hide from an amped-up werewolf. And they still wondered why I wasn't sold on embracing the Immortal inside of me.

"My life sucks."

Sireenia patted my shoulder. "Everything will be fine. I can feel that inside of you too. You already know what you have to do." When she reached the door, she looked back. "She hasn't let go of the human world yet so you won't meet Talia as one of us. She still holds on there."

I closed my eyes when pain sliced through me, like I'd been gutted.

"And Davy?" Sireenia smiled, an ethereal look came over her as she stood with her white hair in a braid over one shoulder and dressed in a white hanging robe. "You mustn't assume the obvious all the time except one thing."

Dread filled me. "And what's that?"

"You're strongest when you're with him. You showed us that now. Go to him. I think you're ready."

"What about the werewolf?"

The door closed behind her, but I heard her answer, "I think you're ready for that too."

My mouth dropped. I hadn't been ready ten minutes ago and now everything changed? And how was I even going to get back?

I gulped. "Saren?"

CHAPTER 16

Saren and I left the castle, walked down a wooded pathway, and then she clasped my arm. "Take us back."

"What? You do it."

"You do it. Sire thinks you're ready so you need to be able to do this. Take us back."

"I have no idea where we are."

"It doesn't matter. You know where you want to go. Take us there."

"But—" My mouth hung open. How was I supposed to do that? Then I heard a voice in my head. It was a whisper and it felt strangely familiar, too familiar. *'Think of where you want to go, where you want to be, then wish it and it will be.'*

"What?!" I snapped, spinning in a circle. The voice was in my head, but it sounded so real. "I thought I was done hearing voices in my head and now someone's back."

Saren grabbed my other arm. "What are you talking about?"

"Someone just told me to wish and it will be. It's annoying. You're all annoying. You want to know why I don't want to be the Immortal, it's because of this! I have voices in my head. I have freaky witch spirits telling me that I can teleport myself somewhere and I have no idea how to do it." But as I spoke, everything started to move around us. We were in the eye of a tornado and time was being sucked around us, whipping, snarling.

Then the voice whispered again, '*She can't hear me, she should not. I am here for you, Davina. I always will be. You are never alone.*'

Okay—creepy. And before I could reflect on that thought, something snapped us away. It was like a hand reached into our vortex and shook us into a different vortex. Before I could shriek from surprise, we'd fallen to the ground and I hissed from the pain.

"What was that?" I turned for Saren, but she wasn't there. "Saren? Where are you? This is not funny. Did you do that?" Scrambling to my feet, I couldn't see or feel her. She wasn't close to me at all. I didn't feel her presence. It was like she was dead, but she was a witch spirit so I wasn't that surprised. Well, a witch spirit with some extra oomph to her.

"We're close."

A gruff voice spoke behind me and I whirled around to see a blonde vampire sitting in front of a fire. She was hunched over with her elbows braced on her knees. A bag was placed behind her. It was slightly open. Some pictures poked out from the bag along with a yellow cardigan and a beaded necklace.

"Fine," she sighed and stood lithely in one motion. When she turned around, I found myself staring into Talia's face, but it wasn't. This was a vampire, not the thread holder. She was older, maybe five years older, but the same hazel eyes stared through me, hardened. Instead of Talia's red hair flying around her, this girl had blonde hair pulled back in a tight bun tucked behind at the base of her head. She bent down and pulled a long sleeve armor shirt over her. The front of it had a black wolf painted over it with green eyes that seemed to see right through me. As I moved to the left, they watched and then followed when I went to the right.

Freaky.

Suddenly, she walked right through me. I gasped, braced for the contact, but nothing happened. The girl walked straight through me as if I was air. Then I realized I was air. I wasn't there in body, but in mind. I had no idea why I would want to be there, but I turned with the intention of following the girl when a shadow jerked away from the fire.

The movement caught my eye and I whirled back around, but I didn't see anything except the flames that waved back and forth in a smooth rhythm. I started to turn again, but there it was. The shadow jerked forward and this time I was able to catch where it went. I focused all my attention on it.

"Who are you?" I asked. Was this an actual shadow or a ghost or a witch spirit?

It didn't say anything. It didn't move. It glimmered there above the bag. Some embers in the fire moved in that moment and flames exploded, the sky was illuminated for a second. I saw a face in the shadow and they looked downwards. It was focused on the bag, so much that I drifted closer so I could look at the bag too. Glancing back up, I could no longer make out the shadow, but I could still feel it. The presence was strong, so strong, and I closed my eyes. I let myself feel what this shadow wanted me to feel.

Urgency. Desperation. And such clear concentration that I was jerked out of my trance-like state. The thing wanted me to look in the bag and if it could've told me in person, it would've been screaming at me.

"Tracey, where are you going?"

I jerked around. She was coming back. Talia's sister was almost to the bag, reaching down.

'Oh god.' I sucked in my breath and snatched the bag before she could. Everything whirled around me again and I knew I'd broken through the vortex. She couldn't see me before, but she did now and she was pissed. Her eyes went from shock to a murderous rage.

"Hi! Sorry!" I squeaked and then closed my eyes again. '*Vacuum away. Vacuum away. Roane. Go to Roane! Go to Roane!*' I tried to command my Immortal insides and as Tracey's rough hands scraped my skin, the wind picked me up again and I was back in the same tornado.

When I landed this time, it took me a minute before I realized where I was. It was quiet, too quiet in the room, but there was loud music below me. It sounded like a bass booming underneath my feet and when I looked around, I saw a couple of leather couches, a bar, a desk, and three walls made from glass. Then I realized that it was the sound of bass under me. I was in Roane's office at the Shoilster. Then I gulped, oh goodness.

Just then the door opened, the bass sounded clearer, and I looked up.

Wren took two steps inside and froze. The papers in her hand ripped apart. She couldn't hide the terror in her eyes before I saw it. And then it was gone. She stood at her highest height and her leather corset creaked from the movement. The papers were forgotten when she moved her hand behind her back.

"What is that?" I lurched forward.

"What are you doing here?" She looked around, but no one was there. The door was closed. There was no escape.

"It's just you and me and whatever you're hiding from me."

"I'm not hiding anything from you."

I narrowed my eyes and studied her. I studied the vein that had started to pop in her neck. "Yes, you are. What's in those papers?"

"Nothing. They're for Roane, not you. And what are you doing here? I should be yelling for him right now."

I swallowed and looked back to her eyes. They were frosty now, but I narrowed mine and went inside of her. It was an old empathic trick. I sensed the disarray inside. Wren was relieved I was back, pissed that she was relieved, and another part was in chaos because she smelled something familiar, too familiar for her to handle.

I pulled out and then sniffed the air. Nothing.

"What do you have?" Her eyes looked frantic.

I lifted the bag. "This? This is what you smelled?"

"Wha—get out of my head!" She grabbed the bag from me. Her long curls whipped against my head as she moved back. "Do you know whose this is?"

"I'm the one who took it. Do you?"

Wren blanched and jerked backwards, stumbling to the door. I watched as she went through it, but gaped as the door shut behind her. The almighty hoity-toity vampiress had just ran from me—me! She was scared of me for some reason. My gaze shifted to the bag. I doubted she was terrified of a bag so that left only one possibility. She knew the owner of the bag. Wren was scared of Tracey, not me. Who was Tracey to Wren? How did they know each other?

"Davy?" Roane was frozen in the doorway. His gaze was riveted to me.

Oh god, he looked good. His hair had been buzzed again, but it was how he was dressed that had my knees buckling. He had on black dress slacks matched with a black soft cotton buttoned shirt tucked inside. Roane looked like a business owner, one that oozed sex appeal from extreme confidence. And he didn't care, which made him even hotter. He looked so different from the college student he'd been in the beginning.

I swallowed, my throat was tight. "Hey," I choked out with a small wave. When I saw that my hand was trembling, I stuffed it behind me.

I didn't know what to say. He didn't move. He didn't speak. And my feet were glued to the floor. Maybe I shouldn't have come. Maybe Sireenia had gotten it wrong and I wasn't my strongest around him. "I shouldn't have come. I'm sorry."

"No!" Roane jerked forward, but stopped. His hand was in the air. He reached out to me, but he didn't move or say anything more. A myriad of emotions flashed over his face before his hand moved back to his side. "Where were you?"

My eyebrows shot up. That was what he settled with? No hug? No kiss? No 'I missed you and was so worried about you?' My blood started to boil. "Are you serious? That's all you have to say to me?" Maybe I hadn't been gone that long? And maybe Roane hadn't missed me as much as I hoped he would.

"I—" He opened his mouth, but shut it without saying anything, again.

The door burst open behind him and Gavin came inside. He flashed me a smile. "Well, well, well. The prodigal superpower is back again. Where've you been, darling?" Then he opened his arms wide to lift me in the air.

Finally. Someone was happy to see me.

He twirled me in a circle.

I laughed and glared at the same time. "Put me down." But it was nice to know someone missed me.

Gavin set me back down and glanced over his shoulder. "Aren't you going to give your girl a kiss? You've been worrying enough to give your immortal body an ulcer. And a splendid body he has, Davy. He really does, but then again, I think you already know this."

I felt him patting my shoulder and knew he was trying to reassure me, but it wasn't helping. Roane still hadn't moved. He seemed normal now, no shock residing. His eyes were clear and focused on me, but I didn't see what I had hoped I would. Gavin was wrong, Roane hadn't missed me. If he was worried, it was about the Immortal being gone. It was all about the Immortal, not me.

"Gavin, can you give us a moment?"

"Sure." Gavin flashed another smile and winked at me before he left.

I remembered being annoyed with him the last time I saw him but now I didn't want him to go. He wore a white track suit that still gave him the athletic look, but somehow he made it look natural. All vampires should dress like that. When the door closed behind him, I wondered what color his track suit would be the next time I saw him. Then Roane cleared his throat and I no longer cared.

"You've been gone for three months." He moved around me to his desk.

We brushed shoulders as he moved past, but it wasn't close enough. I sucked in a breath and felt my body yearn for his touch. When it didn't happen, I felt cheated, but I turned and regarded him. "Has it been that long?"

Roane turned his back to me and looked out over the dance floor. "What happened that day? Gavin was there. He said you were fine. You were with your roommate and a witch. I've spoken to Emily and I've read the police reports from the witch and wolf. None of them know what happened and there's no video of you leaving."

Wow, the police had been called. "Emily's mate has Immortal essence in him. He was made with magic and I had to leave. He would've sensed the Immortal in me and tried to drain me. I might not have been able to control myself and I was scared of what could've happened. I could've killed everybody. So I left."

"Left where?" He turned now with his eyes narrowed.

I tried to sense inside of him, but was blocked. I could've pushed through, but it didn't take away the fact that Roane didn't want me in his head. He was guarded against me and I realized that he didn't trust me. Pain flooded me at that thought. I felt a knife to my gut.

"Where did you go, Davy?"

I sucked in my breath and blinked back tears. It shouldn't hurt that much, but it did.

"Where did you go? You said you left, but there's no footage of you leaving. Did you disappear into thin air? Can you do that now?"

He was so cold. I shivered in his office and wrapped my arms around myself. "It's an Immortal thing that I didn't know I could do. I came back once I figured out how to control it, not that I really can, but I think I'm figuring it out."

"You came back? You came back here?" Roane still stood in front of the glass wall, as far away from me as possible.

"I came here. I wanted to see you. I know that I'm stronger when I'm with you. I can control my powers better." I stopped because he didn't look convinced. He looked alarmed, but what was wrong about that? I hadn't expected any of this from him. He should've been happy I was back. He shouldn't be cautious.

"But where did you go?"

"I don't know, not really. I was in some castle somewhere."

"Alone?"

"I—yes." I had no idea why I kept Saren and Sireenia a secret, but if he was being cautious then I would too.

"And you decided to come back now?"

"No." Why wouldn't he understand? "I couldn't come back

because I didn't know how. I couldn't control my powers and I don't know what to do about Emily's mate. He can't know I'm the Immortal. I don't know why he can't know, but I just know that he can't. It wouldn't be good if he did." And I was rambling like an idiot. *'Smooth move, Davy. Just remind him that you're still a dork and he really won't see what he liked about you before.'*

Roane cracked a grin.

My eyes popped out. "You can hear my thoughts, but you won't let me hear yours?"

Everything about him relaxed in that moment and he came around the desk with a smile. "I had to make sure it was you and not someone else. Jacith is a powerful sorcerer. He could do this. I'm sorry that I hurt you."

"What?" I glared. "Not fun."

But then it didn't matter. Roane moved close and folded me against his chest. He hugged me tight. The fight, the tension, the hurt all rolled out of me in that moment. Everything slipped away and I was wrapped in warmth again. With my hands fisted in his shirt and my forehead pressed against his chest, I mumbled out, "What made up your mind?"

"Only you would worry about me seeing you as a dork. No imposter could be that good." He rested his cheek on the top of my head and held me tighter. "It's good to have you back."

I felt his relief then. He *had* been worried, enough to grow ulcers as Gavin had teased. And then I felt desire burst inside of me. Nothing else mattered. It started low, in the pit of my stomach and spread out. It spread fast, shooting through me and then I was wet between my legs. The need throbbed there. It was powerful, so powerful that I was blind to everything else. Without thinking, I lifted my head, arched my back, and climbed up his body.

Roane grabbed the back of my thighs and anchored them around his waist. His hand caught my neck and tilted my head back. His lips brushed mine and I groaned. I needed more. As he touched them again, it was agonizing. He was gentle when I wanted him to dominate.

"Yep, they're getting along just fine."

Gavin's voice interrupted us and Roane growled. "Out!" His voice was low, so low it sounded like an animal and I knew his vampire side had come to the forefront.

"I'm going to be sick."

Wren wasn't far behind Gavin. The two ignored the warning and came further into the room. Gavin perched on the couch while Wren went to the glass wall and peered out. The door opened one more time and Gregory came through. His shoulders almost didn't fit, but he stooped down and shifted sideways.

'They aren't going anywhere.'

I felt Roane's reluctance as he let me down, but he held my elbow and lifted me to the opposite couch from Gavin. My legs weren't able to stand so I was grateful for his help. As I collapsed on the couch, my heart was racing. I pressed my sweaty palms between my knees and felt them throbbing, pulsating from need. Gavin gave me a knowing look and I ducked my head. I couldn't control my body.

Roane shot me a dark, primal look underneath his eyelids, but turned to the group. "The Immortal took her away. I assume that Emily called out for her mate and he was approaching the room. Davy feared that he would've attacked her and she wouldn't have been able to control herself. She worried that the Immortal in her would've reacted and killed people she didn't want to kill."

"So where was she?" Wren clipped out.

"Davy doesn't know where she was, but she came back once she could figure out how to get back." Roane gazed at the vampiress steadily for a moment before she lowered her gaze. Then he glanced at the rest with authority. "That's all we need to know. I trust her and she's right. The Alpha would've known who she was so Davy did the right thing in disappearing. He still can't know who she is."

Gavin growled, "The wolves want to take over. They always have. It's why they created him and it's why he's here. They know something about the Immortal – otherwise he wouldn't be here. His pack comes from across the ocean."

"Their ancestors originate from where Talia grew up," Gregory said as he watched his master.

Roane didn't blink. "Talia came from a gypsy family. They had no set place."

"Where did her mother die?" I felt all the desire drain from my body. Any talk about Talia would do that. I just felt empty now.

"In Veneto. Talia's roots are the Sinti gypsies. They had settled there when her mother was killed."

"And when the thread went to Talia," Gavin finished.

"Does it matter where he came from? He's here now and he's a pain in the ass. It's all nice and not really lovely that Davy's back, but I don't care about where Roane's ex's mother died or where she became the thread holder or where the Alpha is from. He's here and so is Davy. What's the next step? Hide her?"

"What? No." I couldn't leave my friends.

Roane watched me throughout the conversation and measured me with his eyes. "You said that you could control your powers, can you? What's going to happen when he meets you?"

I gulped as I felt all of their attention on me. The air was heavy in the room. "I think I can. I know I can. It'll be fine when I meet him. It will, I promise. He won't be able to detect anything in me. I won't let him."

"Really?" Wren scoffed. "Because I can 'detect' it right now. You're not the same. You came back weird and there's something extra in your smell."

I wrinkled my nose up. There was? How did I smell now? "What do you mean?"

"It's not lemons, if that's what you're asking." She rolled her eyes. "You're different. That's all I can say."

"You're stronger." Gavin spoke for her. His eyes were grave now and I was reminded of the first and last time I'd met him. He was dangerous then and seemed more dangerous now.

"I am?"

Gregory shifted in the background and remained quiet.

"You were strong before, but you hid it. There's nothing more for you to hide behind. You are just strong now. There's no weakness in you anymore, none that I can see."

"He's right. They're all right." Roane sighed. "You *are* different, Davy. It's why I didn't think you were you, but you said you could control your powers. You're going to have to. Or you will have to stay hidden. No one can know who you are. The Alpha *really* can't know who you are."

"So how are you going to do that?" Wren sat on the edge of Roane's desk.

I looked at her and had no idea how to answer that question.

CHAPTER 17

"Are you sure about this?" Roane asked when he showed me to a guest bedroom at the Shoilster.

So many vampires had come to town to join him that his home was full and the extra rooms at the Alexander were all taken. Even though the Shoilster and Alexander were a nightclub and restaurant, Roane had rooms built into them and tunnels around them. They were perfect to hide the entire army, but he kept a few rooms for his closest allies. Since my room was right next to his, I knew it meant something. They were attached by a door in the wall.

Was I sure? Yes. Did I want to? No. I sighed and turned back. He looked good, so good, but there was so much distance between us. We'd been excited before and had jumped at each other, but I'd had time to remember something that would guarantee more distance between us. Talia.

So I nodded. "Yeah, I'm sure."

"Okay." He glanced at the door. "You know where I'll be if you want to talk."

Talk. Yes. We needed to do some of that too.

"Davy." He sounded hesitant. "I thought we were fine. Before, in the room."

"I know, but I have to wrap my head around things." Not to

mention that I'd forgotten about the day I'd met Gavin when waves had hit me with the same urgency I'd felt by the fire and from the shadow. The shadow pulled me there. It wanted me to find Tracey's bag. It was the same voice that had assaulted me the day before I'd disappeared.

'Tell Roane of my daughter.'

I wasn't stupid. That shadow was connected to Tracey. It was connected to a child. And it was connected to Roane. Common factor? Talia. I'd forgotten about it amidst everything, but it came back to me. As I glanced at my bag, I knew that Roane smelled Tracey from it. Wren had bolted from the room because of it. Why was Roane ignoring it? What did that mean?

"Things?"

I looked back at him. There was sadness to him. I felt the history from it. Oh yes. He knew that I had connected with Tracey. He was aware her bag was in my possession and he knew I had something else to tell him. Did he know it was about Talia? Did he know it was her child?

Oh hell. Why postpone it?

I dumped the bag out on the bed.

"What are you doing?" Roane jerked behind me. There was panic in his voice.

I started to shift through her things.

"Stop." He caught my hand. "Please stop."

I yanked my hand away and kept looking. Clothes. Weapons. A journal. Little remnants here and there. And then my finger touched something small, thin, and I knew it was a picture. I felt it in my gut. This was what she wanted me to find. Intense pain flooded me, dread formed in my stomach, but I gritted my teeth and lifted the photograph.

It was of Talia holding an infant to her cheeks. She was smiling to the camera. Love exuded from her. The baby's eyes were open a fraction, but it was enough. They had the same eyes. All eyes were blue at birth, but this one had hazel eyes. This one was the same as her mother's. That also told me that this child wasn't an ordinary child. There was magic in her.

"Oh my god," Roane said beside me. He took the picture from me and lifted it for closer inspection.

I couldn't watch. I didn't want to see tears in his eyes or feel whatever he was feeling. I just knew that his love for her would be renewed. I couldn't handle it so I turned away. I felt gutted when I spoke. "She came to me before I disappeared. She wanted me to tell you about her child. And she's the one that took me to that bag. It's Tracey's, but you knew that. Wren knew too."

He didn't respond and I felt an overwhelming sense of longing from him. It was too much so I left. Roane needed time alone. Who was I kidding? I knew I shouldn't have left, but I did. As I wiped a tear away and turned down a hallway, I knew that I was running away because I couldn't bear to see the man I loved remember that he loved someone else.

Talia would always be first. That was the truth and I needed to accept it.

I kept going down hallways. I didn't watch or try to remember which way I was headed, but then I found myself at the door to a deck built on the second floor. Some patio tables were set up beside a small garden with a small waterfall that over granite rocks that had been piled from above the over-hanging roof. As I stepped out and felt the moisture in the air, I breathed in deep. I hadn't smelled water since I'd been gone. The castle had been rock and gardens, but no water. I'd missed it.

"Why are you out here?"

I turned and gulped when I saw Gavin at one of the tables. A lit cigarette was between his fingers and a glass of alcohol sat in front of him. He was in the shadows. A sense of brooding clung to him.

I inched a step closer to him. "I needed to clear my head."

"From what?" He tapped his cigarette on the ashtray.

He looked like he wanted to be alone. That was evident, but I didn't know where else to go. I sat down. "From Roane."

"Because?" His eyes were too knowing.

"I just told him that Talia had a child."

"Oh. Wow. That's not something I saw coming." Gavin glanced at the door.

"Please don't leave. I—" I closed my mouth. What was I going to say? That I didn't want to be alone? This was Roane's best friend. He was the person that should be with him, not with me.

"You didn't want to stick around?"

I snorted. "For what?"

My hands were so clammy and I looked down. I wrung them together. That's when I saw I was trembling at the same time. My whole body was shaking. I knew Gavin saw it all.

"It's not his, if that's what you're worried about."

"Huh?"

"Roane can't reproduce. None of us can except for the Mori or humans. She got with one of them to have a kid. You don't need to worry that Roane will take off to find the child. Guaranteed. And if you're worried that he'll pine over her, it won't happen." His eyes were cold as he watched me. Then he lifted his hand and took a drag off the cigarette. "Want my advice?"

I clasped my eyes shut. I readied myself.

"Go back to him. You're the best friend, not me. Trust me on that." Ice clinked in his glass as he took another sip.

There was a haunted look in his brown eyes, a sadness that resonated deep within me. I didn't want it. It wasn't mine to carry and I wanted it gone, but I knew that the pain in him would lessen if I took it into me. After a moment, he lifted his glass. "I can see why my best mate loves you. Not get back there before I do something I'm going to regret."

I grinned. "If I can find my way back."

"You'll be fine, Davy. Trust your gut. It knows where to go."

As I left, something made me pause. Was there something more to his words or—I closed my eyes and told myself to stop. He was right. I knew before I left, but I needed to go back and face Roane no matter the end result. And so, with a deep breath, I smiled goodbye and then tried to trace my way back. It wasn't hard. Every time I took a wrong turn, I opened myself and felt Roane. He was around this corner, then the left in the hallway, and finally after a few more walkways, I found myself at his office.

He sat behind his desk and had turned to watch the club's chaos beneath his feet. The office was dark, but the dance floor's strobe lights flashed through. All sorts of colors illuminated his face.

I didn't know what he was thinking or feeling and I didn't feel into him. He wouldn't like that.

"You came back." His voice was quiet, too quiet.

"Yeah." My own was raspy. "A little birdie told me I should."

A snort escaped him. "I've never heard someone call Gavin a little birdie. Don't think he'd find that complimentary."

"Yeah, well. " And I had no idea what to say. Again.

Roane stood in a fluid motion. His body was tense. "Do you think that I'll never be over her?" As his head lifted up, his eyes caught mine. Piercing. "You think so little of me? That I'll never be able to move past Talia? Is that what you think of me?"

Oh hell. This was not what I expected. "I think that she was a big part of you." What did I think? "I think you still love her and that you always will."

"Talia was a part of my life. A big part of my life, but she wasn't my entire life. She wasn't the reason I woke up. I didn't think of ways every morning to protect her, ways to help her live a better life, ways to make sure that she never felt the pain that so many others would in our world. I didn't start a war to protect her. I didn't make myself ache every day because I missed her so much when I knew that she needed to live a normal life. I didn't kill vampires or humans without a second thought for her. I never did those things for Talia."

My eyes couldn't leave his.

Roane started to come to me. "The elders thought I was growing too close to her so they sent me away. I went. I never argued. I never considered it. I didn't fight for her and I was gone for over a year before I felt her death. And when I felt it, Davy, it didn't hurt. She was where she wanted to be. She was at peace. I loved her, but not like I love you. I love you to the point of starting a war for you. I love you to the point where I want you to be in college. I want you to have as normal of a life as you possibly can. Because one day I know that you'll have to leave all of that. You're going to have to stop being a normal human and come by my side to be the Immortal. I know that you don't want that. I know that you want me, but you want to be normal more. And I'm trying to help you. I am, but it's so goddamn hard when you disappear for three months and I can't do one thing to bring you back to me. And then, suddenly, you're here. You've come back to me and I had nothing to do with it. You brought your-self back. You saved yourself. You did it. Not me. It's a hard pill to swallow when I'm able to protect anybody, but I can't protect you, the one person that I would do anything to save. I can't. And then you tell me about Talia's daughter. I'm reminded that it's another thing I can't give you. I can't have a child with you. And I want to. I want so much to do that. I want to have a normal life with you, but I can't. We can't, but you can have parts that are normal. You can still have a child. I didn't think Immortals could, but she did so you can—"

I stopped him and placed a finger over his lips. They were so tender. And then I replaced my finger with my lips.

It felt right to kiss him again.

Roane picked me up and kicked his door shut at the same time. He sat me down on his desk and his mouth opened. He took control and his tongue swept inside. He demanded entrance and I let him. I felt him rub against me, teasing, capturing. I grabbed onto the back of his head and held myself against him. He groaned as he sucked on my bottom lip.

A knock sounded at the door and Roane growled, "Leave!"

They didn't. They knocked again.

"No." I held him tighter.

"Who is it?"

"It's Gregory." We could hear his hesitation. "There's a guest asking for you. She wishes to enter the premises."

"A guest?" Roane pulled away now.

"No," I whimpered. Our time was here. I wasn't going to let someone stop us.

"I'm sorry." He kissed my forehead and stood back. "I should go. Gregory wouldn't interrupt unless it was important."

"But—" My mouth fell open and I watched him walk towards the door. "This is important!"

Roane flashed me a grin. "Don't worry. I'll be coming right back, quicker than you think and you'd better be naked."

I perked up at that thought.

He was gone then, but it wasn't long before he was back. When he came through the door, a pained look was on his face. I had a brief second to ponder why before the guest poked her head around Roane.

"Kates." My mouth hung open. I knew I should've said something more welcoming, but holy moly.

With a squeal and a skip, she threw her arms around me and hugged me tight. "Davy! It's so good to see you again."

I patted her back. "You left to find someone? Who was it?"

Not to mention, what was with the happy note? When she left, she'd been morose and depressed. She'd gone to search for someone. Now she was back. With a simple white tee shirt and jeans, her hair gleamed bright blonde instead of the dirty locks she'd had before. She looked nothing like the mischievous bad girl from before.

She laughed and pulled away from me. "I lied to you."

Shock. Not.

Kates added, "I made it sound like I needed to deal with my daddy issues and Blue suggested that I should go and find him. I'm not stupid. I knew that she wanted me out of your life. She can't brainwash you when I'm around."

I narrowed my eyes, frowning as I heard more evidence against my old sponsor.

Kates continued, "You're wondering what I was up to, but the truth is that I went on a mission for your boyfriend." She clasped a hand on Roane's shoulder, or she tried to. He moved away at the last moment and Kates' hand fell back to her side. She laughed. "He wanted me to find Lucan and I did!"

Silence met the last bomb she dropped.

I waited a beat. "You what?"

"I found Lucan."

My eyes shot to Roane. "She what?"

He'd been studying me with narrowed eyes and now he moved forward. "Kates, go with Gregory. He'll take you to a room. You can settle down for the night. I'm sure you're tired."

"Not really. I'm amped up. Mind if I hit the club instead?"

"There are vampires down there."

Kates gave me an incredulous look. "You know they're my forte."

"No killing and no screwing," Roane warned. "They've pledged their allegiance to me. I don't want any of them upset that a slayer is in their midst."

"You know I can't kill. I've followed the decree." Kates didn't seem to mind that she was being hurried out of the room. Just as she disappeared through the door, she looked back and winked at me. I relaxed as I saw the same Kates from before.

When the door shut, the mood wasn't the same. I wanted to smash his bones now, not jump them. "You sent her to find your brother?"

"I did."

"And when were you going to tell me this?"

"I wasn't." He didn't seem guilt-ridden by that answer.

I wanted to hurt him. Bad. "What else should you tell me? Anything else that you had my best friend do for you?"

He hesitated, but then answered emotionless, "Blue. I knew your sponsor wasn't being honest with you and I knew she was only trying to get close to Kates to try and control you. I told Kates about Blue, that she's working for Jacith and was sent by him. Her job was to report back to him when you became the Immortal. Kates was supposed to try and get information from Blue, not the other way around. When it wasn't working and when I knew Lucan had gone to the Mori for protection, I sent her to him. I can't get to him there.

They're too strong for me, but she could. She's human and he loves her."

I sucked in my breath. "I thought no one knew I was the Immortal. I didn't think Jacith knew about me."

"There was a prophecy about an empath who would become the Immortal. Jacith doesn't believe in it. He doesn't think the thread-holder can become something more, but he sent her anyways. You know this. You know that Blue worked for him and that she had been picked for you."

I did, but I hadn't realized the extent of her betrayal. Or that Jacith knew about me.

"Davy, you knew when Kates had kidnapped Blue that time. She knew about you then. She knew you were the Immortal. You were in her head. You heard her talk about Jacith. He sent her to you."

"Stop." I held my hands over my ears. I didn't want to hear about another person who had lied to me and betrayed me.

"I'm sorry that I never told you. I didn't want you to get mixed up in all that deceit. I hoped not to involve you and then when I found out Lucan went to the Mori, it seemed like the perfect timing. Kates said that she couldn't get any information from Blue without raising more suspicion. She worried that Blue would start to piece every-thing together. Blue still thinks you're merely a thread-holder. I want her to keep thinking that. I don't want her to raise Jacith's concerns. He thinks he's only sending an army to find the thread-holder. He doesn't think you're an actual threat. That time will come. It's coming soon. I didn't want to fight Lucan and Jacith at the same time so I moved first. I needed someone to get close to my brother. Kates fit the bill. I knew he'd let her get close."

Jacith, Jacith, Jacith. Everything was about this guy and I was starting to hate him. I gritted my teeth.

"I needed to know what Lucan is planning. He didn't just go away. He went somewhere to wait for his next attempt at you. I'm not stupid. I know my brother and I know he has every intention of getting your power. I needed to know what to expect from him so that I could bring the fight to him. I have to take him out first, at least before Jacith comes to us. You understand, right? Tell me you understand."

Did I? Well, I had to. It made sense. That was the problem. So many lies. So much deception. And Roane acted like none of it was personal. It was all business to him, but it wasn't to me. Kates was my best friend. She had lied to me. Roane had lied to me. Blue had lied to me. And this Jacith person had been manipulating me since I'd been born. Everything about this war was personal to me.

"Davy?"

"Stop!" He reached for my arm, but I backed away. "Just stop. I can't. She's my best friend and you sent her away to a lunatic. She's my best friend, Roane! She could've been killed. Lucan could've killed her."

"She's a slayer."

"She's human. She can die."

"Everyone dies."

"I don't. This is about me. Everyone wants something from me. They want me dead or they want to take what's in me. Blue was like a mother to me. I thought of her like that. She was my mother. My own mom died. Did someone do that? Did Blue do that? Did she really die in a car accident? Is Kates really my best friend? Maybe Lucan sent her to me too. And you? Are you who you say you are? Do you actually love me? Or is this all a strategy too?"

A part of me cringed as I heard the hysteria in my voice, but another part of me shut down. I felt myself growing numb. I couldn't handle any more deception, any more lies. Where was the truth? I couldn't find it anymore. I couldn't feel it.

CHAPTER 18

"Shut up."

"What?" I turned.

Roane had an annoyed look in his eyes and he shook his head. "Shut up."

Excuse me?"

"You're not that girl anymore. You're not naïve. You're not being sheltered. And you're in no way being fooled by anyone. Yes, I kept some things from you, but did you really want to know any of that? You knew I had to do things to protect you. You knew Lucan got away. What did you think I was going to do? What did you think about Blue? You knew she's been lying to you and you did nothing."

My mouth fell open.

Roane poured himself a drink, his shoulders tense. "You wanted a hiatus away from this world. I gave that to you. I dealt with the things you didn't want to think about. And your best friend signed up for this gig. She wanted to spy on Blue. She wanted to find Lucan. Unlike you, Kates won't sit back and let things happen to you. She wants to help stop it. Your best friend was looking out for you."

I was about to argue when someone knocked on the door. Both of us turned, but when Gregory looked inside the concern was evident on his face. Roane set aside his glass. "What is it?"

The Viking vampire's eyes darted between us. "We've encountered a scout."

The air in the room shifted. Roane was no longer annoyed. Gregory seemed apologetic and I was stupefied. Roane was out the door before I could think anything else. "I need to deal with this. We'll talk tonight."

The door closed on the last of his message. Okay, it slammed. And I was the irritated one now. Always keeping stuff from me. Before there had been an incoming of Roane warriors, now there was a scout. It all meant the same thing, something that I hadn't had the time to share. The Roane army was close. When I'd zapped in and out from Tracey, my senses knew that they were close. I'd heard the university's tower bell chime in the distance, but I'd been distracted by Talia's ghost and the bag.

A part of me wanted to zap myself to follow Roane, but he would've sensed me. It didn't matter. Lucas didn't want me there and I couldn't do anything to raise further suspicion. So I perused my bedroom once again, but alone this time. The bed was enormous. That wasn't surprising. Roane kept the best for those closest to him and a goliath-sized bed didn't shock me anymore. The silk sheets, the chiffon curtains. All of it set the mood. The image of me with Roane entangled together on those sheets popped in my head. It was so vivid, I had to take a breath and cool down.

"Whatcha thinking, best friend?" Kates drawled. She was propped against the doorframe.

I rolled my eyes and looked for the bathroom. "I'm thinking that it's going to get ugly real soon."

Kates narrowed her eyes and straightened. "You're different. Why are you different?"

Because I was sick and tired of the lies. And because Roane was right. I had no one else to blame. I'd wanted to turn a blind eye. I hadn't wanted to deal with a lot of things. My best friend was one of them and I knew her better than anyone.

"So." I took a deep breath and sat on the bed. When I raised my eyes, I went inside of her. Kates could feel me, but I didn't care. I wanted her to be uncomfortable. "Are you on his side?"

Her green eyes went wide. "What are you talking about?"

"You know."

"I don't."

I knew she was trying to shake me out. It didn't work. "You went to Lucan. You're back. Whose side are you on?"

"Are you kidding me?"

"I think you might be kidding us. You still love Lucan. It's why you went to him. I know it. You know it. I'm not sure if Lucas remembers it. Did you come back to work for him now?"

We stared at each other. Neither of us blinked.

And then Kates threw her arms in the air. "Are you kidding me? You're my best friend. I betrayed the man I loved for you. What do you think? That I'd double cross you this time?"

"Yes."

She drew back. "You think I would betray you?"

"Knowing that I can't die? Yes. Knowing that whatever he has planned probably won't work. Yes. I think you would promise him the moon to get him to take you back."

"I can't believe you." She shook her head. "You think that I'd hand you over?"

"Is that why he sent you back?" My eyes narrowed and I felt how calm her heart was. The beat was steady, on rhythm. There was no erratic pulse. It didn't speed up or panic. And I wasn't sure what that told me, but I knew Kates. I knew what she was capable of. "Or why he allowed you to come back?"

She froze and I had my answer. The guilt was there. It felt like my question had been a key and it slid into the lock. A perfect fit.

Kates knew it too. The fight left her the next moment. "I never had any intentions of actually going against you. If I had to choose between you two, I would choose you. I always have."

"You didn't before."

She closed her eyes and pressed her fingers to her forehead. "You were never, it was never you or him. I thought you were on the sidelines. But then I realized who you were and that it was you Lucan wanted. I made my choice. I made the same choice when I walked back in here."

"But Lucan thinks—"

"Yes." The admission ripped out of her. "He thinks that you trust me and I can convince you to go back with me."

"Were you intending to tell Roane this?"

Kates shuddered and shook her head. "Do you know what he would do to me? If he thought that there was a chance I'd turn on you? You and I both know he'd slaughter me. And he'd do it with a grin on his smug face."

"You love that same smug face."

"As do you!" She surged to her feet.

I gritted my teeth. "Lucas doesn't want to kill me. He's not some psycho who tried to start a civil war to overthrow some decree."

She laughed and threw her arms wide in the air. "Are you listening to yourself? Have you looked around? I've been here five minutes and it already feels like old times."

"What do you mean?"

"Another war's been declared. It's just not from the smug face I like to kiss." Then she quieted. "Lucas might have different intentions, but he's doing the same thing Lucan did. They're brothers, Davy. They're not that different."

My eyes bulged out and my heart started to race. I felt the anger rise in me. "Lucas is nothing like Lucan."

Kates laughed to herself. "Look at us. 'My boyfriend's better than yours.' Really? That's what we've been reduced to?"

I closed my eyes and forced myself to calm down. No matter what she did, I always knew Kates wouldn't want me hurt. She'd push the limits and betray me, but not if it meant that I'd get hurt. That was the final straw with her and I knew it. I still didn't trust her when it came to Lucan. If she could find a way to do what he wanted and be with him where I wouldn't get hurt then she'd do that first. My saving grace was that Lucan did want to kill me, or at least take the thread from me and that would kill me.

Would it? Sireenia had the thread forced out of her. It had killed her, but I was the Immortal. What would happen if someone tried that with me?

"Who are you?"

I pulled away from my thoughts and saw Gavin in the doorway. A mask of contempt was on his face, mixed with hostility. My heart sank. He had heard every word we said.

Gavin narrowed his eyes. I felt the disgust in his voice. "Roane called. He wanted you to know that he won't be back till morning." He raked his eyes over Kates with a sneer on his face. "Something came up."

My best friend smirked and stretched. Her arms stretched wide and lifted her chest up. The entire movement was provocative. "You're new. Whose bed are you staying in tonight?"

"Kates!"

She snorted. "Like he didn't expect some slutty remark from me. From the first word he overheard, he labeled me a whore. Right, whoever you are?"

"This is Roane's best friend."

"I'm Gavin." There was nothing on his face. It was void of emotion now.

"Well la di da." Kates sounded bored. Her eyes flashed at him. "You can go back to your best buddy and report my lie to him. I'm sure he'll be even more indebted to you."

With a growl, Gavin was across the room in a flash. I blinked once and saw him holding Kates against the wall with a hand to her throat. She stared at him in a heated challenge, but no snippy comments passed her lips. They continued to glare at the other.

I cleared my throat. "Put her down?"

My best friend smirked. "He would, but he's enjoying it. Aren't you? You didn't expect to be turned on? And by a vampire slayer too?" Then she grunted and slammed an elbow into his face. The positions were reversed in the next second, but Gavin didn't fight back. He wasn't lifted in the air as she had been, but he stood there. His eyes never left hers.

I felt Kates' surprise as she let go and stepped back.

Then Gavin looked at me. "If you need anything, lift the receiver and speak into it. They'll get whatever you need. Roane wanted you to be comfortable."

As Gavin left, I glanced at Kates and saw a look that I'd never seen on her face. Perplexion.

I grinned as I sat on the bed. "That was fun to watch."

"What?" She rolled her shoulders back, but her eyes were lost.

"Maybe Lucan's not the one for you after all?"

Kates crossed to the bar and poured herself a drink. She downed it in one swallow. "Don't go all fairytale romantic on me. That vampire is definitely not 'the one' for me. He's not 'the one' for anyone. Don't you feel it from him?"

"Feel what?"

She poured another drink. "He's cold to the bone, Davy. He might look pretty on the outside and seem flashy, but he's dark. If I were to choose between him and Lucan, I'll always go Lucan. He's not as dangerous as that one."

I'd never seen Kates this rattled so I slipped inside of her and felt her confusion. She was frozen to the bone and I retreated out of her. It gave me the chills.

"I'm going to go." Kates moved to the door.

"Where are you going?"

She lifted haunted eyes to me. "I'll be back. He's right or Roane's right. Sleep. He'll draw the army away. That's what he's doing right now. You and I go back to Benshire University tomorrow." She flashed me a wolfish grin. "I wonder how Emily's going to welcome me back?"

The joke fell flat. "Where are you going?"

"Don't worry about me. I'll be fine."

"Kates, where are you going? I know that you're going to do something not-good right now. What is it?"

With a hand already on the doorknob, she smiled at me. An odd ray of honesty shone bright from her. I blinked back tears from the power of it.

Her smile turned down at the ends. "I know that I'm not a great person, but I will always be a good friend to you. I will never let you get hurt. Ever. But right now, I have to go do my own thing. I'll be back in the morning. I'm your cover story, Davy. You were gone to help me. I'm sure Roane will have everything in place by tomorrow morning so our story will check out."

She left before I could respond and I was left to sit by myself. I felt more alone at that moment than I'd ever felt my whole life.

WREN EMERGED from the forest behind him and scanned the horizon before them. They were ten miles from town. Lights glimmered behind them and a vast darkness spread out before them. A sneer formed at her lips when she drew beside him. "Tracey's two miles away. I can smell her."

Roane already knew where they were. He couldn't smell a past lover, but he felt them. Their army was intense, built on fury and lies. Some of them were confused. Those vampires followed their leader because they'd been told to, but a majority believed in finding the Immortal and destroying her. He could smell their fear, though many of them weren't aware how deep their terror lay inside of them.

"Jacith is behind this. He's not with them, but his influence is strong over them."

Wren glanced at him. "You think he knows?"

"No." Roane was void of any emotion. "He doesn't know what she is, but he fears it anyways. He knows something has happened. He's stirred something in them, made them fear for their lives if she lives. I don't know if it's from words or magic, but I can feel him among them."

"He's powerful. Maybe he's seen into her already?"

The sword felt heavy slung across his back, but it was where Roane wanted it. Close at hand and ready for when it would be used to kill. He just wasn't ready to kill thousands of what used to be his army.

"Lucas."

Wren surprised him when she spoke his first name. He felt into her, an ability that he'd developed from being intimate with Davy. The vampiress was also scared, but she was in longing. "Go to Tracey. I want her on my side."

"I don't think she'll be converted."

"She will. Tell her that Talia is trying to communicate with the new thread-holder. Tracey will come then."

He felt her shock.

He added, "If she knows that her sister is with us, she'll know that she fights for the wrong side. She can help us."

"And if she doesn't? If she turns on me?"

"She won't with you. If she chooses the Roane Family, she'll send you away, but she'll make sure you're safe."

Wren nodded and left. She moved with a grace that made her invisible and one of the best warriors he had trained. There'd been a moment when he had thought she would've chosen to be at Tracey's side, not his, but now as he watched her vanish into the forest, he was grateful for her loyalty. She was one of his best warriors.

She hadn't been gone long before he felt another's approach. Before Gavin spoke, Roane knew he'd seen Kates.

Gavin spoke in a rough voice. "You could've warned me. I didn't know Davy's best friend was a slayer."

Roane grinned, but the night hid it. "Why would that be important to you?"

"Don't be an ass."

"I thought you were over Isabella."

Gavin let out a ragged breath. "I thought I was too."

Roane waited and knew he'd need a few moments. Gavin would either talk about her or forget the mention of her. He had his answer in the next second.

"Their army is close. What are you planning?"

"I don't want to fight them now. I've sent Wren ahead to convert Tracey to our side."

"But what about the army? They're too close and our numbers aren't enough. We need more vampires." Gavin shifted on his feet. He wanted to fight, purge the memories. Killing would do that.

"Release their scout. He will lead them in the opposite direction."

"And how'd you get him to do that?"

"Jacith isn't the only one who can use magic."

Gavin grinned with a hard look in his eyes. "So you changed his memories."

"It's nice to have a few friendly witches on our side."

"So we wait and make sure they leave?"

Roane stretched his legs out before him. They both sat on the darkened hill. Then Gavin murmured, "What are you going to do about the Bright witch?"

He hesitated for a moment. Roane had felt her when he came to town. He followed Davy to Benshire, but the young witch's presence had been overpowering. She was strong, even with her magic still locked inside of her. The determination he'd seen in her when he had checked on Davy at the library had surprised him. She would unlock her magic and Roane knew Davy, as her friend, would help the witch. It was in her nature. Davy didn't like anything locked away or kept hidden. He just hoped the witch would stand on their side. If she chose their allegiance, she would be more powerful than either she or Davy knew.

He was resigned. "I'm letting that one sort itself out."

CHAPTER 19

When I woke up, the room was dark. It was just me and the darkness. The club had shut down hours ago. A sense of emptiness swept through me, but then a different feeling came and took its place. I knew what had woken me so I sat up and hugged my knees. I pulled the sheets close to my chest. "You're here, aren't you?"

No one else was in the room.

But I felt her and I wanted to see her. I wanted to speak to her, hear her answer back. A sudden intensity took hold of me, starting in my feet and sweeping up. A vacuum had formed and it sucked everything up in me. Then I was inside of it. I squinted as my eyes adjusted. What was dark was light now and I knew the Immortal had answered my wish.

Talia stared back at me, perched on the end of my bed. A woeful look was with her, but when I focused on her, she screamed and jumped back. She vanished from the room, but was back in the next instant. I knew I had caught her so I reeled her back. An invisible hand lurched out of me towards her. She appeared again and was more fearful.

Her red hair floated around her as did the white dress she wore. It was the same outfit she'd worn the night she had jumped. She looked the same as a spirit as she did as a human.

"Can we talk?" I spoke out loud, but when she frowned I thought it instead. *'Can we talk?'*

Her eyes widened again and I felt the panic in her. 'This isn't right. How are you doing this? You're not supposed to be able to do this.'

'I don't think I'll be able to do this again.' I felt her start to calm down and she settled more on the bed. Could a ghost feel comfort?

'Lucan has my child. You've told Lucas?'

'Yes. Well, not about Lucan. I didn't know.'

She nodded. 'What does he plan to do?'

'I have no idea.' Did she know about us?

'Lucan was the one chasing me that night. He and his men. They killed everyone that was there. They were all trying to protect me, but none of them were Lucas. Only he could've fought them off. Lucan took my daughter. He took her and then he wanted to kill me so the thread would jump to her. I couldn't have that. I couldn't condemn her life. But then the thread took over my body and I went to you. I have no idea how I got there, but all of a sudden you were there and I felt it leave me. I knew they didn't see it leave me so you'd be safe. I wanted to warn you about Lucan, about my daughter, but I couldn't. I couldn't say anything.'

She closed her eyes and flinched. Both of us replayed that night as she jumped off the building. The peace had been evident on her face.

That same peace was with her again, but she lifted still-stricken eyes to my face. Sireenia had said Talia hadn't let go of the human world and that something still held her there. It was her daughter.

'I will find your daughter. I will make sure she is safe.'

Her eyes clung to mine. She wanted to believe me. The desperation was evident, but she held back. I knew she didn't trust me so I shifted forward and reached for her hand. I held my breath, but then my fingers touched hers and I let it go in a rush. I could touch a ghost. I could feel her. It was mind-blowing. As I blinked back tears, I couldn't believe it. And then her fingers grasped mine. She tightened the hold and smiled as tears of her own fell too.

'I cannot believe this. You are the true Immortal. You're the one all the prophecies speak of.' Her relief washed over me. *'My daughter's name is*

Lily. I named her after my mother, but I don't know if they've changed it. Her growth will speed up with the Mori. She could be older than seven months, but she will answer to Lily. It's engraved in her and even Lucan can't take that from her. Please find my daughter. Please make sure she's safe.'

I nodded, feeling overwhelmed. I'd grown accustomed to the weirdness that came with being the Immortal. I could do so much, some of it at my control and most of it not, but this time I was taken aback at the intensity I felt from her and how much my body reacted. My heart pounded stronger with each second I held her hand. I had to find Lily. The child was important, more than me, but before I could ask, something changed and Talia was gone.

"No!" I reached for her, but only felt air. She was gone. Not even her spirit lingered and I knew she wouldn't be coming back.

Lily. I had to find her. I had to protect her.

"Hey."

I shrieked, but calmed when Roane put a hand on my shoulder. "I thought—nevermind what I thought." I brushed away my tears and looked at him. Some light shone into the room from the hall and it cast a shadow over his face. His eyes were hooded and the light reflected off his cheekbones. Two plump lips were visible and my heart skipped a beat at the sight of him. I'd forgotten how good he looked.

Anything I was going to say was forgotten. He opened his mouth to speak, but then I licked my lips. His mouth closed. The air changed in that moment. It pulled us both in and things were forgotten. The world was forgotten or maybe I wanted to forget it for a moment. I didn't care; I just knew what I wanted at that moment. Him.

His hand cupped the side of my face. "What's wrong?"

My heart started to pound, but I shook my head. We should talk. There was so much to tell, but I didn't want to. There was always something wrong.

We'd been apart for too long and now that I knew he loved me, that it was me and not her. I reached for him and pulled him close.

His thigh brushed against mine. I closed my eyes and hoped it wouldn't go away. Then his thumb started to caress my cheek and his other hand rested on my chest. He felt my heart pick up speed.

I wanted this. I needed this.

His lips touched mine, but held there. No pressure was applied and then he retreated to close the door. And then with one swift movement, he climbed above me. His thighs cradled mine, but his upper body hovered over me. His lips hadn't moved and I felt my body jerk upwards, starving for his touch. When he held back, I bucked against him. He was torturing me. I felt him between my legs and groaned. It'd been so long.

His thumb still caressed my cheek and then he slammed his lips onto mine. Finally. He took control.

I couldn't think anymore. He slid a hand up my stomach, underneath my shirt. It teased the sides of my breasts and went between up to my neck. As his hand splayed out and grasped my throat, he held my head captive. His tongue swept inside. He went deep, so deep that I could only hold on and let him. My arms wound around his shoulders and my legs wrapped around his waist.

He licked. I nipped. I panted. He claimed. My hands found his shoulders and his went between my legs. One finger slipped inside and I screamed into his throat. Two fingers pumped and my entire body convulsed against him. We blended together. And then what seemed like hours later, I felt him push into me. He filled me and pushed further than I thought my body could handle. I panted and fell onto the bed as Roane stretched me. My arms were pinned down. My legs were under his and he started thrusting.

You're mine.

Through a haze, my eyes found his. Dark with desire, a predatory look was in his eyes and I answered to it. I needed it. And then my mind went blank again as he continued to thrust. He built the fever, thrusting harder and harder until both of us panted. Our hands intertwined as he climaxed. We hurdled over the edge, but before I fell back to sleep, Roane started again. The night was spent savoring each other's body. We explored and rediscovered.

He nuzzled my shoulder hours later. "You should sleep."

I heard the exhaustion in his voice and smiled. My own was raspy. "You should too."

He tightened his arms around me. His mouth lingered on my cheek and I closed my eyes when I heard his voice. "I can't. I came back to check on you. I was supposed to relieve Gavin."

I flipped my body over and pushed against him.

Roane groaned as he closed his eyes. He skimmed a hand down my arm, tracing my leg and then brought it back up to rest underneath my breast. It teased me as he rested it there. I felt him push against me and he slipped inside once again. He held himself still instead of thrusting farther inside. We felt each other. My eyes closed and I rested my forehead against his.

'I should go.' Roane kept his eyes closed as he kissed me.

'I don't want this to end.' It'd been too long.

'I'm planning more nights like this.' His eyes opened again.

In that moment, I felt the world come back. It slammed down as it settled over us. When he pulled out and started dressing, I sat back up with the sheet pulled over me. It wasn't to cover up my body, but to hold off the chill. I'd grown cold again.

Roane pulled on a dark shirt over black pants.

"Where are you going?"

He paused while reaching for a vest that housed enough weapons to make my mouth go dry. Why would he need all those? And then I remembered. I clasped my eyes shut. I didn't want to wonder if he was leaving to kill or just to hunt them. That was what he was best at.

"Davy." Roane sat back down on the bed.

"What?"

He searched my face. "Something happened before I came in. What was it?"

My heart picked up its pace. Dare I tell him about her now? So soon after we'd been together? A vision of us in bed flashed in my mind and my heart clenched. I could still feel him in me. I wanted that again. I didn't want him to leave.

"Where are you going? Can you tell me?"

Roane hesitated. He saw my need, though the need was for something else. "We're watching the Roane Army. A scout should've told them they were headed in the wrong direction. I need to make sure they believe the scout and leave."

"Will they be back?" My throat hurt.

"Yes." He tried to smile at me, but it fell short. "They'll be back. I bought us some more time. I need more men to fight on my side."

"What do I do?"

Now he frowned and pulled away. "Where did Kates go? She's to go back to the university with you. Didn't she tell you?"

"She did." It felt so strange now. We talked of business, as if we hadn't loved each other moments ago. "She said that she was my alibi and that you had stuff set in place to back up the story."

"She was supposed to fill you in."

I jerked a shoulder up. "Her and Gavin had a weird reaction to each other. She took off. She's coming back, but I think she had to go and do—" *'What we just did.'*

A grin peeked out from the corner of his mouth. It felt genuine and I relaxed when I saw it. Roane pulled me close and tucked his head into the crook of my shoulder. *'I know you can feel me pulling away. I'm sorry for that.'*

'Why are you doing it? Why won't you let me inside?'

'Because it distracts me too much. I don't want to do what I need to do. I want to be with you and only you. I'm sorry.'

I knew he was apologizing for something more, but I didn't want to know. Not really. And then I couldn't hold it off any longer. He was going back to war and for once, for the first time, I wondered if everything would be okay. A prick of doubt settled inside of me. I didn't want it there. I didn't want to think of what was to come. Not yet.

"I can go back? Everything will be alright?"

"Yeah." He pulled back. He seemed resigned now. "You can go back."

'For now.'

It wasn't permanent. When he stood and went to the door, a part of me died as he left. I felt it curl up and fall down to the pit of my stomach.

I nodded and closed my eyes as he left. The door shut again, but this time the light shone in from the window. Even though the curtains were closed, the day had started and it had invaded my room. I lay down and could've stayed there in bed for the entire day. A part of me wanted to go back to my old life. I could be normal once again, but it wouldn't last. It was a lie. It was only until I'd have to leave again.

The war was real to me now.

A knock at the door woke me. When I looked at my phone, I saw that I'd been asleep for three hours.

"Yeah?" I croaked.

"It's Kates. Your door is locked." She pounded on it again.

I looked underneath the sheet and saw I was still naked. Thankful that Roane had locked the door; I jumped out and threw on the nearest clothes. When I unlocked the door, I tried to smooth my hair down.

She stepped in, took a breath, and then choked back laughter.

"What?"

"I can smell sex all over you." She rolled her eyes.

I wrinkled my nose up and cringed. "And what'd you do the whole night?" I sniffed and then tried to block her aroma. "It's not just booze I smell on you."

"Yeah, well." Kates shrugged. "Can you blame me?"

As she crossed the room and sat in a chair, I heard the swoosh of her clothes. That's when I looked closer. "Are you serious? You're wearing leather?"

A look of pure delight crossed her face. "Are you kidding me? We're going to be seeing Emily again. Nothing else is appropriate. She hates me, Davy. Don't take that away from me. You know I love her hatred."

I rolled my eyes and pushed back my hair. It blocked my sight and I needed to see. I needed to think too. "She's dating a werewolf now, you know."

Clothes. I needed clothes. Wait, I had clothes. Did I need new ones?

Kates grunted and kicked a bag to me. "I got these for you."

I picked up the bag and looked at it with caution. "I'm not wearing leather."

"It's not, but that look would be hot. Bet you'd get Roane back here in a flash for round two." She gave me a seductive smile. "Don't even act all virtuous right now. I know you want nothing more than to wrap those legs around him and let him dominate you."

I snorted. "Maybe, but we need to talk about Emily. She's not as dumb as you think and she's not as ignorant anymore. She knows witches and werewolves exist. Her mate is one of the strongest there is."

She threw a leg over the side of her chair and struck a sultry pose. "Why do you think I didn't shower? The sex is going to drive him crazy."

Before she had left, I would've made her shower. I would've lectured her on being good and keeping the peace, even though I knew she wouldn't. I didn't say a word now. Instead, I grabbed a towel and walked into the connected bathroom. Then I turned the shower on and stepped underneath the spray.

I needed a shower. I needed to rid myself of the past because I knew that Emily wasn't the only one with questions. Brown. Pippa. Even Blue. They'd all want to know and I'd have to be the best actress in the world. When I moved back into the room, I was dressed and ready to go. Kates narrowed her eyes. I waited for her to say something, but she didn't. She stood at the door and waited in silence.

"We're ready."

CHAPTER 20

Kates cast a worried look to me when we were in the backseat of another black car. Roane always sent the same car for my transportation. I'd grown accustomed to them by now, but I wasn't used to my childhood mate being the one worried about me. It was usually the other way around.

"What?"

"Are you okay?" She reached for my hand resting in the middle of the seat between us and hooked her pinkie finger around mine.

I took a deep breath. "I'll be fine."

"You're different."

She should've noticed the night before. I'd been different since I got back, but I kept my mouth shut and shrugged instead. "I just want to be with Roane."

My answer appeased her and she patted my hand. "I'm sure he'll find time to sneak in a quickie. He'll be calling for you by the end of the night."

The war was coming. It was at our doorstep. It might not have rung the bell, but it would. Our time away from it was short lived and Kates had no idea. She was usually the one who knew what was going on. I had been the one in the dark, blinded by my own denial. But this time, everything had changed.

I felt like I was just biding my time. Waiting.

Then we were at the police station and I took a deep breath. Roane said we should head there first since an official investigation had been opened. When I walked in, the clerk hadn't recognized me, but when I told her my name, the pen in her hand dropped. After a moment, she hurried away and I was shown inside. I was stuck in an interrogation room for over an hour. The detective had sat me down at her desk, but too many people were around. They all wanted to hear and some even asked their own questions so she sat me in a private room. Then Kates was brought in too. She took over most of the questions since she was the reason I'd been gone. My acting skills weren't as honed as hers. She was animated and believable while I didn't give a crap.

When everything checked out, that she had called me to help with her mother who had died and then stayed to help with the funeral planning, the detectives let us go. My case was closed, but I knew the detective still had questions. I heard them. She didn't believe me, but why would someone lie about helping out a friend? Or taking care of a funeral? Or that my phone was broken and I didn't think about replacing it. When she ran my name, nothing had come up. Then she ran Kates and a lot came up, but none of it was substantial. The detective had nothing to keep us and I looked fine. So we walked out and I knew I had part one of the subterfuge down. Part two was Emily and she was going to be the hardest one.

When we arrived at the dorm, Kates cast another look at me and bit her lip. "Maybe I should do the talking."

I snorted and then grabbed my bag. "Come on. She'll never believe us. Let me handle it."

When we went inside, the desk clerk had a similar reaction as to the one in the police station. Instead of her pen dropping, her textbook fell to the floor. A few girls were in the lounge and their conversation halted as they stared. I ignored it all. They'd hear the story soon enough. Gossip was good for some things.

And then I felt it. Or I felt him. His power was overwhelming. It came over me in waves and I staggered back from it.

"Davy?"

I saw Kates' lips move, but I didn't hear her. I couldn't. His power blanketed everything else. I couldn't smell. I couldn't hear. I couldn't feel. I could barely think. It was a dense fog that formed a cement box around me. And I was alone in it. No one else felt it and no one else was aware of it.

How could they not know?

I shook my head and tried to push some of it away, but it didn't matter. His power was too much and I started to panic. I reached out blindly. My hand hit something. I felt movement beside me, but I couldn't discern what had happened.

My heart rate picked up. It pounded in my ears. It was so loud. I wished I couldn't hear in that moment, just for a moment. I couldn't handle any of this.

I tried to scream, but nothing came out. And then the power grew. I felt it coming closer. The walls doubled. I fell to my knees and cradled my head. How was I going to do this? I couldn't move past the front desk in my dorm.

A loud thunder blared in my ears. Then another and another. I turned for the door and strained to see through it, but I couldn't see a storm. It wasn't raining.

"Davy!" Kates' cried out. Her voice was so quiet.

I reached out to her and then gasped. I couldn't find her, but then as my heart picked up its pace. More thunder sounded. It was coming closer. It was now one big crackle in the sky. The boom shook me.

'Suppress your power, Davina,' Saren's voice snapped in my head. *'Suppress it now. He can feel you too. He knows there's something coming and he's hungry for your power. Suppress it all! Wrap it up and lock it in a box. Push that box deep inside of you.'*

Another boom jerked my body aside.

She screamed this time, *'Do it now!'*

And then it happened. I gasped as my own power swirled in a vacuum. A tornado formed inside of me and everything went around and around. I swallowed thickly, my hands were shaking from the effort, but I imagined a blanket. I saw it happening in my mind. The immortal was snarling, but I kept it in the swirl and the blanket wrapped around it. Then it was forced down, down, further down into a box. As it got there, the lid shook. It couldn't contain it, but I gritted my teeth and I snapped the lid in place. It shut with a violent force, but then I pushed it all the way deep in me, further than I could reach.

Then my eyes opened again and I was trembling in place.

"Davy!" Kates screamed at me. She twisted her hand free from my hold and hissed as she examined it. "I'm bleeding! Holy cow!"

"What?" I couldn't stop shaking. "What happened?"

"You went crazy. That's what happened." She shook her hand as she watched me with weary eyes. "What happened to you?"

And then a guy rounded the corner.

He was tall, built lean, and soft in the face. He had the face of a little boy who'd grown into a pretty boy, but his eyes made me pause. They were old, had seen too much for being so young. Then he stopped altogether, his nostrils flared and I felt him sniffing around me. He started low, around my feet, but his eyes held mine. I slipped into him without realizing it. Images of him as a young wolf came back at me. His fur was a golden bronze with white eyes. He was running and playing with Pippa when she had been a pup. The two nipped at each other, licking each others' toes at the end. And then an image of a woman flew at me. Her hand was outstretched to me, her red hair streamed behind her. She wore a similar dress to what I'd seen on Talia. When her eyes found mine, I sucked in a breath. I was horrified. She was Talia's mother, or the essence of her. There was no soul within her. This was only her residue, left in him. This was Emily's boyfriend. This was the Alpha.

I shut it down. I shut the last bit of power down and got out of him before he knew I was there. He wanted to know why I smelled familiar to him, but Kates' scent distracted him. The booze and sex pulled at him like a drug.

When she winked at me, I knew she'd done it on purpose. Then she drawled, "Got a good enough whiff? Are you a horny puppy now? Gonna go hump something?"

He snapped back and bared his teeth.

Kates rolled her eyes. "Please. Unlike vampires, I can kill your kind. There's no decree saying I can't."

He composed himself and stood at his fullest height. Then he smirked." You couldn't handle me, slayer."

"Maybe not alone, but I've got a few friends. You can't hurt me and I've got no such rule. If an animal's attacking me, I have every right to protect myself."

His lip curled upwards in a heated snarl.

I felt his anger start. It was low, but strong. As it rose in him, it grew even more powerful. Then it got to his eyes. The dark brown color had grown black with a silver haze that clouded over the white in his eyes. His eyes had been white as a pup. I was waiting for the full change now. He was within seconds of transforming in the hallway, but then his mate called him.

"Pete?" Emily was walking towards us.

He turned back and held out a hand. "I'm fine. No worries, hon."

Her eyes skimmed past him and fell on me. Her mouth fell open and she paled. "Oh my god."

My eyes widened too. "Don't faint!"

"Davy?" Her voice had grown weak. She wavered on her feet and then leaned against the wall. "What are you? Are you real? Oh my god."

"You already said that." Kates brushed past them to walk into our room.

My feet were still frozen, but I felt Pete's curiosity double.

"Davy? Is that really you?" Emily seemed to be on the brink of tears, but then Pete took her hand and she pushed them down. He steadied her. I saw the connection between them and it was remarkable. Before, she'd been more neurotic and almost hysterical at times. Now she was strong and calm. He did that for her. I could see his strength flow into her. It tripled when their hands touched.

I wasn't the only one who had changed.

"It's me."

"Davy?" A squeal came from behind me before two arms wound themselves around me. Her voice was muffled into my back. "Thank god you're home. I was so worried."

Only one person would react like that. I laughed. "It's nice to see you too, Brown."

She squeezed harder. "I did magic. I created spells. I begged for my sister's help. Nothing. I couldn't find you. And now you're back. My prayer must've worked. I finally had to go to God, though I hope the goddesses don't condemn me. I was at a loss, but it doesn't matter." She let go and then skipped in front of me as she beamed. Brown threw her arms in the air. "You're home! Welcome back."

"Davy?"

I looked back up and saw Pippa in her doorway. She tugged on her two braids in shock. "Are you—is that you?"

Pete turned to her, but she looked away.

I waved a helpless hand in the air. "Hey everyone. I'm back."

Kates stood in my doorway and lifted up the phone. "Can I order pizza? I'm starving."

Pippa looked taken aback. Brown frowned. "Who are you?"

Emily seethed, "Out! Get out! She was gone because of you, wasn't she? Of course, you would do something like this. I bet you wouldn't even let her call home. I bet you said that you did, that you took care of it all. And Davy, being the good friend she is, believed you. It's all your fault."

Everyone was taken aback, even me. Kates looked annoyed, but I caught the amusement in her eyes. When her lips curled up in a malicious smirk, I darted forward and stood between the two. "It's not her fault. Yes, I left because of her. Her mom died, Em. Be nice. And since Kathryn was like a mother to me, I didn't really think to call. I'm really sorry. The funeral took planning. Then her family and my family were there. When it was time to come back, I didn't want to come back. I didn't know how to deal." I lifted both my shoulders up in a helpless shrug. "I'm sorry. I really am."

"Good one on the guilt," Kates murmured under her breath.

"Shut up," I hissed through my teeth.

Emily frowned. "You were gone because of a death?"

Pippa remained quiet and then Brown exclaimed, "We didn't even think about that! We're so stupid. What else would make someone leave so quickly? I wouldn't call if my mum died. Well, I might call Davy now, but I wouldn't call anybody else. No one would care."

I watched my roommate and waited. Did she buy it? Kates was right, I'd added some guilt in the hopes that it would push Emily into accepting the story. I couldn't have her asking any questions. I kept an uneasy eye on her boyfriend. He didn't buy the story, but I hoped he wouldn't say anything. It wasn't his place. He didn't know me or my relationship with Emily.

"I'm sorry, Davy," Pippa spoke in a soft voice. "We didn't even think to call your home."

"We didn't have a number *to* call."

I heard the anguish in my roommate's voice and relaxed. I was a horrible friend. "Maybe we should go to a hotel? I don't want to be a bother. I know that you're probably used to having a single room."

"No," Emily spoke up. "No, please. Stay. I'm sorry." She looked past me. "I'm sorry, Kates."

She sniffed as she opened a bag of chips. "It's no problem." Then she glared at Pete. "I don't want the wolf here. He makes me uncomfortable."

Emily sucked in her breath.

Pippa held a hand to her mouth. Brown opened her mouth and then closed it. Then she repeated the motion.

"I don't believe you—" He surged forward, but Emily caught his arm.

"Honey, stop. Please."

"You're going to let her get away with that?" His hands were fisted at his side. "And I don't buy their story. It sounds fishy to me."

Brown closed her mouth with a snap.

"It doesn't matter." Emily moved close to him. "Even if it isn't true, my roommate's back. I need to be here for her. If Davy went somewhere, it was for a good reason. I know it was."

'She didn't trust me enough to tell me. I can't push her. I care about Davy. I want her to trust me. Please, Pete. Please go.'

'There's something that doesn't smell right about her.'

Emily drew upright. "You can go. Thank you. I'll see you tomorrow for lunch."

The dismissal was swift and harsh, but effective. Pete went, but not without glaring at us. Even Pippa melted away.

Brown bounced past us and into the room. She plucked the bag of chips from Kates' hands and settled on our couch.

"Your boyfriend doesn't like me. Is that going to be a problem?" Kates smirked as Emily followed everyone else inside. She lounged back on our couch.

"What. Huh? No. I don't even like you."

Kates quirked an eyebrow up and winked at me. *'That was easier than I thought. Your holy roommate barely put up a fight.'*

I looked away and stood there. What do I do next?

'Don't pretend you can't hear me. I know you can. I can't hear you, only human and all, but seriously. Emmykins folded like a rag. What's up with that? Where'd her backbone go?'

She had a backbone, but I'd snapped it in two. Manipulation and guilt could confuse almost anyone. When Kates started sending her thoughts to me again, I closed my eyes and blocked her. I already felt bad about lying to Emily and I'd only been back for five minutes. How had I kept up the lie before?

"Davy?" Brown had stopped her chattering. "Are you okay? Your aura looks green."

CHAPTER 21

The afternoon was strained in my room. Emily wanted to murder Kates. Kates enjoyed fueling that fire and Brown was confused by everything. Her eyes were wide as she studied me at moments, and then studied the tension between my roommate and best friend. After awhile, she threw her hands up in surrender and announced we should go drinking.

To my surprise, the other two jumped on board.

Kates suggested a vampire bar, but since I still didn't know if Emily knew they were real, I vetoed that suggestion. Then Emily suggested a werewolf bar and Kates shot that down. The truce was Brown's idea.

"What's the name of it?" Kates narrowed her eyes.

"Bosom's."

Emily's eyebrows shot up and I asked, "Like boobs?"

"No, like, well. Yeah. It's all about sisterly love and stuff." The more we stared at her, the more uncertain Brown became. She was staring at her shoes by the end of that statement.

"It sounds like a witch bar," Kates said in a flat voice.

"It's not a witch bar." But Brown was busy inspecting anything around us. No eye contact.

"Wait!" Emily held up a hand and skirted from the room. She

was back within minutes with a full grin on her face. "I asked the girl across the hall and she recommended a place called Barbwire?"

"Sold," Kates sighed.

I surged to my feet. "I'm good with that one."

Brown frowned. "Where is that place?"

"It doesn't matter. That's where we're going." Kates raked her up and down. "You need a wardrobe change."

She looked down. "What are you talking about? I think I look good."

"For a witch." Kates bent into her own bag and started rummaging around.

"I *am* a witch."

I couldn't help but watch Emily through their exchange. She had seemed uneasy about the witch stuff before I disappeared, but now she didn't blink an eye. I started to wonder if she knew more about the supernatural than she was letting on.

"Not tonight you aren't. If you hang out with me, you gotta look good. None of this stuff." She waved a hand up and down Brown's figure.

Brown looked down at herself. "What do you mean?"

"Nothing." Kates threw an arm around her shoulder and drew her close. "Trust me. I'm going to make you hot. The witch look isn't attractive. You're going to send the guys running away. You want them to come to you."

And make her hot she did. Brown emerged from our room with skintight jeans and a flashy white camisole. Kates wanted her to wear a black bra underneath, but it was vetoed by everyone else. She matched Kates, who wore skintight white pants and a black camisole. When my roommate disappeared with clothes, I was a little scared she would return with her Target outfit from the last time she had gone out with Kates and me. I was wrong and impressed when she came back in loose-fitting white pants and a conservative black tank. She had a classy look to her now. I frowned at my own closet. Kates would want me to look like a slut. Brown wouldn't care and Emily would vote for something similar to her outfit. I ended up with basic jeans and a pink top that ran around my neck, wrapped around the opposite side and looped together in the back.

Kates whistled when I stepped out of the room. "If only Roane could see you now."

I grinned and then stiffened as I sent a furtive look towards my roommate. Emily went rigid for a moment and then relaxed. Brown started to bounce up and down. "Girls' night out. Girls' night out."

She stopped when Kates grabbed her arm. "Chill, girl."

"Oh, okay." But the stupid smile wasn't wiped clean.

Emily fell in step beside me as the other two led the way. She remained quiet all the way until we got to the bar. We followed the directions the girl from across the hall gave us. After we parked five blocks away and crossed over a park, I caught a glimpse of Barbwire. The entire building looked like an old warehouse with a simple red door in the front. A line of people wrapped around the building. There was nothing glamorous about the place, but as we drew closer, I saw someone in line and groaned.

"What?" Emily looked ahead. "Is that Holly from the hotline?"

My joy for the night was gone.

Holly looked the same. Oval face. Pasty skin. Brown eyes that reminded me of an owl. She looked like a librarian intent on getting drunk. She wore a gray skirt and a low-cut white top underneath a matching grey lace vest. When she reached behind and grabbed the arm of a guy, I felt the desire inside of her. Oh yes. The girl was on a mission. Then she looked my way.

And I froze. Adam was with her.

She gasped and a wide smile spread over her face. "Davy?! Is that you?"

Kates asked underneath her breath, "Who's that?"

"She works at the hotline," Emily murmured back.

"Wasn't he the guy that got killed from there too?"

"What?" Brown gasped.

Holly darted our way. Her hand was still attached to Adam's arm and he looked like he had seen a ghost.

Holly clapped her hands together. "How are you, Davy? You never showed up again to cover Adam's shifts. Adam, aren't you going to say hello?"

"Hi, Davy." His eyes darted behind my shoulder.

When he tensed, I knew he had recognized Kates. Then she jostled forward and threw out an arm. "How's it going? I'm Kates, Davy's best friend. Hi, Adam. Remember me?"

He froze. Even his eyes didn't blink.

Holly's bright smile dimmed a bit and she glanced to her date. "Hi, I'm Holly. You know Davy?"

"Best friends. Childhood." Kates threw an arm around my shoulder. Her smile was easy, but her eyes were pinned on Adam.

"Oh. That's great."

Then Brown burst forward. "I'm Sarah, but you can call me Brown. I'm a witch. What are you?"

Holly's eyes threatened to burst out. "What did you say?"

"I'm a witch. I'm not very powerful. Or, well, I barely have any power, but I will. Someday."

Kates muttered under her breath, "You really need to stop telling people that."

Emily moved forward. "I agree. You need to learn some boundaries."

"Boundaries? But she's a friend of Davy's."

"There are different types of friends."

Emily nodded.

"Wait, what?" Holly kept glancing between all of us. Her hand tightened on Adam. "What's going on? Davy?"

Adam looked everywhere and anywhere, just not as us.

"Oh look. It's almost time for you to go in." Kates pointed behind them. When Holly saw the bouncer motioning towards them, she swallowed and then came to a decision. "You can come in with us."

"What? No. That's okay." I shook my head.

"I mean it. The line's really long and they have a limit. Come on. Come in with us."

"What the hell." Kates broke free and led us forward. Holly

seemed uncertain, but then nodded before jumping forward. She motioned to the big guy in black. "They're with us."

When the bouncer's cold eyes passed over us, he paused on me and then nodded. "Sure."

A shiver went down my spine. I felt like he had looked inside of me. As I passed through, I looked back over my shoulder. He was still watching me, but Kates grasped my hand and dragged me the rest of the way. When the door closed she whispered in my ear, "He's one of Lucan's. Don't draw any more attention. He knows me, not you. Let's keep it that way."

I nodded and then was distracted when Adam stopped beside me. When I looked into his eyes, I was shocked. The Adam I knew had been happy and carefree. He had liked me before, but now he feared me.

The old Adam was gone. I had been a part of that.

I didn't say anything. He didn't say anything either, but his eyes went to Kates again. No matter what he'd told the police before, he knew what she had done. I went inside of him and felt how he blamed her for Shelly's death. That's when I knew that no matter how much time he took off, he'd never be over the past.

"Let's get something to drink." Kates gestured towards the bar and then grabbed Brown and Emily. She pulled them around groups and weaved through until they were on the other side of the club. I followed at a more sedate pace, but I couldn't shake the look from Adam's eyes. He watched us go as Holly stood silent beside him. She had a hand over her mouth, but she didn't stop us. When we found an empty table, I saw the relief in Kates' eyes. I wondered why, but then she plopped her purse on the table and took out her clutch. "I'll buy. Save my seat."

Emily scooted onto a high-top stool. "Is this going to be a repeat of the last time all three of us went out? I still don't quite remember what happened that night."

I gritted my teeth and realized that no one had explained she'd been love-bitten by Bennett. But that had been when she hadn't known about vampires and werewolves. Now she knew about werewolves, which reminded me. "How'd you handle it when Pete told you he was a werewolf?"

Emily blinked. She didn't look surprised at the question. "I thought he was nuts at first. And I ran away from him, but then he changed in front of me. I had to believe it after that."

"He changed in front of you? He could control the werewolf?"

She nodded. "It's a part of him. He can change whenever he wants. It's very exciting at times."

"You're okay dating a werewolf?"

"You're okay dating Lucas?" Emily shot back with a hard look in her eyes.

It made me pause. Did she know what he was?

She added, "We never talked about him before you disappeared."

We hadn't. "This is awkward."

Brown scooted off her stool. "I'm going to the bathroom."

Now it was just me and Ems, and there are so many lies I had told her.

I cleared my throat. Emily had a guarded look in her eyes, but she stared right back. So I started, "I met Roane—"

"You call him Roane."

"That's his last name."

"How long?"

"What?"

"How long have you two been together?"

"A few months, I guess. We started a few months ago, but I guess we didn't get together 'together' until yesterday?"

"Yesterday?" Emily gulped and reared back. "I thought you didn't come back until today. You went to see him first?"

"I—" I had no idea what to say now.

Kates appeared with a tray of drinks in hand. She pushed her purse onto my lap and shoved the tray on the table at the same moment. Then she scooted next to me on a stool. "I forgot how grabby guys can be. I've been spending too much time with stiffs.

One guy had his hand down my pants before I could knee him in the balls."

A look of hurt flared in Emily's eyes before she grinned and looked down. As she did, I met Kates' knowing look and knew she had come back at the right time.

I no longer wanted to be there.

"I would recommend no one going to the bathroom without me." Brown returned and pulled up a stool on the other side of Emily. "I have sanitizer with me and you'll want it. I think people were having sex in the stall beside me. And I think a girl was puking in the *other* stall."

Kates choked back a laugh. "Something tells me you're a magnet for fun."

"Fun for you maybe, but not me." Brown reached for a drink and downed it in two swallows. Then she reached for another.

Kates laughed and pulled the tray out of reach before she pointed at Emily. "This girl was wasted the last time we went out. Davy took care of her and so that means it's my turn to take care of the drunk. I don't want to have to take care of you."

"Oh, that's okay. It takes a lot for me to get drunk." Brown tipped her head back and finished the second drink.

"There are seven shots in each of these."

The glass fell to the table from Brown's hand, but Kates' caught it. Her grab was lightning fast and Brown's eyes went wide.

As Kates placed the glass on the table, Emily let out a ragged breath. "Oh wow. That was, that was fast."

Brown had new emotion in her eyes as she watched Kates. "You're really fast, like crazy fast. Oh my—"

Emily grabbed the witch's hand and dragged her off the stool. "I'm going to take her to the dance floor before she goes into too much shock."

"Did you see how fast she was?" We heard Brown ask Emily before they were out of earshot.

Kates turned to me. "So what'd the roommate have to say?"

I shook my head and reached for a glass. "I don't want to go over it."

"It was about Roane?"

"Yeah." Then I took a sip and wrinkled my nose. "This is awful, Kates."

"I know." Kates shook her head. "And that says a lot about the witch. The girl isn't normal. What are you doing hanging out with her?"

I tried another sip, but it tasted too horrible. "I thought you liked her?"

"I do, but she's off. I can't get a good read on her and that makes me nervous. What read do you have on her?"

What read did I have on her? That she was going to be a very powerful witch and sooner than I had thought. But I wasn't going to tell Kates that so I smiled. "She's a good person. I trust her."

"Okay." She lifted her glass and saluted me. "Here's to you and who you pick to surround yourself. I shouldn't complain. You're still talking to me."

"Very true."

As I reached forward to clink my glass with Kates, tingles shot up and down my spine. Someone was watching me. I scanned the club and then backpedaled when I saw a lone female in a narrow hallway. She watched me back and then I realized it was Pippa. When she saw that I'd seen her, she motioned to me.

"I'll be right back." I slid off my stool before Kates could ask me any other questions. As I drew closer, I asked, "Pippa?"

She looked scared. Pale.

"What are you doing here?"

Her eyes glanced over my shoulder. "You're in danger."

"Come again?" When she looked behind me again, I turned as well. Emily and Brown had returned to the table with Kates. All of them were smiling and laughing. "Do you want to go over there?"

Her eyes went wide. "No. I can't. And you shouldn't either. You have to get out of here, Davy."

"Why?"

"Um." She bit her lip and her hands were twisted into the ends of her shirt.

"Pippa, what's going on?" I couldn't look away from her hands. They kept twisting around each other. Something was wrong, horribly wrong. And then I slipped inside of her.

'She has no idea. I don't know how to tell her. Oh god. Why couldn't he leave it alone? He had to go and tell Mother Wolf. What's Emily going to think?'

I grabbed her shoulders. "Pippa! What is wrong? What's happened?"

"It's Pete," she wrung out. "I've been shielding you from Mother Wolf, but he didn't. He went straight to her. I could tell he didn't like you. He knows that you're different. He doesn't know what it is, but neither do I. He went straight to her."

"To who?"

"To Mother Wolf." She took a deep breath. "She sent a small army for you. They're coming here. Now."

I gulped. "How big is a 'small army'?"

"Twenty wolves. Her best fighters."

"And Pete? Is he one of them?" I had no idea what to do if the Alpha was going to attack. Saren helped me evade him once. And after my first encounter with him, I didn't think I could suppress the Immortal again so quickly.

"No, but he'll be watching. They aren't supposed to hurt Emily, but it's hard to control that in a fight. Especially when it includes vampires." As she finished speaking, her eyes went over my shoulder again.

I turned, but I already knew who she meant. Roane stood a few feet from the doorway. Gregory trickled in behind him, followed by Gavin, Wren, and Tracey. Another vampire stood behind her, but all of them stood as one force.

CHAPTER 22

Roane saw me in the next second and jerked his head towards the door. As I grabbed Pippa's hand and pulled her with me, Gavin hurried across the club to grab Kates' arm too. She yanked it back, but when he whispered something in her ear, she relaxed and looked for me. I gestured towards the rest of the group and watched as she switched from best friend to vampire slayer. It was shocking, but also not. Before Gavin found her, Kates had been laughing. A different look now slithered over her face and her eyes sparked in anticipation. She was born to hunt, much like Roane. It was what she loved.

As she met me at the door, chills went down my spine. She was once again the stranger that had kidnapped my friends not long ago. Emily stood behind her with frightened eyes and I knew she recalled the same event. Brown was beside her. She stared in befuddlement at Gregory. Her eyes trailed up his giant form and back down, and then repeated. As the group started outside, Brown scurried to follow him.

Gregory looked at her and his eyes narrowed. The rest of his face was emotionless, but he glanced at me as we followed Roane into a back alley. I shrugged.

Wren and Tracey fanned out to stand at one end of the alley.

They both passed me, but Tracey met my gaze for a brief moment. She was taller than I had realized and wore darkened red armor with her long blonde hair pulled into a braid to fall at her waistline. When she passed Gavin, I saw they were built the same. Tall and muscular. Gavin was lean for a guy, but she was sturdy for a female.

'The wolf told you?'

I looked at Roane, who stared at me with hard eyes. He was brimming in fury, but it was suppressed. He asked again, *'She told you? A pack of wolves are coming. We need to move. I don't want to fight them in town.'*

'The Alpha went to the Mother Wolf and told her about me. I don't know what he said, but he knows I'm different. He doesn't like me. Pippa came to warn me about them. How did you know?'

'Some wolves are loyal to me.' Then Roane barked at Gavin, "We'll cross the park. Kates, you'll drive their car back to the dorm. We'll follow and transport everyone somewhere safe."

Gavin nodded and walked to the front of the alley. Gregory took position next to me and Brown followed behind him. The other vampire trotted back in, past Wren and Tracey towards the group. He swept cold eyes over me and spoke to Roane, "They're coming in fast. If we hurry, we can meet them in the park."

Roane's jaw clenched together, but he gave a brisk nod. As soon as he did, Wren and Tracey rushed past us. Gavin ran with them and they went in three different directions.

"My orders?"

Roane glanced at me and then said to the vampire, "I'm staying with Davy. Gregory, you—"

He jerked his head behind him and everyone looked at Brown, who was nearly pressing into his side. She scurried back a couple steps and gave everyone a sheepish grin. "He's like the jolly green giant, but not green."

"—can stay with the witch," Roane finished with a frown.

Brown perked up. "Gee, thanks. You know I'm a witch."

"Lucas?" The other vampire stood to the side.

"Gregory, keep Emily with you too."

"And the wolf?" Gregory glanced at Pippa, who stood behind the group. She looked unsure.

Roane's eyes hardened. "I'm sure they won't hurt their own."

"Lucas?"

He jerked his head in a nod. "Bastion, circle behind us. Wren, Tracey, and Gavin will set up a perimeter. Anyone who gets through them, Gregory and I can handle. You'll scout around and sweep back. I don't want anyone trying to get us from behind."

"And me?" Kates asked in a firm voice. "I can fight too."

With a smug look, Roane told her, "There's no decree against them."

A bright smile filled her face. The anticipation in her eyes doubled. It sent a shiver down my back as she purred, "That's what I thought."

'Lucas, they're here!' Wren's thought warned the vampires.

As one person, Roane, Gregory, and Bastion jerked around. Emily squeaked. Brown grabbed hold of Gregory's shirt and flew with him. Her body picked up in the air as if she were a balloon. Kates jerked forward, but stopped at the sight. As the vampires disappeared down the alley, she held back.

Kates looked at me. "Your friend is crazy."

I had enough time to shrug before she shot after them. Pippa, Emily, and I were the only ones left in the alley.

"What's going on?" Emily hugged herself tightly.

Pippa stood next to her, but didn't say anything. She looked at me instead. They both looked at me. "What?"

"They're here for you. What's going on?" Emily gave me a 'duh' look. "Are we under attack?"

"Oh my god!" Pippa burst out. "You're not stupid, Emily. You know what's going on. That's why you're not that scared. I can tell when you're scared and you're not."

"What are you talking about?" Emily's lip trembled.

"He just said 'what about the wolf?' and the other guy said 'I doubt they'll hurt their own.' You know we're under attack. They're all acting like they're going to war. What does that mean? That they're going to war! Figure it out, or at least stop acting like you haven't because I know you have. You're just acting like this so that people will take care of you. God forbid that you'd have to fend for yourself."

Pippa started to walk away when Emily cried out, "What do you mean by all of that?"

"Davy!" We turned at the fierce command. Roane stood a few feet away and he gestured to me. "Let's go!"

I looked back. What would happen to Emily and Pippa?

Pippa waved me to go. "I'll take care of Emily. We'll be fine. Be safe."

I opened my mouth to ask if she was sure, but there wasn't enough time.

Roane grabbed me around my waist and flew out of the alley. We were in the park within moments. When he stopped, I was plastered against him and a wolf was in the air. He had leapt in the air with his mouth opened, fangs extended, but Roane reached up, grabbed his hair and flung him across the park. The wolf bounced against a tree. As it snapped in two the wolf threw his head back up and snarled at us. He took off again. Bounding towards us, he tried to go around us this time. Roane bent down and sped towards him. He met him halfway and caught the wolf unaware. With another throw at the same tree, the wolf was impaled on the broken stump. The body twitched and jerked to get free, and a high pitched whimper came from its mouth as it did. Two more wolves snapped to attention. They had been stalking Wren, but whirled around. As one went to its mate the other flew at us.

Roane tucked me behind him. *'Under any circumstance, no powers. You are human and only human. Got it?'*

I gave him a mental salute, but the wolf was on us. Roane ducked underneath the massive jaws, caught him around the neck and twisted. It snapped in two and the giant body fell limp at his feet.

Five wolves froze in place. As one body, they turned and regarded Roane. Wren plunged a dagger into one of their necks.

Gavin took hold of another and threw him, but the other three bounded towards us.

"Gregory!" Roane called out.

The Viking vampire looked up, saw the situation, snapped his wolf in two and took three long-legged strides towards us. He jumped and grabbed me from his leader's arms in mid-air, just as the three wolves ascended on Lucas. Brown smiled at me from underneath Gregory's long arm. She held onto one of his belt loops with a knife in hand.

"Hi, Davy. Isn't this exciting?"

"Brown." I shook my head at her. "You are crazy."

"I tried doing spells, but they didn't work. So then I tried to twist their tails when I caught them. I distracted a few, but one of them just swished me away." She showed me a red welt on her cheek. "It got me good so now I just hold onto Green's belt."

"Green?" I said faintly, but was distracted when Gregory deposited us both of the ground. We were away from the fight now and I expected him to return. He didn't move. I knew his job was now to guard us.

"It's my nickname for him. I think the leader called him Greg, but I like Green." Brown spoke as if we were shopping for a couch.

"Not much fazes you, does it?"

She let out a puff of air. A strand of her hair flew back in place. "Not much, no. You fight. You either live or die. It's easy to know what to do. Other stuff's harder to figure out."

Gregory glanced back and we quieted.

From there we watched the fight unfold. Roane was quicker than the others. He reacted faster and with more strength than the wolves expected. The body count grew around him, but the fight continued. Wren and Tracey had their own system. Wren would distract the wolf and lure it in while Tracey would come behind with the fatal stab. After the first one they killed, I saw that Tracey knew where to hit their heart. The wolves fell instantly. Gavin and the other vampire, the one who Roane had called Bastion, didn't fight with weapons. They threw the wolves around or were thrown by the wolves. Eventually, each of them would have enough of a hold on the necks to snap them. They just weren't as quick at it as Roane.

Kates fought her own way. She punched, twisted, rolled underneath them. I realized that she used her smaller size against them and moved around until they couldn't keep up. That was when she'd bring her gun up and shoot them in the head. Her arm was steady, her feet planted apart. She knew what she was doing and she had no qualms about it.

For some reason, the other vampires didn't bother me when they killed the wolves, but watching Kates brought chills down my back. She was human, but she wasn't at the same time. Was that how I was going to be? Was I going to become like her? I shuddered at the thought, but I knew I couldn't hide much longer.

When only seven remained, the wolves began to disperse. A few tried to drag their fallen comrades with them, but then Roane announced, "We will allow you to take them with you as long as you do not come back. This is my territory. No wolf will come in and take what is mine. Take that message to your Mother Wolf. Tell her that she's mine."

All of them stopped in their tracks and then turned to one in the back with a fur coat of sleek black. He padded forward and lifted piercing blue eyes.

Roane waited and held his gaze.

The wolf lowered his head in submission. The fight was done, simple as that.

I looked to my far right. Pete stood in an alley with his fists bunched at his side. He wanted to go out and fight with them. I felt the immense control it took to keep him where he stood, away from the fight. It was costing him. Sweat poured down his body to puddle around his feet.

His eyes caught mine and he jerked back in surprise.

As I held his gaze, I let him see inside of me. I wanted him to see inside of me. I was strong. I wasn't afraid. And I knew, without a doubt, that I'd have to deal with him at some point. Pete felt all this from me. I didn't let him go too far, not far enough to sense the

Immortal, but I wanted him to know that I wasn't scared of him. The vampires had defended me this time, but there was going to be a time for my fight. I was starting to look forward to that now.

Then Roane stood in front of me and blocked my view. He snarled at Pete, "Leave."

I grabbed Lucas' arm. "No. This is my fight."

"It's not!" He turned on me and grabbed my arms. "It's really not, Davy."

"Yes." I took his fingers and lifted them off my arm. "It really is." But when I moved around him, Pete was already gone.

I was conscious of Brown's gaze. She watched every interaction between Roane and me, but I didn't feel judgment from her gaze. Then she took my hand and I felt her calm slip into me. Immediately, my heart slowed down. Rational thought returned and then I was able to remember Emily and Pippa.

"Where's Emily?"

Kates had come over. She pointed down a hill. "They're safe. The Werewolf Wonder didn't stick around for his mate. I wonder why."

"Because she's not his, not yet." I held Roane's gaze as I spoke, "She's still my friend more than she's his girlfriend."

I moved forward, but Kates stopped me. "She's going to have to pick sides, Davy. Or you're going to have to let her go."

"She's not a part of this. She's not supposed to be a part of it. She shouldn't have even been here."

But then Roane pulled me closer. "Enough." He turned towards Gregory. "Take them to the estate."

"All of them?"

"Wren, Tracey, grab the other two. Yes, all of them."

"Roane," I started.

He turned and walked away. Gavin gave me a soft grin before he followed behind him. Bastion went next and then Gregory spoke up, "Davy?"

Brown patted my arm.

"Yeah," I sighed.

Kates laughed, "Road trip."

"Shut up," I snarled at her before I followed the jolly green giant. Brown was already going after him. Pippa and Emily got into a car with Wren and Tracey while the rest of us climbed into the back of Gregory's car.

"Where are they going?"

Gregory didn't answer.

Kates did. "They're following the werewolves, making sure they leave town."

Why wouldn't they? I should've thought of that in the first place. I rolled my eyes at my own sarcasm. What was my problem? Roane had come to protect me. He did it for me. If he hadn't, I would've used my power and the truth would've been out. Everyone would know it was me. My friends would know too and maybe that was my problem. Maybe I was sick of hiding? Maybe I was tired of being protected like I was some helpless weakling? I wasn't one, not any longer.

I sighed and then settled back in my seat. As I turned to look outside, I bolted back up. Saren stood on a hill. She was watching our car and I knew she'd been watching me the whole time. When our gazes met, she grinned and lifted two fingers in a salute. Then she disappeared and something in me went with her.

It was over. I knew at that moment that my normal life was gone. Werewolves had attacked. Vampires had defended. And one of my guides had stood back because she knew I could handle it on my own.

I couldn't stay out of the war any longer. I was the entire reason for the war.

A tear slipped down my cheek and I felt someone take my hand. Brown gave me a smile and then squeezed my hand. *I might be going out on a limb here, but I'm pretty sure you can hear thoughts. Maybe you can't. If that's the case, then I'm just thinking to myself which is normal. I do that a lot, but I know something's different about you. Maybe this is it or maybe this is a part of it. I don't know. All I know is that whole fight was about you. And the other thing I know is that when I'm not around you, I don't feel the magic in me. Okay. I feel it a little, but I always thought I was just fooling myself. But when I met you, I felt the magic in me. It was the first time I knew it was really there. I always feel it when you're around and that means something. So whatever's going on, I'm always going to be grateful to you. You made me not believe everybody when they said I was crazy.'*

Another tear fell down my cheek.

'Thank you, Davy.' She squeezed my hand once more.

CHAPTER 23

Everyone was quiet when we arrived an hour later. Even Wren seemed withdrawn as she showed the rooms to everyone. Tracey stayed in the foyer, which was big enough for a tennis court, but I felt her eyes. They hadn't left me since we'd arrived and despite the private room I was shown, I still knew she could see me. When someone knocked on my door, I wasn't sure if I should answer. I didn't know if I wanted to talk to Talia's sister or not, but then Kates burst through the door.

"That was a welcoming invite." She flung herself on my bed and flashed me a smirk. "What's your problem? Your honey came to your rescue and now you get to sit back and wait for him to come to bed tonight. I don't know about you, but that would give me the shivers, the *good* shivers."

"I was just attacked by werewolves. Unlike you, I don't find that thrilling."

"You should." Kates sat up. "What's your problem?"

"Have you seen what's going on?" My voice went shrill.

"Have you?" My childhood best friend shook her head and got off the bed. "Davy, this is what happens. We fight. We deal. Then we wait for the next fight. Why are you acting all shocked and bothered by it? Wait. I should've thought of it before, but I didn't." Then she sighed. "You can't deal, can you?"

"Shut up."

"You can't." She stood behind me. "I can't believe it, but you were the one that lit Craig on fire. It's not like this is the first time you've had to deal with something bad."

"Craig wasn't bad. Craig was a nuisance. He didn't mean that my entire life would change. I did what I did so that my life wouldn't change."

Her voice gentled. "You lit him on fire. You burned him alive, Davy. I was there and don't act like you were doing it to save yourself. You were doing it to hurt him. You wanted him dead."

"I didn't kill him. Those hunters—" My voice trembled.

"Those hunters ripped him apart, but he was dying anyway. He was already on fire when they got him. You killed him; they just made it go faster. You're going to have to do worse. You know that, right?"

Could I deal with what I'd done in the past? Craig had been obsessed and a vampire stalking me had made me go crazy. I won't ever deny that, but to acknowledge that I'd made the decision to kill him, I wanted to hide from that reality. I knew it was there. I'd made the decision, but what sort of a human was I if I could do that and then pretend I was still normal? What did that say about me?

"Davy, this is just the beginning." Kates sounded shaken. "I thought you were ready. I thought Roane had been prepping you this whole time, but he hasn't. You aren't ready for anything."

"I'm ready for what I need to be!" I shouted at her, but stopped when someone else knocked on my door.

Emily poked her head inside. "Can we come in?"

"We?" Kates laughed under her breath.

Pippa and Brown followed behind. All three of them looked around the room.

"You have a better room than me," Brown exclaimed. "You could have two bedrooms in this room."

"Three." Pippa gave me a shy smile.

Emily was quiet, but she glared at Kates before she sat in a far corner.

Kates' eyebrows went up. "Could you find a seat farther? In the next room maybe?"

"Kates."

"What?" She looked at me. "The girl's got a problem with me. I'm just pointing out the nonverbals."

"Nonverbals?" Brown's eyes danced between us.

"She glared at me and then sat as far away as possible. You know what that's called? Passive aggressive. I've heard that's not good."

"Leave her alone." I felt a headache coming on.

"Tell her not to glare at me."

"She didn't say anything."

"That's the point. Passive aggressive. She's being passively aggressive with me and it worked. She's got you doing her dirty work."

"That makes sense," Brown murmured as she sat beside me on the bed.

"Thank you."

"I don't like you. You know that." Emily glared again.

"It's like you're blaming me for this. I had nothing to do with it. If you want to blame someone, blame your wolverine, not me."

"What are you talking about?" My roommate stood. "Not all werewolves are connected to each other. They don't all know each other."

"No, but when your honey runs to the Mother after meeting Davy for two seconds and she sends a pack after her, I'd say he had something to do with it."

"Pete had nothing to do with that. And what does this have to do with Davy?"

"Please. Everybody knows it. Even the witch knows."

Brown gave Emily a tentative smile. "He was there."

"Pete would never hurt anybody. He's not like that."

Pippa's eyes went wide and Kates snorted in disbelief.

"What?" Emily looked around. "He wouldn't."

"Do you know that he changes into a werewolf?"

"That doesn't mean he hurts people."

Kates laughed. "I just want to make sure you're not denying that too."

My roommate's face twisted into an angry scowl.

"Ask her." Kates gestured to Pippa. "Weren't they friends since the cradle or something? She's the one who warned Davy."

Emily gasped. "Pippa? Is that true?"

The wolf squirmed. "I think there are things about Pete you may not know about right now."

"Did you warn Davy about the attack?"

Pippa nodded.

"Pete was behind it?"

"I really shouldn't say anything. Pete wants to be the one to explain things. It's not my place."

Kates snorted again. "Way to take the pussy way out. You're not running for office."

Pippa snapped her mouth shut and her cheeks flamed.

"I agree." Emily's eyes were accusatory.

"Hell's frozen over," Kates muttered under her breath with an evil grin on her face. "I think you two should clear the air. It's obvious something's going on between you two."

Both girls grew quiet and glanced at each other, but the door burst open and they shrieked in the next moment.

Kates groaned, "We were just getting to the good stuff."

Wren strode inside. "I could care less. You and you." She pointed to Emily and Pippa. "Come with me."

"Davy?" Emily looked at me in fear.

"It'll be fine. You haven't been kidnapped this time. You're just here for our safety."

My reassurance fell on deaf ears as Emily went pale when Wren and Tracey both grabbed an arm on each girl. They were lifted into the air and carried out the door. The two looked like dolls from the ease each vampire moved them.

When the door closed again, Kates spoke, "I wonder if we'll see them alive again?"

"Kates, shut up!" I pushed her off the bed. "Get out."

She laughed and shook her head. "Come on, Davy. That's a little funny."

"Out." I pointed to the door.

After she gave me a sarcastic eye-roll, she grabbed Brown's arm. "Come on, witch. Let's go find Gregory and see if we can get the Jolly Green Giant to find us some food. I checked the kitchen and it's bare."

Brown followed and I heard her say before the door shut, "Vampires don't eat food."

My headache had gotten worse. I had no idea where Roane was or when he would come to the estate, *if* he would come to this place, but I knew I couldn't do anything at this time. When I closed my eyes, I wasn't sure if I could fall asleep. Maybe I'd rest. So much had happened today.

ROANE DROPPED to the ground after the last werewolf bounded across the field. When Gavin dropped beside him, he turned and held his best friend's gaze for a moment. Neither spoke. Then Bastion sidled up to his other side and threw a cigarette on the ground. His heel ground it out and he spoke, "It's been ten miles. They're gone for good."

Gavin grunted. "Let's hope."

Roane watched over the field. They'd gone, but he knew they'd be back. The Mother Wolf knew about Davy. He wasn't sure what she knew, but she knew she was connected to the Immortal. The Alpha's alarm would've piqued her interest. Even he had felt it as they had fought. The Alpha had hid in an alley, there to make sure his mate went unharmed, but his fear of Davy was strong underneath his fury and concern for Emily.

Roane knew the wolf had been given strict instructions not to join the fight. If the Alpha had fought, then the truce between the Benshire wolves and Roane would've been destroyed. But he hadn't and the Mother Wolf knew sending her own wolves from a different pack wouldn't violate the truce. She had only agreed that Benshire wolves wouldn't claim his territory. The truce had been mediated years ago and Roane hadn't given it much thought since. He'd been too concerned with the impending vampire army, but the number of wolves had been increasing. Their pack still didn't match the vampires' numbers, but it was a two to one ratio now. If they succeeded in getting Davy's powers it could've been a five to one ratio and it wouldn't have mattered. Her power mixed with the Alpha's magic would've made the werewolves unstoppable. The Roane army with Jacith wouldn't have been enough.

"What are you going to do about the Alpha?" Bastion asked. His eyes were cold. "He'll figure out who she is."

"We need to strike first."

Roane knew they were both correct. It was why he had Wren take the roommate and the wolf with Davy and the rest. He wanted them away, far away. If the Alpha came for his mate, the more secluded the better. He wouldn't travel with his pack, he wouldn't dare. Roane wanted to choose when the Alpha would find out Davy was the Immortal and not a thread-holder.

"We will," Roane spoke with an icy calm in his veins.

"He's going to come for his mate. That's the plan."

Gavin didn't blink, but he looked at his best mate in surprise. "That's what you want, isn't it?"

Bastion grinned. "Seems like a good plan to me. He'll come for her—"

"And he'll come alone," Gavin added.

"Then we'll kill him. Even the Alpha can't be a match for the six of us. We're too strong together."

Gavin glanced at Roane. The mask he wore to the world had classic handsome features. Gavin had watched many times as vampires and humans alike had fallen prey to the mask Lucas showed to the world. Noble. Honor. Determination. Those were some of the traits that Roane's conquests had loved about him, but it wasn't often when they glimpsed the darker side of the hunter. He saw it now and knew their own speculations weren't at all close to what Roane had in store for the werewolf. Gavin also knew he'd be wasting his time if he tried to guess more. Roane always surprised him, but this time he worried what the price would be.

"She cares about her roommate." Roane looked at him. His gaze was emotionless, but Gavin still felt fear tug in his gut. Even so, he kept talking, "She's still a human."

Bastion's eyes skirted between the two.

Roane narrowed his. "And your point is?"

"She cares as a human. She won't understand about casualties."

"Anyone who is mated to the Alpha is a casualty. She has to die." Bastion moved back a step.

"Davy's not just a human."

"She hasn't been for awhile, but there's a part of her that still feels like she is. She's going to hold onto those friends tightly because they preserve that side of her. She feels like a human when she's with them."

Roane shook his head. He knew what Gavin warned wasn't to be taken lightly, but he didn't know Davy. He didn't see how she had faced the Alpha in the park. She wanted to fight him and she wanted him to know that she wasn't scared. That confrontation was inevitable, but he hadn't wanted it to happen then. If it had been his choice, the Alpha would've been kept in the dark for another month, maybe more, but Davy had ended those chances. No one stood up to the Alpha unless they had power inside of themselves. No human would *consider* staring down the werewolf and since Davy had, the Alpha would know there was power in her. She let him look inside of her. She wanted him to see that power, but she hadn't shut him off quick enough. The werewolf had sensed more than she realized, but Roane knew. A flare of shock in the Alpha's eyes had been enough for Roane to know. The Alpha already knew she was the thread-holder.

"When he comes, he's not coming just for his mate. He's coming for Davy too."

"The truce," Gavin reminded him.

Roane faced him. His eyes were fierce. "The truce means nothing. We killed too many of her fighters. They'll rise up now. They were going to anyway. It was just a matter of time."

"But the Roane Army—"

"—is the perfect timing for their revolution. They want this land and they want the thread-holder. Now they know who she is. We'll be divided against the army and the wolves. It's perfect timing on her side."

"They'll have to fight the Roane Army then," Bastion spoke.

Roane shook his head. "No, they won't. The army doesn't want this territory. They'll search for the thread-holder. When they won't be able to find her, they'll leave. We'll be destroyed by then and the wolves will stake their claim."

"Why won't they wait it out? Let the Army destroy us and come in afterwards?" Bastion itched for another smoke. He gritted his teeth against the craving. No vampire should be dependent upon something men invented.

"They'll move soon. They know where she is now. And they won't want me to move her where they can't find her."

Gavin knew how Roane cared for Davy, but he wondered if he cared more about keeping the Immortal from his enemies. When the Roane elders hadn't listened to Roane and instead had sent a hunter after him, he knew his best friend had been shattered by the betrayal. Roane had always been loyal to his Family. He had lived and breathed by what the Family wanted. His post as the hunter and then protector of the Family had been the creed that he lived by. When they didn't listen to him and decided to try and destroy the thread-holder, Roane had taken it as a personal attack. Gavin wondered how much his best friend's ego was mixed with protecting Davy.

Then a different enemy popped into his mind and Gavin asked, "And your brother? I know you haven't forgotten about him."

Roane turned cold eyes on him. "I haven't forgotten."

Bastion remained quiet, but he was aware of their tension.

Gavin kept quiet and Lucas instructed, "We'll go back to the estate. Keep on patrol when we're there. I expect Davy's roommate will call her mate soon. I want to be there when he arrives."

Then the three turned as one and sped away. In the night sky, they blended with the ground and were only shadows among the darkness.

I WOKE TO DARKNESS. When I sat up, I knew someone else was in the room with me and I could hear him undressing.

"Roane?"

"Yeah?" He pulled back the covers and slipped underneath. I felt him slide in next to me and then his arms wrapped around me. He tucked me close. I relished the feel of his body against mine. It calmed me.

"Why were you angry with me before?" I yawned as I asked him.

"Because you showed yourself to the Alpha. He knows too much now."

My mouth was pressed against his shoulder as I mumbled, "I'm sorry. I was so angry."

He tightened his arms around me. "I know."

"Did I mess up?"

"A little, but we'll be fine. We can handle it."

"Did they go away? Those wolves?" I tried to keep my eyes open. I wanted to see him, but it was a struggle. They were becoming too heavy.

He kissed my forehead and smoothed my hair back. In a gentle voice, he soothed me. "You can go to sleep. The wolves are long gone by now."

I reached for his hand and entwined our fingers. "What about you? You don't need to sleep that much."

"I'll stay with you for awhile. Go to sleep, Davy. You need it." He pressed another kiss to my forehead and then my shoulder. His arms turned me and he shifted so he spooned me from behind. I felt protected and sheltered in his arms.

"G'night, Davy."

I tried to return it, but I couldn't. My mind had already ventured into dreamland.

CHAPTER 24

When I woke again, Roane was on the edge of the bed. He sat with his elbows on his knees and his hands cradling his head. I scooted beside him and looked at his back. Not long ago, I would've itched to caress it. This day, I felt nothing.

"I'm numb."

He looked at me. "I know."

I lifted haunted eyes to him. "I should feel something. I've tried to fight this. I try to feel something and sometimes I do. I feel guilty. I look at my friends and a part of me doesn't feel like I'm friends with them anymore. What's wrong with me?"

As his hand reached for mine, I heard him sigh. "I feel it too."

"I don't like feeling like this."

"Your mind is preparing you for what's going to happen. Bad things are going to happen."

I didn't want to hear him, but he was right. My body had started to shut down. Emotions weren't going to help me anymore. "I don't like being this way. I'm becoming a robot. I don't even care what's going on anymore. When Kates kidnapped Emily, I was so irate. I was hurt by her betrayal, but now she could betray me again and I wouldn't blink. What does that say about me?"

Roane pulled me to his side and pressed a kiss to my shoulder.

He murmured against my skin, "I think it means that we're going to survive. Whatever happens, we're going to survive."

"I should feel. I don't feel anymore."

He kissed my forehead with a sense of desperation. "We'll get there. I promise."

"What about Emily?" I felt him tense beside me, but I had to ask. "I know Pete is my enemy, but she's in love with him. I saw their connection. It's deep, really deep. And she's my roommate. She was a good friend to me."

He pulled away and stood to cross the room. His voice was distant. "If she's with him, she's with him."

"What about Kates? She still loves Lucan, you know."

Roane's eyes pierced mine. I could feel the struggle in him, but he shoved me out. "I'm sorry. I can't lie to you. You're going to lose friends. What do you want me to say?"

His words whipped me. They stung.

He added, "I am sorry, Davy, but this is what war is. And we're in one. It started with Lucan and then it began again with the wolves. They'll be coming back. I moved us off my territory so that he would come."

"What are you saying?"

"I want the Alpha to come. Then the Roane army will be coming too, and then my brother. We can't survive all of them. Not all of us are even going to survive this first round."

Something in his voice made me cold. I heard everything he said. He said it before, but it was how he did it now. He was trying to tell me something else. He wanted to prepare me for something. I could feel his regret. It went deep, down to his bones, but he wouldn't let me in. He used to let me in. We wouldn't even have to speak out loud, but now he was a stranger again. It seemed so long ago that we had shared a bed.

My gut twisted inside. "What aren't you saying to me?"

Pain flared in his coal eyes, but it was gone quickly. Regret replaced it and then a steel wall slammed over it. He stood upright. "I'm saying to you that you're going to lose some of your friends. I've tried to shelter you from this, but I can't anymore. You're not just a human anymore. You're the reason for all of this and you've been taking a backseat. This is when you stop crying about the war and start becoming a part of it."

"You haven't wanted me to be a part of it." I couldn't believe him.

Roane hissed back, "Because you haven't wanted to step up. You've had this 'poor me' attitude the whole time, even before I met you. I felt it in the library that day and I hated it. You act like a victim. That is what's going to make you a victim."

My mouth fell open; I couldn't form a single thought. How dare he—how dare—He was right. I couldn't fight it anymore because he was right about everything. I had been feeling sorry for myself this whole time.

"You stopped transitioning awhile ago." Roane brought me back. His voice was soft now. "Since you came back from wherever you were, you've been ready. You came back ready. You just didn't want to admit it. That's why you've shut down. That's why you can't feel anything and I know that you've been forcing yourself to ignore it. I could feel that from you too. You don't trust your friends anymore. You want to, but you don't. Stop lying to yourself."

My mouth snapped shut. Each word hurt more than the last. "It's a hard pill to swallow. I hate when things change, especially when I have no control over any of it."

"That's life." His eyes were hard. "Deal with it."

It was then that I really looked at him. He snapped me out of my reverie and brought me back to our reality, to the two of us in that room. I was highly aware of how close he stood to me. And that he only had on a pair of unbuttoned slacks. They had fallen low on his hips. His stomach and groin muscles were defined. Each ridge and line stuck out against his body.

"You've lost weight." My eyes were hungry. I was hungry.

He sighed and ran a hand through his hair. "The last few months haven't been easy on me."

"Do you need to feed?"

Molten heat flared in his eyes. "And become human? I think not, Davy."

I knew that. Of course, I knew that, but I didn't like it.

"What?"

I shook my head. "What if there's a way you could feed from me and not become human? I wanted your brother to become human. Maybe I can control it. You could get power from me."

"I did get power from when you bit me. I got a lot of it. I still have it in me."

"You do?"

He nodded and watched me with a knowing look. I flushed under his perusal. "Sometimes I think you know me better than I know myself."

"Because I do. I love you, Davy." He crossed the room and cupped the side of my face. "How are you feeling now?"

"More normal."

His lips were so close. "You feel better?"

I nodded. My throat was thick. The need for him flared inside of me. I was becoming blind to everything else. "I need you. When we're not on the same page, I can't handle it. I feel disjointed. I'm strongest when I'm with you."

He grinned and dipped down. His lips met mine, but stayed still. I closed my eyes. I waited as my heart pounded loudly in my eardrums. Then his lips brushed against me. "I can help you with that."

Before I had time to respond, he picked me up and threw me on the bed. I shrieked in laughter, but his mouth quickly silenced me. Everything in me hummed in pleasure. His arms went around me. His mouth explored mine. His body demanded everything from me and I gave it to him. As he lifted me higher on the bed and slid inside me, I was blind to anything but him. The world ceased to exist. It was only the two of us.

And then an hour later I rolled over as Roane lay beside me.

"Now I feel really connected to you," I drawled and panted for a minute in silence.

Roane grinned and then groaned as he pressed a quick kiss to my shoulder. He sat up in the next moment. "I'm sorry, but I should go. I have things to do. So do you."

"I do?" I enjoyed watching him getting ready to protect me.

He spoke as he began to dress, "I can't take on three enemies without help."

"You said no powers. They'll know then."

"They already know. They might not know you're the Immortal, but they know you're the thread holder. Maybe it's time they find out the rest." Roane flashed me a grin before he left.

Whatever I'd been feeling before was gone. As I dressed and went in search of the kitchen, I couldn't keep myself from grinning. He did that to me and when I finally found it, Kates looked up and laughed. "You've got the Roane Glow again. Lucky."

Brown smiled and gestured to the table. "They have doughnuts, Davy."

Indeed they did. The kitchen table was filled with cartons of the frosted pastries along with bowls of fruit. Some bread sat beside boxes of cereal and a dish of pancakes was placed in the middle.

Pippa gave me a tentative grin. "They have a chef. He made me an omelet."

Emily was quiet as she sat on a stool by the counter. Kates caught my look and rolled her eyes.

"Davy?" Gavin brandished a metal spatula in the air. "Give me an order. I'm here to please."

"You're the chef?"

He smirked. "I have many skills."

"Okay," I replied as I scooted onto a stool beside Emily. She stiffened and bowed her head. "Surprise me. Whatever you want."

"Anything?" His eyes lit up.

"She just said anything." Kates scowled.

A heated look passed between the two before he jerked away. I heard the control in his voice as he forced a light tone. "You said anything, Davy. Be warned."

I watched Kates, but said to him, "It'll be fine. I'm sure."

She rolled her eyes at me this time, popped a strawberry in her mouth and left the room. Brown watched her go and I saw the same nonjudgmental curiosity from when she'd studied me with Roane before fill her eyes.

"This is a really nice place, Davy. This is your—" Pippa frowned.

"Boyfriend's?" Emily supplied. She looked up again.

My roommate was in love with a werewolf, but she was acting jealous. I thought she was over her crush. "I guess. I've never been here before."

"Lucas seems to own a lot of places."

Though Gavin didn't act any differently, I could feel his interest in the conversation. His hands slowed as he opened an egg.

"Davy."

"Yeah?" I looked back over. Emily had been studying me. "What?"

"So you and Lucas are serious?"

Pippa moved away from the counter, but Brown inched closer. The witch stepped away from the table to round the counter so she was behind me. It was a slow movement, but I knew that Gavin had noticed it. His eyes jerked up once, but went right back to the skillet.

"Why are you asking me about him?"

Emily drew back. "I can't ask you some questions? You lied to me about him, remember?"

"We've gone over this."

Annoyance flashed over her face, but she cleared it quickly. "I thought you were in love with Adam before. I'm just wondering how serious this is. I don't want you hurt again."

She was lying. I knew that much, but this sudden loathing shook me. "I thought you cared about me."

"I do." Emily smiled. "Why do you say that?"

What could I say without making it worse?

"A bitch." Pippa jumped as she spoke.

All eyes turned to her.

"What did you say?"

Pippa jerked to the side. She met Emily's gaze. "A bitch. You're being a bitch."

"Excuse me?"

The wolf crossed her arms and leaned back on her heels. "You heard me."

Kates chuckled behind me and Gavin was all eyes. He didn't hide his attention now.

"I can't believe you. You have some nerve, Pippa! You're the reason we're all here."

"No, I'm not!" she shouted back. "We're here because of Pete. He didn't like Davy and he could tell there was something different about her. He's the one who went to the Mother Wolf. I've been trying to shield Davy from her. I've been trying to protect her. I wanted to protect all of us."

"Why? And what's so special about her? I don't understand any of this." The hysteria in Emily's voice was evident.

Pippa opened her mouth and then clamped it shut. She grabbed the ends of her braids and held on.

"Well?"

She pulled harder on her braids. "I don't know what Davy is, but she's something. I could tell right away. But Pete didn't care. He got mad. He didn't see that she's a person and a good one. And she's your roommate. And she cares about you. He didn't stop to think about any of that."

Emily turned heated eyes to me, but looked back at Pippa. "What are you talking about?!"

A plate was placed beside me gently and I saw that Gavin had a resigned look in his eyes. Then I saw behind him that Wren and Tracey had filed into the room. They stood in the background waiting for an opening. Something had happened.

Roane and Bastion came in next. He jerked his head to the side and motioned for me to come. Before I left, I looked back once more. Brown and Kates both saw where I was going, but neither said a word. When I followed Roane out into the hallway, I heard Pippa explode, "Because it's not right! They want to hurt Davy and I know it's never right when someone is going to get hurt."

Roane reached for my hand and led me into a different room. When the door closed, he didn't say anything for a moment. "The Alpha's coming. He's on his way right now. They're waiting for me to talk to you and then when we go back in, they're going to grab your friends."

"How do you know he's coming right now?"

"Gregory called it in. He was on sentry duty last night. We don't have long. They're coming fast."

"They?"

Roane nodded. "I wanted him to come alone, but he's not. It's going to be a full fight. Your roommate's boyfriend is bringing twice the number. Forty wolves, plus the Alpha. I'm not going to lie to you. Some of your friends won't make it out alive, especially the female wolf."

"Pippa?"

"They see her as a traitor. He's been talking to Emily. He's brainwashed her into thinking you're the enemy and so is the other girl. Emily's no longer Emily anymore."

"That's not true. She still has feelings for you."

He sighed again and leaned back on a desk. He braced against the edge, his arm muscles bulging. "Maybe. Maybe not. She feels lied to. She saw us last night. I'm sure she could see how we feel about each other. You've been lying to her since the beginning and she doesn't understand our side. No one's been talking to her to explain it."

"She should've talked to me."

"She came to your room last night. I think she heard us talking. I knew she was there, but she left. I should've given it more thought."

It didn't matter anymore. What was done was done. I swallowed back the pain and asked, "What do I do?"

"You do what you can." Roane held my face in his hands. He tilted it up so his eyes held mine captive. He'd been guarded before, but now he let me in. The wall lifted and I saw his love. It was clear as day and I had to choke back tears. "I love you, but stay close to me. Okay?"

My throat was thick with emotion. He wiped some tears from my face. Then he pressed a kiss to my forehead and dipped to meet my lips. I pressed against him.

Someone rapped on the door with their knuckles. Bastion poked his head inside. "Gregory's here. We've got five minutes."

Roane straightened and the hunter took over him. He was cold. Ruthless. "Let's go."

"And her?" Bastion nodded to me.

"You don't have to protect me. I'll be fine. I promise."

"Let's go!" Wren shouted from the hallway and then all the vampires sprinted away.

The kitchen had grown quiet when I went back. Kates straightened from the wall. "What's going on?"

"The Alpha is here. He brought forty wolves with him."

Pippa paled. "They're going to kill me."

Emily looked at her sharply. "Don't be stupid. You'll be fine."

"She's right, Emily." My voice was strong. "They're going to kill her. They think she's a traitor."

She flushed. "They're not going to kill her. That's insane, Davy."

"Yes, they will. She chose to protect me against them. Kates, protect Pippa. She's one of ours. Brown, stay with Gregory."

She perked up. "I don't know where he is."

"He came back. We've got three minutes."

"Davy." Emily looked shaken.

"Wake up," Kates barked. "Nothing's the same anymore." She was serious, more serious than I'd ever seen her. "The numbers are unmatched. We're not going to keep a unified front. That means it's going to be every person for herself."

"I'll be fine."

Kates snorted and then turned to me. "Will you?"

She was asking a different question and I nodded. "I'm ready. I'll be fine."

The Immortal stirred inside of me.

CHAPTER 25

We started to scatter, but Roane spoke in my head, *'Davy, stop them.'*

"Wait!"

Everyone froze. Brown tripped.

"Davy?" Kates frowned. "What's going on?"

"Roane said to stop."

"Huh?" Brown looked around. "I can't hear him. Am I defective?"

Kates snorted. "No, girl. Oh my god. They have a mind thing. They can talk to each other in their heads."

Emily scowled and Pippa gave me a dreamy smile.

"I was right!" Brown snapped her fingers in the air. "You heard me in the car, didn't you?"

'Tell them to shut up,' Roane snapped.

I held up a hand and everyone quieted.

'Change of plans. Tracey and Wren are going to cover the south corner. Bastion and Gregory are on the west side. Gavin and I will take the north edge. I need you and your friends to watch the east side of the house. It's a cliff, Davy. Make sure no wolves can climb up from the rocks below.'

'How are we supposed to stop them?'

'I don't know. Use your Immortal power. Figure it out. You'll be fine. There's a slayer with you.'

Use my Immortal stuff. Easier said than done, but he was right. It was time I fought beside them.

"What'd he say?" Kates moved forward a step.

I skimmed the group. Brown looked scared and excited at the same time. Pippa was wary. Emily looked like it was beneath her to be with us and Kates gave nothing away. She was ready to fight. In that moment, I knew everything was going to be okay. It had to be. I'd just gotten this group of friends, even my brainwashed roommate.

Before I replied, I caught a mischievous glimmer in my roommate's eyes. It was masked quickly, but it was there. Then I caught Kates' gaze and nodded in Emily's direction. She understood immediately, shuffled one step to the side, and backhanded the girl. Emily went down hard.

"Ah! What'd you do that for?" Brown slapped her two hands to her cheeks.

Kates snorted. "Like she was really going to help us."

Pippa bit her lip. "She's right. Emily can communicate with Pete. She would've told him everything that was going on with us."

"So what did your lover say?"

"Right." On to business. "We're supposed to guard the east side. He doesn't want any wolves to climb up the cliff."

Pippa's eyes went wide, but Kates smirked. "Have you seen that cliff? A bird wouldn't come that way."

"What do you mean?"

Kates led the way to the east side. When we stepped outside, the entire east side of the house was a stone patio. It extended outwards and around the back of the house. A basketball court could've fit on it. We went to the edge and looked over the cliff. Brown gasped and reeled back. I didn't blame her. My own stomach jumped into my throat at the sight beneath us. Water crashed onto boulders below. The fall would've been two miles down. Huge boulders littered the floor of the ocean. Wind rushed against us at a violent speed.

I could see why a bird wouldn't fly upwards.

"It's a vacuum effect," Kates explained. "Nothing could climb up those walls. They're made completely of rock so it's going to be hard for any werewolf to scale it. If they come up in their human forms, the wind's going to just knock 'em down. Anyone climbing that thing is suicidal."

"He wants to make sure."

She rolled her eyes. "Roane doesn't want you near the action. Forget that. I'm going."

"Me too." Pippa jumped next to Kates. "I'm going to fight too. You guys are protecting me, but my family's bloodline is old."

We all stared at her.

She blushed. "That means I'm stronger than the normal werewolf."

"Ah."

"Gotcha."

"That makes sense now."

"Let's go." Kates started to turn.

"Wait. What about us if werewolves come up?" Then I looked at Emily, who groaned from the lounger that Kates had placed her on. "And what if she wakes up?"

"Really?" She quirked an eyebrow at me. "Put her back to sleep, Miss Almighty."

With a curt gesture to Pippa, they were both gone within an instant.

Brown mused, "Why'd she call you Miss Almighty? Was that metaphorical or rhetorical? Is there a difference? I should look them up when I get home." And then it didn't matter. Brown circled around me with her hands in the air. "I was thinking that I could try some spells. When I'm around you, I feel my magic more. Maybe if I'm connected to you, I might be useful."

"Connected? What do you mean connected?" I moved back a step.

"Our minds. Like meditation. We can chant together."

Suddenly a howl split through the air. Brown grew silent. And the air grew heavy. A somber feeling came over me. I felt him in that howl, the Alpha called to his pack. A second later a unified chorus howled back.

Brown jumped back. Her eyes went wide and her golden skin went white. She grabbed my arm, but I couldn't reassure her. My own heart was pounding.

The essence of Talia's mother was in him. He wasn't holding anything back. That deep magic sparked into me. He could feel me and even as I shook to the core, I couldn't dwell on it. I felt him searching for me. Something shifted and a channel opened to me. I heard him talking to Emily.

"Ems. Emily, are you there?"

When she didn't answer, his anger kicked up a notch.

"That bitch. What'd she do to you?" I heard his growl. *"Wake up!"*

Emily stirred behind us. She rolled over on the lounger, but her eyes stayed shut.

"Davy, this is not fun."

"Was it ever?" I asked through gritted teeth.

"What if I can't do magic? I don't know how else to help."

They howled again. The sound echoed all around. It ricocheted off the rocks. They zapped around us. Brown gasped again and whirled in a tight circle. Her fear was so strong. She was rattled to the bone.

"Brown," I started.

"What?" She glanced everywhere, but at me. She kept jumping in place. The shadows were terrifying her.

It grew dark in the next instant. The light sailed away and the night sky rolled in its place. Only one person had the magic to do that.

"What just happened? This isn't right." Brown clung to me. Her nails dug into my arm.

"It's Pete," I seethed. "It's easier for wolves to hunt at night. Vampires don't see as well as they do."

"I'm really starting to get scared now," she whimpered.

I grew tired of the wolves' antics with their howling. I felt the Immortal kick inside of me and closed my eyes. It was only a matter of time before she burst free. When that happened, there was no going back.

I said again, "Brown."

"What?"

"Look at me."

She grew still and turned. When she did, her eyes widened. "Aren't you scared?"

"No."

"I wet my pants, not in the good way." She shuddered.

"I'm not scared because—" How could I say it?

"Because?"

He howled again. This one was long and drawn out. It was meant for intimidation, but it had the opposite effect on me. The Immortal rattled inside of me now. I could barely hold her back. She wanted out. She wanted his blood. She wanted to reclaim Talia's essence into the rightful body. Mine.

I opened my mouth, but my body shook.

Brown's eyes grew into saucers. She stepped back and her hand let go of my arm.

The Immortal burst free in me. I couldn't hold her in and my eyes switched like a light had been turned on. It now looked like daylight to me. Brown's ashen face was stretched from her fear. I saw the veins in her neck and the blood that pumped into her heart. Everything in her was a colorful three dimensional x-ray.

Pete's howl was cut off. He'd sensed my transition and now he sat back, waiting for the next move. It was mine and I shot off from the patio. I was everywhere at once. I could see all the wolves, how they hunched down behind their hiding spots. Some overlooked the vampires, but most of them still hadn't found where Roane's small army waited. The element of surprise was everything among these two supernatural beings.

Bastion stood behind a tree. His form was camouflaged. I wouldn't have known he was there except for the blood pumping in him. His eyes were closed and he waited. He sensed where they were and they hadn't moved close enough for an attack. Gregory had taken a position behind a boulder. The giant blonde Viking had a bow and arrow in hand, notched and ready to fly. He waited for Bastion's signal.

Then I saw Wren and Tracey. Both knelt down behind a small wall. Each looked graceful, content with their heads bent between their knees. They, like all the others, were waiting. Roane and Gavin stood on separate ends of their area. Unlike the others, they didn't hide. They stood at the tip of their hill. They wanted the attention. They wanted the wolves to come to them.

Roane's head bent and his nostrils flared. He had sensed me. When his head turned towards me, I knew he wanted to see me so I stepped forward.

"What are you doing?"

Gavin tilted his head to the side. "You look good with the white eyes."

I'd forgotten how I looked as the Immortal. I smirked at him. "He wants to be invisible." My anger sparked and magic exploded inside me. "So you will be instead."

Gavin's mouth started to open, but he was gone in the next second. So was Roane. And I knew all the others were too. They were now the invisible ones among the night. Only the wolves remained in true form. I felt Pete's shock when the magic exploded. He knew the thread holder was present, but the new power in the air was a surprise.

Then I bent backwards and my body swooshed to Brown. When I landed behind her, she didn't react. She had no idea I was there so I reached inside of her. My hand found the box where her magic was locked. It was stretched at the seams, ready to explode. My thumb brushed against the lock and the door opened an inch. Magic slipped through and Brown gasped. Her back arched upwards. Her arms shot out. I could see the blood rushing through her. The ends of her fingers tingled and sparks shot out.

The box's lid remained in place. Even as I watched, I saw how it was trying to close again. Magic older than me had put it there. It fought against the Immortal. Something moved in me and I knew it was a response to Brown's box. The magic surrounding it was angered by my interference, but the Immortal's magic was too powerful. I reached back in and lifted it once more. It went open all the way, but when my finger moved away, the lid started to close once again.

"Oh my god," she shrieked and squealed at the same time. In the next moment, she had her eyes closed and was chanting. If I'd been nervous she couldn't control her magic, it would've been for nothing. Brown had complete control over herself. The magic filled her and the paleness of her skin grew into a rosy tan. The fear was gone. She glowed.

"Thank you, Davy," she spoke in the next breath.

A wolf howled in pain. The sound split through the night air.

It had begun.

I lifted my head and was there in the next moment. Wren pulled her sword back and stood over the wolf. Its body quivered in pain underneath her feet. It lifted his head and looked at her, but the fight quickly left its body, its neck slumping back down.

The first kill went to the vampires. Pete's anger exploded into full force. He leapt through the air, right behind Wren and Tracey. Both vampires jumped out of the way, but his mouth was opened. One of his fangs nicked Tracey's leg and she screamed. Her body twisted and convulsed. Poison from him shot through the vampire. Wren screamed and lunged in the air. Her sword was poised above her head, ready to strike, but he turned his head. He waited, ready to open his powerful mouth.

I appeared in that moment. He turned to see me and sniffed into me. His eyes widened. He wasn't ready for what he saw, but it didn't matter. Wren's sword pierced his eye in that moment. Instead of reeling back from pain, he snapped his jaw at her. I threw myself forward and opened my arms. A light from me blinded him and he recoiled.

"What the—" Wren gasped, but he was gone. She ran to Tracey.

I knelt on the other side of her and reached inside. The poison was flowing throughout her entire body. There was a glazed look in her eye and her body began convulsing in a seizure. Her head was thrown back and her body lifted off the ground. When her eyes met mine, I knew she saw me. Wren had no idea I was there. I was invisible to her, but it didn't matter. Tracey's blood saw the thread in me, the same one that had been in her sister and mother before that. I felt her mother's essence battling to get back into me. It wanted to rejoin the Immortal, but it couldn't. It was still locked inside of Pete, but Tracey saw that too.

"Mom?" Her eyes were white around them.

"Tracey, honey, don't go. Stay with me." Wren patted her cheeks.

"You," she gasped. Her tongue got stuck and she repeated the word over and over. Her throat was convulsing at the same time. Her eyes locked onto mine. I couldn't look away.

Wren lifted her head and looked around. Sounds of battle filled the air now. Wolves growled. They whelped. They screamed.

My eyes couldn't leave Tracey's in that moment, so I went into her. My empathic nature shifted and separated from the Immortal. I felt her fear, but I also felt her yearning. She wanted her family back. She loved Wren, but she had returned because of me. I was connected to her sister and she wanted her back. The love she had for her sister and mother was blinding. It brought tears to my eyes. Before I left her, I took some of the fear from her. She calmed and her body lay back down on the ground.

Wren's fear subsided then.

My empathic side connected with the Immortal again and I reached inside of Tracey. I sucked the poison into my hand. Unlike the vampire, the poison bonded with me. It was from the essence of the Immortal and it wanted to be back with its master. When I stood back, Tracey was already healing. I watched as her strength sparked and built. Wren sat back and gaped in relief. Before long, both of them were looking at the other. No words were shared, but they turned as one and jumped at a passing werewolf.

I returned to Brown the next moment and found her bent over the deck's edge. She cast spell after spell below her. Werewolves had braved the treacherous terrain. They were slowly inching their way up. It wouldn't be long before they overcame us.

Brown groaned as she gritted her teeth. Magic sparked from her fingertips. One by one, werewolves fell, but then they got back on the cliff. It was as if she had never hit them. I snapped back to my human form and could feel their magic in the air. The Alpha was keeping them from falling to their deaths.

"Brown," I said.

She gasped. "They won't die. Why won't they die?"

Each spell she sent to them was powerful, but the Alpha's was even more so. My eyes shifted into the Immortal's and then I was able to see through the darkness below. A net had been strung up below them, made of magic. When the wolves were hit by Brown, they fell, but bounced back up. They bounced to a higher place. She was helping them.

I laid a hand on her arm. "Stop."

"I can't. They keep coming."

"His magic is stronger than yours. He put up a net below them. They can't fall through it."

"How do we break it?" Brown wanted to help. I felt the need in her. It was strong. Tears filled her eyes. "I need this, Davy. I need to help. I need to be useful for once. All my life, everyone's laughed at me. I'm tired of it."

I nodded. "Instead of hitting the wolves, shoot below them. I think your magic can undo the net. The wolves will fall then."

She clamped her mouth shut and turned. Her shoulders were squared. And she concentrated with everything she had. She drew up a spell stronger than she had ever imagined. It came out from the depths of her magic and built at a furious rate. I stood back, slightly awed at the gift Brown had. If this was what she could do now, I wondered what she could do when that box was broken in pieces.

"Tres all conte, break the binds he has made. Break the net to fall free. Tres all conte, tres all conte, tres all conte, break the binds he has made. Break the net to fall free. Tres all conte," she repeated. As the power built in her, she narrowed her eyes and the magic blasted from her. The net burst into flame the next moment. It singed the air and crackled. As it fell, the sounds faded. Then a smug look came over Brown's face.

I grinned and stood back. The wolves didn't stand a chance against her.

"Davy!" Gavin shouted at me. I whirled.

CHAPTER 26

When I flashed to Roane and Gavin, I saw the Alpha in mid air. He was lunging with his massive jaw open and ready to tear into Roane, who stood with his back to him. He was facing Gavin, who had another wolf lunging at him.

"No!" I thrust my hands up. Everything stopped in that moment. Both wolves froze in mid-air. Only Roane turned to me.

I walked towards the wolf that was ready to pull Gavin's spine out. After a jerk to the fur underneath his neck, I knew the wolf would fall on the ground. Then I went to the Alpha and stood there.

"No—" Roane started.

I snapped my fingers and time started again. Pete's jaw closed around me instead of Roane.

"No!" I heard Gavin yell in the distance, but I closed my eyes. I felt Pete's surprise, but it didn't matter. He tried not to clamp his teeth together, but everything happened so quickly. He couldn't stop in time. I wanted all my Immortal power to burst within him. I wanted it to be like a bomb. And I wanted to take back Talia's mother's essence. She belonged to me. She wanted to be with me and I wanted to take her with me. As the Immortal's energy built up, I felt her beside me.

Pete struggled. He knew what had happened and was trying to

take it all back. He was trying to open his jaw and unclench what he had accidentally swallowed. It didn't matter. He wasn't the Immortal, though he thought he was. I saw that now. The Mother Wolf had told him that he was the Immortal. He had the essence therefore he was the one all the prophecies foretold.

He had been wrong. He could feel it now.

For a split second, I looked up and saw Talia's mother. Her hair was red like her daughter's and flowed back. Her black dress billowed beneath her hair and blue eyes flashed at me. She smiled and I heard her thoughts, *'It is time for my energy to join the rest. He is not to blame. What was put in him was not his fault or his inspiration. He has been led astray in many ways.'*

It didn't matter. Pete meant to hurt someone I loved. Her pleads wouldn't save him. I pushed forward and let the Immortal explode within him. When it sparked, he reeled backwards and tried to spit me out of his mouth. It didn't matter. I wanted this to happen. It needed to happen. The Alpha's body twisted and convulsed round and round. He tried everything to get me out, but I held firm and then the explosion happened. When it did, his jaw snapped open and I was flung from it. Talia's mother and her essence went with me. She had joined the Immortal and was at peace. As we were thrown in the air, her eyes closed. She laid her hands on her chest and melted away. Then I felt her join the Immortal.

We landed on the ground a few feet away. Pete was flung across the hill. Roane and Gavin had fallen back too. I was beside them before they awakened.

A sudden tingling on my neck made me look over. Pippa stood above Pete's body. She watched him. Somehow she knew what had happened, though I didn't know how. I didn't care at that moment.

I stepped towards her. "Let him be."

"He loved her," she wrung out. Her eyes didn't leave his form as he lay on the ground, writhing in pain.

I watched as she knelt at his feet.

"He's not the same, Pippa," I warned her.

It didn't matter.

She shook her head and ran a finger over his forehead. "No matter what he's been told, he loved her. He's lost Emily as well as the trust he had in Mother Wolf. You don't understand the betrayal he's feeling." She looked up with tears in her eyes. "He was supposed to become my mate. She changed that. She changed everything."

Pippa closed her eyes. The wolf spirit within her went into him. I closed my eyes and followed. Where I went, I wasn't expecting what I saw. The two were pups again and they were playing in a field. Pippa tripped him with her large paws and Pete grinned crookedly, tongue hanging out as he bounded towards her. He stumbled over his own paws, but the two rolled over each other in the grass. Though in wolf form, their joy was evident. Both grinned and whimpered in excitement until the air cooled. They stopped in the next second and lifted their heads to gaze at the far corner of the woods.

An older woman in black garb floated out of the trees. She held a long arm with a finger pointed to them. As a spell started to spew from her mouth, I lunged at her. Black eyes widened and whirled to me before I fell on her. All her battles were won or lost through words and magic. I grinned in enjoyment as I wrapped both hands around her neck and lifted her head free. The fight was over. Her body slumped to the ground, both pups breathed in relief, and her head melted in my hands. It became a puddle of black gunk and I dropped it in disgust.

I felt Pippa's approval, but was back in my real form the next moment. She was still bent over his body. The air sizzled with relief instead of despair and I breathed more lightly.

Roane grasped my elbow and frowned. "What just happened?"

"I have no idea." I smiled at him. "But I think it was good."

He cast a concerned look at the two wolves. "Are you sure?"

"It's for the best. I promise."

Pippa looked up now. She brushed tears away. "Everything's better now. She can't touch him again."

"Mother Wolf?"

She jerked her head up in a nod. "That was her inside him. She was trying to come back in and fix him. She underestimated you." A laugh sputtered from her. "Who knew you could do that? You stopped her, Davy. Thank you."

Pete still lay on the ground unconscious. He had curled into a fetal position.

"Is he going to be okay?"

Pippa shook her head. "I have no idea, but I'll take him back with me."

"To school?" Alarms went off in my head. If Emily went back there too, how would that go?

"No." A grave look entered her eyes. "I'll take him back to my family. I won't be returning to Benshire again."

"Huh?"

"I come from the old wolves. We want to remain hidden. We don't want to war against the vampires. We'll never win. That was her agenda for the last hundred years, but now that the Alpha doesn't exist anymore, we'll make our stand. You shouldn't have to worry about us anymore."

When she turned to leave with a determined glint in her eyes, I was taken aback. There was fierceness in the female wolf that I'd never witnessed before. She was like a new person, but one that I already respected.

"How are you going to move him?" But as I asked, the words died in my throat. Wolves emerged from the shadows surrounding us. Their green eyes glowed in the night. I jerked forward, but Roane caught my arm. He pulled me back.

He murmured in my ear, "They're allies."

"How do you know?"

"She called them."

"Pippa?"

I whirled back to where she was greeting one of the larger wolves. He had shaggy grey fur. His old age was evident, but his eyes looked through me. In wolf form, he towered over Pippa. He would've stood a foot higher than even the Alpha's wolf form. As more wolves moved to the unconscious wolf, a sense of ancestry filled the air. I felt it surrounding us and knew it came from them. They were old, wise, and strong.

I was grateful that they had chosen the side they had. If we had gone against them, I wasn't sure who would've won.

Pippa turned back and approached with the older wolf beside her. Pete had been transported away. Fresh tears filled her eyes when she stopped before me and then she threw her arms around me. As she hugged me tight, she whispered, "Thank you so much, Davy. For everything. I don't know what we would've done if you hadn't helped us."

All this because of the essence in Pete? That was all they needed from me?

She smiled. "We didn't know it was possible to separate it from him. If we had and if I'd been more certain that you were the Immortal, I would've asked you right away."

"What?"

A carefree laugh broke from her and she wiped more tears away. "I came to Benshire for my family. We knew the Immortal was here. I was supposed to find you, but I didn't know it was you until now. I still can't quite believe it. I didn't even really like you."

"I know. You loved Emily. You guys were bosom buddies."

"I sensed her mate in her, but it wasn't Pete, at least not this Pete. This Pete is supposed to be mine." Her face sobered at that thought.

I asked, "What about the mateline? Are you able to recover it so he'll be your mate again?"

She shook her head. "I have no idea. That's old magic. No one would dare interfere with something like that, but Mother Wolf has become impervious and foolish. This will anger the Elders greatly. Matelines are never to be manipulated and now that it's been done, we'll have to see what other damage she did."

"About her, is she dead now?"

"No. You just stopped her magic from getting to Pete again. You put up a block within him. I'm sure the Elder wolves will move on her soon. She's weak now." She smiled again. "Thank you, Davy. You have helped so much. I can't express our gratitude in words."

The elder wolf dropped his mouth to her neck. His eyes locked with hers and Pippa nodded a second later. "This is Christane. He's my Elder and he wants you to know that the Christane family is indebted to you. If you ever need us, we will come."

Elders. Christane family. All this ancestry among the wolves. It was getting overwhelming.

"Davy?" Pippa frowned.

"Sorry. Yes. That sounds nice." I lifted a shoulder up in an awkward shrug. "All this is new to me. I've never had a werewolf feel like they owed me something. I'm just used to him," I jerked a thumb beside me. "He's always telling me to lay low and be quiet."

Roane barked out a laugh, but moved forward. "Thank you, Christane. I am indebted to you as well."

The wolf lowered his massive head to the ground and then turned as one with Pippa. She melted into her white wolf form and soon they vanished from our eyes. It wasn't long before I felt all the wolves disappear and then I turned to Roane. "Why are you indebted to him?"

"They came to show their allegiance to me."

"They came because of Pippa."

"She called them, but they were here to fight on my behalf. If you hadn't stepped in and taken care of Pete, it would've been worse. If the Christane bloodline had fought with me, they would've showed their loyalty to a vampire. That would've meant declaring their own war on the Mother Wolf."

I shuddered at the thought of her. "She sounds like a bitch."

Roane put his arm around my shoulder and drew me close. "Well, she's their problem now."

Gavin approached and flashed a grin. "Is this the official victory walk?"

I felt Roane tense. "For now."

"One victory down, two more to go?" As we treaded down the hill and neared the estate, Kates darted to meet us. Her eyes were gleaming and her chest was heaving. A glow appeared over her skin.

She lifted a hand. "They've gone. All of them. What happened?"

"Davy took care of the Alpha," Gavin responded in a curt voice.

Annoyance flared in her eyes, but she didn't bite back.

"Wren and Tracey are waiting for us in the hall. Bastion and Gregory will follow and make sure the other wolves don't double back." Roane's hand slipped to my waist. His thumb started to rub the side of my hip.

When we entered the house, the two female vampires stood from their table. Brown panted from her seat. She gave me a loopy smile. "I can't stand. My legs have turned into goo. They're all melty. I did magic. Can you believe it?"

I couldn't contain a smile. "I knew you had it in you."

"Oh man." She slumped back. "I feel drunk. Is this normal?"

"Where's the traitor?" Kates looked around in contempt.

Brown tried to lift her arm, but dropped it on the table. "She's still out there, snoring away. They didn't take her with them and they could've. A few of the wolves got around me, but then they all ran away. I must be awesome."

"The wolf?" Wren spoke for the first time. She shifted in her stance and I saw pain flare in her body. She couldn't contain a grimace.

"She was a Christane wolf. She left with them." Roane narrowed his eyes. "You should rest, Wren. Heal. Tracey, take her to your room. Everyone should go to their rooms to clean up and rest."

"What?" Gavin lifted his head. "No party? We should be celebrating."

"We will." Roane's eyes glimmered in amusement. "But no one is fit for that right now." His hand spread out over the small of my back. "Let's enjoy our rest first."

Gavin and Kates shot a look at each other, but quickly looked away. I pursed my lips at that. It wasn't the first time there had been a spark between the two, but then Roane urged me in front of him and I didn't care. I wanted my bed. I wanted him. And I wanted a night away from the war.

Her eyes snapped open when she felt the defeat. The magic had been destroyed, banned from the Alpha. When she tried to go back in, a block was set in place. There was no way she could get past it, but then an explosion occurred and her magic was thrown back at her. It slammed into her and recoiled onto itself. She felt it quaking and knew the tremors were from fear. As she gritted her teeth, her anger rose swiftly. Something had not gone to plan and she was determined to figure out what it was, who it was. No one banished her.

The door burst open and a servant rushed inside. "Mother, what has happened?"

It was then she realized the room was shaking. She wasn't surprised. The rage in her was tightly controlled, but when she stood and turned, the appearance of Gailith made her pause. A bruise was forming on the top of his head; blood spilled from it and soaked his shirt. One of the lenses in the small glasses he always wore had a crack and his hair was matted from his blood.

"What happened to you?" She tried to keep the disgust from her voice. Servants wanted to be cared for. Everyone wanted to be cared for. They found it comforting. They were pathetic.

He hesitated and ran a hand through his hair. It caught on the blood and he withdrew it quickly to tuck behind his back. "Was there an earthquake?"

"What do you mean?"

"The whole house, Mother. It's been shaking for the last few minutes. Many of the servants died."

"Why?" Had her rage been so suppressed?

"They're human, Mother."

She couldn't hold back her disgust any longer and snapped, "What are you talking about? Why would my servants die from a small earthquake?"

"It wasn't small. This is the only room that's still standing."

Her eyes widened and she couldn't speak for a moment. Nothing and no one ever surprised her, but it had happened twice in the space of two minutes. She hated that. Someone was more powerful than her. The wolf inside her raged to get out. It needed to kill, but she took a deep breath and calmed herself. More deaths would not satisfy her. She needed to know what had become of the thread holder. That would satisfy her. She had gone to great lengths to get close, but if it had all been for nothing.

She clamped her eyes closed at the thought of the possible repercussions. "Are the wolves okay?"

He jerked his head in a nod. "Yes, ma'am."

"Ma'am?"

"Mother Wolf. Yes, the wolves were able to escape. I got away because one of them carried me out."

She narrowed her eyes and turned back to the window. Her home had been built during the Civil War. It had been made to survive anything, but she had not considered her own power. Never would she have imagined that she'd hurt something she had built and nurtured. But she had hurt it. Sheds that had surrounded the plantation were in pieces on the ground. Someone made her do this and that someone needed to be dealt with.

"Gailith, I want you to go to someone."

"Who, Mother?"

Her eyes were flat when she looked back. "The vampires."

He paled and his hand jerked to clench around his shirt. Filth. Everything about him was filthy. "You're human. They'll love you."

He closed his eyes and bent his head.

She smirked. They were pathetic, all of them, which is why she knew the thread holder had been underestimated. She had underestimated the girl, so Jacith must've also.

"You will go to Durres to see the Romah Family."

His body started to shake.

"There is a powerful sorcerer there. His name is Jacith."

Her nostrils flared as she smelled his fear. It wasn't long before his bladder emptied itself. It trickled down his leg and pooled on the floor. His head hung in shame, but he couldn't stop himself.

She could barely keep herself from killing him. Worthless humans. They couldn't do anything, much less refrain from wetting themselves. If she asked this of him, how did she know he'd succeed? Maybe a wolf would be better? But no, as she watched him through narrowed eyes, she reconsidered. A human was a perfect messenger and gift. Jacith would see him as one and that he had been one of her servants would mean something to him. The sorcerer was stupid in that way, but he had his uses. And he was powerful. He would be angry to find out the existence of a thread holder who could use the Immortal's powers. It was his fault. He should clean this mess up himself.

"You need to go and tell him what happened to the Alpha. The thread holder destroyed his precious experiment. Tell him this and then return home, Gailith."

He jerked his head in another nod and bolted from the room.

As she sat back down in her chair, she took a deep breath. Everything would have to be rebuilt.

"You're sending a servant to Jacith? He won't be returning, you know that."

She turned and a smile spread over her face. "Hello, Christian. Did you come to make sure I was okay?"

He was tall and muscular with piercing black eyes. That wasn't what attracted her to him. It was the wolf inside of him. He was the inspiration behind the Alpha. Christian Christane was the reigning Alpha wolf for his family. He had many grandfathers still alive, but he was their leader. A union between her family and his would cement the werewolves' dominance over the vampires. No creature could stand against power such as theirs and Christian was raw power in himself. As she watched, she saw it thriving within his body.

She licked her lips.

"No, Caralie. I came to tell you that my family knows what you did. You took the mate that was supposed to be for my little sister and joined him to another. You should not manipulate magic like that. It's old, older than your family."

"Older than yours too."

"Yes," he clipped out. "Older than my family, this is why the Elders have called a meeting."

He wasn't there to flirt. He never was, but there was gravity in his voice. Her inner wolf stirred. It sensed something that she hadn't yet. She stood and gave him a sultry smile. "What are you saying?"

His disdain for her flared. "The Christane Family will be separating themselves from yours. We no longer have to sit back and let you do what you want. We're going to stop you, Caralie. Your fight is now against us."

Her smile vanished.

His nostrils flared once more. "Good luck."

GAVIN HELPED Emily to a bedroom close to ours. She snored when he picked her up and she was still snoring as Roane and I lay in bed. It was a few hours later and the sound kept me awake. When I rolled over, I saw that Roane was too. His eyes were open and he stared back at me with an arm on my hip.

We hadn't talked much when we got to the room. Both of us had showered and then crawled under the sheets. I had rolled to my side as he spooned me from behind. His arm hadn't moved the whole time.

"Why can't we sleep?" I asked now.

A ghost of a smile filtered over his face. "Because of the adrenaline."

"I bet no one can sleep."

"I wanted to be alone with you."

My heart skipped a beat. No matter how many times he said it, I knew I'd always love hearing statements like that from him. "You don't want to make love?"

"I wanted to hold you tonight."

I rolled over so I was facing him. His arm slipped behind me and he pulled me tighter against him. One of my legs slipped between his and my hand found his to hold. Our fingers interlaced and I closed my eyes. I wanted to savor the feeling of holding his hand.

But I knew it wouldn't last and I asked, "You're leaving tonight, aren't you?"

His arm tightened around me for a moment. I heard the regret in his voice. "I have to go. The Roane Family could've doubled back."

I bit back tears, but I couldn't fight the wave of sadness that washed over me. He was always leaving. "When?"

"In a few minutes." He hesitated a moment. "Bastion's been waiting for me. Once I return and learn how things are, I will come back or I'll send for you."

"I can't go back to a normal life, Roane." My eyes searched his. He must know this. "I can't be the college student anymore. Too many people know about me. Pippa, the wolves." Who else?

He nodded and pressed a tender kiss to my forehead. "I know. Trust me, I know."

"I'm coming back. I'm going to be at your side. We're stronger together than we are apart."

He held my gaze for a moment, a long moment. The minute stretched into another and then a third. My heart pounded the whole time and I held my breath. Was he going to accept my plea? He couldn't protect me any longer. I had to start fighting on my own.

It was time for everyone to learn who I was. I felt it in my bones and I felt the thirst within me. I wanted to fight.

"I know, Davy. You don't have to worry, I'm going back to check on everybody. If the Roane Family has returned, I won't risk my best warriors. I'll go alone. Don't worry. If I need you guys, you'll be the first to know. Gavin and the rest have strict instructions to never leave your side. Think of them as your personal entourage."

"Great," I groaned. "Wren is part of my entourage."

"She's not so bad," he teased. "She might act tough, but she's grown a little fond of you. I can tell."

No matter what he said, that vampire was still tough. She might be happy with Tracey among the group, but I knew if or when things went south between them, Wren would blame me. There was nothing logical about my speculation, just a gut feeling.

"Tracey asked if she could speak with you."

I took a breath. She wanted me to tell her about her mother and sister. Did Talia want me to tell her about the child?

"Roane, do you think I should tell her about Talia's daughter?"

There was silence for a moment and then he murmured, "I think Tracey would be indebted to you for the rest of your life if you did."

"So should I tell her?"

"If you were Talia and you had a child, would you want your sister to be told?"

I closed my eyes as a wave of sadness washed over me. "I would want her to be told."

"There's your answer. And Davy?"

"Hmmm?" I looked up.

He kissed me softly and whispered against my lips, "Can we not talk anymore?"

"Why?" But the sudden darkening in his eyes told me and I felt my own desire leap in response.

"I think you know why," he responded, his eyes half closed already. Then he reached for me and it wasn't long before both of us were groaning.

It was an hour later before we could even move from the bed.

When I thought of going to the bathroom, my mind screamed in protest. My bladder didn't agree and I tore myself from the bed to dash for the bathroom. When I came back, Roane was sitting on the edge of the bed. The blankets pooled around his waist and the Roane tattoo was prominent on his arm.

I traced it as I sat beside him. "You're not a Roane anymore." It felt weird to say that.

He glanced at me and then lifted one of my legs onto his lap. As he caressed my thigh, he murmured, "I'll always be a Roane. I'm just not on their side with this one."

"You think you will be in the future? Can you go back to them?"

"They're wrong about you. I hope they figure that out, but history is filled with moments when leaders make wrong decisions. They rarely apologize."

I was about to say something about how they should apologize, but someone knocked on the door. Roane was across the room in a flash. He stuck his head out and then he looked back. "Gregory spotted a new army approaching. I have to go."

I stood and dressed as he did the same.

He stopped with his jeans in one hand. "What are you doing?"

"I'm going to walk you out." And then I thought, *'I love you, Lucas.'*

His head snapped up in shock and he was across the room the next instant. His mouth ground against mine and I felt myself being lifted up. My legs wound around his waist and I held on. We couldn't get enough of each other, but then we heard another knock at the door.

He groaned as he pulled back, but whispered against my lips, "I love you too."

Both of us dressed after that and walked down the hallway hand in hand. When we got to a small door, we stepped out and saw a car waiting there. Bastion and Gregory were conversing on the side, but both looked up. They stood at attention, ready for their orders. Roane jerked his head to the side. Bastion got into the vehicle as Gregory ducked his massive head and went into the estate. A moment later Gavin came back outside and waited next to us.

Roane pulled me against his chest for a hug.

After we kissed again, he thought, *'I will be back soon or I'll call for you. Stay with Gavin or Wren. They are to protect you from now on.'*

'Be safe.'

He nodded and kissed me one last time. His lips lingered over mine as I clung to him. Every instinct in my body told me not to let go. Something bad was going to happen. I knew it. I felt it, and so did Roane. His eyes darkened and I knew he had heard my thoughts, but it didn't matter. He needed to go and be the leader. We had another battle to fight.

As he stepped back, Roane shared a look with Gavin. They both nodded and then he was in the vehicle and it pulled away. The night air had a chill that I hadn't felt before. It wrapped around me and I hugged myself as a shiver wracked my body.

Gavin touched the back of my elbow. "We should go in."

I nodded, dazed. Roane had gone. I knew he had to, but it was different when I felt it. He urged me inside and the door shut behind us. It seemed to slam with extra force, but Gavin didn't react. I stumbled.

"He'll be fine."

I looked up. Gavin watched me with concern. He said again, "Roane's the toughest ass I know. If anyone is going to be fine, it's him. He's just gone for now. He'll be back within the week."

That didn't reassure me. It should've, but it didn't. Then we walked into the kitchen and found Gregory in the kitchen. Brown was slumped down at the table. She gave me a sloppy smile. "Heya, Davy. I still can't walk."

"Big man." Gavin slapped a hand on the Viking's back. "What are you making?"

"Pancakes and scrambled eggs." Both of the vampires grimaced in disgust, but Gregory shook his head. "Sarah insists this is appropriate food for humans. This is what she wanted."

Brown laughed. "It's the middle of the night and I feel like we just had a rave party. That food is what we need. Right, Davy?"

My eyes danced in delight. "What else would we want to eat?"

"Blood," Gavin and Gregory spoke at the same time.

I rolled my eyes. "We're not vampires. We're human."

"Speaking of vampires and humans," Brown spoke up. "What's going to happen with school?"

"What do you mean?"

"I was excited to go back to college, but then I was thinking about all the vampires coming to town. There's going to be a huge fight, right? I mean, there was already one with those werewolves in the park. How are the humans not going to know what's going on? Isn't it going to be too big to hide?"

Both vampires became still at her question and that was when I knew the answer. "It won't be hidden."

Gavin turned apologetic eyes to me.

I gulped. "Benshire is going to be destroyed, isn't it?"

No answer again, but that was my answer. A part of my heart fell. I had wanted to think a small part of normalcy wouldn't be wiped away, but that didn't seem to be the case. My life wasn't the only one that would change. Everyone's life was going to change.

Then Kates walked into the room. She moved in a stiff manner and had an odd expression on her face. Her eyes found mine, but she turned away quickly. When her jaw clenched and moved back and forth, I saw that her teeth were grinding against each other. She did that when something was wrong.

I sat up straight. "What is it?"

Gavin's head snapped up. Gregory paused in his cooking and Brown grew quiet.

Kates' eyes darted between all of us and she jerked her head. "What are you talking about? What are you guys doing?"

I narrowed my eyes. Something was wrong, very wrong. I stood up. "What did you do, Kates?"

Suddenly there was an explosion in the air, except there was no fire. Nothing blew up. No one was thrown backwards and no smoke filled the air, but I knew it was an explosion. I felt it and it staggered me. I fell backwards, but no one else did. They looked at me. In slow motion, I saw all of their different expressions. Gavin started to reach for me. Brown's mouth started to open and Gregory's eyes shifted over my shoulder. Kates never moved. She already knew. I turned my head slowly.

Roane walked into the room with a cocky swagger. His mouth was twisted in a smirk and his eyes held an evil glint. His hair was long. It reached below his ears and was tucked back. There was no fear in his eyes. There was nothing in his eyes. Then everything clicked in my brain.

This wasn't Roane. This was Lucan.

My eyes whirled back to Kates' and she looked away. She bit her lip and ducked her head down in shame. Then Lucan threw his arms out wide. "Hello everyone! It's good to see you all."

"What?" Brown looked at Gregory for explanation, but he and Gavin both couldn't move. They seemed frozen in place. As I tried, I found that I couldn't move either. Whatever had exploded in the air worked magic on all of us. Brown started to lift her hand, but I shot her a pleading look.

'Brown, don't move.'

Her eyes went wide. 'Holy crap, I can hear you!'

'Don't move.'

'Why? What's going on?'

'That's not Roane. It's his twin brother, his evil twin brother.'

'This is like a soap opera.'

'He used magic. None of us can do anything.'

'I can.'

'I think it's because you're human. So is Kates.'

'Davy, what should I do?'

'Nothing.' This was important for her to understand. 'He can't know that you have magic.'

'I don't have much. I think I used it all up.'

I closed my eyes in frustration for a moment. I couldn't tell her that the box inside her had closed again. *'Brown, this is really important.'*

'What's going to happen?'

Fear started to creep into her thoughts and I felt it in her emotions. It began to choke her, but I couldn't think about that. *'He's going to take me. I don't know what he'll do to Gavin or Gregory, but I hope he'll let you go.'*

'Davy,' she whimpered. *'I'm getting scared.'*

'You have to get to Roane. Tell him what happened and that Lucan used magic against us. Tell him that Kates knew about it.'

Vampires came into the room behind Lucan. They swarmed everywhere, searching for something. A moment later, they returned with Wren and Tracey held captive. Both female vampires struggled against their captors, but it didn't make a difference. When they set foot in the kitchen, they were frozen like the rest of us.

Lucan clipped out, "Is that everyone?"

A vampire snapped to attention before him. "He's not here."

He let out a deep breath. "I don't know if I'm disappointed or relieved." Then he swung his dark gaze towards me. "Where'd your lover go?"

I narrowed my eyes at him and dared him to enter my mind. Whatever magic held my body immobile didn't affect my thoughts. As we stared each other down, I felt the Immortal rally in anger inside of me. She was angry and she wanted to hurt him. Rage filled me and I tasted revenge in my mouth. I didn't know what I could do, but I knew I could do something if he entered my mind.

Lucan came to a decision and jerked his head around. "Fine. They go with us then."

One of the vampires reached for Brown and lifted her in the air. She squealed and he asked, "The human?"

Lucan looked at Kates in question. She spoke in a bored voice, "Leave her. She's nothing."

The vampire dropped Brown and everyone swept out of the estate. All of us were placed in different vehicles. I was put in the backseat with Kates across from me and Lucan beside me. One other vampire sat beside Kates and we started off.

My best friend refused to meet my gaze. I swallowed hard and realized that she'd known the whole time. Had this been her intention since she came back? I had been handed to her lover on a silver platter. Did she choose to wait until Roane was gone? Or until we were all weakened from our battle against the Alpha?

When her eyes finally found mine, I saw sadness in them. I didn't care. I narrowed mine and opened a channel in her mind so she could hear my thoughts. *'You don't know what you've done, but you will. I will kill you myself.'*

Kates didn't look surprised, but she thought back, *'Not everything is how it seems, Davy.'*

'You better hope not.'

It was days later before I realized where we'd been taken, and my heart sank.

DAVINA

TIJAN

To all the readers who loved Davy from the beginning and stuck with me, waiting for Davina! You guys are amazing and have been so supportive.
Thank you for being patient.
I truly hope you'll love the conclusion.

CHAPTER 1

They started the chanting again, and I closed my eyes before I bent my forehead to rest on my arms. Would it ever end? They'd been trying for six months now, or so it seemed. I had tried to keep count, but every day melted into the next. Some of the times when I would wake, I didn't know if it was the same day or a different one. There were six flies instead of two on the sandwich some vampire slid into my cell. I hadn't touched it then and still hadn't, but I guessed that an entire day had gone by. With every day, the flies multiplied in numbers. Tomorrow there would be twelve or fourteen.

"There, there, no appetite for the human-no-longer?"

Lucan squatted next to my head outside my cell. He wrapped a hand around one of the bars and bent low to peer into my eyes.

I didn't flinch or look away. "I'm still human, Lucan."

"No, you aren't. You would've been dead a long time ago."

I sighed. It was the only thing I could do. Time and time again, his witches would chant. He'd get excited, as human as he ever was, and he'd stand by for The Immortal thread. It had been his plan since I turned him into a human. He wanted the power so he was determined to get it. He really thought he could be the next thread-holder; he refused to believe there would be no more thread-holders. It was only The Immortal now. I had tried to explain this to him, but since there was no lore about The Immortal, he never believed me.

And then one day, I grew tired of the torture, and said to him, "Do you miss him?"

Lucan grew still beside me. He loved to sit beside me and feel my pain. I knew every time he thought they would break me, when the thread would join him, but it never happened. He still sat beside me every day.

"You two look so much alike."

"Shut up."

I thought it would take more for his reaction. "Roane is all about duty. He's sworn to protect people who he feels are right no matter who it's against."

"Shut up," he snarled again.

"He'll come after you, you know."

Lucan shot to his feet, but he didn't go anywhere. He didn't leave. He didn't threaten. He just stood there and waited.

"He loves me. Do you think he won't come for me now?" I saw how he stood there. "Do you think he won't go against you for me?"

He jerked on his feet, but settled back.

I said further, "He loves me, Lucan. He loves me more than he does you. You've hurt me. You continually hurt me, and that's only going to make it worse for you. Every time you hurt me, he'll hate you more for it. Are you ready for that? Can you handle his hatred?"

"Shut up," he whispered this time. It had been a snarl before, but not now.

My eyes glinted in triumph, but I knew it was short-lived. He'd do what he would do. Lucan was like Roane. Both believed in their own courses, and neither would change for anyone. They both felt they were right.

It was now a matter of who would win, and my heart was on my lover.

"Again!" he roared, and the chanting began again.

I rested my forehead against one of the metal bars. The pain would start in a few seconds.

ROANE

ROANE JERKED his head up when his office door slammed open. His senses should've alerted him before the intruder had breached his inner sanctum, but when he saw who stood before him, he knew why they hadn't. She wasn't human. He sniffed the air and knew she wasn't a vampire either, nor a werewolf.

He stood slowly. "What are you?"

The girl cocked her head to the side. She had long black hair with blue tips. A large mark covered the side of her face and she stood in a warrior's stance in blue leather. She stood confident. A sword was slung across her back.

She sneered at him, "I am Saren. I am not from your world."

"What are you?"

"I am not from your world; it is not your business. I am here to help you rescue Davy."

"Davy? What do you know about her?"

She stepped back, a slow and methodical step. "She was taken by your brother, and she's held in a fortress. He's surrounded himself with Mori vampires. You have no hope of getting in there and getting her out."

"But you do?"

Her chin raised a fraction of an inch. "I am only visible to your eyes because I choose it. Do not push me, Vampire."

"How do you know Davy is there?"

"Because I am more than you can understand." She cocked her head to the side in a defiant stance.

Lucas regarded her. He didn't know who she was, but she was

there. And she had information about Davy. He had little choice but to accept her word. He also smelled the sense of recognition. She did know Davy. He felt it in his gut, and she was as concerned as he was. All other questions would have to wait.

He jerked his head in a nod. "Tell me what you know."

"You have power, but your Hunter tattoo is turned off. I can sense how your powers are leaving you. You're going to need help. You can't depend on me, but I will be there. I will hold my own. I will be the one to find Davy. You will follow behind with help."

"My help?" He moved around his desk. "My best warriors were taken with her."

"Except for your fastest one and you have already sent a request to the Christane wolves."

His nostrils flared, and Roane stopped abruptly. "How do you know that?"

"I am not of your world. Do I need to repeat everything I say to you? Davy is being held—"

He waved her off. "I heard that part, but when you say 'I'm not from this world,' it doesn't explain how you knew that I'd sent word to Christian."

"Christian Christane is your friend. He is a powerful Alpha Werewolf. It would make sense for you to enlist his assistance. All members of your army are needed here." She tilted her head to the side with an absent look in her eye.

A corner of his mouth curved down. This thing wasn't something he had foreseen. "If you know Davy, why didn't she tell me about you?"

"Because I told her not to." She turned and started to leave.

Lucas jerked forward. "Wait. Where are you going? How do I get in touch with you?"

"You don't." She left the room and never looked back.

His door never opened.

Lucas sat back down and remembered a time when Talia had been the ghost Davy could see. She'd talked to her, but this Saren was something different. Then he sighed and picked up his phone. It seemed that he'd need more than the Christane wolves.

BROWN

BROWN HELD her breath and rubbed her shaky hands down her legs. Vampires roamed past her and stood before her as she inched down the hallway. Davy's boyfriend had called for her and a car had picked her up when they ended the call. Now she was back in the bar she had once been excited to go to. Her legs wavered, and she hoped she wouldn't lose her bladder this time.

She glanced around and found herself hoping for a glimpse of the Viking giant, but then, as a sea of vampires parted and Roane moved forward to greet her, she saw the strain on his face and remembered what had happened.

Gregory was gone, along with all her friends.

She struggled to keep a tear from falling and tried to steady her chin, but her lip trembled anyway.

Roane's eyes skimmed over her; his eyes were sharp as a hawk's. Brown knew that he saw it all. He probably heard how her heart started to race.

"My office?" He spoke in a gravelly voice.

Thick with emotion, Brown moved ahead of him as he held out an arm, down a hallway.

As they moved away from the crowd, she noticed glances that nearly every vampire cast her way. Before they moved into his office, a few of the lingering ones in the hallway glanced also, but their eyes moved over her shoulder. They weren't watching her. They were watching Roane. She saw respect in them, and all of them stood taller. They squared their shoulders back when Roane moved past.

This was their leader. She had never considered him before, during the brief moments when she heard him converse with Davy, but she was overwhelmed with butterflies now. Her palms got a little sweaty and her eyes went wide. When he closed the door behind him, the air seemed so intimate, so private. No wonder Davy was head over heels.

This vampire was unlike any others that she had met, not that she knew many. There had been that one with orange hair—never mind. She wasn't there to daydream. And Davy's boyfriend started to look impatient, like he was waiting for something. Then it clicked.

"Did you ask me something?"

A shadow of a smile graced his features. It transformed him. He had seemed intimidating before, but with that slight hint of amusement, his features were breathtaking. Sharp cheeks, intense eyes, a full mouth, and that cleft in his chin.

Brown swallowed and looked away. Davy's boyfriend. She needed to keep telling herself that.

Then, again, she realized the room was heavy in silence.

She closed her eyes in frustration. "I'm sorry. What did you say again?"

The smile faded, and he clipped out, "Have you worked on your magic since the attack?"

Her stomach twisted over. The 'attack' had been months ago, long, long months ago. Every day she tried to get her magic back, but nothing worked. Even the slight amount she could use before was gone. She felt human, *only* human. No magic. Nothing. She was useless.

"No, I haven't. I've been trying, but I think I used it all up. I don't think there's any more in me." Her lip trembled.

Roane narrowed his eyes. From what Davy had said, the girl had an unlimited supply, getting to it was another matter.

"Somehow," he murmured, "I don't think that's the case. Keep trying."

She glanced from under her eyelids and quickly looked away. "My sister is the one with magic. Only one of us gets the family blessing."

"Look." He sighed. His hand curled around the back of the chair he stood behind. "You have magic. Davy said that it's in you. I trust her. You should, too."

She squeaked, and her eyes widened. "I do! I trust Davy with my life or I would if she were here. When is she coming back?"

He never blinked, and he never looked away.

She hung her head. "I was wondering if you had found her." She looked back up. Hope shimmered over her face. "I'd like to help. Can I help?"

"If you have magic. That's why I called you here."

"Oh! Yeah, that makes sense. I was wondering, well, I wasn't wondering but I don't know. I mean . . . I'll keep trying. I'll always keep trying. I feel it's there. Davy said it is, and I do trust her. She's my best friend. I know she has that other girl as her best friend, but she sorta betrayed her, so I don't trust—"

"Stop. Talking."

She clamped her mouth shut.

"It's why I called you. Your magic is blocked, and I have another witch for you to meet. He might be able to unblock your magic."

"Really?"

He nodded and the door opened. A man with long brown hair, frizzy and curly, floated into the room. He wore a gray tunic, and long strings of beads wrapped around his neck. A jewel was placed above his lip, underneath his nose. His eyes were dark, and black makeup was encased around them. He studied her, up and down.

"Mavic, this is Sarah Bright."

She thrust out a hand. "You can call me Brown."

The man ignored the offered hand and turned his head. "You insult me, Changeling. I am no more a witch than you are a blood-sucking creature." The young man gave her a gentle smile. "I am a sorcerer, but Lucas refuses to acknowledge my status. He feels it is too threatening to the world."

He brushed back a wave of curls and tucked it over his shoulder. He offered his hand and Brown gasped when they touched. A night sky filled her vision with shooting stars that soared at her. Underneath them the ocean roared and waves crashed against each other. Her nose twitched. A whiff of a campfire mixed with incense teased her nostrils.

"You're a sorcerer?" Goodness.

He nodded and then cast Roane a hard look. "You didn't tell me she was a Bright."

"Does it matter?" Roane held his gaze steadily.

A look passed between the two, and Mavic sighed. "I guess not."

"She has magic that needs to be unlocked. You said you're the best."

"You tease me, Lucas. I should curse you for that."

Roane laughed and patted him on the back. "This will be your biggest challenge. Imagine how your reputation will soar if you've freed a Bright witch."

"There will be ramifications."

A hard look came to him. "She's friends with the thread-holder. That can't be coincidental."

"Then the thread-holder should free her."

"She's a thread-holder. The Immortal powers are not available to her. You know how they are."

The sorcerer gave him a grim look. "You insult me again, Roane. Stories of an Immortal have been in the wind and much more as of late. Why do you ask for my help if you continue to insult my ability?"

Roane sighed. "It's not your abilities I am insulting. It's you."

Brown closed her eyes and hung her head. She dared not make a sound. The air was thick with tension; tension that she knew not to ignite. Not the slightest movement.

Mavic sighed again. "Why do I put up with your disrespect? I have many who worship my teachings. Many who would give their siblings' lives to learn from my hands."

Roane took one step closer. His eyes never moved away and he gave him the slightest smirk. "You are here because you dare not make me an enemy, and we all know how you love gossip. You've been given a window to see if those slight murmurs of an Immortal are true. We both know your ego is not so grand that it will get in the way of even the possibility of meeting an Immortal."

Brown counted her breaths. One. Two. Three. Neither man spoke. Neither man moved.

"The witch will come to my dwelling. I will train her there."

"You will train her here."

"Lucas, I cannot. All my supplies, all my books, everything is at my home."

"You packed a bag. You knew I wouldn't allow it. She will remain here and she will be under watch." Roane stepped close, so close his nose nearly touched the sorcerer's. "If you harm her or my men in any way, I will hunt you down." His eyes turned lethal. "And I am the best there is." He stepped back and cast a sweeping gaze over both of them. "Start her training now. I want it done as soon as possible."

And with those parting words, he swept out the door. Two vampires entered behind him. They both took their guarding position, just inside the room.

Mavic lifted closed fists in the air and cursed under his tongue.

Brown frowned, it was in a language she had never heard, but she wanted to learn it. She wanted desperately to know everything this sorcerer knew, even if Roane didn't trust him. If she was going to get her magic back to help Davy, this witch was her best shot. She gave him a bright smile. "Where do we start?"

CHAPTER 2

Everything was a blur when I opened my eyes. Then the light blasted me and I screamed, lurching backwards in retreat. Anything would do to hide from it. I had to get away. My skin started to boil from the inside out. I felt it starting to peel away, layer by layer. That light, it was all because of the light.

A deep baritone laughed. He was enjoying my pain.

Lucan.

I gritted my teeth and tried to think of a retort, anything to shut him up. But then, I realized it wasn't him. He annoyed me, but this voice hurt me. When he laughed again, pain flared through my body. Millions of tiny knives were slicing through my skin. Each one took its time. I screamed again and tried to writhe away, from him, from the light, from everything.

It hurt to breathe. The knives pierced my throat. I drew in a breath, and they slid deeper.

Then, nothing. Everything stopped.

I gasped and shot upright. There was no one in the room with me. My cage was still in the center, encased in darkness. There was no light anywhere.

The door opened and Lucan strolled inside, a satisfied smirk on his face. Blood was on his hands, but he made no move to wipe them clean.

"What new game was that?" I rasped out.

"What game?" He lifted his head and inhaled deeply.

I caught a whiff of the blood, and my stomach knotted. That was Kates's blood. I didn't want to know how that had happened, what sick game they played with each other, or even how I knew it was hers.

"What game?" he repeated and came closer to my cage.

I glanced at the door. "Do you have a new witch on your staff? One that can do that?"

I expected them to come in. They usually traipsed behind him, ready with chanting spells. The door stayed closed today.

Lucan frowned. "What are you talking about?"

Though my Immortal powers had been stripped away, my empathic abilities were still a part of me. I felt into him and read his confusion. A dark suspicion was starting to form in him and an ugly smirk appeared again. I wanted to jerk out, but I didn't. I needed to know whatever he thought, though painful and disgusting it would be.

"It's working. The thread is starting to unravel. She's starting to inflict her own pain, delusions, too. Sarach never told me this would be the first step. It has to be the beginning."

"You will never get the thread. The sooner you realize that, maybe you can figure out a way to kill me."

His smirk vanished. "You are a mere thread-holder. It will work. I've forced the thread out of others, I can do it again."

"They were thread-holders. I am not. I am The Immortal."

His hands curled around my cage bars and he leaned forward. His face pressed between two bars and his smile was blinding. He looked so much like Lucas at that moment, handsome with sparkling eyes alive with life. My heart skipped a beat, and pain of a different sort speared through me. It hurt to breathe again.

Lucan reveled, "If you were The Immortal, my witches couldn't touch you. You are not The Immortal. You cannot be because there is no Immortal. No human can handle that amount of power. Your body cannot endure it. You are more powerful than the others. I will give you that, but don't think that it's not because Lucas's blood is in you. You drank from him. It's the only reason you have more power than the others do. That is all."

How did he know that?

He laughed. "It was written all over your face." His voice became husky, intimate. "I know my own brother. He's always shared blood with his lovers. It gives him a connection that humans could never experience, not without vampire blood."

I swallowed back the pain. I wasn't just some lover to Roane. I knew I wasn't. "The Immortal thread has only been in humans, it has *only* ever been in humans. No vampire-wannabe is going to get it. And that won't be you. You're not good enough. The thread picks the person it goes to. If, by some miracle, you do get the thread out of me, it won't go to you."

"I'm the only human here."

"Besides Kates."

He moved back and raised a hand to the side of his cheek. Her blood trailed across his lips, and his tongue swept out to lick her blood from the rest of his hand. "That'll be remedied soon enough. Thanks for pointing that out, Kates's best friend."

My stomach dropped again. "What a nice boyfriend you are. You get her to betray her best friend and then you kill her. No matter what she's told you, I know her. She doesn't want to be a vampire. She's a slayer. Everything inside of her wants to kill your kind. That's what she was built for."

A dark hint of amusement filled his eyes, and he turned to stroll out. "Who said she was going to become a vampire?"

I rushed forward, smashing against the cage. I needed to get out. Gritting my teeth, I closed my eyes and concentrated. I needed to be free. Free. Be free. The cage never gave way. Lucan's laugh raised a notch, and the door slammed shut behind him. I could still hear him as he went down the hallway. The laughter faded, but my chest still rose up and down sharply. No matter what she'd done,

Kates didn't deserve to be killed at his hands. By my hands, but not his.

———

GAVIN RESISTED the urge to break through the bars. He could hear her screams. Every day, every night, every hour. He heard them, and he couldn't do anything about it.

"You can't help her." Gregory sat forward on the bunk bed. He watched his cellmate pacing. "And get away from those bars. I don't want a repeat of the last time."

Wren laughed huskily from across the hall. "Oh, come now. Burning vampire flesh. What's a better smell than that? I know it helps me meditate. What about you, Trace?"

The tall blonde vampire glanced from her leaning stance, but didn't respond. She crossed her arms and looked back through the small window again. A bored look was on her face, but her eyes were sharp. From their basement position, their windows allowed them to see foot level of the ground above. It seemed like millions and millions of Mori moved past their dungeon.

Wren sighed and stood to stretch. Her black leather stretched with her. As she arched her back with her breasts pointed in the air, she glanced backwards.

Tracey never looked away from the window.

Wren sighed again, but this time in disgust. "Give it up, Gavin. You can't help Davy. None of us can, and unless you have magic in that tight ass of yours, there's no way we're breaking out of here."

"Why do the Mori have magic? Why can't we?"

Gregory's bunk groaned in protest when he pushed down to stand, but when he stepped forward, a deep thud came from the ground.

"Stop." Tracey looked now. "The Mori didn't build this place for vampires of your size. They're light footed and slender in build."

"Yeah," Wren bit out. "You could help us escape, make the bars crumble. Let's not do that."

Tracey shot her a look. "He could bring the entire building down, and who knows who he might kill in the process."

The dark-haired dominatrix bared her fangs at her cellmate.

"You are being immature, Arwena."

"Shut up, you two," Gavin snapped and started to pace again. "It's been months, and you two have been at each other's throat the whole time. I thought you were lovers, you used to love each other."

"'Used to' is the operative phrase." Wren sat on her bunk bed. Her shoulders slumped forward. All fight seemed to have left her in that moment.

A strand of golden hair fell over her shoulder and as she moved it back in place, Tracey flashed her deep blue eyes at her lover. A small frown appeared, but she didn't allow it to last long. Wren seemed to be losing her fight every day they remained in captivity. And the regal Roane warrior knew one thing; they would all need to keep their rest for when they would fight free. They would get free. They had to. She glanced back out the window. If anything, she'd get free to find Talia's daughter. She knew Lucan had taken her a year ago. She would have to be there, somewhere. She would find her sister's child and take back what was left of her family.

Gavin had been watching the blonde. He saw the thoughts fly through her head, and then he saw when she dismissed Wren's emotions. His own eyes hardened. He growled, "It doesn't matter, Wren. Maybe you're better off."

Tracey's chin tightened, but she never looked away from the window.

Gregory's jaw clenched as well and he sat back down. His bunk shifted underneath his weight once more.

Gavin turned back and saw how his friend's shoulders drooped. A sad expression came over him, and he knew the blonde Viking was missing the scatter-brained witch, for not the first time.

He stopped pacing and stood there, in front of the bars. They hummed with magic, and though his fingers itched to tear them apart, he knew he couldn't.

Then he heard her scream again, and he gritted his teeth. One of these days he would find a way. He would help Davy. He had to.

DAVY

WHEN THE LAST scream left me, my body collapsed on the ground. The witches had been chanting again. This time, with each of their chants, my body lifted off the floor and rose in the air. I had fought it at first, rallying The Immortal inside of me to fight back. Nothing worked. No magic could leave my body. So now I let them try. I let them fling my body back and forth, up and down, upside down at times. I no longer cared.

It never worked. They never won.

They left again, quieted and confused.

I rolled over and tried to lift myself up. My arms fell underneath my weight and my face slammed back down. My nose hit the bottom of the cage with force and I groaned, but the pain was almost welcoming. It was nothing compared to what I'd endured. When I pushed myself to a sitting position, I felt the blood that came from my nose. I touched it with gentle fingers and found that it still remained intact. I hadn't broken my own face, yet.

A soft laugh escaped at that thought, but I groaned instantly from the pain.

"You have hurt yourself."

My head whipped up, but no one was there. There was no Lucan to taunt me.

"What is this?" I asked. It'd been a long time since I had a voice speak to me in my own head.

He laughed. *"I am not The Immortal speaking to you."*

My shoulders sagged forward. "That'd be more helpful."

He laughed again, softly. *"They have been trying hard, have they not? The thread must be buried deep inside of you.*"

"Can you help me?"

There was silence.

I heard my own breathing. In and out. Inhale, exhale. They were shallow breaths. They grew shallower by the second.

Then I heard his response. "I cannot."

"You're powerful enough to speak to me, to see what they are doing, but not enough to free me? What kind of a sorcerer are you?" My tone was loathsome.

There was a sharp intake of air and a powerful explosion immediately after. The force of it threw me against the far wall of my cage. For the first time, I didn't feel the impact. As soon as my body fell down to the metal bars, I lifted my head once more and gazed around. He had gone. I knew that, but my eyes quickly searched for anything. And then I saw it. A small amount of smoke still floated in the air, near the top corner of the room. He had been watching from there and the next time he came, and I knew he would.

The door crashed open, and Lucan raced inside. "What was that?"

I frowned. I would've expected him to be angry, but as I searched his face, there was no rage. When I felt into him, there was concern, but no anger. I murmured softly, "It was nothing."

"Don't lie to me!" He grabbed the cage and lifted it, shaking it.

My eyes grew wide. My cage was big enough to encase an entire bedroom and he lifted it without breaking a sweat. There was no resistance, as if he lifted a bag of books.

Lucan set my cage back down immediately and backed away. His eyes caught and held onto mine.

"You are not a normal human." I rushed to the end of the cage beside him. "What are you? What have you done?"

He was quiet, staring back at me. Then he left, just as quietly.

When the door closed behind him, I sat back. He wasn't human. He was more. I didn't know what that meant, but it meant something. I felt it in my bones. I could use that to help me escape. I just had to figure out how first.

CHAPTER 3

The voice never came back. It seemed like a month had passed. And Lucan stopped taunting me. He stopped coming to sit by me. I didn't know if they corresponded, but something had happened. Perhaps his magical palace wasn't so magical after all. Perhaps the enchanted Mori weren't so impervious. I didn't know, but after that day, things weren't the same. Lucan wasn't so mad crazy. He had stopped enjoying my pain.

The witches continued their chanting spells, and he still insisted the thread could be pulled out of me, but I caught his stares a few times. He was scared, but he wasn't scared of me. It had to be whatever had happened to me, whoever that voice had been.

Then one day, Lucan sat beside me again.

I tensed and waited as the witches left again. Was this the day he started taunting again?

"I can see why my brother loves you."

I laughed. "Really?"

He didn't look at me, but sat beside and stared at the wall ahead of us. It was bleak, made of cement, and the night had fallen. The room had grown dark; soon the cold would come.

"You're beautiful. You don't know it so you're not a high maintenance girl."

"You can tell that here?"

"I could tell before, and you were Kates's friend. They both love you—"

I gritted my teeth. My fingernails pressed into the palm of my hand. It wouldn't be long before blood would start to drip down.

He continued, "—He loves you because you love him. Even now, you see his face every day, but you don't flinch. You hate me with passion. You should've broken by now. You should be pleading with me, begging for your life. You haven't done any of it."

I clenched my jaw. Blood splattered onto my legs now. It made its way slowly down to the floor.

"Lucas was the quiet one when we grew up. Did he tell you that? Mmmm. I suppose not. I was the outspoken one, the leader. We had a group of friends and they did whatever I told them to do. Lucas didn't like it. He said that I didn't think ahead at times. He might've been right. I know he thought he was, but I never cared. I could've thought ahead, but there was no fun with that. There was no adventure. We weren't tested then. We couldn't rally and see who we could really be." He laughed softly. "Our friends were weak. I never cared about them, but I loved watching my brother. Every time we'd get in trouble, Lucas would make everything okay. He always stepped in and got us out of trouble. He grew and grew every day. He became who he is today because of me. I made him. I created him."

"A Roane vampire sired him."

He sighed and stretched out his legs. "He has their blood. He became a vampire because of them, but he's the man he is because of me."

"Because he fixed your problems?"

"Because I tested him. Every time he didn't think we could come back from whatever trouble we were in, but we did. He always found a way. I did that. I raised him."

"You're crazy."

"I love my brother. He's the only one I love."

"And he's going to kill you." I looked over.

He did, too. Our gazes met.

I finished on a harsh note, "Because he loves me. He doesn't love you."

I waited. He'd become the enraged vampire again, but it never came. Instead, he smiled at me. "I would be honored if he was the one to kill me, but it won't happen. He's not coming, Davy."

I looked away.

He leaned closer. His voice whispered to me, it teased over my skin. "He would've been here by now if he was coming. On the night I came for you, the Roane Army was at Benshire. They attacked the town when we were leaving. My brother is dead."

This was a new torture. It had to be. "What are you doing?"

He stood and looked down at me.

I couldn't look away. He wasn't telling the truth. He couldn't have been. Roane was alive.

I felt it. I felt *him*.

Lucan smirked. "You can be with him. Just give me the thread." He squatted at my head. "You see, I've started to think that maybe you're the one holding onto the thread. I thought before that it was attached to you, but it's the other way around. Isn't it? You won't let go of it, because of my brother. You think he only loves you because of the thread, don't you?"

Shame filled me, but I couldn't look away, not even when a tear came to my eye.

His voice grew soft again. "He loved Talia. She had the thread. He loved you. You had the thread. But you see that now it doesn't matter. You don't need the thread. And if you give it up, you can be with him again. He's waiting for you, Davy. He's been watching the whole time, waiting for you. He wants to be with you again."

My stomach dropped. I'd been dormant for so long. My empathic abilities had died two weeks ago. I'd grown numb, but something sparked again. It was as if a hibernating monster had been poked too many times. It was starting to stir again. The Immortal was still inside of me. She was unable to get out, but she was there. She was angry again.

My body started to shake.

He didn't notice. "I know my brother. He'll still love you. If he had been alive, it might've been a problem. You know, if you hadn't had the thread in you. Then again, he wouldn't have even noticed you. There's really nothing breathtaking about you. You're beautiful, or you were before, but I think it was the thread that made you beautiful. I saw you before, too, when you went onto that roof with Talia. There wasn't anything special about you. Meek. Dull. Your body is boring, but the thread makes you shine. Even now, you still shine."

My hands started to jerk. My arms were starting to flail out. She was coming. She was rising.

"He will love you in the afterlife. If you die now, you'll have his love forever. But if you don't, it's a matter of time. The thread will leave you anyway. I will get it one of these days. I can feel how close I am. Give it up, Davy. Let it go. Let go and you can have my brother again. You can be in his arms again."

I was rising. My feet lifted off the floor, the toes barely touched. I stared at him. Waiting.

Lucan smirked to himself and lifted a hand to push through his hair. Silk strands of black hair slid against his fingers. They fell back in place, slightly ruffled. The bottoms touched underneath his ears. "I never told you before. I thought you'd die too soon and I had to get myself ready, but I'm ready now. I've been ready. It seems you aren't. You can't let go so I'm giving you that last push. It's time to let go, Davy. My brother will love you in the afterlife, thread or no thread. He won't care anymore. He's dead."

Something hot shot through my core. It jerked my body upright. My arms flew out to the sides and my back arched upward. The cage was big, but I slammed against the top. My chest, chin, and nose smashed against it.

Lucan was finally quiet.

Then my body started to shake again. The fury was white hot. My blood was boiling.

"*Kill him,*" a voice hissed in my head.

"I can't," I gasped out loud.

She hissed back, "*You can. The channel is there. Open it. Do it.*"

"I don't know how!"

"Kill him! You want to kill him."

Lucan was yelling in the distance, but the voice hissed over him. She wanted to break free. She wanted to murder, maim. Her hold over my body wasn't like it'd been before. The Immortal had been a part of me, but it had always been me. Davy. I was in charge of myself, but this element was something different. Her fury and power was so much, she wanted to overtake me.

Something flashed in her eyes. A white light blinded me, and she smiled at herself. It was evil, filled with rage, and she reached inside. Her hand stretched out and started to cup something in the center of me, possibly my soul. The white light began to become infused with it. It was absorbing it. She was taking control.

Then she was jerked away. The white light slammed back into darkness, and my body crashed to the floor.

My head rolled to the side. Lucan's shoes were in front of me. I heard the witches behind him, but I heard her whisper to me, *"We will be free. Vengeance will be ours."*

Then there was nothing.

SAREN

SAREN JERKED BACKWARDS. Her feet slid against the floor, but the pull stopped as quickly as it had happened. She closed her eyes and reached out to Sireenia. *"What has happened?"*

"The Immortal is impatient and angry. She is trying to break free on her own."

Saren's head moved to the side. *"The Mori magic will not allow that."*

"Not yet, no."

"Then what would happen if she continues to try?"

Saren heard the sadness in her sister's thoughts. "Davy will die. The Immortal will become its own entity."

"Then what?"

"Chaos."

Saren sighed and thought to her, *"I will stop it."*

"We are all fused together. You are our body and we are the spirit together. Go to our last sister. She needs us, more than ever now."

"No, child, you must open all your senses." Mavic's frustration was heavy.

Saren returned to her body form and looked to a field below her. The little witch was learning from the traitor sorcerer. They had taken camp in a valley protected by the Independent Army. He was attempting to help the little witch open her mind, body, and soul. Even from her vantage point above them, Saren knew he was only achieving with her ears. The little witch was listening, but she wasn't doing anything else.

The wind picked up at the moment and swept Saren's black, blue-tipped hair behind her. Her sword was clasped tightly in front of her, as if she would jump into battle that very moment. Then she sighed. Questions flew around in her head, and she knew the right person to answer them was not in that valley. Though, she would deal with the traitor later, and she would enjoy that moment.

Bastion returned from his scouting route and stood beside Roane. He waited until his arrival was acknowledged before he informed his leader, "They are coming. Due south and headed at a quick pace. They will be here within the hour."

Roane nodded. Grim. He knew his friend had more on his mind. "You don't approve of this alliance?"

Bastion chose his words wisely. "The Christane wolves are honorable."

"You don't approve of Christian?"

"He loved her as well."

Then Roane smiled, for the first time in four months. "And you think he still holds a grudge?"

Bastion looked away and stood tall. His lean form showcased his muscles, all developed to help him as the fastest vampire any had seen. His buzzed head had a black feather tattooed on the right side. The left side showed another tattoo written in a language he had spoken to no one. Lucas once asked, but Bastion responded that only one person would know the meaning of that tattoo. He had never spoken of it again. Lucas had never asked.

Over the last four months, Lucas depended more and more on his fastest warrior. He was tempted to ask again about the tattoo, but he always held his tongue. Bastion would share if he chose to.

The vampire responded now, "I think he could love this one, too."

Lucas was not normally taken aback, but his eyes widened a mere fraction. "You think he will fall in love with Davy?"

"You two have similar tastes." Bastion moved over, a slight inch.

"Christian fell in love with Talia because he spent two summers with her. I was gone, training for the Roane Army. He will not fall for Davy, and even if he did, it doesn't matter. He knows she is mine."

"I hope as well."

Lucas frowned at him. "If that is my biggest worry, then I gladly embrace it. I am more worried about finding her alive."

"She's alive." Confidence emanated from the lean warrior.

"You are sure of that?"

Bastion nodded his head in an abrupt movement. "You would feel it if she were not."

"And as of yet, I have not felt it." Then Roane frowned. He cast a sweeping look to his left and searched into the shadows. They stood in a valley, alone for miles except for his men, but a slight tingle warned him of a new arrival. And then, though nothing moved and no one reacted, he knew this new person was coming toward him. When a shadow separated from the rest of the night, he knew who it was. She had evaded Bastion's scouting.

Saren approached. She had watched as the vampire felt her

arrival. Not many could detect her, let alone know before she wanted them to. This vampire had gone up a notch in her opinion, but she should've expected as much. Davy would choose her love wisely.

Roane spoke first, "Do you share in Bastion's concerns?"

Saren's nostrils flared.

Bastion's head whipped to the side. His own flared, but in a different emotion.

Her voice was curt. "I care not about your human emotions. Love or jealousy, both are wasteful to non-human species."

"Such as yourself?"

Her eyes narrowed, but not before a flame leapt in them.

Roane didn't react, but the sight made him pause. This thing was becoming more and more than he knew what to do about. His gut was telling him that she was a fighter, probably the best he would ever see. An ally like her was priceless, but her presence didn't sit well with him. He couldn't factor her in, she was a variable given to him, perhaps a gift or perhaps a curse. They would all have to wait and see.

Bastion spoke, "They are here."

"They moved faster than you thought."

"I said within the hour."

"It's been a minute."

Saren's eyes skirted between the two. She tilted her head to the side. "Do you always argue as comrades? Is this another wasteful emotion?"

Roane's arm shot out before she could react. His hand grabbed her throat and lifted her in the air. He growled, "I don't know who or what you are, but the only reason I don't kill you is because I can smell her on you. And I can smell that you're as scared for her as I am." He settled her back on her feet. "So you can keep your ridicule to yourself. I am in no mood to hear it."

Her eyes were cool as she reached up and untangled his hand from her throat, one finger at a time. Their gaze never broke, but the flame increased in her eyes. The fire touched the air and the smell of smoke swept around them. When his hand was free, she moved back one step. "You will not touch me again, vampire. The only reason I have not killed your kind is because I know how she cares for you. If she did not, I would slaughter all of you."

"You don't like vampires." Roane nodded, but his gaze shifted to the tree line before them. He had smelled the werewolves when they were five miles away and they were near now, very near.

"I don't like anything."

"You like Davy."

Saren's lips clamped shut, and then she took a whiff of the air and turned. Her arms were flexed, ready for a fight, and her legs were bent, ready to leap forward. The wolves had arrived. They sat watching them, their heads outside the tree line and their bodies hidden in the shadows. All of them were in their wolf forms except a group in the center. The young man was Christian Christane, leader of the Christane Pack. The young girl smelled of Davy. Saren knew this had been the girl that Davy considered a friend, who had helped her. The other two, both older men, reeked of their power. They were ancient wolves, each a lineage amongst themselves. Still, though they were old and powerful, both adhered to the younger man. They remained behind as the other two moved forward.

Roane stepped forward to meet them.

CHAPTER 4

Christian Christane stepped forward with blond locks that the wind whipped back and forth. He had blue eyes, as clear as the aqua colored Mediterranean, and he strode forward with confidence and authority that emanated from him. Large muscular shoulders and a trimmed waist, not many men could measure against the Alpha Christane, but many would try. An air of sharp intelligence gave others an impression that Christian didn't care what others thought of him; the only item of importance was what he thought about others. What he deemed is what was.

Pippa approached behind her brother by a step. Her reddish hair was no longer worn in two braids, but flowed freely around her face. It tossed around her shoulders, the same as her brother's, but both ignored it. As they continued to approach Davy's boyfriend, her fingers twitched. She lifted her hand to adjust her coveralls strap, but they stopped short on her shoulders. She no longer wore those coveralls anymore. When she had returned home, their older sister burned every piece of clothing Pippa owned. Her closet now housed clothing that she had only ever seen on models, such as now as she wore a white cashmere sweater that showcased her slender body over custom tailored jeans.

Pippa no longer looked like the awkward freshman she had

been. Lola Christane wanted her little sister to be the beautiful woman that she knew was in there. Unfortunately, at tense moments like these, Pippa longed for her coveralls and braids. She would've felt more comfortable.

"Pip?" Christian stopped and glanced over his shoulder. He could feel his sister's nerves.

She forced herself to relax. "I'm fine. I'll be fine."

He patted her on the arm. "We'll find your friend. Roane is the best hunter I know."

She nodded. "I know."

Then they turned together, Pippa beside him, and stared across a space of fifteen feet.

Roane, Bastion, and Saren stared back.

Christian's eyes swept over the blue-leathered girl and frowned. He couldn't remember this vampire, and from the condescension on her face, he knew he would've.

He nodded to her and asked, "Have you sired a new warrior?"

Roane narrowed his eyes and stepped forward. He blocked the Alpha's view of her. "Thank you for coming, Christian."

His blue eyes snapped to Roane's. "As if I had a choice. I could not ignore my sister's friendship with this new thread-holder."

Roane's lips curved upward, but the half grin was gone in a second. His face was emotionless again. "Of course."

"Of course."

"It is nice to see you again, Pippa." Roane's voice was guarded, his body tense and on alert.

She gave him a tentative smile and said faintly, "I'm sorry about Davy."

A dark emotion flashed in Roane's eyes, but it was gone again instantly. As Christian watched, if he hadn't been told by Pippa how much the Hunter cared for his lover he wouldn't have been able to judge it for himself. Lucas Roane had never given him any window to his emotions. At one point the two might've called themselves friends, but it'd been shattered. While he respected Lucas Roane, he would never trust him enough to let down his own guard.

Christian spoke curtly, "Should we be going then?"

"How many wolves have you brought?"

His eyes narrowed further. "Around forty."

The blue-leathered girl sneered at him. "He has seventy-five men. Only thirty have come forward to intimidate us, but he has more behind them. He wasn't going to let you know about the last forty-five."

"How do you know that?"

Her eyes narrowed, and a flame leapt in them. "I counted, dog."

Bastion glanced at Roane, both hid their amusement as Christian threw his head back in a snarl. His body flipped in the air, and a werewolf with sleek white fur landed in front of them. He pounced on Saren, ready to hold her captive with his large paws. She reacted before he could grab her and leapt higher in the air. Her knees bent forward and her arms stretched out as she lifted higher and higher in the air.

Christian roughly landed on the ground, but his head reared back, and he was after her in the next second.

"Christian!" Pippa yipped at him.

He looked back, and his werewolf transformed back to his human form. Two of his men ran forward, and he emerged from behind them with clothes on instantly. When he stood in his place beside his sister again, Saren returned to her place.

Roane looked at her. "You are not helping here. Leave."

She growled.

"Now!"

Pippa shifted on her feet and clasped her hands as the two were locked in a staring battle. After a moment, the girl warned, "I will be back, vampire. You will need my assistance."

"I'm sure we will. Come back. Later."

Saren took one step backwards and vanished from their sight.

Pippa's eyes went wide, and she gasped.

Christian's eyes narrowed even further. "Who was that?"

Roane sounded weary. "She is an ally. She cares for Davy, as we all do."

"She knows Davy?" Pippa's voice squeaked.

"I will not travel with an ally I do not trust."

Roane studied him a moment. "You don't trust me, but you will fight for my cause."

Christian fell silent, studying him in return.

Bastion moved forward a step, closer to his leader.

Roane didn't look away.

Pippa stepped between them and held up her hands. "I don't know the history between you two, but I can see now that there is some. But I'm here for Davy. Chris, you know how much I care for her. She's the only friend I have."

"You have other friends."

She sighed. "They aren't my true friends. They're nice to me because you're my brother, because I'm a Christane wolf. Davy liked me even when she thought I was there to hurt her. I respect her, and we need to go help her. She gave us Pete back, Chris. Don't forget what she's done for you, too."

At the reminder, his shoulders relaxed a bit. "My sister is right. We should start. Traveling to the Mori will be long and taxing. We don't have time to fight amongst ourselves."

Roane extended his hand.

After a pause, Christian reached for it. They clasped their hands around each other's wrists and shook once, a firm and final shake. Pippa watched the two and felt something new in the air. It was something powerful, hopeful, inspiring. It filled her with new energy, a new adrenaline rush of excitement. And something told her that she'd see more moments such as this to come, many more.

DAVY

When I opened my eyes, I was still on the floor. Some new food had been placed in a dish beside me, but too many flies buzzed around it. The smell of citrusy garbage made my stomach clench and vomit regurgitated out of me. I hadn't the energy to move, and so it came out as a cough, then it dribbled down my chin to fall on the floor. I couldn't move away and I couldn't stop when another cough shook my body. More vomit came out, then another and another cough. Each time it was slower than the last and each time my body shook harder and harder.

My stomach was violently assaulting my body. I was helpless to stop it. After an hour of it, my eyes started to droop. The unconscious started to beckon me. Slowly, so slowly, I heard my breaths grow shorter, shallower, and then—

"Wake up!" a voice boomed.

My eyes snapped open, and I jerked upright. A scream ripped from my throat from the pain in my limbs. A butcher knife felt like it was embedded in my spine with little knives and razors inside my body, all over. Each ligament felt like they were being cut with each movement I made.

"Who—" I doubled over, and another wave of nausea hit me. Fresh vomit spewed out again.

Then the door opened. When I tried to lift my head, another scream came out of me again. My neck felt paralyzed. I couldn't move it. A pair of shoes came to my head and they squatted down.

I had expected Lucan, but this was a female. She had long red hair, brown eyes, and white skin. A memory flashed in my head, and I remembered the Mori, when they had followed Bennett to my college. She looked like them. This was one of them.

Her eyes were blank as she watched me, then she reached through the cage and touched my head. It was a gentle touch. If I hadn't watched her do it, I wouldn't have felt the touch. But then a surge of heat raced through me. My heart started pumping fast. I gasped as my back arched again, my lungs filled with something warm, and every ligament of my body tingled.

She said softly, "I have given you life now, stand."

And I could. It was a miracle. Then I remembered. "Magic."

She stood as I did, my eyes parallel to her the entire time until I was able to stand tall again. When I squared my shoulders back, the Mori did the same. When I took a deep breath, the vampire copied again. She was copying everything I did.

"What are you doing?"

"What are you doing?" She stepped closer and wrapped a hand around one of the bars. Her head tilted to the side, all the way until I thought she would turn her head upside down.

"I'm a prisoner. What are you?"

She touched her chest. "I am Jiyama."

"You are a Mori."

"I am Jiyama. You are prisoner."

I frowned. "My name is Davy. Your name is Jiyama—"

"—name."

"—You are a Mori. I am a human."

"You are a prisoner."

"No, I'm a human—"

"Human. Davy. Prisoner."

"Yes." I surged forward eagerly. She was getting it.

"I am human, prisoner. Jiyama."

"No." She sighed. "You are a vampire."

Her lips lifted, and fangs appeared.

"Yes, see. You're a vampire. I'm a human."

The fangs slipped back in their place, and she closed her mouth. "Davy. Jiyama."

"Oh God." This was going to take a while.

The door burst open again, and Lucan stomped in. "Jiyama, what are you doing? Get away from her."

She turned, but not before I saw her grin. "I am learning English."

He stopped and frowned at her.

I expected him to rip into her, chastise her, but when he said nothing, her mouth dropped open. Instead he looked at her in confusion, like she was a puzzle that he couldn't figure out.

When he continued to stare at her, a laugh ripped out of me. "I can't believe this."

His eyes grew dark, and he pointed a finger at me. "You shut up. You don't understand a thing. Jiyama, we need to go."

She turned back and reached through the bars again. "Davy. Prisoner."

The same surge of warmth spread through me again. I gasped and my vision blurred this time. She had healed me before, but this time her magic helped me. Life—something took root in me. The Immortal stirred inside of me, wakened once more. I seized the magic and absorbed it eagerly.

"Don't!" Lucan yelled.

Jiyama jerked away, but I grabbed her hand before she could pull it out. I yanked her back to me.

Jiyama yelped, but I was blind from greed. I needed more of that magic. The Immortal's power was starting to build again. It was spreading through me. The more Mori magic I felt, the more my power rose. This time I wasn't afraid of it. I could do something with this magic. The channel could be opened again. If only—

"No." Lucan caught my hand.

I salivated for more, but crashed against the cage.

Jiyama stared at me. Her face still looked blank, but something was stirring in her eyes. They had turned from brown to red, a dark red. "I gave you a gift. Something you could not have had, you have now." She looked down. "But you must protect your gift." She held her hand out, and another burst of magic came from her. It shot through me, sealing something, but The Immortal slammed against me. She wanted to get out. She wanted the Mori.

"Stop!" Lucan pulled her back. "Jiyama, leave. This is not the one you can learn English from. I have others." He placed a hand between her shoulders and led her to the door.

She went, but looked back over her shoulder. "Others?"

He nodded. "They are below. They are not dangerous. This one is dangerous. Do not come here again."

She finally nodded and went into the hallway. His shoulders sagged in relief as he shut the door.

I held onto the cage bars. "You are not their leader, are you?"

His shoulders tensed immediately before he swung to face her. Resigned.

I saw his answer. He didn't have to say a word. A smile came to my face and I couldn't stop it. I didn't want to stop it. "You are a guest, aren't you? They have no idea who I am, who the others are, or that we're even here. What are you to them?"

Lucan frowned at me, studying me. "The Mori saved me years ago. Lucas nearly killed me once. They found me and took me in. They healed me and became my family when my real family turned on me."

"You don't really believe that, do you?" I laughed. "They have no idea who you are, what you're trying to do."

"What am I trying to do, Davy?" he asked, softly. A keen look came to him, and he started to advance forward. With each step, he asked, "What is it that you think I'm really trying to do?"

"Kill me. Take ultimate power from me. Rule all the vampires."

He stopped, but sent me a dark look. "I am trying to better the vampire race. I am trying to make it so that we don't have to hide anymore. Humans can know that we live among them. We won't have to worry about a war with the werewolves. We will be safe, once and for all. And yes, that means the Mori, too. They can finally come out of their hiding. They can show the world who they are."

"You're mad," I murmured. "I don't think you even know anymore what you want."

Everything changed in that instant. His shoulders stood upright. His smirk came back, and he gave me a radiant smile. "I want The Immortal thread. And I won't stop before I get it, Davy. One way or another, I will figure out how to rip it out of you. When I do, you will die slowly, painfully, and I will enjoy watching it."

CHAPTER 5

There was no sound, no change in the air. I didn't smell anything new, and the hairs on the back of my neck didn't stand up, but when I lifted my head, I knew who I would see. And I was right.

Jiyama stood in front of the cage. There was a determined look in her eyes, and she squared her jaw as she reached through the cage to me.

I stood from my sitting position and stepped close.

The Immortal slammed inside of me. She wanted the Mori. She was salivating like a newborn vampire for blood.

I held her back. "What are you doing?"

Everything in me wanted to go closer, to grab her hands, and take what I could. The Immortal was snarling, an angry tornado, but I stood firm. What would happen if I took those hands? The Immortal wanted it so bad, I wasn't sure I could control myself. And that was when I realized I was scared. Not of myself or the situation, I was scared when The Immortal would take over, and in the next second, I admitted a second truth to myself. The Immortal *would* take over. I didn't know when, I didn't know how, but she would.

She was too strong, and she was no longer a part of me. She had separated from me.

Her eyes flashed, and she jerked forward. Her hands caught mine, and before I could react to pull away, The Immortal surged inside of me. She burst through our connection, and I saw the Mori's head get thrown back. Her mouth opened wide, and a bright light burst from her. Her eyeballs were like flashlights, and even her fingertips burst forth with light. It was a blinding white light.

"Your magic and mine are sister threads."

I frowned. It was the Mori. She was in my head, and her English was perfect.

"It's our connection. I have obtained everything from you, as you have taken from me."

Images flew at me, of Jiyama as a child. The first time she found a dead body, but it wasn't dead. It was Lucan. She poked it and kicked at his foot. He rolled over and her heart stopped. Then she yelled for her father and his men picked up the weird man's body and took him home with them. There was another image when she was older, twelve maybe. She sat at a bonfire and was trying to stitch something together. Lucan sat beside and showed her how to do it. He was gentle, patient, and kind.

He wasn't the Lucan that I knew.

Then she grew older. Lucan was always with them. He taught her many things about the other world, how to read in other languages except for one. English. He showed her books, and as she read them every night, they were from the human world. He told her nothing of the other vampire species. And then he was gone.

My last image was when she stood and watched him go. He gave her a gentle smile and kissed her cheek. Jiyama wrapped both her arms around him and lifted high on her tiptoes. She pressed against him and told him in their language that she loved him. He swept back her hair and promised he'd come back. Then he kissed her on the mouth.

As I hurled around inside of her, I couldn't believe this was the Lucan I knew. If he'd been like that with me, I might've fallen in love, too.

Okay—reality check. I shuddered. That would've never happened.

"He is not the monster you feel he is."

I jerked my eyes back to her. Our hands were still clasped together. The Immortal was back inside of me and purring like a cat that had gotten the cream, and Jiyama's eyes had a white rim around them now. They'd been so dark before.

"You don't know how I know him." My eyes were darting all over. Did she know? Could she read my mind now? I didn't like this one bit.

Her mouth tightened. *"You have an incredible power inside of you. Our magic comes from the earth. Yours come from the life itself. It is a new power, no one is aware it exists."*

"Except for all the thread-holders before me."

She tilted her head to the side and chewed on a lip. *"What are you concerned for?"*

"You want a quick answer or the real one?"

"You fear Lucan."

"He's not good, Jiyama."

She stepped back. When our hands let go, the connection was gone. It was instant, and I reeled inside from it. The Immortal blared again, angry once more. She wanted the connection back.

"He's good to me and my family."

I grew silent. She didn't want to hear about the real Lucan and from what I saw inside of her, what I felt—she was in love with him. It was powerful and it gripped her so tightly. Then the door burst open and Lucan strode inside.

"What are you doing in here, Jiyama?"

She turned and gave him a faint smile. "You shouldn't have kept her from us."

He drew up short and watched her warily.

"You want to know what he's doing?"

"Davy—"

"He's trying to kill me."

Jiyama turned to me with intent eyes.

"He wants to take that power out of me, and if he succeeds, I'm dead. He doesn't care. If he's this good and great person, the one that you love so much, would he do that?"

"A man should be ruthless to protect his loved ones."

I snorted. "Are you blind? Or just dumb? Your family saved his life. You have power in you that he wants. Of course, he's not going to show you the real Lucan. He's ruthless, but he's also a psychopath. Every day his witches come in here and torture me. Every day." I swung my gaze around. "And where's Kates? Does she know about her? Why do I always smell her blood on you?"

"Enough!" Lucan growled as he launched himself at me. He ripped open the cage and was inside the next instant. His hands wrapped around my throat as he flew us against the back end. When the cage tipped over and his hands loosened a fraction, I shot my hand against his chest.

"Stop."

Then everything halted.

My heart skipped a beat, and I blinked. Nothing moved. No one breathed, no one twitched. Nothing. I'd frozen time again and I turned toward Jiyama. Her eyes were wide, fearful, but her hands remained at her side.

She wasn't scared. I wedged myself out of Lucan's hold and edged closer to her. There was a look in her eyes, deep in them. Confidence. A shiver broke over me and something whispered in the back of my mind that I hadn't uncovered the tip of the power inside of her. But from what I had seen and felt, it sent chills down my back.

"Uh." Lucan's finger cracked the air. He was fighting against the time freeze.

I didn't have much more of it so I whirled around and was in the hallway. Everyone stood in place. I had done that. It hadn't been contained to only my room. Then, with my heart pounding, a loud rushing sound in my ears, I stopped and tried to concentrate.

I needed to find the rest. Even Kates. The Immortal rattled inside of me. A small burst of air came from me. It formed a tiny cloud and as it started down the hallway, it bounced back to me. Slowly, with my heart pounding and my limbs shaking, I started to follow.

It took me down another hallway, through door after door, until a last one opened. A dark stairway led downstairs and I went down, weak in the knees. These were the moments when I needed Roane to hold my hand. He would know where to go, how to do it, and I would never feel my fear.

I felt it now. It railed inside of me. And that was when I realized I had merged with The Immortal, but it was only a tiny bit. She was angry and hissing inside of me. She was screaming for me to hurry, but I didn't. I inched downwards, step after step, and prayed the time freeze wouldn't loosen.

It wasn't far after that until the small cloud darted around another corner. There they were.

Gavin and Gregory were held on one side while Tracey and Wren were across from them. They seemed so tired. My heart pounded even more and I hurried past them. Nothing. There were more cages, but none with Kates. Where was Kates? And why did I care? But something told me it wasn't right. She should've—he had her blood on him. Every day, he came to me with her blood on him. I shuddered as I remembered the look of twisted delight in his eyes. What was he doing with her?

Oh goddess. What do I do?

I ran back to them and tried to open the door. Nothing. It didn't even jar against my force and I closed my eyes in defeat. My blood was pumping furiously through me and I sagged against the cage. I couldn't do it. I couldn't do anything.

"I can."

I steeled myself and shook my head. There had to be another way.

"I can free them. You know this."

I whimpered to myself, "No. There has to be another way. Not like this—"

"Let me, Davy!" The Immortal screamed and lunged herself at

me. I gasped and my arms flew out. She was battling for control again, and she was winning.

"No!"

"*Yes!*" She lunged again. And again. Each time she drove farther into me.

As I readied myself for another launch, I already knew the battle was done. So I turned my head in slow motion and looked at Gavin. Worry lines circled his eyes. His shoulders had drooped, maybe in frustration? His own surrender? I swallowed a painful knot in my throat. I hadn't considered what torture they had done to them. Then there was a bleak emotion in me. Did I want to know? Would that give The Immortal more power over me? The angrier I got, the weaker in my compassion I became, the stronger she grew. She was taking over.

"*Now!*"

And it was done. Everything shot through me at once. Visions blasted in my head. Lucan had cracked another finger through the time freeze. Jiyama was freed, but she watched him in a calm curiosity. I felt Gavin's fury and his determination. Gregory was worried for his friend, who sat in front of him. Wren was anguished. I felt her fear for Roane, her loyalty to him, and the love for the blonde vampiress beside her. And Tracey—she shifted inside of herself and met my gaze. She was frozen on the outside, but she was aware in the inside.

She gave me a haunted smile. A tear slipped down. "*My niece is here. Leave me.*"

I jerked in shock. We were communicating on another level of consciousness. "*We can't leave you behind.*"

"*I will be fine. Tell Wren that I love her.*" She bowed her head to me. "*I must stay for my niece. Talia would want me to do this.*"

It was done. She had decided. I nodded. "*This is why you came to us, isn't it? To find Talia's daughter?*"

Tracey gave me a sad smile. "*It is, but it was healing for me to connect with Wren once more.*"

"*Once more.*"

There it was, the finality. I had no idea what was going to happen in the future, if we would become free or not, but I felt it. Tracey wouldn't be returning, no matter the outcome. She had another road to follow.

It went without saying. I said it anyway. *"Wren loves you."*

"She does, but she needs Roane more than my love." She glanced over and would've caressed the other vampiress's head if she could've. *"Her belief in him grounds her. She needs that and she knows it. She'll always choose him over me."*

Tick. Tick. Tick.

I felt the clock beneath our feet. The time was coming. I had to make my move. I had to do it now.

The Immortal rallied again. She snarled at Tracey, *"Leave us. You do not help, you will only hinder."*

Tracey's eyes shuddered, but she surged away in retreat.

I felt Lucan's anger. It was broiling to the top. Soon he would break through the time freeze so I hurried to the cage, closed my eyes and let go.

The Immortal gleamed as she lifted a hand. There wasn't a command, just the will. The door unlocked and Gavin and Gregory were also unlocked from the time freeze.

"Wha—Davy!" Gavin launched himself forward and started to scoop me up.

My eyes flashed at him and he braked. The Immortal's whites shined at him and he took a breath.

Then I waved my hand to the other door. Wren was unfrozen. Her head jerked up, and her nostrils flared. A wild look shifted over her, and her fangs protruded at me.

Then she stopped and turned back.

Tracey was still frozen.

She swung her head to me. "Undo her."

The Immortal sneered at her. "She wishes to remain. So be it."

"Undo her!" Her hands lifted, and her body started to arch.

She would've thrown herself on me, but I waved a hand. Her body slammed to the wall from my will. When she would've fallen to the ground, I lifted my palm. She rose in the air, and my grip was at her throat. "She remains for her niece. You knew this."

She snarled again. "Unfreeze her—I will not—"

"You will." I let her body fall to the ground with a thump. "Or you will die. I will not go against her wishes, not when they rally with one of my sisters."

"Sisters?" Gavin murmured behind me.

Then I felt the crack beginning. The time freeze thread was starting to unravel. "We must go or all will be lost."

"Kates?"

I clasped my eyes shut a moment. The Immortal allowed me this weakness. Something broke inside of me. "We must leave her. I don't know where she is—"

"Davy!"

Lucan was coming.

I whirled to Gavin and gasped, "I'm weakening. I can't—"

Gregory was at the door, then through it. Gavin started to follow, but turned back. He saw the problem and with a hardened mask over his face, he swept past me. Picking up Wren, he carried her to the door. I started forward, still leaving Tracey frozen when Wren shouted, "At least let her escape on her own, or do whatever she wants. At least—" The growl melted into a forlorn look. As Gavin paused, right before the door, her shoulders dropped. She finished, "At least, let her decide."

I felt inside of myself. I didn't have much magic, but I nodded. "Go!" I yelled at them and unfroze Tracey at the same time.

She jerked out of place, but she knew what was going on. A resolved expression crossed her face. She nodded to me. "Go."

"Wren is—"

"Go." She surged forward.

I wavered on my feet. The magic was leaving me so quickly. My knees were weakening, an entire wave of exhaustion was rising up over me. It was going to crash soon. I felt its impending arrival.

The blonde vampire saw my dilemma and she cursed under her breath. I felt Lucan coming. He was roaring my name through the building, making even the cages shake from his fury. I looked back at the door. I knew then, I wouldn't be able to make it. If Gregory, Gavin, and Wren got free, that was good. I wasn't going to be with them. I had nothing in me to evade Lucan and his army.

Then, abruptly, Tracey soared to me. She grabbed me up and was running with me. I looked up at her. Her head was down and focused, but as she darted through the door, her eyes shifted to mine. She was getting me to safety. I nodded, thinking in my head, *"I'm sorry."*

Her lips pressed together. She didn't say anything, but I felt the sadness inside of her, and she thought to me, *"Rest, Davy. I'll carry you the way."*

We raced down a hallway and soared past a door. I was so tired. The wave was crashing down on me, but I lifted my head. I felt Lucan coming toward me. He sensed my presence. He knew we were going fast, but Tracey wasn't fast enough. He was coming—the door exploded in the air and he was there. He was barreling after us. I closed my eyes and transcended above us. The Immortal was quiet, more than she had been the entire time. I didn't have enough energy for this, so I knew she was doing this.

We weren't as one anymore. We were almost two separate beings, and she felt my distress. She was lifting me up. My body was in Tracey's arms, but I was up and I could see Lucan racing to catch up.

We were doomed. He was faster than Tracey was, but I had to try to help. I had to try, at least.

"Rest, Davy." I felt The Immortal's words. The anger was there, but held off. It was as if she knew I had tried, and then, my head started to fall back. I watched myself as my body grew limp in Tracey's arms. She glanced down, her alarm picked up, but she didn't stop. Her fear gave her a small boost of speed, but it still wasn't enough.

Lucan was almost there.

"Davy." The Immortal was at my side again. She laid a hand on my shoulder. *"Rest."*

And, as if her words had magic over myself, the world started to grow black. My eyelids fell, suddenly so tired, but I saw The Immortal gazing down where I was in Tracey's arms. Wind began to pick up. The walls of the hallway started moving around, and then we were gone.

I had fallen asleep.

CHAPTER 6

Christian stared across the bonfire at the man he never understood. Lucas Roane was a vampire. They were all alike, but this one never did as he predicted. He loved a woman. He left her. He lost her, so he fell in love with the new thread. Next he chose to declare a war for the woman. And when she was taken from him, the old vampire he knew would've found another woman. This Lucas Roane sought an alliance with his enemy. They went together for this Immortal, for the woman the legendary Hunter thought he loved.

And then he glanced to his side. His sister sat there, content, as she munched on a chicken leg he roasted over the fire for her. Pippa was the younger sister no one understood. She scurried away from fights, hid in the shadows when confronted, and was so eager to escape away to a school far away. Then she called for them and she wasn't the same woman. She had grown. She stood upright when spoken to, she met each attack with her own fierceness, and she rallied them all when she heard a friend was in need.

It was the same woman. They both loved the same woman, though not in the same way.

Christian looked down at his lap and gripped his water again.

His confusion didn't matter. He would go to this woman. He would rescue her and he would do it without protest. His sister believed in this woman and he would forever be grateful. He was given a new sister, one who loved herself, was proud of herself, and who made him proud as well. He would fight for whoever managed that feat.

"You're thinking too loud." Pippa glanced up as she bit into the chicken leg again. She grinned.

"That's what being older and wiser means. We think a lot." He draped an arm around her shoulder and pulled her close. A tender smile came to him. "Good thing I have you with me."

She nudged him with her elbow. "I keep you on your toes."

"You do."

"I do." She was solemn as she held her older brother's gaze.

From across the fire, Lucas watched the exchange. A part of him tore inside, but there was no outward reaction. He sat as a statue and his face never moved. He was a stone, had been since Davy was taken. But something softened in him as well. Davy would've liked to see her friend happy, and she seemed to be with her older brother.

And then a woosh sounded behind him. Saren took the seat beside him. Her blue leather crinkled in protest as she lowered to the piece of tree. She glanced at him, looked where he watched, and sighed in disgust.

"You humans are all the same," she snorted, rolling her eyes.

Lucas gave her a restrained look. "I am a vampire."

"You're still human."

"I eat humans."

"You drink blood. It is different. You still feel. You let those feelings overtake you. You're still human." She nodded across the fire. "As are they. They are worse."

"How so?"

"Vampires act like they're better than humans, but they know deep down they aren't. They're worse. You all are vain and weak, but werewolves feel their arrogance is fulfilled. They think they're the greatest creatures on earth, all because they are still human, they have mortal lives if they want them, and they think they're in control of everything." She snickered. "Davy always talked how wolves were the best to be around. They repressed everything; she didn't have to feel their emotions."

A grin teased over his face. "That sounds like her."

She mirrored his amusement, but looked over and it faded. She stared with an intensity now. It drew him to ask, "What?"

Her mouth tightened. "Why did you leave the witch with Mavic?"

His jaw slackened at her words and he whirled to her. It happened so fast, faster than in the blink of an eye, and his hand clasped onto her arm. "How did you know about him?"

She never blinked. "I've been watching you since Davy insisted she was in love with you. She was a fool," she spat out. "You're both fools."

His fingers loosened. Just a little. "What do you know about Mavic?"

"He is a traitor. He is the worst scum underneath the dirt on my shoes. I want to squash him into the earth until his loins burst and his body bleeds dry. I want to—"

He lifted his hand free. "Okay. I got it."

She drew upright. The embers in her eyes burst into flame. "What are your plans for the traitor sorcerer?"

Roane shot her an annoyed look. "I'd still like to know how you could stalk me without me knowing about it."

"I did not stalk." She squared her shoulders back. "I do not stalk."

One of his eyelids twitched.

She frowned. "I hunted you. I did not stalk you. Hunt. That's more . . ."

Bastion stuck his head around. "Less creepy?"

Her shoulders dropped. "Yes. I am not creepy."

The two vampires shared a look.

"What?" She looked from one to the other.

Bastion shrugged. "You're a bit creepy."

"I am not."

"Yeah. Yeah, you are. Sorry to break the news."

She took a deep breath. Her chin lifted and she sat to her fullest height. "I am the representative of my clan. I am here to help a fellow sister, the followers of my sister, and I—." She clamped her mouth shut.

Bastion raised an eyebrow. "Yes?"

Her shoulders sagged down again. "Nothing."

Roane grinned. "You're creepy, but in a good way."

"Thanks." She lifted her head again.

The two shared a slight smile, and Bastion groaned. "I'm getting the creeps now."

"What is the plan?" The question was almost thrown from the other side of the bonfire like a challenge. The small exchange between Saren and the two vampires was interrupted, and the small moment of a slight break in tension was sniffed away like it wasn't supposed to have been there in the first place.

Roan straightened, remembering how Christian Christane had once taken the woman he loved. A dark emotion took root inside of him. He wouldn't allow that to happen again. He didn't fear for the same repetition, but that he'd lose Davy because of the Alpha wolf. That would not happen, and the wolf sensed the deep determination. It was like an old rivalry, once buried was awoken again. His nostrils flared, knowing the near loathing was there. He couldn't do anything about it, and the two weren't on speaking terms. They couldn't speak about Talia, at least.

Pippa glanced up at him, picking up the undercurrents. She pressed her lips together and let out a small growl. She looked at both and said one word. "Davy."

Roane and her brother received the message. The small flare-up dampened immediately, but it was still there. It was a back burner turned to simmer. It was still hot and still dangerous if left ignored.

Saren narrowed her eyes. She harrumphed. "Foolish human emotions."

No one responded, but she stood, and as she stepped away from the fire, she vanished.

Roane continued to stare across the dancing flames at the werewolf. Neither looked away.

CHAPTER 7
DAVY

I woke up on a bed and lifted my head, or I would've. My neck wouldn't move. Stabbing pain sliced through me, and I cried out. My body instantly locked up, and I started trembling, sending even more stabbing pain through me.

"Davy."

Gavin rushed inside, the sound of something was shoved aside, like a tarp. He added, "You're awake? Are you okay?"

"Yeah. I'm—" I couldn't talk. My teeth were grinding together.

He laid a hand on my arm and said, "You've been out for three days. Rest."

"Wha-a-at happened?"

"You."

Me? I frowned at him, trying to remember. The Immortal was with me, she told me to sleep, and I was watching from above. "Lucan was going to catch us."

"You teleported Tracey and yourself. We only just found you guys yesterday. Tracey was exhausted by the time we did. She'd been standing guard over you."

"Teleported?"

He nodded, grim. "You sent the both of you to the highest mountain. We're twenty miles from the Mori camp. Wren's the one that kept us going to find you. She said she could feel Tracey and used her scent. She tracked you guys."

He thought I did this. I didn't. The Immortal did it, and I tried to sense her right now, but I couldn't. It was like she wasn't even inside of me. All I felt was nothing. Exhaustion. Pain. That was it.

Gavin added, "It must've taken it out of you."

"Yeah." I looked away. "It must've."

He gestured around, but I could only see above. It was a dark wall of rock. Gavin said, "We brought you into this cave. We used a tarp we found by a riverbed not far from here. It's used to block out the cold for you."

For you. Those two words—they were all vampires. The cold didn't matter to them, but I was human. I was The Immortal, or I thought I still was.

"Is she awake?"

I tensed, hearing Wren outside. She was angry. I could feel it coming off her in waves.

Gavin studied me. "Are you up for her?"

No. I said, "I need answers."

He nodded, then left my side. The tarp was lifted and he spoke to them, "She's in pain. I don't think she can take too much."

"She's The Immortal. She can take more than any of us." She shoved at the tarp, coming inside. I didn't move my head over. My neck would've seized up again, but her anger became stronger. As she stood over me, glaring down, it was blanketing on top of me, and I struggled to push through it all.

This wasn't normal. This was my empathic side. This was how it had been when I still struggled to control my senses. Since becoming The Immortal, I hadn't had this problem. Everything was easily controlled, even kept at bay so I could pull it forth as I pleased.

Something was wrong.

"What happened back there?"

"Wren." Tracey came inside. "Don't berate her. She needs rest, not to be interrogated."

"I don't care." She twisted back to look at her. "She brought you both here. Why? How? Was it The Immortal power in her? Is Lucan coming for us? Does he know our location? Do we even know our location? We need answers."

"And we'll get them." Tracey touched her lover's arm. Her voice gentled. "But not now. I was carrying her body. Her body, Wren. Not her, but a body. Her heart stopped."

My eyes snapped to her, and I jerked upright.

Oh.

Shit.

I held my breath, knowing what was coming—and yep, there it was. A crest of new pain crashed onto me, and I stifled a scream. I bit down on my lip, but I was wailing on the inside.

"Davy?"

I shook my head, holding a hand up to Gavin. I'd be fine. Answers. Answers. I focused on that. Wren wanted answers, well, so did I. I waited out the pain, then lifted my gaze to Tracey's, and I asked one word. "Stopped?"

She nodded. "I thought you died. I was carrying you when you suddenly stopped breathing."

"And you continued to hold her?"

Tracey shot Wren a dark look. "I wasn't going to let him have her body. She wasn't slowing me down."

"But you said they were going to catch you," Wren spoke.

Tracey nodded. "They would've, but then," her hand lifted toward me, "we were on this mountain."

"I was dead?"

"You weren't alive."

I couldn't—I'd been dead. Had The Immortal left me? Was I only an empath now? A cold shiver of panic wound down my spine, but I shook it off. I wouldn't start thinking about that, not until I knew for certain. "How long?"

"A day."

"A day?" I was gutted. I was dead for an entire day?

"She's The Immortal. How is that possible?"

Tracey looked at Wren. "I don't know. I didn't think it was, but she had no heartbeat. But she's alive again, so I guess it doesn't matter."

But she didn't sound so certain. Neither was I. I always had a heartbeat. Always. Not having one—I didn't want to not be a human. I'd completely become The Immortal then and I knew that wasn't right. I needed to hold onto my humanity as long as I could. A heartbeat was part of that.

"Davy," Gavin said.

I looked to him.

He said, "We need to decide our next move."

Wren snorted. "Leave. Get back to Roane as fast as possible."

Gavin didn't look at her. He was waiting for me, and I knew what the unspoken question was. Kates. We had left her behind.

Raw emotion rose up, threatening to choke me. Like the panic, I shoved it away. I needed a clear head. "Where is Gregory?"

Tracey answered, "He's on point, watching."

"We're twenty miles away. I think we're safe, for now." Wren threw both a disgusted look. Her anger melted into pure impatience.

I nodded. Okay. So this was the decision that had to be made. "We go back—"

"Go back?" Wren echoed me. "To die?"

I ignored her and finished, "—for Kates or we continue forward, hopefully toward Roane."

"Can you sense him?"

I couldn't even sense The Immortal, much less my lover. I wasn't going to say that, though. I shook my head. "I'm too tired, I think."

"You need to rest," Tracey said.

"We need to move." Wren shook her head at both of them. "We move or die. Those are the options we have."

"Not if we have her at full strength." Gavin indicated me. "If we have an Immortal at full strength, we can fight back."

"We're in Mori territory. They're going to find us."

He shook his head. "It's Davy's call. We do what she wants."

"I want to go back." Tracey cut through any more argument. Wren's mouth hung open, and before she could say anything, Tracey added, "I wanted to stay behind. My niece is there. I want to know her."

"Your niece?"

Tracey looked at me and said, "If you go back for Kates, I'll go with you. I'll fight at your side."

"As will I." Gavin stepped beside her. The two were in solidarity and both turned to Wren.

She shook her head. "We'll die."

"Not if she can rest."

Wren clipped out, "We go to Roane. He's coming for us. He'll have an army with him. We can go back for the traitor and your niece, but with him. We'll have numbers on our side." Her voice rose. "We'll have a fighting chance. These are Mori vampires. You guys are forgetting that. They're not like us. We're lucky we got free at all. They're a force all at once. They fight as one being. We'll never win, with or without a rested Immortal on our side."

She was right. I looked to Gavin and Tracey. They both knew she was right, but they'd do what I said. They believed in me the way they believed in Roane. The same loyalty Wren felt for her leader hadn't transferred to me, but it didn't matter. Even though Gregory wasn't in the cave with us, he would do what I said. That was his way.

It was my call, and as Wren turned to me, reluctance written all over her face, I knew she knew it as well.

I said, "Let's rest. For now." That was all I could say.

CHAPTER 8
ROANE

"Vampire."

Two days earlier, Roane would've been surprised at the sudden appearance of Davy's blue-clad mysterious friend, but as he was standing on the cliff, overlooking the camp, he was starting to recognize when she'd appear. A slight buzzing would fill the air and feeling the same sensations this time, he merely looked over as she was standing next to him. The wind was fierce where they stood, high above the others, so her blue-tipped black hair was immediately flowing behind her. She gazed out over the cliff's edge. "You take point up here because of the wind, not just because of the view."

It wasn't a statement, and Roane didn't respond. He was up there for other reasons. Yes, he could smell any enemy approaching better from there, and yes, he could see beyond their camp better, but he was also up there because it would've been a spot that Davy would've loved. It was the highest vantage point where he could see as far as possible, and if she was within range and if she happened to send him a signal, he wanted to be in the best possible spot to see it.

As it was, he gazed back over the horizon and it was only mountains, trees, and a river's glimmer sparkling from the moonlight's reflection. There was nothing in the distance, nothing that he was hoping to see.

"Who are you looking for?"

He gazed back at her and still didn't answer.

Saren narrowed her eyes and folded her arms over her chest. Her leather made a swooshing sound as her arms rubbed over the material. "Answer, Vampire."

"Why?"

Her head cocked to the side. "What do you mean why? I asked you a question."

Roane was growing tired of her impatience and condescension. Seeing her reaction, he hid a grin, but answered, "I don't owe you answers to anything, so why would I start reporting to you now?"

Her eyebrows furrowed together and the corners of her mouth curved down. "I do not understand what is going on right now. What is happening?"

He sighed. "I'm giving you 'attitude.'"

"Why?"

"Because you're not my boss." Roane shook his head, turning back to continue searching the land beyond them. He hadn't had a boss for a while. Going rogue from the Hunters' Line was freeing, but nerve-wracking. He knew they would come for him, along with Jacith's army. And, suddenly, as if feeling them hot on his trail, he almost imagined seeing them moving along the trees. They would've been moving silently, like ghosts, approaching their camp with near perfection. He knew they weren't out there, not yet, but they were coming. Their camp had been traveling at a fierce speed, but they needed to rest. One more night of rest, then another full week of going hard. The vampires could handle it. They were letting the wolves catch up.

And Saren must've felt the same because she said, "We shouldn't stay long. Davy is in trouble. I sought you out to remind you of the importanc—"

Roane had a hand at her throat before she could finish that sentence. Her eyes widened from the quick turn of events, and she looked down at the arm. Before she could respond, Roane leaned forward and growled, "Do you think I don't know?"

"We must keep going." She spoke stiffly, her eyes lifting and holding Roane's gaze. A fire started in her eyes. It sparked, but it was pulled down to a simmer. It was there. It was burning. The flames were bright, but she was keeping it contained. "The Immortal thread is separating from Davy. The sooner we get there, the better."

Roane tilted his head to the side. The growl was still there, but he muted it. His hand dropped, releasing her suddenly. A normal being would've fallen from the abrupt departure, but Saren held still. He asked, "What do you mean? The thread is separating? I didn't think that was possible."

"It's the witches."

"The witches?"

"I was able to connect to Davy, and the last time was when *your brother*," she spat the last two words, "had a coven working to pull the thread out of Davy."

Roane wasn't surprised to hear that Lucan was trying to pull the thread out of Davy, but he was surprised about two other items. His nostrils flared. "You can connect to her?" His hand started to curve again. He wanted to grip her by the throat once more and squeeze until she gave him all the information she had. She was keeping this from him, keeping a part of Davy from him. He was close to becoming murderous, but he kept his arm next to his side. He had to, or he'd kill the other being, whatever Saren was.

She didn't answer. It was her turn to become silent.

He asked the second question. "Is that possible?" If the thread left Davy, she'd die. She told him that herself, but hearing that it could be ripped out of her—he couldn't think of the possibilities. If he did, he would leave this army and get to her on his own. Nothing and no one would get between them, even his own allies.

"No."

He relaxed. Slightly.

She added, "Not normally because Davy merged with the thread.

She became The Immortal, but the witches are strong. They're powerful and they've been able to unbalance the merge."

Roane shook his head. "What does this mean?"

She hesitated.

For the first time since he met her, Saren looked uncertain. That sent a slice of panic through him. If she was nervous . . . No. Even before the thought entered his mind, he turned it off. He had to stay with his army. He couldn't arrive without them. Lucan had an army of Mori. He wouldn't be any help to Davy if he showed up alone.

"Speak!" he snapped.

"This means." She lifted her head back up, rolling her shoulders back to a ready position. "We don't know."

"We?" The more she talked, the more Roane was questioning why she was needed. "Who else are you connected to?"

"My sisters." She closed her eyes. The flame disappeared for a second, but when her eyelids lifted, Roane saw thousands of flames in them. It wasn't just hers. And they were all different colors. Blue. Pale green. Sunlight yellow. A pastel shade of pink. They were all there and they were waving back and forth as one unit. The longer he stared at them, the stronger they grew. They began to take over Saren, moving past her eyes and moving along the rest of her body. Within seconds, her entire body was lit up with all of the colors, then the flames began to sizzle and meet the air. When they stopped, she was standing in front of him, completely on fire.

She spoke, but it wasn't her voice. It was thousands of voices, all speaking as one. "We are one. The past, the present, and are awaiting our future sister."

"Roane shook his head. "What? What are you?"

"We are the last carriers. Each of us has had the thread inside of us."

That meant Talia was there.

And, as if reading his mind, Saren's body shifted. The blue leather changed into a shimmering white dress and her blue-tipped black hair transformed into deep auburn curls. The flame didn't lessen or change, but it was Talia's body in front of him.

"Are you—" His eyes roamed over her, taking in every aspect of her. The small dimple in her cheek, the curve of her waist where his hand used to rest so many times. "Talia?"

She nodded, a small and impish grin appearing. "It's me. Saren stepped back and is allowing me to come through, but it's not for long. We're all here, Lucas. All of us together. It's such a glorious event."

"Glorious?" The end of his mouth dipped down.

"It is. All of the thread-holders are united, and we've been waiting."

"For what?"

"For one purpose."

"And that is?"

"To help the last thread-holder. She will need us when she battles the only threat to The Immortal line."

"Jacith," Roane breathed out. His own flame of fury started inside. He knew the sorcerer was mounting allies against them. "Is he close?"

"He's close to Davy. He's talked with her."

His fury lit up, like gasoline had been thrown onto it. "He was close to her?"

"Only his spirit. Not in body. He can't do much to her, not unless he's in closer proximity. There are some limits to Jacith's power."

"But he's tried to hurt her?"

"Not yet. She was weakened from the witches. He's underestimating her right now."

His rage lessened, just a bit. "How do you know all of this?"

"Because we watch, Lucas. All of us together. We're everywhere, watching, listening, protecting. Saren is the one chosen to be here in body, but we've all connected as one."

Roane had been around enough in the world to know that every being, no matter how powerful, had limitations. The Immortal was no exception. While that was in the back of his mind, he asked, "Christian is here. Would you like to talk to him?"

"No." The impish smile returned. She lifted and pressed her

hand to the side of his face. She cupped his cheek. "I came forth because of you. Thank you, Lucas. Thank you for loving me. Thank you for loving Davy as a separate entity. And thank you for taking in my sister."

"Tracey?" But as he said the name, he knew that was who Talia meant.

She nodded, a wistful sound coming from her. "She will find my child and raise her. When she does, and when you're reunited with Davy, I'd like to come forth again. I'd like to talk to Davy and my sister."

He nodded. The wolf would be pissed when he told him that Talia could've spoken to him and declined. Roane was looking forward to passing along the message.

"I must go now." Talia waved a hand at herself. "Saren is balking by how long this is taking. We wanted to show you that we're all together. We're here to help Davy and to be reassured. We will be victorious. You don't have to worry. I know you still will, but we, also, are watching out for your soul mate."

"Thank you, Talia."

She nodded, her eyes growing fond. As if she couldn't help herself, she leaned forward, then wavered. She paused, but her eyes grew determined and she closed the distance between them. Her hand fell from the side of his face to his chest and she leaned forward until her lips pressed against his cheek. She whispered, "Be assured, Lucas. Not all is as it seems. You will have more on your side than you realize."

Still standing there, he felt a tear fall from her eyes onto his cheek, but he felt her distancing. It was changing again. And as soon as Saren had taken over the body, her eyebrows arched high and she sucked in her breath, realizing the closeness Talia had been standing. Her eyebrows snapped down and a scowl formed, but before she could spew something out, Roane's hand was at her throat.

He did what he'd wanted to do since he met her.

He snapped her neck and let her body fall.

CHAPTER 9
DAVY

I was up shit creek.

It had been three days since I woke from our escape and in those times, it was me, myself, and I. A.k.a. no Immortal. I hadn't tried to use any powers, just because I didn't know if I was ready to admit we were sans Immortal powers. I didn't want Wren to use that as an excuse to make us leave completely to find Roane. It wasn't that I didn't want to see Lucas. I did. Badly. It was Kates. No matter how she betrayed us, I could still hear her screams. They'd been bloodcurdling and I knew they'd haunt my nightmares. I needed to know what happened. If Lucan forced her to betray us or if she did the backstabbing all of her own free will.

Either way—I needed to know, and we weren't going anywhere till I did.

Gavin lifted up the tarp and peered inside. When he saw that I wasn't lying in bed, his eyes warmed and he came in, carrying some logs in his hands. "You're sitting up."

I nodded. "I am. I was considering doing some yoga planks even."

He stared at me and cocked his head to the side. A beat passed, then he nodded. "You're teasing me." He grinned.

"Yes, Gavin." I wish I hadn't been. "I was joking. No. Sitting up is the best I can do right now."

"That's good." He put the logs in the corner before placing the last one in the fire pit. "Your body needs to rest as long as possible."

"Wren doesn't think so."

Gavin was somber. "Yeah." He sighed. "She fears the Mori will find us, and we can't defend ourselves properly against them."

Which was true, and I could be putting them in even more danger. I needed to tell Gavin, at least one person about my problem, but I didn't know how he'd react. As he turned and left again, I knew I needed to figure out what was going on with me. At least, to know my limitations, if I had any powers or if it was just my empathic self, like the old days.

I closed my eyes and tried to sense—well, anything.

I needed to know that the thread was still in me and that I hadn't let everyone down, but as I tried to feel outside of myself, I was picking up Gavin's restlessness. He was anxious, wary, and fearful. There was a small amount of concern emanating from him. I knew it was about me, and I tried to pick up his thoughts.

There was nothing.

I couldn't hear his thoughts, and holy crappola, that sucked.

Okay. Power from The Immortal was gone. What else was gone, and I kept sensing farther out until I hit Gregory. He was farther away like he was on point, and as I slipped inside of him, nothing. I was met with a cement-like wall. He was feeling stuff. I could pick it up, but it was slight like the tiniest of ripples on a smooth surface. That was when I realized that he was just waiting.

I pulled away from him, searching for the other two, but I couldn't find them.

Without realizing it, I was up and moving out of the cave. I lifted up the tarp and stepped outside. I could feel Gavin's surprise, but he didn't say anything. I kept going, past where I felt Gregory standing, guarding. I wasn't really seeing as I walked forward. I was fully focused on my empathic abilities. I trusted that extra sense to help guide me, and I was moving beyond the camp. I kept going until I felt a cold breeze against my face and heard the sounds of water rushing past me.

I was by a river, but there was still no Wren or Tracey. Gregory and Gavin were trailing behind me, but both kept quiet. They were letting me do my thing. It was later. I wasn't sure how far I walked, perhaps half a mile when I picked up the first traces of anger.

Wren.

I thought that immediately, but no—I was wrong. It was Tracey. Talia's daughter flashed in my mind, and two things happened at once. An overwhelming surge of relief crashed down on me. My knees buckled from how strong it was, but I caught myself. I needed to know what else I could still do. Tracey was thinking about her niece, then I felt how torn she was. She wanted to leave, and I heard her thought, *"I should leave tonight. Davy is too spent. It's not fair for the human child. She shouldn't tax herself—"* Her thought abruptly stopped, and I cried out.

Was it me? Had that brief power left me again? But no, I grew aware of another vampire. This one had even more rage, mixed with love, yearning, and misery that had me blinking back tears.

This was Wren.

The two began to converse, but when it turned personal, I left. Wren knew Tracey was planning to leave. She didn't want her to go. That was the last I heard before I returned back to myself and looked around for the first time.

I turned around. Gavin and Gregory were standing with their backs to each other. Both had a hand on the swords they wore, ready to pull them out for a fight if necessary. They had been guarding me.

"I'm sorry," I said to both.

Gavin's hand fell from his sword. He shook his head. "Don't be. It was good to see you out and about again. I was starting to worry."

I nodded to him. "I know you were."

He laughed.

I let the sound wash over me. It was refreshing to hear it because it was genuine. It wasn't forced or restrained. In that one brief moment, there wasn't the weight of the world on us. I heard all of that from Gavin, and I was envious. I wanted that brief respite, and I wanted to experience it in Lucas's arms, but that wasn't going to happen.

"Did you find Wren and Tracey?"

"I did. They aren't far." But I wasn't sure. I gazed around. I couldn't see any traces of our camp either. "Where are we?"

"A mile from camp." Gavin gestured to the other side of the river. "Those two are a mile farther. I'm surprised you didn't see them, though. You were only sensing them?"

I scratched my forehead. This was the opening I needed. I could reveal the truth about The Immortal, but even as quickly as I realized I should tell them, I knew I wasn't going to. The words died in my throat and instead, I said, "Yeah. I was using my empathic ability." I gave him a reassuring smile. "I'm still trying to let myself rest."

Gavin nodded, accepting my answer and started back up the trail. "We should get back. We're safer from a higher vantage point."

As he took the lead, I watched him, and my gaze went past Gregory's. I was going to keep watching Gavin, but I saw a knowing look in Gregory's eyes. Our gazes caught and held, and for the first time in a really long time, I felt exposed. I felt like he could see through me, like Roane used to be able to.

He knew.

I don't know how he knew, but he did.

He said, quietly so Gavin wouldn't hear, "Just keep resting." There was more unspoken to his statement, and I felt it. I needed to rest, but if my powers didn't come back fully—a decision would have to be made.

He added, looking down the river, "The Mori, when they come, will be coming from there."

A knot formed in my stomach.

He said, "They'll come so far, sensing outward with their sonar ways. Then, when they find that they're close to us, they'll fan out and come at us from all angles. They'll be on us before we'll know. That's how they are. They move as one being and they strike as one. No one has bested a Mori vampire. We got out because of you. I don't know if you realize you helped us, but you did. There was a whole group of them, and we strolled right past them, like we were invisible. Only one being that could do that." He nodded to me. "You." His eyes narrowed, inspecting me. "And judging by the shock on your face, you had no idea, did you? You helped us, and you helped you and Tracey. It'd make sense if you were taxed."

That knot doubled. Taxed, was that all it was? I hoped so. God, did I hope so.

"But they'll be coming."

I looked down. We didn't have long. That was what he was saying. "One more day."

"You think you can handle an entire Mori army in one day?"

I felt slapped by his disbelief, but it was because he was right. I wouldn't . . . I'd have to go alone. I couldn't take them with me into danger. I could cloak myself. If the Mori hadn't realized they were there, three very powerful vampires, maybe I could do the same for myself. I could wait one more day, work on being able to cloak myself, and once that happened—I'd leave on my own. That was what I would do.

I looked back up and said, letting the Goliath-sized vampire see the truth, "One more day, then we'll go."

"For what it's worth," he said quietly. "I'm rooting we won't have to leave."

The knot moved up to my throat, forming into a lump. I whispered back, "Me, too."

THE MEETING WAS SET in a back corner of a restaurant. As the wolves strode past them, in their human forms, the customers were clueless to the danger so close to them. They laughed, drank, ate, and conversed. They flirted. Others fought. All were clueless, except a few. As the wolves walked by, one after another, they surrounded the most important wolf, their Mother Wolf.

She was dressed in a white dress with a blue robe covering. It wasn't a robe that one would wear at home. It wasn't comfortable or made with the purpose not to be seen. This robe was extravagant. It was made of silk with gold trimmings lining the edges. As it draped over her head, a jewel hung from the tip and it dangled above her forehead. The other wolves kept their eyes forward. They weren't there to play with humans. The lesser ones, the human servants, were at the end of the line. Their heads were bent forward, and their shoulders were slumped down. One was right behind Mother Wolf, holding the end of her robe and dress so it didn't get dirty from the floor.

A hostess led them, but she didn't hold any menus. Her head was held high, and she walked with purpose. She wasn't in fear of the wolves, though she knew who they were. She had been told to stand at the front of the restaurant and wait for the other supernatural beings. And as the wolves came into the restaurant, the other human hostesses shrank back. They didn't know what beings the wolves were, but they knew they were something other than human. The power came off them in waves. The only reason the other customers were clueless was because a spell had been cast over the customers. They almost didn't even see the impressive parade except a couple that came in, after the spell was cast. They felt the power immediately, and while they were seated in the back, their eyes were huge by the time the wolves went past their table. Neither moved, reacting on a primal instinct inside of them. They knew they were the prey among predators, and as the wolves went past, they shrunk down in their seats. Their hands trembled, holding onto each other in their laps.

They were ignored. And as the last servant went past them, the couple got up and ran out of the restaurant.

The Mother Wolf turned at the doorway, right before entering the back room, and watched their departure. The corners of her eyes crinkled up and her lip twitched into a faint smile, but as quick as it appeared, it disappeared. A stoic expression settled back in place, but her insides were amused. She forgot how some humans were. It'd been so long since she was around these new humans, ones that knew nothing of their existence and only were aware of their own lives. They were self-absorbed and ignorant, thinking they were safe in their daily lives. They were not. The rest of her wolves had stopped and were waiting for her. She went into the back room, but she had a brief thought in the back of her mind. Perhaps it would do to send her wolves out to this new world, maybe every now and then. It would be good to remind humans how weak and powerless they were. They could do with the reminder.

Then, she turned and faced why they had arrived in this very busy city, and to a restaurant that the world thought was trendy. She saw the sorcerer. He stood in the back, still in the shadows, but she felt his power and it was equal to hers. He came from the oldest and most powerful vampire family, and normally, he would be her enemy.

Right now, on this day, he was her friend, and she smiled. "Hello, Jacith."

CHAPTER 10
ROANE

Roane felt her arriving, just like the last time on the cliff, but he felt her rage more than the slight buzzing in the air. When she did appear, he was scouting ahead of the group on a higher embankment, and he dodged the impending attack.

"Vampire!" Saren roared, flying through the air.

She regrouped and came at him again.

He ducked one more time. As her hand jabbed at him, he bent backwards so he was almost horizontal to the ground. Saren flew up in the air again and kicked out with her leg. This time, as he started to come back up, she clipped him in the head, but he was unfazed. He reached up and caught her ankle, twisting her body in the air again.

Saren gasped from the surprising speed of his reaction, but countered once again. She dipped backwards, jerking her foot out of his hand and she followed through, doing a backwards roundhouse. As she righted so she was standing on her feet, her second foot swiped out at Roane. He caught that one, too, but instead of trying to throw her, he shoved her away from him.

She landed on her feet, her knees buckled, her arms out in a ready stance. "You killed me."

"I snapped your neck. There's a difference."

The flame in her eyes sparked up. "Oh? Please unveil the difference to me."

"You're Immortal. Snapping your neck did nothing to you." He smirked at her. "But it did me a world of difference. Thank you. I had a whole day away from you."

The flame lit up, overtaking her entire eyes, and it burned the air. "And if you were attacked while I was gone?"

Roane drew back, startled. His eyes narrowed. "I would've slaughtered them like anyone else. You think you're that needed? Trust me. We did fine without you, and we'll do so again."

"You have no idea—" she started.

He cut her off, shaking his head. "Don't. You're here as a tag along. That's it. You need the army to rescue Davy. We don't need you. Let's get that straight."

She stared at him, and as she did, the flames doubled in size. But then, they stopped. They drew back and simmered so only a light smattering of smoke showed. She said, almost saddened now, "You're wrong, Vampire. I am more needed than you realize."

Grass was stepped on in the distance, and both went silent, looking toward where the sound came from. A second piece of grass was crushed, then a third. Both remained silent, now on high alert as predators, as they waited for the newcomer. Whoever it was, kept coming. They seemed unheeded by the sudden lull in voices. As one unit, without looking at the other, each drew to opposite sides of where the new arrival would appear. Both moved silent, as if touching air when they moved, and drew their weapons. Saren held a sword across her chest, her head dipped low, and her eyes downcast. Roane pulled out a knife, but kept it tucked against his arm. He waited with his arms down at his side.

The person continued toward them.

Roane lifted his head, filling his nose with as many smells as he could get. It was a werewolf, but he couldn't identify what family. If it were a Christane wolf, he'd only maim him. No wolf should be on his path, unless sent there because Christian didn't trust him. If it were an enemy line, he'd do the same. The wolf would be brought back to camp for interrogation, but when the person stepped forward, now between them, Roane held back. It was Christian himself. But Saren didn't hold back. She launched forward. Christian twisted and caught her. He fell back from her momentum, but tossed her over his head.

"Wolf," she snarled, her nostrils flaring, as she hurled toward a tree, caught it, and flung herself right back at him.

Christian wasn't ready for the quick counter-attack. She kicked him right in the chest, and he went down once again. This time, instead of being bucked off, she remained on his chest. Her feet were planted there and she knelt down, her sword immediately placed in position. The sharp edge of it pressed up against his carotid artery, and she knelt down, a warning hiss from her, "Move, Wolf. I dare you."

Christian started to retort, but the words caught and held in his throat. He looked to Roane instead and sighed. "This is my greeting by both of you?"

Roane had tucked his knife away during their scuffle, and he held his hands up now. A slight grin was on his face. "We needed to know the hierarchy. Now we know."

"Hierarchy?" Christian echoed, a scowl forming.

"I am above you." Saren pressed her sword against his throat before jumping off him. She sprung backwards in the air, looking as if invisible strings suddenly yanked her from him. She lowered herself to the ground a few feet away, sheathing her sword back in place, strung across her back. She gestured from herself to Roane. "And the vampire and I are equal for now."

Christian got up to his feet, dusting off his pants. "I held back, whatever you are. Get that right."

"Right." She smirked, folding her arms over her chest. "Let us get on with it. Our group approaches, and we're supposed to be scouting ahead." She sent that last statement to Roane, a flare of disapproval in her tone.

Roane narrowed his eyes at her. "You're making me want to snap your neck again. For a while there, I didn't want to. Funny how that emotion is never far for long."

Christian hid a grin.

The flames lit up again, but they were contained. They only filled half of her eyes, waving together in sync. "I'm sure we'll have another disagreement. You can try at that point, but until then, I suggest you remember the reason you're scouting ahead." She stepped toward him, dropping her voice. "For Davy, remember?"

He was scouting ahead to keep the group safe, but he got her meaning. This was all about Davy.

Christian sensed the new tension and cleared his throat. "That's why I'm here." He looked at Roane. "Another family of wolves is coming."

Roane frowned. "Who?"

"They come from Mother Wolf."

Roane had killed their Alpha, but the younger wolf was second in line to the female wolf. "She's allied with Jacith."

Christian nodded. "More than likely."

"How close?"

"Half a day behind us."

Roane said, "Then we keep going. I'm going to fall behind to watch them. I want to study my opponent first."

"I'll go with you."

"No." Roane shook his head, speaking to Christian. "You keep ahead. We'll switch our teams. You had your wolves trailing us, and my vampires were scouting ahead. I'll pull my team to trail behind. Your guys go ahead this time."

"They're wolves—" Christian started to argue.

"And they'll react to other wolves," Roane interrupted him. His tone was firm. The decision was made. "They won't be expecting vampires."

"If they bite you—" Christian warned.

"Then nothing. A wolf bite doesn't kill us." Roane started back to the group.

Christian turned, watching him go. He called after him, "Since when?"

Roane threw over his shoulder, "Since ever. You need to rip us apart to kill us." He kicked forward with a sudden surge of speed. He was moving faster than the other two could see, and when he was gone from eyesight, and from within hearing distance, Christian looked at the blue-leather girl.

She was watching him back. She saw the questions forming and shook her head. "I still will not explain who I am to you. No one except one needs to know."

"Why do I get a feeling that Lucas is that one?"

"Because he was. He's the leader. You pretend you are, and may tell yourself that you are, but he's the true leader. Even myself, as I am a more evolved being than he is, must acknowledge that he has the power in this situation. Your men follow you. You follow him. His men follow him. He is the one who needed to know." Her top lip lifted in a sneer. "And even now, I am regretting revealing myself to him."

"Why did you?"

Christian was more than curious about the girl. She wasn't a witch. He thought that was all she was at first, but he was wrong. Witches didn't fight like she did, and if there was an impasse between herself and Roane, which he doubted there was, then that said more about her fighting abilities than he found from his own little skirmish with her. He held back, as he assumed Lucas had as well. They wouldn't really know who the better fighter was until there was a day, it was kill the other or die. Only that day would show the true winner, and as long as they were allies, Christian knew it wouldn't come.

Saren answered his question, "Because he needed to know. He needed to know who else was on his side before we arrive in the Mori territory." She waited, feeling the wolf's desire for more information. He was like the vampire. He didn't like not knowing, either if she was truly an ally or an enemy in sheep's clothing. He was also sensing the familiarity of Talia through her. His previous lover's essence lingered with her, since coming forth to talk with the vampire, but the wolf knew her on a carnal level. Saren said nothing, though. She wasn't lying. Only one needed to know. That was it if another knew that one past Immortal thread-holder was still on this plane, linked to all of the past thread-holders, she would become the hunted. Within her own self, she held the power of a complete army, and when she would be reunited with Davy, that power would be doubled. The true Immortal was an army on her own as well, but the wolf still didn't realize how powerful Davy could be. He, like so many others, was just becoming aware of an actual Immortal. Davy was a new entity. When she faced against Jacith, it would be realized the depths of her power, and that would change everything.

But Saren said none of this to the wolf. It wasn't her place to tell. She did ask, "Can I be of service of to you, Wolf?"

Christian held back a slight laugh. The girl was feisty, and he was starting to enjoy that. He shook his head. "No. I'm just curious about you. That is all."

"I know." And with those words, Saren stepped back by a tree and vanished from his eyesight. She was still there. She was still watching him, but he couldn't see her. He couldn't sense her or smell her either, and because of that advantage, Saren waited until he left. She followed him, because even though the vampire seemed to trust that the Christane Alpha would play along, she didn't. She sensed a darker turmoil inside him and wanted to find out the reason for it. Would he actually be the vampire's ally or would he turn on him at some point? If he turned, Saren would be there first. She would have to kill the wolf then, hopefully before the vampire realized he'd been betrayed. It was her gift to Davy. She knew she would want the vampire protected at any cost.

That was the other reason she was among them, to do Davy's bidding, as much as to help rescue The Immortal.

CHAPTER 11
DAVY

It was time to go.

Wren and Tracey had returned to camp and acted normal. There'd been no sign of their earlier fight. Gavin and Gregory didn't say a word either. Everyone went on like normal, waiting for me. As for myself, I rested and spent the entire night trying to cloak myself. I prayed. I wept. I tried talking to myself. Nothing worked, or so I thought. It wasn't until around three in the morning when I found out that I had been cloaked the entire time. Gavin brought wood inside for the fire, couldn't find me, and raised the alarm. As everyone was leaving camp to look for me, I ran outside of the cave and started flailing my arms around. I yelled at them. I was there, but nothing worked until I was following Gavin down a wooded path and he abruptly turned around. He barreled into me, but once he hit me, he froze.

"Davy?" he whispered out.

"It's me." I jumped in front of him again.

Nothing. No reaction.

I poked him in the side. This was when I realized I was cloaked, and I scrunched up my forehead, summoning the strength to now uncloak myself.

"Look." Gregory turned a cautious eye around him, skimming the woods. "If that's you, poke me again."

I did, right in the fleshy stomach his giant size had. I was expecting something like the Pillsbury doughboy, but I got The Rock instead. He was solid muscle, and I said, "Ouch."

"Ouch?" His eyebrows shot up.

My head jerked up to his. "You can hear me?"

His eyes were trained on where I was, but he still wasn't looking at me. He was looking through me. I gritted my teeth. This was becoming annoying. I had convinced myself that I could control my powers. I don't know if that was true or not, but here I was. I was a fledgling newbie once again, not even able to let my friends see me when I wanted them to.

Suddenly, I had enough. I yelled in my head, *"REVEAL!"* And poof! I felt something snap in the air, and in me.

Gregory's eyes snapped to attention. "I can see you." His hand came to rest on my shoulder. "You're here. Thank God. I thought I was going nuts."

I shook my head. I was glad I could be seen again, but still frustrated. Was that what it took? I had to scream it in my head? I bit down on my lip.

Wait.

"LET ME SEE ROANE!"

Another burst of energy in the air, and Gregory was gone.

"Vampire!" I heard Saren's scream in the air, and my heart lurched to the bottom of my throat. I twisted around. I thought Gregory had disappeared, but it was me. I wasn't on a wooded path. I was high up. I could feel the cool draft of a breeze and closing my eyes, I sensed from where I was. There was a sudden drop in elevation ten yards from me. I was high up on a cliff somewhere.

Then I felt him.

I started to take a step out, to find Saren, but I felt Roane's laugh. He hadn't laughed aloud, but it was inside of him. It washed over me and for a moment, I soaked it in. It was like a warm blanket on a cold night. I wanted to grab him, pull him over me, and hold on forever.

"Lucas," I whispered, starting forward. Getting over the shock, I felt Saren's fury right after. It was overwhelming the rest. I was starting to lose my connection to Roane, but then a hand clamped on me, and I was jerked backwards.

I looked up to Gregory's furrowed eyebrows. He asked, "Where'd you go?"

"What?"

No, no, no. Rising panic was threatening to choke me. I looked around. My head was whipping back and forth. Roane—he'd been close. Saren was angry with him—I had to find both of them. I started forward, but Gregory held me back.

He said, "Oh no. Were you practicing some invisibility spell or something? You were here, then you weren't."

"Oh my God," I muttered. My knees started to tremble. I'd been so close.

"Try again."

I stilled. That was The Immortal. She was still with me. Relief like I had never experienced coursed through me, and I did fall.

"Where were you?"

"I was here. You silenced me."

"I did?"

"Davy." Gregory broke through the conversation.

I shot a hand up. "Stop." Then, I closed my eyes and concentrated on The Immortal. She was here, and she was talking to me. I was slowly gathering my strength and abilities. That was what this meant. Had to be.

"You always had them."

"I did?" I cocked my head to the side, but the words never left my lips. I asked The Immortal this.

She answered, *"You were angry with me. I was becoming too much for you, so you silenced me. It was just recently that you allowed me to talk again. I'm not happy with you."*

I laughed. *"You're not happy with me? You were trying to take over."*

I felt her shrug. *"You weren't doing anything. Something had to be done."*

"I wasn't doing anything? Me?"

"Yes. You."

My teeth were still grinding against each other. She was self-righteous, looking down on me for being a captive. I said back to her, I couldn't do a thing. *"The witches—"*

"Could've been killed," she interrupted me.

"What? How?"

"Next time they try, because they will try again. Let them have me. I will go to them, but I will infect them. One by one, I'll move through all of them. I'll soak up all their power, and I'll return to you. Don't fight it next time."

"Fight it?" She was delusional. How was I supposed to know to do that?

"You should trust me." A calming and reassuring wave passed from her to myself. *"You are The Immortal, Davy. I am merely a part of you. I will never be taken from you, and I will always return to you. It's as if you would be loaning me to them, but* a darker and sinister feeling came from her next, *remember that any that I go to, I will poison. All will fall beneath me. All will fall beneath you."*

I gulped. That sounded ominous.

I felt her withdrawing, but she whispered again, *"Remember. All will fall."*

"All will fall?" I echoed her.

"Good." Gregory clapped me on the shoulder. "Let's use that, whatever it was, and go with it. Come on. Let's return to the others. You can let them know you're one with your Immortal self again."

He started back, but I couldn't move. I was rooted in place, gazing around. I'd been so close to Roane. I heard his laugh. He'd been amused by Saren. I wanted to go back there, and I realized now that I had been there. It was a brief instant, and I could go back. The Immortal powers were awakening in me again, but as soon as I thought that, I knew I couldn't.

My original plan to leave on my own was here now.

"Davy?" Gregory called from farther down the path. "Are you coming?"

"Yes." I coughed, clearing my throat. "Coming." My legs moved on automatic pilot. My body was with them, as we went back to camp, and as I explained that I had accidentally cloaked myself, but my mind was ahead. I was planning my route back to the Mori village, and a few hours later, as the vampires fell asleep, it was time to go.

I packed a bag of food, pulled on a coat that Tracey gave me, and cast a sleeping spell. They were already asleep, but this ensured that they wouldn't wake when I left. Even though my powers were coming back to me, I was learning I needed not to assert them. I would tire, and I wouldn't have them when I needed them. Because of this, as the others snored, I walked out and left them behind.

KATES DOUBLED OVER, coughing up blood. She gazed down at it. A good solid pool of it had formed beneath her hands. She wanted to disappear in it. She wanted the torture done and over with, so her body could fall in the blood and become one with it.

"Come now," Lucan taunted her, coming to stand over her and gazing down. He lifted an eyebrow and shook his head, an ugly smirk appearing. "You wish to leave me? That's not the Kates I know." His eyes darkened, turning lustful, as he ran a hand down her arm. She recoiled, feeling even more disgust rising up as his laugh grew louder. He said, "We used to have such fun, Kates. Where'd that girl go? I miss that girl."

Her teeth were clattering together, but she tried to seethe out, "That girl left when you compelled me to betray all my friends."

"Oh yeah." He withdrew his hand from her and shook his head, still laughing. "I figured that would be a wrench in our relationship."

"You're an asshole."

Her insult came out with less heat than she wanted, but she couldn't muster up the extra oomph. He had taken her life in his hands, ending it, having the witches give it back, then torturing it out of her again so many times that she was almost a shell. Any fire she still had in her had been reduced to one small coal. Even that, she didn't know if she could light it up. She didn't have the strength anymore.

"Okay. Come on." He flipped her back up and slammed her onto a table so she was face first, lying on her stomach.

Her eyes almost bulged out. Renewed panic had her fighting against his hold, but it didn't matter. Lucan was stronger than her. Always had been, and always would be. He swatted her hands away and restrained her again, pulling each one tight into leather binding that was almost cutting off her blood flow. It never mattered to Lucan. He didn't need her alive or the blood flowing in her body. He pulled the restraints to the side of the table so her arms and legs had her spread eagle on it. Then he squatted down so he was at eye level with her.

He grinned at her, almost leering. "How's that feel?" Without waiting for a response, he stood up and ran a hand up the back of her arm, across her shoulder, and down her back. It was left exposed to him. He had ripped the shirt from her so it hung over her in rags. He took a moment to enjoy the whipped marks on her back. He enjoyed having her in this position. She tried to fight him before. She hadn't wanted to lead Davy and the rest into his trap, making them powerless to him. She even tried to break free from him, running to jump off the cliff near his brother's house. That had shaken him. Knowing that Kates tried to take her own life, rather than help deliver her best friend and new friends to his hands, but he would've rather known it then and not later. Because of it, that sealed her fate.

Since arriving back to the Mori, Kates had become his favorite toy to play with. When he wanted a drink, she was here for him. When he wanted something else, far more sinister, she was still there, and thinking about that now, his hand drew down to her naked waist. She wore her jeans. He had allowed that, but his hand caressed over her ass. He grew hard, remembering the times they had in the bedroom and when he would take her from behind.

He hadn't done that again, not since she made her loyalties

known, but he was tempted. Taking her against her will had been a game they had liked to play before. His nostrils flared, feeling his body's blood pumping through him, remembering the feel of his dick inside of her. His hand curved around one of her ass cheeks, and she whimpered.

He chuckled. He smelled her fear in the air, but he chided softly, "Even now, even after all I've done to you, you still want me." His hand squeezed the other cheek.

"No." She tried to shake her head, but couldn't because of the restraints.

"Yes." His hand moved lower, falling to the curve of her ass, and he kept going. He was about to touch the core of her when the door opened. His head whipped up, then he jumped back as if burned. "Jiyama," he rasped out.

The Mori vampiress stood there, showing no emotion, but her eyes darkened. He felt her instant anger, and she moved into the room. "You would touch her against her will?"

He didn't respond.

"The human told me you were torturing this one." Her eyes glanced down to Kates on the table.

Lucan narrowed his eyes. He didn't like what he was seeing or what he was hearing. "You're a vampire."

"So?"

She was challenging him. Lucan frowned. Jiyama had never challenged him before. He scratched his forehead. "What are you doing here?"

"She told me you were doing this." Jiyama pointed to Kates and the table. "She said you had a lover here, and you were torturing her."

"She's for me to play with. Why are you judging me for this?"

"Because it's wrong."

Lucan's frown deepened. This wasn't the Jiyama he knew. "You're a vampire. You drink from humans. This," he pointed to Kates, "is nothing out of the ordinary. I've seen you out there, Jiyama. You enjoy playing with your meals."

"She's not a meal for you." Jiyama continued to gaze at him. "Anymore."

His jaw clenched. "This is The Immortal's power over you. You gave her your power, and she infected you because of it."

"No." Jiyama shook her head. "You have this human here because you still feel for her. You're going to turn her."

That last sentence came out like an accusation. Lucan tilted his head to the side. His hand came up to rest against his cheek. He needed a moment to realize what was happening here. Jiyama was jealous. He thought it was disapproval, but it wasn't. She had loved him since finding him at an early age. It was assumed among her family and the rest of the Mori clan that he would wed her, but she never pushed him. Lucan had enjoyed his freedom. Going where he wanted. Being with who he wanted, and she was right. As she said the words, he realized that was the real reason he kept Kates around.

He was going to turn her, but not till he was done having fun with her.

His eyes closed to slits, watching Jiyama carefully. She was the predator to Kates in that moment. He could see the words forming in her mind. She was going to kill Kates. He saw the intention on her face, and he forced himself to speak casually. She couldn't know the extent of his wishes, not for Kates. He said, "She is still of use to me."

"Why?" Jiyama still looked down at Kates. "The Immortal is gone. She will not come back."

He shook his head, softening his tone. "She will." His hand lifted.

Jiyama's eyes snapped to it.

He caught himself, but still lowered it to touch the back of Kates's calf. He had been about to caress it, but instead he touched the tip of his finger to her skin. His nail cut into it, filling the air with fresh blood. Jiyama's gaze was focused on that now, floating toward him and the blood. Her nostrils flared and he knew Kates's blood had done exactly what he wanted. She wanted to feed now, not to kill his ex-girlfriend.

As Jiyama stood next to him, pressing into his side, he added, "The Immortal will return for her."

"Why?" But the Mori vampiress wasn't listening. She was too distracted by the blood. Lucan pressed harder into Kates's leg and more blood spilled out. He knew the power it had over Jiyama. This was slayer blood. It was the best kind to a vampire. The slayers used to use their own blood to entrap vampires and in a way, maybe that was still happening. Lucan remembered being ensnared by Kates. Perhaps that was why he still wanted to keep her.

If he didn't obtain The Immortal thread, he would become a vampire again. That was when he would turn Kates, but he wanted to be the one to do it. He wanted to be her sire, to have that connection with her for eternity. And part of that was keeping her alive—for now. If Jiyama killed her, she might take Kates's body away. He needed her body to have the witches bring her back to life, and if Jiyama turned Kates herself, he didn't know if she could be turned back to human without Davy's assistance. Too many variables had entered the room when Jiyama found Kates. Lucan wanted to control everything, so he needed to distract Jiyama and then remove her as soon as possible.

He ran a hand up Jiyama's arm, feeling the shudder that he created in her, and his hand cupped the back of her neck. Jiyama started to tremble against him, her small breasts rubbing against his chest. He lowered his head, his mouth right next to her ear, and he whispered, "Drink, Jiyama. Taste what vampires have thirsted over for centuries. Taste a slayer's blood."

He smelled her wanton desire in the air. He knew she was close. One taste and Jiyama would forget everything she saw in this room. The feeding would overpower her. He pressed her head down, pushing her close to Kates's blood. His finger cut more into Kates's skin. The slayer didn't move, and he looked up—she had passed out.

Probably for the best, he thought as he grinned, his mouth still so close to Jiyama. He pressed a kiss to her ear and whispered to her, "Quench yourself, Jiyama. It's like nothing you've tasted before."

Her body kept trembling against his, but he felt the instant she gave in. Her fangs came out, and she drew in a deep breath, before lunging for Kates's leg. He pulled his finger away just as her teeth sank in, and she drank. As she kept drinking, Lucan ran a hand down Jiyama's back, enjoying this moment. His vampire lover was feasting on his human lover, and as she kept going, he moved to the back of Jiyama.

She groaned, moving against him. He knew what she wanted. It was what he wanted as well, and as she kept drinking, he lifted up her dress and lowered his pants. He slipped inside of her, thrusting deep as she arched her back from the pleasure.

Grabbing ahold of her slim hips, Lucan pulled out, only to thrust back in. He fucked her hard, and once Kates would be willing, he couldn't wait to do the same to her again.

CHAPTER 12
DAVY

I was hurrying.

The farther I could get away from the others, before they realized my disappearance, the better. The spell I cast should keep them asleep for an additional few hours. Long enough so they couldn't catch up if they dared to try. Every hour, I gave myself some Immortal speed, zooming through the woods, but I stopped almost as soon as I started. I didn't want to wear myself out. I was still hoping to keep regrouping The Immortal powers, but once I got to another mountain and came to a cliff's edge, I knew I needed to use a bit more than I planned.

Mustering up an extra amount of energy, I felt the world falling away. I looked down. It wasn't the world. It was me. I was lifting myself in the air and over the deep ravine until I landed on the other side. Once landing on my feet, I let out the breath I'd been holding and tried to stop any powers that I might've still been using, any leftover. Once I was sure I had completely stopped, I looked up. I needed to head over this mountain, but I knew there was so many more to go. I felt the Mori and Kates. It was low in my gut, but it was like an anchor deep inside of me. It was pulling me toward them.

I was going for Kates, but I was going to kill Lucan. He couldn't be allowed to remain alive. He'd keep coming. He'd keep trying to hurt me, hurt Lucas, hurt anyone else that I loved.

There was another battle coming. I felt Jacith's presence. He was over my shoulder, watching me, studying me, and I knew that he would arrive soon. But first, head ducked down, I started up the embankment. I needed to kill Lucan first.

———

"She's gone!"

Wren ripped down the tarp and raced outside. She repeated, "Davy's gone."

The rest of the vampires were awake and on their feet instantly. Gavin reached for his sword, but there were no enemies to fight. He forced his hand to release the weapon as he gazed around. "What are you talking about?"

"No." Tracey shook her head. "Wren is right. Davy is gone. I can't hear her heartbeat anywhere."

Gavin stifled a curse. Lucas would be furious about this. Davy wasn't helpless, but she still didn't know the full force of her powers, and she had struggled. She used too much of her powers helping them escape. They shouldn't have been able to get away from the Mori, but they had. They all knew it had been because of Davy, and she'd been exhausted since.

His anger started to mount. They had to find her. They had to stop her, or at least slow her down. She couldn't go back unassisted.

Gregory began picking up his weapons and the rest of what little they had around the camp.

Gavin asked, "What are you doing?"

The giant vampire stopped and gave him a hard look. "What do you think? We have to go after her."

"No." Wren drew both of their gazes.

Gavin took a step toward her. "What did you say?"

She raised her chin up. "I'm not going." Her eyes cooled. "She made her choice, to go without us. I'm going to find Lucas. It's time we returned to our leader's side."

"He would want us to aid Davy."

"Then I'll get that order from him." Wren reached down and grabbed the bow and her satchel of arrows. She fitted both over her back, pulling her arm through the strap. "I'm going this way."

"Davy went that way." Gavin pointed the opposite direction.

"I'm going, Gavin." Wren's tone was final. "I'm sorry, but I have to go where I feel I'm supposed to be. Lucas needs us. He'll move at a faster rate if we are at his side."

A low and primal growl came from deep in Gavin's throat, and he started forward. If he had to force her to go with them, he would. His hands were in the air, ready to battle his sister vampire when Tracey stepped between them. "I'll go with you."

Everyone paused.

Gavin realized she meant him at the same time Wren did. His eyes widened in surprise, but Wren let out her own growl. "Are you kidding me?" she snapped at her. "I thought you had come to your senses."

Tracey held Gavin's gaze for a moment longer. She thought in her head to him, *"Give me a moment. I need to say my goodbyes to her."*

With Tracey's decision, Gavin looked to Gregory. He asked, "And you?"

"The Immortal promised me she'd help my daughter." He had picked up his sword, but he sheathed it now. "I'll go to be at her side."

It was decided then.

All three of them, Tracey, Gavin, and Gregory all turned as one and regarded Wren. Her mouth fell open, and she looked to all of them slowly. She gutted out, "Are you kidding me?"

"We've made our choice, Wren."

She shook her head. "You all are wrong. You're abandoning our leader."

"Lucas would want us to help The Immortal." Tracey reached out to touch her arm.

Wren twisted away, her eyes flashing in anger, and she hissed back, "Do not lie to me. You're not going to help the human. They are." The last two words were spat out as she pointed to the other two. "They go for her, but not you. At least, give me that consideration. You're going for a whole other reason."

"Wren—" Tracey stopped. Wren wouldn't listen to reason, Tracey saw that now. There was nothing else to be discussed. The goodbye would be pointless. Wren would leave in anger. She wouldn't be able to hear anything else. She had reached out for her, but her hand fell back to her side now. She couldn't shake the forbidding feeling that was the summation of their relationship. They could've been together again. They could've been a force to be reckoned with, but it was only Wren's way. If she didn't go to be at her side, there would be no going together. Tracey's head hung down. She said quietly, "I have to go for my niece. I have to try."

"Your niece is a Mori. She will only hate you. She will never love you."

Her words stabbed at Tracey, and she sucked in her breath. Closing her eyes a moment, the blonde vampiress choked out, "That is something I hope does not come to fruition. I have to try, Arwena."

"Stop," Wren hissed out, her hand clenched around the end of her own sword. She didn't pull it out. Her hand fell to it out of habit. It was what she held when she was in battle. And right now, as her lover was leaving her, she felt very much in battle. She shook her head. They were being foolish. The human didn't want them. She always thought she was better than the rest, that her powers made her more valuable, and perhaps they did. But, Wren knew her place was beside her leader. Her place had always been there, no matter whom he might've sent her to protect.

It was done. The three she considered family remained in one line, and she took a step backwards. She rasped out, "So be it."

"Wren—"

She'd been about to turn and leave, but she stopped at Gavin's words. She looked back. He added, his eyes looking bleak, "Be safe. Fast travels."

Her entire body was tense, but she forced her head to nod. "To you, too." She hesitated, then added, "Brother." She looked to Tracey, who had a tear in her eye. Wren bowed her head to her, saying, "Sister, too."

Sister.

Tracey closed her eyes, feeling the acknowledgement for what it was. Their relationship was done. Sister. Not lover. She murmured back, "To you, too. Sister."

But it didn't matter. Wren was gone.

CHAPTER 13

ROANE

The wolves moved underneath them.

There was a path in the valley where they walked two by two in a line. They were in their human form, but there were others that panned out to the side. They melted among the trees and mountainside. Those were in their wolf form and as they moved past the trees where they were perched, their bows and arrows already readied and aimed, they weren't sniffing for vampires above them. They were sniffing for the Christane wolves.

Lucas glanced over to Bastion, who was in the tree next to him. They'd been in position for two days now. His army and Christian's were ahead of them. They were still trekking toward the Mori territories. Lucas and Bastion would catch up. They'd have to, and Roane had started to worry. He wasn't sure if they dared stay any longer, hoping for a glimpse of their enemy from behind. It was the last morning they held back. He'd been about to suggest covering the fire and catching up to their group, when they heard the first scout behind them.

They turned, and a wolf was there.

The wolf hadn't expected to find vampires. He recoiled immediately. He started to dash back to his allies, but Bastion and Roane moved as if one unit. Both leapt for the wolf. Bastion came from the left side. Roane was on the right and as the wolf turned back, prepared to meet their onslaught head-on, Roane didn't let a battle ensue. He grabbed both sides of the head, rooted his feet in the ground and ripped it right off. As it came clear off, Bastion grabbed the body and threw it into the fire.

They had to move fast after that.

The body and head were both destroyed in the flames, but they needed to cover up the smell so Bastion gathered sage and dumped it on the fire. When it wasn't enough, he dumped more. Roane knew they needed to leave if they were going to get in position before the rest of their enemy showed, so they lit the entire camp on fire. It would spread far and wide and leave no trace of a wolf at all.

A day later, as they were still moving to meet the oncoming army, the skies split open and down-poured. The fire would be doused. Lucas hoped there'd be no remnant of the wolf at all, and now, watching as the enemy wolves passed them, he knew they hadn't found any body. Word would spread once they did.

He waited, frozen in place against the tree, as the last of the wolves passed by. Once they moved along, he and Bastion still waited half a day. It was nearing the time when they needed to jump back to the ground and start following behind, but Lucas didn't move from his position. There was no reason to wait. They had sentries trailing behind, just like their own group, and those had already gone beneath them, but Lucas didn't emerge from his hidden spot.

He knew Bastion was waiting. He would follow his leader's movement.

Roane still waited.

Then, he shook his head. He was wasting time. His hand relaxed around the bow's string where his arrow was notched and ready, but he sensed their presence. He didn't hear them, see them, or smell them. They were like him, almost invisible to the senses, but he felt them.

Looking down, moving as if they were ghosts, was another army. They were vampires, like him, but they were dressed in black ninja-style robes. Some had their hoods pulled low over their heads with a gold lining around them. Others had their hoods back and their ears were adorned with gold chains. Roane knew of only one army that had worn similar gold colors like these—the Romah Family.

He looked over and met Bastion's gaze.

They were severely outnumbered, and this army was the oldest and therefore the strongest there was. He hadn't realized how many wolves Mother Wolf would send, but as the Romah Army kept going past them, and they had to wait up there another entire day, he knew his army with Christian's would be overpowered. They didn't have enough. They'd only be able to contend against them if they had Davy at her fullest strength.

"Roane."

He whipped his gaze to Bastion's. The silent thought sent to him could've been picked up by another, but he saw Bastion's gaze was trained on the ground.

A foreboding sense began to fill him and it increased as his gaze turned to see what Bastion was riveted by.

There, in the middle of five Goliath-sized wolves and four Romah guards in full armor, was a woman.

He knew who she was.

This was Mother Wolf, the one that Christian told him about. She was stunning. Black hair fell free and loose past her shoulders. She wore a blue and silver robe. The colors were striking, matching the air of strength she was emanating. Her eyes were dark. Her lips were bright red, curved into a half smile, and her head was raised in a confident and authoritative manner, but that wasn't all that clung to her—magic. He felt it in the air. Older magic that he never felt was in the air, and as they progressed below them without sensing their presence, Roane was surprised.

If anyone would've felt him, it would've been her, but it hadn't happened. They waited another half day before dropping back down to the ground. Once they did, both vampires groaned from the impact. Their legs had hardened into stone from the lack of movement. Both had gone without blood for days. There was no point to talk. Both needed sustenance if they were going to get around the army and back to theirs. Christian would need to know Mother Wolf was with the army, and she was protected by Romah vampires, but hearing a leaf stepped on in the distance, Roane lifted his head up and smelled the air. It was deer—that meant blood for them.

Both vampires took off and were on the deer within moments.

Both fed because both knew their days ahead would be grim.

———

DAVY

ALL RIGHT.

I had to admit to myself that the idea of going alone was ambitious and honorable. It also sucked. I was hungry. My feet were bleeding. My back was sore, and my hands were almost frozen. The first leg of the trip had been glorious. I used my Immortal speed and zipped over any cliff that needed an extra boost to cover. My head had been high and my shoulders were firm. That lasted a day. I was on day four and because I was doing all this the 'human' way, I had an entire mountain still to cover. I didn't know why I'd been so eager to blast us so far away with my Immortal powers before, but like Gavin said—we'd been safe.

Oh yes.

We were safe. We'd been four mountains over safe. I was cursing myself, just like I'd been the last day, when I heard a sound that I didn't think I'd hear again.

"You doofus! We need that to burn the Mary Jane."

Humans.

Glorious, doofus-saying, Mary-Jane smoking, humans.

I almost doubled over in relief. The mere sound of that voice slammed an old sense of reality back into me, one where I had been human, somewhat normal, and I hadn't been interrogated, tortured, wounded, or hunted by a supernatural being, or an entire army of supernatural beings.

I was so overwhelmed that I was frozen in place as two guys stumbled past the clearing and onto the same path that I was on.

I was there, standing with my hand wrapped around a walking stick, and my eyes so damn wide a flying saucer could've entered them. I knew I must've been a sight. I'd alternated between shivering and sweating over the last day and a half. I still didn't want to use any more of The Immortal powers than necessary, and because I wasn't expecting to find anyone so close to me, I hadn't resurrected the cloaking spell. I was still stunned. I hadn't even thought about making myself invisible.

These two guys, one was tall and lanky, with a bright green rain jacket and glasses on his face, and the other was an inch shorter and pudgier, wearing a matching jacket, stared at me. They both had hiking boots and had large hiking bags strapped to their backs. They were dumbfounded.

Then, one broke out, a wide smile appearing, "Hey! Are you a hallucination?"

The taller one frowned and smacked the shorter on the back of his head. "If we're both seeing her, I doubt it." He paused, his frown deepened, and he took his glasses off. After cleaning them, he put them back on and leaned forward. "Nope. She's still there."

"Hey!" The shorter one pumped his hand in the air. "What's your name? Do you speak English? I'm Spencer."

"Of course she speaks English," the taller one muttered, but stopped and scratched behind his ear. "Wait. She might not."

At the same time, Spencer twisted around and muttered to him, without moving his lips, "You don't know that. This place has some strange folks in it. She could be from some native tribe or something."

"She's wearing jeans."

"Oh yeah." Spencer nodded to himself, his smile brightening even more. "What's your name?" He jerked a thumb over his shoulder. "This is Cal. We're here on holiday. We're hiking through these parts before heading back to the States. Figured this was a trip of a lifetime. We were nearby in Brunsby on a semester visa, but that's done for in a week. You on holiday, too? Wait." He glanced around, narrowing his eyes and pursing his lips in concentration. "Where's your group? You're not alone, are you?"

This was absurd. Both were from America, and both were high. A laugh started deep in my throat and before long, it doubled in volume. I couldn't contain it. They were hiking. They were on holiday. They thought I was a student.

I was so very far from just a student.

Drifting closer, warming to me from my laughter, the taller one chuckled, too. "I know we're a sight. We got separated from our group yesterday. We haven't washed or eaten anything except a little marijuana that Spencer had left over. And side note, if that's all you have to eat, don't do it. The munchies are making me go crazy. Spencer won't let me eat any of our food. Rainforest tree bark started to look a lot more appetizing than the pine trees back home. Say," his eyes focused on me again, "You haven't seen any other U.S. students, have you?"

No, no. Just vampires. That was all.

My shoulders were still shaking, and I shook my head back and forth. I was trying to form a coherent word, but the hilarity of the situation was still hitting me. A few tears leaked from my eyes, and my cheeks were starting to ache from the laughter.

"What's your name?" Spencer's lips were still curved up, but any slight chuckle he might've let out had dwindled. The bright smile he had was no longer. It lessened and a look of alarm was starting to enter his gaze. "You haven't said yet."

"Da—" I was Davy. The nickname of Davy didn't pertain to me anymore. It hadn't for so long, since my first torture session, but I heard myself saying, "Davy," to these two strangers. I wanted to be Davy again, even if it was for a brief moment in time. I could be that girl with no big responsibilities, where I only had to worry about being empathic. I suddenly missed that girl a whole ton.

"Davy." Spencer pumped his head up and down, his lips tugging into a smile again. "That's an awesome name."

The taller one glanced up to the darkening sky. "Well. I hate to admit it, but I think we're going to be lost for another day. It's going to be nighttime soon."

Spencer looked pained. He repeated the earlier question again. "You haven't seen any other Americans, have you?"

I shook my head, growing somber. They were lost and I had one last mountain to cross before being back in Mori territory. I could feel their magic. It was growing more and more the closer I got. I also knew that I didn't have long before the others caught up to me, whoever it was that was coming after me. Gavin. Gregory. Tracey. Any of those three or none of them. I didn't figure Wren would come. Seeing that these guys were looking around to put their bags down, I spoke up, "Uh."

They stopped and looked at me.

I gulped suddenly. What was I doing? I should send them on their way, but I said instead, "There's still some light, and it was a full moon last night. It'll be one again tonight. We can keep going."

"You know where you're going?"

The taller one asked that. I forgot his name.

"Cal," the shorter one said, "I don't know."

Cal was the tall one. Spencer was the shorter guy. C and S. I nodded to myself. That was how I'd remember their names.

Cal was saying, gesturing to me, ". . . I think we should. She knows where she's going, or she looks like she knows. Let's go with her, and maybe we'll find our group."

I cleared my throat, drawing their attention. "I'm headed over that mountain behind you. I-uh—I have a friend over there. I need to get to her."

Spencer frowned at where I pointed and he scratched behind his ear. "I'm pretty sure that's where we came from over the last two days."

Cal's head bobbed up and down. "Hey, yeah. I think you're right.

Wait." He twisted around to the mountain I just came from. "Fuck. I have no clue. They all look the same."

"Well." Spencer grimaced, his hand falling back to his side. "Let's just go with her."

"You can't." I corrected, "I mean, not all the way. My friend—there's dangerous people where I'm going. You can come with me part of the way, but not all the way."

"Oh." Both gave me alarming looks.

I didn't want to go alone anymore, but they couldn't go all the way with me. The Mori would kill them, if they hadn't already killed their group. But if they went alone—I didn't know if that was safe either. My allies and I were the only ones I knew that wouldn't harm them. Whoever these guys were, whatever fucked-up kind of karma that put them in the middle of this war, I needed to protect them. Or I had to try, at least.

The decision was made then.

I nodded at them. "You should come with me, at least as far as its safe. If you find your group, I'll keep going it alone."

Cal cocked his head to the side. "What are you doing out here?"

Saving my potential ex-best friend.

Saving the world.

Saving myself.

None of those answers sufficed. I only said, "Just looking for a friend."

The small surprise both had when they first saw me was wearing off. I didn't know if it was my doom and gloom attitude that I couldn't seem to shake, or if the Mary Jane was wearing off. Either way, both seemed more wary of me than they had been in the beginning.

Or maybe they were just realizing the absolutely fucked-up situation they were in.

I was going with the latter, and with that cheerful thought, I started up the trail, and after a few moments of hesitation, they did as well.

CHAPTER 14

My two new besties and I hiked most of the night. The full moon gave us enough light until we got to a large canopy of trees. No light got through so we were forced to camp out. Cal and Spencer had large hiking bags, and they came in handy. They had an extra blanket, and when they pulled out a tarp, and after securing it between two trees, I snuggled into their makeshift hammock. It was blissful.

Sleeping in the cave had been—well, I'd been out of it. I don't know if it was restful, but this was. I almost professed my love for these two lost hikers, but sleep overtook me, and it wasn't till morning when I woke again.

Once my eyelids opened, I felt The Immortal again.

It was amazing. It was fabulous. It was about-freaking-time!

I jerked to a sitting position. The blanket fell to my lap and I could feel everything. We were half a mile away from a river. I could sense the fish in there, all the berries on the way that we could eat. Beyond the river, was Mori territory. I thought it didn't start till after the mountain, but we were just on the precipice of it. The steep incline for the mountain started right behind the river, and as I realized that, alarm bells started ringing in my head. My brief moment of euphoria was snatched away.

I couldn't go over that river with these guys. We must've gone farther than I expected last night, and we discussed our plans before sleeping last night. We were supposed to trek around the last mountain, then they were going to head north where they thought their group was, and I was going to keep going east to where the Mori were.

"Morning!" Spencer held a hand up, bent over by the fire. He was stirring a pot over it. His hair was wet and he had a changed his clothing. Seeing my lingering gaze on his hair, he grinned and pointed to the top of his head. "I took a quick dip. There's a river half a mile thatta way." Twisting around, he pointed in the direction I hoped he wouldn't have. I'd been hoping he said there was a different river. I could've led them that way instead, but nope. He'd been closer to the Mori than I ever wanted him to be.

I took a beat and pushed the small panic aside, then I smelled coffee.

Wait—coffee? I sniffed the air, and scrambled out of the tarp. "Oh my God." I started for him.

Spencer's grin spread. There was an extra pan sitting at the bottom of his feet and he moved back. "Yep. Instant coffee." He lifted a spoon of it and poured it into a thermos he'd taken out of his bag. I couldn't even let him fill it. I grabbed it after the first scoop and guzzled it. "Oh hey." He laughed, taken aback by my quickness. He blinked a couple times. "You must've been out here longer than you thought, huh?"

I closed my eyes, savoring the taste of the coffee grounds. I stuck my nose into the cup and inhaled the aroma of it. My euphoria was back, and I held the thermos back to him, a dreamy smile on my face. "I declare it here and now. I love you."

"You love me?" he teased back, taking the cup from me.

"And I'll worship you forever if you have more in there I can drink."

"Ha!" He was already reaching for the pan. "I'll take you up on that. I got my heart crushed before going on this trip. Knowing one girl worships me does wonders for my ego." He poured three more scoops into the thermos before the spoon scraped the bottom of the pan. "Oh." He peered inside, and grimaced. "It's half full. Sorry about that."

He held it out to me, and I took it, sinking down to the ground beside him. Good God. Being The Immortal should've allowed me to make coffee out of nothing. I needed to work on that magic. Screw protecting vampires or Kates. I needed to look out for my caffeine needs first.

"Hey," he called out, turned behind us. "Did you bring more water? Davy loves coffee, apparently."

I glanced over my shoulder at the same time I heard shoes breaking a twig. Cal was coming back from the river. His hair was wet as well, and he had changed his clothes, too. Both guys were up and ready to go.

Fuck.

"Oh yeah?" Cal ran a hand through his hair, shaking some of the water out. A towel was thrown over his shoulder and he flipped up the end to dry his face. He lifted up his other hand, holding a bucket. "Good thing I brought extra. I figured we'd need it for the pans, too."

"Sweet ass." Spencer shifted around, still bent down, and took the water from him once he got to the fire. He pointed to the other pan he'd been stirring. "I splurged this morning. I made the grits."

"You did?" Cal grabbed his bag and sank down on the other side of the fire. He glanced at me. "Spencer is pulling out all the stops if he made the grits. We were saving it for a celebration day."

Spencer snorted. "Yeah, when we weren't lost anymore." He pointed to me with a wooden spoon. "And thanks to her, we won't be. Since she came from the west, and knows what's east of us, we're pretty sure where our group is. We won't be lost for long."

Aaaaand that was my cue. They couldn't go past the river. "Hey, um." I lowered the coffee cup. "You know. We could wander north from here. We don't need to go over the river just yet."

"The fuck?"

Cal shared in Spencer's sentiment, frowning instantly. "Why?"

"I mean, we might've overshot our destination a bit. I mean,"

Fucking A. I was horrible at lying. I felt my cheeks growing red. "Well, I mean, I recognize that river."

The two guys shared a look. Both furrowed their eyebrows forward.

Spencer echoed my words, "You 'recognize' the river—"

"—that you haven't seen yet?" Cal finished for him.

I couldn't squirm under their gazes. "Yeah." I shrugged, glancing down at the cup on the ground. "How many rivers are there? And I recognize this area, too." I gestured to the trees around us. "We're closer than we realized. I think you guys need to head straight north." I paused a beat, swallowing over a knot in my throat. "And, you know, maybe steer clear of the river if possible?"

Shit. Shit. Shit.

I used to be so good at being evasive. Who would've known I'd be wishing for the days when I had kept so much secret?

The guys glanced at each other again before Cal cleared his throat. "We've not run across another river as large as that one, and I know we crossed a river the same size before, so I think we should stick to the original plan. Cross the river, go around the mountain, and split up on the other side."

"No," I cried out before clamping a hand over my mouth. Seriously. I would've sucked at espionage. "I mean." I scratched behind my ear. "I really don't think it's safe, you guys."

"But you're going over it, aren't you?" Spencer narrowed his eyes.

"Um." I averted mine.

Cal stood slowly, grabbing his bag. "I think we should stick to the original plan, like I just said."

"No." Spencer shook his head.

"Spencer," Cal started.

Spencer held a hand out to him, stopping him. His gaze was still firmly pinned on me. "What were you going to do?" Spencer asked me. "Were you going to double-back and cross then? Were you going to lead us somewhere else?"

Cal's frown deepened. His hand wrapped tighter around his bag. "You mean, like into a trap?"

Oh fuck.

At the *T* word, I knew I was done for. Suspicion jumped to both of them. Spencer stood and as he did, Cal moved back a step. Spencer went right with him. They were both regarding me like I'd stolen their pot.

"Come on, guys." I jumped to my feet, too.

"Yeah," Spencer shot back. "Come on, yourself."

"Tell the truth."

I was caught. I'd backed myself into a corner, and both weren't backing down.

"Use me."

Of course, The Immortal would pop up here. Nope. Not going to do it. I shoved that thought away.

"You're wasting time. Let me take over. I can get in their heads and make them do what you want."

"Nope." I shook my head.

Spencer and Cal saw the motion, and both of their eyebrows lifted.

Cal asked, "No what? What was that for?"

"Uh."

"Use me, Davy. This is ridiculous. You're being foolish. They're both humans."

"I'm human!" I shot back at her.

"No." She said it so calmly, so—I gulped—final. *"You're not and you know it. You're clinging to a past that's not with you anymore. You need to let go of your humanity."*

I scoffed in outrage. Let go of my humanity? *She* was being ridiculous.

Cal and Spencer heard the sound I made and the suspicion was turning toward doubt, like I'd grown two heads and they didn't know what to make of me. Spencer checked his pocket and pulled out a baggie. He was checking if the pot was still there. Reassured it was, he put it back, and his eyebrows bunched together even more.

"Davy. You're indulging these two humans. You don't have time to be

kind. Let me take over. They'll go to safety, and we can be back in the Mori camp."

"*Why do you even want to go back there?*"

She was silent.

I almost laughed out loud. Of course, she was silent now. The witches had separated us enough where I couldn't read her thoughts, but she knew my every wish, thought, and feeling. It wasn't fair.

But then I felt a growl coming from inside of me. It was from the farthest part of me, deeper than my consciousness had ever been in touch with. It was her. I angered her.

"*Witch,*" I thought.

Her anger doubled. It grew in volume and strength.

That was why she wanted to go back. "*You want vengeance?*" I asked her.

"*No. You want vengeance. I am you. You are me. We are as one. Don't fool yourself into pretending you're the 'good' one. You want to taste their blood every bit as I do. That's why we're going back, Davy. We're not going for your traitorous friend. It's time you were honest with yourself, just like how these two hikers came to be in the first place.*"

"*What?*" I snarled at her, whipping my head to the side as if I could see her.

I sensed Cal and Spencer's growing caution, but for once I was in sync with The Immortal. They were human. Lying to them could be easily done. I had a more important fight to deal with now.

"*Tell me!*" I yelled at her.

There was nothing. Just silence. She was there. I felt her, but she was pouting. No—that wasn't right. She was waiting.

"*What are you waiting for? Tell me the truth.*"

Fury and impatience ebbed into resignation. The first two emotions slid away like a wall inside of me, opening up to the back room where she was. I felt her honesty then, and she said, "*It was you, Davy.*"

"Me what?"

"*You brought them here.*"

I didn't respond. I couldn't. That was preposterous. But I couldn't argue with her, because as soon as she said those words, I felt it inside of myself. She was right. I backtracked in my memory, looping back over the last two days. I was walking through the woods. I was tired, hungry, alone—there. I felt the instant I did it. I had stepped the wrong way on a rock and my foot went one way while my ankle went the other. I cried out, grabbed onto my ankle, and I wished for someone else in that split second to come. I wanted to be normal, not in that place where I was traipsing back to vampire territories.

I wanted someone that reminded me of my humanity, where I was normal again.

The Immortal reached out for me. As I mended my own ankle, she found a group of hikers. She picked up two and brought them so they were right in my path. They didn't even know it themselves, but I made them get lost. Their group wasn't even in this same area. They'd been in another country.

I had done that.

The Immortal did it on a whim.

I gaped at them now, feeling the guilt coursing through me. I choked out, "I am so sorry."

"You're sorry?" Spencer echoed me again. "For what?"

"I did this."

They shared another look, and both edged back one more step. Spencer asked, "Did what?"

"I brought you here." And I had to take them back, but I didn't know how.

"What do you mean, you brought us here?" Cal spoke this time.

I couldn't explain. I shook my head. "Come on." I grabbed my bag, turning toward the river. "When we get there, I'll fix it. I'll have to, somehow."

"Not to be mean, but you're sounding like a nutcase."

Cal nodded in agreement. "I second that. You're not making any sense."

"Let's go." I pointed ahead. "When we get to the river, I'll explain everything." Regret flared up. "I owe you that much, at least."

"You owe us?"

I wasn't listening anymore. I started for the river, and the other two scrambled to get all their stuff together. I should've helped, but I used the extra time to try to send them back. Once they were ready and walking behind me, I knew it was going to be harder than I imagined. The entire trek to the river was in silence. I kept trying to send them back, but once I heard the sounds of the water rushing ahead of us, I had to admit the truth. I had little to no control over my powers again. Getting both of them back to their group, an entire country over, was beyond my capabilities. The only way I could do it was if it was on a whim, just how I brought them here in the first place. I needed to wish both of them back there, and the closer we drew to the water, I kept trying. Nothing happened. They were still with me.

I was frustrated, and I had no idea what to do now. They couldn't go into Mori territory with me. I never looked at the river. I knew we were there. I'd have to cross it and they couldn't, and I was gearing myself up for a fight when I turned around and looked up at them.

They weren't looking at me.

Both of them were frozen in place, their eyes wide and fixed on a spot behind me.

"Whoa," Spencer said under his breath.

Cal closed his mouth, but a vein bulged out in his neck. Fear that I hadn't experienced since before Lucan took me blasted from him. I gasped, falling back from the intensity of it, and I felt Spencer's fear mixing with Cal's before I whirled around.

And, right there, standing on the other side of the river, was the reason.

Three Mori vampires stared back at me.

CHAPTER 15

Three things happened at the same time.

The Mori lunged for us, leaping the river in one bound. Cal and Spencer wet their pants. And I flung my arms out at the same time a scream ripped from my throat. With it and the motion of my arms, two spells burst from me at once. One swept behind, picking up Cal and Spencer and carrying them far back to where it was safe. The other came from the scream, and it slammed the three vampires backwards. They fell the same distance that I threw Cal and Spencer, and both groups landed at the same time.

Cal and Spencer had to scramble back to their feet, but they stayed back.

The vampires did neither. As soon as they touched down on ground, their feet firmly planted in place, all three launched at me once again.

I was ready.

My arms swept forward, pulling the same power I cast Cal and Spencer backwards, I propelled it forward. It hit the vampires back once again, but they fought this time. They were prepared for my onslaught and magic sparked from one of them, breaking my spell in half. It still moved them back, but not far enough.

They were too quick and too powerful.

They were on me within seconds, and I could only stare at them as they leapt over the river. They were in the air, and their fangs were out. Their mouths were open, and they'd be on me—then they were shoved back once more, but not by me. I didn't have a spell ready to throw back.

I had a second's warning as a deep roar sounded from behind me, before three bodies leapt over me, meeting the Mori vampires in the air.

Gregory, Gavin, and Tracey each grabbed a Mori, and all three pairs crashed to the ground in a wrestling fervor.

"Whoa," one of the guys muttered behind me.

I didn't glance back. I couldn't look away from the others. If there was an opening, I had to help. And, as if reading my mind, Gavin flipped his Mori over his head. The other vampire fell to the ground, not far from me. I ran over, my hand in the air and a spell ready to cast when the Mori was back on his feet. He was back in the air, hitting at Gavin. The punch was blocked, but the Mori was back in the air, his knees bent toward his chest and his feet ready. He slammed into Gavin, this time on the top as the two were on the ground. After that, everything began to blur. The vampires were too fast.

I recognized Tracey's growl and whipped to where they were. She and her opponent were close to Cal and Spencer, too close. Any second, they would be hit or used as a hostage.

I ran for them and yelled at the same time, "Get back."

They both jerked backwards, eyes wide, faces pale, and beads of sweat on both of their foreheads. Spencer pointed to Tracey, who heard my voice and kicked her Mori in the opposite direction. She stopped once and looked to me. Our gazes caught, and I nodded at her. Her eyes narrowed, and her fangs showed, then she turned and leapt in the air, landing on her Mori.

"Who are they?" Spencer grabbed my arm.

Cal surged to my other side. "Yeah. Were those fangs on that chick?"

I couldn't answer. I didn't know what to say, not yet anyway.

"Davy."

I shrugged off Spencer's hold and said to him, "When this is done. I'll tell you everything when this is done."

"When the crazy, freakish fighters are done fighting?" he shot back.

Cal frowned at Spencer, but didn't say anything against him. His Adam's apple bobbed up and down as he surveyed the battles once again.

"Davy!" Spencer's hand wasn't on my arm anymore, but he stepped close. His presence was demanding answers.

"When it's safe," I hissed at him.

"We should be running for our lives, not waiting to see who wins."

Cal added, "Let's go. They're all freaks."

"Sounds good to me."

Before they could leave, I grabbed both of their arms, and because I knew there'd be no words to explain everything, I showed them. Using The Immortal's power, I slipped into their minds. Okay. When I say that I slipped, it was more like I burst through their door and charged my way in. I showed them everything using my memories, of when I first became an empath, of when I lit a vampire on fire, how I enjoyed watching him burn, when I went to college and tried to be normal. They were there when I first met Roane, my first college date that Roane ended coming along with, how I kissed him to distract him, later when we kissed more in a professor's office, and the first time I realized I was The Immortal. After that, the memories were coming in quick spurts and all at once. I introduced them to Brown, to Kates, to the werewolf, to who Jacith is supposed to be, to Pippa, and lastly they were shown my time in the cage. They were there when I was tortured by the witches, and again when we escaped. The last memory they were shown was when I stumbled upon them in the forest.

I released their arms before anything else could slip through. I didn't want them to hear the conversation I had with The Immortal and how I learned it was my fault they were pulled from their group.

"Whoa. Holy—" That was all Spencer got out before he ran a few feet away and bent over, throwing up.

Cal didn't look too far from the same. He raised his arm and pressed it over his mouth, but his face turned a slight shade of green.

"You going to throw up, too?"

He started to shake his head, but as he did, his eyes bulged out, his cheeks puffed up, and his entire top half of his body lurched upward. He sprinted next to Spencer, and the two were throwing up in sync.

I sighed. Maybe I shouldn't have done that.

"Friends of yours?" Gavin was behind me. He was sweating, bloody, and his chest was heaving up and down.

I grinned, though I didn't feel it. "Apparently, I'm not so in control of my powers as I used to be."

He frowned at me. "Were you ever?"

I shrugged. "I thought I was better."

A deep and ferocious roar came from behind us and we looked over, just in time, as Gregory stopped, grabbed the wounded Mori in front of him on both sides of his head, and he twisted the head completely off. The body fell back to the ground with a thud, but Gregory wasn't done. Tracey yelled at him as she lit her Mori on fire. She tossed the lighter to the Goliath-sized vampire, and Gregory lit the head on fire instantly. He dropped it on the ground as he lit the rest of the body on fire, too.

Both of them, Gregory and Tracey, looked at where Gavin had left his Mori on the ground.

He hadn't burned the body, but it wasn't needed. The body had been pulled apart, literally. Arms, fingers, legs, parts of its stomach and chest were scattered all around the beach.

Gavin remarked, "I was mad."

Gregory grunted. "Got that."

Tracey didn't reply, but she began to gather the body parts. Gregory did the same until every part of the Mori were thrown in one burning pile. By that time, Cal and Spencer were done throwing up and we gathered around the fire. It wasn't enough. The flame should've been higher, and without thinking, I held my hands out and began to mutter a spell. The fire began to grow.

"Who-a," someone muttered.

I didn't care. Every last part of them had to become ash and even then, the pile of ashes would need to be spread all over. I didn't know the Mori lore and how to kill them, but I wasn't taking a chance. I kept chanting and the flames doubled in size. A white twinge started to grow on the outskirts of the fire, but that was from The Immortal. I couldn't see myself, but I knew my eyes had changed to The Immortal white. I kept them lowered so no one could see them until the Mori were completely gone. Then, as the last piece of ash fell to the pile, I raised my hands and made a motion to the left. A strong gust of wind swept through the clearing where we were and picked up the ashes. I sent them off, directing where I wanted them spread, and once I was content, knowing they would never return and never come back to life, I stopped.

I could still feel The Immortal in my blood. She was on an adrenaline high, like she was intoxicated. I was buzzing, but I still waited until an ounce of calmness settled over me. Cal and Spencer had come up behind us, and I turned to look at Tracey, so my back was to the hikers.

I asked in my head, "Are my eyes still white?"

She answered back, "You're fine."

Reassured, I looked back over the group.

All of them were staring at me with mixed emotions. Cal and Spencer looked like they were crapping their pants, while Gavin was closed off. I felt his anger. It was just underneath the surface. He was keeping it contained until the humans were dealt with. Gregory and Tracey had similar reactions. I felt the awe in both, but they were also resigned. They were waiting for Gavin and me to fight, then to keep on with whatever we decided.

I grinned slightly, but felt regret, too. "I shouldn't have left."

That was all Gavin needed. He erupted, "YOU THINK?"

"AGH!"

Cal and Spencer fell back again, their fear spiking once again.

I took a breath and held a hand out to Gavin. "You didn't need to come."

He bristled back. "You had three Mori about to rip your spine out, and you're telling me we didn't have to come?"

Tracey said quietly, "You knew we would."

"You cast a sleeping spell over us."

I stiffened, hearing the accusation coming from Gregory. I started, "I'm sorry—"

"Wren is alone," Gavin interrupted. His eyes were narrowed to slits, and his jaw clenched. "She continued to Roane."

"I didn't ask you to come with me," I argued back. My blood started to pump again. "I came here on my own."

"To do what?"

His words felt like a slap in the face. I winced. "To save Kates."

"You're lying to them."

I closed my eyes. This is not the time.

"Too bad," The Immortal snarled at me. *"You're going to have let me talk. You have to stop lying to them."*

"Davy?"

I shook my head at Gavin, turning half away from them.

"They can smell your lies."

I grew still, hearing her answer. It was simple and given to me so calmly. I asked, *"What?"*

"If you want to be rid of them, stop lying. Believe your truth. They'll smell that instead and will do what you want."

"I want them to be safe."

"So send them to safety."

I frowned. *"What are you talking about?"*

"It'll cost you, but it'll be worth it. Send them back to Roane. They'll be safe with him. They won't be with you."

"I don't have enough strength."

She laughed at me. *"You do. You've been restoring it since you woke. You just have to tap into it."*

"What have I been using since I woke?"

"You have a back channel of power. It's all stored up. It's where I'm

speaking to you from. You are me. I am you. I am this back section of power. Open up your mind and let me in."

"*I . . . can't . . .*" I was going to say I didn't know how to do that, but it wasn't true. I did. It was the same way I had gotten into Cal and Spencer's minds. I had my own door closed off to myself. I just needed to find it and burst through it, but thinking about it, I hesitated.

"*Come on, Davy,*" she started to chide.

"Stop it!" I screamed back, the words coming from my throat as well. My heart was pounding. I could feel her wanting to get in. That was when I realized it—that door wasn't keeping me out, it was keeping her in. It was keeping The Immortal from completely taking over me.

"Davy?"

I didn't know who said my name, but I looked to Gavin. Seeing concern and his anger lessening, I almost whimpered. "It's The Immortal. She's trying to take over."

A wave of alarm swept over all of them.

Gavin froze in place and asked, his voice dipping low, "*What* did you say?"

ROANE

ROANE AND BASTION had been tailing the Romah army for three days. They were trying to go around them, moving higher on the mountains to give the entire army a wide berth and their progress was painstakingly slow. More than once they were almost discovered and each time, Roane worried about what they'd have to do if that happened. No matter the consequences, whoever discovered them would have to be murdered. If the body was found, that could start a war before he was ready for it. The only plan he had was one he didn't want to do. It put them at risk as well, but so far, he hadn't needed to put it into play.

So far.

They were high up, at the highest line of trees on the mountain-side. If they broke free from their cover, they'd be seen from below and every time there was a clearing, both had to drop to the ground and crawl across, going as fast as possible.

They weren't moving as fast as Roane wanted. They needed to get ahead, but the break hadn't come for them. The Romah army didn't rest. They slept in shifts. While some would walk, the others would sleep on some makeshift carts. The awake ones would pull them ahead, then switch places and progress even further. The weight of their comrades slowed them down, but not enough.

They were being assisted with magic. Roane felt it in the air. It was covering all of them and it was a problem. It'd be a problem in the future as well. He wasn't sure where the magic came from, but he knew it was there and he knew it was protecting and helping them to go at an unnaturally faster pace.

He and Bastion were running, sprinting from tree to tree, when suddenly they felt a shift in the air. Both vampires froze as one, looking like statues now.

"Do you see anything?" he asked Bastion in his head.

Bastion leaned forward and his nostrils flared. He closed his eyes and smelled the air, like a wolf would do. Roane knew the answer was nothing before Bastion thought to him, *"No. Whoever it is, is beyond the next ridge."*

He edged farther. Instead of their break-neck speed, he and Bastion snuck ahead, keeping to the trees for camouflage. They were going at a snail's pace now. He wanted to see whoever or whatever it was before they saw them, and as they cleared the hill, both froze in place. A wolf scout was thirty feet in front of them, resting against a tree. Its head was down with closed eyes, and the wolf panted for a moment. In and out. It sounded like it was struggling for breath, but that was from the speed the group was traveling at. Even the wolves were tired.

Roane thought to Bastion, "*Hold. The wolf will move forward.*"

Bastion didn't move an inch. "*The wolf will keep moving ahead of us. We're stuck behind him.*"

Roane grimaced. There was no way around it. If the wolf didn't move down, but kept going straight ahead of them, he knew Bastion was right. A confrontation was imminent. He was about to signal Bastion to move around when a wolf's howl filled the air. The wolf in front of them immediately responded. His eyes opened and his head fell back. A long howl ripped from deep in its throat and the two vampires shared a look. From the intensity of closeness of this howl, both knew they wouldn't forget the sound. It was haunting, sounding from a deep sorrow.

As the wolf finished, he lumbered forward. His head went back down, and he took two quick breaths before bounding ahead.

"*He's keeping to the same path.*"

Roane nodded, knowing what Bastion meant. They had to kill the wolf. Giving him the signal, Bastion took off to the left as Roane sprinted forward. Instead of going upward, Bastion would circle around the wolf, coming from below. The wolf would sense Roane's presence and prepare for an attack, assuming a second opponent, if there were one, would circle up and out of the army's territory.

That would be his death then.

But before Bastion could go far, the wolf ripped through the foliage, coming straight at them. Roane felt the wolf's surprise. He had doubled back, not knowing what he'd find, and before he could call for help, both of them were on the wolf.

As Roane impaled the wolf, drawing his sword and shoving it deep into his enemy's chest, a sadness filled him. He had come to know that creatures such as this one followed orders. That was their only reason for its death. If he had been born or turned by the Christane bloodline, his blood wouldn't have been spilled on the ground that morning. But this wolf hadn't been and because of that one fact, Roane reached in and yanked out its heart.

The sword harmed him, but it wouldn't kill him. His own touch delivered that fatal blow and as he stood there, with the heart still beating in his grasp, he said a small prayer honoring its death. Bastion was beside him, and without saying a word, both knew what had to be done. One by one, they took the heart and spread its blood all over them. It would aid in their travels and they could move at a faster rate. They would smell as one of their enemy's own, which would turn an invisible eye to them. The wolves wouldn't be looking at their own.

Once they were done, both completely covered in its blood, Roane put the heart back. It was his way of paying homage to the wolf, giving back its heart. After that, knowing they only had limited time before they realized one of their own was dead, Roane and Bastion sprinted ahead. This time, they could move farther down the hill. They didn't need to travel along the highest tip of the ridge. The wolves were scouting the mountains, and their noses would allow them camouflage.

It was time they made up their lost time.

As they ran forward, weaving around trees and giving every wolf ahead of them a wide berth, Roane glanced down. The army had changed their positioning. The Mother Wolf was in the middle of her men, along with Romah guards behind her.

They were nearing his army. They wouldn't risk leaving their leader in the back. It was too vulnerable of a position. She was more guarded this way and for a brief second, Roane knew he could fly down and rip her heart out, as he had one of her brethren just now. It would be a suicide killing, but for the briefest of moments, he considered it. It would be a harsh blow to this army, one that could assist in their victory, but Bastion reached back and grabbed Roane. He pulled him forward with him, and as he did, the moment was gone.

Roane knew he'd have to find an opening later. He couldn't regret that moment.

CHAPTER 16

Roane and Bastion were nearing their camp. Roane could sense his own men and knowing it was safer, they began killing the wolves and any Romah guards they came upon as they made their way out of enemy territory, closing the gap into their own. They still needed to cover twenty miles, but once they came upon the last of the Romah scouts, and let their bodies fall to the ground behind them, they slowed their pace. They still kept to a brisk speed, but this was their resting time. Once they hit their encampment, he knew their army would have to pick up its own speed to stay ahead of their enemy.

They cleared a tree line, and he sensed an attack from behind. Roane twisted around, his sword drawn before he realized the body hurdling at him was a Christane wolf.

"Halt!" a voice cried out in a commanding tone.

The wolf couldn't, but Roane tucked his sword down and ducked, evading the wolf's attack. It hit the ground where he had been standing, but rolled once and was immediately on its feet and rounding to attack again.

"Stop." Roane held a hand out, showing his Hunter hand symbol. "I'm one of yours."

"It's the Hunter." The same voice from before materialized out of a foliage. It was Christian. He lifted his head, sniffing the air, and he frowned at Roane. "You reek."

"Your rival's blood." As he spoke, Roane signaled to Bastion to keep ahead. Once the other vampire took off, with instructions to ready the rest of their men to move forward at a faster rate, Roane fell in step with Christian. The other wolf moved back to its hidden post, ready to attack anyone else that followed them. Roane said, "It camouflaged us the last few miles. I sent Bastion ahead. The group needs to go faster."

"Roane—"

"They're moving faster than us. Your Mother Wolf is in the middle of their group. She's protected by her wolves and Romah vampires. We need to get ahead and get Davy on our side if we're going to stand a chance. Or—"

"Roane—"

He ignored Christian, continuing to talk as they grew closer to the main camp. "And I couldn't find Jacith. He's not traveling with his family, but he's a sorcerer. I'm sure he'll be with them at the battle line."

"Lucas!"

"What?"

He twisted around, a fierce frown on his face. They had just cleared the last opening, leading to where the others had all congregated. Christian wanted to say something, and he stopped to listen, finally, but he felt one of his own coming toward him. He paused, distracted from whatever Christian was saying when he looked. It was one of his that shouldn't be there. He hadn't felt her for so long, since she was taken, and as he searched for her, or whoever it was, Christian's words broke through his concentration the same time he spotted her.

"—Wren is here."

She paused on her path. Vampires had stepped aside to let her pass, but she stopped, and her chest lifted. She took in a breath before she tucked her hands behind her, but he saw how they trembled. The usual defiance wasn't there. Instead, she was hesitant, and he sensed the guilt through their blood connection.

He asked her in his head, *"Why are you fearful of me?"*

Her eyes widened at his question and she swallowed, her eyes glancing to the side for a moment. Her head lowered, but then her shoulders rolled back and she lifted her eyes once more. As they found his, they were strong once again. Her normal flare was back, and she replied, *"Because I left them behind."*

Roane started for her. The relief at seeing her faded into alarm. She braced herself for him and as he drew abreast, he grabbed her arm and propelled her with him. There were no tents assembled, but Roane didn't say a word until he pulled her far enough from the group so no wolf could overhear. As soon as they moved out of earshot, he released her and asked in his head so no nearby vampire could eavesdrop on their thoughts as well, *"You left them? What do you mean you left them?"*

"She's safe. Davy is safe."

"You guys got free?"

"Yes." She didn't answer for a split second, then, *"Davy got us all free. I don't know how because she didn't have her magic, but then she did. She carried us twenty miles away."*

"Why aren't they with you?" But he knew, as soon as he asked. He answered for her, *"Because Davy went back, didn't she?"*

"She didn't get Kates out. Davy went back for her."

No. Roane knew that wasn't the truth. She wouldn't have gone for her traitorous best friend. That would be an added benefit, perhaps, but he knew the real reason Davy was going back. For Lucan. She wanted to kill his brother so he wouldn't have to. He looked to Wren. He kept his thoughts barred from her before he asked her now, *"How far?"*

"Five miles away. I can take you to her."

He nodded, though he knew the chances of catching up to Davy before she got to the Mori was low. Still. They had to try. He spoke out loud, "You'll show me on a map where you were and we'll go from there. We won't return to the same spot. Davy will be ahead of us. We have to try to intercept them."

"I will."

He started to return, but glanced back. He frowned. "Was there more?"

"I wanted to return to my leader's side."

He sensed her fear come back, and the guilt made sense then. She left Davy's side to return to his. Reaching out, he gave her arm a slight squeeze. "The others remained with her?"

Wren nodded, feeling her first wave of relief since they escaped the Mori. "Yes. Gavin, Gregory, and Tracey went to find her. Davy left us behind. She didn't want to endanger anyone."

For the first time in a long time, Roane allowed a half-grin to show on his face. "Of course she did." His hand squeezed her arm once again before dropping back to his side. "You came back. That will help us figure out where to intercept her. You did good, Wren, but rest as quick as you can. We need to proceed as soon as possible."

She nodded, and he left her behind to find Saren. He needed to know where Jacith was, and he had a hunch Davy's Immortal sister could help him with that information.

DAVY

THEIR GROUP VENTURED across the river and into Mori territory. If Davy hadn't seen the Mori vampires before, she would've known the instant she stepped from the water and onto land. She felt the magic all over. It was in the ground, the trees, even the rocks. The air had a shimmer of it even and she breathed it in, but got another shock. It was her magic. It bonded to her and she realized it must've been left from when she carried her group from Lucan's captivity. Enough magic must've burst out of her, that it was only now moving to the outskirts of their land.

Gavin noticed her reaction. "What is it?"

"I feel my magic."

"What do you mean?"

"It's like a rock that's thrown in water. It causes waves to emanate from it. My magic, what I used to get us out of here before, it was like that. Instead of a rock, though, it was like I dropped an entire mountain in the ocean."

Gavin turned back to look at the river. "And you didn't sense it on the other side?"

"Their lands are protected. They use magic anyway, and they want to keep what is theirs already. They have a barrier. It's why my magic won't extend over the river, and it's why I didn't sense the Mori vampires. Their essence was blocked because of the barrier."

"Oh whoa."

Davy glanced to the side, farther down the river where Cal and Spencer were crossing. Tracey was with them. She had a sturdy arm around both of them and carried them so the river's current didn't sweep them away. Spencer had just stepped down on the ground, and those words had been his reaction. He was human, but even he felt the magic, too.

A knot formed in her throat. They were going to be changed because of their presence among the Mori. She didn't know how, but she knew it wouldn't be for the better. They were humans and she had brought them into this war. After reuniting with Gavin, Gregory, and Tracey, they hadn't moved into the Mori land for a few days. They stayed, camping on their side of the river, while they decided their next move. After hearing that Wren went back to Lucas, Davy knew what would happen. He would use Wren's information about where they had been and he would try to intercept them before they got back to Lucan. She didn't want that to happen. Davy wanted to infiltrate the Mori, cloak herself, so she could kill Lucan herself. She wanted to save Lucas this demon. If he had to murder his own brother, she knew it would haunt him for the rest of his life. The closer she got to Lucan, the more her real desire grew. It wasn't just to retrieve Kates. It was more about enacting vengeance. Kates was fast becoming an after-thought, but it was one she needed to cling to. It would save her humanity, or that was how she was feeling. When she thought about Lucan, The Immortal grew in strength inside of her. When she remembered her best friend, the human side of her sparked alive again.

But she hadn't shared any of this with Gavin or the others. She just let them know there was a battle inside of her. The Immortal wanted to take over, but she was holding it at bay. They had been reassured it wouldn't happen, that she had a handle on it, but the longer they camped near the Mori, the more her blood lust for Lucan grew and the stronger The Immortal was becoming.

Finally, after waiting a few days where Davy wasn't able to send the two humans back to their group, they decided to keep going. She hoped at some point she could send them back, but now they were on Mori lands, she knew their death was imminent. Even if they stayed behind, they were smack in the middle of a vampire and werewolf war. They'd be dead by someone's hand, so it was voted on by everyone, and it was unanimous. Cal and Spencer were to be brought with them, and they'd remain protected by their group of three vampires and one Immortal that wasn't in control of anything anymore.

"Davy?"

She tore her gaze from Cal and Spencer. Gavin had been trying to talk to her. She blinked a few times, as if waking up. "What?"

He gave her a half-grin, seeing where her attention had been. "They'll be fine. We'll protect them. Don't worry."

He had no idea. A doomed feeling was in her stomach, and it was growing, but she only replied back, "Yeah. You're right."

But he wasn't right. She felt their death in her already. In fact, she felt all of their deaths. The only one who wouldn't die was her, but she wished for it because what was going to happen was much worse than death.

"Are we going?" He gestured ahead to a walking path that led through the trees.

"Yeah." She started forward, falling in line behind Gregory who had taken the lead. "Let's go."

Her head went back down, and she began chanting in her head. She was connecting to the magic she had left in the Mori land. It had been waiting for her return and it gathered inside of her now. As they progressed into the forest, she cast a cloaking spell over all of them.

She didn't need to worry about tiring out. It was the opposite here. The Immortal was so much stronger. She needed to use her energy, to try to keep *her* at bay. They wouldn't realize it, but as they made their way farther into the Mori lands, they were completely invisible to the magical breed of supernatural vampires. It wouldn't be until later, much later, that they would realize the cost of returning to enemy territory would have on them.

CHAPTER 17

BROWN

The Bright witch chewed on her lip and wrung her hands together. Mavic had been helping her 'become one' with her inside magic. He explained, many times, if she could burrow deep inside of herself, she could release her family's power within herself. It sounded easy enough. Get one with thyself and pop that lock except it still hadn't happened. Every time he cast a spell that would help her become in tune with herself, something went awry. The first couple of times, his magic bounced off her and spread throughout the room. Objects that weren't supposed to be alive came alive. A couch began singing a One Direction song once. Mavic zapped the couch a.s.a.p., quicker than Brown wanted. She enjoyed the song, but when a lamp started doing the Whip and Nae song, complete with dancing, he cut off all those efforts.

The next few weeks were spent where he blasted her with magic. Instead of having her awaken inside, he was trying to do the deed himself. All that ended horribly too. His own magic cut back inside of himself and he ended with a nosebleed that could've filled a small pond. Brown felt bad after seeing that side effect. She could live with the dancing couches and lamps, but seeing her trainer in physical pain, she had to keep reminding herself of the end goal to stop from calling it quits.

Help Davy.

That was her reason to keep going. She had to help her friend, no matter how many nosebleeds Mavic endured. It wasn't until the last week where they finally made progress. He had her drink a concoction. When she asked what it was, he wouldn't tell her. He pushed the cup against her lips and growled, "Drink."

She did.

Davy's vampire boyfriend brought this guy to help her so she had to trust him. She closed her eyes and drank the bitter tasting liquid. It churned her stomach, making her feel nauseous, but Mavic clamped his hand over her mouth and began uttering words under his breath. He was spelling the liquid and she began to sputter, feeling it spark to life inside of her. Her body seized, wanting it out of her. Her stomach began to spasm, trying to push it all back up, but even when it hit her mouth again, ready to spew outwards, her lips wouldn't open. They'd been spelled shut. The liquid kept trying to break free, but nothing. Her mouth wouldn't open and a scream built up inside of her. It was like cement hitting cement. Pain sliced through her, then backed up and rammed through her over and over again. She was bleeding inside. She tasted it among the bile, but Mavic was undisturbed. His hand remained over her mouth, and his head went down. He kept the same chant until her body surrendered.

The liquid began to seep inside of her, merging with her body's organs and down to the cellular level. It was becoming one with her, and casting one last chant, Mavic backed up. He held his hand still in the air, but it wavered. He was ready to slam it against her mouth again if need be, but as he watched, he saw the transformation begin.

The spell was working how it should've. It was moving throughout the witch. It was a physical structure, therefore it couldn't be spelled from her like all the other magic he cast, but it could root out wherever her magic was locked up. It was supposed to find the location inside of her and it would help unlock it. He knew The Immortal had been able to do the same, but with The Immortal's power. His wasn't as strong, but if anything would help, this would, or he hoped. His choices of getting her magic unlocked were fast depleting.

Brown watched him as he watched her, but she was held immobile. She couldn't move, not during whatever was going on with her body still happening. She felt the change inside of her. The liquid found her core, and it settled there. It was her spiritual core, where her magic was, and she closed her eyes, suddenly knowing what was going to happen.

The magic he forced inside of her was going to do a full-on assault where her magic was, to open it up. She knew it was going to be painful, and she had a second to brace herself.

Then it began, and a scream erupted from deep inside of her, lifting her body in the air.

THE
BATTLES

CHAPTER 18
LUCAN

He stared down at Kates's bloodied body. He had broken her so many times, mended her, and then broke her again. As it was now, she was done. He saw that she was at the edge. She had no will, no fight, nothing more.

He withdrew from the table that he tossed her onto it and grabbed a washcloth. Wiping at the blood left on his hands, he washed himself clean and glanced over when the door opened to the room.

Jiyama stood there, her eyes going to Kates's broken body first. An emotion akin to sympathy flashed in her gaze before she said, "Three of our men never returned from their mission. They're believed to be dead."

Davy . . .

His jaw hardened. "Did the Healers go out?"

She nodded, her head bowed to the ground. "Their essence was last sensed at the river. It is believed they died there."

He frowned, distracted for a moment by Jiyama's actions. She was acting like a demure little girl. He ground his teeth against each other before asking, "Why are you acting like this?"

She stiffened and her hands tucked under her long sleeves. "I feel remorse. I think."

"You think?"

She lifted her head then, and a pained expression was there. Her gaze trailed to Kates before she said, softly, "I've only felt wonder. I've wondered about life, about who Davy was, about the magic inside of her, about the world beyond these lands, about life as a human, but I have never felt this sensation inside of me." Her hand, fisted around her sleeve, lifted and pressed between her breasts. She kept it clutched tight to herself. "I have never wondered about the side of life, about right versus wrong, but this—" her hand left her chest and indicated Kates, who hadn't moved or made a sound. "I feel almost like crying. I've never experienced that emotion." She lifted haunted eyes to Lucan, her bottom lip falling open. "Why is that?"

Anger filled him, but he bit back a curse and moved to the vampiress. Cupping the side of her face, he made sure his tone was soft as well. "That just means you are evolving. That is all."

Her eyes traced back to Kates. "I feel a pit in my stomach. I have only felt the fullness of blood in there." Her eyebrows pinched together. "I do not like this emotion."

"It's because you've spent too much time near humans."

A brightness filled her eyes. She asked him, "It's because of them?"

He nodded, leaning forward to brush his lips over her forehead. "Yes. Right and wrong, guilt and sadness, those are all human emotions. You've spent too much time near them with Davy before and now this one." He moved, adjusting her so his back was to Kates. He was blocking Jiyama from looking at her, and he pressed another gentle kiss to the Mori vampire. "They are a unique species, wracked with silly emotions. It's like a cancer to them, one that they don't realize is something to be expunged. They almost worship these sensations."

Her hand lifted up and grabbed onto his arms. "They do?" She was pressing her forehead tight to his lips. Her entire body was against his.

"They do. I didn't realize their 'humanity' could infect you."

"Humanity?"

"Hmm mmm." He nodded, clasping her to him still. "It's their sickness. I'm plagued with it too, but once I have The Immortal thread in me, I won't suffer from it anymore."

"You think Davy suffers this same sickness?" She pulled back, leaving enough space to look up at him.

Lucan paused, sensing there was more to her question other than curiosity. He frowned slightly, still holding her head in his hands. After a few beats, he asked, almost gruffly, "Why do you ask?"

Her hand fell to his chest, and she stepped to the side to see Kates again. "Davy said they were friends. If she is sick as well, I can't imagine what she would feel knowing what we have done to this human."

His frown deepened. "Why are you saying this, Jiyama?"

She stepped completely away from him. Her hands fell from his chest and balled into fists around her long sleeves once more. "The Immortal was good. I knew that as soon as I touched her. I don't know what this 'sickness' is that you're talking about, but it was different for Davy. I remember that. She was like honeyed blood. She was alluring to me. I had to go back and experience her again, but it wasn't her blood I wanted." A stricken wonder entered her gaze. "I wanted to give her my magic. I wanted to help her, and I haven't been able to get that out of my head. I keep thinking about our time with this one." She stepped forward and touched the table near Kates's leg. "I don't think she would be happy with what we did. She cared about this one. I knew that when I touched her. Lucan," she looked back to him. "I don't think we should have done what we did."

"No, Jiyama." He shook his head and moved once more so he was between her and the table. His hands lifted to her head again and he cupped her cheeks. "You're sick. That's all this is."

"I don't understand the sickness, but I remember how I felt when I helped The Immortal—"

He cut her off, saying, "And that will be me soon. I will become The Immortal. Remember? You will be helping me again. You can experience the same feeling with me, too."

"You want to become a vampire once again."

"No. I'll have to stay as a human if I become The Immortal."

She shook her head. "The Immortal will only go to a female. That's what they said—" She broke off, her eyes wide and startled. She jerked backwards from his touch. "I—"

A deathly stillness came over Lucan. He cocked his head to the side and narrowed his eyes. "They said? Who is they?"

She took another step backwards.

He took the same step toward her. "Who have you been talking to, Jiyama?" His tone was so soft, eerily soft.

"The child."

"The child?" He stepped back, his thoughts whirling, but then it clicked. He took Talia's child with him. She had been given to a Mori family to be raised. It was decided that he would not raise her and he had forgotten about the child till then. Then, it began to click with what else Jiyama had said. "You've been to the child's home?"

She nodded. "I was curious, Lucan. I wanted to know more about The Immortal and about Davy. I was not used to this feeling, wanting to know but not having the answers given to me. The child is still human. I thought she could explain more to me."

A human child within close proximity and a female one at that. No. He had completely forgotten about the girl. She came from an Immortal thread-holder already. Once the thread would leave Davy, it wouldn't bounce to him. There hadn't been a male thread-holder, but he had been determined to become the first. No other human within close distance, it would have to go to him, but now he realized his mistake. He had planned to turn Kates when the witches told him Davy was close to losing the thread, but the child—it would've gone to the child then.

The family.

He was trying to remember whom the child had been given to. They were going to let her grow as a normal human until she got to the age she wanted to be at for eternity. He was recalling all of the meetings now. She hadn't been born a Mori. If she were turned, she wouldn't continue to grow as the Mori vampires did. There'd been so much debate about the child, they had been furious he brought the human into their lands in the first place, but then a woman fell in love with the girl. She volunteered to raise her, and the husband . . .

"Who took her in?" he muttered under his breath. His hand turned into a fist, and he rapped it against the table. "Who was that?"

His questions were spoken out loud before he realized how they sounded, and he felt Jiyama's withdrawal immediately. The air grew cold as she stepped away, a scowl instantly on her face.

"Jiyama." He reached for her. "It's not how it sounds—"

She clipped her head from side to side. "No." Her eyebrows bunched together again. The corners of her mouth dipped down even more. "I felt your intentions just now. You want to murder the child. That goes against the Mori. You must not touch a child. Ever."

His anger rolled into fury, but he kept it contained. He knew he was broadcasting his emotions. Jiyama was in tune with the earth and all sensations rolled together. She could feel his rage even though he was trying to keep it blanketed. She just hadn't sensed how much rage he had. He was still trying to keep it locked inside of him. As her eyes became hard and accusing, he knew he was failing.

He knew what he had to do then, but he wouldn't think about it. If he did, she would know. He couldn't let himself experience that sadness, because he really did love her.

"Jiyama," he said quietly. "I need to thank you."

She paused, thrown from his change in demeanor. "Thank me?"

He nodded, tucking all his hostility aside. He reminded himself that he would become The Immortal. Davy was close. She had to be. No one else would be able to kill three Mori vampires, unless they came upon an army. All would happen as it should. He would find Davy, because she was coming for her friend. She would try to rescue Kates, and he would grab her then. He would use the child to distract her. Everything would work wonderfully, and as he let himself believe his thoughts, a peace settled inside of him.

Jiyama felt the peace, and she started to look more reassured.

He went to her, closing the distance between them. They were lovers and he held her face for the third time that day. He leaned down until his forehead rested against hers and he breathed out, "I would've completely forgotten about Talia's child, if you hadn't reminded me."

Her eyes widened, but before she could recoil—he snapped her neck.

He let her body fall to the floor, and he murmured, "And then all would've been in vain. So thank you, Jiyama, for you saved my plans after all." And then, knowing he would have to burn her body to kill her completely, he reached down and hoisted her up. He carried her to where he had kept Davy imprisoned and tossed her body onto the fire in the corner. No one would think to check this room. It was considered forbidden because it was used to hold captives, and they would never consider checking the ashes for any Mori essence.

Lighting the fire, he waited until Jiyama was burned beyond recognition, and then he left, knowing the fire would die down on its own.

He had an Immortal child to hunt down now, but once he stepped into the hallway, a Mori guard came rushing toward him. "Lucan." The guard stopped, his chest heaving. "There are two armies approaching our lands."

Lucas.

Lucan narrowed his eyes. "Who are they?"

"One is your brother, but the other army have their own magic." He stepped back and gestured down the hallway. "The Archon requests your presence."

The Archon was the Mori leader and Jiyama's father.

Lucan nodded and proceeded ahead of the guard, but this wasn't good.

This wasn't good at all.

CHAPTER 19
ROANE

"This is ridiculous."

Saren appeared next to Roane, who was perched in a tree and watching as five Benshire wolves were combing the trees a mile away. They were doing what he and the Christane wolves had already done. They arrived at the river three days earlier. On the other side were the Mori lands, but a protection spell was cast as soon as they tried to cross the water. Two wolves exploded in thin air and since then, no one ventured across. Because they couldn't move forward, Roane and the Christane wolves set up their camp and scouted their perimeter. They arrived three days ahead of the Benshire wolves and the Romah vampires. It was why Roane was in place and was disguised when the Benshire wolves would move underneath him.

He shot Saren a dirty look. "I'm trying to hide here."

She waved a hand and snapped her fingers. Immediately, Roane felt the difference. They were blanketed in place. It was like being on the inside of an invisible plastic bubble, but the plastic was rock solid. He asked, "What is this?"

"I shielded us. We can talk. They won't hear us, smell us, or see us."

"It's like a cloaking spell?"

"Cloaking is harder. This one was easier, takes less of my strength to keep it up, but if the wolves try to climb this tree, they'll know we're here."

"The plan is to sneak behind and kill them, one by one."

She nodded. "I'll wait until they move far enough ahead. We can both slip behind them."

His eyes narrowed. "You're going to help?"

She'd been absent for the last week of their trip. Once Wren arrived, Saren disappeared. Roane didn't know why and he wasn't the only one who realized it. Christian asked one night as well, but Roane couldn't tell him the reason. He had a feeling it had something to do with Davy, but he wasn't sure, and he didn't know if he even wanted to ask.

"Are you asking me why I've been gone?"

"I guess I am, yeah."

Two Benshire wolves were almost directly underneath them. Roane's instincts quieted him, but he knew the spell would protect them. Davy's magic was strong, and he knew Saren was connected to the same power. The other three wolves spread farther down. They were all in one line, a hundred yards between each of them. The other three wouldn't react fast enough. He could jump down and take care of both wolves before they'd be on him, but he still waited. One paused to sniff the tree where he sat.

He met Saren's gaze. She had quieted as well and was watching alongside him. He asked in his head, *"Does that spell protect my trail as well?"*

When there was no answer, he had the answer.

Roane nodded to himself. It was time. He reached and pulled out one of his daggers. It would do better in such close quarters against an enemy.

Then, Saren held up her fingers. She counted down, from three . . . two . . . on one, the air exploded. The spell was lifted and both leapt down from their spots. The wolf reacted too late. He'd been too startled.

As soon as he realized they were there, Roane was already in front of him. Saren landed behind him, and as the wolf glanced back, taking note of his surroundings, Roane plunged his dagger into his heart.

It was an instant death, but as quick as they were on this wolf, the second was on them. Roane had enough time to pull the dagger out and turn around. The second wolf was in the air and leaping onto him. Before its claws and teeth could pierce him, Saren slammed into it from the side. The two fell onto the ground and rolled once, then twice before coming to a stop, but Roane didn't wait. He wasn't watching as a bystander. He leapt in the air with them and as soon as they came to a stop, he waited long enough for Saren to roll free from the wolf before he was on the wolf's back. It reared up, trying to pull him off, but it couldn't. Roane was too fast. His hand went back as he plunged the dagger into another wolf. This time he was coming from the back so he used his entire body strength and weight to drive the dagger all the way into the body, ripping through skin, cartilage, and organs.

Roane held on, pushing it into the wolf, who was wriggling around. The wolf was trying to dislodge Roane, but he held on. He was vulnerable, though, and seeing his situation, Saren readied on her feet.

She drew her sword and braced because the other three wolves were coming. They were moving at a faster speed than normal, and they were on them before she could blink a couple times.

A silver-maned one leapt right at her. His mouth was open and his fangs ready. The other two, an all black-haired one and another black with a white strip running from under his head and down his torso, went for Roane, but as she swung the sword up and sliced across the wolf's nose, one of them turned to help. There were now two against Saren and one trying to bite into Roane, to pull him off.

Saren couldn't help him.

She swung the sword, but it only grazed across the silver wolf. He pulled his head back in time, but recoiled in pain.

Roane had been watching and he saw the smoke that rose from the silver wolf's gaping hole.

The sword was spelled as well. He didn't know with what, but he didn't care. Then, he was brought back to attention when the white-striped wolf bit into his back—or tried. Roane saw the teeth coming and yanked out his dagger. He couldn't keep pushing for the heart. Pulling his weapon free, he swung it at the striped wolf. It did the same as Saren's sword. It only grazed the wolf, who pulled back in time.

Roane fell to his feet and rounded.

The two wolves held back, regarding him. The first one was hurt badly and was panting for breath. He was falling down, even as Roane surveyed the scene. There was no element of surprise anymore. It would be a head-on confrontation. Hearing a sudden roar from behind him, he knew Saren was holding her own.

Then, he saw his opening.

The hurt wolf looked at his comrade and in that split second, Roane shot forward, kicking off the tree behind him for an extra burst of speed. He slid to the ground, coming up underneath the hurt one, but he didn't stop. He slid all the way under the wolf and as he did, he plunged the dagger into the heart, releasing it as he kept going. Coming to a stop, he watched as the wolf fell to the ground, impaling the dagger further into the body. Roane had a split moment where he grimaced before he realized a worse danger.

The striped wolf stopped, lifted its head, and howled. The bellow sent chills down Roane's spine. It was haunting, but there was more to this howl. He heard other wolf howls, but this one held more power.

"It's Jacith." Saren stepped next to him, wiping her sword against the grass to clean the blood from her sword. "The wolf's call traveled farther and imprinted its urgency on the rest of the Benshire wolves. They'll be here faster than normal."

And that left them with one option.

As the striped wolf ended the call, he lowered his head and regarded both of them.

It was a standoff between them now. The wolf couldn't kill both of them, but when he didn't leave, Roane knew the wolf was willing to die. He wasn't running.

Respect for this one wolf grew in him, but as he shared a look with Saren, he knew what had to be done.

She nodded, swinging her sword up, and both of them launched ahead.

The wolf met them, but it was a similar exchange as the first wolf. Saren jumped higher than Roane, landing behind the wolf. He twisted his neck to try to nip at her legs, but that was his mistake. As he did, Roane pushed ahead with an extra boost of speed and used that momentum to ram his dagger into its heart.

But, unlike the other two, this wolf didn't fall to the ground.

He didn't lunge for Roane either. He stood there, panting for breath, as both Saren and Roane waited.

The wolf did nothing.

Roane looked, but no blood fell from the wound.

"He's been protected," Saren gasped, her eyes widening.

"What does that mean?"

"That means we run." She rushed forward. The wolf tried to bite her, but she evaded him and as soon as her hand touched Roane's arm—he felt them coming.

He was pulled backwards into what felt like an invisible vacuum and Saren gritted her teeth, still pushing forward into whatever she had woven for them. Roane watched from where they had left. The wolf started after them, and behind him, more wolves appeared suddenly.

Saren waved behind her. As she did, the hole vanished.

They stumbled to the ground. There were no wolves around.

"What just happened?"

Saren stopped and took a breath. She reached for him again.

Roane caught her hand and held it in place, an inch above his arm. He asked again, "What just happened?"

"It was Jacith." Saren pulled her hand free and reattached it to his arm. "I only pulled you a mile away. He was aiding them. They'll be on us again if I don't get us farther away."

Alarm spiked in him as she grabbed his arm, and the same invisible vacuum effect happened. They landed again. Saren took a breath, then grabbed his arm again. They kept doing this until they landed outside their own encampment. She was doing it to save her power, only using it in short bursts. Once they were done, she closed her eyes and bent forward, resting her hands on her legs. She was the one panting for breath now, much how the wolves had before.

Roane knew they were safe so he started, "Was Jacith there with them?"

She nodded and opened her eyes. They were strained as she answered, "Yes. I watched their army before and his body wasn't with them, but he was there. Or he was in close proximity."

"I don't understand what you mean."

"He's powerful enough to project his magic, but he can only go so far. And it's only so powerful. The closer his body is to where he is projecting, the more power he has, and back there, his magic was very, very powerful. It was too much. The magic alone would've killed me. I knew he had spelled the wolves so they were unnaturally strong and faster, but that was him. That wasn't the power he had already given them."

Roane was reeling. Jacith was here. He had come for Davy.

Saren felt his urgency and panic rise and she held a hand up, stopping him. "Davy will have enough power to beat him. That is why I'm here after all."

"But if he can get to her—"

"He can't. The protection spell the Mori put up isn't for us or the other army. It's against Jacith. They feel his magic, too. They don't want him within their lands either."

"Can they defeat him?"

Saren lifted up a shoulder. "I don't know. The Mori have ancient magic, but I'm unsure about how powerful they are or if they even want to war against him. They're already with Lucan."

Roane stifled a groan. He clipped out. "My brother is with them, not the other way around."

"What do you mean?"

"The Mori are relatively peaceful. They don't leave their lands, but they did with him. I can't help to wonder if they've been told the full truth of why they held Davy in captivity."

She narrowed her eyes at him. "You think they don't know?"

"I don't know. Talia said not everything is as it seems. I'm wondering if that's what she meant."

"Maybe."

"Roane!"

Wren was coming down the path toward them.

Roane said under his breath, before the other vampire could reach them, "Don't tell the others about Jacith. They don't think he's here."

Saren glanced at him, a question lurking deep in her depths, but she didn't respond.

SAREN

As THE FEMALE vampire got to their side, Saren stepped back and tucked her head down. The Christane wolves should be aware of what they are going against, but this vampire that Davy loved had proven his intelligence. He must have a reason for her silence. However, she was uneasy. She needed to move ahead and find her Immortal sister. The sooner she could merge her power to Davy, the better for her sister, but as the days had been progressing Saren found herself more and more reluctant to leave these group of warriors.

They were simpletons. They were weak, but spending time in their presence was like a sickness. An infatuation grew for them. She found herself wanting to protect them, to aid in their survival. It was because of Davy. Her sister would want her to make sure this vampire lived. Saren tried to reassure herself it was because of the true Immortal—that was why she hadn't left them to enter the Mori land.

Roane and his comrades weren't aware, but the protection spell wasn't cast to keep Saren out. She had already crossed the water and explored a day's trek inwards before she realized the others were kept outside.

As Roane moved forward to intercept the female vampire, Saren felt it was time to pull herself away from this group and so, as she thought it, she vanished from their sight.

Sireenia felt her presence and greeted her. "I have missed you, sister."

They were on their plane, though Saren kept a window open. She could watch Davy's vampire and materialize if her presence was needed. She said to her other sister now, "Jacith is near them."

"Yes. He didn't travel with his army. He went somewhere first."

Saren heard the fear in her voice. "We aren't aware where he went?"

"He cloaked himself, even to us."

"How is that possible?"

Sireenia didn't respond, not at first. It was a beat later when she said, "We don't know."

CHAPTER 20

DAVY

Davy realized she had cloaked their entire group the first time they ran into a Mori. It was unexpected, and none of them realized the other vampire was there until they stepped around a tree. The Mori was right there, in the middle of a path. Davy froze while the others drew their weapons. The humans were behind them so they didn't know what was going on, but as soon as Davy thought about casting a spell, it didn't matter.

The Mori never reacted.

Wearing a dark brown robe, the hood was pulled over its head. Davy couldn't sense if it was female or male. Its back was to them, but they bent down and picked up a flower. It turned halfway to them, and they watched as she sniffed the yellow flower.

There was still no reaction.

"We're cloaked." Tracey put her sword away and turned to Davy. "Have we been cloaked the whole time?"

"Um."

Gavin twisted to her, too. He raised an eyebrow. "You don't know?"

"I remember wanting to protect all of us and I thought as we left the river that I wanted us to be invisible, but I didn't know I actually cast a spell."

Tracey moved closer. "There's five of us. My sister had a hard time cloaking one individual and she could only keep it up for a few moments." Fear, wonder, and another emotion, one that Davy didn't like seeing and one she didn't want to identify, flashed in the vampiress's eyes. "We've been traveling for days."

"Are you going to wear yourself out?"

Davy stepped back. The question was almost hurled at her from Gavin. She shook her head and held up her hands. "I didn't even realize I was doing it." She couldn't keep them in the dark anymore. They had to know what danger they were walking into with her. "I'm not in control of my powers."

"I thought they were coming back just fine."

That was what she had told Gavin earlier when she relayed The Immortal's wish to take over. Once that slipped out, Davy instantly regretted revealing that truth. They looked at her like she was an atomic bomb waiting go to go off, one she couldn't diffuse herself. She lied after that. She made it sound like she was in control, that she could hold off The Immortal, that there was nothing to be worried about.

"Did you lie to us?"

Davy nodded, waiting for Gavin's response.

What she got was instant anger. It slammed to his surface and she felt it, stepping back from reflex. But, balling her hands into fists, she stopped herself from taking another step. He had reason to be upset. They all did. She hung her head. "I'm sorry. I—"

"So what."

The three looked over. Gregory had joined the conversation. His plump lips pressed together, and he was putting his own sword away, too. He added, swinging his head to look at both vampires, "There's nothing you can do about it. The only choice you have is not to travel with her."

"You've known?" Gavin's tone was accusing.

Gregory didn't answer, not at first. A beat of silence passed before he nodded. "I did."

"When?"

"Since a day after she woke up in the cave."

Tracey went rigid. She resembled a warrior statue, made in stone while Gavin's nostrils flared. He hissed, "Are you kidding me?"

Gregory was unmoving. "She didn't even have powers at that time."

Davy gulped as the others looked at her. She turned away. She didn't want to see the shock and outrage. She didn't want to see the disappointment.

Gregory said further, "She's got her powers back, but we can't act surprised. We all heard her screaming. Who knows what Lucan's witches did to her."

Davy still couldn't bring herself to turn to them. She cared, more than she should've—perhaps, but they would be the first affirmation that she was different. She couldn't see that look in their eyes, like she was less than human, like she wasn't human at all.

"Uh." *Cough*. "Dudes."

Hearing Spencer's voice, a rush of relief went through her. These were the humans she had pulled to her, because she wished for them, because she needed a reminder of how to be a human. Spencer just fulfilled that desire for her and her lips twitched, forming a grin.

He went on to say, "So we don't hear you guys, but there's a monk smelling a flower dead ahead of us. Should we, be like, doing something about the dude?"

"I think that's a girl." Cal shuffled forward and craned his head, looking around them. "Yep. She's a girl."

"Yeah?" Spencer's excitement was obvious. "Is she hot?"

"I can't tell. She's got a robe on." Cal started to edge out from behind them.

"Stop." Tracey pushed him back. "You're back there for safety."

He pointed around her. "Either the chick nun is deaf and blind or there's something funky going on for her not to see us. I think we're safe."

"Cal." Spencer pulled him back. His voice dipped low. "We gotta do what they say. They're not human."

Cal said back, his voice dipping just as low, "I don't think that chick is either."

"Great."

"Why do I have a feeling we're not going to get out of this alive?"

The more the two humans conversed, the more guilt Davy was feeling.

"*Get off your high horse.*"

The Immortal was laughing at her. "*They're lucky to be brought on this path with you.*"

"*Stop,*" Davy said to her.

"*No. I mean it. Their lives were useless. Humans are weak and pathetic. They'll probably be turned into vampires. If you don't send them back to safety, the others will change them. They'll do it to save their lives and when that happens, the two humans will get the best thing possible. They'll have power and immortality.*"

"Losing one's humanity is not a gift. It's a curse."

"*Having humanity is a curse. Look at you. Once you give in, you won't feel any pain. There'll be no more guilt, no more shame, self-loathing. None of that. You'll be free. We'll be free and we can do anything we want.*"

"Stop . . ." But as she tried to muster the strength to shut The Immortal up, Davy found there was none. Her strength was depleting, at least against her own inner demon.

"*That's what you think of me?*"

Davy shot back, "*Aren't you? You're not human.*"

"*I'm not weak. There's a difference.*"

"Humans are weak."

The Immortal snorted. "*Right.*"

"They aren't."

"*Yeah. Sure.*"

Davy growled, her hands back into fists, and she lashed back, "*Being human is strong. It's courage. It's strength. It's moral.*"

The Immortal interrupted, saying, "*It's pain. It's misery. It's heartache. It's loneliness. It's suffering. It's being selfish. It's opening up your heart and only getting hurt in response. It's helping others and having them turn their back on you. It's loving and being cheated on. It's giving, then getting betrayed. It's foolish. You're not human anymore, Davy.*"

"*Shut up.*"

"*Admit it. The sooner you do, the freer you'll become. The stronger you'll become.*"

"*Shut up.*"

"*You've already started to turn your humanity off. I don't understand why you won't admit it. You don't feel pain. You don't feel misery. You don't feel fatigue. In fact, you're impatient. The others are slowing you down. You can go faster, farther, beyond any of them. They're an anchor to your abilities, but you won't leave them—*"

"*SHUT UP!*"

A surge of power and magic burst inside of her, and as it happened, Davy knew instantly it was a mistake. She wanted to silence The Immortal—she silenced her magic instead . . .

She looked up, and the Mori was staring right at her.

"Oops."

"What?" Tracey whipped around, her hand grabbing onto her sword.

Davy couldn't look away from the Mori. She didn't move. In a normal situation, she should've fled or at least attacked with a spell. She did neither. Something was holding her in place, and she continued to hold the Mori's gaze.

She was drawing the vampire into her mind.

Tracey and the others knew they could be seen by now and had their weapons drawn. Davy flung her hands out and barked, "No! Don't move."

"*Who are you?*" the Mori asked in her mind. She had beautiful doe eyes, high cheekbones, a heart-shaped jawline that curved to petite pink lips. She didn't stand in Davy's mind with the robe. The Mori female was in a white dress and nothing else. No makeup. No shoes. No socks. She was barefoot, and her long black hair swung freely as she gazed around her surroundings. A small line appeared in her forehead. "*Where am I?*"

"*My mind.*"

"Your mind?"

This Mori wasn't the enemy. Davy felt goodness from her. She wasn't a warrior that would instantly kill. That was why Davy was drawn to her, pulling her into her mind. It was a safe place, for both of them.

Davy asked, taking a step toward the vampiress, *"Do you know who I am?"*

She gazed around once more, the corners of her mouth pressing in. *"You're The Immortal thread-holder. No one else would have the power to pull one, such as myself, into your mind. I'm a priestess for my people. My own powers have not been challenged by more than a handful."*

She was a big deal. Davy nodded. She got it. *"What's your name?"*

"Yaeyn." The vampiress added, *"Jiyama spoke about you. She said your magic was addicting. She yearned to touch it again."*

"Jiyama helped us. My friends and I could escape because of her. I'd like to thank her someday."

"She's missing."

Davy frowned. *"What?"*

"She's gone. No one can sense her essence anywhere. That's why I'm out here. I thought perhaps she went in search for you." Yaeyn turned around and regarded the others. *"I am not seeing her with you."*

The one Mori that Davy hoped could help them was gone. She— there was nothing she could do about that. *"Lucan loved her."*

Yaeyn nodded. *"She loved him as well. It is troubling. No one can find where my sister went, even Lucan himself. He was the last to have spoken to her."*

A dark cloud of suspicion lined the bottom of her stomach. Davy wondered, but that didn't make sense. Lucan loved her. She witnessed their exchange herself. If he did something, then that would be on him. It would be another reason to make him suffer.

Yaeyn said, *"I hear rumbling."* She focused on Davy. *"That is you. That's your anger."* She inclined her head, a soft question coming from her, *"Lucan was to wed my sister. Why would he harm her?"*

"I don't know, but the Lucan you know isn't the Lucan I know." The rumbling in Davy grew, shaking, sending Yaeyn from side to side.

She held her hands out, trying to steady herself, but the beautiful landscape that Davy had sculpted for the Mori turned to the inside of a volcano. The heat was rising, more and more, and Davy was ready to explode.

"Kill her," The Immortal hissed.

Yaeyn's head whipped around. *"Who was that?"*

Davy was standing in front of the Mori, but another presence stepped beside her. She knew, before looking, that it was The Immortal. It was herself.

Yaeyn's eyes widened, and she took a step backwards. *"They unhinged the thread. You are no longer merged."*

"Kill her," The Immortal said again, ignoring the Mori. *"Take her power for yours. We can use it instead of using the power you're restoring for Jacith. Take her power, Davy."*

"No." Davy shook her head, but her voice was quiet.

Yaeyn started looking around. *"Release me, Thread-Holder. Release me now."*

It was too late, though. The Mori sensed what Davy already knew, it was why she released The Immortal to stand next to her. Her power was still locked up, but Davy knew what she would do. She needed the extra encouragement or she didn't think she could go through with it.

She was going to kill the Mori.

They were all attached. It was why they called each other sister and brother. If she took this Mori's essence, it was a gateway into their community. She would be connected to all of them and she could yield that connection as she pleased. She could slip into their minds. She could tell them what to think, feel, do, and so much more.

Yaeyn whispered, shaking her head, *"Don't do this, Davy of the Thread-Holder. Jiyama said you had good in you. She longed to assist you. She wanted to be your friend."*

Davy snorted. *"She loved Lucan. Her judgment's off."*

"I can feel it in you, too." Yaeyn's eyes were piercing, pleading with her. *"It's why I didn't attack or flee. My reflexes are faster than yours are. I*

feel what she felt. You are good. You are pure. Do not listen to the evil in you." She gazed with scorn at The Immortal. "*This one is power hungry. She wants to take control over you, and she'll swallow your soul whole to do that. She won't hesitate. Don't let the darkness win.*"

But as the Mori was talking, The Immortal reached over. She clasped her hand onto Davy's, who turned her palm around. They were now palm to palm, and their fingers intertwined. They were the most connected in a long time, before Davy merged with her back at Roane's restaurant.

"*This is good. This is the right thing to do.*" The Immortal spoke quietly to her, clasping her hand tight.

"*No, Davy.*" Yaeyn thrust a hand out, as if to grab ahold of Davy.

Davy closed her eyes and hung her head.

"*Block her out. Don't listen to her. You need her essence. It will help you against the Mori and Jacith. You'll be able to find Kates.*"

Davy still hesitated.

"*The Mori captured you. They assisted Lucan with taking the others and torturing you. You can use her essence and her power. When we're done, you can let her essence go. It can rest with her family.*" The Immortal squeezed her hands. "*We have to, Davy. It's no longer you and me. It's us. We have to do this.*" She paused a beat, then added, "*This will save Lucas, too.*"

The last sentence was enough. Davy was wavering, but her mind was made up. She shut her emotions off and started to chant.

She concentrated on the words. Magic hadn't been an effort for her before. The effort had been in trying to control her power, but since Lucan's witches, it was like she was learning everything new. And this spell, drawing the Mori's essence, was beyond anything she had done knowingly.

"*Davy!*"

The Immortal moved so she was directly in front of Davy. Her back was to the Mori, and she tucked her head next to Davy's. She took Davy's other hand, and she began to chant with her. They both spoke at the same time, in the same breath, with the same focus and attention.

"*Davy,*" Yaeyn yelled once again. "*I know there is good in you. Please don't do this. I'm one of my people's leaders. They will be devastated by my death—*"

Enough!" The Immortal slammed a hand behind her, and in a moment, she snapped Yaeyn's neck. Her hand returned to Davy's, and she squeezed it hard. "*Hurry. We can still take her essence. It hasn't depleted to the earth yet.*"

They worked together, as one mind, one mouth, and when it was done, a peace settled over Davy. She opened her eyes, but she was back in her own body once again. She wasn't in her mind and she looked down.

The Mori was at her feet. Her eyes were wide open with death in them, and her mouth was open, like she had been gasping for breath.

"I can feel them." Davy didn't turn to the others. She said, "I can feel all of them. I know where they are."

Gavin gestured to the Mori. "What about her?"

Davy didn't look. She only said, "She would've killed us. I was protecting us." And with that, she stepped over the body.

CHAPTER 21
ROANE

As soon as Roane walked into the encampment, the Christane wolves knew. He still wore Benshire blood on him, and it wasn't long after that before Christian issued the order. They were marching on their enemy.

"You'll lose."

Christian was leaving his tent, his sword ready. Pippa was next to him, and as Roane said those words, she stood next to her brother. Both regarded him with resolved faces. They were going to war. The order had been issued. They were ready.

Christian snapped, "You brought us here. This is why we're here."

"They're being helped by Jacith—"

"And we're supposed to have The Immortal on our side," Christian's voice bellowed. "Where is she?"

"Brother," Pippa said. Her head turned up, regarding him.

He ignored her, glaring at Roane. "You're the leader, but you come in here wearing our enemy's blood." He gestured around them. "Look at my men. If you wanted a battle cry, you got one. The smell worked them into a frenzy. They must have blood of their own now. They have to spill their enemy's blood for themselves."

"We have to wait." But as Roane said it, he knew they wouldn't.

He smelled the wolves' blood thirst. It was intoxicating, even to himself. It was bringing the Hunter in him alive again, the Hunter that he thought was long gone. Even now, as Christian started to speak, Roane wasn't paying attention. The Hunter mark on him started to burn. It was awakening and he closed his eyes. He needed to allow it to return. He had been stripped of his Hunter privilege, but for a reason unknown to him, it was being returned to him. He was no longer only powerful because of Davy's blood, but because of his ancestry.

". . . We have no choice," Christian was saying.

Pippa added, "We have to go."

Roane didn't look at her. He hadn't paid attention to the wolf that was Davy's friend. It hurt too much, remembering the times when Davy fought for this one, proclaimed she was friend and not foe. That had been when Davy was safe, not like now. She'd been gone for so long.

Wren stepped next to him. "The witch is gone, but we'll fight with you." She glanced to Roane, then back to Christian. "It's why we all came here."

"It's not time." Roane shook his head, but he knew it was pointless. They were going. They had waited too long.

"It's time, Lucas Roane, Hunter of the Hunters' bloodline." Christian spoke to him, but he wasn't paying attention anymore. His gaze was directed beyond Roane's shoulder and he turned to see all of the wolves there. They were waiting. Then, one by one, they began to change into their wolf form. When they were all done, they turned as one and formed a line. Two by two, they began to leave. Roane stepped back with Bastion and Wren. As they watched, Christian and Pippa transformed as well and followed their bloodline.

They were going to war.

Wren said, when they left, "It's not enough. They'll all die."

Roane asked Bastion, "You sent your man?"

Bastion nodded. "I did."

"Would he have had time?"

"I don't know." Bastion took a breath, hesitation on his face, but it cleared. He was the fastest of Roane's men. "I could go, if you want me to."

"What?" Wren's head whipped around. "You are not thinking what I think you're thinking. You are not leaving. Are you?"

"I can go. He would be there by now, but coming back—"

They needed help. Roane realized that as soon as he saw how many Benshire wolves and Romah vampires there were. He had his own men, and he sensed them now. They heard the exchange. They knew the wolves were heading out, but they were waiting for their own leader. Roane didn't want to send his men to fight. They would die. There were too many Romah vampires. They were older, and they had magic. Davy was their ace in the sleeve, but they couldn't get to her.

"Roane."

He glanced down to the ground. Wren spoke his name, standing beside him, and he knew why. He felt his men. They had come, standing not far, and he knew why they were there. It was the same reason they came on this journey with him. It was time to fight. It was that simple. The wolves, who had come to be their ally, were going. They would go to their deaths. They didn't have Davy, but he couldn't put it off any longer.

It was time.

He turned around. Wren turned with him. Bastion was on his other side. It was too late. If he sent Bastion, he wouldn't get back in time. No matter what, the war was here and it had already started.

He spoke quietly, but every vampire heard him as he said, "We came to fight."

The excitement and adrenaline filled the air. Each vampire was on high alert.

Wren said, "We're ready."

Roane nodded. "Then we fight."

He turned and led his men to join the Christane wolves. So be it who fell and who lived at the end.

DAVY

SHE COULD FEEL THE MORI. She knew exactly where they were, even the little babies in the mothers' wombs, and she walked toward them. Her feet glided soundlessly over the forest as she kept moving forward. Davy walked and walked. She wasn't aware of the time, the weather, even where she was. She could've been walking on a cliff's edge and she would've kept going.

Everything was tuned out, except for the Mori.

The Mori meant more magic, more power. And as she kept going, she moved with a serene and ethereal quality to her. Gavin, Gregory, and Tracey followed behind. They were no longer guarding her. They were merely trailing now. It was as if they didn't exist, and more than once the three vampires shared a worried look. This was a Davy that they didn't know, and while the humans didn't know the old carefree Davy, they reacted on a primal level to this new Davy as well. They were silent and had grown pale. Their bodies started to tremble from the exertion they were being put through. Showers erupted in the sky and drenched their group. The two humans shivered. They accepted blankets that the vampires offered, but when Cal's teeth's chattering overpowered the sound of his own heartbeat, Gavin knew they had to stop.

"Davy." He reached for her. "We have to stop."

A part of him felt she wouldn't, but when she did, he was surprised. Some hope sparked in him. His senses were telling him she wasn't human anymore, had slowly been transitioning in that direction, but since killing the Mori, he could see The Immortal's power over her. As he stared at her, he could only see small traces of the old Davy.

Her chocolate almond eyes, that usually danced and laughed,

were dead. There was no life in them anymore. Her cheeks, that would pink and plump up whenever she would grin at something Lucas said or if she was caught staring at Gavin's best friend, they barely moved. The color was gone. A white, almost tranquil, glimmer had formed over her skin.

"Why?"

She asked that one word, but instead of the impatience or even understanding that the old Davy would have, she sounded careless. It was like she was curious, as if the idea of exhaustion was a new concept to her.

He gritted his teeth and tried to quell his anger.

Davy's eyes sharpened. Her head tilted to the side and the age-old hierarchy was switched. He was no longer the predator that every vampire was to a human. He was her prey. Gavin knew it, and Davy knew it. A faint grin teased at the corner of her mouth, but it only remained a faint glimmer. Her eyes remained cold and soulless.

He shifted to the back of his heel. "The humans need to rest."

Davy stepped aside so she could see Cal and Spencer. As her dead gaze left him, Gavin could breathe. He'd been under her attention, which was a spell in itself now. He had to do something. This couldn't continue. She would be gone and the allegiance he owed his best friend, to watch over his lover wouldn't be upheld. He would be letting Lucas down. He couldn't do that. As Davy continued to study the humans, Gavin cast a quick look at Tracey and Gregory. He saw similar unsettled looks in their faces.

"You are too tired?" Davy asked Cal and Spencer.

Neither answered. They glanced behind them, tucking their hands against their sides. Their shoulders hunched down, like they were trying to make themselves seem smaller. They wanted to run from her.

Davy's eyes narrowed. "You are not too tired? Why are you not answering me?"

Gavin cleared his throat. His hand went to his sword, but he only gripped the handle. He didn't pull it out. "Davy, this is enough."

She looked back. He braced himself, knowing how her gaze now felt, and as it settled on him, he felt all his breath being stolen. It was being drawn out of him, slowly, and at a torturous rate. Her eyes fell to his sword and though there was no reaction on her face, he felt her attention sharpen.

She asked, "You would use that on me?"

"You're different. You're almost unrecognizable."

He searched her face, but nothing. There was no response. There wasn't even anger.

Her face remained flat as she asked, "How so?"

"Come on," Tracey burst out. She surged forward, throwing her hands out. "Look at you. You're not even like us anymore. We have emotions and with you—there's nothing. You're cut off. You're empty. You're—"

"Bat shit crazy," Spencer supplied, moving forward.

Cal snorted behind him. "Ditto on that. I used to think she was hot."

"Yeah." Spencer said over his shoulder to him, "If you're into Terminator Dominatrix."

Davy was quiet, but she asked, "I'm like a robot?"

"No." Cal and Spencer started to talk at the same time. Gavin threw both a look. "Shut up."

They did.

He turned back to Davy and held a hand out toward her. "Davy, this isn't you. This is The Immortal taking over you. It's happening. What you didn't want to happen, losing yourself to her, it's happening. You're losing your humanity."

He waited, almost hoping for a murderous reaction from her.

"My humanity?"

He closed his eyes. She was gone. That one question was spoken as if she'd been asked the weather. There was nothing left. He saw that now. His anger buried deep in him, but alongside it was an anchor, pulling it low and helping to drive it further inside of him. She was gone. He had let Lucas down.

He cast a sideways look to Tracey and Gregory. A deep sadness clung to both.

She was gone.

"Davy—" Gavin cleared his throat.

"The humans are tired. That's what you're saying."

She didn't get it. So much more happened here than just those few words, but he nodded. He felt a heavy weight on his shoulder, heavier than he ever remembered experiencing before. He murmured, so softly, "Yes, Davy. They're tired. They can't keep up with you."

"Then stay here with them." She angled her head to the side again. "Or kill them."

"Dude!" Spencer cried out. "What the fuck?"

Cal groaned. "Why do I get the feeling this isn't going to end well?"

Davy started toward them. "If you cannot keep up, you're no longer useful. I can relieve your pain right now." Her hand stretched out, a single finger pointing toward them.

Both jumped back. Their hands came up, and they were shaking their heads. Their arms began waving back and forth in front of them.

"No, no."

"That's okay. Thanks, though."

Spencer added, "We're good." He coughed, hitting his chest. "We can keep going. No problem here."

"Pretend we're not human."

The anchor stopped. It was all the way to the bottom of his feet, but Gavin knew what had to be done. He let go of the sword. He couldn't plunge it into Davy. He couldn't do that, not yet anyway, but she had to be handled. She stepped toward the humans and he moved behind her.

Spencer gave her a thumbs-up sign. "Really. We're good. We'll march all night."

Cal nodded, his eyes gleaming from fear. "Yep. Me, too. All night."

Davy shook her head. She said quietly, "No. I can help you. You're human. I remember what that feels like. So much pain. So much misery. You feel worthless half the time and then struggle to even feel that much the other half. It's a disease."

"Oh God." Spencer gulped. He backed away as Davy advanced. Cal was right with him. "Really. I like my humanity."

Cal jerked his head up and down. "Me, too. Lots of pain. I live for that shit."

"No, you don't." Davy let out a sigh. Sympathy laced it. "You were high when I met you. Both of you. You sought other planes of consciousness. No one does that if they're happy. They seek to escape life. They seek to distract themselves. It's why you went on your study abroad in the first place. I felt your reasons, in both of you. You wanted to get out of your home. You wanted to travel, seek new and exciting places to be. You were searching for yourself. That's what you were doing. No, no." She stopped in front of them. As they cowered, she seemed to grow in size. She didn't move, but she was suddenly looming over them.

Gavin kept with her, moving as she did. She couldn't know he was right behind her. He moved as silent as she did.

She paused, gazing at the humans for another second. "I used to want what you have. I wanted to cling to my humanity desperately, but I was wrong. It's so much more freeing this way. There's no sadness, no regret. You'll see what I'm talking about. The others know. They understand."

Spencer and Cal shrunk down. "Come on, Davy. Can we —please no."

Spencer didn't say a word. He saw what was coming and clasped his eyes shut. Sucking in a breath, he started to envision somewhere else, somewhere safe. He hoped to be there whenever this psycho bitch did whatever she was going to do.

Davy lifted her arms up. She closed her eyes, too, and started to say the words.

And Gavin moved.

His hands grasped both sides of her face, and as she stiffened in reflex, he snapped her neck. He let her fall. He didn't catch her. This wasn't a normal being. Another vampire and he knew they would have a few hours before they woke. This was Davy. She was something entirely else, and he had no idea how long she'd be out.

He turned to Tracey and Gregory, saying, "We have to go. Now."

They both nodded, and in the blink of an eye, the vampires were gone. They snatched the humans with them.

Davy's body was left on the ground.

———

DAVY'S EYES SNAPPED OPEN, but she didn't move from the ground. She remained there, staring at the sky, as she realized what happened.

"Well." The Immortal sat next to her, her legs crisscrossed. "I can't say that I didn't think this was going to happen."

Davy turned her head to the side. She knew only she could see The Immortal, dressed just as herself, but she didn't care. In fact, as she remembered Gavin snapping her neck and the others were gone now, she didn't care about that either.

In fact, she didn't care to comment back to The Immortal so she remained there and looked back to the sky.

She used to care.

Why had she cared?

What had she cared about?

It was nagging her, in the back of her mind, but she couldn't remember. Humanity. That was what she had been talking to the humans about when Gavin broke her neck. Was that what it was? Was that what was missing from her now?

"I'm dead," she spoke out loud, as much to herself as to The Immortal.

"Yep." The Immortal sighed, sounding impatient. "You are. Welcome to the official world of Immortality."

"My human body is dead."

"And you're still here. Still talking. Still breathing, well—" The

Immortal leaned over and pressed her ear to Davy's chest. She paused, then straightened back up. "—you don't need breath anymore, but you're still breathing because that's what is natural to your body."

"Like vampires."

"I guess." The Immortal let out another sharp sigh, glancing around. "I think we should get going. The Mori aren't far now. We can get there before nightfall."

Yes. That was what Davy had been thinking about—the Mori. She needed to get there. She needed to take their magic. She wanted their power too. That was all she'd been focused on before, but now, she had a moment to rethink. Her neck being snapped wasn't something to be taken lightly. This was important. It meant something important. Or it should.

Davy moved her head, her eyes finding The Immortal again.

She was just like herself. Her brown hair was longer. Her dark eyes were watching her back, but while Davy felt shut off inside, The Immortal's eyes had a glimmer of rage, impatience, and thirst. She wanted more. She needed more. She was going to demand more. Davy was separate from The Immortal right now. Before they had been walking side by side. Their hands had grazed each other's. Davy knew the others couldn't see The Immortal, but she was among them as much as they were. But there was distance between herself and The Immortal right now. Davy could think for herself, or so she thought.

She mused to herself, "What if I stayed here?"

"That's a joke, right?"

Davy shook her head. The sky was clear, but some stars were starting to show. It'd be dark in a few hours. She could do it. She could stay there. She could watch the rest of the stars appear and she could wait, do whatever she wanted. The Mori weren't leaving. No one was going anywhere. She could do as Gavin had requested for the humans. She could rest—that was what she would've done before.

She had been human before.

She would've needed to sleep as well, just like Cal and Spencer.

Davy frowned, marring the lines on her forehead. She brought them to her for the very reason she just tried to kill them for. Humanity. Weakness. Emotions. She had been trying to hold onto it, but it was gone.

She knew that now.

Inside was nothing. She felt nothing. She knew that when she would stand and resume her journey for the Mori, The Immortal would walk with her. She would become infected with The Immortal's wishes once again. Hunger. Need. Thirst. That was all The Immortal wanted, but Davy needed to remember what had guided her before all of this.

She was losing herself, and she was in a place right now where she needed to remember who she used to be. Who she used to be was vital. Davy knew that and she closed her eyes, trying to dig deep into herself. She needed to find that girl once more.

"We need to go."

"No." Davy kept searching. Somehow she had switched places with The Immortal. The human she used to be was locked away. Where had she gone? "I think I'll rest."

"Why? You don't need to rest. You're not a weakling anymore. You're not controlled by the same needs as them."

The Immortal was getting riled up. Davy almost smiled, but she masked her amusement.

"Davy!"

"No." Davy shook her head. "I'm going to stay a moment. I'd like to pretend I'm normal again."

"Why?"

"I don't know." She was honest. "But I feel it's important, so that's what I'm going to do." She rolled her head to the side. If steam could've left The Immortal's head, an entire cloud of it would've exploded from her. Her cheeks puffed out and her lips pursed together, she was about to argue, but Davy held up a hand. She motioned it to the side and because she willed it, The Immortal's neck was snapped.

The invisible being didn't drop to the ground next to her. No. She disappeared, that was it, but Davy closed her eyes and did as she said she would. She was going to rest and she was going to try to remember why she started this journey in the first place.

The Immortal would be back, but for now, it was nice to have silence.

CHAPTER 22

"What just happened back there?"

Gavin ignored the human's question. They were still rushing back. He growled, holding onto whichever human he had grabbed. "We have to keep moving."

Tracey was sprinting next to him, holding onto the second human. "The Immortal is no longer our ally. We have to return to our leader."

"What?"

Spencer was held within Gavin's grasp and he looked over, able to meet Cal's gaze even though they were traveling faster than a race car. He shrugged in response to his friend's question. The vampires knew where they were going. All he cared about was that he hadn't died, because he was pretty sure that was what psycho chick had been about to do. Taking their humanity was code for, I want to kill you, bitches. As long as they were away from her, he was golden pie.

Until they got to the river.

When they stopped and saw what was happening, Spencer squeaked, "Can we go back to the psycho chick?"

Cal's hand shot in the air. "I second that."

Before them, right on the river's bank, was the battleground. Wolves were running at each other, tearing each other apart. Gavin leapt out of the path of two wrestling each other. They careened past him, right into the water, and both scrambled back to the bank, but the one on top ripped into the other's throat. Landing on his feet, in a crouching position, Gavin threw his head back. His vampire senses were on full alert. They didn't have time to stand there and take in the bloody and violent scene. They needed to identify allies from enemies and they needed to do it fast.

He yelled out to Tracey and Gregory, "Guard the humans. Roane is here."

Both vampires already had their weapons drawn. A wolf turned on them, leaping in the air. Tracey evaded it and sliced the sword through the wolf's throat. He fell to the ground, right at Spencer and Cal's feet.

"Holy—" Spencer started, his mouth gaping wide open.

Cal let out a harrowing groan and clenched his teeth together. "I suddenly feel warm. " He asked Spencer, "Why would I feel warm right now?"

Spencer shook his head. "Did you piss yourself? Because I think I just did."

Gregory grabbed the wolf's feet and threw it in the air. It landed clear across the embankment, and as it did, it drew the attention from a large group of feuding wolves. Those that were fighting, stopped, sniffed the air, and turned their heads until they were staring at the newcomers.

"Yep," Cal muttered. "Definitely soiled myself there."

A wolf was in mid-air sailing right past them when Gregory grabbed it. He held it up by its throat and leaned in close to growl, "What bloodline are you from?"

The wolf had a silver mane with a black streak around the eyes. It tried to bite him. Gregory adjusted his hold, bracing his arm on the other side of the wolf's neck when Gavin yelled out, "Stop. That's a Christane wolf." His eyes were almost beaming as he looked at Tracey. "Christian Christane was Davy's friend's brother. Right?"

Tracey frowned. She shared it with Gregory, who asked, "So I shouldn't kill the wolf?"

As he held him, another wolf bounded up and pulled the wolf free. Gregory turned to reach for it again, but the rescuing wolf was there. It snarled at Gregory, but it was a soft snarl. There wasn't enough heat behind it to warrant that it was a threat.

The two wolves backed away and then ran to their allies.

Tracey stood close to Cal and Spencer, her sword in front of her. She kept her back to them, shielding them. Gregory and Gavin did the same.

She threw over her shoulder, "We need to identify who are allies and quick."

Gavin clipped his head in a nod. "I agree." He was scanning the battleground. Dead wolves were all over the ground, but as quickly as they arrived, the battle on their bank was already ending. The last wolves that were alive dashed off, going around a bend, and sounds from another battle were heard. Howls. Screeches. Whimpers. Shouts. Screams. They heard all of that, but there was a low rumbling in the distance, too. It sounded like thunder from far away, but it wasn't. As Gavin gripped his sword tighter, he took a step forward. He could feel the rumbling. It was coming from beneath them. It was in the ground, and he felt its magic.

It was strong, maybe too strong for them.

"There are vampires over there." Tracey was moving forward. "I can feel them."

Gavin hurried ahead, but didn't try to draw her back. They went together, hurrying at the same pace. Cal and Spencer jogged behind and Gregory brought up the rear. Right before turning the corner, Tracey melted into the foliage. Gavin was right behind her. The rest fell in line.

"Where are we going?" Spencer asked the group.

None of the vampires answered. All were tense, silent, and scanning their surroundings.

Spencer glanced at Cal, who shrugged and replied, "I dunno. Looking for friends?"

"Shut up," Tracey clipped out. "Both of you."

They kept moving into the forest. There were vampires hidden within the forest. Gavin, Tracey, and Gregory could feel them, but they couldn't identify if they were friend or foe. As they kept moving forward, each was waiting for an enemy to attack, but none happened until they were deep into the forest. The battle sounds lessened behind them, and each vampire started to loosen their hold on their weapons, just a bit.

Suddenly, all three whipped around until they were facing east.

Cal and Spencer were shoved behind them.

Gavin lowered his head, focusing every sense he had on who was coming. "A vampire."

Tracey and Gregory didn't reply. They both knew. All three were trying to identify who it was, but they were coming fast and they weren't being cautious. Whoever it was wasn't trying to hide their approach. Sounds of them whipping past trees, leaves, grass, leaping over logs, they all heard those tiny sounds. It was deafening to a vampire and then the assailant crashed through the last foliage.

They leapt over the entire group and kept going. They never stopped.

"Who—" Gavin's head snapped, watching the vampire. He had two seconds to decide and he did. He yelled over his shoulder, "I'm going after him." He sheathed his sword across his back and before anyone could argue, he was gone. The same sounds came in his wake as he sped after the vampire.

Gregory growled, "He shouldn't have done that."

Tracey threw him a dark look. "What do you expect? We have to find our allies. We need to find Roane."

There was another crashing sound from the forest. It was coming from where the battle was, and both vampires turned once again. It was the same as before. A vampire was coming at them. They knew it. They couldn't hide. They had humans with them. It would've been useless. Any vampire could smell a human. There was no point in hiding.

"We're like sitting ducks."

Tracey gave Gregory another annoyed look, but pressed her lips together. She couldn't argue with him. All she could do was get ready and she was.

Twenty yards.

Eighteen.

Twelve.

Eight.

The vampire was moving faster than the other one.

Five.

One—she leapt as the new vampire soared through the air. The first knew they were there and jumped over them already, but this one landed before them. The new vampire was going to stop, land where they stood, and push off against the ground for more speed. As he came through the last of the trees and brush, his eyes went wide at seeing them, but Tracey was attacking before he saw her, too.

She thrust out her arm, hit him across the chest with it, and rotated swiftly so her other arm was wrapped around the vampire's head. She snapped the neck before she stopped to see who it was, and when the body fell to the ground, her knee was going to his chest. Then, she saw his face.

Horror filled her and she leapt backwards. "Oh no."

Gregory looked and grunted. "Good one, Tracey."

It was Bastion.

CHAPTER 23
DAVY

Davy knew there was something wrong with her.

The Immortal was still silent. Davy had shut her off with an extra boost of power. She was surprised for how long the mute spell was working, but she wasn't complaining. It was nice to be walking with only herself. No vampires among her. No judgments. No disapproval. No quiet condescension. And no voice in her head. When The Immortal was awake, Davy felt her persuasion. She knew she was being pulled in one way, but she wasn't sure of the direction now. All she knew, as she paused with only one more hill to go before she would arrive at the Mori community, was that she wasn't the old Davy anymore.

She tried to remember who that girl had been. There'd been a reason why she was taken captive. She only remembered the torture. The witches had pulled the thread so it was separated from her. And Lucan—it was Lucan who had taken her. He wanted the thread, but there was more.

She frowned, dipping her head down. She couldn't remember the other reason anymore. A faint stirring began in her. She didn't like this feeling, of being turned off to the real soul inside of her. A solid plastic wall had been erected in her and she was shut off from everything that made her *her*.

Davy. She didn't know who that person was anymore.

She closed her eyes and commanded, *"Remind me."*

A memory stirred. *"He'll come after you, you know."*

Lucan shot to his feet, but he didn't go anywhere. He didn't leave. He didn't threaten. He just stood there and waited.

She remembered that conversation—there'd been a guy. No, he was more than just a guy.

"He loves me. Do you think he won't come for me now?" I saw how he stood there. *"Do you think he won't go against you for me?"*

Lucas Roane.

She remembered him now. He was Lucan's twin brother. Lucas turned on his brother to save her. He protected her, and then Lucan came into his brother's house and took her. He took her and all of her friends too.

But no.

Davy needed to remember. She had a purpose before. It hadn't been about power.

It was about friendship, love, trust, making her loved ones safe.

Pippa, the wolf. Brown, the witch. Kates, the best friend. There were others, but those three were her human friends.

Gavin, Gregory, Wren, and Tracey—they were Roane's vampires. They followed him.

She remembered their first kiss.

As if I had no control over my actions, I watched my own hands grasp the front of his shirt roughly. Roane didn't have time to react before I pushed against him and slammed my lips over his. After that I felt like something unlocked inside of me. My eyes snapped shut, and I pressed harder against Roane. As kisses went, it was forced and impersonal.

And another time, when they were together. Then I felt Roane's hand slide around to the back of my neck, and he took a breath before he took over the kiss.

He moved his hand from my leg and slowly reached to untangle my hands from my hair. I gasped as the last finger was detangled, and then my fingers desperately sought his shoulders. He slid in, and I surged forward to wrap my arms tighter around him.

"You have to bear something that you didn't choose. I understand, Davy. I understand it more than you think." Roane tucked his head against mine. His lips brushed the tip of my ear. *"I know what it's like to have your life suddenly change, and it's not what you decided. I do understand that."*

I frowned.

His hand curved around my neck, and I felt the cool touch of his lips when he pressed a kiss to my ear. "You can do this, Davy. We'll figure everything else out." She remembered the last time she saw him.

Roane pulled me into his chest for a hug. After we kissed again, he thought, "I will be back soon or I'll call for you. Stay with Gavin or Wren. They are to protect you from now on."

"Be safe."

He nodded and kissed me a last time. His lips lingered over mine as I clung to him. Every instinct in my body told me not to let him go. Something bad was going to happen. I knew it. I felt it, but so did Roane.

He was the reason she was fighting. He preceded the need for power, before The Immortal became her own entity.

Davy faltered, stopping on the very top ridge of the hill. The Mori were spread before her. There were five hidden in trees a few yards away. They would see her, but she wasn't ready. She didn't want to go in there being detached from herself so she cloaked herself. She needed more time, just a bit more, and she needed to remember this vampire that the human inside of her loved so much.

She ordered in her head, *"Take me to him."*

The air popped, and she was there.

He was standing in front of her, peering out over a cliff as a war waged on beneath his feet. She didn't care about who was fighting. There was blood, sweat, and death all over. Many already died and many more would succumb to the afterlife. She wasn't there for any of them. She moved forward, still cloaked, as she stood beside him.

This man, this vampire, was the reason the girl inside of her lived. She felt her yelling, trying to break free. Even the sight of him, so close and within reach, had her humanity fighting like she had never fought before.

She wanted him.

The rage was whipping through her. It wasn't rage at him or where they were. It was rage at herself. The human was raging to take control once again, but no, that didn't make sense. She wasn't The Immortal. She wasn't the human. She was the in between. Davy cocked her head to the side and lifted a hand. The in-between was curious about this vampire. She wanted to touch him, and as she lifted a hand and extended it to him, the human grew silent. This was what the real Davy yearned for, to be complete with him once again.

Her fingers touched his cheekbone and held there.

He was beautiful.

His eyes were fierce. He had high cheekbones, a strong jaw, lips that Davy wanted to touch, and a warrior's body. Broad shoulders. A trim waist. Fresh blood was all over him, coating of dried blood underneath, but as she looked over him, she saw it wasn't his blood. She found herself wanting to make sure. She wanted to clean him, double-checking that none seeped from a wound on his perfect body.

As she had that thought, she realized that she thirsted for his body. She wanted to touch him, press against him, feel his arms wrap around her. Those lips—her gaze went back to them. She couldn't look away, and she stepped toward him. Her heart began beating, faster and faster. Her mouth was suddenly parched.

She wanted to touch her lips to his.

As if she had cast a spell onto herself, the battle melted away. It was only this vampire and herself.

She drew closer.

Her hand slid down to the side of his mouth, and she was directly in front of him. She stood on tiptoes—her breath held—she needed to feel this man again. Then, with her heart pounding to be freed from her chest, she touched her lips to his. It was soft. This was foreign to her, but the human inside wanted more. She demanded a harder touch, and Davy found herself answering. She pressed closer to him, and as she did, he felt her.

Her eyes widened, as she knew the instant he grew aware of her.

His hands grasped her arms. He stiffened in shock, and just as she feared he would pull away, he took control of the kiss. He caught the sides of her face and moved for a better angle to meet her. He breathed against her mouth, "Davina."

She didn't reply. She closed her eyes and sighed inwardly as he grasped her in his arms. Lifting her, her legs wound around his waist, and he stepped away from the fight. "Davina," he gasped again, but then he pressed her against a tree. "My God—I don't care." His mouth opened, demanding hers to do the same and his tongue slid inside. The brush of him against her was a caress and Davy wound her arms around his neck. She arched her back into the tree, pushing her breasts toward him. She hungered for more. She wanted his touch in the center of her. The human was clambering to get closer and Davy answered.

Her hands went to the side of his face and held him.

He kept kissing her. He was claiming her.

Me. He was claiming *me.*

"*No!*" The Immortal rose up. "*You cannot have her!*"

The Immortal slammed her backwards.

"Davy!" Roane roared, moving with her. He didn't know how she came to him. He didn't care to question it, but he had her. He wanted her back. He had to have her. Whatever was going on inside of her, he needed to grasp her. He had to be her anchor. He could tell that she was losing herself. He reached out for her and Davy tried to grasp his hand, but The Immortal growled, and broke through the barrier inside of Davy.

She gasped.

The power was immense. It spilled out inside of her, coating her insides with its power. It was a burst of cold air. It felt alien, but refreshing, and then it was over. As soon the floodgates opened, she was drowning. There was no chance of a fight inside of her. The power overwhelmed her, instantly suffocating her. Davy was gone. She had lost. The Immortal was free inside of her—her body bent in half. Her back arched upward, and as it did, her body flew in the air.

She flew.

Her entire body transformed. Her body was going up in the air, flying, and her hair billowed out, turning into a black color. A white dress covered her now, and her hands flung backwards. She pushed up into the sky, going higher and higher until she was above the entire foray below.

All of them stopped. The woman in white had taken over the battle, but as Roane watched, she stopped in mid-air and looked down.

A rumbling started in the distance.

Everyone stopped.

CHAPTER 24
THE IMMORTAL

This was her world.

The Immortal relished this sudden experience. She was free. She was alive. She was in control and she gazed down upon the war beneath her. Simpletons. The lot of them. All of them were weak. She wrinkled her nose. Here she was in the air and looking down on them. She was above them.

She was a god to them.

She couldn't believe this was the world Davy honored above everything else. She wanted to be one of those weaklings. No. It was worse. These creatures were more powerful than humans. Davy wanted to be the lowest of the beings.

Never.

Determination coursed through her and as she gazed beneath her, The Immortal's hands formed into fists. She would never be replaced. The human in her would never become human again. Davy's destiny was linked with hers. She would not allow it. She would never go back into the shell, contained as a thread, jumping from one less than worthy human to another. All of them. They were all *stupid*. Everything they believed was wrong.

"Davy?"

She looked over to the cliff. Lucas Roane, the vampire that Davy loved. He was the vampire Talia loved as well, but he had no idea where their love for him was created. He would need to understand. Even now, while she was still acclimating to her new freedom, her body felt a stirring in her core. Her body wanted this vampire, but that was no surprise to her.

Everyone had stopped to gaze upon her, like the goddess she was. They felt her power. There were pockets among them, places where one person had more power than the other, but none matched her. She could feel her superiority over them, so they were ignored. For now.

She lowered herself so she was a few feet from the vampire Davy loved, and she cocked her head to the side. A small grin formed. He didn't move. He didn't dare. She sensed the horror in him. It was recoiling inside, pulling him from her. It was the body's instinct for survival.

She did not come in peace, and his body was trying to pull him as far from her as possible, but still, he didn't go.

Her eyes narrowed. "I can feel what is going on inside of you."

Roane remained frozen in place. This couldn't be. No, no. This couldn't—he choked out, "Davy?"

She shook her head, slowly, and almost gently. "You know I am no longer her." She took a step toward him. Her feet were bare, but she felt no pain. The ground was covered in blood, dirt, rocks, and she felt none of it. She only felt her power. Her dress glided over her body as she walked another step forward.

He jerked backwards. His eyes were piercing. A nerve bulged out from his neck. "Stop right there."

"Now, Lucas," she chided, wagging a finger from side to side. "You know I am not a being you can command. If anyone should know how powerful I am, it must be you." She sent him visions of their past. The first memory was when he realized the thread had jumped to Talia. The second when he watched her bring their dead mother back to life. The third, when Talia stood behind her sister. Her hand was up and she was going to attempt the same event. Tracey was turned into a vampire and Talia wanted to make her human. Lucas stopped her, but The Immortal remembered that moment. She wanted Talia to try. She wanted to test the boundaries of her power, see how far she could go. He stopped her, though, and the two made love. The Immortal made him remember that night. When he slipped inside the thread-holder, held her, and cupped her face. He gazed down into Talia's eyes, but it wasn't Talia he was looking at. It was her.

He loved The Immortal, just as he fell in love with the next thread-holder.

She relished that feeling now. When she slipped into Davy. It was right. The body was right. There was power already in the human, more than she could've imagined, and as soon as the thread was inside of the empath, The Immortal knew she found the right body. At last.

She pushed that memory into Roane's head, too. She wanted him to experience the moment he lost the next thread-holder, because he had. As soon as the thread was inside of Davy, it was over.

Davy was hers.

He fell in love with her vessel once again, and still, even as she pushed more memories into his mind, she knew he wouldn't realize it.

He was in love with her, not the vessel.

Memory after memory, she shoved them all into his mind. Every time she was there. Every time he was feeling her power, not the thread-holder. Her. The last vision was when he drank from Davy's blood. He was drinking her, not Davy. It was her, mixed in the vessel's blood, that filled him and gave him power.

She stood just before him now, her hand still in the air. "Do you feel me?"

His eyes rolled inside and he bent over, falling to his knees. She pulled at her power that was still in his blood. The Roane Hunter-line had turned off his connection to the Hunters. He could no longer sense them, but she felt a faint stirring of them. She felt his Hunter tattoo. It sparked alive and that meant one thing, the Hunters were near. He was still not connected to them. They feared he was too powerful, but his tattoo was burning. It only burned when other Hunters were nearby.

"No," she murmured. She was lost in thought.

Lucas was reliving that moment when he drank from Davy. It was on a loop, repeating over and over again. As he was blind to everything else, she cupped the side of his face. He looked up at her, but he still couldn't see her. She pressed her wrist to his mouth and urged, "Drink."

The other Roane was turned into a human, but that was because Davy wanted it.

Lucas didn't fight her. He gripped her arm and his fangs sank deep into her skin. He was drinking her blood and more of her power went into him. It mixed with the other remnants of her power and everything became more inside of him. He was more. He was more of a vampire. He was more of a Hunter. He was more of her lover. He loved her more. His strength was more.

His power was more, and he was her creature now.

She traced the side of his face as he kept drinking. Her own love for him filled her. She could feel Davy protesting in her. She didn't want this to happen, not while The Immortal was in control, but the human was the one contained now.

The Immortal smiled. Still holding her lover's head to her wrist, she gazed out over the battleground.

She felt Jacith's magic. It was underneath the warring vampires and werewolves. He was there, but he was hiding. He had sensed she was near and he was cloaking himself from her. Even now, she searched each and every being below. Some of them were connected to him. She felt his magic in them. He had given his magic to them. He was aiding one side to win against the other. As she thought this, Roane sank his teeth deeper into her. She looked down, confused.

"Can you hear my thoughts?"

He drank harder, faster.

He could. She had taken over his mind, but that was his response to her.

He wanted her to help his side. She felt him imploring her. He wasn't thinking it, but somewhere his consciousness was reaching out to her. She felt his desires as if they were hers, and for his friends and loved ones to win was one of the most important.

She needed to consider it. If one side won over the other, how would it benefit her? Or would it not? It was Jacith's side versus Roane's. If Jacith won, her eyes narrowed—she had to locate him. She needed to understand what he wanted from her.

She focused on the battle again, waving a hand so she and Roane were cloaked. A group of vampires broke away from the rest. They were racing to find Roane, but they weren't of too much concern. She would stop them once they arrived. The rest resumed their fighting, and she used this distraction to go from one creature to the other.

Jacith had covered his tracks. His magic was disguised inside of his creatures. She had to go from one to another, one at a time, and sink deep into each of them to find the amount of power he had given to each.

Vampires. Werewolves—she found that the wolves were given new power. The vampires held his power, but it was buried deep. Their power and magic had been with them for centuries. Each had been weaned off. It was their own power now, there was no line back to him and that was what she needed to find him.

She focused on the wolves. She went from one to the other, until she had searched the last of the wolves. They were all linked, but there had to be a line back to him. She needed to find the one that held Jacith's power.

Wait.

She stopped and lifted her head. The answer was in herself. Davy would know. Closing her eyes, she began to shift through her own memories. Lucas was still drinking from her and she continued to hold his head in the palm of her hand. *"Davy, Davy. What do you know?"*

"Fuck you!"

Her mouth lifted in a grin. *"Oh, how I've missed your spunk."*

"My spunk? Here's some more spunk."

Davy began fighting her.

The Immortal frowned. She was distracted and released Lucas from her hold. She rallied, focusing all her attention on the human in her. *"You would dare to fight me?"*

"I'd dare to do more. You took my body, you psycho narcissistic bitch."

"And I will take more. I will take your life," The Immortal sparked back at her. *"Remember that I hold the power of your loved ones in my hand, literally. You will do better to work with me than against me."*

The human wasn't happy. The Immoral felt Davy wanting to fight back, but what she spoke was the truth. The human needed her to help her friends.

"The Mother Wolf."

The Immortal frowned. *"The Mother Wolf?"*

"That's the answer. She's the big bad mother Alpha. I'm guessing she's the key to Jacith. She's a psycho bitch like you, so you better kill her. Don't become besties or something. She'll try to take your power."

The Immortal chuckled softly. No one could take her power. No one was a match to her anymore. She thought, *"Thank you, my human."* Then, she released Davy from her thoughts and pushed her back, as far back into the back of her mind as possible. It was the same jail that she herself had been locked in. Then she opened her eyes once more. She turned again to the battleground before her.

Instead of resuming her search for this Mother Wolf, she saw that Lucas wasn't kneeling before her anymore. She turned, and he was behind her. An army of his vampires behind him. All of them were staring at her, and she could sense their fear and rage all at the same time.

They wanted to kill her.

She smiled. *"I don't fear you."*

Lucas growled, *"You should."* But he was conflicted. She saw the damage that all his memories had done to him. He loved her, or he loved the vessel, but he wasn't sure anymore.

"You shouldn't question yourself. You know who you truly love, Lucas." Her voice dropping to an intimate whisper. Her words acted like a

caress to him, trailing over him and filling his mind with the memory of when he made love to Davy. But it was her. He was feeling The Immortal, not the human anymore. He felt The Immortal's power in the vision.

"Stop." He turned away, breaking the connection from her. "Get out of my head."

She whispered, her voice sounding as loud as thunder in his mind alone, *"I cannot. You love me. It was never her."*

He pressed his hands over his ears and roared, "GET OUT!"

His friends started forward, reacting to his plea. They each had varied expressions. Alarm. Fear. Awe. Some were captivated by her, but none of them were a threat.

As they raced around their leader for her, she stepped backwards. Her feet touched air, but she lifted her arms and she was airborne once more. They stopped on the edge of the cliff. There was a woman snarling at her. Her chest was heaving. Her rage was clear and she wanted to murder The Immortal.

"Wren," The Immortal spoke, pulling her name from Davy's memories. "You are in love with Lucas."

The vampire's eyes narrowed and she reached for her, but The Immortal moved back again. She was out of the vampire's reach unless she stepped off the cliff. "There, there," she taunted her. "You cannot fly, the last I remembered."

"I'm going to kill you."

"Yes. You wished the same thing to the human who I share this body with." The Immortal tilted her head to the side. "But you cannot harm either of us. We are both too powerful for you, and you hate it." She flicked her eyes up and down the vampire's body.

She was strong. Long black hair. Fierce dark eyes. Ruby red lips. She had hate and a yearning for power not so unlike The Immortal. She chided, sighing, "I wish that the prophecy had been changed. If I could've merged with you, I think both of us would've been happy with the result."

But no, she had a human in her.

"Davy!"

A new voice sounded and The Immortal lifted herself higher. The voice came from behind the throng in front of her. It was a werewolf, and as she recognized her, she felt Davy fighting once again. This was a friend to her human.

"Pippa."

"Davy." The younger wolf rushed forward. Her sleek hair blowing in the wind. She had recently transformed back to her human body so her clothes were torn. They hung limply from her. The werewolf paid no attention. "Davy, please."

The Immortal didn't say a word. Sympathy filled her and she frowned. Where had that emotion come from? She wasn't keen to human emotions.

Davy. The answer was clear to her. The human in her still had power over her senses. Perhaps that was why she didn't wish to harm this wolf.

She needed to leave. She had to get away from Davy's friends. They had power over her, power that she didn't want anyone to have. She turned her back to the group on the cliff. She could feel Lucas's confusion still. They were linked now, linked even more than they ever had been, but she had to deal with Jacith. He was a problem she didn't want to regret not stopping as soon as she could.

The Mother Wolf. She needed to find her first.

She flew then, searching for her prey.

CHAPTER 25

ROANE

"**R**oane."

As soon as The Immortal was gone, Wren dashed to her leader's side. Falling to her knees, she placed a hand on his shoulder. He was pale and trembling. The Immortal had been inside his head. She frowned, worrying about how to help him. What damage had Davy's Immortality done to Roane?

"I'm okay." Lucas touched her hand and raked his other hand over his face. He could feel her. He could see through her eyes as she soared over the trees now. He needed a block to her. He couldn't let her know what he sensed when she had been accosting him with visions of time with Talia and Davy. Sensing that Wren was about to question him, he held a hand up. "Don't ask me questions. She's in my head still. I can't tell you anything."

Wren pulled her hand free and hastily retreated a step. The vampiress's eyebrows were arched high. The others heard his words and followed her lead. They all looked in fear at their leader now.

He couldn't think.

The Immortal was moving farther away. Their link was lessening, but it was still there. He could feel The Immortal's essence in him. It was pure power and he drew in a sharp breath, feeling his body acclimate to the sudden surge in him. It was overwhelming, but he couldn't do a thing to stop The Immortal right now. Turning to the battle, he could do something there instead.

"Lucas!"

Christian Christane had arrived. He pushed his way through Roane's vampires and stopped next to his sister. Glancing at Pippa, he paused a moment. Their heads bent together. She was filling him in on what happened. When she was done, a different expression crossed the Alpha Werewolf's features. It was close to sympathy, but there was caution as well. His eyes held to Roane's with a wariness Lucas felt in his bones.

Christian was gazing at him as if he were an enemy.

He was so far from that, or he hoped to be. Before Christian could speak, Lucas shook his head. "She gave me power. A lot of it. We can use that and launch another attack."

"They're retreating below. We can follow to where their camp is."

Roane nodded. He signaled for Wren to come to him. She did, so did Pippa and her brother. He spoke, already feeling a grave distance starting between him and them. He would be their enemy soon. The Immortal was in his head, and she just proved that she couldn't be trusted.

He said, "She's in my head. She can feel me, but she's distracted right now. Her power is immense and I don't know how long I'll be able to hold onto my own will. Right now, I'm your ally. You can use me against our enemies, but don't trust me."

Pippa's bottom lip trembled. "Davy's gone?"

She wasn't. He felt her inside of The Immortal, but he said, "There's little hope of getting her back."

"Your brother."

They all turned to Wren. She raised her chin up and squared her shoulders back. Her hands went behind her back and her legs stood apart. She took on a soldier's pose. "He used witches to separate the thread from Davy. He could help, perhaps, in weakening her now."

Christian's nostrils flared. Anger pitted deep inside of him. "Are you joking? He's the reason this entire war is happening."

Wren stiffened, but she didn't back down. "He wants the thread.

Now that she's loose, he'll be scared of her. He caused her pain. I heard the screams. I've no doubt that he'll be more fearful of The Immortal than he will be of us."

"It's a shot."

Christian's head jerked back to Lucas. "You can't be serious?"

He was, so very much so, but there was more Roane needed to say. He couldn't. She would sense his intentions. As it was, he was trying to keep his thoughts clear. The Immortal couldn't know what he was planning, but while she was in his head, he was in hers. He was there. Davy was there too. It was something, at least.

"Roane."

His name was being called and Lucas looked over. What he saw had him closing his eyes as a surge of hope filled him. He shoved it down, almost as soon as it appeared. Bastion pointed behind him, to Gavin, Tracey, and Gregory. There were two others and he could smell the humanity on them. Before going over to greet them, he turned away. The less The Immortal knew, the better.

He said to Wren, "Fill them in. I will lead a charge to where the Romah and Benshire wolves are holed up. That was their first wave. I know there's more farther in the forest."

"After that?"

Lucas hesitated. "After that, I will venture to my brother, but you must head there yourself. Without me."

"Why?"

"The less all of you have to do with me, the better." He could feel The Immortal still flying. She was nearing wherever she wanted to go. She was intent on her target, and he was taking advantage of his distraction, but he knew there were limits. He couldn't risk too much. He held onto Wren's hand and whispered urgently to her, "I will fight. We can win now. The Immortal is seeking The Mother Wolf. After that, I will seek out my brother. He's our only hope in getting Davy back."

Wren went still. Her eyes sought and held onto his.

He saw the fear appear and he swallowed hard. Wren was never scared. She was only angry or hurt, seeing that vulnerability in one of his most loyal now caused his anger to flicker alive. He had it contained, along with all of his emotions, but as it broke free, that was one emotion he wanted to feel. It would blanket the rest. If he was furious, The Immortal would accept that. She wouldn't search for what else was in his mind.

He started to step away. His head lowered, and he was going to leave without speaking to his friends. He didn't want to, but The Immortal couldn't know they were alive. The less she knew, the safer everyone was.

"Roane." Wren grabbed him again.

He heard the dip in her voice, how it grew husky, and his chest tightened at the sympathy he knew would be in her eyes. He couldn't look at her.

"I have to go."

"But Da—"

He pulled away and rasped out, "I know." He had to stop her. She couldn't say Davy's name, because Davy wasn't really lost. She couldn't be. He couldn't think that way. His voice hardened. "I have to go to kill our enemies."

She started to reach for him again, but he went to the edge and dropped to the bottom. Sensing their leader, his men that had been on the battleground turned toward him. They didn't know yet, but they soon would that he was no longer their leader. He was compromised, but until he really was under The Immortal's power, he had one more battle to wage.

Pulling out his sword, he started in the direction that he saw The Immortal fly. She was seeking The Mother Wolf, that was where the rest of their enemies would be. He didn't look behind him, but he registered that the Christane wolves were turning to follow him. Christian and Pippa had followed him, as everyone did.

Wren, Bastion, and the new arrivals remained behind. They had their own mission.

IT WAS DONE. Roane felt it in his gut. The Immortal had won, and he hadn't even known there was a fight for Davy until she was smack in front of him, kissing him. He knew she was different, but he didn't care. It was Davy. She was finally in front of him. He could hold her. He could taste her, touch her, inhale her. But, it had been too good to be true. There'd been something off about her, he felt that in the back of his mind, but he turned it off. He didn't want to question how Davy came to be. He was just glad she was there.

Then the other shoe dropped. It wasn't her.

And now, as he led his army into the forest with his sword ready in his hand, The Immortal was swirling around inside of himself. He wasn't sure if it was even him in there, or just her. He felt under her control, but there was a small tunnel. He felt Davy before. She was still in The Immortal. If he could get to her, if there was a way of breaking her free, he had to take it, but for now—they crested the last hill and below them, they could hear the screams.

The Immortal had already arrived.

It was chaos. Hundreds of Benshire wolves were dead on the ground. The image was almost as bad as the battleground they just left, but there was an army missing. Roane searched the woods. The Romah vampires were there. It wasn't just the Benshire line. Jacith had brought his oldest and most powerful vampire family.

"No!"

Christian and Pippa stood next to him, but the rest of the Christane wolves streamed around them. They began to attack the rest that still lived, but before the first could lunge in the air, a bloodcurdling scream went through the air. It went through everyone, sending chills down their spines.

At the top of the next ridge stood The Immortal and The Mother Wolf. One in her white dress and the other in her blue robe.

A deep roar ripped from Christian. "No. She's mine to kill." He surged forward. "NO!"

Davy looked over at them. He hated to call her that, but he loathed to keep referring to her as The Immortal. It was a grand title that she didn't deserve. She wasn't grand. She wasn't anything except a monster, who took the real Davy away.

She was holding The Mother Wolf up with one hand at her throat. Genuine confusion flashed over her features as she looked from Christian to the woman in her grip. She held her up higher. "You wish to kill this one?"

Pippa started crying. Lucas heard her sniffling from the other side of her brother. He closed his eyes—this stranger who had Davy's body was so cold.

Anger was mounting in Christian and he nodded, stiffly. "Yes." His tone softened, but only a little bit. He was holding back the rage.

The Immortal—Roane couldn't call her Davy. It was too painful to think of her name—met his gaze. She was weighing her options. Her head tilted to the side and her long dark hair swept over her face from the wind. She was impervious to the weather. It was normally hot and humid where they were in Central America, but a cold front moved into the air. The temperature dipped low. The werewolves and vampires, who were impervious to weather as well, were starting to shiver. And through it all, The Immortal was immune to all of it, even the blood that seeped around her bare feet.

He looked around—so many bodies, so much death. The river would run red from the blood that night, but this was what they all signed up for.

War. Death. Carnage.

The Immortal still hadn't decided what to do with The Mother Wolf. She turned back and brought the older woman closer to her. She was studying her like she was a new creature for her to understand.

"No." Roane started forward.

Recognizing his voice, The Immortal looked again. More confusion crossed her face, but she didn't say anything. She held her comment and waited.

"What are you doing?" Christian reached for Roane.

"I'm going over there."

"No, Lucas."

"Don't. Please."

The last was a whimper from Pippa, Davy's friend. Roane's stomach clenched, but he moved out of Christian's reach. Lowering his voice, he said, "I'm going to her. Someone has to try to contain her."

"Contain that?" Christian's statement was a whip, lashing at him.

"Yes." She was too powerful to allow on her own, and he had no idea if he could control her. He could try, at least. He had to try. "None of ours can get hurt."

"One of ours already did." Pippa was glaring at Davy's body. Her own growl began to build in the back of her throat.

Roane started forward again, but he said as a goodbye, "I'll ask her to leave The Mother Wolf for you, but return home after that."

"Lucas—"

"I mean it!" He glared at them before turning away once again. "Leave. Go home." "*Go and be alive,*" he thought before crossing the distance until the next ridge.

The Immortal was waiting. She had heard his thought and she asked now, in his head still, "*Is that what you think will happen? You will die.*"

He faltered just beneath the hill she stood upon. He held her gaze, never wavering. "*Either my body will die or my soul will. Either way, all is lost.*"

"*Nothing is lost. It's just a new life. That is all.*"

Everything was lost, but he held back those words. She heard them, a darkness flashing in her eyes, but both let it go. He gestured to The Mother Wolf. "*My friend has come this entire way to kill her.*"

He remembered the stories spoken about The Mother Wolf.

"*The Alpha went to The Mother Wolf,*" Pippa said.

The Mother Wolf knew about Davy. She was connected to The Immortal.

He remembered when he first saw her. There, in the middle of five Goliath-sized wolves and four Romah guards in full armor, was a woman. He knew who she was.

This was The Mother Wolf, the one that Christian told him about. She was stunning. Black hair fell free and loose past her shoulders. She wore a blue and silver robe. The colors were striking, matching the air of strength she was emanating. Her eyes were dark. Her lips were bright red, curved into a half smile, and her head was raised in a confident and authoritative manner, but that wasn't all that clung to her—magic.

She had been so powerful then. And now, her arms hung limply, her head fell back as if she were a doll, and her eyes were dull. They were almost lifeless. The Immortal had done this. It was a shock.

She was nothing now. She was weak.

The enormity of The Immortal's power shouldn't have surprised him, but it did. And with each action that showed even more power, a part of his hope died inside of him. Swallowing painfully, he asked, "Why did you go after her?"

"She has his magic." The Immortal peered at The Mother Wolf again. "It's inside of her. He planted it in her and I need to follow it to where he is. He must die. He is the only one who could be troublesome to me."

Roane continued to feel his insides spilling out over him. "You mean he's the only one who could match your power."

"No." She snapped back to attention. "Never. He is no match. He is beneath me. It's why he is hiding. All his magic, it's everywhere. It's in the wolves. It's in his vampires. It's in the ground." A light gleamed in her eyes. "The ground. He's underground." She focused on Mother Wolf and placed her hand between the woman's breasts. The Immortal leaned closer, peering where her hand was and she began to say under her breath, "You are in her. I can feel your magic. There is a path. I must follow where it goes."

As the last word was spoken,=, the air shifted.

Roane could feel a heaviness, as if something was poured into the atmosphere around them. Then, The Immortal uttered one word, "Ignite," and an explosion happened. He covered his eyes. The light was blinding, but when he looked back, Mother Wolf was hanging in the air. The Immortal had suspended her there and a light shone from inside of her. A string, or a line, moved out from Mother Wolf's body and he turned, tracing it all the way down the hill they stood on, through the valley of the second battle, and past where Christian and Pippa stood.

The Immortal came down to stand beside him. She was watching the trail. "It goes back to the water. He is back there."

She started forward.

A surrealness had come over everyone. There were few of the Benshire werewolves alive, but those who still survived ceased fighting Christian's pack. As The Immortal walked past them, they moved apart. An opening cleared for her and she left, either unmoved or indifferent to the fear that everyone had for her.

He looked back to The Mother Wolf, but she was still in the air. There was no fight left in her.

Christian and Pippa hurried to his side once The Immortal was gone from their eyesight. Christian peered up at his enemy. The corners of his mouth turned down, and he remarked, "The victory in battle has lost its appeal."

Pippa looked up at him. "You need to kill her. You can't let her live through this."

Christian's frown deepened. Roane could hear the regret in his voice when he replied, "I won't, but it's not an honorable death anymore. I'm merely ending her suffering."

"*Roane.*" The Immortal spoke in his head. "*Come.*"

He had to go, but he said to Christian, "Thank you for being my ally."

Pippa moved around so she could see him squarely. "You're leaving?"

"*Roane.*"

"The Immortal." He gestured in the direction she had gone. "She's calling me."

"That's annoying," Christian bit out.

Roane laughed. There was nothing else to do. There were no other reactions to feel. All he could do was laugh, because at the very least, it was annoying.

He rested a hand on the Alpha Wolf's shoulder and lowered his head in a small bow. "Our time has come to an end. I hope to see you on the other side one day."

He started to pull back, but Christian covered his hand with his. It was a rare gesture, but before Roane could do anything or say anything, the Alpha Wolf pulled him in for a hug. It was brief. Each clapped the other on the back; they had come a long way. There'd been mistrust and a reluctant aligning with each other. They loved the same woman, but now they were on the same side. They had another similar enemy.

Christian stepped back. "Go get your woman back."

Roane swallowed a lump.

He couldn't think about her. Those thoughts were erased and he stepped aside to face Pippa. "Thank you. I know you came to help your friend."

Tears were trailing down her face. The younger wolf lifted a hand and wiped at some of them, but they were replaced with new tears. Roane didn't think they would end soon, and he had to admit that he wished he could cry alongside her. Instead, he murmured, "If I can, I will save her."

"You are lying to them," The Immortal chided him. *"You know she is lost. Do not give them false hope."*

He thought back, *"They will fight otherwise. I am saving their lives."*

He waited, but there was silence from her end. Pippa hugged him, and then he left them. He walked on the same path The Immortal had gone, and once he was gone from their eyesight, he heard one last bloodcurdling scream.

The Mother Wolf was dead.

CHAPTER 26
LUCAN

He stood at the highest point among the Mori lands.

The winds had shifted. What he thought was his greatest enemy was now his greatest ally. Another Mori came to stand beside him and he spoke, knowing it was Jiyama's father, "The thread has become her own entity."

The elder Mori glanced at him. There was a pause and the air was heavy with tension. It was known that Jiyama was gone. Her body was never found. None sensed where her essence was, and stories of how another Mori was killed at the hands of The Immortal had spread fast. Another Mori witnessed the murder, but he had retreated to share the information. He hadn't engaged. When the rest of the Mori realized their new danger, a council had been called. Warriors were placed near the outer edge of their land to report back the events that were unveiling beyond their river's boundary.

Lucan heard about the transformation, and he was told how The Immortal had seemingly cast a spell over his brother.

Jiyama's father, Jeoji, asked, "What will happen now?"

Lucan grunted. "If I had to guess, my brother's friends will want to come here." Jeoji turned to him, but Lucan added, "We created this. We unbalanced the thread inside of her. They'll want us to help fix it."

"We?" A warning growl. "You created this problem. We had nothing to do with this."

Lucan turned and faced the Mori's leader. They were face-to-face, eye-to-eye, and while one held all the power and magic of a Mori vampire, the other was more dangerous. Lucan was human. He remained in his weak vessel because of one thing: the thread. He wanted that thread inside of him, and he knew that he would be told of visitors traveling their way. What he predicted would come true. His brother's friends would seek him out, and he would help them because at this moment, their wishes co-aligned. All of them wanted The Immortal contained. Afterwards, that was another issue, but he said to Jeoji now, "Do not play the ignorant fool. I was one of you. You and your men traveled with me in search of the thread. You and your men, my brothers too, helped me capture my brother's lover. You have known since the beginning my wish for the thread. It is why you allowed the child to come into this clan. Do not act innocent. You have shed blood, just as I have."

Jeoji was older, wiser, but he knew Lucan spoke the truth. Blame fell on his shoulders, perhaps more because he never stopped this one. "My daughter loved you." He let that sentence hang between them. His daughter, who was missing. His daughter, who had been so curious about the thread-holder. His daughter, who would never leave without telling him or her mother. His daughter, who he thought would marry this man standing in front of him.

His regrets were deep, and he added one more to the pile. He pulled his robe tighter over himself and glanced to where the war was still going on. "We have heard their screams. We can smell their blood. We can even feel their pain, and all of them were wiped out by one being that we set free. Capturing The Immortal is on our shoulders. We will assist you by whatever means you find necessary. That creature must not be allowed to remain alive."

There was an unspoken message between them, and Lucan accepted it. There was no proof, but Jeoji suspected him of his daughter's death. They would help him take The Immortal down, but afterwards he would be cast out. It was the way of their clan. He'd be exiled once again, but it wouldn't matter.

Lucan would get the thread. He would get that power, even if he would die in the process. It had become his sole obsession. He turned to go, but said over his shoulder, "Lower the shield. Allow my brother's friends in."

CHAPTER 27
ROANE

He trailed behind The Immortal. She kept going, past the first battlegrounds and farther down the beach. The Mother Wolf was killed, but the line that led them to Jacith still existed. He didn't know how that was, but he didn't question it. The less he thought, the better, but he couldn't stop waves of grief from crashing over him. They came one at a time and every one was suffocating. He couldn't breathe so he kept going, sometimes blindly. He kept going. This thing, whatever she was, continued ahead. He knew she was aware of the suffering inside of him, but she paid him no attention.

"It is not because I do not care." She paused, and turned so she could see him from one eye.

He stopped, but he said nothing.

She kept going, "It's because there was no other way. You don't comprehend it. No one does."

"Comprehend what?"

"My existence."

They were coming to a waterfall. Roane heard the water falling earlier, but the sound was nearly deafening now, even to him. Still, he could hear her fine as she walked around a pile of large boulders. They were setting out on the bank, and as she circled them, he saw there was a trail that led underneath the waterfall.

"He's undergound." Her words came back to him, and he understood. Jacith was beneath everything. He was in the cave below the waterfall. The Hunter in him was telling him to pull back, proceed with caution, but The Immortal didn't have the same instincts. She walked freely without a care for herself. She spoke with the same freedom, speaking loudly, "Since I was created, I was always contained and hidden within a human. My creator did that because humans were thought to have the compassion to restrict me. That wasn't true. What they had to restrict me was their weakness. I couldn't exist if they did, and since it was their body, they were the host. They contained me. All that changed with Lucan and his coven. They weren't pulling me free of Davy. They were changing her. She was turning into something that wasn't human anymore. When that happened, I was able to get a foothold in her. I've been steadily gaining a foothold in her ever since."

She dipped underneath the water and held a hand up. There was nothing hanging to be lit, but small bursts of fire floated in the air, lighting their way.

He asked as he followed, stepping onto the damp rock path, "What did you mean before? What is it that no one understands?"

She paused. Just beyond her shoulder, the light was brighter as if they were about to step into a large opening in the cave. A low baritone voice was chanting in there, and Roane could feel the magic all around him. It was thick, sending shivers up and down his back. The hair on his neck stood up, but this was The Immortal's show. If she wasn't worried, he didn't think he needed to be.

Or he hoped.

Her eyes flicked over his face before the corner of her lip lifted up. "It was never about me becoming one with Davy. It was either me *or* her. That was the question. Always."

He frowned. "What do you mean?"

"I couldn't exist if she did."

She waited, letting that statement linger.

Roane cocked his head to the side. His frown deepened. Understanding and horror dawned on him at the same time. "You—you were planning this the whole time." He felt gutted.

Her slight grin turned smug and she stepped around the corner into the larger open area. "You are right." Her gaze trailed to the man chanting in the middle of the cave.

Roane couldn't move forward. Everything in him was locked in place. He needed to run, but he was the Hunter. He was a vampire. He was Lucas Roane. He did not run, but right there, in the realization that The Immortal had been planning this move all along, he knew survival meant running.

He jerked around, as if he were actually going to go. He tried making himself.

He couldn't.

The Immortal laughed. It was a soft graze against his ears and he winced, instantly hating the sound. "You've been looking for Jacith. You said it was because he was the only one equal to you, but—" He couldn't bring himself to say the rest. His gut was saying otherwise. One didn't seek out their enemies first. No. One would seek out an ally first, and she'd been seeking out the sorcerer since she came to be.

This wasn't enemy territory to her.

She wasn't cowering. She wasn't sneaking. She wasn't even being cautious.

She stood, right in front of one of the most feared sorcerers since Roane had been alive and there was no fear.

He finished as all of his insides threatened to spill out of him, "He's not your enemy, is he?"

"No." A full smile stretched on her face, and she turned around.

Jacith had his eyes closed. He was wearing a similar robe as The Mother Wolf, blue and silver. The hood was pulled low over his face so his eyes were shielded, but his power was immense. It rippled through the cave. His arms were stretched out as he continued to chant, he allowed them to continue their conversation, until he sensed The Immortal's attention. His eyes opened and a smile appeared on his face.

The sight sickened Roane.

Jacith lowered his arms and his head at the same time. He bowed to The Immortal. "As we meet at last."

He held a hand out, and The Immortal took it, letting him hold it as he looked back up. She echoed, "As we meet at last."

The two shared a smile before Jacith removed his hood.

Roane had never met him, but he heard about him. Everyone had. Jacith was tall in his vampire body, but once the hood left his head, he grew in height. He stood at another four inches, towering over the both of them. His hair was black and gray, all mixed together and his eyes were a clear blue. A white line shone around his irises, but Roane had a dreaded guess that that was The Immortal's influence over him. She was assisting him with magic in some way.

"Lucas Roane." Jacith tucked his hands to his chest, his robe's sleeves hanging low to the ground. He moved around The Immortal and approached. He scanned him up and down. "You are every bit as powerful as she said you would be."

Roane needed to get out of there. As fast as possible. He began to move backwards, an inch at time.

The Immortal studied him alongside Jacith. She folded her arms over her chest and nodded. "He is. The Hunters are close by. His tattoo is alive. I can feel it." She glanced to him. "Can you?"

Jacith's eyes narrowed, a mere fraction of an inch. "Of course, I can."

"Really?" Her grin turned smug, just the slightest hint. "He has power. We can draw from it."

As she spoke those words, Jacith's eyes lit up. An eager gleam grew bright, and he moved forward. Roane went still. He was a prey to the sorcerer. He was focused on getting out of there, but at the cold sliver that rang down his back, he reassessed the situation. Hunters. His tattoo. They could draw his power, the last shoe dropped then.

"You promised him my power." Roane didn't even ask. He knew that was what happened. It was the only thing that made sense.

Surprise and pride flashed over her features. "You're smart, Lucas. Yes, I did."

"All that you said before, about how I loved you, all of that was a lie."

"No. That was the truth. You do love me. I've been drawing you to me for decades. The thread-holder before Talia would've found you, too, if she had been smart enough to realize her wishes weren't her own." She spoke dryly, a wry twist at her lips, "She was more accustomed to females so when she began dreaming of you, she knew something was wrong." Her eyes grew hard. "But I will have my time with that thread-holder. I know she is waiting. Her time is soon, but until then, everything else was a lie." She shook her head. "I don't love you, Lucas. I'm not a crazy, besotted weakling like the others. You have power. You have lots of power and you will be giving all of that power to Jacith." She glanced at the sorcerer. "He was very keen to get his hands on you. That was my part of the deal. I was to deliver you to him."

"How?"

Roane wasn't sure he wanted to know, but he asked anyway.

"Your brother helped so much, but I needed more power to break free from Davy. Every time she was unconscious, and there were a lot of times your brother's coven made her pass out from pain, I called onto Jacith. I drew him to me. He loaned his power to me and here I am, returning it to him. You. You are my payout."

"This is a joke, right?"

Jacith was advancing on him. His sick delight was making Roane's stomach roll over. He couldn't defeat the sorcerer and he knew he couldn't defeat The Immortal. A brief thought of ending it his way, his power intact, flashed through his mind.

"Don't!"

He met her gaze. *"Why not?"*

"Because—" she glanced to Jacith, but his back was completely to her. He was focused only on Roane. Her eyes narrowed and a cold wall fell over her face. She thought back to him, *"Because you were my bait for him. That's why."*

"Bait?" He couldn't keep up with the changes. A new alliance was popping up every other minute. He asked her in his mind, *"What do you mean by bait?"*

"Wait." Her voice was calming. *"You will see."*

As Jacith grew closer, Roane was backed up into the wall. He didn't feel the cold wetness of the rock behind him. Jacith's eagerness was rolling over him, overwhelming him. The sorcerer reached up and gripped Roane around the throat. At the contact, Roane gasped. His blood was on fire. Every inch of him was burned and he felt his insides being sucked out. Jacith was drawing on his power.

No matter what she said, this was the end.

Roane closed his eyes. He didn't know if the sorcerer was in his head or not, but he made himself think of Davy. He tried to talk to her. *"Davy. I love you. Can you hear me?"* As he spoke, his hand reached for a dagger tucked behind his back. His hand found the handle and wrapped around it, gripping it tight. A tear slipped from his eye. *"Davy, I don't know if you can hear me or not, but no matter our ending, we'll have the next life together. A new chapter. I promise."*

He imagined she was there. She was standing in front of him. He could hold her. He could rest his forehead to hers and whisper, *"I love you so very much, to the deepest parts of my soul. You, Davina, you make me an honorable man. You are why I have fought in this life and you are why I will continue to the next. I love you, wherever you are."*

She was there, gripping his hands with hers. Her tears mixed with his and she whispered back, kissing him at the same time, *"I love you, too. I will be there. I'm waiting for you, Lucas. Come to me. Come to me."*

They were kissing. They were hugging. They were happy—and at the last thought, he pulled his dagger out and plunged it into Jacith's stomach. The sorcerer jerked back, a thunderous roar ripping from him. Lucas was unfazed. He pushed up from the wall and held onto the dagger with a better hold, then he pushed it as deep as he could. His hand was inside of the vampire, and knowing it wouldn't be enough, he thrust his other hand and wrapped his fingers around Jacith's heart.

No creature could live without a beating heart.

He yanked it out.

The body crumbled to the floor, but his other hand held onto the dagger. The Immortal screamed, and in the midst of it all, Lucas held the sorcerer's heart in his hand and the dagger in his other. A feral smile adorned his face as he met The Immortal's horrified eyes.

He said, "Oops."

He threw the dagger at her.

"**N**O!"
She deflected the dagger.

It flew right at her, would've landed smack center in her chest, but The Immortal lifted her hand. The dagger stopped and flew right back at him, except it sheathed itself into the cave wall behind it. Roane froze, his eyes wide at how quick her response was. She rushed to Jacith's side, and placed her hands on his chest.

Roane didn't say a word. She could've killed him with the dagger, but didn't. She could still kill him, but after that one scream, she was concentrating. Resting on her knees, her eyes closed, she remained perfectly still.

Roane stood there. He needed to run, but he stayed. He needed to see what she was doing, and when a black coloring formed under her hand and began to move up her arms, he had a good idea. She was absorbing all of Jacith's power.

Roane turned to go. It was time, but before he could even form the thought, she opened her eyes, pure black, and said, "Stay."

An invisible wall slammed in place. He couldn't get through. Hitting it only hurt his hand. It felt like ten cement walls glued together. Vampire strength couldn't stand up against magic. He waited, leaning against the wall as The Immortal continued to pull the rest of Jacith's magic into her. When she was done, the black coloring was gone except as she stood and opened her eyes once more. They were still black.

Her hair billowed out behind her. She didn't say a word and Roane didn't think she could. The magic was settling inside of her, and another few seconds, her normal chocolate brown eyes snapped back into place. Her hair rested against her back again and her normal coloring came to her face.

Jacith was different. He was a corpse with a giant hole in the chest. A second later, his body burst into flames. He really was dead now. He couldn't come back from that.

Roane grunted. "If I knew it would've been that easy to kill him, I would've done it a long time ago."

"You're a fool," The Immortal spat at him, waving her hand in the air again.

The invisible wall fell from behind him and Roane caught himself. She swept past him, and he followed behind. "What do you mean?" He was waiting for the wrath to come out on him, but she kept heading back toward the waterfall.

She said over her shoulder, "Everyone has a weakness. Jacith's was just like a normal vampire. You had to get close to him in order to kill him, and that was my mistake."

He was still waiting for her wrath.

Sensing his thought, she said, "I wanted to kill Jacith. That was why I gave you my power."

Wait.

"What?"

She glanced back, rolled her eyes, and turned back. "Everything I've said to you was a lie since I broke free. Everything, Lucas."

"You told me that I loved you."

She said, "You don't."

"You told me that Jacith was your enemy."

"He wasn't, but he was at the same time."

"You told me that you were going to offer me to him as a payback."

"I was. That was my plan."

He frowned and stopped walking. "I don't understand."

"You don't have to." She kept going. When he didn't resume following, she gestured to him and commanded, "Come."

His feet and legs started moving. Roane had no control over them. He sighed. There was a lot that he couldn't control anymore, but the one thing he could—his murderous rage. He wanted to kill.

He wanted to kill *her*.

LUCAN

LUCAN STOOD UNDERNEATH A TREE, just behind his brother's friends and downwind from them. They were all lying toward the top of a hill, peering at the Mori on the other side. He had been notified of their presence and circled around, taking a tunnel underneath so he could sneak up, but as they all lay plastered to the ground, he didn't have to be stealth.

They were talking too much. A blind elephant could've have snuck up on them.

"So," one of the humans cleared his throat, speaking up. He pointed over the hill. "Just so I get this straight, the four of you were captured by this dude in there."

No one responded. A beat passed and Gavin said, "Yes."

"He tortured you guys—"

"He tortured Davy."

The human nodded. "The psycho chick that killed that one other cute chick, right?"

Wren glared at him. "Do you have a point?"

"Yeah. I mean, why are we heading back there when we should be leaving?" The human propped himself up on his elbow, lying on his side. The other human was still behind him, but he was facing the rest of the others.

Lucan frowned. There didn't seem to be fear on this human, just curiosity and a dry sarcasm. He sniffed the air. There was another smell to him, too. He couldn't place the smell, but it clung to both of the humans heavily.

Gavin hissed, motioning with his hand. "Get back down. Now."

"Okay." The human rolled to his back and folded his hands over his chest. He gazed up at the sky. "But back to my point. Tell me again why we're seeking out some dude who wants to kill all of you guys."

"Because he doesn't care about us. He cares about the thread." Gavin sat up. His voice raised to a normal volume. "And because that means we have the same enemy."

"What are you doing?" Wren yanked him back down.

"Wren," Gavin started, sitting up and staring behind them.

The last human muttered, "I could go for a smoke. Seriously. Seeking out another bad guy's got me jonesing hardcore."

His friend threw him a grin, kicking his feet. "Don't stress, Cal. The way I figure it we're hanging out with a bunch of vampires."

"We're going into another group of vampires," the one called Cal groaned. "And they aren't friendly."

"But we just escaped an entire army of other vamps and werewolves. Like, holy shit, vampires and werewolves. No one will believe us, but we saw those things."

"We're going to die, Spencer." He shot him a dark look.

"Yeah." Spencer shrugged. "But we sure have lived, haven't we?"

"Shut up," Wren growled at both of them. "We either move or we leave. We need to do something to help Lucas."

Gavin, still looking into the trees behind them, said, "Wren—"

"Let's go." Wren collected her sword and crouched to a crawling position. She could maneuver over the hill, continuing to slink toward the village.

Gavin stood up and Lucan grinned. His brother's best friend was staring right at him, and as the others gasped in shock, Lucan stepped forward. He said, "Welcome." All of them jumped to their feet, grabbing for their weapons, and he turned his smile toward the two on the end. "You brought more humans. My friends will welcome their dinner tonight."

Cal frowned and scratched behind his ear. "Say what?"

CHAPTER 29
ROANE

They'd been walking through the forest until it got dark. Roane kept waiting for her to fly away, or go invisible, or do something magical, but she never did. She trekked ahead of him, walking as if she were a human, until they came to a clearing. She stopped and gazed around, sighing. "I suppose we can sleep here tonight."

His eyebrows pinched together. "You sleep?"

"No." She waved her hand in the air and a bonfire appeared. Two sleeping bags were on the floor, on either side of the fire. She dropped down on one of them and crossed her legs. "But you do."

His head moved back an inch. He couldn't bring himself to give her a compliment. She was being nice.

"What?" She laughed. "You're surprised I might have a soul in me? I was inside of Davy for a year. Some of her niceness rubbed off on me."

She had Davy's face. Davy's voice and right now, as she was staring at the fire, it was like she was Davy. His stomach clenched. This was not Davy, and he couldn't forget that. Ever.

She rolled her eyes, lying down on her side. Her hands tucked under her head, acting like a pillow. "I'm not her, but I'm not that bad either, Lucas Roane of the Hunters."

He grunted, dropping down onto the other sleeping bag. "You replaced my girlfriend. I think you are."

Her eyes found his through the fire. A dark and sober expression filled them. "When it comes to the question of you or someone else existing, you might be surprised at the lengths you'll go to live."

"You're not a person."

"And yet here I am." She rolled to her back. "Talking like a person. Breathing. Feeling. I think I'm more human than you are, even."

She was lying. She had no soul. Davy had been the soul in her. He continued to study her, and she let him. He didn't need to sleep that much, maybe a few hours if even that, but after a while his eyes closed, and he slept.

"Lucas."

He stood up. Everything around him was dark, but that was Davy. She was crying. More sobs came from her, and he called out, "Davy? Where are you?"

"Lucas?"

The crying stopped. Her voice grew clearer. "Lucas!"

"I'm here. Where are you?"

"Here." And suddenly, she was. She was smack in front of him. Her dark hair lay straight down her shoulders and her eyes were wide. "What are you doing here?" She touched his shoulders and patted him. "Are you real? Are you really here?"

"Davy." He closed his eyes and groaned. She was right in front of him. He could touch her. Taking her hands in his, he pulled her close and tucked his forehead to the crook of her neck and shoulders. He clasped her tight. "Oh my God. I can feel you."

Her arms wrapped tightly around him and she pressed up on her toes. Her whole body moved even closer against his.

He savored this. He had her. Finally. He could hug her, kiss her, feel her, taste her, inhale her.

"Oh my God."

He felt her tears against his shoulder. He only wanted to hold her longer.

"Oh my God," she repeated. More tears. "Is this a dream?"

Yes. He was asleep. If this was real or not, he didn't want to question it. He just wanted to draw strength from it. If only in his dreams, if that were the only place he could see her, it would be enough. It would be more than enough.

"This is a dream." Her tears lessened. She pulled away, but he held on. He didn't want her to pull all the way away. She leaned back so she could look into his eyes. What he saw there had his rage going again. She knew this moment wouldn't last. He would leave again. She said, "Lucas, if this is real or not, you have to know about her."

He shook his head. "Stop, Davy. I just want to hold you. I don't want to think of her."

She stepped farther back. Her hands fell to his arms. Her fingers dug in, holding onto him with a cement grip. "No, but you have to. This is important. She's going to destroy the only person who is a threat to her. She's an innocent."

He leaned back. "An innocent? She'll never be innocent."

"No. You don't understand." She clenched onto him even harder. Her fingers were turning white. "You think she's all powerful. You think there's no hope, but there is. Someone is missing. Who is missing? Ask yourself why they're missing? And she's not the innocent, but the innocent is the key. There are people coming. They will help. People you have forgotten about. People that you started in motion. Remember, Lucas. Think, Lucas."

Wind started blowing around them. It was growing faster, starting to tug at him. Their time was ending. He was getting pulled away.

He didn't want that. He wanted to only savor her.

"Lucas!" She framed his face with her hands. The wind was like a tornado. It tripled in power and she was yelling so he could hear her. "I can come back! You can bring me back!"

The wind was too much. It was a vacuum. He was pulled away and their hands held onto each other. He was in the air, but still, his fingers laced with hers. She was trying to keep him there, but right before he was yanked backwards, she yelled again, "Bring me back!"

He was gone.

His eyes snapped open and he jerked upright. "Did you do that?"

The Immortal was on her sleeping bag. It was light out, and she turned her head lazily to him. "Do what?"

"My dream. Davy." His breathing was ragged. "Did you do that?"

Her eyebrows knotted together and the corners of her lip curved down a bit. She sat up, straightening her dress. "No, but now I'm intrigued. What did you dream about?"

"Why do you lie?"

Her eyebrows arched high. "I'm not. I really want to know now. What did she say?" A half grin teased at her lips. "Did she tell you of my demise?"

"Someone is missing . . . the innocent is the key. There are people coming. They will help. People you have forgotten about. People that you started in motion. Remember, Lucas. Think, Lucas."

Davy's words haunted him. They were ricocheting around him, and they felt so real. Her desperation was still with him. He could feel it. He could feel her.

He sat back down.

Davy had been there. Whether real or not, she was there. She was giving him a message. He shook his head and lifted his gaze. The Immortal was watching him. Her eyes were piercing. He asked, *"Are you in my head?"*

She didn't respond. Her lips pressed together, then she stood up. "Let's go. We've rested long enough. Neither of us is human. We don't need that much sleep."

She wasn't in his head anymore. She started forward, but that realization echoed strong inside of him. She wasn't in his head, and she was pissed about it. Then, did he dare hope, that could mean that Davy had been real?

He swallowed hard, painfully, but hope bloomed inside of his chest. It was small, but it was there.

He could bring her back.

SOMEONE MISSING.

An innocent.

And people were coming back.

That was Davy's message to him, and Roane tried to decipher it. Who was missing? Davy. Everyone. Himself. He couldn't wrap his mind around who she meant and the innocent—no one was innocent. And who was coming back? She was insistent that there was hope, but as he followed The Immortal, he couldn't figure out who Davy meant. The one person who had enough power to defeat The Immortal was Jacith and he was dead. Thinking about it, Roane could've cursed himself. He hadn't been thinking, but The Immortal was in his head. He couldn't have been thinking ahead. She would've known then.

"Okay." They'd been steadily winding up around a mountain and The Immortal stopped. She stepped out on an edge. "We're here."

He looked to where she was gazing and was surprised. "That's the Mori village?"

His mind was racing. Why had she come here? What did this mean? He glanced sideways to her. "Are you here for my brother?"

Her eyes narrowed, but a hint of a grin flashed over her face. It was a glimmer, and it was gone just as quick as it showed. "No, but your brother could become an annoying pest." She leaned forward and said, "Silence. I need to hear."

She was listening to the entire village. He should've been surprised, but nothing surprised him anymore, not when it came to this creature. She could bend the world's rules. She could be in his head. She could do almost anything. It was hard to imagine that Davy could be brought back, and yet, The Immortal was no longer in his head. A small victory happened, and she hadn't gotten into his head since. She had stopped many times on their trek, and she kept glancing back at him. She was trying to understand what happened, how she was locked out. Frustration rippled off her, and he basked in it, but all that was gone as she was eavesdropping on his brother's allies.

"Your friends are there," she murmured.

Alarm spiked in him.

She waved a hand at him. "Of course, they're there. They want to free you." She shot him a warning look. "They won't succeed. They're harmless, right now."

His friends weren't being held captive. She would've told him if they were. That meant they were there on their own accord. They were there to work with his brother, like he told them to do. He needed to distract her.

"Why are we here? If you're not here for my brother, who then?"

She frowned.

He asked further, "My brother's witches? He has a coven. Are you here for vengeance? I can't imagine they're an actual threat to you, not if Jacith hadn't been. He was the most powerful sorcerer on the earth—"

"I know what you're doing." She cut him off. "And it won't work." She turned back for the trail. "I found what I needed to find."

"What?"

She ignored him and began around the mountain once more. Roane fell in line behind her and they walked in silence until they got to the other side of the mountain. He was mulling everything on his mind when she stopped again. He could hear the sounds of children laughing not far from them. He judged they were a quarter of a mile away. Too close for his liking. She shouldn't be this close, not to children, but he couldn't stop her. *Yet.* He could hear Davy's voice in his head. Yet, but he would.

She closed her eyes, bowed her head, and a second later the air became overwhelming. It pressed down on him, and he couldn't move. He opened his mouth to ask what was going on, but no sound came out. She looked at him and spoke. Her voice sounded like she was on the other side of a wall. He could barely make it out.

"You can't come with me any further."

"*Why?*" He tried yelling. No sound still came out. He was yelling in his own head.

"You're cloaked. No one will know you're here. They can't sense you either. I will be back once I'm done."

A foreboding sensation tunneled low in him. It was spreading fast and growing in urgency. *"Don't."* But it was useless. She turned her back and left for the village.

All he could do was yell, but no one heard him.

CHAPTER 30
TRACEY

Talia had been her sister. Their bloodline was among other thread-holders. She was honored to be Talia's sister. She always had been even when she was taken and hidden by the Roane family. She knew Talia loved Lucas Roane, but she knew that Talia had loved the werewolf as well. Both loves had been true and unconditional. Talia was a gentle soul. She was beautiful in spirit and body. Tracey understood why both men became besotted with her.

And now, as she watched her niece kicking a ball around, she saw similar traits in her. A soft smile spread over her face. It felt alien. Her cheeks were stiff. She hadn't smiled in so long, but this was right. She had come all this way for her niece. Her mission had been the correct one. No matter what happened, she would remain at her side. She would guard this child with her life.

"She looks like her mother?"

Her niece's mother, the Mori who adopted her, sat beside Tracey. Her name was Suhnah, which meant sunny and warm in their language. She explained it to Tracey the first night she welcomed her into her home. When Lucan brought all of them into the village, their reception was much different than the first time. They were captives then. They were visitors now. And being able to walk among the Mori freely, she realized they were good people. They just weren't aware of Lucan's evilness, but that would be corrected soon.

The Immortal was coming. Tracey felt it in her gut. And she was coming for her niece. When The Immortal would arrive, Tracey didn't know what would happen, but she knew there would be chaos, death, and misery. Lucan would no doubt unveil his true self. He wanted the thread for himself, but the thread would never go to a man. It could only go to a female and the Mori had kept her niece human. Suhnah told her that they wouldn't turn her into a true Mori vampire until she decided what age she wanted to be for eternity. They thought that would be her future. That's what they wished anyways. Tracey hoped her niece had a future at this point.

"Lily!" Suhnah called, standing up from where they were sitting on the grass. "It is time for your meal."

Lily stopped in mid-kick. Her cheeks were rosy and her eyes were elated. Her blonde hair was in a mess, sweat-darkening streaks near her forehead, but to Tracey, she had never looked more alive than ever. This was the magic of humans. This was why they were to be treasured and cherished. They were alive in the truest form.

Their heart beat. Their blood warmed their faces. They had a child-like naivety that never left them. Tracey felt the same quality from Davy, even until the end. It was there, like a light that had been dimmed, but it was still there. Tracey yearned for that never to happen to her niece. She always wanted her light to burn bright, no matter what forces of evil were at bay.

"Are you thinking of your sister?" Suhnah asked, holding her arms open as Lily came running. A giggle escaped her niece and she stopped, breathing hard, but smiling so widely as Suhnah closed her arms, folding a robe around her child.

At the mention of 'sister,' some of the glee left Lily. She gazed up at Tracey, like she had since she first arrived as a guest in their home. No words had been exchanged. Suhnah told her that they never explained her connection to a thread-holder or that Tracey was her aunt through blood, but she knew. A look of wonder showed over

Lily's face every time she focused on Tracey. She knew deep down, whether she spoke the words or not. Lily knew Tracey was her aunt.

She took her hand, tipping her head back so she could look all the way up the bigger vampire. "You're missing my mommy."

Suhnah gasped, but Tracey felt a burning behind her eyes. She was trying not to cry. "You know who I am."

Lily nodded. Her little hand squeezed Tracey's. "But you know that I knew." Her cheeks puffed out. The color had started to fade, but it pinked again. "My mommy comes to see me. She told me about how nice you are. You came all this way to protect me."

Suhnah's head lifted. She stared at Tracey intensely. "Protect her? From who?"

"The other lady that broke them out, Mom."

The burning moved to her throat. Tracey felt a lump forming. Her niece was trying to reassure her Mori mother, but she looked back to her and when their gazes collided, she knew that the child was aware of so much more than she should've been. Tracey knelt down. Her hands rested on Lily's tiny shoulders. "What do you know about that lady?"

"She's here." Her voice dipped low. She glanced over her shoulder, as if looking for her to arrive right then and there. "She's coming because she's scared that I'll take the thread from her."

"What do you mean? She is the thread."

"Yeah, but if she's turned, she'll come into me. She won't exist anymore. She'll just be the thread again."

Tracey's mind was spinning. There'd been talks about how to stop The Immortal, but no one had come up with anything legit. All the ideas were too outlandish and failure was a certainty. None had considered asking the child. She had to know more, so much more, but she forced herself to speak calmly. She didn't want to alarm her niece. "Lily, do you know how to stop The Immortal?"

At the mention of her, Lily's face grew alarmed. Her eyes rounded. The ends of her mouth grew tight and her neck stiffened. She looked like she couldn't breathe, but she only shook her head in a clipped motion from right to left and back again. A whispered, "No," came out.

"Stop it." Suhnah rushed forward and pulled Lily away. She lifted her up. Lily buried her head into her Mori mother's neck and held on tight. A whimpering sounded from her. It was low and sent shivers through Tracey, but her niece knew. Her niece knew about The Immortal. She knew she was coming for her. She knew about Tracey. She knew about Talia. She wanted to ask more, know more, but she bit her words back. She wouldn't find anything out that way.

Tracey stepped back and lifted her hands up. "I'm sorry." She faltered, feeling an ominous sadness weighing down on her chest. She was going to lose her niece. Her end was coming, but she didn't know when.

"If you don't mind, I think you should stay with the others for the night." Suhnah cupped the back of Lily's head. Her eyes flashed in anger. "There's a room for you. We can talk tomorrow about what happened today."

Tracey nodded. "Okay."

Suhnah walked away, and she couldn't do a thing to stop her. The ominous feeling grew, and all she could do was watch. Lily lifted her head. The tears were dried up already, but she held her aunt's gaze as she was carried away.

Tracey let out a soft sigh. "Talia, if there's a time for you to perform a miracle and help me save your child, it's now. Help me keep her alive."

———

TALIA HEARD HER SISTER. She was on the other side. A barrier was between her and the living, but she was there. She knew what was coming and unlike those still alive, she could see what was coming.

Saren stepped next to her, watching Tracey who was watching her niece. "We'll stop her."

Talia glanced at her, sadness emanating from every cell of her spirit. "I hope so. I really hope so."

"The Immortal knows about us. She must've been the one to tell Jacith about us. She'll come for the child and then she'll come for us."

Another thread-holder sister joined them. Others were there as well. One by one, they all came to stand on the other side of that veil. All watched the child and all knew, their end was near.

Sireenia said, "She is the last thread-holder. That means something."

No one looked at her. No one wanted to remind her that it could mean all their spirit deaths were coming, because more than likely, that was the ending for their prophecy. It was their death and not The Immortal's.

Saren was the vessel chosen to fight for them, but it wasn't time yet. She was waiting, and as they remained there, she was coming.

The Immortal had arrived.

CHAPTER 31
ROANE

Lucas was stuck, literally.

She froze him in place and all he could do was wait. No matter how much force he tried to break through her invisible boundary, he couldn't. And he was cloaked, but if he did break free, he'd figure a way around being invisible. Another day, another time Davy would've been laughing with glee. She would've loved being invisible. All the pranks she could've pulled on everyone, even her human friends that annoyed her. She really loved torturing them.

He started to grin, imagining it. Then, he was brought back to reality with a resounding crash. There was no Davy and there soon wouldn't be if he didn't do something about it. She said he could break her free. He had to try, but his Hunters' tattoo burned at that moment. It had been burning more and more since the battle. The Immortal said it was because the Hunters were nearby, but it was a lie. They kicked him out and turned off his connection to their power. The tattoo was alive because of her. That was the only reason that made sense, but it was scalding him now.

He tipped his head back and a roar erupted from him. The pain was blinding, even to him. He glanced around, but there was no Immortal. She wasn't there, so what was happening?

Then, he heard, "Lucas Roane of the Roane bloodline." A deep and bellowing voice spoke from behind him. He turned around, but there wasn't one person. There were a dozen or more.

Shock had him speechless. He got over that real fast, though and scowled. "Blackstock."

Blackstock was the elder of the Hunters' line. He vowed to protect humans from vampires. It was the terms for why the slayers were discontinued. Too many slayers went rogue, and the Hunters were created. He was old, even for being a vampire, and he had gray hair. Not many vampires had gray hair. It spoke to his eternity. He was close to the end that he chose. Gray hair appeared only when a vampire wanted to die.

He folded his hands together. "You've been feeling your connection again?"

He meant the Hunter tattoo. Roane continued to scowl. "I'm guessing that's why you can see me."

"It is. We activated your connection when we learned of your new mission."

"My mission?" Roane clipped out. "You wanted me to kill Davy."

"We had good reason for your order. She is too powerful now."

"I know."

"This is what we feared. A creature too great to exist on our plane."

Lucas groaned. He used to be more professional, but that was when he had been regarded as their best Hunter, before they told him to kill the woman he loved. Since then, since going rogue, he wasn't feeling any inclination to be polite. "Tell me something I don't know." He shot Blackstock a dark look. "Tell me something that's useful." He punched at the invisible wall holding him in place. "Get me out of here. That'd be useful!"

Blackstock frowned, but glanced over his shoulders. The other Hunters nodded. "We will try."

"How?"

"We will give you all of our power."

Roane was stunned. That much power . . . he looked at all of them. There were sixteen Hunters standing there and no one was blinking an eye. There was no hesitation. All were ready, merely staring back at him, and waiting for when it was time.

He said, "This is why you came, isn't it?"

Blackstock nodded. "We had to know what side you were on so we came. We waited. We watched and now, we know. It is time."

He had no words. "You will die."

"It is worth dying for. The Immortal cannot be allowed to live. You must kill her."

"But—"

"There is no time, Lucas of the Roane Bloodline. There is only one more who was created to hold the thread. The Immortal is looking for the child now. She will kill her, and when that happens, there is no more hope." He raised his hands up. It was the signal. All the Hunters placed their hands on the shoulder of the Hunter before them. The two behind Blackstock both touched his shoulders. They were all physically connected and at the last touch, Lucas doubled over again. His tattoo was a line of fire. It was burning, singeing the air, and the pain was slicing through him. It felt like his tattoo was trying to pull him apart.

There was no more time wasted. Blackstock immediately began chanting, and as he kept going, one by one the Hunters began to fall to the ground. It was the last line. They started on the left and went to the right. One down. Two. Three. Four. Then, five, six, seven. Lucas couldn't do anything except watch and count them. Eight. Nine. Ten.

Six left.

They had gotten to the second line of Hunters behind Blackstock. Eleven. Twelve. Thirteen.

It was the last two behind Blackstock.

He kept chanting. Lucas's tattoo was one huge flame. He ceased feeling anything except being burned alive, but he knew it would stop. The higher the flame went meant another Hunter had fallen.

Fourteen.

Fifteen.

It was down to one. Blackstock stopped. He was the last and he lifted his head. His eyes were complete fire. It reminded him of Saren . . . Saren? Lucas frowned. A nagging emotion started, but he couldn't focus on that. Blackstock spoke, "With these last words, I will pass along the last Hunters' power to you. We have lived our lives. We have fulfilled our missions. Our new purpose is to live through you."

"Blackstock." Lucas didn't know what to say. Everything in him was searing pain, but he felt like he should say something. "I'm sorry it came to this."

"It would've come to pass no matter what course of actions you chose. As long as a thread-holder exists, The Immortal would've tried to come alive. It is no one's fault." He paused. The older vampire hesitated, just slightly, before he lifted his head even higher. "Are you ready?"

Lucas nodded. He wasn't asking him. Blackstock was asking himself. It was time for him to die and he said the words needed. As the last one left his mouth, his head fell back. His arms spread out, palms faced to the sky. A burst of light left him, making his body appear like it was going to blow up, but it shot up in the air and then back down right away. It burst through the invisible barrier and slammed into Roane. He cried out, feeling all of their power inside of him. It was too much. His body couldn't contain it. He was going to explode. All would be lost, but as he thought that, it was done.

He was the last Hunter. The power settled into him and he could only stand and watch as one by one, the Hunters' bodies died. They withered to corpses, and then to bones, and then to dust. They became one with the earth.

A last wind raced across the land, sweeping them up, and it grazed over Roane. It was his last goodbye to them, and with that, as they were carried to be scattered over the lands, Roane was alone.

He saw his sword had fallen to the ground. He bent to pick it up, and as he did, another voice spoke, "You got amped up, I see."

It was Saren, but instead of the usual sneer on her face, there was wariness. He finished picking up his sword and sheathed it into place. "You've been missing." She was the one Davy talked about.

She didn't come closer. She remained ten yards away and shifted so her knees were bent and she was on the tips of her toes. She was ready to bolt or fight if necessary. Lucas registered her stance. "Are you fearful of me?"

"She was in your head. She could be speaking through you right now."

She—The Immortal.

It wasn't meant as an insult, but Lucas still felt it was one. His eyes flashed in irritation. "I was never under her control."

"You drank from her. You could've been."

"She forced me to, but I was never under her control. I was still myself."

"She was in your body and your head."

She was. Lucas couldn't argue that. "She's not anymore. Davy did something. I don't know what, but The Immortal isn't in my head anymore. I'm not connected at all to her now."

At the mention of Davy, Saren's head popped up. Her eyes grew more alert. "Davy? You've been in contact with her?"

He nodded. "I don't know how. It was when I was sleeping, but when I woke up, The Immortal wasn't in my head."

"How'd she react to that?"

"She didn't really, but I could tell it bothered her." He shrugged. "It's probably why she didn't let me go with her."

"What else did Davy say?"

"That someone is missing. She said something about being turned and an innocent one." Talia's child. Blackstock said the child, but it all clicked with Lucas right then. Talia's child was here. She was the next thread-holder. It was why they had come to the Mori village in the first place. He couldn't think about Talia's child being murdered. He said to Saren, "You've been missing. Why?"

Saren didn't answer at first. She gazed at him, seemingly studying him for something, Then, she sighed and replied, "Jacith was aware of us. He had cloaked himself to my sisters and me. We didn't proceed until we knew the reason."

"It was The Immortal."

"Yes." Saren nodded, her eyes downcast. "We saw all that transpired. It was alarming to find out that The Immortal betrayed Davy and our sisters. You killed him too early, though."

Lucas frowned. "What do you mean?"

"She was going to use him to help destroy our line. We think that is why she allied with him. That, and because she needed more power to burst free from Davy. Those were the two reasons."

"She said she was going to offer me to him. He wanted the Hunters' power for himself."

"No." She shook her head, moving closer to him. Whatever had been holding her back diminished. Her shoulders relaxed, her words came more freely, and the old Saren spark was revived. He saw the flame light up her eyes, and as she spoke, it burned more and more. "We think that was a ruse. We think she took you and connected you two to keep watch if anyone would plot against her. You are the glue. She knew you sent your friends ahead to plan how to save Davy, but if anyone is able to bring her back, it would be you. We think that was the real reason she took you with her."

"But Jacith."

"If he killed you, her blood would've been in him. She would've had even better access to his power, and he wouldn't have known. We think that was the real plan for her to use him and then destroy him when she didn't need him anymore."

"So she would've killed me?" Lucas's head moved back. That thought didn't sit well with him. "That bitch."

Saren cracked a grin. "Yeah, well, that bitch is going to kill one of my sisters. We will need your help to stop her."

Talia's child. Roane focused again. "What's the plan?"

She didn't skip a beat. "You."

CHAPTER 32

They felt her coming.

The winds moved with her. The grass turned toward her. The sun dipped low, as if to light her path better. Clouds formed in the sky, circling over the Mori village. Animals raced for shelter, and a chill went down everyone's backs because they could all feel her power.

The Immortal walked across the grass for where the Mori children played. Suhnah was halfway back to their home when she stopped. She turned, holding Lily, and fear slivered through her like she had never experienced before.

Tracey couldn't move, not at first. The same fear everyone felt was paralyzing her, but then her instincts kicked in and she placed herself in The Immortal's path. She raised her chin up, challenging, and said, "You will not go any further."

The Immortal stopped a few feet away and cocked her head to the side. Her eyes ran over the warrior vampire and then she grinned. "You are Talia's sister. At last, we meet." The way The Immortal stood there, her hair billowing from the wind, flying behind her and around her, the image was beautiful, but chilling at the same time. Her white dress was clean, as if she wasn't a creature of the world. It was like she was above them, a god among them, but

Tracey knew that wasn't right. She was beneath them. She had been created and stuffed inside a human to keep her powers controlled. She was a murderer.

The Immortal laughed softly. She shook her head. "You are wrong, Tracey, sister to Talia. I'm fighting for my existence. That is all. You would do the same."

"I wouldn't," she growled back.

"You would." The Immortal's voice dipped to a low warning. "You would kill anything that stood in your way of living. It is the very essence of who you are."

"What are you talking about?"

"You are a vampire. You take blood from those living to live yourself."

"I do not kill them."

"You would if you were starving. You wouldn't be able to control yourself and you would justify it later when you were of sound mind. You had to live. They were the weaker species. It is the hierarchy of life."

She was right. Tracey hated it, but she had killed. When she first turned, before she could control herself, and though she felt guilt, it hadn't stayed with her long. She was fighting to live. "Shut up."

The Immortal laughed again. The sound was eerie. "You're angry because you know I am right. I am only trying to live."

"You are life itself. You will live even if you are inside another human."

"That is not life. That is surviving. That is entrapment." Her eyes flashed in anger. She drew closer, and as she did, the winds picked up. They slammed behind her, rushing past and assaulting Tracey. The Immortal added, "I am only trying to exist. That is all."

"It won't be enough."

Others were gathering. The longer they spoke, Tracey saw more and more Mori standing around them to watch. All had fear in their eyes. All had a sense of helplessness. Tracey couldn't stomach it. They weren't even going to fight. It came down to her and her alone. Her gut twisted into a knot and the ends were yanked savagely, tightening. For a moment, she felt tears swimming in her eyes. This was the end. She couldn't do anything except try, but she had to. Suhnah had taken her niece away. Tracey only hoped they were hiding the child as she stalled The Immortal.

"But you are not."

She heard The Immortal, and her heart sank. "What do you mean?"

The Immortal tapped her head. "I can hear your thoughts, if you didn't realize it already. They are not hiding the child." She bobbed her head down, indicating behind Tracey's shoulder.

Tracey turned and that knot withered and died.

Suhnah was bringing Lily to them.

"No!" She held her hand out. "Don't. Run. Hide. Try something to save Lily."

Suhnah stopped, still holding onto the child tightly, but The Immortal crooked a finger. She made a motioning signal to her. "Come, Suhnah. Bring me the child." She said to Tracey as Suhnah did as she commanded, "There is no more fight. They can all sense it. They are offering a sacrifice instead for their livelihood."

"How do you know?" Tracey couldn't speak. Her throat was raw. "You can't know." But it was. She saw the resignation and defeat in Suhnah. The Mori vampiress was crying. Tears streamed down her face in a steady line, but she never faltered. She closed the distance until she was right in front of her child's would-be murderer.

"No," Tracey whimpered. She had to try and she shot forward. She reached for Lily. She was going to rip her from Suhnah's arms and run as fast as possible. It wouldn't be enough, but at least she had tried. At least someone had fought back, but her hand only grazed over Lily's leg before she was yanked backwards.

"NO!" The Immortal lifted her in the air. She didn't touch her. She merely held a hand up. The higher the hand went, the higher Tracey was in the air and she turned her hand. She released Tracey from her hold and the warrior vampire was flung to the ground, yards away. Her body broke through the crowd of Mori. They jumped aside so she wouldn't crash into any of them and once she fell to the ground, she tasted blood in her mouth. She rolled over, coughing it out. The Mori closed the gap behind her. She was aware of this in the back of her mind, and she wasn't paying attention to it. The need to try again, to save her niece, was the only thing forefront on her mind, but when she raised herself back up, she realized the Mori wouldn't let her pass. They remained strong, keeping their backs to her. She tried to move past another one, but it was the same. They moved to block her. She couldn't penetrate the circle anymore.

"Stay back."

A hand came to her shoulder and she was lifted once again and moved backwards. A growl ripped from her throat, and she turned, ready to fight, but it wasn't who held her in place. It was the person beside who told her to stay back.

Lucan held her in place, but her eyes fell to the human beside him and she fell back in surprise. "The witch?"

Brown waved, smiling self-consciously. She tucked her hair behind her ears and grabbed her other hand in front of her, pulling and twisting at her sleeves. "Heya. You're Tracey. I remember you."

It was the human witch that Davy was friends with. Tracey said, "You were left behind. Lucas—"

"Lucas put her with Mavic to train her magic."

"Your magic was locked to you."

Brown nodded, dropping her voice to a whisper, "It was. Mavic helped unlock it, and he's been helping me hone it more."

"But why?" She wasn't enough. Tracey knew it would take more than one Bright witch. She turned to Lucan. "Tell me there is more. Tell me you have a plan."

Lucas's twin brother glared at her, his forehead wrinkling and he narrowed his eyes at her. "I would ask you to stop being insulting to me. Right now, you can stop."

Tracey didn't dare hope. "There's more than her?" There had to be, or all was lost. Davy was gone. Her niece was gone. "Lucan, tell me—" She grasped onto him with desperate hands.

"Tracey, stop." Wren ran up to them and pulled her lover's hands away. She held them in her own and said to her, "It's not. There's more. I promise." She twisted back to Lucan. "Do it. Now. We can't wait."

But Lucan wasn't paying attention. Brown and a man in a robe stood beside him. Tracey guessed this was Mavic. She had never heard of the sorcerer, but he was rumored to be the second most powerful, second to Jacith. Some of her dread lifted as she recognized him and hope flickered inside of her. It was small, so small, but it was there. Tears streamed freely from her eyes now. She must've looked as Suhnah had, but she would never relinquish to The Immortal. Never.

She held onto Wren's hands now. "Wren," she gasped.

"I know." Wren pulled her close so their bodies touched. She rested her forehead against Tracey's. "Just hold on. Hold on."

"It's not done." More tears. She gave her lover a watery smile.

"It's not done," Wren soothed her. One of her hands released her and wrapped around Tracey's shoulders. She held the blonde warrior to her chest and ran her hand down her hair. "It's not done. I promise. There's more to come, much, much more."

And then, a new sudden burst of wind ripped across the lands.

Lucan let out a breath. "It's time."

Tracey watched from the crowd. The Mori allowed her to see now, knowing she wouldn't rush in anymore. The Immortal reached for Lily. Both mother and daughter's faces were wet. They were crying steadily, but Lily didn't fight. It broke Tracey's heart. She couldn't imagine the fear her niece was experiencing, but the little girl wore a brave front. Despite the tears, her eyes gleamed with a fierce determination and her hands were balled into tight little fists. When The Immortal pulled her into her arms, Lily didn't wrap her legs or arms around the other. She held limp, making her body dead weight for The Immortal. A twinge of pride tunneled deep into Tracey's chest.

She brushed her own tears away and held onto Wren's hand tighter.

Their roles switched in that moment. Tracey was the solid one.

She had been their foundation and Wren was the feisty, more emotional one. Wren was her rock that day. She held her hand and as Tracey couldn't look away from her niece, she continued to smooth a hand down Tracey's hair and back. She was reassuring her, or trying, but the truth was that no one knew what was going to happen.

Even Lucan, who glanced to Mavic and Brown. Both nodded. Both were ready, but they still waited. Mavic felt the thread-holders arriving. He knew the entire line of sisters was going to show, and he felt another power traveling with them. He didn't know who or what that was, and he refrained from telling Lucan. There'd be questions he could not answer, but when they were on the outskirts of the Mori, he lifted a hand to Lucan's shoulder.

Lucan touched Wren's shoulder, who was already touching Tracey. The Mori nearest Tracey touched her shoulder and one by one, a Mori would touch the shoulder of the next one and so forth. Tracey stopped crying. She stopped feeling so helpless, and her tears dried up. Her hope flared brighter. They were all going to fight. She realized that as all the Mori became connected to each other. When they were done, the only Mori who wasn't touching another was Suhnah. It came full circle, rounding back until it was Brown's turn. The last Mori placed his hand on her shoulder, and then they all began to chant.

We are.

We will be.

As one.

Together.

We will

cast out

the imposter.

They repeated those words softly under their breath.

Tracey couldn't help herself. She called in her mind, *"Lily, look at me."*

"I am."

Tracey's eyes snapped open. Her niece was staring right at her and there was no fear. There was only happiness. Her tears dried up too and she added to her aunt, *"I'm going to see my momma. I am so excited, Tracey."*

Tracey gasped silently. Her mother. Talia. Lily was going to die. That was what she meant and she started to say, *"No, Lily. Not that way—"*

"Yes!" Lily cried out. She thrust her hand over The Immortal's shoulder. "Look!"

CHAPTER 33

DAVY

Davy felt them.

She could feel her sisters there. They were with Lucas, who was connected to all the Hunters before him. The Mori were as one being, along with Brown and Mavic. There were so many, but they were all needed. All against one. It was what was needed and as The Immortal turned, distracted, Davy stood up inside of her. She was pushed to the farthest regions of The Immortal's mind, but she was still there. It wasn't over. Not yet.

SAREN STOOD BESIDE HIM, and they strode forward.

They had remained hidden, cloaked from The Immortal until the last second. Everything was set in place. They continued walking forward and he knew the instant the invisible spell fell away. They appeared, a foot, a leg, both legs, the torso, then the arms, shoulders and finally their heads. The full bodies were now visible and The Immortal turned at the child's cry of 'look!' Her eyes first gleamed in amusement. Her top lip curved up in a mocking grin, but her eyes trailed past Saren and soon filled with horror.

"No," she shook her head, saying quietly.

"Yes!" Saren growled.

Lucas glanced behind him and started. All of the thread-holders were there. They weren't in their bodies, but they stood as if ghosts. They were there, though. That was all that mattered, and they were standing behind Saren. He realized now what it meant that she was their vessel. He had the Hunters' power in him and she had all of their power inside of her.

The crowd moved to the left of Saren. The Mori were all still connected, but they were able to maneuver so two that were forgotten came forward.

Brown and Mavic. Lucan followed behind them. Lucas's eyes went flat at seeing his brother, but that was a battle for another time.

Lucan caught his gaze and wore a mirrored mocking grin that The Immortal had moments before. It was as if to say, "Later, brother. Later."

Lucas stifled the growl and swung his head to focus on The Immortal again.

She congregated to them. "What is this?" Her eyes trailed over everyone, seeing the touching hands of the Mori before landing on Lucas. She jerked forward, a growl coming from her. "What is this?"

"It's over." Saren drew her sword. "That's what this is."

"No."

"Yes." And Saren attacked, but as she did, all the thread-holders launched with her. They rained down on The Immortal. It was a whirlwind after that. The Immortal was covered in ghost forms and the wind picked up, swirling around them like a tornado. Lucas stood back. He wasn't sure if he should wade in or hold back, but when he heard the first cry, he knew that wasn't The Immortal. No matter how much he hated it, she still had Davy's voice. He would've recognized her cry no matter how far away.

He started forward.

"Wait." A hand touched him. It was soft and warm. It was gentle, too.

Brown was there, her eyes were open, but he only saw the whites.

Her eyes had rolled into the back of her mind. He said, "Tell me that's magic."

"It is." Her hand clasped tighter onto him. "I am connecting you to everyone to fight her."

"I can't fight if I'm being held back."

"I know. I'm connecting to you mentally." A shift happened inside of him, like a room appeared and the door swung open to let thousands inside. He gasped, but he heard her say, "And I'm done. Go. Fight. Get Davy."

That was all he needed to hear. Gripping his sword, he waded in through the winds.

The Immortal and Saren were trading blows. One would hit, the other retaliated. It would repeat, over and over again. He had to push through more winds and more of the thread-holder sisters. They were there right alongside their sister. They were urging her on, chanting words of magic to her. The Immortal was growing frustrated. She couldn't strike Saren down, but when Saren swung the sword to her head, she grabbed it and yanked it out of her hands.

Saren cried out, losing her weapon.

"Finally," The Immortal growled and swung it herself.

It would've come down on Saren, who was dazed, but Lucas blocked it with his own sword.

"No!" Furious dark eyes snapped to his. They widened at his arrival. "I was going to let you live."

He kicked her sword away and grunted, "You were going to let Jacith kill me."

"Well." She shrugged, rounding back and steadying on her feet. "I was, but then I liked your company after all."

"Bitch," he snarled.

"Vampire," she shot back.

His eyes jumped to hers. Shock spread quickly through him. It was the same insult, said with the same venom that Davy first held for him. He looked into The Immortal's eyes. *Davy?* The Immortal's eyes lit up. A literal light filled them and he heard back in his mind, *"It's me. She can't concentrate on me, but I'm slowing her down. Each time she swings or tries to send magic out, I block her. She hasn't figured out what's going on, but she can't stop me anyway. She's losing her hold. Keep going!"*

He swung his own sword, and The Immortal blocked him, rounding to hit him across his face. It was a slap, but with her strength, it was a launch backwards.

"Vampire!"

He thought it was The Immortal, but it was Saren instead. She jumped in the air, grabbing a dagger that was tucked against his back and she thrust out, slicing The Immortal. It was going to slash her throat, but The Immortal evaded. It cut her arm instead and another unearthly growl came from The Immortal, who retaliated. She swung the sword out. It was quick enough to graze Saren's cheeks.

Blood had been spilled on both ends.

Lucas rebounded and both Saren and he were swinging at The Immortal. They struck at the same time. The Immortal was cut by both, but her efforts doubled. They fought like that, trading blows, until Lucas had lost track of time. He felt like he had been fighting for hours. His body was growing weaker so he closed his eyes and pulled forth more of his power. The Hunters were there. He felt them rallying inside and when he opened his eyes again, he felt all of them with him. He swung, but they were all swinging with him.

His sword hit hers. It held and he leaned forward, pushing on it. He was going to overpower her. He had to.

Sensing the renewed strength, she dropped her sword and hit at him with magic. "Enough!" she roared.

The magic hit him like a two-ton semi. It hit him hard and he was winded. He could see, but he couldn't stop her as she turned on Saren. The wind went to her feet and began circling her. It picked up speed as it started up over her feet, her calves, her legs, her waist. She was drawing power from the ground.

She was going to kill Saren. He felt her intent and tried to help. "No!" he yelled.

It was too late.

The Immortal shot Saren with a blast of magic.

The blue-leathered warrior fell back, stunned by the hit. Her eyes rolled to the side and she began to fall.

"No!"

Lucas thought that was him. He was shouting in his mind, but it wasn't. It was the other sisters. They surged ahead and Talia stepped into Saren's body. He blinked by the sudden transformation. The blue leather was gone, and instead the red hair grew and a similar white dress formed over the thread-holder.

The Immortal stepped back, shocked, too.

"MOM!"

Talia's eyes widened. She paled and turned. The Immortal did as well. Lucas saw the little girl run past him. He didn't know what had happened to her. The Immortal must've placed her down, but she ran right by him. Her arms and legs were pumping as hard as she could and her eyes and mouth were flat, looking determined. "MOM! Mom!"

"No!" Talia gasped.

She lifted horrified eyes to Lucas. "Stop her—"

But she was past him. It was too late. Talia moved to scoop her daughter up, but The Immortal was there. She grabbed the child before Talia could and swung her away. She lifted up in the air and laughed down. "It is too late now. I will end all of this foolishness."

"NO!"

The Immortal placed a hand against the child's cheek and closed her eyes.

"No, no, no." Talia was whimpering. "She can't kill her. It's all over for us then."

"Lucas!"

He heard Davy shouting to him. *"What?"*

"Throw Talia up here."

"What?"

Talia turned to him, hearing him. "What?"

He ignored her. *"What, Davy?"*

"Throw my sister up here. Just do it. The child has a knife. She's going

to plunge it into my body. The Immortal's distracted. Now's your chance to free me."

"Davy, I don't know—"

"DO IT!"

So, he did. He hurried to Talia. "I'm only doing what I'm told." His fingers wrapped around her arm and he circled once, gaining enough momentum and then he let loose. Talia was launched in the air.

"Mom!" The child saw her coming and like Davy said, she pulled out a dagger that was inside of her shirt. He recognized it as one that he had given Wren as a gift. Then, right as The Immortal saw it, it was too late. It was plunged into her stomach.

"NOOOO!" she screamed, crashing back down to the ground, but he didn't have time to figure why that one cut held so much more power than the others. The Immortal's body was writhing on the ground and he stepped forward. A hand touched his. Brown was beside him. She said, "They need magic for this so hope you're ready."

"Wha—"

Again. He didn't have time to question anything. He was over-taken by her magic, but it wasn't just hers. He sensed all of the Mori as one. He sensed his friends. Gavin. Gregory. Wren. Tracey. Bastion. They were all connected. His brother, too. Mavic. Everyone. A moment later, he felt all the thread-holders, too. Brown must've connected to them, or to Talia, and they were all being channeled into him.

"Come in, Lucas!" Davy was calling him. He was on another plane. He wasn't in his body form anymore. He had become his mind, but he followed her voice. *"Davy, lead me!"* he shouted back.

"I am. I'm pulling you to me."

He stepped forward, feeling intense power all around him. It wasn't his. It wasn't Davy's. It was angry, but it was distracted. It was blind to him until he was in front of Davy. He reached for her hand. Relief pouring through him. *"Davy!"*

His hand went through hers. He frowned, pulling it back. *"I can't touch you."*

"I know." She was concentrating on his hand, her eyebrow bunched together. Her mouth turned down and she said, with authority in her voice, *"But I'm going to grab you."*

He waited, holding his hand up, and as he held his breath, she started to lift her hand to his. He felt an immense pressure pushing back against him, but he held strong. Davy was breaking through whatever was holding her in.

A gasp.

He heard it in his ear. It wasn't him. It wasn't Davy.

A reeling sensation zipped around them. An anchor began to sink inside of him. The Immortal knew what they were doing.

"Davy, you have to hur—" Her fingers touched his and the last of his sentence fell from his lips, *"—ry."*

That was all the connection she needed. Her eyes closed and he felt the power radiate from her. It was like a blanket coming from her, one thread at a time. It was covering The Immortal around them and he felt a shift in gravity. They were going down.

Davy's palm fit against his. She tightened her hold on him and grunted out, pain laced in her tone, *"It's working. She's weakening."*

She kept breaking through the barrier until her other hand was holding onto his, then her arms, her elbows, her legs, her knees, her feet, her waist, then her entire body. They were crashing to the ground. It was The Immortal, not them. He realized that now until he was holding Davy in his arms again. As the entirety of her body fit against his, perfectly and how it always had, he was back in his own mind. He was in his own body and he really was holding Davy.

She opened her eyes. Tears burst forth, and she smiled at him. "Hi."

Hi. She said hi. Lucas felt a stupid grin on his face. He grabbed her face, rested his forehead to hers, and asked, "Is it done?"

Her smile spread as wide as his and she nodded, bobbing their heads together. "Yeah." Happy tears slid down her face. "It really is."

She grasped his head too and dipped so her lips met his. One kiss. Two. Three—he couldn't let go. It'd been so long, so damn long. He groaned, his hands going around her. He pulled her in. He just wanted to hold her and reassure himself that she wasn't going anywhere anymore.

"I'm here," she gasped against his lips. "I'm not going anywhere. She can't break free. She doesn't have the power. I do. I'll never let her have it again."

As they kept kissing and hugging, they began to hear sounds of sobbing. He didn't want to pull away, but he did with reluctance.

Lily was kneeling on the ground beside Talia. Tracey was next to her, and Wren was standing on Tracey's other side.

"Momma." Lily stroked Talia's cheek. She bent down and pressed her forehead to her mother's. She whispered, "Momma, I love you."

"Talia." Tracey was moaning, rocking back and forth. Her hand went to touch her sister's cheek, then lifted away. She started to touch her niece's cheek, but her hand raised once again and began to go back to her sister. She couldn't decide who to touch and in the end, she merely bent forward and pressed her forehead to Talia's stomach. She grabbed ahold of her on both sides and cried.

Wren let out a soft breath and stroked Tracey's back.

"Oh no." Davy's hand found Lucas's. "They're gone."

Brown stepped forward. She told Davy and Lucas, "They gave their power to Davy—"

Davy finished, "I needed more. I couldn't break through the barrier. They gave everything to me so I could. It cost them." She lifted her haunted gaze to him. "They died so I could live."

"No." Brown grabbed one of Davy's hands. She held it to her chest. "They died so The Immortal would be defeated. If it was another thread-holder, if it was another time, you would've done the same."

"I'm alive, though." Tears were fast falling down Davy's face again but the celebration had gone. There were losses to mourn.

"And they won't be forgotten," Brown said. She readjusted her hold on Davy's hand, holding even tighter. "I promise, Davy. They will never be forgotten. We will remember. We will live for them now."

Lucan joined the circle. His face was a mask. His lips were in a flat line. His eyebrows were fixed. He wore a bland expression before he turned to Brown. "I hate to strike while there are grieving ones here." He lifted his eyes to his brother. A smirk showed and a chill sliced through Lucas once again.

He growled, his hands forming fists. "What are you doing, Lucan?"

"Well." He let out a frustrated breath. "You see, everyone forgot why I was helping. I mean, yes. Take down The Immortal. Hear, hear. All cheers for her demise, but," he cringed, smiling at the same time. "No one thought about the afterwards, and well . . ." His hand gestured to Talia and to Davy. "I have to strike while I can, and the time is now."

He stared at Davy, but Brown gasped. Her head flew back and her chest arched up. Her hands spread out. She cried out, "Davy!"

"Brown!"

"There's pain." A bloodcurdling scream ripped from her. She cried out, hoarsely, "Something's happening inside of me. I can't—oh my God! I can't—Davy!"

"What?" Davy grabbed both of her hands. "What is going on? Lucan! Stop it. Whatever you're doing, stop it!"

Lucas started for his brother, but he was grabbed and hauled backwards. Five Mori warriors restrained him. He scanned the group, and all of his warriors were being held back by Mori. A high-pitched scream sounded from Lily as she was picked up and handed off to her mother. "Mom!" She hit at the Mori mother, but her futile attempts were ignored. She was whisked away.

Tracey kicked out. She tried to break free, an animal-like growl coming from her. She couldn't. She was too weak. So was everyone else, Lucas himself, and his eyes found Davy's, too. She was the weakest of all.

All that power, everything that had been given to them would be for nothing.

Lucan double-crossed them. As Brown kept screaming, Mavic moved around so he was standing in front of Brown and Davy both.

"Yes. Yes." Lucan stood in front of his twin. His breath was hot as he was laughing. "You're starting to piece it all together now, aren't you? You were my way of breaking the thread from existence, but you're my enemy. You were my weapons against her and it all couldn't have worked better for me if I had planned it myself." He leaned close and said softly, "Thank you, brother. Thank you for putting one of my own coven members in touch with a Bright witch. Thank you for allowing him to mold her into his own weapon, because you see, her magic wasn't released at all. No, no. He's not able to perform miracles, but he was able to channel other magic inside of her. She was the trusted one. She was sent here to help you and one of mine traveled with her. So while she was in The Immortal's head with you and Davy, she thought she was helping you free Davy, but she wasn't. Her magic wasn't created to do that. Her magic was weakening Davy so that now I can kill her. Finally. The thread will jump to Brown, and then right to me. It's all been planned. I'll get what I wanted. I'll be the first and only male thread-holder. I'll be the final thread-holder."

His brother's delight repulsed him.

Lucas shook his head. If the thread were pulled from her, she would die. The thread made her immortal and as he watched, it was happening. Brown was connected to Davy still and Mavic was performing a spell on both. Davy's skin was literally jerking. The thread was going to be ripped from inside of her.

Think, Lucas. He had to think. He had to calm down and just think!

Turned. That was the last piece that Davy told him in his dream. Everything else had come true. The innocent. The forgotten. The one would come back, but she said she would have to be turned.

His brother had everything planned.

But what if she died *before* the spell was completed? That would stop it from going to his brother. No. The thought sickened him. Davy wanted to be human. That was all she dreamt about, to be normal. He couldn't . . . no, no. He couldn't take that away, but as he continued to watch—he couldn't see any other way. Davy would die. He had no doubt his brother would kill everyone else.

He had to do it.

He closed his eyes and focused. He needed to call upon all the Hunters again, but there was other power in him still. The Immortal gave him her power. He used most of it up, but he still felt it in him. He needed to use all of it. He had to make it count.

"Davy," he thought.

Her eyes found his, so terrified.

He said, *"I'm going to kill you."*

"What?"

"Don't be afraid. I have to do it. It's the only way."

She nodded, moving her head only a tiny bit. She was held captive by the spell, but at her signal, Roane erupted into motion. He launched himself backwards and then jumped over his five captors. They were too slow. Everyone was too slow.

He was at Davy's side within the blink of an eye and in the next, his fangs were in her neck. There had been blood trickling down his arm and he raised his thumb to her lips. He brushed it over her mouth, and her tongue darted out to swallow a drop. His other hand grasped the back of her neck, and as she drank, he told her, *"Turn, Davy. Turn for me."*

He snapped her neck.

CHAPTER 34
DAVY

They told me I slept for three days and I started laughing. Three days. How cliché was that, but it was true. It had been three days since my final death. And I say final because it felt like I had died a thousand times over, but three days ago had been my last time. I was no longer The Immortal. I was no longer even a thread-holder. I wasn't empathic, and I wasn't a human.

I was a vampire.

Lucas told me when he killed me, the thread jumped out of me. It hadn't been in enough time for Lucan's spell to do whatever it had intended to do. It went straight to the nearest thread-holder, Lily. Talia's little girl was the newest and according to a prophecy that I never knew about, she was the last thread-holder. Tracey explained that Lily would always be the thread-holder. She doubted anyone would try to separate the thread again, not after word spread far and wide how powerful The Immortal had been.

I felt horrible. I felt Talia's second death. I felt all of my sisters' second deaths, but in the moment I hadn't realized what the impending doom was that I was feeling. I had been selfish. I had been so happy to be in Lucas's arms again, for real, but Tracey reassured me that Lily isn't a normal thread-holder. Apparently she was still able to see her other sisters, Talia too. Because she grew up among the Mori, who had their own magic, her body wasn't normal. I was thankful to hear the sisters still lived on another plane, but I wouldn't see Saren again or hear her annoying voice in my head.

It was done. All of it. Even Lucan.

When she became the thread, Lily saw Jiyama's death. She told the Mori leader that Lucan killed her and where he had deposited the body. Any assistance Lucan got from the Mori was done. Apparently, there had been suspicion, but there was proof now. One of their own saw it. Lucan was hauled into their prison while Lucas and the rest of us were treated as guests. Tracey laughed. The Mori were never going to harm any of us, but they were following what Lucan had promised—that they still needed to complete what they had originally set to do, which is to destroy the thread. They weren't aware of Lucan's secret plan of putting the thread into himself. They were ashamed once they found out the truth. Kates was set free, as well. It was realized that Lucan forced her to turn on us. When the others discovered the torture she endured from Lucan, she was welcomed back, but I knew it would be a long time till she was trusted.

I was in bed waiting for Lucas to come back. He went to see his brother, one last time, and we were leaving for home the next day. Lucan was going to be executed at the same time, but Lucas didn't want to stay for it. He knew it would happen. That was good enough for him. All the killing had been too much. He had kissed me and told me, "I just want to get home. I want to get you home. Finally."

Home.

I never thought I would be going home again. That night, the first night that I woke as a vampire, Lucas made love to me. I cried the whole time because I never thought I would be in his arms again. I never thought I would have a second chance at life.

The opening to our tent lifted, and Roane slipped inside. I sat up and smiled. "Goddess." I shook my head. "I will never get used to seeing you. I'll never take it for granted. I will never," I paused as he came over, a grin teasing the corners of his lips and I laid back. He started to fall on top of me, but switched to rest beside me. One of his elbows propped him up and his eyes traced all over me, from my eyes, forehead, cheeks, and to my lips. He lingered there. "I will never take it for granted myself." He leaned down and touched his lips to mine.

I sighed, happily. It was like coming home. I caught the side of his face and whispered, "Have I told you how much I love you?"

He nodded, moving his lips over mine. "Say it again. I like hearing it."

"I love you."

His eyes darkened, and he shifted so he was lying on top of me. "And again." His mouth dipped to my throat.

An ache was forming between my legs. I knew he would soon be there, filling me, making me feel whole again, and I sighed as his lips moved up my jawline to find my mouth again. "I love you."

"And again." He kissed me. Long. Lingering. And so damn lovingly.

"I love you." I would never stop telling him, just like he had done the same to me the night before.

After he was inside of me, after we were moving together, after we reminded each other that we could still touch one another, he lifted his head and gazed down. "You mentioned last night that you wanted a new name?"

I laughed, arching my back and pressing against him. "Is now the right time for this?"

He smiled down at me. "I want to know what name to call you when I make you scream tonight."

"Oh my God." I laughed, but then sobered up. "Davina."

"Davina?"

I nodded. It was my full name, one that I hated, but I was different. I was changed. I was no longer the happy and giddy college girl, only hoping to deal with being empathic. I would find that girl again, but it would be a while. It might be a long while, but it felt right. My hands splayed out over the side of his face. I looked up into his depths as he gazed down to mine. I murmured, "It's a new life for me. I'm no longer Davy. She died when The

Immortal took hold of me, but I can still be Davina. That's my name."

"Okay." He leaned down, and his lips lovingly moved over mine. "Have I told you how much I love you today, Davina?"

I laughed and then relished as he proceeded to, over and over again. We were still showing our love for each other as the sun dipped down, the moon came out, and still when the early morning started to peek out again.

When it was morning, I fell asleep, but there were no more worries anymore. I was in Roane's arms again and I knew if I stayed there, all could be handled. When we woke, we packed up. The rest of our group was waiting for us. The goodbyes were spoken. Lily hugged me tightly and I barely managed to hold back tears. She was such a little girl, but I was reassured that she was protected by an entire village. Tracey and Wren said goodbye. Wren decided to stay with the Mori. She would help protect the newest thread-holder and she wouldn't have to leave her lover again. There was a special goodbye between Lucas and Wren. She had been one of his best warriors for centuries. She would be missed, but it was a good good-bye, not a sad one. He was holding back some of his own tears as he stepped next to me and took my hand. After the last goodbye, the Mori headed for the center of their village. The bells began to toll. Lucan's execution was near. As the Mori headed past us, we walked the other way.

We left.

We were outside of the village, and the bells had almost faded when a sudden cheer filled the air.

We all stopped. Gavin, Bastion, and Brown. Gregory found his daughter, so she came with us. We glanced back, and then to Lucas.

His brother was dead.

We traveled another mile when we heard a bush rustling. Both Gavin and Bastion drew their swords, but then we heard, "Hey, man. Shit. What's with the swords? I thought we were all friends."

"Yeah," a second voice crawled out. "You told us to stay put and we did. We've been chilling for a week and holy cripes," a pair of eyes found me and widened, "the psycho bitch is back."

It was Cal and Spencer.

Gavin's mouth fell open. He groaned, hitting his hand to his forehead. "We completely forgot about these guys."

Lucas frowned. "Who are these guys?"

All eyes came to me and I laughed, nervously. "So, it's a long story, you see."

And, as we continued home, I held his hand and told him everything that happened, and it was a long story indeed, but it was a good story. In fact, it was a great story and while Spencer and Cal were finally sent home, I knew this was a story that I would tell our child. The one thing I never told anyone since the beginning was that I was pregnant, and even though I was a vampire now, with Mori magic in me, I was able to give birth to a healthy little girl.

We named her Saren.

EPILOGUE

Lucas said the wedding could be in his restaurant or the new hotel he bought, but the idea of being indoors hadn't sat right with me. It hadn't sat right with me ever since we returned to Benshire. Being captured by Lucan and then again by The Immortal, I'd been yearning more and more to remain outside. It was wintertime, but I still did. The winter didn't touch me, which was one of the nicer qualities about being a vampire. Still. I was transitioning to my new state in life. I was free. I was a vampire. I was going to be a wife, and feeling my hair getting tugged, I looked down at the best transition in my life. I was a mother.

Saren waved her plump hands in the air and started to tip back, laughing. She didn't go far. I had her tucked in my arm so her head hit my arm lightly, but she loved it. Peals of more laughter filled the air.

"Is she hungry?"

Pippa asked the question, eager, but Brown was right next to her. Since we got back, Brown had been wonderful. She'd been by my side the entire time, making sure I was okay. Pippa came for Saren's birth, and she stuck around. She was going to try college again. So was Brown. Both had dropped out because of my captivity. I knew that was the elephant in the room. They wanted me to go with them, but neither asked yet. Vampires could go. It's where I met Lucas. We could walk in the light. We could do almost everything a human did, but it was different.

I had to mourn not being a human. Going to college—it would be in my face every day. I would never grow old, weak, diseased and I was an idiot. I was grieving? I was a vampire. They were always gorgeous and since my transformation, I'd gotten the gloss over too. It wasn't that my looks were totally changed, but my skin was clearer. My eyes darker. My hair was shinier. I was already slender, but I became more toned.

Saren started kicking her legs and gurgling.

This one, my hold on her tightened, she was worth it. Everything. If I hadn't spent so much time with the Mori, Lucas's sperm in me wouldn't have taken root. I was human, but he wasn't. It was their magic, just being in their lands, that helped make Saren possible.

"You should get your dress on." Pippa came forward. Her hands were already up and she was smiling at Saren. "I'll take the little one."

Brown jumped beside her. "I can't wait. A bridesmaid. I'm a bridesmaid. I've never been a bridesmaid."

Pippa slid her hands under Saren and stepped back with her. She grinned at Brown. "You're a Bright bridesmaid."

"And you." Brown clapped her on the shoulder. "You're a werewolf bridesmaid. I can't wait till I get drunk. You're nursing, Davy—in a . . ." She trailed off, glancing away.

That was another transition.

I told her, "It's fine, Brown. You're not the only one. Trust me."

Pippa groaned, rocking Saren back and forth. "Oh yeah. I've been calling her Davy since I arrived."

Both sobered and gazed at me. Brown sighed. "It's not that we don't want to call you Davina."

They were torn. They loved Davy. I was alive. I reached for both of their hands and squeezed them. "I'm different. I know, but I'll get back to my old self."

The Immortal.

Lucan.

Losing my humanity—the last year before Lucas broke me free had been hard, but I felt the old me coming back. The old me *would* come back. I squeezed once more. "I love you guys, and you are helping the old Davy spark to life again. Thank you. And thank you for being a part of my wedding."

"Well, hell yeah. Of course." Brown gestured outside my bedroom window. We were back at Lucas's house, the one by the cliff where Lucan captured us in the first place. There weren't great memories, but each night Lucas helped push those bad ones away as he made new ones with me. And there was land. There was lots and lots of land. I didn't feel so 'constricted' here. The cliff was where the wedding would take place. Emily was the wedding planner and she was utilizing everyone to help. The entire backyard was transformed so it looked like a magical forest. Trees had been relocated and spelled to grow tall. Flowers hung everywhere. Logs made up the seats. It didn't look like it was next to a cliff at all. And within a few hours, it would be filled with vampires, werewolves, witches, and a few humans (those who were either clueless or brave.) There would be a few slayers as well. A group of them were waiting for us when we returned. They took Kates with them. I knew they were going to help her heal. Her time in captivity had been the worst of all of us. There'd been a few correspondents between the two of us. We were both getting better, and I was excited to see her again. She'd been my childhood nolstage. I wanted to get to know my best friend once again, well not my real best friend. That was Lucas now, but Kates held a special place in my heart. She always would.

Brown said, "This wedding is a dream wedding and hello, Roane in a tuxedo." She fanned herself. "Swoon right there."

Pippa frowned. "He's going to be her husband."

"But he's gorgeous. I can see. I can appreciate." Brown nudged Pippa with her shoulder. "Just like I can appreciate the hotness of your brother. Hubba hubba. Come to me Christian Christane." She leaned over and grabbed Saren's thumb, but paused and asked, "Does he have to be betrothed to another werewolf? Is that a thing?

What about a witch? You think I got a shot? He can be my Alpha any night of the week."

Pippa's frown deepened and she turned, giving Brown a curt response. Brown retaliated, another laughing joke. It had been like this over the last few months and I sighed, listening, but I loved it. The teases were flying. The jokes were sent back and forth. Pippa would huff about something, and Brown would follow with one more outrageous suggestion, all the while trying to hide her grin.

This was normal. This had been my life, and I knew it would be again.

The old Davy was rearing up. She wanted to join in, but the slight tease I had was held back. If I joined in with the joking, they would be quieted in shock. Then, they'd want more. They'd start looking for the old Davy every minute, every hour, every time they were around me and she wasn't there. Not yet. But she was coming. I felt her in me again.

I turned back to the window and gazed down. Roane was there, listening to Emily who was pointing at a post that was covered with flowers. Her hand movements were sharp, and his frown grew, even as I watched.

Emily never wanted to bother me with anything, so she bothered him. I thought it was hilarious.

"*Having fun?*" I asked him.

He looked up, knowing exactly where I was. He thought back, "*Your old roommate still drives me crazy.*"

"*Remember when she had a crush on you?*"

He groaned. "*I was using her to get to you. I should've known better.*"

Resting a hand to the window frame, I leaned closer. I teased back, "*Oh, come on. Don't be so hard on yourself. You're a stud.*"

"*Don't start.*"

I laughed under my breath. "*You're the last living Hunter. You're a legend, Lucas.*"

"*Davina.*" He sighed.

I was loving the sweet torment. "*I know you're a legend in my mind. A legend in bed.*"

His eyes flashed a warning. *"If you keep going, I'll come up there and show you how legendary you can be, too."*

My hands curled around the frame. *"Promise?"*

He groaned again, shaking his head. Emily quieted, and stared at him blankly. Her eyes trailed up, following his, and when she saw me, understanding flared over her face. She lifted a hand, giving me an impish grin, and said, "I'll let you two be alone. Davina, dress."

I opened the window and hollered down, "Aye, aye, Staff Sergeant."

I didn't think, but as soon as the words left my mouth, I cringed. Emily's eyes widened and she sucked in her breath. That was the old Davy. Sarcastic. Teasing. Still grimacing, I waved back. "I will. Thank you, Emily."

A sheen of tears showed and her hand waved again. Her smile softened. "I'll be up in a bit. Your hair looks beautiful."

She darted around Lucas, hurrying and waving at someone else. Lucas was still there, and my eyes found his again. He asked, *"You okay?"*

I nodded. *"I am."*

"I love you."

Warmth rushed through me. *"I love you, too."*

"You're going to be my wife in an hour."

I gave him a half-grin. *"You have an hour to run away. You've been warned."*

"Never." His eyes glittered, his love shone brightly there. *"Never, Davina of the Roane Bloodline. You are mine forever. You are in my heart. You are in my soul. We are of one now."*

Saren shrieked behind me and both of us grinned at the other.

Roane thought to me, *"One day we'll explain why she'll age older than us."*

I barked out a laugh. *"It's a hell of a story."*

"Yes," he answered. *"It was, wasn't it?"*

I held his gaze and let out a soft sigh. He was right. It really was.

THE END

**If you enjoyed the Davy Harwood trilogy, please consider leaving a
review! They truly help so much.
For more stories, go to:
www.tijansbooks.com**

ACKNOWLEDGMENTS

Wow! I can't believe I'm writing this part, and for this book. This series was one of my first that I was really proud of. I had written other stories before Davy, but all of them were while I was trying to 'learn' how to write. Davy was the first story where I felt ready. I didn't know what I was ready for. I had no idea what to do after I wrote the story, but I was ready for something. I was so proud of myself. I had gone up another level in writing. Man. Davy was always so near and dear to me. I want to thank all the readers that started with me in my Fictionpress days, followed me to Livejournal, and stuck with me when I began publishing. I know so many of you have been waiting years for this conclusion. I truly hope I did it justice.

Thank you to the Tijanettes! You, ladies, make me smile daily! Thank you to the admins, to my betas, to my editors, proofreaders, to my formatter, to my agent. Thank you to Erica Adams and Ali Oop. I know both of you have really cheered for Davy and it always meant so much to me. Thank you to all my author friends who I might've pasted something in their inbox to quick read over for me, or patted me on the back when I needed it. Thank you, thank you, thank you. I don't know if I can say it enough.

ALSO BY TIJAN

More Paranormal Standalones:

Evil

Micaela's Big Bad

Mafia novels:

Carter Reed Series

Cole

Bennett Mafia

Jonah Bennett

Canary

More of the Fallen Crest/Roussou world:

Fallen Crest/Roussou Universe

Fallen Crest Series

Crew Series

The Boy I Grew Up With (standalone)

Rich Prick (standalone)

Nate

Kess

Other series:

Davy Harwood Series (paranormal)

Broken and Screwed Series (YA/NA)

Jaded Series (YA/NA suspense)

The Insiders (trilogy)

Sports Romance Standalones:

Enemies

Teardrop Shot

Hate To Love You

The Not-Outcast

Young Adult Standalones:

Ryan's Bed

A Whole New Crowd

Brady Remington Landed Me in Jail

College Standalones:

Antistepbrother

Kian

Contemporary Romances:

Bad Boy Brody

Home Tears

Fighter

Rockstar Romance Standalone:

Sustain

An MC short story:

Kess

More books to come!